THE TALENTED FAIRY TALES

THE COMPLETE SERIES

S.C. GRAYSON

Copyright © 2024 by S.C. Grayson

All rights reserved.

No part of this publication may be reproduced, distributed, or transmitted in any form or by any means, including photocopying, recording, or other electronic or mechanical methods, without the prior written permission of the publisher, except as permitted by U.S. copyright law. For permission requests, contact author@scgrayson.com.

The story, all names, characters, and incidents portrayed in this production are fictitious. No identification with actual persons (living or deceased), places, buildings, and products is intended or should be inferred.

Edited by Lisa Green and Crab Editing

Book Cover by Covers by Jules

Case Laminate Design by Megan Van Dyke

Interior Illustrations by Lulybot

Contents

Beauty and the Blade

Little Red Shadow

The Hood and his Thief

The Gardener and the Sharpshooter:
A Kristoff and Gregor Prequel Story

Beauty and the Blade

Book One

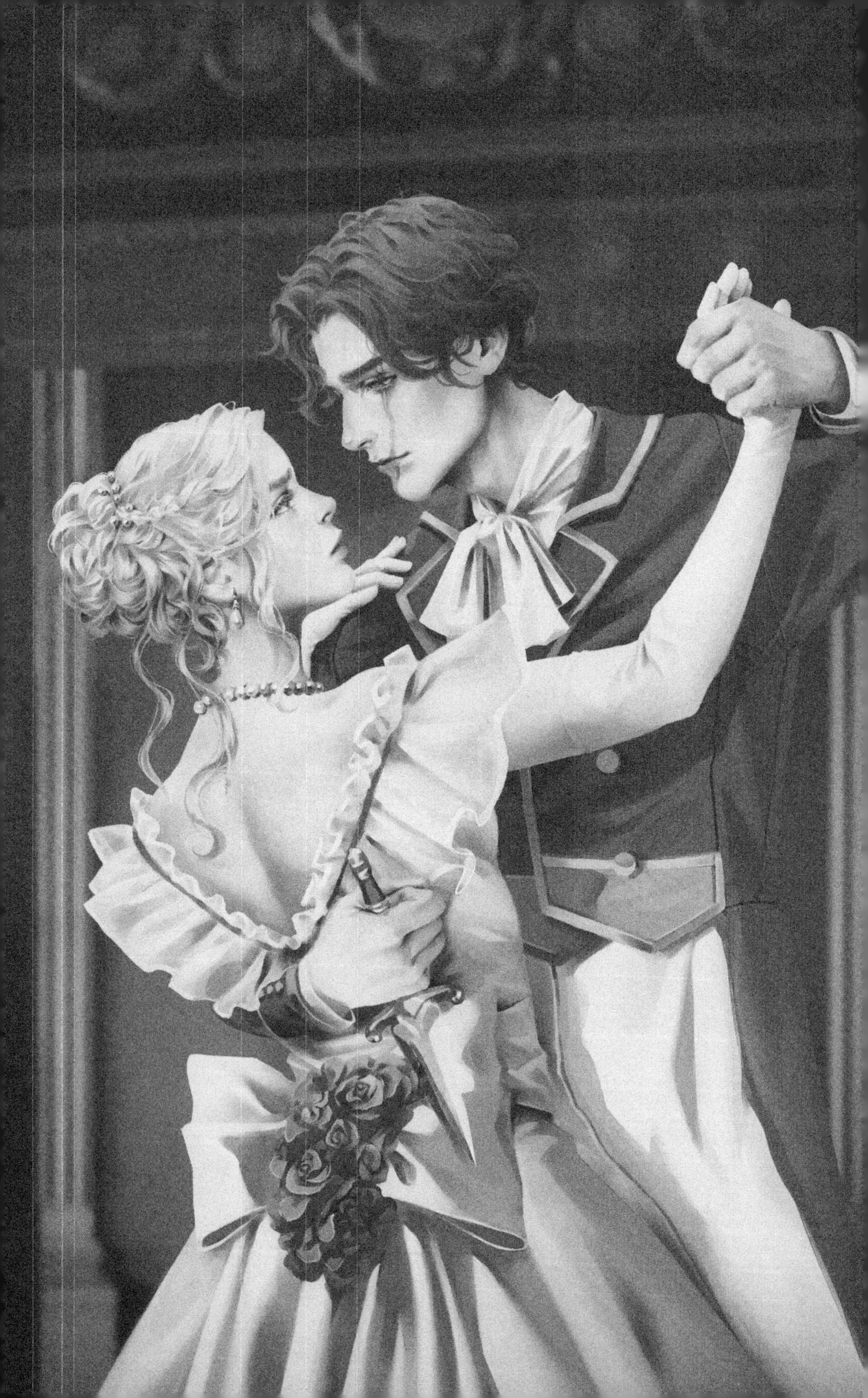

Chapter One

As Contessa prepared for her wedding, there were no tittering bridesmaids to remark on the fashion of her gown or to gossip about what eligible bachelors they might dance with at the celebration. There was only her maid, Ada, solemnly buttoning up her gown. Despite the decadent lace dripping off the wide sleeves of her dress, Contessa couldn't escape the feeling that she was a knight donning armor for battle as Ada tightened her corset.

Ada drew Contessa from her imaginings as she began pinning the veil to the crown of her head, the ivory of the lace only a few shades lighter than her silvery blonde hair. It was the same veil her mother had worn on her wedding day, and Contessa couldn't help but feel comforted by the thought of her. After all, if it weren't for her, Contessa wouldn't be getting married today at all. Ada lowered the blusher over her face like a knight's visor before combat. She was ready.

Contessa emerged from her room to find her father waiting on the landing. As soon as she stepped out the door, his gaze darted over her form, taking in every detail as if he were cataloguing evidence for a police report.

"Yes, you'll do nicely. Every bit the beautiful bride that rabid dog bargained for." Her father's tone was clipped and business-like, as usual, even in his approval of her. After all, this wedding was the first step in a plan that was as much his as hers.

Her father turned on his heel and marched towards the front door. Once Contessa picked up her hem and maneuvered her skirts down the stairs as well, they made their way to the carriage that waited for them on the cobblestoned street.

The ride to the church was blessedly short. Only the harsh clop of hooves on the cobbles and the clatter of wheels broke the silence in the carriage. Contessa pushed back the curtain in the window to peer out into the gray city streets of London. People paused to watch the carriage pass, knowing it belonged to the chief of the Royal Police from the crest on the side. The closest bystanders smiled and waved at Contessa as they wove their way from the upper city towards the spires of the palace and the church at the top of the hill. As Contessa looked longer, though, she noticed people peering from darkened doorways and curtained windows, their faces shadowed with fear.

It seemed that the respect commanded by Chief Cook was laced with a healthy dose of apprehension. The number of Cursed—or Talented as they had once been called—he had sent to the gallows in the Inquiries kept the city safe, even as it frightened many. And the fear burdening the people of London was only made heavier by the growing rumors of the King's illness.

Only when the carriage jerked to a halt in front of the church did Contessa's father speak.

"This is the last moment we have to talk openly. From here on, you must appear to be the perfect and demure wife. You cannot expose your true motivation in marrying Mr. Woodrow to anybody, or you risk your safety."

Contessa nodded, already having heard this information a dozen times but unwilling to interrupt her father to tell him so.

"We're lucky to have this opportunity to get you so close to Mr. Woodrow. We can't afford to squander it. It's incredibly fortunate that he took a liking to the way you looked and was rash enough to want to marry you despite you being my daughter." Her father's hard gray eyes softened fractionally as he continued. "It's no wonder, though, with you looking so much like your mother. She always was so beautiful. I'm glad you take after her. Remember, we're doing this for her, Connie."

At his words, steel snaked its way into Contessa's spine. The use of her mother's nickname for her brought back memories of smile lines and gentle lullabies—brighter times, before her father had become consumed with his work in the Inquiries. No matter what lay ahead, she could be strong if she remembered her mother's laughter, her light.

"We're doing this for her," Contessa echoed.

Her father smiled tightly. "She would be so proud of you."

Together, they stepped out of the coach and made their way into the church. Organ music swelled within as they pushed open the double doors to the Sanctuary. At the end of the aisle, she could just make out the horrifically scarred face of her groom, but it wasn't his disfigurement that imbued icy hatred into Contessa's veins.

Waiting for her at the end of the aisle was the man who had murdered her mother.

For a wedding with so much riding on it, the ceremony was unremarkable. Contessa kept her eyes fixed on the golden buttons of her groom's waistcoat as the priest's words washed over her like the droning of mosquitos. She almost snorted when she found the gilded buttons were emblazoned with a rearing lion. Her groom mocked the authorities desperate to arrest him by paying homage to the name people called him in fearful whispers on the street.

It was said that, when he was young, he'd challenged the former leader of the Lion gang to a fight. The man had pinned Nathanial down and tried to claw his eye out, but Nathanial had bitten his finger clean off. It was the fight that left him with the name everybody in London called him in hushed tones: the Beast.

The priest reached the end of his lengthy homily and moved on to the vows. Contessa was pleased her voice didn't waver when she said, "I do," although it did come out stony. Her father stiffened infinitesimally.

To Contessa's surprise, her groom's vow came out equally cold. She had expected enthusiasm from the man who had suggested the marriage to begin with. After all, he'd approached her father to ask for her hand after only laying eyes on her once—without even speaking to her. Surely, he was pleased to wed such a lovely bride if he had been willing to have the Chief of the Royal Police for a father-in-law just to have her. Maybe Contessa's bitterness had put him off.

Contessa didn't have any more time to ponder Mr. Woodrow's motivations as the ceremony moved to the exchanging of rings. She succeeded in not flinching as he took her left hand in his to slide a simple gold band onto her finger. Mr. Woodrow withdrew his touch quickly, but not before she spotted a myriad of scars crisscrossing his knuckles. She'd spent so much time concerned with his disfigured face, she hadn't considered the possibility that he was similarly marked elsewhere.

With the rings exchanged, the only part of the ceremony left was the moment Contessa had been dreading the most. The guests applauded, but the sound rang hollow in the vastness of the sanctuary, echoing sparsely among the rafters.

Mr. Woodrow lifted the veil from Contessa's face, and she found she could no longer get away with fixing her gaze on his buttons. She steeled herself and lifted her eyes to see the face of her husband up close for the first time.

Contessa understood why people called him the Beast. His legendary scar overtook most of his face, a gnarled rope of tissue running from the left side of his chin to the right side of his forehead and into the edges of his shaggy auburn hair. It pulled up the right side of his lips to create a permanent snarl and bisected his right eye so it squinted until its hardened hazel was barely visible.

Contessa was so taken off guard by the expression in his good eye that she'd forgotten why she was looking at his face so closely until he leaned in. As much as Contessa had known the kiss was coming, the feeling that washed over her at the sensation of his mouth on hers caught her by surprise. She was used to her anger for her mother's murderer freezing the blood in her veins. Now she felt unbearably hot, fire taking the place of jagged ice at the base of her spine. Perhaps her rage demanded action instead of steely resolve as she stood so close to the object of her hatred.

The roughness of his scar scraped her lips, and the warmth of his breath brushed her face. Then it was over as quickly as it began, the kiss leaving only a simmering warmth in its wake. Contessa felt rooted to the spot until the Beast took her hand to lead her down the aisle to the celebrations and the night beyond.

The wedding meal wasn't as dreary as it could have been, given the general solemnity of the rest of the day. White roses bedecked the ballroom, and flickering candlelight lent a surreal look to the room. Lilacs peaked through the windows, blooming on the bushes in the adjacent park. Contessa had to admit it was a lovely venue, if not as grand as the palace ballroom would have been. Her father made no secret of his resentment for not being able to host the celebration in one of the London palace's smaller ballrooms, as he would have before he lost his position as the King's personal bodyguard. However, Contessa preferred the less ostentatious location.

Contessa endeavored to enjoy a piece of cake, but she was constantly aware of the man at her side, the same way she would be aware of a sharp pebble that had worked its way into her boot.

The Beast sat up perfectly straight, hands fisted on the table. Contessa found herself staring at the untouched piece of cake in front of him. His lack of celebratory mood perplexed her. Perhaps the realities of having the chief of the Royal Police as a father-in-law were setting in. There were a lot of officers in the room after all.

The Beast's uneaten dessert was cleared, and his chair scraped harshly against the wooden floor as he stood. A scarred hand appeared in her line of vision and Contessa realized she was going to have to take it to participate in their first dance. She took her time folding her napkin before placing her hand in his much larger one. Rough calluses rubbed against her palm as he led her onto the dance floor.

The orchestra began to play a waltz, and the Beast placed his other hand on her waist. The warmth of his skin seeping through her dress was at odds with the shiver that ran up her spine. Contessa managed not to recoil from his touch and placed her own hand on his shoulder. Once again, she found herself inspecting the buttons of the Beast's waistcoat, noticing how they strained across his powerful chest when he lifted his arms.

As they began to move to the music, something became clear: both Contessa and the Beast were horrendous dancers. Contessa had never spent the time mastering dance beyond the basics, avoiding balls to convince her father she wasn't as girlish and silly as her peers. If Contessa had hoped the Beast was skilled enough at leading to disguise her incompetence, she was in for a disappointment. Within the first few bars, he had stepped on her toes twice, which was quite a feat considering the width of her skirts. Although Contessa hadn't given it much thought before, it occurred to her that being the secret ruler of the most feared gang in London didn't leave one with time for dancing.

The only good thing to be said for the waltz was that it was blessedly short. Contessa found herself whisked into the arms of her father for a stiff, but thankfully, more elegant dance. It wasn't long before she found herself tossed around between distant relatives and high-ranking members of the Royal Police. They all wished her well until she found herself in a set of arms she felt more comfortable in than the rest.

"Joey," Contessa sighed, relaxing for the first time in hours, "Thank goodness."

He succeeded in turning her around the floor without stepping on her toes. He was used to her poor dance skills and had adjusted after many gavottes that left him limping. "I'm glad I finally stole you away. It was much harder than it should have been for your father's protege to get a turn. I must say, I had hoped attending the wedding of a friend who might as well be my sister would be emotional in the joyous way, instead of anxiety inducing."

Contessa tried to scowl at his indiscretion but found she was too glad to see a friendly face to commit to the expression.

"It's very kind of you to wish me well," Contessa responded politely as they passed a distant relative from the country who was staring at them.

"Wish you good luck is more like it," Joseph responded, seemingly oblivious to the danger Contessa would be in if their plot was discovered. "Hopefully, you can find the evidence we need and be a sympathetic young widow within a month."

Contessa squirmed at the casual mention of a man's death, even if he was a murderer. "You make this sound as easy as a walk in the park."

"It will be easy for you," Joseph encouraged. "Nobody expects girls as pretty as you to be capable of treachery. You look too angelic to be plotting. That's what I thought before you beat me at chess ten times in a row."

Contessa furrowed her brow. "Historically, aren't the beautiful women the dangerous ones? Using their feminine wiles to bring down powerful men?"

"You read too much," Joseph scolded with no real disapproval. After all, he was the one that lent her novels to supplement the vast tomes of history and politics kept in her father's library.

Contessa opened her mouth to retort that she hadn't had as much time to read as she would have liked recently, but Joseph jumped in before she could speak. He leaned in close to whisper in her ear, "Please come home soon. I don't want defeating an enemy to come at the cost of losing a friend."

Contessa swallowed. Having to stay away from Joseph meant losing the only confidante she had. As her father's protégé, though, Contessa doubted the Beast would take too kindly to him.

"Just think, seeing me less means losing at chess less often." Contessa tried for levity, but it fell flat.

The music ended, forcing them to step apart. Contessa tried to draw strength from the encouraging smile Joseph gave her, but it was ruined by the telltale creases between his brows as he sketched a polite bow. Be careful, he mouthed before turning to weave his way back through the guests. His dark head retreated, leaving Contessa to feel alone in the crowded ballroom.

She was jolted out of her reverie by a tug on the full sleeve of her gown. She startled to find her new husband at her elbow. His gaze followed where hers had been, and her heart froze at the thought that he may have overheard their conversation. It resumed beating when she saw his expression was not angry but merely pensive. His disfigurement made it hard to be sure, though.

"The festivities are winding down. You should distribute your flowers to your friends before we leave."

This was the first time she'd heard his voice besides when he'd said, "I do," and she'd been too busy inspecting his buttons at that moment to pay attention. It wasn't what she anticipated. She'd thought somebody of his appearance and reputation would have a coarse, grating voice, evocative of the monster she knew him to be. Instead, he had a smooth tenor, sounding much younger than she had expected. She didn't know how old he was. Before this moment, she hadn't even thought to ask.

Finding the Beast still staring at her, she looked down at the bouquet in his outstretched hand.

"Oh, well," she hedged. "I don't have any bridesmaids to give flowers to. I have some cousins here, but I don't know any of them well."

The Beast's face twisted into an expression she couldn't identify on his unorthodox features, but it smoothed itself out again just as fast.

"Good. I never did like the tradition anyways."

He took her elbow to guide her through the crowds of well-wishers to the exit. Contessa's attention narrowed to the point where his fingers touched her arm, an electrifying feeling making her freeze before she remembered she was supposed to be walking. As she allowed herself to be led through the grand room, the cake she had eaten turned to lead in her stomach. She'd been so distracted by surviving the festivities that she'd managed to keep her mind off what came after the celebration. Now, though, the heat of her husband's hand seeping through the sleeve of her dress was an inescapable reminder that she would no longer be able to keep him at arm's length. By the time she stepped up into the Beast's carriage,

Contessa was beginning to think her wedding cake might make a reappearance based on the churning in her gut.

The coach she arranged her skirts in was a good degree smaller than her father's carriage, although the benches and curtains were luxurious in their upholstery. Contessa found her voluminous dress dominated the confined space. She wasn't even sure the Beast would fit. He stepped up into the coach after her and managed to wedge himself onto the bench across from her. In the enclosed space, his frame looked wider and more hulking, and Contessa found herself shrinking back against her seat. In the darkness of the evening, the shadows cast by the ridges of his scar were even more pronounced on his face.

Contessa clenched her jaw and looked the Beast full in the face. If this plan was going to work, he was going to have to believe her a willing participant in their marriage. The only nerves she could show were those expected of any young woman on her wedding night.

To Contessa's surprise, the Beast looked away first, cramming his considerable bulk into the far corner of the coach so his coattails didn't so much as brush the ruffles of her dress. As the carriage lurched into motion, he pulled back the curtain on the window to peer out into the night. Contessa settled for staring at her hands where they rested in her lap, rearranging them into a more relaxed position when she found them gripping her skirts with white knuckles. Only the clatter of wheels broke the silence. It seemed as though she was not going to have a conversation with the man before she shared his bed. His physical presence seemed to make the space grow warmer, causing sweat to prickle the skin at the nape of Contessa's neck.

She tried to convince herself it was a blessing he didn't expect her to speak, for it would be difficult to hide her disdain. It should be a consolation that she didn't have to converse with the criminal who had murdered her mother. Still, she found it impossible to stay silent.

"It was a lovely party."

The Beast's head snapped around, and he fixed her with an incomprehensible look. "Do you generally enjoy parties?"

"No," she admitted, caught off guard by his question.

There was a long pause while he considered her answer. Contessa resisted the urge to return to the study of her fingernails.

"Neither do I," he said flatly, before turning back to watch the passing street.

Contessa followed his gaze to find the manicured green of the park had given way to the elegant rows of houses in the wealthier districts of London. She knew the Beast's home was in the upper city, although not as close to the palace as her father's. The Royal Police were very familiar with his residence, given that her father had men watching it night and day. Despite his efforts, the Royal Police had been unable to find evidence confirming Nathanial Woodrow's identity as the leader of the notorious street gang, the Lions. Still, the entire city whispered he was the Beast, cutthroat gang leader and ruthless murderer. The only reason nobody could prosecute him was that nobody who saw him left the scene alive. Instead, he left a trail of corpses with three slashes cut across their face—the calling card of the Lions.

The carriage trundled to a stop. Contessa was surprised to find herself looking at a house featuring a cheery blue front door and a row of neatly trimmed hydrangea bushes out front. She chided herself for her disbelief. The Beast wouldn't keep the heads of his enemies on pikes or have a dozen thugs armed with crowbars waiting outside his front door. That was why he hadn't been caught. His facade was so immaculate that nobody could pin down any proof of his crimes. Contessa was walking into the lion's den to find the evidence everybody else had failed to get.

She just hadn't expected the lion's den to have a front door the color of a clear sky.

Contessa followed the Beast out of the carriage and trailed him up to the front door. Before he could even reach for the knob, the door sprang open to reveal a woman in a neat gray dress and white cap. She looked to be a few years younger than Contessa and was currently bouncing on her toes, trying to look over the Beast's shoulder.

"Welcome home, sir," the woman offered. She stepped aside to let him in, although her gaze remained fixed on Contessa behind him.

The Beast ignored her behavior, stepping inside and immediately shrugging off his coat. Contessa followed after him.

"Take her to the rose room and see to it she is prepared for bed," was the Beast's only greeting before he stomped off into the house, tossing his coat over the back of a chaise lounge as he passed.

The maid didn't seem concerned by her employer's behavior, her attention already on Contessa. She appeared to be quivering in excitement, her curls bouncing where they spilled from her cap and onto her round face.

"Oh, aren't you lovely! No wonder Mr. Woodrow was in such a rush to marry you," she exclaimed, looking Contessa up and down. "Oh, and you still have your flowers! Let me take those so we can get you a vase of water. They'll be a nice touch to add to your room. Liven the place up a little bit."

Contessa numbly handed her bouquet off to the girl, surprised by her bubbly demeanor. Meanwhile, the maid was practically skipping up the stairs, keeping up an impressive stream of chatter as she went, commenting on everything from the fashion of Contessa's dress to the weather. She acted oblivious to the fact she was working for a monster who was currently prowling through the downstairs, waiting to devour Contessa.

As Contessa followed the maid, she took the opportunity to examine her new personal prison. While the outside of the home had been welcoming, the inside of the house was sparse. All the furniture was good quality, but none of it drew the eye. A few generic landscapes decorated the vast walls, but there were no signs of the homeowner's tastes or preferences. It lent the place a sense that it was simply inhabited and not really lived in.

As they reached the top of the stairs, the women turned to the left down a darkened hallway until the maid pushed open a door.

"This will be you room, Mrs. Woodrow."

Contessa startled at the use of her new name but schooled her features quickly. "Thank you, Miss..."

"Pinsberry," the maid supplied, "but I'd prefer it if you would call me Julia."

Contessa stepped into the room and wrinkled her nose. The entirety of the room was wallpapered in a print of small red roses. The blotches of crimson on a cream background made Contessa think of drops of blood. She shivered.

Julia didn't notice Contessa's displeasure, herding her towards an intricately carved dressing table. Contessa kept herself from looking towards the bed against the other wall, richly hung with thematic crimson drapes.

"We call this room the rose room. Mr. Woodrow suggested this one for you himself."

Contessa exhaled sharply through her nose as Julia began to unpin her hair. Of course, a man who married a woman he had never spoken to would put her in a room that resembled an overgrown garden. It was odd he hadn't brought her to his own room. Although considering the Beast didn't know her at all, maybe he desired to keep his space to himself and keep her elsewhere for his amusement. Contessa took a few moments to even her breathing at the thought.

Julia's ability to chatter endlessly extended through Contessa's nighttime preparations. As she brushed her hair and changed into her nightclothes, Contessa listened, hoping she might start uncovering hints about the Beast and where she might find evidence of his crimes. Contessa was left disappointed, although she found the maid's energy to be infectious. She'd never spent significant time around women her age, and she welcomed the distraction of Julia's company in her current predicament. While the wedding had been nothing more than an act, it was refreshing to hear Julia gush over every detail of her flowers and her dress.

Once Contessa was perched on the edge of the bed, Julia left with a quick curtsy and a friendly, "Goodnight, Mrs. Woodrow."

As the door clicked shut behind Julia, a heavy silence descended in the room. Contessa strained to hear movement in the hallway, but there was no noise except

Julia's receding footsteps. Her earlier tension had returned tenfold now that she was alone, and her fingers gripped the fine fabric of her nightdress until her knuckles blanched. She tried to distract herself from the thundering of her heart by counting the gaudy red flowers on the wallpaper. She couldn't keep herself from listening for heavy footsteps in the hall, though, as she waited to be devoured by the Beast.

Chapter Two

Contessa woke to sunlight streaming through windows covered by scarlet drapes, turning everything in the room an unearthly shade of red. Shivers shook her body as she found herself curled in a tight ball on her side, hugging her knees. She was still lying on top of the coverlet, never having climbed under it the night before.

As her consciousness returned to her, she pushed herself up and looked around in confusion. It took Contessa a moment to register her surroundings, realizing she was not in the bedroom she'd slept in since she was a small girl.

Awareness chased the last vestiges of sleep from her mind, and Contessa jolted to her feet. She couldn't remember the Beast coming to her bedroom last night. She looked down at herself, trying to discern what had happened. She found her nightdress undisturbed, and her hair still neatly plaited over one shoulder, just as Julia had left it. Whipping her head around to double check, she found that she was indeed alone in the bedroom.

Contessa furrowed her brows in confusion before icy terror shot through her veins. Her true intentions must have been found out. That's why the Beast hadn't come to her the night before; he was furious with her deception. Soon, Contessa would find her throat slit at his hands, just as her mother's had been.

She took a step forward, preparing to search the room for something to defend herself with. Something sharp would be best, but a heavy candlestick might do the trick. Contessa wouldn't go down without adding another scar to the Beast's horrific face.

The door to the bedroom sprang open before she could take more than two steps. Contessa's hands flew up in preparation to defend herself, but she let them fall to her sides when it was not the Beast but Julia who traipsed through the door. Her wide smile just peeked over the fluffy magenta bundle in her arms.

"Good morning, Mrs. Woodrow," Julia greeted, giving no sign that anything was amiss. "You're up early! I thought you would want a bit of a lie-in after yesterday's excitement, but apparently not. I thought I heard you get up, and I realized I hadn't shown you how to ring the bell to summon me. I apologize if you've been waiting long."

"Not at all," Contessa responded, keeping her distance for fear this was all some elaborate plot to catch her off guard.

Julia simply approached her and shook out the bundle in her arms. It revealed itself to be a gown, which the maid laid across the covers of the bed. Contessa grimaced as the magenta clashed violently with the red coverlet.

"Mr. Woodrow ordered a set of dresses for you as a wedding present, but this is the only one that's arrived so far," Julia explained as she set to work getting Contessa out of her nightdress. "He has no sense of fashion, so he told the dressmaker to outfit you in whatever the most popular styles are. The color is so lovely. It'll be gorgeous with that pale hair of yours."

By the time Contessa was laced into the fuchsia monstrosity, she was forced to disagree with her maid. While the general shape of the dress was flattering, that was the only positive feature Contessa could find. The ribbons and bows and ruffles made Contessa think of last night's wedding cake. She prayed the rest of the dresses would show a touch more restraint.

Contessa schooled the distaste from her face as Julia wove a matching ribbon through her hair. The maid seemed to be enjoying styling Contessa so much, she didn't have the heart to ruin her fun.

"Oh my, you're so lovely," Julia tittered. "I've never gotten to dress a lady as beautiful and stylish as you. Not that I've dressed many ladies at all before. I mostly just learned how to style hair by practicing on all my friends."

"You're quite good at it," Contessa praised her honestly, twisting her head to get a better look at the maid's handiwork. While the color of the ribbon wasn't Contessa's favorite, she had to admit the way her hair was piled on top of her head made her neck appear impossibly long. A few choice ringlets framed Contessa's heart-shaped face, accentuating her gray eyes, the only physical feature she'd inherited from her father.

"Oh, thank you." Julia bounced on her toes. "I've always wanted to be a lady's maid. I was so worried I wouldn't be any good at it."

"How did you come to be working as my lady's maid then?"

"Oh well, I was working for a friend of Mr. Woodrow's." Julia twisted her apron between her fingers. "When it became clear that Mr. Woodrow would need a maid for you, his friend mentioned my interest. Put in a good word for me, as it were."

"So, you were a maid for a friend of Mr. Woodrow's?"

"Something like that," Julia responded, looking down at her feet.

Contessa's eyes narrowed as she scrutinized her maid in the mirror. The woman's nervousness betrayed that there was more to the story than a simple reference. Perhaps there was a link to her employer's illicit activities. Still, it seemed cruel to interrogate the maid when her involvement was likely minimal and possibly involuntary. Contessa would use Julia as a last resort for collecting evidence.

"That was very kind of your former employer," Contessa settled on as a response.

Julia nodded and changed the subject. "Well now that you're all dressed, I'm sure that you're absolutely famished. Let me show you down to the dining room for some breakfast, Mrs. Woodrow."

Contessa let the subject drop and followed the girl downstairs into the living areas of the house. As Julia directed Contessa into the dining room, she glanced around for the Beast, but he was nowhere to be found. Instead, a sandy-haired man about her own age entered the room and pulled out a chair.

"Good morning, Mrs. Woodrow," he said, indicating she should take a seat.

Contessa slid into the proffered chair. "Thank you, and who might you be?"

"Mr. Topps at your service, but you may call me Gregor," the man offered, picking up the teapot.

Contessa was surprised that both servants preferred to be called by their first name, but she supposed that when you murdered people for a living, you didn't have to stand on ceremony with your household staff.

"Will Mr. Woodrow be joining us?" Contessa ventured.

"Oh no, he left early this morning," Gregor commented, as if this wasn't out of the ordinary as he served her breakfast.

"I see." Once her plate was filled, Gregor stepped back and asked, "Will that be all, Mrs. Woodrow?"

Contessa dismissed both him and Julia but didn't start eating. Her stomach tangled into knots, and she didn't feel putting food in it would help the situation. Why had the Beast gone to all the trouble to marry her, then not joined her in bed the night before? Now he was completely absent. If he was regretting his decision, it was going to make her mission to discover the truth of his crimes more difficult. If he wouldn't even speak to her, gaining his trust was out of the question.

Maybe it had nothing to do with her at all. Maybe some matter of business had come up. Surely that was it. She would be able to winnow his secrets out of him as soon as he handled whatever matter had stolen his attention.

Contessa began picking at the food in front of her. If she were to make any good of this situation, it wouldn't do to have her fainting in the middle of the day. She didn't know who the cook was, but the meal was excellent. Even the bacon was perfectly chewy, just how she liked it. Before she knew it, Contessa had cleared her plate.

Neither Gregor nor Julia reappeared to clear the table, so she made her way out of the dining room. There was still no sign of anybody else. It wouldn't hurt to have a look around, especially if the Beast wasn't there. Perhaps she could find some piece of evidence and bring the man to justice without even speaking to him.

Contessa set off through the living room, poking at cushions and pulling open drawers. It wasn't as if she expected a bloody murder weapon to tumble out from a hidden compartment, but Contessa still found them shockingly empty. The drawers were devoid of any personal effects, not even a matchbook to be found lying about.

She moved through the drawing room and the parlor with similar findings. In fact, the cushions on the sofas and chairs were so smooth, it looked as if they had never been sat on. The only significant thing Contessa was able to discern was that whoever decorated the house was fond of flowers. In every room she passed, she spotted multiple vases of fresh flowers, all blooming so beautifully that it must have cost a fortune. It seemed odd in a house that barely appeared inhabited otherwise.

When Contessa reached the hallway in the back of the house, she was greeted by a dark wooden door. She hadn't found an office yet, and of all the rooms she might investigate, it seemed an office was the most likely to contain useful evidence. Maybe some records of his underhanded business dealings or letters from accomplices. After all, the Beast had accumulated wealth so rapidly that it set off the initial rumors of his criminal activity. Gossip claimed that nobody could be that fortunate with investments without having meddled. Still, no one managed to find anything incriminating. He had never even been seen entering a gambling hall, which, while legal, tended to be crawling with gangsters with unnaturally good luck.

Contessa strode towards the closed door, hoping to finally confirm the years of rumors. Her heart sank when she found it locked. Of course it was locked. The Beast didn't trust her enough to leave her alone with all his potential evidence, and he was right not to.

Somebody cleared their throat behind her. She whirled around so quickly she nearly tripped on her ridiculous skirts and toppled over. After correcting her balance, she looked up to find Gregor staring at her and wearing a bemused expression.

"May I help you find something, Mrs. Woodrow?" he asked, his tone polite but still managing to convey that he didn't approve of her walking around trying random doors.

"I just thought I'd explore my new home a bit. Get to know the place a bit better." Contessa stepped away from the locked door.

"Well, is there anything I can get you to entertain you for the afternoon?" Gregor offered, once again implying there were more suitable activities for her than poking around in his employer's belongings.

"I do like to read."

"I could show you to the library," Gregor suggested, although he looked amused for reasons Contessa couldn't puzzle out.

When he led her through a door at the top of the stairs, the reason for Gregor's earlier amusement became clear. While the room obviously was a library, for the walls were lined with bookshelves and there were several comfortable looking chairs scattered about, it was not filled with books. Instead, the shelves lay barren. Contessa got the impression that if she were to run her fingers across them, they would come away caked with dust.

She caught Gregor's eye and he smiled sheepishly, his honey brown eyes sympathetic.

"Mr. Woodrow hasn't gotten around to stocking the library. He's a busy man," Gregor offered.

Contessa took the opportunity to pry. "It would seem so. What business did he have that was urgent enough to call him away the day after his wedding?"

"I wouldn't know." Gregor pointedly avoided Contessa's narrowed gaze. "But I'm sure he wouldn't mind if you took the liberty of acquiring some books."

"That would be nice," Contessa lied. She didn't intend to be around long enough to build him a worthy collection. "Do you have a newspaper I could read in the meantime?"

Reading the paper was a practical habit her father had instilled in her as soon as she could read. Contessa didn't intend to let it go by the wayside because of her current predicament.

Gregor fetched her the paper and suggested she might like to read it in the garden. Contessa agreed, hoping the sight of the open sky might make her feel less like an exotic bird in a cage.

As Contessa stepped out of the back door and into the hazy city sunshine, she found the gardens might as well have been in a different world than the interior of the house. Where the inside had seemed completely devoid of life, here it overflowed. Plants bloomed everywhere. Full hedges lined a brick path to a trickling fountain in the middle of the courtyard, and flowering vines adorned the wrought iron fence surrounding the small lawn. Rose bushes of every variety filled the beds, and there were even some flowers which Contessa had never seen outside of a greenhouse.

It struck Contessa how different this was from the garden outside her own home. Where that garden had been neatly trimmed until the hedges took on unnatural shapes, this garden was bordering on overgrown in a way that made it seem anything but neglected. It was a perfect sanctuary from the austerity of the house.

Contessa settled herself on the edge of the fountain, fanning her skirts around her to sit more comfortably. She turned to the newspaper and opened it on her lap, frowning immediately.

The headline announced a set of public executions that would take place within the week. The Inquiries had uncovered three more Cursed wreaking havoc in the streets. Apparently, one of the offenders was capable of conversing with birds and was using it to spy on and blackmail officials for the Scorpions, another one of the street gangs. Contessa felt a mixed bolt of concern and pride upon reading that Joseph had been responsible for his arrest. Another Cursed could summon bright lights that could blind an opponent in combat, and a third was accused of using her ability to murder her husband.

Contessa shifted in her seat, dreading another set of executions. She hated magic as much as anybody else, but she never enjoyed watching the hangings. The fearful eyes and twitching legs of the sentenced always made Contessa want to look away. She never did, though. She could hear her father's voice in her head telling her the hangings were a show of strength—that they made London safer. They ensured there would never be another assassination attempt like the one that killed King Royce, the current King's father. It hadn't been the first time the Talented, as they had been referred to then, had threatened the monarchy, either, with a group supposedly responsible for the end of the Stuart line with the murder of Queen Anne. The resulting chaos had nearly torn England apart before the Royce family managed to reunite the country under the crown once more.

As Contessa flipped through the rest of the paper, her sympathy for the accused lessened further. The Scorpions had burned down a house in the middle city, the owner and his wife locked inside as the flames burned an unnatural shade of blue. Two nights ago, a family had been found dead in their home, turned to stone by another one of the Cursed.

This was why the Inquiries had to continue. The gangs were full to bursting with Talented who used their powers for fear and destruction. Her father was right—they must be stopped and brought to justice.

Chief Cook made it his life's work to stop the Cursed's reign of terror, working tirelessly since the assassination of King Royce. He had been King Royce's bodyguard, standing watch outside his bedroom as one of the Cursed used their power of invisibility and slit the King's throat in the night. It had lost her father his reputation, his status, his job, forcing him to be demoted into the Royal Police. In his new position, he led the Inquiries with unmatched fervor, to root out and destroy the Cursed—to make sure nobody else had all their hard work destroyed by a perversion of nature.

When one particular gang had come knocking for revenge, and Contessa's mother had paid the price, Chief Cook had thrown himself into his work with even more vigor. That was why Contessa had attended every execution in the last five years, and why she was sitting here in the home of the most notorious gang leader of them all.

By the time Contessa finished the newspaper, the sun in the sky was no longer sufficient to thaw the ice in her veins. The descriptions of the atrocities committed by the gangs had renewed her purpose. She would stop this monster, and she would avenge her mother.

Still, she would have to keep her wits about her if she was to succeed. Contessa took a few fortifying breaths and looked around the garden to calm her pounding heart. It still seemed so odd that the Beast would have a sanctuary this lovely, especially when the rest of his home was so bleak.

That night, Contessa mentioned her observations about the garden to Julia.

"The garden is all Gregor," Julia responded, brushing Contessa's hair until it fell in pale ripples past her shoulder blades. "Mr. Woodrow doesn't spend much time thinking about the house, but he's given run on the landscaping to Gregor. He loves all things gardening. I do wish somebody would liven up the inside of the house, though. Maybe you could help."

Contessa met the maid's eyes in the mirror over her shoulder and softened at her optimism. "I doubt Mr. Woodrow would appreciate me interfering in his home. He seems like a…volatile man."

"I don't think he'd even notice much if you spruced the place up. He spends most of his time either out of the house or locked up in his office in the back."

Contessa stayed quiet, hoping Julia might give her a hint of how to gain entry to the office, but she was disappointed.

"I'm sure you know best, though, Mrs. Woodrow, being so sharp and classy," Julia said, tying off the plait she'd woven Contessa's hair into for bed.

As Contessa perched herself on the edge of the bed once more, Julia curtsied and left the room with a cheerful goodnight. Though the Beast had been called away the evening before, Contessa was convinced he would pay her bed a visit sooner rather than later. Why else would he marry her and dress her up like a ridiculous paper doll if not to take advantage of her appearance? Again, Contessa listened for footsteps in the hall until her eyes drifted closed of their own accord.

Chapter Three

The next three days in the Beast's house passed similarly to the first. Contessa woke and was dressed by Julia. Each morning her dress was more horrendous than the last, but Contessa found herself thankful none of them were the same magenta as the first. Still, the third dress was a canary yellow that did nothing positive for her complexion and only served to make her look mildly jaundiced.

It turned out not to matter how sallow Contessa's clothes made her look because she saw nobody but Julia and Gregor. She was beginning to think she'd dreamed up the Beast's existence entirely as she sat out in the back garden and read the paper. She was reassured of her purpose in the den of her enemy, though, when she read about a series of raids at the harbor by the Lions. Gang members had burned three ships and left several police officers dead in the harbor with three slashes cut across their faces. Contessa let out a sigh of relief when she skimmed the names of the dead and found none that she recognized.

What was odd about the raids was that the police couldn't identify what the target of the attack had been. The gang had crept in and caused a large amount of chaos, then left just as quickly without having stolen anything. It was peculiar, but then again, that was the way with the Cursed. They used their power to cause pain and spread fear, while decent folk were just trying to live their lives.

The raid on the docks must have been why her new husband had been absent. It seemed violence and death were more important to him than getting to know his new bride. Contessa couldn't say she was surprised. Although, she wasn't sure if she was relieved he had been missing or disappointed she hadn't been able to make more progress on her mission.

Every day she went through her same routine of searching the house for clues, and every day, she came up just as empty-handed as the last. She tried the dark wooden door at the back of the house, and each day she was less surprised to find it locked. It felt like the door stood between more than her and an office. It stood as a barrier between her and her way home. It stood between her and revenge.

At night, Contessa sat up for as long as she could, spine rigid and ears pricked for footsteps outside her door. Dread kept her alert late into the night, and each morning, she woke up both relieved and concerned that she would never get her chance to earn her target's trust.

On the fourth day, the routine changed jarringly. Contessa walked into the dining room and nearly crashed face-first into the table. Sitting in the seat opposite hers was the Beast himself, tearing into a piece of buttered toast as if it had personally offended him. His deformity pulled at his mouth in such a way that made him chew with his mouth partially open, and he sprayed crumbs across his plate as he ate.

Contessa looked on in horror for the briefest moment before she remembered her role and composed herself.

"Good morning," she greeted him in what she hoped was a polite but not forcibly cheery tone.

The Beast jumped as if he too hadn't been expecting a companion, and his hand sprang to his belt. Finding no weapon there, it came back to rest on the table in a fist as he responded with a "Good morning" of his own. He turned back to his toast without even making eye contact.

Contessa must have displeased him at the wedding if he couldn't even look at her. Perhaps he had been intoxicated when he had asked her father for her hand in marriage. But then it wouldn't make sense that he had gone through with it. He certainly didn't seem the type of man to have a strict sense of honor. No, his displeasure must stem from something Contessa herself had done. Maybe she wasn't as beautiful as he had first thought, or perhaps she hadn't been guarded enough with her hostility towards him.

Now Contessa did her best to school her expression into the vacant but pleased look so many men seemed to favor. She also made a note to try to acquire clothing in more flattering shades. Her father would hate Contessa fussing over her appearance, and it twisted something in her gut to make herself try to appear vapid and suggestable. She reminded herself it was all a means to an end.

Still, as she served herself porridge, her efforts seemed to be in vain. The Beast continued to keep his eyes firmly fixed on his plate. With an internal sigh, she dug in and hoped the conversation would improve.

"You don't take any honey or milk on your porridge?"

Contessa jumped for the second time that morning and glanced up. Her husband still wasn't looking at her face, but his eyes were firmly fixed on her spoon. She supposed it was an improvement.

"I've always eaten it plain. I never really considered trying it any other way," Contessa replied.

The Beast made a noncommittal noise and turned his face back to his plate, although his mangled brow was now wrinkled like he was trying to solve a complicated puzzle. Contessa concluded he had earned his nickname not only from his appearance, but from his unappealing manners.

He didn't speak again until Contessa laid down her spoon across her empty bowl. Then he motioned to Gregor, who Contessa hadn't noticed was stationed somewhere off her shoulder, and asked him to bring around the carriage.

"Where are we going, Mr. Woodrow?" Contessa asked once Gregor had left, pleased her voice continued to sound friendly.

"The executions."

"The executions?" Contessa failed to hide the distaste from her voice. She'd hoped she wouldn't have to attend considering she wasn't currently under her father's roof, but she was mistaken.

"Yes. You would have read about them in the papers." The Beast's tone made it clear that there was no doubt in his mind she'd been reading the news. Even if he hadn't been home, he wasn't ignorant of Contessa's activities.

Of course, a murderer would want to watch his competitors' demise. Contessa wasn't sure why her attendance was expected, but she decided not to ask. After all, this was her first opportunity to observe the man since their wedding.

Contessa simply nodded and braced herself for the day.

If Contessa hadn't been to any executions before, she would have thought she would stand out in the crowd wearing a garish shade of purple at such a somber occasion. However, as usual, the crowd was clad in all manner of bright colors, and even her hat bedecked with feathers didn't seem out of the ordinary for the occasion.

The crowd bristled excitedly, and loud chatter filled the square surrounding the gallows. Contessa avoided looking at the stark wooden platform in the center of the courtyard, looming over the crowd in judgement.

Public executions had gone out of fashion, having been seen as barbaric. But after the last king was assassinated by a Cursed, there had been public outcry. The masses demanded to see justice done, and her father had been at the head of the charge. So, the gallows had been constructed and the Inquiries began.

Contessa scanned the crowd in favor of looking at the wooden platform. A lump formed in her throat as she saw children among those gathered in the square. Her father had brought her to her first execution at the age of seventeen, just after her mother had died, but there were some in the crowd much younger than that.

The Beast stood next to Contessa. He was so still she might have mistaken him for a statue if not for the slight stretch of his waistcoat when he breathed. His presence next to her only served to worsen the churning in her gut.

Trying to ignore her husband's tension, she returned to scanning the crowd. She managed to spot her father standing with the rest of the Royal Police at the front of the square. His salt and pepper hair was parted so meticulously that Contessa was sure his manservant must have used a ruler, and his moustache was polished so it shone in the thin sunlight. He was every inch the Chief dutifully protecting his citizens from the threat of the Talented.

Standing next to her father was Joseph, and Contessa allowed herself to be comforted by the sight of a friendly face. He was currently laughing at something the officer to his right had said, his crooked smile reminding her of sunny days and playing pranks on each other.

Contessa was ripped from her contemplation by the jeering of the crowd as three figures were marched onto the platform. Contessa stayed silent and forced herself to look each of the convicted in the face. While the front of the crowd where Contessa usually stood with her father heckled and mocked the accused, she noticed that more people in the back where she stood now stayed quiet.

The first two figures who stepped onto the gallows were the image of the Cursed everybody had in their minds: burly men wearing fierce scowls and looking like the stuff of children's nightmares. Contessa squinted to see the tattoo on one of their forearms, indicating his membership in the Scorpions.

The third gave Contessa pause. The woman couldn't have been any older than Contessa herself, a slight thing who stumbled up the wooden steps to the gallows. Her trembling was visible even from this distance, and red rimmed the woman's swollen eyes.

As the charges against each of the sentenced were read, the Beast reached up and removed his top hat. Contessa peeked at him out of the corner of her eye, but the Beast's eyes remained fixed on the sentenced. A muscle twitched near his jaw under his warped skin.

Contessa returned her attention to the platform as the executioner stepped forward to fasten the rope around the necks of the sentenced. The woman was still shaking, but she didn't speak or beg. She kept her eyes straight ahead and lifted her chin as the noose was slipped over her head.

Contessa dug her nails into her palms and gritted her teeth as she waited for the executioner to pull the lever that would bring three lives to a sudden end. There was a ringing in her ears that made it difficult to hear the noises of the crowd, but she'd long since trained herself not to look away.

After a moment that seemed to last forever, the executioner pulled the lever, and the three victims dropped to their deaths. The necks of the two gang members snapped immediately with cracks that Contessa could hear over the ringing in her ears. The woman's weight was insufficient to break her neck, and she dangled, jerking sickeningly as the life was choked out of her.

The moment went on for an eternity before Joseph stepped forward, wrapped his arms around the woman's legs, and jerked down decisively. Joseph had confided in Contessa that he hated watching the lighter criminals strangle to death nearly as much as she did. At the sound of the woman's neck snapping, the Beast jerked. His reaction was enough to distract Contessa from the horror of the moment. She wouldn't have expected somebody with so much blood on their hands to flinch at one more death. Still, as she peeked at the face of her husband, she found it was white as a sheet. Even the usually reddened tissue of his scar had turned pale.

Feeling as if she shouldn't be watching his distress for some reason, Contessa looked forward once more to find her father looking directly at her. He began weaving his way through the milling crowd towards her, the sea of people parting to let his distinguished figure through.

"Excuse me for a moment, Mr. Woodrow," Contessa asked, hoping it wouldn't raise too much suspicion for her to have a few words with her father.

The Beast grunted and stayed rooted to the spot, which Contessa took as assent, and she set off through the crowd to meet her father.

As soon as father and daughter reached each other, Chief Cook grabbed Contessa's wrist to pull her close, murmuring in her ear, "Have you made any progress?"

Contessa shook her head infinitesimally, eyes darting about to ensure they weren't being observed. The crowd seemed entirely preoccupied, chatting excitedly about the gruesome executions.

"I've tried, but he doesn't even speak with me. It makes it difficult to gain his trust."

Chief Cook's moustache ruffled as he blew out a disappointed breath. "Surely, I've trained you to be resourceful enough to try other methods. What about looking through his belongings?"

"He keeps everything in his office, which is always locked. I can hardly convince him he doesn't need to if we never converse," Contessa's eyes continued to dart around the crowd as she spoke as quietly as possible.

Chief Cook shook the wrist he was holding, rattling her bones. "Then pick the lock, girl. Those pins in your hair can do more than make you look fashionable, you know."

He was right, but Contessa had hoped to avoid something so risky. Picking locks was time consuming, and the chances she would be caught in the act seemed high. Still, Contessa had all the training of a police detective. Her father had made sure she was prepared for exactly this eventuality. She wouldn't let him down.

"Alright, I'll do it as soon as possible," she promised, and Chief Cook's eyes softened.

"Good. You're doing me so proud, Connie. I'm glad to see you safe and whole." His hand slid from her wrist to her hand, where he gave it a tight squeeze.

Contessa's usual steely resolve returned at his words. After several disheartening days in her new home, her father's encouragement was just what her soul needed. If he believed in her, then she would complete her mission and come back home with her mother avenged.

The moment was broken when Chief Cook pulled his hand from her own, "The devil is looking for you right now, and he's motioning for his carriage. Get back to him before he gets suspicious."

"I won't let you down," Contessa promised before turning and picking her way back through the crowd. Sure enough, her husband stood at the edge of the square where Gregor had just pulled the carriage up. His eyes scanned the crowd for her and caught hers just as she separated herself from the edge of the masses.

Once again, Contessa was surprised by the contrast of their warm hazel to his ravaged features. The intensity of his gaze almost made her trip over her hem, but she matched his stare with the piercing glare she'd learned from her father. He blinked and turned back to the carriage. He climbed in before she reached him, leaving Gregor to help her into the coach.

Once they were settled inside, the coach jerked into motion, bouncing and jostling over the cobbles.

"How was your father?" the Beast asked, fixing her in his gaze once more like a predator sighting his prey.

Ice slid into Contessa's gut, but she didn't back down.

"He is in excellent health. Thank you for asking."

The Beast exhaled sharply through his nose in what might have passed for a sign of amusement.

"I'm sure he is. Today must have been a proud day for the Royal Police." As much as Contessa had been having difficulty reading him, the disdain in his tone was clear.

"Of course, as it is a proud day for us all when murderous gangsters are brought to justice." Her tone was insipidly sweet, like sugar hiding the bitterness of poison.

Contessa had been sure her statement would have stoked his rage, but instead, the Beast blinked as if perplexed and then turned to the window. Silence fell, and Contessa felt unbalanced, despite having landed a verbal blow against the Beast.

She didn't have time to dwell on the hollow victory as the Beast interrupted.

"Stop!" He shouted, banging his fist against the roof. "Stop the carriage, Gregor!"

The sudden halt caused Contessa to nearly tumble off the bench, but she caught herself. Her hands landed on the seat where the Beast had been sitting half a second before, but he had already thrown himself out the door. Contessa took a second to follow him, yanking on her dress as it caught on the steps. By the time her feet hit the ground, the Beast was already darting around the corner of a house into an alley. Contessa ran after him, feet slipping on the cobbles and internally cursing the dainty slippers that came with the dress. She didn't even know why she was chasing the Beast, but there was a buzzing in her head clouding her reason. He had sounded so urgent.

Contessa rounded the corner just in time to see the Beast grabbing a man by the front of his tattered shirt, dragging him away from a lady huddled against the wall and clutching a parasol like a weapon. As the Beast backed the man up, he stuck out a leg behind the thug, making him lose his footing. As the thug slipped, the Beast used the hand twisted in his shirt to bodily lift him and throw him down. His back hit the ground with a painful thud. The noise finally chased the buzzing from Contessa's mind, and she darted over to the woman.

"Are you alright?" Contessa asked, arriving at her elbow.

"I think so," she said shakily. "He was after my purse, but you arrived so fast, I hadn't even screamed..."

Contessa followed the woman's gaze to where the Beast knelt next to the thug, still wheezing for breath after his violent introduction to the ground. The Beast leaned in and whispered something to the man. Contessa couldn't hear what it was, but the effect was immediate. The man blanched and struggled to his feet, stumbling and tripping out of the alley before he had fully stood.

"Thank you, sir!" said the woman at Contessa's elbow.

The Beast stood, brushing off his coat and turning around.

The woman drew breath as if to continue, but the words turned into a choked noise in her throat when she saw his face.

"I—I must be going," the woman stammered, before beating a hasty retreat out of the alley. She walked close to the wall, trying to keep as much distance between her and the Beast as possible, before nearly running around the corner.

The Beast didn't acknowledge her reaction, taking a moment to straighten his cuffs. Contessa stood quietly, watching a rapid transformation of the man in front of her from feral Beast back into the man she'd stood next to at the execution. Picking up his hat from where it had fallen on the ground, he dusted it off before jerking his chin to indicate they should head back to the carriage.

Gregor didn't comment on their short stop, clucking the horse back into motion. Contessa herself couldn't help replaying the moment the Beast had picked up the thug and bodily thrown him to the ground. Remembering the way his muscles had flexed in his back and imagining the strength it would take, Contessa shivered. Her face and chest felt hot at the thought. It must be the fear of knowing she was living with an enemy this dangerous. She'd known it before, but the actual demonstration of the Beast's power caused a much more visceral reaction.

What she didn't understand was why he'd stopped the attacker at all. Perhaps he'd recognized the member from a rival gang and didn't want them stealing the Lion's quarry. How he had even known about the attack was another issue. Perhaps there had been a commotion and Contessa had been too lost in thought to hear it. Contessa shook herself. Whatever the Beast's motivation for stopping that offense, her job here was to find evidence of his own crimes.

Chapter Four

Contessa sat up longer than usual that night, convinced her husband would finally visit her bed. After all, she'd finally seen him today for the first time since their wedding. She knew he was no longer otherwise occupied. Still, the clock ticked on in the silence, and she remained alone in her chambers.

What she'd begun to suspect now became clear in her mind; the Beast didn't intend to bed her at all. Perhaps he had married her simply to torment her father. Not only could the police not pin him down for his crimes, but he could steal away first the Chief's wife and then his daughter.

Contessa slid off the bed and began pacing. While the days were still warm, the night was cool, and the wooden floor chilled her bare feet. Contessa welcomed the cold as it kept her alert and helped her think.

Her hopes of gaining her husband's trust had been thoroughly dashed. It seemed the only choice left to her was force—far from Contessa's preferred method, but she was capable enough.

Making up her mind, she strode to her dressing table and pulled out several hair pins. Then she donned her dressing gown and slipped out her bedroom door, silent as a shadow.

She tiptoed down the hall, listening at every turn for signs of life. This wasn't a task she wanted to undertake if the Beast was awake in any of these rooms, but her ears met only silence.

She crept down the stairs, alert for any signs of life on the lower level. If the house seemed devoid of life during the day, it was positively macabre in the still of the night. The ticking of a grandfather clock echoed loudly through the living space. Long shadows distorted the room until even Contessa, in all her practicality, could have been convinced the place was haunted.

Finally, she arrived at the locked door in the back of the house. Its dark wood loomed larger than life in the shadows of the night, and Contessa chided herself for letting her dramatic sensibilities get the best of her.

Sinking to her knees, she pulled the hairpins out of her pocket and got to work. It was slow going, and Contessa kept pausing to listen for the click of tumblers and signs of life in the house. After long, tense minutes, the last tumbler finally fell, and the door swung open on blessedly silent hinges.

Groping about, Contessa managed to locate a lamp and matches on a sideboard near the door. She memorized their position in her mind so she could replace them before moving to light them. After a few seconds of struggle, she managed to cast a dim light in the office.

She made her way to the center of the room where a desk dominated most of the large room. As she lifted the lantern higher to get a better view, she gasped as the light caught on a gleaming piece of metal. Lying in the center of the desk was a knife, flat enough to slip into a boot but long enough to easily deliver a killing blow.

The sight made the blood run cold in Contessa's veins, but she continued to scan the desk. As much as Contessa's heart hammered at the sight of the knife, simply owning a weapon was not enough proof to warrant an arrest. Still, a dark voice in the back of Contessa's mind wondered if that very blade had slit her mother's throat.

The rest of the desk was unremarkable, sporting only a few fountain pens and a handsome malachite paperweight. Just as Contessa was reaching to open one of the top drawers, she heard a sound almost like a growl behind her.

She whirled around, her stomach dropping sickeningly, to find the Beast standing with his hand braced against the doorframe, effectively blocking her way out. Her mouth opened but no sound came out. She'd been found, and now she would meet the same end as her mother. She would fail her father, and she would never get to see Joseph again.

"I suppose this is what I get for not giving you a proper tour of your new home."

Contessa opened and closed her mouth a few times. She was unsure what she'd expected the Beast to say, but it hadn't been that.

"I'm a curious person," she eventually settled on as a response.

Contessa could hear his exhale, but she couldn't make out any change in his expression in the dim light.

"Let's have a drink," the Beast said before turning and stalking out of the office.

Contessa blinked at his broad back a few times then followed him. She supposed she could have grabbed the knife from the desk next to her and charged at him, but she knew it would be futile. The Beast wouldn't turn his back on her if she posed any sort of threat to him.

He led them to the living room where he set about lighting more lamps while Contessa stood in the middle of the room awkwardly hugging her dressing robe around herself. Now that she was slightly less concerned with her impending death, she was far more aware of her state of undress. Goose bumps crawled up her spine as the Beast glanced at her.

Once the lanterns were lit, the Beast turned to the sideboard where there was a single decanter filled with amber liquid. He poured two glasses and turned back to her.

"Here," he handed Contessa a glass before throwing himself down in the nearest armchair.

She continued to stand there, dumbly staring at the glass in her hand.

"Drink. I'm not trying to poison you," he said, taking a sip from his own glass in demonstration. "Unless you don't like whiskey, in which case I'm afraid I don't have anything to offer you."

"Whiskey is fine," Contessa responded, perching herself on the edge of a nearby settee and taking a delicate sip. She raised her eyebrows as she found it was the same brand Joseph had pilfered from his father's cupboard on several occasions to drink with her in secret. It wasn't an expensive brand, surprisingly modest for somebody as wealthy as the Beast. Despite the odd situation, she found the familiar warmth calmed her.

"So," the Beast bit out the word as if he were having great difficulty formulating exactly what to say. "I think it's time we stop beating around the fact we don't have a traditional marriage."

"That's an interesting way of describing our situation," Contessa said, her formerly sweet demeanor nowhere to be found. Considering he had caught her breaking into his office, it seemed all pretense of earning his trust was thoroughly destroyed.

"And how would you rather I phrase our situation?"

"How about being honest about the fact I've been sold off to a Beast?" Contessa's frustration at her continued failure was getting the better of her, and her voice was bitingly cold.

The Beast's twisted eyebrow shot up in surprise at her use of his notorious nickname. "An ungrateful spitfire like you is no walk in the park," he shot back.

Contessa floundered for a response. It was bold of him to assume she should be grateful he had deigned to marry her. The only thing he had done for her was dress her in hideous clothing and relieve her of her mother.

The Beast took the opportunity of her silence to continue. "I can't give back the opportunities you've lost. But considering we are stuck with each other; what do you say we endeavor to not make each other's lives a living hell? I've tried to stay out of your way, but today I couldn't help but notice some signs of...hostility from you."

Contessa suppressed a derisive snort. She would love to make his life a living hell, but it was more important for her to bring him to justice.

"I'd love to put our hostility to rest." She silently added that she would like their hostility to end with him on trial for murder.

"Then we're in agreement," he said before taking a long sip of his whiskey.

Contessa took the opportunity to observe the man. He was still fully dressed despite the late hour, but he seemed exhausted. Where he had always sat rigidly in her presence, now he was slouched in his chair in a way that almost looked defeated. There was a purpling circle as dark as a bruise under his good eye and his unruly auburn hair was even more wild than usual.

"Are your rooms to your liking?" he asked suddenly.

She stuck with the theme of honesty for the evening as she answered, "Not particularly. I've always hated roses."

The Beast tilted his head. "I would have thought red roses were your favorite based on the frequency with which your suitors had them delivered to your house."

Contessa was unsurprised that he had been having her house watched, just as her father was watching his. His reconnaissance must have been thorough to notice the flowers from her few admirers before her father shooed them away.

"That's because men always assume women want red roses, considering they are the flower of Aphrodite. Everybody thinks women want to be associated with the Goddess of love and beauty."

"And what Goddess would you rather be compared to?" he asked.

Contessa swirled the amber liquid in her glass as she weighed her answer. "Nemesis, the Goddess of retribution."

The Beast's eyes appeared to be a glittering gold in the light of the oil lamps as he raised his drink in a toast. "To revenge."

"To revenge," Contessa echoed, lifting hers in return.

The Beast drained his remaining whiskey in a single swallow and Contessa watched his Adam's apple bob in the dim light. Then he set his glass down on the floor and pushed to his feet. He began to stalk out of the room, but he paused in the doorway. The lighting was such that Contessa could only make out his silhouette, his powerful shoulders taking up the entire doorframe. Contessa's skin tingled.

"I would recommend you don't go through my things anymore. I assure you that you will end up in far more trouble that you bargained for." Despite the implications of his statement, the Beast's tone remained conversational. He slipped down the hall without waiting for any response from Contessa.

Contessa stayed in her seat nursing her whiskey long after he had disappeared. When she did eventually make her way up to the rose room, she didn't sit up and wait, but slipped under the covers and went straight to sleep.

Despite her escapades the night before, Contessa woke as soon as the sun began peeking in the window. Her body was too regimented to sleep in much past dawn unless she was deathly ill.

Today, Julia dressed her in a sky-blue dress edged with delicate white lace. The sleeves were far too voluminous for Contessa's usual taste, but the color was an improvement.

Julia tittered and gossiped as usual while braiding Contessa's hair in a crown around her head. It seemed she was unaware of Contessa's transgressions the night before—or if she was, then she was a far better liar than Contessa ever would have guessed. Something about the girl gave Contessa the impression she would struggle to be anything but completely genuine.

Contessa picked at her cuticles as she sat at her dressing table, a habit her father had broken her of years ago. Now she picked until a bubble of blood formed on her thumb as she pulled at a hangnail.

Working her way out of her current predicament would be a complicated game of chess. She'd wasted her opportunity to search the Beast's office. Now that he knew she could pick the lock, he would set more protections on his documents. The plan of using her womanly wiles on him had apparently never been an option at all, which was a revelation as perplexing as it was relieving. Admitting defeat was not an option Contessa was willing to consider. She couldn't contemplate her father's disappointment should she fail to collect incriminating information. Not to mention she was officially married. She wouldn't be free until her husband was hanged for his crimes. The thought made Contessa shudder after yesterday's executions.

She was left with no time to examine her predicament further. As she entered the dining room, she found a figure already occupying her usual seat. Her immediate reaction was to think she'd seen more of her husband in the past day than in the first five days of their marriage put together. She then realized the back of the head she was staring at was covered in black curls instead of the Beast's auburn mane.

Gregor was currently pouring the man tea as he told some raucous tale, gesticulating widely. The story was apparently so engaging that Gregor didn't notice the teacup overflowing until steaming water spilled over his hands.

Gregor yelped and nearly dropped the teapot, and Contessa moved to grab it from him. The mysterious man beat her to it. He snatched the pot from Gregor and grabbed a napkin to tend to his scalded hands before Contessa had even taken a step forward.

"Are you alright, Gregor?" Contessa asked, taking a napkin from another place setting to mop at the spreading spill.

Gregor nodded, his round face turning beet red as the man dried his hands with the napkin.

"Really, I'm fine," Gregor stammered. "Just let me grab another cloth to clean the spill and boil you some more water."

He snatched up the teapot and beat a hasty retreat, looking mortified by a simple spill.

"He's an odd duck, that one," said the man, and Contessa recognized a slight lilt to his words that placed him as being from the northern part of the continent.

He turned away from the door Gregor had exited to face Contessa where she was still working to contain the spill with a thin napkin. He immediately let out a low whistle upon seeing her.

"And you are a pretty little bird. Nate failed to mention how lovely his wife was when he told me he was getting married."

Contessa gave up on managing the spill and turned her full attention to her surprise breakfast companion. Taking in his appearance, she finally had an image in her head for what an author meant when they described a character as a handsome rogue. His curls were messy in a way that appeared to be perpetually windswept, and his eyes held a twinkle as he fixed Contessa with a crooked smile.

"Mister Kristoff Mainsworth at your service," he introduced himself, offering an outstretched hand to Contessa in greeting. Several rings sparkled on each finger.

As Contessa reached out to shake his hand, she caught a glimpse of tattooed ink encircling Kristoff's wrist beneath his cuff. The rounded *r*'s in his accent lent his speech a distinctly friendly air, and Contessa couldn't help the smile tugging at her mouth as she introduced herself in return.

"Contessa C—er, Woodrow. May I ask what brings you to our home this morning?"

Kristoff slid back into his chair and resumed buttering his toast, which had escaped the flood of hot water.

"Oh, I'm a business associate of Nate's. I stopped by this morning to give him some help with his affairs." Kristoff brandished the butter knife with an unconcerned air as he spoke. "I always like to stay for breakfast after our meetings. Gives me more opportunities to torment poor Gregor."

It took Contessa a moment to comprehend that Kristoff was referring to the Beast when he called him Nate. Still, she perked up immediately upon hearing he was a business associate.

Looking more closely at his appearance, she could see scars across his knuckles and could just spot the gleaming handle of a revolver poking out from his belt.

She knew what type of business associate her husband might have. While she'd recently hit a dead end in her investigation, she saw another avenue as she looked at Kristoff's open smile.

"I see. And what kind of work do you do for Mr. Woodrow?" she asked with wide, innocent eyes as she reached to serve herself some porridge.

"This and that." Kristoff looked at her with narrowed eyes as he took a bite of toast.

"Well, you must be instrumental if you're here this early. You're the first guest I've seen in the week I've been here," Contessa flattered.

"Mrs. Woodrow, Nate may not have mentioned that you had the face of an angel, but he did say you were sharp as a whip." Kristoff waggled his piece of toast at her. "You will be getting no information out of me."

Contessa managed to look taken aback even as she internally cursed. "I'm sure I don't know what you mean, I was just curious as to the nature of your work."

"Oh, you know exactly what I mean, but if we are all going to play the idiot here, I'll humor you. I just deal with day-to-day aspects of Nate's business so he can focus on the big picture of his work." Kristoff finished off his toast and spoke with his mouth full. "And that is all the details you'll be getting out of me, so don't go pressing for more."

"I suppose it makes sense," Contessa quipped back. "Mr. Woodrow is too high and mighty now to really get his hands dirty, but you look far too concerned with your appearance to be the hired muscle. You're stuck being the middle management."

Kristoff choked on his last swallow of toast and had to cough enthusiastically before responding with a chuckle. "No wonder Nate has been keeping so busy recently. He certainly has his hands full here."

If Contessa wasn't going to get information on the Beast's gang involvement from Kristoff, then perhaps she could at least unravel the mystery of why the man had married her at all.

"You can't possibly mean his hands have been full with me. We've scarcely spoken since our wedding day."

A crease formed between Kristoff's arched brows as he responded, "Well, that's too bad. He may have finally met his match in you."

Contessa suppressed a frown of her own at the comment. "Yes, well, if he didn't want to have anything to do with me, then why go to the trouble of marrying me?"

"For the same reason that you agreed to it." Kristoff fixed her with a knowing look, and Contessa stiffened in her seat.

She'd thought she was the one trying to get behind enemy lines, but it might be the other way around. Still, he was doing a rather unsatisfactory job of gaining information on her father. Contessa opened her mouth to quip about how the Beast would have no such satisfaction from her, but at that moment, Gregor returned with a fresh teapot and Kristoff became thoroughly distracted.

"Ahh, Gregor, you've returned," he said, gesturing broadly. "You must let me take a closer look at those talented hands of yours. Can't have that green thumb impeded by any nasty burns."

Gregor regained his earlier flush, and Contessa smiled into her porridge.

Kristoff left shortly after breakfast, and he spent the rest of the meal too busy flirting relentlessly with Gregor for Contessa to weasel any other hints from him. Contessa would have felt bad for Gregor if she hadn't thought he was enjoying the attention.

Once she was alone again, Contessa was briefly at a loss for what to do. She eventually settled for her usual routine of finding the newspaper and heading out into the garden to read.

She was settled in her spot on the rim of the fountain, the paper spread across her lap in the sunshine, when a shadow fell across the page. She looked up from the article she was reading about how a physician from the Southern Continent had arrived to treat the king's illness, to see the face of the Beast looming over her. She resisted the urge to immediately jump to her feet. Instead, she asked politely, "Is there something I can help you with, Mr. Woodrow?"

"I was looking for the newspaper. Gregor said you had it."

"Well, he was right. I'm reading it right now," she said, looking back down at the article, not in a particularly accommodating mood. If she wasn't going to weasel information out of him, she saw no purpose in being nice to a murderer.

The shadow didn't move from over Contessa. The Beast's hands clenched and unclenched at the edge of her vision. Good. Let him feel a fraction of the frustration this marriage had caused her.

"Standing over me isn't going to make me read any faster," she commented without looking up.

There were a few seconds of stillness until the Beast moved away. Instead of heading down the path back to the house, however, he simply moved to the side and sat down on the edge of the fountain a few feet from Contessa.

Contessa flipped the page, but her eyes scanned over the same sentence several times.

"So, this is what you do all day?" the Beast finally broke the silence.

Dropping the pretense of reading, Contessa looked up to find him staring at her with his head tilted to the side. Contessa was still unsure of her ability to read his expressions. His scar made him seem constantly hostile. Or maybe that really was his expression, and the scar just enhanced the effect.

Remembering his question, she answered, "Well, it's not as though you've given me many options to entertain myself with around here."

This creases between his brows deepened.

"What do ladies like you do to entertain yourselves?"

Contessa considered his question, finding it an odd thing to ask. "I personally read a lot of books."

The Beast exhaled sharply through his nose, clearly spotting her predicament there. "Aren't there other things you like to do to pass the time?"

"Don't you dare suggest I embroider cushions. Not every young lady enjoys straining her eyes over a needle and thread."

The Beast huffed again in what could have passed for a laugh had his face managed more than a slight grimace. "No, you don't strike me as the type to embroider. You have to enjoy something besides reading, though."

"I do. I play a lot of chess, and I like a good walk in the park." Contessa thought wistfully of spending Joseph's afternoons off in the parlor laughing over a chess board and the rolling pathways of the Grand Park. She'd been cooped up in this sterile house for too long.

"I have a chess board," the Beast offered.

"That's rather unhelpful if I don't have anybody to play against. I learned long ago that I can't stay objective enough to play against myself," Contessa pointed out.

The Beast fixed her with a thoughtful stare. "I can play."

"Then perhaps we should see who the better strategist is."

The silence between them stretched. He broke the it first.

"Why haven't you gone for a walk in the park if you enjoy them?"

Contessa opened her mouth to answer but paused. She'd thought the answer was obvious. Realizing her mouth was hanging open like a fish, she shut it with an audible snap.

"I married you; I didn't kidnap you," said the Beast, having the nerve to sound disgruntled by her assumption that her mother's murderer might have hostile intentions.

"That was rather unclear when you married me and then refused to speak to me," Contessa retorted and then winced. She wasn't sure why she made it sound like she wished he would speak to her. Maybe a week in a foreign house barely seeing anybody but Julia and Gregor had begun to affect her head.

The Beast considered her for a moment. She waited for him to snap and say something in his defense. Instead, he said, "If you ask Gregor, he'll bring around the carriage to take you to the park."

Contessa just nodded in thanks. After a moment, the Beast stood, straightening his cuffs before heading back down the garden path.

"Wait," Contessa said before she could stop herself. "You can have this now." She held out the paper for him to take.

He stared at the offering in her outstretched hand for long enough that Contessa almost pulled it back. Then he took it with an inclination of his head before turning back to the house.

Contessa watched his receding form, feeling as though every conversation with him confused her more than the last.

Chapter Five

Contessa was surprised to find that she would have company for dinner as well. Gregor was just placing a bowl of pea soup in front of Contessa when the Beast stalked into the dining room and threw himself down into the chair across the table. He grunted something that may have been a greeting as he did.

Gregor, for his part, didn't seem perturbed, and moved to fetch another place setting. Contessa peeked through her lashes as she blew on her soup to cool it. She didn't speak. The Beast didn't object to the silence and set about ladling a large amount of soup into his bowl as soon as Gregor set it in front of him.

As they ate, the silence was only broken by the slurping the Beast made as he spooned soup into his crooked mouth. Contessa was used to quiet meals, her father not being particularly loquacious. This silence, however, made her sit up so straight she felt as if she might float off her chair.

As the meal ended, Gregor brought the Beast a glass of whiskey. Contessa prepared to excuse herself from the table and the silence that put her on edge. Before she could stand up, the Beast spoke.

"I thought we could play that round of chess this evening."

He sounded almost uncertain, as if the fact he was asking her surprised him as well.

Against her better judgement, Contessa nodded in assent. If she couldn't beat this man at his own game to bring him to justice, then she certainly would enjoy beating him at chess.

He pushed from his seat and moved around her to lead the way out of the dining room. As he brushed by her, he passed close enough she could smell the whiskey that clung to his breath. The hair on the back of Contessa's neck stood up and she took a step back.

The Beast led the way to the parlor where there was indeed a Chess board on a low table. She thought she would have noticed it during her earlier investigations, but perhaps the Beast usually kept it in his office. He perched himself on stool near the table, and Contessa arranged her skirts around her on the end of a chaise lounge opposite him. As the Beast leaned forward to ensure the tiles were properly arranged on the board, Contessa couldn't help but think that his large form looked a little ridiculous crowded onto the small wooden stool, his powerful build making it seem like furniture for children. Perhaps he could have taken her seat, but Contessa wasn't one to argue with him if he was determined to be uncomfortable.

Once the board was set up, the Beast jerked his head towards her, indicating she should make a move since she was sitting closest to the white pieces. Contessa picked a simple first move, hoping for him to underestimate her. He responded as she hoped he would, and the game was afoot.

They played in silence, but Contessa took pleasure in the sharp exhales of surprise she was able to elicit from the Beast with her strategy. She almost smirked when he ran a wide hand through his hair in frustration, but she schooled her face to neutrality.

Contessa found herself enjoying the match despite herself. It reminded her of evenings spent playing chess with her father. He had taught her to play at a very young age and always encouraged her to sharpen her strategic mind. She could still remember her mother scolding her father when he won repetitively, but he insisted she wouldn't learn otherwise.

Now she could best her father nearly half the time, and her current adversary wasn't nearly as skilled. The Beast hadn't even finished half his whiskey by the time she had him on the ropes.

"Oh dear, it looks like I've backed you into a corner here," Contessa commented in feigned surprise as she executed her final strategy.

The Beast looked up at her with one brow lifted.

"I wonder how that happened," he mused in a tone that made it clear he wasn't shocked in the slightest.

Contessa was loath to admit she was disappointed he didn't rage at his defeat. She'd hoped making him angry would make her feel less frustrated at her current predicament. Instead, he took a long sip of whiskey and calmly accepted his fate.

"You play very well," he commented, clearing the board.

"My father taught me."

Any sense of a truce that had fallen between the two immediately vanished as the Beast's eyes snapped up to hers, flashing gold in the dimming lamplight.

"Of course, your father would train his daughter to be a sharp one."

"It's fortunate for me that he did."

A beat of silence passed before Contessa pushed to her feet saying politely, "I'm afraid I must be going to bed now. Thank you for the match, though. It was certainly enlightening."

Contessa turned to go in a rustle of skirts, but not before she caught the hard glint in her opponent's eyes. She swept from the room feeling smug. By the time she got to her rooms, her victorious glow had faded. A game of chess had been a temporary outlet from her frustration, but it still didn't get her any closer to justice.

The Beast seemed to have developed a vested interest in besting Contessa at chess. For the next two nights, after dinner, he would materialize with a glass of whiskey in hand and challenge her to a match. Contessa accepted each time, telling herself it was a chance to get to know her adversary better. Indeed, Contessa began to be able to read the signs of his frustration as he played—the way he gnawed at his bottom lip and the heavy exhales through his nose when Contessa thwarted him.

They played mostly in silence, broken by only short bits of conversation. Contessa debated trying to talk more, thinking perhaps she could get him to let some important piece of information slip. The silence, though, seemed to be an integral part of a small truce they had created, and Contessa was inexplicably hesitant to violate it.

One of their brief conversations occurred when Contessa had managed to knock over her teacup with the oversized puff of her sleeve. She cursed in a way that would make her father scowl, and the Beast's eyes shot up from the board at her expletives.

Contessa tried to mop the spreading stain from her skirts with her handkerchief, but it was no use.

"Well, this one wasn't my color to begin with," she mused, tucking the soiled handkerchief away.

The Beast scowled at her periwinkle skirts. "The dressmaker assured me this color is what all the ladies are wearing."

Contessa was taken aback that the Beast had conversed with a dressmaker. She couldn't picture him entering a dress shop at all.

"Be that as it may, pastels make me feel like a porcelain doll."

"What colors do you prefer?"

Contessa found it odd that they were talking about something as mundane as favorite colors, but she supposed stranger things must have happened.

"Gray," she responded honestly. "And blue."

The Beast considered her with a tilted head. "The same color as your eyes," he commented thoughtfully.

If the conversation had been unusual before, it felt downright bizarre now. The Beast seemed to feel similarly and quickly turned his attention back to the game board. Contessa found herself distracted by his implementation of a new strategy and pushed the comment to the back of her mind for further consideration.

Two days later, she was dressed in an elegant day dress made of gunmetal gray silk, and she was forced to consider whether the color choice was a coincidence.

Contessa resolved to ask the Beast about the dress that evening over their nightly game of chess. However, he didn't appear as she finished dinner to challenge her to a match. Presumably, he was delayed, so Contessa moved herself to the parlor to set up the board herself.

By the time the board was set, he still hadn't materialized. Contessa had nothing better to do than sit and wait. Settling back on the chaise lounge, she considered her strategy for the coming game. With the Beast's increasing prowess, she would have to employ more sophisticated tactics. As she contemplated, the candles burned lower and lower. Eventually, they burned out, but Contessa didn't notice, for she had dozed off.

Contessa was woken by the sound of a child crying out. It took her a moment to place the noise, for it wasn't something she was accustomed to hearing. As soon as she recognized it, though, she jerked awake, sitting bolt upright amongst her rumpled skirts.

The noise of the crying child was the loudest, but it was accompanied by the pounding of footsteps and panicked words in a distinctive northern brogue. Just as Contessa recognized the voice, Kristoff rounded the corner into the parlor, and she located the source of the wailing. Bundled in the man's arms was a child, no older than seven or eight, based on his size. The child was wearing the grubby clothes of an urchin, but the shoulders were darkened by blood dripping from his scalp. He was howling and clutching to Kristoff's shirt sleeves, marking the crisp white fabric with crimson handprints.

Contessa leapt to her feet. Kristoff looked slightly taken aback to find her in the parlor, but the expression didn't last long. He strode over to the chaise Contessa had been dozing on and gently laid his cargo down.

Even as he arranged the screaming child carefully on the cushions, he barked at Contessa, "Find Gregor. Out back, in the garden."

Without another thought, Contessa hiked up her skirts and dashed from the room. As she flew around the corner into the back of the house, she saw something that made her heart skip a beat.

The door to the office was flung wide open.

Contessa skidded to a halt in front of the open doorway. The desk lay beyond the threshold, a few papers scattered across its surface. She made to step inside, see what clues the papers might hold.

Her foot hovered in the air before she could enter the forbidden room. In her mind flashed the image of the young boy in the living room, dark blood dripping down his face.

Cursing internally, Contessa whirled in place and sprinted towards the back door to the garden. Bursting out into the night air, she spotted Gregor kneeling in a bed of hydrangeas.

"Gregor," Contessa shouted, heaving for breath in her too tight corset after her brief sprint. "It's Kristoff, there's a child in the parlor, he's bleeding."

Gregor, looking concerned but less surprised than Contessa might have thought, shot to his feet before she could get Kristoff's name out. He brushed his muddy hands off on his work apron as he rushed towards the house.

"Apply pressure to the wound, I'll be right there with my kit," he instructed, pushing through the back door.

Contessa ran back to the parlor, pointedly avoiding looking at the temptation of the open office door. When she arrived back in the parlor, she found Kristoff already trying to staunch the bleeding with his bare hands. The child was still whimpering and squirming, but he had stopped screaming. Sliding to her knees next to him, Contessa could see the blood was coming from a long, jagged graze across the boy's forehead and into his hairline. Gathering up a handful of her skirts, Contessa pressed the gray silk against the wound, the fabric instantly turning dark and heavy.

Kristoff glanced over at her with a grateful expression, wiping his reddened hands on his pants. Just then, Gregor pushed into the room, carrying a leather case. Kristoff sprang to his feet to give up his space next to the boy. Contessa pulled her hands away so Gregor could inspect the injury.

He hissed between his teeth at the ripped skin.

"Bullet graze?" he asked as he began pulling supplies out of his leather case.

"Broken cable," came Kristoff's voice from over her shoulder. "One of the machines was hit by a stray bullet in the escape, and the broken wire caught him across the face."

Contessa looked at the child in front of her again as he spoke, taking in the gnarled hands of a laborer in a textile factory.

Gregor nodded in understanding as he pulled out a bottle and began pouring the contents on some rags. A harsh chemical smell filled Contessa's nose.

"I'll need to clean this and then stitch it up. Somebody will have to hold him steady."

At Gregor's words, the child began to wail anew, flailing his arms and batting at Gregor and Contessa where they knelt. Contessa slid onto the chaise, pulling the child's head into her lap as she did so and stroking his hair gently away from his wound.

She shot a pointed look at Gregor as she began to speak, indicating he should work quickly.

"You've been so brave," Contessa cooed. "What's your name, brave one?"

"P-Paul." The boy's lower lip trembled as Gregor approached him with an antiseptic-soaked rag. He flinched as the cloth touched his wound, but Contessa placed her hands on either side of his face and held him firmly in place.

"Well, Paul, I'm Contessa Woodrow, and I'm so sorry we had to meet under such painful circumstances. You are in good hands now though, and Gregor is going to fix you up perfectly." As she finished, Contessa shot Gregor a look that made it clear he needed to deliver on her promises. He nodded once and set back to cleaning the wound.

"You're Mr. Woodrow's wife," the child said, his eyes becoming round, and he seemed to relax into her lap just a touch.

"Yes," Contessa said, eyeing the needle and thread Gregor was pulling out of his kit and tightening her grip, "and I'm going to help you. Your parents must be worried sick about you."

As Contessa spoke, Kristoff begin to shake his head, but it was too late.

"I-I don't have any parents," Paul stammered. "It's just me and my little sister, Olivia."

The boy's eyes widened even further as if he had just remembered something important. He began to squirm in Contessa's lap as he yelled, "Olivia! Where is she? We were running and then..."

Contessa tried holding the boy still and stroking his hair, but he remained distraught until a familiar voice sounded near the door.

"She's safe with the others, and a tough little thing too."

Contessa's looked up to find the Beast standing in the doorway looking disheveled. His overcoat had a long rip on the sleeve, and his hair was even messier than usual, but he seemed uninjured. His gaze was trained on the little boy in Contessa's lap, and his eyes were softer than Contessa had ever seen them. Maybe it was just the dim lighting.

The boy calmed his squirming, but Contessa knew the worst was yet to come, so she returned her attention to him.

"I'm sure your sister would be very impressed with how courageous you're being. Do you think you could be brave for just a little bit longer?" Contessa encouraged the boy.

The boy nodded, and Gregor began to approach him with the needle. Contessa held his head firmly in her hands but let her thumb stroke through his hair in reassurance. She heard a rustle next to her and glanced up to find the Beast had also settled on his knees beside the chaise. He took one of the boy's small hands in both of his large ones, and despite the difference in size, in that moment, Contessa couldn't help but notice the similarities in their scarred fingers.

Her attention was drawn back to the boy when he screeched in pain as Gregor began to make his first stitch. He attempted to jerk away, but between Contessa and the Beast, they managed to hold him steady. Contessa cooed out soothing nonsense as best she could between gritted teeth. The cut was not as severe as it had initially appeared once the blood had been cleared away, but it still looked painful. To everybody's relief, the boy had fallen unconscious by the time Gregor was making his third stitch.

The room was silent as Gregor worked, and Contessa remained still with the boy's head cradled in her lap while he finished. The Beast didn't move, either, Paul's hand still clasped in his. Contessa snuck glances at him out of the corner of her eye and could see the muscles in his jaw clenched under his uneven skin. His eyes didn't waver from the boy's face the entire time.

When Gregor had tied off the last stitch, the entire room breathed a collective sigh of relief. Gregor mopped away the blood with a clean rag to reveal a neat line of sutures marching across Paul's forehead and into his hairline.

"The cut was pretty jagged. It will leave a scar. It should heal quickly, though," Gregor commented as he packed up his kit.

"With luck, it will just make him look dashing when he's older," Kristoff commented.

Contessa couldn't help the way her eyes flicked over the Beast's own scar, hard won in the fight for the leadership of the Lions. Thankfully, Paul's wouldn't be nearly as severe.

The whole room seemed to shake itself from its reverie as the Beast spoke.

"We need to get him out of here, Kristoff. Take him out the back and bring him to the rendezvous point with the rest of them. Rhosyn will make sure he's taken care of from there."

Kristoff stepped forward and lifted Paul out of Contessa's lap as if he weighed nothing more than a house cat. He arranged the boy so his head didn't loll. Then Kristoff made to leave the room, but before he did, he leaned towards Gregor and whispered something Contessa couldn't hear. Then they both left, leaving her alone in the now deafening silence with the Beast.

Contessa stared down at her lap, the silk now completely darkened with blood.

She contemplated her stained dress as she waited for the Beast to break the silence, but he remained quiet. He stared at his own bloody and scarred hands as if they might hold the secrets of the universe.

Contessa was so full of questions that, eventually, one burst forth.

"What happened to Paul's parents?"

Perhaps it wasn't the most urgent question, but she couldn't banish the pain she'd felt when Paul had said it was only him and his sister. Losing one parent had nearly ruined her. Losing both wasn't something Contessa wanted to consider.

The Beast looked up from his hands, tilting his head as he responded. "The same thing that happened to the parents of all the factory children."

When Contessa showed no signs of comprehension, he elaborated.

"They were hanged in the Inquiries."

The air rushed from Contessa's lungs of its own accord until she felt hollowed out. Her vision narrowed at the edges and wavered until the sight of the living room was that of a different one, five years earlier. The blood on her hands was no longer Paul's, but her mother's.

She could still feel her mother's head cradled in her arms as she screamed for her father. She'd found her on the ground. The blood that poured out of her mother's ruined throat seeped into her flaxen hair, which had tumbled out of its elaborate rolls as if yanked by violent hands. More blood trickled out of three scratches raked across her mother's cheek. Contessa would never forget the look in her mother's eyes as the light faded out of them. It was one of pure rage. Rage that Contessa had absorbed into herself until her life had been consumed by the need for revenge against her mother's murderer as well as all the rest of the Cursed in the city.

Now, Contessa found herself drawn out of her terrible vision by the warm hand of the murderer himself. It rested softly on her shoulder, and Contessa realized he hadn't touched her at all since the dance on their wedding day.

When her husband's hazel eyes met hers, Contessa was surprised to find they didn't fill her with the rage she normally felt when she thought of her mother's murder. Instead, she just felt incredibly sad. She had lost a single parent to the Cursed, but how many orphans had the Inquiries left? Those children had been forced to endure watching their parents dying in public executions, in front of a crowd who was glad for their death. Perhaps those orphans were just as full of anger as Contessa, ready for vengeance that would make more orphans.

It left Contessa feeling cold to her soul. The Beast removed his hand from her shoulder as quickly as he had placed it there.

"I feel awful for them," Contessa murmured.

"You weren't the one who murdered their parents."

That wasn't exactly true. She might not have pulled the lever that sent them plummeting to their death, but her father was the one sending them to their executions. She'd stood in the crowd as they died, just as full of fear as the rest of the spectators.

"What happens to the orphans?"

Contessa needed to know. As uncomfortable as the executions had often made her feel, she hadn't stopped to consider the dangerous gangsters being hanged might have children of their own.

"Most of them start working in factories, trying to make enough money to eat. They eventually fall into enough debt that they aren't much better than slaves, worked to the bone, punished for falling behind." The Beast's eyes were pointed towards Contessa, but she got the impression he was far away as he spoke.

"And where do you and Kristoff fit into all of this?"

"We try to give the children…another option in life," he answered.

Contessa's heart sunk. It was out of the frying pan and into the fire for these children. Rescued from the harsh factory life only to be thrown into a life of crime in the gangs, likely ending with their own hanging. She didn't know why she'd hoped for something better from the Beast.

She found her eyes drawn to his scarred hands still resting on the lounge and covered in Paul's blood. Part of her itched to reach out and touch them, to wipe them clean and soothe the scars. Not all the marks could be from knife fights, and she pictured the small boy's hand clutched tightly in his own.

While the textile factories offered harsh working conditions, the street gangs couldn't be much better.

Contessa's head whirled. She needed to take a step back, regroup, and develop a new plan of attack. She pushed to her feet and attempted to smooth her now ruined skirts.

"I think I need to retire for the evening," she offered, desperate for a chance to think on her own.

The Beast just nodded and remained kneeling on the floor. It was odd to have her mother's murderer in such a vulnerable position before her. It was something she'd envisioned many times, usually with him begging for her forgiveness. Now that she was here, though, it felt vastly different than she had imagined.

Banishing the thought from her mind, Contessa turned to leave the room. Just as she was about to step into the hallway, she heard a voice behind her.

"Thank you for your help tonight, Contessa."

She glanced over her shoulder.

"It was no trouble at all, Mr. Woodrow."

She made her way upstairs to her rose infested bedroom, thoughts of everything that Mr. Woodrow had told her swirling in her now troubled mind.

Chapter Six

The next morning at breakfast, Contessa was greeted by a neat, white envelope waiting for her at her usual seat. Her heart sped up in her chest as she recognized the green wax seal emblazoned with a set of scales that belonged to her father. If he was taking the risk to write to her in Mr. Woodrow's house, it must be of utmost importance.

Contessa endeavored to eat her porridge at a normal pace, not wanting to appear too anxious. She tucked the letter into her dress to read once she made her way out into the privacy of the garden. She preferred not to read it here, where Gregor might enter and see something untoward over her shoulder.

By the time Contessa had arranged herself on the fountain in the back courtyard, she had to keep herself from ripping into the letter like a child opening a present. She broke the wax seal with quick fingers, letting her eyes rove the page and take in her father's aggressively neat and angular handwriting.

She'd known her father wouldn't put any explicit information about her mission in the letter. Her brow furrowed as she read. She'd been prepared to decipher a hidden message artfully concealed in seemingly mundane news. Instead, the page held nothing more than a short note telling her the weather tomorrow was supposed to be ideal for a stroll in the park.

Contessa's brow smoothed once again. Her father was suggesting she go to the park so she could converse with him in person. It wouldn't be seen as unusual for Contessa to go for a stroll with her father, although they would still have to be careful not to be overheard.

The sun managed to warm Contessa's face, even through the parasol she carried. She would just as soon have gone without the lacey accessory, but Julia had been so pleased it matched her hat that Contessa had been persuaded to take it with her. Now she was glad of the shade it offered as she squinted, searching the shrub-lined paths of the park for her father. She ambled along as casually as she could for a minute before spotting his angular silhouette standing alone, contemplating a nearby fountain with his hands clasped behind his back. As Contessa stepped up beside him, he glanced at her out of the corner of his eyes.

"What on earth are you wearing?" he asked.

Contessa glanced down at her dress and grimaced. It was exactly the type of frivolous ensemble her father would look down his nose at.

"Mr. Woodrow bought this dress for me," she answered, smoothing the skirts as best she could, wishing she could make them take up less space in the tight alcove.

"Perfectly predictable. That Beast would like to show off the money he stole through blood by having ostentatious taste," her father scoffed.

Contessa considered the sparse house with the blue door and thought maybe the ostentatious taste was that of the dressmaker and not Mr. Woodrow's. She kept that observation to herself as her father continued.

"What progress have you made? I assume I have received no evidence because you have been unable to communicate with me, so I took the liberty of making you an opportunity."

Clasping her hands in front of her, Contessa responded, "I have been working to find evidence, but progress is slow. He is not as trusting as his proposal may have initially led us to believe."

Chief Cook sniffed. "He is a violent man ruled by his baser urges. Surely, after sharing his bed for two weeks, you must have gotten some small piece of information out of him."

"He is more cunning than you give him credit for," Contessa retorted, for some reason feeling loathe to speak to her father about the fact she hadn't been warming Mr. Woodrow's bed.

"Are you defending the man?"

Contessa's spine went rigid. "I'm simply stating why I have had to be more cautious in my approach."

Chief Cook sighed, the action ruffling his moustache. "Well, I am glad you're being careful. I do want my daughter home in one piece at the end of this."

Contessa relaxed her hands where they had fisted in the folds of her dress. Her father was simply pressing her because he was anxious to get her home. Being back in her own element did sound appealing. The world within the walls of Mr. Woodrow's house had begun to turn her head.

"Father," Contessa began, needing to find some clarity in the confusion, "what happens when those hung in the Inquiries have children?"

Chief Cook's gaze darted over to his daughter. "What an odd question. I would think most of them go to work in the factories. The factory owners will look after them and pay them an honest living until they are old enough to learn another trade."

Contessa nodded, staying silent as her brain integrated her father's response.

"Why do you ask? Has this got something to do with Mr. Woodrow?"

Contessa opened her mouth to tell him what had brought on her question, but the breath caught in her chest. She remembered Paul's scared face and scarred hands and couldn't bring herself to admit the whole story. If she told her father about Paul, he might be found and punished for running away from the factory.

Instead, Contessa told a half truth.

"I think Mr. Woodrow might use the children of the Cursed as a recruiting ground for his gang." Contessa mentally patted herself on the back for her carefully crafted response. Now her father could work to prevent children from being forced into the gangs, but Paul and his sister wouldn't be hunted down and made an example of.

Chief Cook smoothed his moustache in thought.

"Interesting. It makes sense I suppose. It explains why the Lions seem to always have endless numbers. I'll see what I can do about these children, make sure they don't get pulled into a life of crime."

The tension in Contessa's chest ebbed a bit. Her father might be harsh, but everything he did was to serve the Kingdom. If he was going to protect the children from the hardships of lives on the streets, then they would be safe.

"Thank you for that information. You have done well after all," her Father praised, reaching out to squeeze her hand briefly.

Contessa squeezed back. "I must go before Mr. Woodrow's man misses me."

"Then go and keep using that sharp wit of yours. It will get you home in no time."

Contessa did as she was bid, glancing over her shoulder at her father one last time before stepping around a topiary and back onto the main path. Here she blended in with others enjoying the nice weather. She spotted couples strolling arm in arm, and her heart squeezed. She looked away and began walking around the loop, back towards where Gregor waited for her, but a hand reached out and yanked her into a gap in the hedges.

"Joey!" Contessa scolded when she saw who had grabbed her, adrenaline fizzling in her veins.

"Chief Cook said you were safe, but I had to know for myself." Joseph held her by the shoulders, scrutinizing her from head to toe.

"I'm fine," she reassured, happy to see him—happy to have a friend as her world grew more complicated.

"Then what's happened?" Joseph pressed. "What's taking you so long?"

Contessa sighed. "Things are more complicated than I thought. Mr. Woodrow...he's not exactly who I thought he was."

"He's not the Beast?" Joseph's eyebrows shot up.

"He is," Contessa hedged, "but he's not what I was expecting beneath the façade."

Joseph's grip on her shoulders tightened. "Are you defending him? Saying he's not a monster?"

"No," Contessa shook her head, "but there's more to the story than his crimes."

Joseph released her shoulders as if they had burned him, taking a step back.

"He's broken the law, committed *murder*. Nobody is above the law, no matter their infraction and no matter their reasons."

For a moment, Contessa saw her father's fervor in Joseph's eyes, and she stammered.

"It's not that…" Contessa trailed off, trying to communicate to Joseph how nothing was turning out how she expected.

"Remember who's side you're on." Joseph's voice was cool. "The Royal Police are trying to keep London safe. Don't let the Beast change you."

Joseph turned on his heel and ducked back onto the path, leaving Contessa feeling lost. Maybe he was right, and everything was as black and white as he said it was. Still, she couldn't rid herself of the feeling of Paul's blood on her hands.

Chapter Seven

At dinner that night, Contessa found the table set not with two place settings but three. Already seated at one of them was Kristoff. He sat slouched jauntily to one side, his feet propped up on the chair beside him and absently twirling a silver fork in one hand. Upon Contessa's entrance to the dining room, though, he leapt to his feet.

"Ah, the lovely and ever poised Mrs. Woodrow," he said, taking one of her hands in both of his and bowing over it in truly dramatic fashion. "What a pleasure it is to be joining you for the evening meal."

Contessa felt a smile tugging at the corners of her lips despite herself. The man could charm a teakettle.

Just then, Mr. Woodrow stalked into the room. His eyes darted quickly over the scene in front of him before saying, "Stop terrorizing her, Kristoff."

Contessa was surprised to find he didn't bark the phrase like a command, but his voice was light as if he were used to Kristoff's antics and they had ceased to bother him long ago.

Kristoff did as he was bid and resumed his seat, but not before throwing Contessa an exaggerated wink.

Contessa and Mr. Woodrow also moved to their places, and Gregor stepped in to begin serving the meal. Kristoff's eyes roved quickly over Gregor, and Kristoff opened his mouth to say something. Seeing the wicked glint in Kristoff's eye, Contessa determined it would be in the best interest of Gregor's poor nerves to interrupt him.

"To what do we owe the pleasure of your company, Kristoff?"

Kristoff turned his attention away from Gregor and to Contessa.

"You mean besides the fact that eating dinner with Nate night after night must get incredibly boring, and I thought it time to save you from that torturous monotony? I had some business to attend to that ran late, and I wasn't going to be able to make it to my own home in time for supper, so I decided to stay."

"Working this late on a Sunday? You must be uncommonly dedicated," Contessa commented as she accepted a bowl of onion soup from Gregor.

"On the contrary, if I had my way, I wouldn't be keeping these long hours. It's Nate over here and his utter disbelief in leisure that keeps my nose to the grindstone. Maybe if he learned to lighten up a touch then I would not suffer so," Kristoff said, clutching his chest in mock drama.

Mr. Woodrow glared at him over his spoon, but Contessa sensed no real malice in his gaze. For her part, she'd never imagined that anybody would dare tease the most notorious mass murderer in the city, yet here Kristoff was. She'd never considered the possibility that Mr. Woodrow might have friends.

They made an odd set, Mr. Woodrow's constant tension and surliness clashing with the twinkle in Kristoff's eyes suggesting he saw most things as a joke. Still, something about the way they mirrored each other signaled to Contessa that they had shared a life-long friendship—something Contessa herself had never experienced.

"Why, Nate, when was the last time you did something purely for your enjoyment?" Kristoff prodded.

Mr. Woodrow paused in the middle of a slurp of soup and furrowed his brow.

"I've played chess with Mrs. Woodrow most nights," he defended, sounding offended by Kristoff's asserting that he didn't know how to have fun.

"You only do that because I forced you to admit you have nothing else amusing to do in this house," Contessa argued. While their nightly games had certainly been preferable to boredom, she'd gotten the impression they were engaging in them as a test of wits rather than a form of entertainment.

"I have been enjoying our nightly games." Mr. Woodrow tilted his head, sounding honestly wounded.

Contessa struggled to formulate a response. The best she came up with was a soft "Oh."

Kristoff sipped his own soup, pointedly staring over the spoon at Mr. Woodrow. Mr. Woodrow in turn shot him an indecipherable look, but Contessa was saved from her puzzlement by the return of Gregor with the next course.

The rest of the meal passed without incident, Kristoff and Contessa chatting idly about articles she'd read in the newspaper. They spent a while discussing whether they thought the King would survive the fever he was suffering from and another few minutes examining the merits of each of his sons as successors.

They stayed pointedly away from any news that involved gang violence or police activity. While Contessa still knew her role in this house was to gather evidence of gang activity, she found she genuinely enjoyed Kristoff's company. There would be other opportunities to ferret out incriminating details, so for now, she allowed herself to enjoy some of the first real conversation she'd had in weeks.

To her surprise, Mr. Woodrow also offered his opinion from time to time. He seemed much more at ease in the presence of his friend. Contessa reminded herself that he was a young man, not much older than herself, and not just the figure of legend he had built himself up to be on the streets of London. The realization made Contessa shift uncomfortably in her seat.

When the plates had been cleared from the table, Gregor came in and delivered Mr. Woodrow his customary glass of whiskey. He turned to offer one to Kristoff as well, but Kristoff waved him away.

"Today has been a long day. I think I should be getting home. You two enjoy yourselves, though." He looked pointedly at Mr. Woodrow who shot him an inscrutable look over the top of his glass.

Kristoff turned to Contessa, giving her a small bow as he said his good-byes.

"Maybe I'll work late and stay for dinner more often, just for the pleasure of your company."

"I might enjoy that," conceded Contessa, inclining her head to him.

With that, Kristoff took his top hat from Gregor and swept from the room. Contessa could have sworn he gave the manservant a wink as he left.

The room grew noticeably quieter with the lack of Kristoff's presence, but some of the levity he brought remained, hovering in the air.

"Would you like to continue with another game of chess tonight?" Mr. Woodrow broke the silence. "I would hate to think you were only feigning interest in our matches out of a sense of duty."

"Well, I am your wife," Contessa shot back, but her tone lacked its usual venom.

Mr. Woodrow exhaled in amusement but gave her a look that said he knew perfectly well what she'd meant.

"I would actually enjoy a game of chess tonight," Contessa admitted.

Mr. Woodrow nodded and made to lead the way from the dining room. As he rounded the table towards the door, he reached out and snagged the decanter of whiskey and another cut crystal glass from the table.

When they arrived in the parlor with the chess set, Mr. Woodrow poured a few fingers of whiskey into the glass and handed it to Contessa.

She took the offering but tilted her head curiously.

"Most people could use a drink after having dinner with Kristoff," he offered by way of explanation.

Contessa let out a small giggle as she took the glass, then froze immediately. It was an odd feeling to giggle like a gossiping flirt, and she realized she hadn't laughed in weeks. The noise felt foreign in her throat, and she stole a glance at Mr. Woodrow.

His expression surprised her more than her own laughter. While Contessa often had trouble interpreting the expressions on his scarred face, the look he wore now was unmistakably a smile. It was a small thing, just curving up the corner of his mouth and crinkling his good eye, but something about it made the way his scar warped his face appear less grotesque.

Contessa quickly looked away and began arranging the tiles on the circular board.

They began as usual, in silence, but the whiskey Contessa sipped against her better judgement must have turned her head. Soon, she looked down at the board and found Mr. Woodrow had decimated her strategy. She tried quickly to salvage her pieces' formation, but it looked to be a lost cause.

"You've improved immensely," she commented, trying not to sound petulant as he took one of her knights.

"I have Kristoff to thank, actually."

"Kristoff?" Contessa asked as she managed to move a rook to safety, if only temporarily.

"Yes, I told him of our games. He suggested I try implementing a different strategy. Something a little less aggressive that involves my pieces working together more," he explained, quickly circumventing her escape strategy.

Contessa knew they were no longer just speaking of chess, but she wasn't sure what Mr. Woodrow was suggesting.

"It seems to be working for you," she hedged, "but doesn't that force some of the pieces to compromise their strengths?"

"Maybe it is worth compromising for the greater good."

"It depends what kind of game you are playing," Contessa countered, feeling as if she was losing her footing in the conversation and the chess match.

"And what kind of game are you playing, Mrs. Woodrow?"

Contessa looked up from the board to find Mr. Woodrow looking at her, not with hostility, but with genuine curiosity, as if she were a puzzle with a missing piece. She chewed the inside of her cheek for a moment before answering.

"Justice."

"Then we play the same game," he responded, his voice soft.

She shook her head. "It doesn't count if we play for the opposite team."

"There is only one team when it comes to justice," Mr. Woodrow said, making a final move to corner her king and win the match.

Contessa turned her attention back to the board in front of her, taking in her scattered tiles. It felt like an accurate reflection of her brain right now. Her mind was filled with scattered images flicking through her consciousness. Her father staring up at the gallows with fervor on his face. Joseph, insisting that there was no gray area. Her mother's eyes, angry and empty. The bloodstain left on the skirt of the gray dress.

"If there is only one side, then why is so much blood spilt?" Contessa wondered aloud.

"Seeking justice can be a dangerous profession," Mr. Woodrow's fingers brushed over his scar for the briefest of moments. Still, it was enough to make Contessa wonder if the tales about how he had gotten it were true. It was possible he had earned it in a street fight, but gossip and rumors had been known to be untrue.

Contessa stayed silent as she considered his words, and Mr. Woodrow sighed.

"I know you're smart, Mrs. Woodrow," he paused to throw back the last of the whiskey in his glass. "Just use that impressive intellect of yours to think on what I've said."

With that, Mr. Woodrow pressed to his feet and inclined his head to her before leaving the room. Contessa stayed frozen on the stool she occupied in front of the chess board. She looked at the chair Mr. Woodrow had just vacated. It was in the same place the chaise lounge had previously occupied, but the new wingback armchair was noticeably free of stains.

Perhaps that was why the furniture in the house was so impersonal, so it could be burned and replaced if it suddenly became evidence in a crime. Contessa thought it much more likely that the furniture was generic because nobody had spent time in the living area of the house before she'd moved in. Maybe Contessa should consider trying to liven the place up a little bit if she was going to be inhabiting it much longer.

Contessa shook herself at the thought. She was not here to become a society housewife. She was here to... Well, truthfully, she wasn't sure what she was doing anymore. She couldn't endorse the activities of murdering thugs, but she was forced to reconcile with the fact that their breaking children out of forced labor in the factories might be doing some good. Not to mention that she liked Kristoff far too well to believe him to be capable of the degree of the violence that was always attributed to the Lions.

Pressing to her feet, Contessa resolved not to think of these confusing issues until she'd slept the last traces of whiskey out of her system. She would need her full wits about her to devise a plan reconciling all her interests.

Contessa considered heading upstairs and climbing directly into her bed but dismissed the idea. Her head was still spinning and, for some reason, she kept picturing the way Mr. Woodrow's face had looked when he smiled. It wouldn't do to have him appearing in her dreams. She would go for a quick turn about the garden to clear her head before going to sleep.

Contessa headed to the back of the house and out into the garden. She passed the entrance to the office that had taunted her, and lamplight flickered through the crack beneath the door. It seemed that Mr. Woodrow had returned to his work after their game. She paused for a moment as she passed the office but then continued out the door to the back garden.

She took a breath of the still night air, and instantly, her twirling mind began to slow. The night was quiet, the only sound to be heard the clop of horse hooves from the street in the distance and the trickling of the fountain.

The cool of the night was refreshing in comparison to the warm weather they had been having and it made Contessa's problems seem much smaller. She began to make her way towards the center of the garden, thinking it would be nice to sit and listen to the splash of water for a moment. As she walked, the wind blew through the trees, rustling the nearby leaves. In fact, Contessa mused that the wind sounded almost like a blissful sigh as it moved through the plants.

As Contessa rounded the bend in the garden path, she understood why this comparison had occurred to her. Her favorite perch on the edge of the fountain was already occupied by Gregor and Kristoff, who were sitting very close together indeed. Gregor's hands were fisted in the lapels of Kristoff's coat, rumpling the fine fabric and pulling him in close. Kristoff, for his part, seemed equally enthusiastic, one hand cupping Gregor's face and the other brushing through his hair as their lips pressed together.

Contessa took a step back and gasped softly, but the noise came out louder than she intended. Gregor pulled back, and even in the dim light, Contessa could make out the look of horror on his crimson face. Kristoff sprang to his feet and took a few strides towards Contessa, his palms outstretched placatingly.

"Wait, please. Please don't think poorly of Gregor," Kristoff begged. "This was all my doing, I swear."

Contessa shook her head. "I...I don't think poorly of either of you. I was just caught off guard."

Kristoff relaxed a touch, but Gregor continued to look mortified, burying his head in his hands. Kristoff continued, "I'm sorry. I shouldn't have cornered Gregor while he was working. Please forgive me, it won't happen again."

Now that Contessa had recovered from her initial shock, she had the wherewithal to arch her eyebrows at Kristoff's promise.

"Alright, well, it may happen again," Kristoff conceded as he sensed that Contessa was not going to faint in horror at their actions, "but I will ensure it does not happen in a place where you might unwittingly wander by us."

Contessa raised her chin but couldn't help the upward twist of her lips as she responded, "See that you do."

"With that, I should be going," Kristoff said, straightening his rumpled jacket. He sketched a dramatic bow to Contessa before striding off down the garden path. Gregor didn't look up during this entire exchange but remained seated on the fountain with his hands concealing his face.

Contessa sighed before making her way to the fountain and settling herself on the edge next to Gregor. As she sat, Gregor parted his fingers so that his round blue eyes could peek out between them. Contessa remained silent, patiently waiting for Gregor to speak first.

Eventually, he let his hands drop and looked up at Contessa. He opened and closed his mouth a few times before saying, "I wasn't avoiding my work or anything, Mrs. Woodrow, I promise."

Resisting the urge to shoot him a disbelieving look, Contessa said, "With the way you and Julia keep things running around here, I would say you probably could use a night off."

Gregor nodded and looked down at his twisting hands.

"I'm more concerned about Kristoff's relentless pursuit of you. If he made you at all uncom—"

"I was the one to kiss him, Mrs. Woodrow."

"Oh. Well. In that case, I suppose there is nothing more for us to discuss," Contessa said, about to make her way to her feet, but Gregor stopped her.

"Please don't think poorly of me, Mrs. Woodrow."

Contessa settled herself back down on the fountain edge and cocked her head at Gregor. "I wouldn't think poorly of you for stealing a kiss after work. We're all adults here, Gregor."

Gregor relaxed in his seat next to her, some of the redness draining from his face. "Very wise, Mrs. Woodrow. No wonder Mr. Woodrow seems to get on with you so well."

Contessa suppressed a snort at Gregor's politeness. Still, as she pictured the way her father's face would purple with rage at what she had come upon in the garden, she could understand Gregor's hesitance. It served as a perfect reminder that her father hadn't always been right about everything. Pushing to her feet she said, "On that note, I think I will be heading to bed. I came out here to clear my head, but I sense that you need the refreshing air more than I do."

Gregor nodded. "Goodnight, Mrs. Woodrow, and thank you."

Chapter Eight

Contessa spent the next day fretting over what she would say to Mr. Woodrow when she saw him. As she sat in the garden struggling to focus on the newspaper in front of her, she came to realize that she didn't know exactly what she'd been offered when he'd implied they should cooperate.

Mr. Woodrow had vaguely suggested that joining forces might be beneficial, but he hadn't been clear what he wanted. It seemed illogical to think he might be proposing the daughter of one of his victims help his gang in their violent pursuits. However, he seemed to be aware the plight of the children in the factories had struck a nerve with her. He was going about helping them in his own way, but perhaps with Contessa's aid, they could do more.

Besides, being part of Mr. Woodrow's work might get her access to solid proof of his crimes.

As Contessa readied herself for dinner, she still hadn't settled on exactly what she was going to say to Mr. Woodrow regarding his proposal. It was a supremely uncomfortable feeling for somebody who was used to having a plan, but she found this a more difficult issue than she had faced in the past.

However, as Contessa entered the dining room that evening, it appeared she would have a temporary reprieve. There was only one place setting at the table. Mr. Woodrow didn't materialize as Contessa finished her meal either, and she breathed a sigh of relief, although it was accompanied by a pang of disappointment in her chest. She had to admit that her nights spent over a chess board with Mr. Woodrow were much more diverting than evenings spent alone in the empty house. Once again, Contessa lamented the lack of good reading material. Maybe she should learn to embroider after all.

After a cup of tea, Contessa ended up heading to bed early, if only for the pleasure of Julia's company as she readied her for sleep. Contessa had continued to ask Julia bits about herself, and Julia had begun questioning Contessa about herself in turn. Julia lingered over Contessa's hair just so they could converse a bit longer.

When Julia eventually left, Contessa climbed into the crimson fourposter bed and turned down her lamp. In the darkness, she pondered the silhouettes of the roses adorning her wallpaper. The flowers made her think of Gregor, of how smitten he seemed with Kristoff. It made her wonder what it would feel like to kiss somebody like that.

Contessa jolted awake to a banging noise. She sat bolt upright, head whipping side to side in search of danger.

Her thoughts cleared as the noise came again and she realized it was simply somebody knocking on her door, if rather insistently. Contessa pulled on her dressing gown before padding over to the door and cracking it open. When she peeked into the hall, her jaw dropped in shock, and she immediately threw it wide.

Standing in the hallway was Mr. Woodrow, dressed in shirtsleeves and looking rather the worse for wear. His hair stood out at all angles, and he swayed slightly where he stood, holding on to the doorframe for support. Most shockingly, his shirt was splattered in something dark. In the dim light of the hallway, Contessa couldn't be completely sure, but she thought it was blood.

"What happened?" she gasped. She might know the answer, but she was more concerned with why he had chosen to show up at her bedroom door in this state.

"Don't worry, most of the blood isn't mine," he responded, trying to sound nonchalant even as he gritted his teeth.

Before Contessa could respond, he swayed again where he stood. Contessa found herself reaching out automatically to steady him, her hands landing on his firm shoulders.

"I do need some assistance, though," he said, taking an unsteady step forward. Contessa moved to his side and let him lean on her as they made their way to the bed. He was much larger than her, so it was an awkward affair, but they made it until he could sit on the edge.

"The wound is on my back," Mr. Woodrow said tightly. "I don't know how bad it is because I can't see it."

"I thought you said most of the blood wasn't yours," Contessa pointed out.

"Most of it, not all of it," he countered, his hands moving to the top button of the shirt to undo it.

Contessa's face suddenly grew hot, and she floundered. "What about Gregor? He's the one with the medical kit. I only know the basics."

Mr. Woodrow's fingers paused but remained hovering over the button at his neck. "I happen to know that Kristoff took Gregor out for the evening. If you'd rather me tend to my wounds myself, though, I can leave."

Contessa didn't argue with that, with the assistance he had needed to get to the bed, she doubted he could get far on his own at this point. The fact of the matter was, she had her sworn enemy injured in front of her, giving her the option to do nothing. She could let him suffer alone and possibly die from his injuries.

She was already shaking her head. If he was going to suffer for his crimes, it was going to be after a fair trial, not bleeding out on her bed while she watched.

"I'll help you as best I can, although it might not be much."

Mr. Woodrow nodded and resumed unbuttoning his shirt, the top of a muscled chest coming into view. Contessa ripped her gaze away from him, trying not to stare, but it seemed she didn't know where else to look. She decided to busy herself with lighting the lamps so she would be able to inspect his injuries properly.

By the time she was finished, Mr. Woodrow had completely removed his shirt and angled himself on her bed so his back was to her. She was unsurprised to see his pale skin was not smooth, but dotted with thin white scars, and even a pink one that looked like it may be more recently healed. Most noticeable right now were the series of deep scratches running across his left shoulder blade and down to his mid back. They were still oozing, but it appeared he hadn't been lying about most of the blood on his shirt not being his.

Contessa picked her way closer and perched herself on the edge of the bed next to him. He bowed his head so she could get a better look, and she leaned in to inspect the wounds. This close, she could smell the sweat and blood that clung to him, as well as something darker and more earthy. She found herself inhaling deeply.

Brushing those thoughts from her mind, she focused in on the task before her. In the deepest wound, she thought she caught sight of something glimmering.

"Is it possible there are pieces of glass in these wounds?" she questioned.

"It's possible," he conceded. "I think Gregor has some tools in his kit you could use to get it out. He should have left it downstairs."

He directed Contessa to where the kit would have been left, and she scurried from the room to retrieve it. She was grateful for the moment alone to clear her head after the shocking turn her night had taken. Mr. Woodrow was now shirtless in her bed, although it wasn't in the context she'd thought it would be when she'd married him. Perhaps more surprising was the fact that she was voluntarily helping him.

She hurried back up the stairs with the leather case clutched in her hands. When she pushed through the door back into her bedroom, she found Mr. Woodrow had laid down on the bed. He was on his stomach with his hands folded under his forehead so Contessa would have good access to his injuries. She found she was glad of the positioning, for at this angle, she couldn't look at his face.

Contessa could simply treat the injuries before her without having to think about who the torso belonged to.

Contessa settled herself on the edge of the bed, opening the kit and laying out the tools. She found a pair of pointed tweezers and a long needle that would serve her purposes admirably.

With her tools selected, she turned back to Mr. Woodrow. Blood trickled from his wounds and dripping onto the already red comforter, making it nearly black. Contessa leaned in and placed her hand on his side to steady herself as she selected her starting point. At the contact, Mr. Woodrow jumped. The movement caused the muscles in his back to tense, driving the glass deeper into his skin. He grunted in pain and Contessa jerked her hand back.

"I'm ok. Your hands are just cold." Mr. Woodrow's voice came out muffled from being facedown in the pillow.

Looking at the project before her, Contessa knew he had a lot worse than cold hands coming.

"I'm going to touch you again. Try to hold still," she directed.

As Mr. Woodrow nodded into the pillows, Contessa slipped off her dressing robe and set it on the covers beside her to collect the shards of glass. The cool of the air chilled her skin to goose bumps, and she felt strangely exposed even though Mr. Woodrow couldn't see her from his current position.

When Contessa placed her hand on him again, Mr. Woodrow did a better job of not moving, but she could still see tension across the top of his shoulders, causing the muscles there to cord and bunch.

She began with the shallowest of cuts, picking out the most easily visible fragments first. Mr. Woodrow hissed into the pillow but remained still. The muscles under her hand twitched with the effort. As she began to reach for deeper fragments of glass, she needed a better view. She scooted closer to see until the side of her hip was pressed flush against Mr. Woodrow's ribs. She was overly conscious of his body heat seeping through her thin nightdress, and soon she found she was no longer chilled.

As Contessa finished cleaning the first cut, the silence in the room was thick, broken only by Mr. Woodrow's breathing, which was so measured that Contessa was sure he must be counting his breaths to manage the pain.

Before Contessa began working on the second wound, Mr. Woodrow said into the pillow, "Could you...talk?"

"Talk?" she echoed in confusion.

"Just... to give me something else to think about," Mr. Woodrow said haltingly.

Contessa furrowed her brow before an image came to mind—her mother perched on her bedside when she was ill, singing the sweetest melodies to distract young Contessa from the feverish ache in her bones. The songs told of princesses or knights, and Contessa became so engaged in them that the pains eased until she drifted off to sleep.

Contessa didn't have a singing voice that would calm anybody, so as she picked the first shard of glass out of the next wound, she blurted out the first thought in her head.

"My mother used to sing to me to distract me when I was sick."

"What kind of songs would she sing?" Mr. Woodrow asked through gritted teeth.

Contessa plunged ahead, too distracted by the delicate extraction of a particularly tricky piece of glass to think how odd it was to be telling stories of her mother to the man who was responsible for her death.

"Made up songs about dragons and heroes. They always made me feel better and lulled me off to sleep."

The jagged piece of glass finally pulled free of Mr. Woodrow's skin with a wet sound, and he let out a soft groan as she dropped the crimson-stained shard onto her dressing gown. Contessa rambled on as she investigated to make sure she'd removed all debris from the second cut.

"She was always singing around the house, as she embroidered or brushed my hair. Everybody always paused in what they were doing to listen, her voice was that beautiful. I swear the very sun seemed to shine brighter as she sang."

Contessa ensured the second cut was cleared. Mr. Woodrow's muscles trembled under her touch, and a slight sheen of sweat formed on his back with the effort it was taking him to hold still. She unconsciously ran her hand over his uninjured shoulder, trying to soothe him into relaxing.

Now it was time to move on to the largest cut, across the thick muscle of Mr. Woodrow's upper back. There were several small fragments of glass embedded in the edges of the gruesome wound, with one large shard protruding from the center, glistening red with blood.

"She sounds lovely."

Contessa had been so concerned with examining the task before her that she'd lost the thread of the conversation.

"She was," Contessa murmured as she used the tweezers to remove the smaller pieces of debris.

"You must take after her," Mr. Woodrow grunted into the pillow.

Her hand froze in midair, the tweezers poised above the largest shard as she processed what Mr. Woodrow had said. To buy herself time to respond, she grasped the glass and gently began to pull at it.

In response to her actions, Mr. Woodrow twitched and let out a choked grunt before going limp. It seemed that the pain of the process had finally become too much, and he had fallen unconscious. He must have been delirious during their entire conversation. It would explain that last odd comment.

With Contessa's attention now completely free to focus on the task before her, she set to work on the last shard. She ended up having to employ a needle to dig out the base of the glass while tugging with the tweezers in her other hand. After long minutes, a piece of glass the length of her little finger came free of his back with a wet squelch.

Mr. Woodrow's back now clean of debris, Contessa pulled some ointment and a piece of cloth from the kit beside her and set to cleaning and bandaging the wounds. Her work wasn't as neat as Gregor's, but by the time she'd finished, the cuts were no longer oozing blood.

Contessa admired her handiwork for a moment before realizing the predicament she was in. Mr. Woodrow was unconscious in her bed, and he was too large for her to possibly move on her own, much less without disturbing his injuries.

With a sigh, she bundled up the glass in her ruined dressing gown and brought it over to her dressing table. With Mr. Woodrow's body no longer warm against her side, she began to shiver. She grabbed the blanket from the foot of the bed to wrap around her shoulders. Before she moved away, she paused, contemplating Mr. Woodrow's bare torso laid across the coverlet. She hesitated only a moment before folding the quilt over, covering him up.

Then she made her way to the window seat and settled herself there to wait through the long night until Mr. Woodrow awoke.

Contessa woke to find she could barely move her head, her neck impossibly stiff after spending the night dozing in the window seat. She was momentarily confused as to why she was propped against the cool glass that overlooked the street before she remembered the events of the night before.

She jerked away from the window and looked towards the bed, half expecting to find it empty. Instead, Mr. Woodrow occupied the same spot he had last night. During the night, he had rolled onto his side, so he faced the window where Contessa sat. His face was pillowed on his hand, and his mouth hung slightly open. The entire effect would have been less than intimidating, had the coverlet not slid down around his waist as he slept. In the dim light, the shadows under his muscles were exaggerated, accentuating his wide shoulders and thick chest.

Contessa swallowed, pulling the blanket tighter around herself even though she felt uncharacteristically warm. She had to remind herself not to be embarrassed by the situation. They were technically married. She'd seen as much of his body the night before, but she'd been too distracted by the blood and the glass to take in what the rest of him looked like.

The thought brought Contessa back to last night, and she remembered that Mr. Woodrow was still wounded. She pressed to her feet and padded over to the bed. She expected the creaking of the floor to wake Mr. Woodrow, expecting somebody of his profession to be a light sleeper, but he didn't stir.

As she drew closer to the bed, she could make out a dull purple circle under his good eye. It made her think of how he was already out in the morning before she came down for breakfast, even though she was a habitually early riser. He often went to his office after their nightly game of chess. Perhaps it was no wonder that he slept like the dead.

When Contessa sat down on the side of the bed, the movement jostled Mr. Woodrow enough to finally make him stir. When his eyes fluttered open, they looked momentarily wild, darting around the room as his shoulders tensed. His gaze landed on Contessa after a moment, and his shoulders relaxed although he still looked wary.

"I just came over to check your bandages, see if they need to be changed."

Seeming to remember why he was here, he shook his head and pushed himself to sit. His wince was slight but unmistakable.

"No need. Gregor should be back by now, and I can have him take a look. And if he's not, I will have to have a talk with Kristoff about not getting in the way of my employee's work."

Contessa nodded. Gregor would be far more help than she was.

"Thank you for your help last night. I would be in sorry shape without you," Mr. Woodrow went on, cocking his head as he spoke, like he was as confused by her actions as she was.

"You're welcome, Mr. Woodrow."

He made a face as he swung his feet to floor.

"You don't have to call me that you know," he said, his voice tight with discomfort as he stood.

"Mr. Woodrow?" Contessa asked, taken aback. "What else would I call you?"

"You can just call me Nate. Everybody else does," he paused as he considered for a moment. "At least, that's what people call me to my face."

It seemed odd to call her husband by such a nickname, but then again, this whole situation was turning out to be rather odd.

"Alright Nate," she tested the name out. "Then I would prefer it if you wouldn't call me Mrs. Woodrow as well."

Nate picked up his soiled shirt off the ground and examined it as he spoke.

"Then what should I call you? I can't very well go back to calling you Ms. Cook."

Seeming to decide the shirt was not worth salvaging, Nate threw it over his shoulder.

Contessa chewed her lip. "Well, then you can call me Contessa."

"You're calling me Nate, not Nathanial. That hardly seems even," Nate countered. "What about a nickname? I think Connie would suit you nicely."

Contessa's breath hitched, and she folded her arms over her chest.

"Do you not like Connie? If not that, then maybe Tessa?"

She shook her head. "No, I like Connie. It's just…that is what my mother always called me. Very few people call me that anymore." She met Mr. Woodrow's curious eyes as she spoke, and she expected to be filled with rage at the memory of her mother. Instead of the normal fury rising up in her chest, there was a hollow sort of sadness in the space her heart occupied.

"It's a lovely name. It suits you."

Contessa nodded. "Then Connie it is."

"Well, thank you, Connie," Nate said as he turned to go. "I'm going to go find Gregor before he gets busy preparing breakfast."

He made his way to the door but paused on the threshold for a moment. He turned his head back, not fully looking at her.

"I'm sorry about your mother."

The words were so soft Contessa wasn't sure she heard them correctly, but they almost knocked her off the bed as Nate disappeared around the corner. If she'd been perplexed by her emotions yesterday, the events of the last eight hours were enough to make her feel as if she were drowning.

She sat on the bed for a long time before she rang for Julia. As she contemplated, her eyes roamed over the rumpled and bloody sheets. It reminded her of her question to Mr. Woodrow the prior night. If they were fighting for justice, then why must so much blood be spilled?

Chapter Nine

The seat across from Contessa's was already filled when she entered the dining room for dinner that evening. She jumped when she walked in to find Nate, even though she'd spent all day thinking about him, replaying his words in her mind. She nodded, not sure what she wanted to say despite all her ruminating and sat down to dinner. She was halfway through dutifully spooning her portion of split pea soup into her mouth when Nate broke the silence.

"Is the color of that dress more to your liking?"

Contessa froze with her spoon halfway to her mouth, momentarily dumbstruck by his attempts at conversation. She glanced down at her sleeve, which was indeed an icy blue of a simple cut, mercifully free of lace and bows.

"Yes," she answered simply before pushing her spoon into her mouth without another word. Nate didn't attempt to press her for more of a response, but she could feel his sharp eyes on her through the rest of her meal, even though she pointedly avoided looking at him. In fact, she avoided looking at anything in particular, choosing instead to vacantly stare at her plate and chew her food without tasting it.

"I want to do something to help," Contessa blurted out, the thoughts that had been bubbling in her head finally bursting forth. The troubles of London might have been more complicated than she'd originally thought, but she was done sitting on the sidelines.

Nate looked up hopefully, opening his mouth to respond, but Contessa cut him off before he could speak.

"It doesn't mean that I'm on your side, though, and you would do well to remember that."

"What if I'm on your side?" Nate asked.

"I know for a fact that you aren't."

Nate's good eye narrowed, but he didn't press the matter.

"I'll make some arrangements then. See how you might be able to aid some orphans without brushing up against anything too...unsavory."

Contessa nodded and pushed to her feet, the events of the night before and the lack of sleep finally crashing down on her and making her feel drained. She turned to leave and head to the sanctuary of her bedroom, but before she turned into the hallway, Nate spoke behind her.

"It's a shame your mother hasn't gotten to see what you've grown into."

Contessa stopped but didn't face Nate as she asked, "Oh, and what am I?"

"Whatever you want to be."

Contessa left the room without responding, but she was glad Nate hadn't been able to see her reaction as she blinked hastily.

Apparently, the arrangements Nate had to make for their newly developed partnership were involved, because Contessa didn't see him at all the next day. She couldn't decide whether or not she was glad about it, and when she tried to discern her feelings on the matter, she only succeeded in giving herself a headache. This seemed to be a theme for the day, as Contessa only managed to spin her thoughts in endless circles. Even she had lost sight of her goals.

Contessa didn't fetch the newspaper from Gregor for her afternoon reading in the garden. It seemed Gregor had noticed the break in her routine, and when she entered the dining room for dinner, the paper was neatly folded at her usual place. On top of it was a letter sealed with green wax embossed with scales. She furrowed her brow but ate before heading upstairs to read both the letter and the paper.

Sitting on her bed, Contessa cracked the seal open to find that this note from her father was just as short as the last. All it said was that he was anxious to see her at the executions tomorrow. Contessa hadn't known there were executions scheduled, but she'd been too distracted to read the paper today. She had no way of knowing if Nate planned on attending tomorrow. Still, since he had watched the last executions, it served to reason he would do the same tomorrow.

On the other hand, maybe they shouldn't attend tomorrow. Contessa shook the thought from her head immediately. Of course, she would follow her father's instructions. Her main goal was still to bring criminals to justice, even if she was doing what was necessary to help the people of London in the meantime.

Contessa would make sure they attended the executions tomorrow and hear the information her father had for her. Maybe it would mean she could be free of this marriage soon and return to her father's house. However, as Contessa lay down to sleep, she knew going home wouldn't mean she could put everything she'd learned behind her.

It seemed Contessa shouldn't have worried about the plans for attending the execution, for no sooner had she finished her breakfast than Gregor announced he was going to pull the carriage around. Nate entered the dining room just as Gregor left, looking solemn in all black and holding a smart top hat in his hands. It made Contessa wince at her own attire, a canary yellow dress bedecked with a series of oversized bows. It seemed outright disrespectful to wear such a garment to an execution, but she hadn't thought to request a different outfit when Julia dressed her that morning.

Nate broke her from her thoughts by clearing his throat.

"You know, you can stay here if you'd prefer."

Contessa blinked.

"Oh, no it's alright. It would not do for a wife to make her husband attend such an event alone."

It was the first excuse Contessa could come up with for her insistence on attending. She knew Nate could tell she didn't enjoy watching people hang. He tilted his head and looked at her with something like softness—if his face had been capable of such an expression—before turning to lead her out to the carriage.

As the carriage lurched forward and clattered through the streets towards the main square, Contessa watched Nate's hands twist his hat in a white-knuckled grip. She nearly asked him why he insisted on attending the executions when they obviously caused him such distress. However, as she opened her mouth, the image of his white, sweat-soaked face from the last time flashed before her eyes, and it suddenly felt like much too personal of a question for a man she'd already gotten to know better than she'd ever intended to.

They remained silent the entire ride, even as they pulled up to the square and Nate stepped down out of the carriage. This time, though, instead of letting Gregor help her out of the carriage, Nate turned back and offered his hand as Contessa stepped down. It was a small thing, but it made the idea of the coming horror a little more bearable than it had been last time, when she'd felt as alone as humanly possible.

They wove their way towards a spot in the rear of the square, not too close to the looming scaffold, but giving them a clear sightline to the proceedings. Contessa avoided looking towards the front of the square where the police officers stood lined up at attention. Still, in the brief glance she spared them when she arrived, she couldn't help but notice that Joseph stood in the place of honor next to her father. His words about being on the wrong side played unbidden in her head. She tried not to think about what he would say about her offering to help Nate.

Contessa also couldn't bear to look at the rest of the assembling crowd, who once again dressed more like they were attending a party than anything else. The ones who were solemn hung back or peeked out of shuttered windows. Contessa stared straight ahead at the scaffold in the center of the square. Its stark height only served to add to Contessa's growing sense of foreboding. She always dreaded the hangings, but this time was worse than usual, a gnawing sensation in the pit of her stomach growing until she felt like she was facing the gallows herself today. Heart pounding in her ears, she resisted the urge to rock from foot to foot and search around frantically for some sort of threat.

Taking deep breaths, Contessa tried to calm herself with thoughts of her father's firm hand when it came to security. He would have dealt with any threats to the execution—unless there was something different this time. He had insisted it was important for her and Nate to be here. Her mind raced with possibilities.

Contessa was ripped from her anxiety by a firm hand on her shoulder.

"Connie, what is it?"

Contessa jerked in surprise as she glanced at Nate, who was looking her up and down like she was unwell. Giving how she felt, he might be right.

"I...I don't know." Contessa's voice came out thinner than ever before. "I feel...afraid."

Nate's good eyebrow shot up, and Contessa was just as startled as he was at her admission.

"You can go wait in the carriage," Nate offered. "You don't have to watch, and I'll come join you afterwards."

Just as Contessa became sure this was a good idea, she was struck by the sudden need to not be alone.

"No," she said, much of her usual firmness returning to her voice. "No, you have to come with me. We need to leave."

Nate hesitated, his brow furrowing even further. Not having the patience to wait for him to make up his mind, Contessa grabbed his hand and began forcibly towing him through the crowd. This seemed to make Nate's decision for him, and he didn't resist, instead trotting to catch up with Contessa as she marched across the square. Now that she was moving, some of the tension in the pit of Contessa's stomach eased, but she couldn't stop her eyes from darting this way and that, still on high alert.

What felt like ages later but was only a few moments, the pair emerged from the crowd at the edge of the square and turned to make their way towards the carriage. No sooner had Contessa let out the breath she'd been holding and dropped Nate's hand, there was the earsplitting bang of a gunshot.

Contessa's hands flew to her ears as she whirled around to find the source of the noise. She turned just in time to see the hangman tip over face first on the scaffolding, a bloody bullet hole exactly in the middle of his forehead. People instantly began screaming and pointing at the spot where Contessa and Nate had been standing not a minute earlier. Before Contessa could spot the gunner, a firm grip on her elbow yanked her around the corner.

Nate continued to tug on her arm even as Contessa stumbled over her skirts, pushing through a door and yanking her through behind him. The sounds of screaming and chaos in the square were dulled as Nate slammed the door behind them and threw the bolt.

As soon as they were alone in the darkness, Nate swore colorfully. It was the type of language that was supposed to offend ladies like herself, but Contessa didn't blush as she echoed similar sentiments in her own head.

"Where have you brought us?" Contessa asked when he paused for breath.

Nate seemed to compose himself at the reminder of her presence and took a steadying breath.

"It's a storeroom. I've used it as a hideout before."

Contessa vaguely thought about trying to figure out what storeroom this was so she could track it down later, but that train of thought quickly took a backseat in her mind as Nate began swearing again. He clearly was beyond worrying about admitting to criminal activity at this point.

"Are you hurt?" Contessa ventured.

"No, but this is bad."

Now that Contessa's eyes had adjusted to the darkness, she could see Nate plunging his hands into his hair in frustration.

"That gunshot came from right where we had been standing, and I'm the first person people would want to implicate in the disturbance of an execution. Especially when they thought the people being executed were Lions. It's like somebody..."

"Tried to frame you," Contessa finished for him, her mind racing again. "My father wanted..." She kept herself from finishing the thought...that her father had wanted to make sure he was at the execution that day. She shoved the suspicion aside to turn back to the issue at hand.

"Do you think we were seen there?" she asked.

Nate let out a sound almost akin to a growl.

"I'm not exactly hard to recognize. People will be willing to testify against me, and I don't exactly have an alibi."

"You would if you were seen somewhere else," Contessa suggested. "Right now, we should go somewhere very public and pretend as if we don't know what's happened. It could sow enough doubt that whoever framed you would have to risk looking like a liar in court."

Even as Contessa spoke, she had to wonder why she was doing this. Of course, if Nate had been seen at the crime scene, then so had she. She didn't want to be implicated.

"We need to be seen somewhere with lots of high society people that any accuser wouldn't want to cross," she continued.

"Strolling in the park?" Nate suggested.

"No, we need something more high profile." Contessa wracked her brain before another announcement from the newspaper the day before presented itself to her. "There is a public ball at Snowberry Hall. It's far enough from here that it wouldn't seem suspicious, but close enough to get there quickly. Although if we take the carriage, it will be obvious we are just arriving and haven't been there the whole time. Maybe—"

"That much, I do have a solution for," Nate cut in, already striding further into the darkened space. She trailed behind him, struggling to keep her skirts from snagging on the cramped shelves and crates in the darkness.

By the time Contessa caught up with Nate, she could hear the dull scraping of something heavy sliding across the stone floor and just make out Nate's broad shoulders flexing as he shifted a huge flour barrel. Before Contessa could ask what they needed that much flour for, Nate bent down and opened what appeared to be a hidden panel in the bit of wall.

"Is that…"

"A secret tunnel, yes. I'll explain later, but right now, time is of the essence."

Contessa snapped her mouth shut but added another topic to the long list of questions that needed answering when they got home—if they managed to make it there without being arrested, that was.

As Nate stepped into the tunnel, he reached back to her, and it took Contessa a beat to realize what he wanted. Her fingers wavered in midair for a moment as it struck her that this was not just the choice to take her husband's hand. This was the choice to help him evade arrest—an arrest for something that, for once, he hadn't done.

"It's dark inside, and I know the way," said Nate as way of explanation when he noticed her hesitation, his hand drooping slightly as if he were about to withdraw it.

Before he could return his arm to his side, Contessa reached out and grabbed it. A moment later, when Nate had shut the panel behind him, she was glad to be holding onto him. She couldn't see more than a few inches in front of her, and while she didn't fear the dark, it would have been disconcerting if she didn't have the warm roughness of Nate's hand to ground her.

She had no more than a moment to contemplate the blackness before Nate pulled on her hand and they began hurtling through the tunnels at breakneck speed. The pace at which Nate turned invisible corners and navigated the few steps up and down, warning Contessa of the upcoming obstacles, made it clear he was no stranger to this particular passage. She would have speculated more had she not been so focused on keeping her footing.

As quickly as they had traversed the tunnels, Nate stopped, causing Contessa to run headlong into his back. It was like crashing into a mountain, and Contessa caught the briefest whiff of sweat and earth before righting herself and smoothing her dress. She was pleasantly surprised by how fast they had arrived, getting to the ball in nearly half the time they would've if they had gone through the streets.

Nate didn't comment on their collision, instead standing stock still as if listening for something.

"This panel should let us out in one of the rear hallways of Snowberry Hall," he whispered. "I don't think I hear anybody out there, so we should be safe to go in."

Light seeped in through a hairline crack as Nate pressed some hidden panel to open the wall. They were greeted by the distant sounds of music and merriment but heard no voices in the immediate vicinity. Nate pressed the panel open, and they slipped out into an empty hallway, forcing Contessa to blink rapidly in the sunlight streaming in through the high windows on the opposite wall.

She only had a moment to let her eyes adjust before Nate was marching down the hall towards the laughter and voices in the ballroom.

"Better be seen as soon as possible if this is going to work," Nate grumbled, about to lead them around the corner into the open ballroom.

Contessa darted after him, grabbing his elbow.

"Wait! We need to look like we've been here for a while and have an excuse for why we're suddenly appearing out of a back hallway."

Nate looked quizzical.

"And what excuse could we have for skulking around a back hallway that wouldn't raise even more suspicion?"

"Not all skulking means you've committed a crime," Contessa snapped. "Act like you've been kissing me."

Nate purpled for a moment before giving her a single jerky nod. Seeming to catch on to what Contessa was getting at, he tugged at his cravat, making it look crinkled and askew.

"You should mess up your hair and..." Nate chewed on his words for a moment, "giggle or something."

Not one usually prone to giggling, Contessa found herself surprised by how easily a high-pitched laugh bubbled up in the back of her throat. Perhaps it was the hysteria of the whole situation, or perhaps it was how embarrassed somebody as notorious as Nathanial Woodrow seemed by the prospect of stealing a private moment with his wife at a ball.

Taking advantage of her momentary girlishness, Contessa leaned herself into Nate's side, and they ducked around the corner into the ballroom. It was too easy to relax into the arm he threw around her waist, and another giggle burst past her lips. Nate, for his part, gave her what appeared to be his best try at a devilish grin, but it sat rather oddly on his face and came off as a grimace.

They found the ballroom crowded and lively, and Contessa worked on weaving them through the chattering crowds in as visible a way as possible. Suddenly, she was grateful for the prominent color of her dress, as everybody she passed spared her a glance. The room grew momentarily quieter as the musicians in the corner finished their song, and the couples on the floor bowed and curtsied to each other.

Suddenly struck by an idea, Contessa tugged Nate towards the emptying space in the middle of the floor.

"We're going to dance," she announced, directing them as close as she could get to the center of the room.

Agreeable to all her suggestions so far, Nate seemed to have reached his limit as he balked.

"That can't possibly be a good idea. Don't you remember... You know neither of us can dance."

"But everybody watches the dance floor, and they're sure to remember we were here if we dance. And not to worry, the worse we dance, the more memorable it will be," Contessa stated as she positioned them across from each other.

At that moment, the musicians played the opening notes of a gavotte, and Nate mumbled under his breath, "This is about to be the most memorable dance in the history of London."

As it turned out, Nate may have been right. Only through sheer adrenaline and a steel will did both Nate and Contessa manage to stay upright for the next several minutes. While the waltz at their wedding had been far from graceful, at least it had been short and slow. Their combined inexperience with dancing was magnified tenfold with the livelier dance, and the matter was further complicated by the fact they now had to navigate around the other couples occupying the dance floor. Owing to the amount of minor collisions they caused, Contessa had no doubt everybody in the ballroom had noticed them by the time the musicians brought the dance to a close.

Somewhat breathless, Contessa offered Nate a polite curtsy at the conclusion of the dance. Nate surprised her by taking her hand and pressing a kiss to the knuckles, but she realized such a gesture would probably be expected for a married couple out for an afternoon of merriment. Still, the rough feeling of the scar across his lips brushing her skin came as a shock and she almost jumped. Then the moment was over, and he led her to the side of the dance floor.

"Now that we've thoroughly embarrassed ourselves, can you promise me we will never do that again?" Nate grumbled, producing a handkerchief to blot his now damp brow.

"Believe me, I took no pleasure in it either, but I'm sure anybody here will be able to testify that we were dancing at the ball this afternoon," whispered Contessa, so as not to be overheard, as she fanned herself with a hand. She glanced around, finding there were indeed several influential socialites in their vicinity.

Still, Nate looked uncomfortable in the crowd, shifting from foot to foot and fussing with his cravat as if it was strangling him.

"I think we've been here quite long enough to make an appearance," he grumbled again.

"Indeed, it is rather warm in here," Contessa said for the benefit of anybody who might be listening. "Perhaps it's time to go home and rest."

As they wove their way through the crowd and pushed out of the exit, Contessa's heart sank. There was a line of carriages in the circular drive of the public ballroom, but of course, their own black coach was nowhere to be found. Nate seemed to have the exact same realization and let out a sound halfway between a sigh and a growl.

"I'm not entirely sure my feet can handle a walk home in these shoes after that dance," Contessa admitted.

Nate looked down towards where her feet were hidden by the hem of her dress and frowned.

"Damn impractical things," he muttered. "Come with me, I may have a solution."

He led Contessa to the edge of the drive where it met a side street. It was deserted except for a small group of children rolling a ball between themselves. Nate leaned on the wall and shoved his hands in his pockets, suddenly looking the picture of casual ease, the exact opposite of his demeanor in the ballroom.

He let out a low whistle, and the heads of several of the children popped up. The instant she spotted him, a round faced little girl sprang to her feet and skipped over to them.

"Nate!" She squeaked as she approached. "Whatcha doing round these parts? You haven't visited in ages!"

"I know. I've been busy. You've gotten big while I've been gone, though, Poppy. Not letting John push you around too much I hope?" Nate answered with easy familiarity.

The girl, Poppy, responded with a wide smile, revealing missing front teeth. "No, sir."

"That's my girl," Nate praised. "You think you could do me a favor? Gregor is with our carriage over by the town square. You think you could fetch him for me?"

The girl nodded vigorously, bouncing on her toes. "You got it Nate! I'll be back with him right quick!"

Poppy took off down the side street at a headlong sprint.

Nate finally turned back to Contessa, who had been watching the whole exchange in fascination, feeling oddly like an outsider. Now that he was looking at her, she cocked her head and raised an eyebrow.

"You probably don't want to know," Nate offered by way of response, rubbing the good side of his face wearily.

"Oh, I've decided there are a good number of things I do want to know after the day we've had," Contessa said, folding her arms.

"That's fair enough, but can we at least wait until we're at home and can do it over a glass of whiskey?" Nate conceded, looking exhausted.

"Alright, but don't think I'm going to let this drop."

"I wouldn't dream of it."

Silence fell as they returned to the drive to wait for Gregor and the carriage. It seemed Poppy was good to her word, and it wasn't long before there was a clatter of hooves and the familiar coach pulled into the drive, Poppy perched next to Gregor on the driver's seat. As it came to a halt in front of Contessa and Nate, the girl hopped down and gave them another wide grin.

"As promised, Nate!" She gestured proudly to the carriage.

"You've become quite the fast runner." Nate fished a copper piece out of his pocket and flipped it to the girl, who snatched it deftly out of the air. Poppy pocketed the coin and disappeared around the corner, presumably to rejoin her group of friends.

Contessa and Nate made to enter the carriage, and Gregor immediately opened his mouth to bombard them with questions. Nate held up a hand to silence him.

"Save it until we're home, Gregor."

As the horses clattered over the cobblestones to the safety of the house, the thought dominating Contessa's mind was which of her questions she wanted answered first.

Chapter Ten

When they arrived back at the house, Gregor attempted to fuss over Contessa and Nate like an overbearing mother hen, but Contessa wasn't having it. At some point, Nate would have to explain to him how they had gotten away safely, but for now, it seemed Gregor could tell they were breathing and without major injury, so that would have to be enough. Now was the time for a frank conversation with her husband.

Nate seemed to be of like mind, dismissing Gregor in a way that would have been firm had it not been interspersed with assurances they were safe and he would explain later. Gregor glanced at Contessa, and his eyes lit with understanding. She was overdue on a lot of explanations. Once Gregor had reluctantly retreated in the direction of the gardens, Nate led Contessa to the back of the house. Contessa was almost shocked when they stopped in front of the locked door to his office, but it was hardly the oddest thing that had happened today.

Nate produced a key from a hidden pocket on the inside of his waistcoat and used it to open the door, gesturing for Contessa to lead the way inside. She looked around as she stepped past him, getting her first good look at the space while not fearful of being discovered. It looked much like it had when she had been there last, though without the wicked knife on the desk. In the sunlight shining in from a small window, Contessa could now see the room was painted in a pale blue, the shelves filled with all sorts of trinkets from globes to pen stands. Contessa couldn't help but notice that these too were noticeably empty of books.

A clinking of glass drew Contessa's attention, and she turned to find that, true to his word, Nate was pulling a decanter of whiskey off one of the shelves and pouring a healthy amount into two cut crystal glasses.

"I normally save this for special occasions but," Nate shrugged one shoulder as he passed her a glass, "today feels like as good a day as any to celebrate being alive."

"As well as out of prison," Contessa commented as she plucked the glass from his fingers and gave it a sniff. It smelled richly of cloves and oak, and Contessa gave an appreciative hum.

"I'm likely only going to stay out of prison due to your quick thinking. There were quite a few people that could testify we were at that ball. Influential people that somebody wanting to frame me wouldn't want to cross in court." Nate swirled his glass thoughtfully, watching the amber liquid slosh against the sides as he spoke. "Although they probably wouldn't come forward just to defend me. It's probably your presence as the chief's daughter that saved my skin."

Contessa hummed noncommittally as she perched herself on the wooden chair across from the desk, keeping her focus on smoothing her skirts. She ignored the implied question in Nate's comment. If he was hoping to coax some admission as to why she'd helped him, he was going to have to be far more direct.

Seeming to sense Contessa's reticence, Nate sat himself on top of his desk as he continued, "You know, you probably wouldn't have been implicated if I had been framed for the disturbance at the execution. Nobody would want to testify against the daughter of the chief, even if you had been at the scene of a crime. The same notoriety that would have saved you is exactly what I have to thank for not being in custody right now."

"Are we sure you were being framed?" Contessa deflected. "We had to assume the worst in the moment, but it could have all been a coincidence."

Nate shook his head.

"No, it's all too much to be sheer happenstance. The paper said the Talented being hanged were from the Lions, but I'd never seen those people before in my life. I originally thought it was a mistake, but..."

"Careful, it might sound like you are admitting to being associated with the Lion gang," Contessa commented with an arched brow.

Nate fixed her with a flat stare, his eyes penetrating as he asked, "Are we really going to play this game still, after what we've just been through? Dancing around facts we both know is getting exhausting, and I have a hard time believing you're going to turn me in for it when you just helped me escape arrest."

Contessa shifted in her seat. "Well, that was for a crime you didn't commit. Who is to say I might feel differently when you are actually guilty?"

"Your father seems to have no such scruples," Nate snorted into his glass.

Contessa opened her mouth to argue that they had no way of knowing her father was behind the set up but then snapped it shut again, remembering her father's insistence that Nate attend the executions. She pursed her lips, and her inner turmoil didn't go unnoticed by Nate.

"I'm glad to see you're no longer set on defending your father," he commented. "Although I imagine it must be hard to try to impress a father who would so thoroughly disapprove of you if he truly knew you."

"What is that supposed to imply?" Contessa snapped, her cheeks growing hot. Helping Nate was causing her enough turmoil without him rubbing the salt of her betraying her family in the wound.

Nate blinked.

"Your father has made it his life's mission to wipe out the Talented," he said slowly.

"And what of it?"

"But..." Nate's brow furrowed. "You're Talented. You must have had to hide it from your father your whole life."

Contessa blinked once, then again. Then she shook her head, as if that could force Nate's words to make sense.

"How could you possibly think I'm Cursed?"

"Only the Royal Police call us Cursed," Nate snorted derisively, "but I know because I'm Talented, and I could sense it on you the moment I saw you."

Contessa stared at Nate silently, hoping she would detect some hint of a lie on his twisted face, but she found he only looked as confused as she felt.

"That's why I asked to marry you," Nate continued, as if all of this should have been obvious. "I wanted to give you a chance to get away from your father before he found out and you were endangered. It wasn't an elegant solution, but it was the best thing I could come up with on short notice. I assumed you agreed to marry me because you knew you needed to get out of your father's house."

Contessa shook her head dumbly, mind feeling dull as a spoon as she tried to process his words.

Nate sighed and scrubbed his face with a large hand. "That would explain the hatred I felt rolling off you when we were first married. I must have truly seemed like the Beast everybody calls me for asking to marry somebody I had never even spoken to."

This finally snapped Contessa out of the trance that seemed to have overtaken her.

"You think that's why I hate you?"

Nate drew back as if Contessa had slapped him.

"Of course. If you thought I wanted to marry you without even knowing you just because of how you looked—"

"Your shallowness is the least of my concern when I'm married to an actual murderer!"

Nate chewed on his lips looking hurt, but still appeared rather confused.

"People have died in the attacks of my gangs before, yes, but only those that enslave children or worse. I've never murdered anybody in cold blood before, though."

Contessa didn't know she'd jumped to her feet.

"That's not what it looked like when my mother bled out in my arms with three slashes cut across her face!"

The glass slipped from Contessa's fingers and shattered on the floor, shards going everywhere and liquid splattering the hem of her dress. The crash seemed unnaturally loud in the total silence following Contessa's shouting.

"You think I murdered your mother?" Nate asked quietly, as if he was explaining this fact to himself more than asking her for confirmation.

Contessa was still trembling, but she managed to make her voice firm as she spoke.

"*That* is why I agreed to marry you. So I could be the one to bring down my mother's killer from the inside. And then everything got all turned around, and I've ended up helping you, and I don't know how I can live with myself for it." Contessa's eyes burned but she refused to let herself cry.

Nate looked as if he had been turned into a statue, and the silence stretched long as Contessa tried to swallow down her tears. She clenched her fists at her side to try and control her shaking, but to no avail.

"I didn't murder your mother."

Contessa swallowed until she could speak again.

"Why would I believe that?"

"Because I don't cut slashes into people's faces."

There was silence again as Contessa stared.

"Why don't you sit down, and I can explain," Nate said, his voice the gentlest she'd ever heard it, as if he were approaching a wild animal.

Contessa sank back down onto her chair. Her legs shook so hard they wouldn't have held her upright for much longer anyways.

Nate shifted so he faced her fully from his perch on the desk, one long leg folded in front of him as the other dangled down towards the floor. He took a long gulp from his glass before he began.

"I grew up working in the factories with the rest of the orphans on the street. I assumed my parents had been killed in the Inquires, but I never knew. Either way, my own Talent started to display itself when I was about twelve, and I knew I wouldn't be able to hide it forever. So, a group of other factory workers—some

Talented, some not—made a plan to run away. To live on the streets where we thought we would have a better chance of hiding our Talents from the authorities and where we would be free of the brutal working conditions. Kristoff was one of the boys who escaped with me. When we were finally free, I started to lead the band of children. You see, I can use my Talent to sense people's intentions and feelings.

"For a while, I used it to gamble for money to feed us, and I always won because I could tell when people were bluffing. Eventually, we started running bigger cons, and I began investing our earnings in endeavors I could sense would be successful. That's how I made my fortune, and the Lions formed from that original group of escaped factory children.

"As we became more successful, we started going back to get the other children out of the factory. I used my abilities to sense Talented children among the workers, and we tried to get them out before they, too, were discovered and hanged. During the escapes, though, several of the Lions started getting more and more violent. They killed the foremen and factory owners for revenge for the way they treated us, and they began leaving the slashes on their victims' faces.

"Eventually, I confronted them, telling them it was our mission to free the workers, not to get revenge. There was a huge fight, and they ended up leaving the Lions to go join other gangs, but by then, people had already associated that signature with us. Other gangs have used the slashes ever since to push responsibility for their crimes onto us. I've never tried to stop it, because the fear associated with the Lions gives all our members a certain degree of protection."

Contessa didn't realize she'd been holding her breath while Nate spoke until she tried to speak and found herself breathless. She panted for a moment before asking, "So, my mother..."

"I'm sorry," Nate said, his eyes full of sympathy, "I didn't even know I had been blamed for it. It could have been any one of the rival gangs who likes to frame us for their violence."

It couldn't possibly be true. Her world was being turned inside out, and she no longer knew which way was up.

"You didn't kill my mother, and I'm Cursed."

"Talented." Nate corrected her patiently, apparently willing to let her repeat her questions again and again until she believed the answers.

"What is my Talent?"

Nate shook his head as he responded. "I'm afraid I don't know. My Talent doesn't work like that. It's far more general, sort of an extra sense that gives me vague intentions. For example, I could sense you hated me, but I had no clue as to why. I can also sense the presence of a Talent, but never what it is. I've learned to hone my skills over time, so I can sense lying or fear, but I'm still far from being able to read minds."

"I guess that would explain how you were able to make such strategic investments and amass wealth so quickly," Contessa mused absently. The shock faded, instead being replaced by a pleasant warm numbness. She seemed to be experiencing some sort of acceptance of the truth without absorbing any of the facts into her reality yet.

Nate, apparently, could use his Talent to sense her state and offered gently, "This has been a lot to process. Why don't I get Gregor to make us a pot of tea to settle your nerves?"

At the glare Contessa shot him, Nate held up his hands placatingly and amended, "Not that you're hysterical or anything. It's just been a long day, and the whiskey hasn't seemed to have the desired effect."

Contessa, content that she didn't appear to be somebody in dire need of having their nerves settled, pursed her lips and nodded her assent.

Nate slid from the desk and ducked from the room with a quick assurance that he would be back as soon as he found Gregor. Grateful for a moment to collect herself, Contessa slumped in her chair and buried her face in her hands. She tried to start at the beginning of their conversation, picking through each comment and organizing each bit of new information, desperately trying to reconcile all this new content with her present world view and failing miserably. She abandoned that pursuit almost immediately in favor of making a mental list of questions she still needed to ask Nate. While this task was much easier, she hadn't made it through more than two questions before a bell chimed, echoing loudly through the house.

Contessa shot upright in her seat, frozen. In the entire time she'd been living in the house, not a single visitor had rung the front bell, and the sound startled her. No sooner had the echoing faded than the bell chimed again, somehow managing to sound more urgent even though the tone was the same.

Contessa sprung to her feet and strode through the house, picking her skirts up to walk faster. All she could think of was that, after all the trouble they had gone to, the police were coming to arrest Nate for the disturbance at the execution anyways. While the question of how she felt about Nate's guilt in light of the new information echoed unanswered in her head, she was sure she would let him be convicted of something he hadn't done when she'd gone to such lengths to get him an alibi.

Picking up her pace, Contessa slid around the corner into the front hall, hoping that if she was the one to answer the door, she could have a chance to use her influence to talk the officers out of making the arrest. She was already forming arguments in her mind when she yanked the door open, only to draw up short as she found her father standing on the front step, completely alone.

Contessa would have expected him to bring reinforcements when arresting such a notorious man, but she didn't have time to ponder further as her father instantly grabbed her wrist and yanked her onto the front porch. His nails bit into her skin, and Contessa barely managed to suppress a yelp of surprise as she stumbled onto the stoop.

"What part of 'be at the executions' did you not understand?" he demanded.

When Contessa had regained her balance, she looked up to find her father's face purpling under his neat moustache, and she schooled her features into neutral surprise as quickly as she could manage.

"Well, Mr. Woodrow wanted to go to the public ball, and I thought it might be a good opportunity to gain his tru—"

"You thought?" Her father's grip on her wrist tightened even further, and Contessa ground her teeth as her father continued. "This wasn't the time for thinking, Contessa. This was the time for doing as you were told. I could have had you home and your mother's murderer at the gallows in a week, but then I found out you were at a public ball today. *Dancing* of all things."

Her father's voice was a low hiss, but Contessa's eyes still widened at the fact he would talk about such things so openly. His rage was making a vein in his temple throb, reinforcing the idea he wasn't thinking rationally.

"I didn't want to draw Mr. Woodrow's suspicion by being too insistent," Contessa tried to reason as she attempted to pull her wrist from her father's grasp, but he seemed beyond reason.

"I thought you had the iron will necessary to pull this off, but when the time came, you were nothing more than a cowering damsel."

At this, Contessa did manage to wrench herself out of his grasp and was opening her mouth to say something she was sure to regret when Nate ducked around the door.

"There you are, darling! I just returned from making our tea when I found you had disappeared. I was afraid you had gotten bashful on me."

Nate stepped onto the stoop and put a hand on Contessa's waist, pulling her a step closer to him and away from her father.

"How nice of you to visit," Nate commented to Chief Cook, wearing a broad smile that made his features appear less disfigured. "I know Connie here misses you terribly, it must do her good to see you."

Her father stiffened at the use of the familiar nickname, and he offered a single sharp nod, keeping his lips set in a firm line.

"Contessa and I just got back from an afternoon of dancing," Nate continued in a voice so convincingly friendly that Contessa now understood how he had conned his way into such wealth. "Nothing like a little revelry to remind me how beautiful my wife is and make me want to hurry her home."

Nate pulled Contessa a few inches closer to him as he spoke, and she allowed the familiarity, hoping it would hide the fact she was still trembling with rage. She allowed him to back them towards the still open door, trying to seem natural even as her father stood so stiffly that she could have been convinced he was made of stone.

"I must insist on continuing to monopolize my wife's evening, but I'll be sure to have my man bring her around to your house for tea this week," Nate continued to explain easily even as he led them back inside the safety of the house. "It was so kind of you to pay a visit."

Contessa caught one last look at her father's dumbstruck face before Nate quickly shut the door between them. Now that she could no longer see her father, Contessa's rage quickly faded, and she felt deflated. The panic that had been propping her up when she answered the door left her all at once, and now she felt like a puppet whose strings had been cut.

Nate's arm around her waist tightened, making Contessa realize she'd been making him support some of her weight in her sudden exhaustion. She regained her footing and stepped away from him, instantly regretting the loss of warmth and support.

For his part, Nate hurriedly smoothed his clothes, seeming surprisingly embarrassed by the situation, considering Contessa had already seen him without his shirt.

"I'm sorry about that," said Nate. "I could sense your rage across the house, and I thought it would be better to interrupt before you accidentally incriminated yourself. Wouldn't want you to spoil all the hard work you put into making us appear innocent."

Contessa nodded dumbly, but Nate was still looking at her like he expected some sort of answer, so she said the first thing that came to her mind.

"I'd like to go to bed."

Nate blinked.

"Oh, yes. Of course. Today has been quite eventful. Nothing of what we have discussed can't wait until morning. I'll send Julia up."

Contessa nodded again, offering Nate a quiet thank you.

Before Contessa turned to head up the stairs, Nate raised his hand halfway, and Contessa was unsure if he meant to pat her shoulder or grab her hand. Before she could decide, he let it drop back to his side again.

"We can figure things out in the morning. Get some rest, Connie."

On her way up the stairs, Contessa couldn't help but feel comforted by the use of her old nickname.

Chapter Eleven

Contessa considered how wise a woman her mother had been when she told her there was nothing like a good night's sleep to set things right. Already halfway through a large breakfast, Contessa was feeling much more herself, and her mind was already methodically replaying each minute of the day before and scouring it for important bits of information.

Still, one discovery kept circling to the front of Contessa's thoughts, no matter how hard she tried to think of other things. Nate hadn't killed her mother. Her father's skeptical voice played in her head, telling her that a Beast like Nate wouldn't hesitate to lie if it meant he could manipulate her more easily, but the voice grew softer and softer as she contemplated. Instead, Nate's soft apology from several nights ago grew louder in its place, and Contessa felt Nate's innocence was the puzzle piece she'd been missing throughout their marriage. Still, she had so many questions lingering in her mind that Contessa only managed to stay to finish her breakfast through extensive self-discipline.

Contessa was saved from her own impatience just as she was serving herself a second bowl of porridge by the entrance of Kristoff and Nate. Their arrival was signaled before they rounded the doorway by Kristoff's bombastic laugh, and Contessa was momentarily curious what Nate could have said that was so funny.

Immediately upon catching sight of Contessa, Kristoff crossed the room to her and snatched up one of her hands in both of his.

"My dear Mrs. Woodrow, I owe you my deepest gratitude," Kristoff said as he bowed over her hand with a flourish.

"What for?"

"I hear that it was your quick thinking that saved Nate here from arrest yesterday," Nate continued, releasing Contessa's hand and throwing himself into the chair next to hers. "Normally, it's my job to keep him out of too much trouble, but I'm glad you do such a good job in my stead when I'm not there." Nate, meanwhile, sat himself down across the table from Contessa with none of Kristoff's easy grace and frowned.

"And how, Kristoff, are you supposed to be the one keeping me out of trouble when you're the one making the trouble in the first place?" Nate asked as he forked four pieces of toast onto his plate.

"Ignore him," Kristoff said with a wave of his hand. "He's just grumpy I insisted he get a good night's sleep after yesterday's excitement when he would have rather been running around the city trying to get more information on who set him up."

"But we already know it was my father who tried to frame you, right?"

Nate had just torn into a heavily buttered piece of toast and was forced to chew quickly, spraying crumbs onto his plate, until he could swallow and answer. "Yes, but he couldn't very well use his own officers to pull off an illegal operation like that. He must have had help from outside the law."

Kristoff thumbed the revolver at his hip as he cut in. "When you're lucky enough to be as influential as Nate here, you have a lot of enemies. The trick is to figure out who hates you so much they would work with law enforcement to take you down. My money is on the Rattlesnakes. They've wanted to see the Lion's fall ever since Two-Faced Thomas became one of Caleb's lieutenants."

Contessa's mind still stuck on one thing as she interrupted. "You are saying my father is cooperating with the gangs? But...he hates the gangs. It doesn't make sense."

"If what you told me last night is true, and he thinks that I murdered his wife, I'm surprised it took him this long to come to this," Nate said with a grimace. "If he was willing to marry his own daughter off to a man he considered a monster just to bring me down, then he must be desperate."

A voice in the back of Contessa's mind told her to defend her father, but then she pictured the way his nails had dug into her wrist the night before, and she bit her lip.

"Speaking of the setup that is your marriage," Kristoff interjected, and Contessa imagined she saw Nate flinch out of the corner of her eye. "I heard you found out about your Talent yesterday. Any idea what it is?"

"Yes, apparently everybody knew about it but me," Contessa shot back. "And before you start grilling me, I think it's my turn to ask some questions. There are still many things left unanswered after last night."

Nate gestured for her to continue, and Contessa pursed her lips as she considered where to start. She ended up turning to Kristoff and asking, "If Nate is Talented, and the gang formed from a group of Talented factory children, what's your Talent?"

Kristoff chuckled. "I'm afraid my only talent is being a gifted sharpshooter, and that's not any sort of magical ability, just years of practice. I ended up here by following through on Nate's daring plans."

"But you've dedicated your life to rescuing Talented children?"

Kristoff shrugged. "Nate used his Talent to save me many a beating when we were in the factory, sensing what foremen were in a bad mood and which would be lenient with us if we asked for an extra bit of food. I realized then that Talents could be used for good, a realization which has been reinforced time and time again over the years. I mean, look at Gregor's garden. How could the Talent to make plants grow so beautifully be born of ill, and why should Gregor have to worry about hanging just for making flowers bloom?"

Contessa blinked, envisioning the garden she read the paper in every day in a new light. Gregor was not at all what she pictured when she thought of a violent gangster using their unnatural abilities for personal gain, but perhaps she'd been misled. Perhaps her own Talent would be something just as lovely.

"So, what do you do besides free Talented children from work in the factories?"

This time, it was Nate who answered. "Very quickly into our mission, we learned that freeing the children is the easiest part of the operation. The problem is figuring out what to do with them after they're free. The Lions give them a sort of...home...to grow up in. We give them the skills they need to survive on the streets, and as they get older, they run jobs for the money to feed the little ones—normally, small things like pickpocketing and learning to deal rigged hands at the gambling tables. Although, occasionally, they'll run bigger cons on people who we feel have wealth that could benefit from—redistribution."

Contessa scrunched up her face at the thought of children having to deal crooked card games to feed themselves, and her face didn't escape Kristoff's notice.

"Perhaps we should focus on how we feed the children and give them a family, instead of the illicit activities."

Contessa shook her head. "It's not that. It's just...sad."

"The kids have the best life we can give them," Nate interjected softly. "They all take care of each other, and the older ones look out for the younger ones like their own siblings."

Contessa glanced across the table and met Nate's eyes, wondering if he could sense she'd always wanted a younger sibling of her own. Shaking herself from that thought, Contessa pushed on.

"So, say I were sympathetic to your cause," Contessa started, and she thought she saw a flash of happiness in Nate's eyes. "Where would I fit into this whole operation?"

"Where would you want to fit in?"

Contessa glanced back down at her uneaten toast and resisted the urge to begin shredding it with her fingers as she thought out loud.

"I doubt I'm a person who should be helping run cons, for too many reasons to list right now. But I do think I'd like..." Contessa pictured little Poppy running to fetch the carriage. "I'd like to meet the children. See what I might be able to do for them."

"That can be arranged," Kristoff said with a dazzling grin. "Rhosyn will be thrilled to meet you. She's jealous I've gotten to meet the woman who's been giving Nate here so much trouble, and she hasn't gotten a chance to congratulate you yet."

Contessa opened her mouth to ask who Rhosyn was but then paused, hearing an odd ringing sound.

"We could go this afternoon if you're feeling up to it. I have to stop by the warehouses anyway for business, and I could bring you..." Nate trailed off as Contessa waved her hand at him for silence, trying to hear the ringing better.

It became clear in a matter of seconds, as Nate and Kristoff looked on in confusion, that the ringing Contessa was sensing wasn't a noise at all. Still, the sensation of vibration in Contessa's skull persisted as she looked around for the source of the disturbance. Her heart beat louder in her chest as she failed to find any sort of reason for the buzzing in her head, until her eyes landed on Kristoff.

Without her mouth asking permission from her brain, Contessa said, "I think you should leave, Kristoff."

"And here I thought you enjoyed the pleasure of my company, but—" Kristoff started, clapping his hand to his chest in exaggerated offense. Contessa cut him off before he could finish his thought.

"I'm serious. You need to leave right now."

Kristoff glanced over to Nate incredulously, but Nate was looking at Contessa, his sharp eyes narrowed.

"I think you should listen to her. Leave, and we'll catch up to you later."

To his credit, Kristoff pushed to his feet without complaint, even as he continued to look supremely confused, and headed for the door.

"Not the front door," Contessa blurted without thinking once again.

Kristoff paused for the barest of moments before Nate interjected again. "Let's go to my office. We'll get out that way."

Nate led them out of the side door to the dining room, and Kristoff strode after him towards the back office. Gathering her skirts, Contessa rustled down the hallway behind them, confused as to why they were going to the office and still oddly unshakable in her conviction that Kristoff should already be gone by now.

As Contessa rounded the doorframe to the back office, she found Nate and Kristoff braced against the solid desk, inching it across the wooden floor with a heavy scrape. For all the desk's substantial size, the two men slid it several feet across the room in a matter of moments. Nate fell to his knees in the spot the desk had just occupied, feeling the floorboards for just a moment before pressing some unknown notch, causing a panel in the floor to spring up. Contessa's mouth hung open as Nate swung the panel open to reveal a tunnel identical to the one they had taken to the ball the day before. Kristoff didn't seem nearly as surprised by this revelation and hopped down into the tunnel without a moment's hesitation.

"Go. We'll meet you at the den this evening," Nate assured him before slamming the panel closed and plunging Kristoff into darkness.

No sooner had the panel clicked shut when there was a *bang* from the far end of the house, as if a door had been slammed open hard enough to rattle the walls, followed by shouting voices.

"Help me move this back into place," Nate hissed, already bracing a shoulder against the desk and sliding one end of it back into position.

Contessa braced her own hands on the end closer to her and shoved with the entire weight of her body, and it began to scrape across the floor, albeit much slower than it had when Kristoff and Nate moved the desk together. The wooden legs stuttered across the floorboards at an agonizing pace as pounding footsteps grew louder and Contessa began to be able to make out the voices now echoing through the house.

"London Royal Police here for Kristoff Mainsworth. Show yourself!"

The voices sounded as if they were just around the corner when the desk finally slid back in place over the trap door. Nate and Contessa straightened up and dashed out into the hallway towards the source of the commotion, shutting the door behind them as subtly as possible. The latch had barely clicked when a stampede of Royal Police rounded the last corner into the back hall, led by none other than Joseph.

"Halt!" Joseph shouted, as if Nate and Contessa were not already standing completely still in the hallway of their own home. Contessa resisted the urge to raise her hands in surrender while simultaneously suppressing the desire to give him a hostile glare, knowing it would not help with whatever sort of trouble they were in. The animosity in his returned gaze made her heart shudder with loss. She could find none of their former friendship in his expression.

"We have reason to believe that you are harboring one Kristoff Mainsworth," Joseph barked, "Turn him over immediately or face charges as accomplices!"

"Mr. Mainsworth?" Nate asked with a confused tilt of his head. "Why, I haven't seen him in almost a fortnight. What led you to believe he's here? Don't tell me he broke in!"

Joseph hesitated, deflating a bit, as if he had expected Nate to throw a punch and was disappointed by his casual denial. Still, Joseph puffed up his chest and continued with renewed bluster. "He was seen entering your house early this morning. If he has left, you have to tell us where he has gone."

"I assure you, it was just my lovely wife and I sharing breakfast this morning. We had no company. Isn't that right, Connie?"

Contessa was so busy watching Joseph's face drain of color at Nate's words that she almost forgot she needed to speak as well.

"Oh, of course," Contessa nodded. "Although, we would be happy to let you look around."

Nate's shoulders tensed next to Contessa for the barest of moments at her suggestion, quickly falling back into casual ease, almost as if Nate was more comfortable facing down the police than sharing dinner with his new wife. Come to think of it, he probably was.

Joseph signaled to the men standing dutifully at his back.

"Search the entire house. Look for open windows or a back door he might have left through."

Contessa fought to remain relaxed as the stomping of boots spread through the house, battling the feeling that her space was somehow being invaded, even though she was used to officers stomping through her home at her father's house. Instead, she put on a cold smile and offered sweetly, "Why don't I show you through the house, Joseph. Help you on your search."

With that, Contessa brushed past Joseph towards the front of the house, feeling him trail reluctantly. Contessa led the way to the living room, determined to show Joseph through the house and get him out of there.

They rounded the corner, out of sight of where Nate was casually hindering the search of the other police officers by attempting to be helpful. Joseph cornered Contessa immediately.

"Where is he hiding him? If you tell me, then I won't have you charged as an accomplice as well." Joseph's eyes were fanatical as he interrogated her. "We'll charge him either way. Make up evidence if we have to."

Contessa's face heated. "You lecture me about right and wrong while you spit in the face of justice and a fair trial?"

Joseph's expression twisted in fury, and for a second, he looked just like her father the night before.

"You've been here too long. The Beast has poisoned your mind. Confused you."

Contessa trembled with rage. "I'm not confused. I'm thinking for myself. Maybe you should consider who really has the poisoned mind here."

Joseph looked at her for a moment longer, all color drained from his high cheekbones, before letting out a sort of choked grunt, turning on his heel, and striding from the room.

The rest of the inspection went quickly, Joseph directing the team to comb the house in such a manner it seemed as if he could barely stand to be breathing the same air as Contessa. Nate even let the officers into his back office, and Contessa held her breath as Joseph tore through the drawers, even going so far as to tap at them to check for false bottoms, but he came up empty-handed. Not even a single piece of paperwork.

At last, Contessa accompanied the group of officers to the front door, having no concrete evidence that Kristoff had even entered the house in the first place.

As he walked out onto the front step, Joseph turned to look back over his shoulder to where Contessa and Nate stood in the doorway and said, "I'll tell your father you send your regards."

The way he said it made it seem like a threat, but Contessa squared her shoulders and simply said, "See that you do."

Joseph marched down to the street where the officer's horses waited for them, and Contessa shut the door and slumped with her back against it, letting out a breath as if she'd been holding it the entire time Joseph had been in the house. Perhaps she had.

She glanced up at Nate, who was staring down at her with his good brow creased. Contessa squinted up at him and pushed herself back up into a more dignified posture.

"You're looking at me as if you want to investigate me too," she commented. "Not the reaction I was hoping for considering I just saved our skins again."

Nate cocked his head as if he hadn't heard her.

"How did you know the police officers were coming?"

"I didn't betray Kristoff if that's what you mean," Contessa snapped, but Nate seemed unperturbed.

"I know that. He already told me he was afraid he was spotted at a break-in last night. What I want to know is how you knew the police would be ambushing him here this morning?"

Contessa glanced down and smoothed her already neat skirts.

"I didn't know. I just had...a feeling, like a dog before a storm."

"Was it the same as when we were at the executions yesterday?"

Contessa blinked, thinking back to the sudden panic she'd felt standing in the crowd yesterday. The way her heart suddenly started pounding in her ribcage just as it had today. She nodded silently as she gazed up at Nate, who was beginning to look as if he had successfully put together his puzzle.

"Have you had things like that happen before?" he asked.

"Not since I was a child. It faded as I got older, but I was always a scared child, thinking something bad was going to happen," Contessa admitted, trying not to think about the buzzing feeling and pounding heart that had caused her to run downstairs one night, only to find her mother lying in a pool of blood.

"Fear is rarely so accurate," Nate commented.

Contessa squinted at him.

"What are you saying?"

"I'm saying we may have just figured out what your Talent is."

She opened her mouth to retort that being afraid was hardly a talent, but then she thought of how adamant she'd been that Kristoff needed to leave. Of how sure she'd been yesterday that Nate had to escape the executions with her.

"So, my Talent is being able to sense when people are in danger?"

"It may be. We'll need to test it out. Find out what it's limits are and how exact it can be."

Contessa nodded even as she pursed her lips. "I feel as if I have been short-changed with my gift if I just have a sense of impending doom, when other people get to fly."

"You would be surprised." The good corner of Nate's mouth pulled up in a wry smile, "Flashy, impressive abilities don't always turn out to be the most useful. My ability seems mild at first, but I've been able to put it to good use over the years, and it's allowed me to keep it a secret relatively easily. Not to mention that I could feel your 'sense of impending doom' both today and yesterday. It was very useful in persuading me that you hadn't just lost your mind."

"You would have thought I had lost my mind?"

Nate looked abashed.

"I mean, not exactly. You just have been completely on guard for the past weeks, and it seemed likely you might crack at some point."

Contessa offered Nate a hand gesture of a very unladylike nature that she'd picked up from some of her father's lower ranking officers. Nate let out a low chuckle, and Contessa realized she hadn't heard him laugh before. It was a pleasant sound.

Nate turned to walk towards the back of the house and gestured for Contessa to follow.

"Come on," he said. "Let's go fill Kristoff in on what happened."

"Will he still be hiding in the tunnel below your desk?"

Nate shook his head. "No, he'll have used the tunnel to head to the warehouse the Lions use as their home base. I thought I would take you there so you can see our operation like you wanted."

"So, these tunnels..."

Nate shrugged a shoulder. "When we were younger, I could tell a thief was lying about how he broke into some houses. I got him to show me the tunnel he used. Kristoff and I spent months mapping them all out, and we've been careful to keep the knowledge well guarded. When the Lions eventually formed, I chose to build my house here because of this entrance. I use it to come and go from the Lion's other safehouses without being spotted. It's probably the reason your father has never caught me."

Contessa nodded. It suddenly made much more sense that the Royal Police had never managed to catch the infamous Beast even though they had a guard on his house for the last several years.

Once they entered the office, Contessa and Nate worked to push the desk back out of the way, and Nate opened the secret panel once more.

He hopped down into the dark entrance without hesitation before turning and offering a hand up to Contessa.

"Are you ready to meet the Lions?" Nate asked.

Contessa held her breath and nodded before reaching to take Nate's outstretched hand. Then she jumped down into the tunnel and the darkness waiting beyond.

Chapter Twelve

Contessa wasn't sure what she'd expected of the Lion's den, but it certainly wasn't what greeted her when Nate ushered her through another hidden panel in a wall. The first thing that struck her, as she blinked to regain her sight in the warm lamplight, was the sound of children laughing. No sooner had Nate stepped into the large open space and shut the door behind them than several children noticed their presence.

"Nate! It's Nate!" a chorus of voices sounded, and instantly, they were surrounded by a sea of upturned and grinning faces.

Nate himself smiled back just as broadly, none of the reserved silence from their meals together in evidence now, as he greeted the children by name and affectionately ruffled a number of bouncing heads. Contessa felt the corners of her mouth pulling up despite herself.

"Alright, alright, let Connie here through. We have business to attend to," Nate said once he had completed his greetings.

Immediately, a hush fell over the group, and Contessa heard a few whispered snippets of "Mrs. Woodrow" and "a proper lady".

Nate distracted her from the flush now spreading across her cheeks by ushering her across the space and letting her get a better glimpse of their surroundings. They were in a vast storeroom of a warehouse, but it wasn't at all the dank and rat-infested place Contessa had envisioned when she thought of the buildings down by the dock. Instead, it was warm and lined with neat rows of child-sized bunks. There were even a few roughly carved wooden toys in sight.

Seated on one of the beds was a girl older than the rest, if Contessa was to judge by her size. For now, all she could see was a mass of red hair as the girl looked down to talk to a small boy beside her.

"Rhosyn," Nate called, and immediately the girl looked up.

Her eyes landed on Contessa, holding a glint that showed even more mischief than Kristoff's smirk. Contessa liked her the moment she grinned broadly, revealing crooked front teeth.

"Nate! You've finally decided you're not too embarrassed of me to introduce me to your wife," Rhosyn bounded up with too long legs and slung a lanky arm around Nate's shoulders with ease. He seemed to be used to the gesture, even though Contessa had never seen him display physical affection before.

"Contessa, this is Rhosyn. She does, well, everything that Kristoff and I can't around here," Nate introduced, extricating himself from Rhosyn's embrace.

"That's me. Nursemaid, universal big sister, and pickpocket extraordinaire, although don't be telling your father that last bit." As Rhosyn spoke, Contessa could hear the hint of the round vowels that marked her as being from the North. "I hear you've gotten our boys here out of two close scrapes in as many days."

"That's why we're here. Can we talk in your office?" Nate said, jerking his head towards a nearby door.

Her "office" turned out to be little more than an adjacent storeroom with overturned barrels for seats and an empty box serving as a makeshift desk. Still, the wall served to give them some privacy from the chatter of the dozen or so children in the next room.

"So, give me all the details on what's happened with the execution and the raid on your house," Rhosyn said as she settled herself on a barrel with the stilted grace of a young woman who had recently come into her full height and hadn't yet figured out how to maneuver her limbs. "All I've gotten are jumbled reports from a panicked Gregor and an assurance that you would tell me more from Kristoff on his way through."

"Kristoff has left already?" Nate asked.

"He passed through to let me know he had been compromised and to grab some supplies before heading on to one of the safe houses," Rhosyn explained. "Said he was going to lie low for a while. What exactly was he running from, though?"

Nate quickly recounted the events of the last two days. While he was speaking, Contessa caught Rhosyn stealing a few appraising glances at her, but she tried her best to keep her full attention on Nate's story.

"And now Connie wants to help with the children, so I brought her here to you. You know best what they need," Nate finished.

Rhosyn tapped her chin.

"I want to know more about this Talent of Contessa's, for starters," she said, raising an inquisitive brow towards Contessa.

"That makes two of us," Contessa said honestly.

"I have some ideas on how we might be able to test it out," Rhosyn commented as she leaned back on her stool and shoved her hands in the pockets of her skirt.

"Oh, like what?"

"Like this!"

Faster than Contessa could flinch, Rhosyn had drawn her hand out of her pocket and lobbed something straight at Contessa's face. Just before it struck Contessa's nose, Nate's hand shot out and snatched it out of the air.

"What was that about?" Nate barked as he looked at the object in his hand, finding it to be a wooden ball children would play with.

Rhosyn shrugged but looked apologetic.

"I wanted to see if she could sense it coming before I threw it," she explained.

"I think my Talent gives me advance warning of danger, not faster reflexes," Contessa said, her tone succeeding at sounding delicate even as her pulse fought to return to its normal pace.

"I guess now we know for sure," Rhosyn said.

"Next time, though, can we try to test Connie's powers in a way that doesn't risk breaking her nose?" Nate chimed in, tossing the ball back at Rhosyn, who plucked it easily out of the air.

"I knew you wouldn't let it break her nose," Rhosyn said with a wicked grin. "Your wife is far too pretty for that, wouldn't you say, Nate?"

Nate coughed forcefully. "Of course, she's lovely, but that's not the point."

Contessa's eyebrows shot up, and Rhosyn looked positively thrilled. Noticing their reactions, Nate jumped to change the subject.

"So how do you think Contessa would best be able to help with the children?"

Rhosyn considered Contessa.

"With your Talent, you'd make an awfully useful lookout. You could help us on some of our liberation missions."

Contessa blanched and resisted the urge to stammer inarticulately as she reached for the proper words. Nate saved her before she could speak.

"I think Contessa would rather avoid being so...hands-on with the less savory parts of our operations."

Rhosyn peered at Contessa with narrowed eyes and huffed noncommittally.

"I guess I should let you get yourself acquainted with our herd of little ones then. See what you think you might be able to do to improve their situation."

When the trio reentered the room where the children stayed, they found themselves mobbed again, although this time in a slightly more orderly fashion. Rhosyn introduced Contessa to each child by name, although Nate seemed to know them all already and was quickly drawn off by one child or another who wanted to show him some game they had dreamed up.

As the next child stepped into Contessa's line of view, she caught sight of a partially healed scar cutting across a familiar brow.

"Paul!" Contessa crouched down so she could be at eye level with him. The color in his cheeks was much better than the last time she'd seen him, and he even offered her a small smile.

"You are looking so well. And who is this with you?" Contessa asked, catching sight of a younger girl's face with Paul's same round cheeks peeking out around his shoulder.

"This is my sister, Olivia. Come on, Olivia, this is Mrs. Woodrow, the nice lady I told you about."

Olivia continued to stare but didn't step out from behind the shelter of her older brother. Contessa outstretched a hand towards the girl, hoping to coax her out, but instead the girl jumped back, situating herself more firmly behind Paul.

"Sorry, ma'am. She's still afraid of grown-ups. Not used to everybody being so nice to us," Paul said, "but you're one of the good ones. You and Nate."

At his words, Contessa glanced over to the corner where Nate was entertaining a group of young ones, only to see him completely engulfed in giggling children. He had one perched on his shoulders and pulling enthusiastically at his auburn hair, another had latched onto his leg like some sort of monkey, and he was clutching a third child upside down by the ankles. Contessa would have found it barbaric if the child in question wasn't whooping and laughing as if it were the most fun he'd had in his life.

A throat cleared next to her, and Contessa looked up from where she crouched in front of Paul to find Rhosyn contemplating her with a raised eyebrow. Contessa straightened from where she knelt on the floor, smoothing her skirts as Paul and his sister drifted over to the laughing crowd of children at Nate's feet.

"A lot of them are pretty shy at first," Rhosyn said as they watched Nate hoist another child into the air, the children having decided they all wanted a turn at being swung about. "I mean, I definitely was. It's hard to change your mindset when you're used to being afraid of being beaten all the time."

Contessa glanced at Rhosyn out of the corner of her eye, noticing the way she held her head with confidence, even though she must have been several years younger than Contessa.

"I take it the Lions...liberated you from a factory as well?"

Rhosyn nodded. "I was in the first group they ever went back for... I grew up with Nate and Kristoff as sort of older brothers, and as much as I adore them, it was...sort of a mess. They were good at running schemes and breaking children out, but what do seventeen-year-old boys know about raising dozens of children? So, I've stuck around to help manage the littler ones."

"What about the other children that were rescued with you? Where did they go?" Contessa asked.

"They mostly stayed with the gang. Helped run our gambling operations and go on liberation missions, although they moved out of this warehouse. We've got a few houses full of Lions in the lower city. I do try to get some of them who want a different life out, but it can be hard. Julia, your lady's maid, was one of the older girls living here. Looks like she's adjusted well, if she was the one that did those braids."

Contessa reached up to pat her hair, which Julia had woven several small white flowers into this morning. Contessa had been inclined to comment that they seemed more appropriate for a special occasion than a day in the house, but she was glad she hadn't.

"She's lovely. It's been nice to have her around," Contessa commented honestly.

"I'm sure she loves it, although the girls here miss having their hair braided constantly," Rhosyn chuckled. "I've tried to do it for them, but I'm clearly no good."

Rhosyn gestured at her own mass of unruly curls, most of which had already managed to escape the leather thong she'd attempted to tie it back with.

Contessa smiled. "I would offer to help you, but I'm embarrassed to admit that I can't even do my own hair. My mother always brushed it for me when I was young, and then... Well, then I always had a lady's maid to do it for me."

Rhosyn wrinkled her nose, but there was no real malice to the expression. "All of you great ladies. You'll have to learn to brush your children's hair soon. It'll only be a matter of time until there are a bunch of little Woodrow's running about this place with the way Nate loves children."

Contessa choked on her own tongue. "Our marriage... I mean...that seems highly unlikely."

Rhosyn shoved her hands in her pockets and shrugged as if she didn't notice Contessa's sudden ineloquence. "Tell that to Nate, with the way stares at you when he thinks you aren't looking."

"I think the best word to describe that look is vexation," Contessa argued.

"Yes, and I myself wouldn't want to marry a man that I couldn't vex on a daily basis. But then again, I don't know how these noble marriages are supposed to work."

Contessa squinted at Rhosyn, only to find her eyes twinkling mischievously over her smattering of freckles. Contessa chuckled as she turned her attention back to Nate, who was on his knees having his own hair braided by one of the older girls with a look of the greatest forbearance. As Contessa watched, Olivia began inching out from behind her brother, obviously curious. Nate caught sight of her and held out a hand with a smile. Olivia paused before inching forward once again like a scared kitten. Nate kept his hand outstretched patiently as she slowly reached for it. When her hand finally landed in his, his smile broadened, and Olivia offered him the slightest upturn of her lips, tucking her chin to her chest bashfully.

"I'm glad to see Nate coaxing her out of her shell," Rhosyn commented. "She's been having a hard time adjusting. She has so many nightmares, I've barely gotten any sleep in the past week from sitting up with her, trying to assure her that she's safe. Her brother's escape was rather traumatic—you saw his injury. A couple men were shot, and well, that's a terrible thing for a child to see."

Contessa's throat tightened, and she swallowed a few times to steady her voice before asking, "Do you think if they'd had a good lookout, a fight could have been avoided?"

"Are you, daughter of the Commander of the Royal Police, offering to be a lookout for a liberation mission?"

Contessa opened her mouth and then closed it. If her father, the man who would give his life for king and country, would bend the rules to achieve his ends, maybe the spirit of the law was more important than the letter.

"If it would be only watching for trouble. I don't want to do any breaking in, and I'm not committing any violence," Contessa conceded.

"I wouldn't throw you into a fight, but you know I'm going to have to train you in at least the bare minimum of self-defense," Rhosyn pointed out. "I don't think Nate would ever let me run another mission if anything happened to his lovely wife."

Contessa pursed her lips but didn't argue. Rhosyn, for all her maturity, was committed to romanticizing her marriage of convenience. Contessa got the impression that arguing with the girl would get her nowhere.

"Alright, when would this be starting?" Contessa settled for asking.

"I have some time tomorrow afternoon. Meet me here then and we can get started, and by the King's bloomers, wear something more practical."

Contessa looked down at her full, frilly skirts.

"Gladly."

Contessa picked her way through the tunnel behind Nate, squinting to make out any obstacles in the flickering light from the lantern he held.

"Watch yourself. There is a little step up here," he shot over his shoulder, not breaking his stride. Despite the jagged floor, he never lost his footing, clearly having traversed these tunnels so often he could have managed in complete darkness.

It was probably easier to navigate without having to constantly lift your skirts out of the way.

As Contessa picked her way across the uneven floor, she chose her words carefully. "You seem to be a favorite of the children."

A gruff sigh came from the tunnel in front of her.

"I think the children idealize me a bit too much, just because I organize the gang that broke them free."

"That, and you seem to have a way with them you know."

There was a long pause broken only by the scraping of their feet, and Contessa wished she could see Nate's face.

"I wish I could spend more time with them," came Nate's eventual reply. "I guess I wish I could give them more of an actual family. I remember being their age, and well... We do the best we can for them, but I know it isn't enough."

"Anybody who has seen them with you and Rhosyn would know they see you as family."

Nate's head dipped as he walked in front of her, and she thought he was probably pleased that his face was hidden.

"Is—is a family something you want?"

While Contessa managed by sheer luck not to trip, she knew she didn't school her face into neutrality fast enough to hide her red cheeks had Nate been facing her.

"I hadn't given it much thought," she hedged.

Nate gave a noncommittal grunt but didn't reply. As they walked a little bit farther in silence, something about the flickering lamp made the scene oddly intimate. She thought of Nate holding his hand out to Olivia, and she opened her mouth.

"I guess at one point, when I thought... Well, when I thought my future was going to go differently, I assumed there would be children. I guess I was always so focused on what my father wanted from me—to be quick-witted and well-read. A girl who thought about finding a husband and having a family all the time didn't really fit in that picture."

Nate exhaled in a way that might have been amused. "Funny, I always thought a quick-witted woman would make the best sort of mother."

Contessa ducked her head as they came to the end of the passage, and Nate cracked the trapdoor above them that would lead into his office. He turned back to Contessa to help her up, but she paused. The dim light made it easy to be brave, and she wasn't quite ready to leave it yet.

"Are children something you want?" she asked.

The light from above only shone on the scarred half of Nate's face, making it difficult to read his reaction.

"If I could make a child feel safe, then…yes, I think I would like children," Nate snorted, but there was no mirth behind it. "Although I doubt I make many children feel safe with a face like this. I think they just find me to be a novelty."

Contessa cocked her head. She'd never heard Nate discuss his scar before. It was a looming presence they were both aware of but felt odd to mention.

"Well, I think it shows how brave you are," Contessa defended. "That you fought a rival gang leader to keep your own safe."

Nate shook his head. "That's a nice story that serves to make me a more menacing figure, but that's not how I ended up like this."

Contessa cocked her head, giving him time to continue if he wished.

"It was when Kristoff and I were escaping from the factory we worked in as kids. We sneaked down from the loft where the children slept and were creeping across the production floor when the supervisor spotted us. We were almost to the door, so I pulled over one of the big machines behind us to block his way so he couldn't chase us. When it hit the ground, it broke, and a jagged bit of the metal hit me across the face. I don't remember too much after that, but Kristoff pretty much had to drag me the rest of the way. I wasn't brave, I was just another scared kid." Nate's voice dropped to barely above a whisper. "If we had known Gregor then, he might have been able to patch it up, but we had nothing. We didn't even have a clean cloth to wash it with, and the wound got infected. It eventually cleared and healed itself, but..." Nate gestured vaguely to his face.

Contessa swallowed hard. "Well, maybe it's a mark of how much of a survivor you are."

Nate huffed. "A pretty platitude to be sure, but it has no bearing on somebody who can sense the feelings of those around him. I know people are afraid when they see my face, even if they hide it from their expression. I say let them be afraid if it keeps them out of my way so I can make sure this doesn't happen to any more children."

Contessa looked down, seeing Nate's fist clenching and unclenching at his side. When she glanced back up, Nate's one visible eye was scrutinizing her.

"I'm not afraid of you," Contessa murmured.

"I know," Nate replied. "You never were. When we first met, I sensed rage, even hatred coming off you. But never fear."

In the tight space of the tunnel, Contessa and Nate stood close enough she could see the flickering lamplight reflected in his eyes. Contessa raised her hand, slowly enough that Nate could pull away if he chose to. Instead, he stood perfectly still, not breaking eye contact, as her fingers moved towards his cheek. As lightly as she could, she dragged her fingertips over the ridges of his cheek. Nate's eyelids fluttered, but otherwise, he didn't move at all. Contessa almost asked him if he had feeling in his scar, but she didn't want to disturb the silence between them. She didn't even think she was breathing. As her fingers brushed across his cheek, they traveled to the jagged corner of his mouth, and he let out a sharp exhale, the warmth tickling her wrist. It startled her enough that she drew her hand back an inch, and the moment was broken.

Nate turned towards the trapdoor and hauled himself out before reaching back down to help Contessa up. She did notice, though, that he didn't try to move away from her as hurriedly as he had the time before, as if she were going to scold him if his hand lingered an instant too long.

"Well, you better rest up," Nate commented as they stood awkwardly in the middle of the office, seemingly at a loss for what to do with themselves after the intimacy of their conversation. "Rhosyn told me you are going to start training with her tomorrow. If I know her as well as I think I do, you have quite a day ahead of you tomorrow."

Contessa nodded and bid Nate goodnight before heading up to her bedroom to get ready for sleep. Even as Julia brushed her hair for the night, Contessa could feel the cool ridges of Nate's scar under her fingertips.

Chapter Thirteen

Contessa stared at the articles of clothing laid across the coverlet in front of her and mused that it was a roundabout way of getting what she wished for. She plucked at the gray trousers Nate had dug up for her. She did prefer the color and lack of ruffles, even if the idea of pants made her blush.

There was no point in putting off the inevitable any longer, so she slid on the pants and soft linen shirt. Both were too big, and she had to roll up the cuffs of her trousers a few times to avoid tripping over them. Turning to inspect herself in the mirror, Contessa bit back a laugh. She thought the new clothes would have made her seem like a proper gang member, but it looked like her face had been transposed onto the body of a street urchin. The twist of braids on the top of her head looked preposterous, even though it was one of the simpler arrangements she'd worn recently.

Contessa took a deep breath to brace herself before heading out of her room and nearly jumped at how much freedom her ribcage had to expand. She almost missed the bracing feeling of a tightly laced bodice.

Walking downstairs, Contessa tried to ignore the way the fabric rubbed against her legs with every stride. As she descended the last steps, Nate rounded the corner into the hall, immediately pulling up short and blinking.

"What is it?" Contessa asked, glancing down at herself to make sure the shirt was buttoned. "Did I put them on wrong?"

"No, not at all," reassured Nate, recovering himself. "It's just a different look."

Contessa resisted the urge to smooth her absent skirts. "It's an adjustment. It's strange having so much fabric touching my legs."

Nate tilted his head. "But your skirts have to have ten times as much fabric as those pants."

"Yes, but they aren't nearly as close to my skin."

Nate nodded his understanding and they stood for a moment in silence. Nate seemed like he didn't know where to look until he cleared his throat.

"Shall we be going?"

Contessa nodded, and they headed back to the office to enter the tunnel. As she walked through the hall in front of him, she continued to think about how much less fabric covered her legs and tried not to imagine what Nate could see walking behind her.

As Contessa approached the doorway to Rhosyn's office, a scraping sound came from inside. As she poked her head around the corner, she found Rhosyn pushing the barrels she used as chairs to edges of the room. She straightened and smiled when she spotted Contessa, blowing a loose curl from her face.

"Well look at you!" Rhosyn said, gesturing for Contessa to come in. "I barely recognized you without all the skirts. It looks like you were hiding a nice pair of legs under all those ruffles, though!"

Contessa knew her father's moustache would bristle at such an improper compliment, but Contessa found herself smiling at Rhosyn's infectious energy.

"Apparently, this is the proper attire for liberation missions, so I better get used to it."

"But you won't be going on any liberation missions until we get you trained up a bit." Rhosyn pointed a stern finger at Contessa. "The plan is to keep you out of the line of fire and just have you signal if any danger is coming, but you never know what's going to happen on a job, and things can change in an instant."

Contessa nodded soberly and stepped into the open circle of floor in the middle of the room.

"Let's start with a few basic self-defense maneuvers," Rhosyn instructed. "The key is to strike where they aren't expecting it and always go for the weak points. Then again, when you're small like you and me, they rarely expect you to strike at all."

Rhosyn's smile was wicked, and Contessa knew she was in for an exhausting afternoon.

Several hours later, Contessa sat slumped against a barrel, all traces of her normally rigid posture gone, her sense of propriety chased away by the intense exercise. She fanned herself with a hand and tried to pick off the pieces of loose hair plastered to her sweaty neck.

Rhosyn, on the other hand, stood in the middle of the room, bouncing lightly on the balls of her feet. The flush on her freckled cheeks served to make her look invigorated, where Contessa was sure she looked like an overripe tomato.

"That was fun, and you did well!" Rhosyn complimented.

Contessa simply narrowed her eyes at Rhosyn and continued to fan herself.

"Seriously, you did better than I would have expected for a proper lady. And you didn't ask to stop as soon as you started sweating."

Contessa pursed her lips but didn't object, even though the first lesson hadn't been particularly productive. She'd only escaped a few of the holds that Rhosyn demonstrated, even though she knew the girl was grabbing her lightly. Contessa would have little chance of actually escaping if a rival gangster were to catch her unawares.

As if she read her thoughts, Rhosyn continued. "The good news is that, with your Talent, you should be able to sense danger coming and avoid combat altogether."

"That's the most encouraging thing you've said so far," Contessa commented.

Rhosyn chuckled and offered Contessa a callused hand to pull her to her feet.

"Do you have time to stay for a bit, or do you need to get back?"

Rhosyn's tone was casual, but a shred of hope flickered in her eyes. She wondered how long it had been since Rhosyn had spent time with a woman close to her own age.

"I'm not in any rush," Contessa replied as she allowed herself to be hauled off the barrel, "I don't normally see Nate until after dinner anyways, so I am at your disposal."

"Good. I have something to show you."

A stack of boxes made a rough scraping sound as Rhosyn pushed them aside to reveal a series of metal rungs in the wall. The ladder led up to a door in the ceiling Contessa hadn't noticed before. Rhosyn led the way up the ladder, Contessa following more slowly. The rungs carried them through an attic space, until Rhosyn opened another hatch and revealed a patch of gray sky.

After easily pulling herself up, Rhosyn reached back to help Contessa, who was currently concluding she was going to need more upper body strength if she was going to continue to spend time with the younger woman. All thoughts of weak arms left her mind, though, when a cool breeze blew across Contessa's face, and she looked out at the view from the roof of the warehouse.

The building was in the industrial district down by the river, which Contessa had known already, but from here, she saw it was on the Southern edge of this section of warehouses. The rooftop had an unobstructed view of the port where merchant ships docked and unloaded. She watched as one vessel set off down the wide river to the sea, a plume of smoke leaving a trail in its wake. Up this high, above the pollution of the city, Contessa imagined she could smell salt on the breeze, even though the ocean was half a day's journey away.

Rhosyn took a deep breath of the fresh air as she settled herself comfortably on the rooftop, leaning back on her elbows. Contessa arranged herself next to the girl, neatly tucking her legs to one side as they watched the harbor together.

They sat in companionable silence for a moment as Contessa surveyed the neat rows of warehouses and factories in the industrial district from this angle, a few smokestacks letting out clouds of smog that faded into the gray sky and blurred the sunshine filtering through the clouds, softening the harsh edges of the city.

It soothed something in Contessa to relax in someone else's presence like this—something she hadn't had since the last afternoon she spent with Joseph before her wedding. With how things were with him now, it seemed possible they'd never have this type of easy companionship again. Finding this sense of peace with Rhosyn now gave her hope that her future might hold more friendship than she had lost.

"I know the lower part of London can be...treacherous," Contessa observed, "but from up here, it almost looks peaceful."

Rhosyn closed her eyes and tilted her face up to the sky.

"That's why I like it on the roof. When handling the kids and running jobs gets to be too much, this is my escape. I come up here and watch the ships come and go. I like to imagine what it would be like to be on one of them, traveling to one of the far-off places they may be heading."

Contessa peered at the girl out of the corner of her eye. "You have an awful lot of responsibility on your shoulders for someone so young."

Rhosyn shrugged. "No one to blame for that but myself. When I was first taken in by the Lions, I told myself that as soon as I could take care of myself, I'd leave to make my own way in the world. But, when the time came, I couldn't do it. I watched all the kids coming in after me, and I knew they needed somebody looking after them, teaching them how to make it on these streets. So, I volunteered to stay, and Kristoff and Nate have treated me like family, so I can't complain. I just...I feel like I owe it to them to pay it forward, even though they would never say that to me."

Contessa watched another ship pull into the wharves, workers scurrying around like ants to bring it to the docks to unload its haul.

"What did you want to do before you decided to stay with the Lions?"

Rhosyn paused, licking her lips.

"I wanted to be a sailor, like my father. I told myself I was going to captain my own ship someday. I guess I take after him and feel a connection to the sea. He was blessed by the sea itself and could read the winds to bring his ships safely to port every time. He was the helmsman of a merchant vessel, and after he predicted a few storms too accurately, well...you can guess what happened next."

Contessa swallowed and looked down at her hands, rearranging them in her lap.

Rhosyn's lips twisted wryly as she continued. "That was a girlhood dream, though, and the world has its own agenda. Nobody has times for fantasies anymore. How about you? What were your childhood plans?"

Contessa pursed her lips. "I'm not sure there was a place for dreams in my father's house. My goals were always to sharpen my mind, convince my father I wasn't too girly to be useful, and help father catch my mother's killer. I guess none of those things worked out, as I'm currently not speaking with my father, am married to his biggest rival, and was totally wrong about who killed my mother."

Rhosyn chuckled, and Contessa herself smiled at the irony of it.

"So now that your old plans have flown the coop, any new dreams?"

Contessa cocked her head.

"You know, I'm not sure," Contessa chewed on her tongue, uncomfortable with the feeling of not having an articulate answer for every question. "I've never had a time in my life where I didn't know exactly what I wanted—or at least what I was supposed to want. It's odd making a new place for myself outside of the forces that always drove me before."

Rhosyn considered Contessa, her green eyes sharp enough that Contessa felt like they could see beyond her words.

"Well, I have a feeling once you do decide what you want your life to look like, there won't be much that could get in your way."

Contessa pulled up short as she entered Rhosyn's office after a week of training when she saw the barrels in the middle of the room. Twin knives, almost as long as her forearm, gleamed against the knotted wood of the makeshift table. Rhosyn looked up from her work sharpening a similar set of knives and grinned at the stricken look on Contessa's face.

"I thought we'd try something a little different today and put some weapons in your hands. It's good for you to know how to escape if somebody grabs you, but you can only do so much damage with your bare hands. Besides, I highly doubt you want to train in hand-to-hand combat to join the brawling rings."

Contessa stepped closer to the weapons and looked down at them skeptically, even as she knew that Rhosyn had a point.

"Be that as it may, you really think it's wise for me to fight with knives?"

Rhosyn considered her, squinting.

"Well, you don't strike me as the type to be a sharpshooter. And knives are easy to carry without being noticed. I mean, think of how many you could hide under those skirts you normally wear. Not to mention, I'm sure the appeal of a nice thigh sheath wouldn't be lost on your husband."

Contessa looked up to shoot Rhosyn an icy glare, but the girl was undeterred as she continued.

"Speaking of Nate, he's the one who suggested knives for you in the first place. Told me to use these to train you with. If I'm not mistaken, these were his when he was younger."

Contessa looked back down at the blades in front of her, noting their simple design and marks of wear around the handle, where Nate's hands would have gripped them countless times.

"If these were his, what does he fight with now?" Contessa asked.

"Oh, he's still the best knife fighter I know, but I believe Kristoff got him a full new set for his twentieth birthday, so all his knives could match, and these are just a pair." Rhosyn snorted. "It's probably been years since Nate has left the house with less than six knives strapped to him somewhere."

Contessa raised her brows. She'd always found it a bit odd that she never saw Nate with a weapon on him, but now she realized it was a testament to how discreet knives could be if one knew what they were doing.

"Well, these are lovely and all," Contessa commented, reaching down to run her finger down the length of one of the knives but stopping herself before she could touch it. "But I feel like I'm more likely to slice myself with them than harm an attacker."

Rhosyn rolled her eyes in exasperation as she pushed herself up from her seat and walked over to where Contessa stood, picking up the knives she was contemplating.

"That's why I'm going to teach you how to use them. I promise, you're in good hands. I teach all the children how to defend themselves, and I learned from Nate himself. Although, I fancy I'm a bit of a better teacher. He's so comfortable holding a knife I don't think he even knows how to communicate with somebody who hasn't done it before anymore."

Contessa chewed her lip and nodded slowly. Rhosyn tossed the knives expertly, flipping them around in her hands to offer them to Contessa handle first.

"Let's start by figuring out what grip you're the most comfortable with."

After some experimentation with Rhosyn's guidance, Contessa settled the knives in her hands, left hand holding the blade point forward and the right with the grip reversed, the blade pointing out from the side of her littlest finger. Rhosyn, looked amused as Contessa got comfortable with the grip.

"What? Is this wrong?"

"No, not at all," Rhosyn shrugged a shoulder. "That's just the exact same way Nate likes to fight."

Contessa looked at the blades in her hands, thinking about her husband fighting with them similarly.

"Must be the knives," Contessa said.

"Of course, must be the knives," Rhosyn agreed sagely. Then she settled into a fighting stance in demonstration.

"Remember, the first step in knife fighting is to have fun and be yourself."

The knife slipped from Contessa's sweat slicked palm and hit the ground inches from Rhosyn's foot with a clatter.

Rhosyn, to her credit, didn't flinch. She bent to pick up the blade with a dry comment. "I hadn't thought we'd get to throwing knives until next week."

Contessa covered her face with a hand, thankful she'd managed to make it this far without anybody losing a digit. She let Rhosyn pluck the other blade from her hand, as the younger girl seemed to pick up on her frustration.

"Why don't we stop here for today? We've come far for only having been working together a week, and you're doing well."

Contessa narrowed her eyes at Rhosyn.

"You know I'm not."

Rhosyn scrunched her nose as she replied, "Well, there is a chance I've taught ten-year-olds who have picked this up faster, but I wasn't expecting to turn a proper lady into a street brawler in the blink of an eye."

Contessa snorted at the girl's honesty. "Well, I'm not sure I'm a proper lady. I can't dance or embroider either."

"No matter what you are, you are still making progress," Rhosyn said and tossed Contessa a cloth to wipe her face. "It won't be long until you'll be ready to tag along on a liberation mission. It's not like you need to be a master fighter to be a lookout."

"That's good, because I'm beat," Contessa mopped her face and grimaced at the feeling of sweat crusted on her brow.

"Hmm. Maybe we should take a break from fighting for the sake of your muscles. Do something fun and teach you to crack locks or pick pockets?"

Contessa waved her off as she hobbled over to a barrel and slumped down onto it. "My father already made sure I could pick any lock, and I don't see myself getting much good out of being able to lift purses."

"Wait, your father taught you how to pick locks but gave absolutely no training in self-defense?" Rhosyn folded her arms as she looked at Contessa in disbelief.

"Yes, well, I guess he thought espionage was far more ladylike than brawling."

"Your father looked down on you for being girly and then insisted you still be ladylike? Sounds impossible to please."

Contessa couldn't suppress a choked giggle at how concisely Rhosyn had summed up the struggle of her entire youth.

Rhosyn chuckled. "Well, then let me teach you how to pick a pocket."

Contessa opened her mouth to argue she didn't think she needed to learn how to commit larceny, but Rhosyn cut her off.

"I'm the best there is, and it would be rude of you not to let me show off a bit. Besides, maybe this could be useful in your espionage. You never know when you might need to get an important letter for evidence or something."

While she frowned, Contessa couldn't help being affected by the pleading look in Rhosyn's eyes.

"Fine," Contessa sighed. "Show me some of your tricks, but remember, this is just for fun."

"Good," Rhosyn grinned. "Because I nicked this out of your pocket, and it would be awkward if you didn't approve."

Rhosyn flicked a small golden object into the air, and Contessa's reached out to catch it, bobbling it a few times before finally gaining control of the item. She opened her hand to look at what she'd caught.

"My wedding ring. How on earth..."

Rhosyn looked smug. "I know you put it in your pocket when you train, but you should be careful. It would be a tragedy if you were to lose it."

Contessa wrinkled her nose as she slipped the ring back onto her finger where she hoped Rhosyn wouldn't be able to get to it as easily.

"I don't even know why I continue to wear it."

Now it was Rhosyn's turn to frown.

"What do you mean? You're married. Nate would be put out if you didn't wear it."

Contessa looked up at the younger girl. "Rhosyn, you have to know that Nate and I don't have a traditional marriage. I mean, I'm the daughter of a man who wants to see him dead."

Rhosyn continued to frown as though vexed by the idea that Contessa and Nate may have ended up married for reasons other than true love.

"Well, maybe if you want to impress him," Rhosyn suggested, "you can use one of my tricks to lift something from his pocket."

Contessa debated for a second whether it would be a better argument to point out that she didn't feel the need to impress him at all, or to mention that she doubted thievery was a particularly endearing form of flirtation. Instead, she decided to let the subject drop.

"Alright." Contessa smiled. "Show me what you know."

Gregor was just serving Contessa her cup of tea after dinner when she heard heavy footsteps behind her. She twisted in her seat to find Nate's frame filling the doorway to the dining room, his hand fiddling with the knot on his cravat.

"Oh, good. I had hoped I would catch you before you went upstairs for the evening," he said.

Contessa picked up her gently steaming teacup. "Well, then, your timing was impeccable."

Nate continued to stand in the doorway silently, and Contessa raised her brow at him as she blew on the surface of her tea.

"What was it you wanted to ask me?" she prompted.

"Oh, yes. I know we haven't played chess together in a while, since things have gotten so crazy. But, well, I was hoping you would join me for a game tonight. I understand if you are tired from your day with Rhosyn, though."

The corner of Contessa's mouth twitched up. "On the contrary, training with Rhosyn has hurt my pride. I think it would be good for me to spend some time beating you at chess."

Nate's good eye crinkled in what Contessa had come to recognize as amusement, and he gestured for her to lead the way into the living room.

They settled into the rhythm of the game after a few turns, but the air seemed lighter than when they had played in the past. Perhaps it was more enjoyable to play as friends than as adversaries trying to outwit one another. Contessa caught herself at that thought. Friends? She wasn't sure if they had become friends, although it seemed like it might be a nice thing to be, considering they were married. Something about the word rubbed her the wrong way, though. Contessa peeked up at Nate, who was considering his next move, absently chewing on the nail of his thumb.

Catching her looking he asked, "How is training going with Rhosyn? I know she planned to start you with knives this week."

As Contessa watched Nate move his tile into the path of one of her own, she commented, "Well, I think the best that can be said for it is that I managed to come home with all my fingers still attached."

Nate huffed. "I suppose it's only normal you aren't naturally outstanding at it. It would be unfair for you to be fantastic at everything."

Contessa straightened from where she'd bent over the chess set contemplating her next move to find Nate's ears reddened. He snatched up his glass from a nearby table and took a sizeable gulp of the brown liquid within, avoiding eye contact. Something about his expression made her think about what Rhosyn had said about impressing him.

Contessa turned her attention back to the board and made her move.

"I guess you are right. You have to be better than me at something, since it clearly isn't chess." Contessa knocked over his king with her knight, indicating she'd won the game.

Nate scowled.

It's probably for the best we finished anyways. You'll need your sleep if what you're saying about your knife fighting is true."

Nate pushed up from his chair and held out a hand to help Contessa up from her low stool. She took it, but as Nate pulled her to her feet, her tired leg muscles protested, and she stumbled. She threw her arm out for balance, and her hand landed on Nate's waist, her fingers just brushing the edge of his pocket, before she quickly righted herself.

"Are you alright?" Nate asked, reaching out as if to steady her but not quite touching her.

"My muscles just aren't used to this much work," Contessa said, smoothing her skirts as she set herself to rights. "Like I said, I find personal combat quite difficult. Although I will say that Rhosyn and I have found one thing I'm good at."

"Oh, and what is that?"

Contessa held up her prize with a grin.

"Pickpocketing."

Nate blinked at the object in her hand.

"Wait, that's mine. How did you—" He clapped a hand to his face. "Oh, Rhosyn. She's creating a monster. It's like there are two of her now."

Contessa chuckled as she turned her attention to the object in her hand, not having had a chance to get a close look at it before. It was a metal rectangle with intricate engravings, and closer inspection showed a small catch on the side. Contessa pressed it and jumped when a blade the length of one of her fingers sprang free.

Nate huffed and reached for the knife.

"It's just my spare blade," he explained as he took it from her and closed it again. "It's too small to be great in a fight, but you can still stab people with it. Not to mention thugs never expect me to have one more in my pocket."

"One more?" Contessa asked. "Rhosyn said you usually carry six knives, but that seems like a lot. Is that true?"

Nate shifted as he slid the blade back into his pocket and patted it to make sure Contessa hadn't managed to slide anything else from it.

"Six? Well, no. I don't carry six."

"I knew she had to be exaggerating…"

Contessa trailed off as Nate looked down at his feet.

"Wait, you can't possibly carry more than six knives, can you?"

"Well, to be fair, not all of them are very large…"

"How many knives do you carry?" Contessa demanded.

"That's not a very polite question you know," Nate countered.

"Oh, come now. It's not like I'm asking a lady how old she is."

Nate sighed heavily.

"Nine." He paused thoughtfully. "As well as a pistol, if you must know, but I rarely use that."

Contessa looked him up and down several times, trying to place where he could keep them all.

"Even when you're in your own house? Doesn't that seem a bit excessive?"

Nate shrugged. "If they are going to call me the Beast, I may as well have some teeth. Not to mention, it turns out I need to have my guard up even in my own home because my wife is a thief who won't hesitate to grab things from my pocket." He shot her a pointed look, and she held her hands up in surrender.

"But to be honest, I hadn't been carrying this many blades until the past few weeks, but with everything so uncertain..." Nate chewed his bottom lip, and Contessa bit back a question, hoping for him to elaborate on his own.

Shaking himself from him contemplation, he said, "Well, I'm not sure if carrying more knives really makes any difference, but at least the weight of them on my body makes me feel like I'm doing something."

The resigned look on Nate's face only seemed to accentuate the tired circle under his unscarred eye, and Contessa had the sudden urge to reach out and touch his arm in comfort. She gripped her hand at her side and instead contented herself with trying to be useful.

"What's made things so uncertain that you feel the need to be so well armed?" Contessa asked.

"I'm sure you're informed about the controversies regarding the potential succession, with the way you read the papers," Nate explained.

Contessa furrowed her brow. "I mean, of course, but what does that have to do with your...business?"

Nate sighed. "As you would have heard, the people of the lower city prefer Prince Byron for the throne. They think Prince Albert prioritizes parties over the people. They're probably right, considering he's shown absolutely no interest in politics. It doesn't sit well with the people of the lower city who are barely scraping by to see Prince Albert be so...frivolous. I was sure he was going to abdicate, but he hasn't yet. Every day the king creeps closer to his deathbed while Prince Albert remains heir, the people of the lower city get more restless. As talk of violence increased, the Royal Police doubled their watch in the lower city, trying to stem any riots. The streets are crawling with officers, day and night. You can't take two steps without bumping into one."

"Ah, well," Contessa said dryly, "I suppose that would make any criminal activity more difficult."

Nate pulled a face that made it clear he had considered rolling his eyes at her. "It's not just strictly illegal activities, either. We only make a fraction of our money off pickpocketing and bigger heists. Most of the funds the Lions use to function comes from the money we skim at the gambling houses. Now the unrest has scared away most of our casual patrons. We've had to spread out over almost twice our usual area to get enough income to feed everybody."

Contessa pursed her lips thoughtfully.

"Well, why not go back into investing, like you did when you were younger to establish yourself in the upper city?" Contessa suggested.

Nate considered her, his head tilted. "I've thought about it you know, but now that most of the world at least suspects me of running most of the criminal underworld, it's hard to get into straight business. People expect all my financial choices to be crooked. Nobody believes I've just been lucky."

"Well, lucky may be a strong word for it," Contessa pointed out, "considering you used your supernatural perception to guide your investments."

Nate's eye crinkled in amusement. "Well, that too. Although, honestly, I only invested the first time so I could gain status. I keep this house and position so I can appear in circles where I can get leads on our next hit. Most of the men who own warehouses that use child laborers are rich and talk too much for their own good at clubs."

Contessa huffed. "Yes, I'm well aware." She repressed memories of escaping conversations with businessmen twice her age trying to impress her with their wealth, focusing on the topic at hand.

"Well," she ventured haltingly, "if you did ever want to get into honest business again, I might be able to lend my small influence in giving it some legitimacy."

"You know, that's not a half bad idea," Nate mused. "Although it would take time to build credibility. We'd have to come up with a solution for the Lion's income in the meantime."

Contessa bit her bottom lip. "Maybe I could accompany you to the lower city some time and see if I could help some of the gambling houses with their strategies."

"You would want to come to one of the Lions' gambling houses?" Nate asked, taking a step back.

"I've literally run from law enforcement with you," Contessa pointed out. "I don't know why this is that surprising to you."

"Be that as it may, you surprise me nearly every day, Connie."

It may have just been a flicker of the lamplight, but there was a softness in Nate's eyes that made Contessa look down and smooth her skirts.

"Well," she said softly, "if I'm going to be up for a trip into the wilds of the lower city, then I should get my rest."

Contessa moved to retire for the evening, but before she rounded the corner to make her way upstairs, she glanced back to find Nate standing right where she'd left him, looking down at the chess board in contemplation.

Chapter Fourteen

The gambling hall wasn't what Contessa had envisioned. As she stood in the doorway, she was greeted by warm lamplight illuminating round tables crowded together in way that might even be described as cozy. It was a far cry from the dingy gray room where she usually envisioned thugs tossing dice. There was even a fireplace in one corner casting a warmth that was welcome after the drizzle out in the street.

"Is something the matter?" Nate asked from her side, noticing she hadn't moved away from the entrance.

Contessa shook her head as she propped her umbrella against the doorframe. "It's just so...cute."

Nate's eye crinkled in amusement. "You know, we do try to make sure not everything we do projects the feeling of illicit activities. I mean, gambling isn't even illegal."

Contessa narrowed her eyes. "Be that as it may, I'm sure the amount your dealers skim isn't exactly above board."

Nate shrugged a shoulder. "That's not the point. We try to make this a place where people want to spend their time and money. At a dingy dice den, you only get the people that can't stop gambling even if they want to, and they don't have much money to take."

As Contessa and Nate pushed farther into the space, a few youths looked up from their tasks cleaning tables and sweeping floors to raise a hand in greeting at Nate. Several sets of eyes widened as they spotted her, but none of them said anything about her presence.

Nate weaved between the tables towards a small bar on one side, "Unfortunately, our best efforts at making this a place where people want to stay hasn't been great at getting them in off the streets. The most lucrative patrons from the middle city haven't been coming down to the lower city to gamble at all. They see it as a ticking time bomb."

Contessa ran her fingers over the scarred wood of the bar as she contemplated. "Have you considered sending some of your people up to taverns in the middle city as plants? Have them talk the place up? They could even try to bring groups of people down here themselves to make them feel like it's safe."

Nate tapped his blunt fingers on the bar top. "Right now, we only put plants in the other gambling halls in the lower city, but that's not a half bad idea." Nate cocked his head at her. "You're remarkably good at this sort of thing for a woman who grew up on the right side of the law."

"Yes, well, I spent my life being taught how to spot crooked business tactics, so I do know a thing or two," Contessa waved Nate off, not wanting to examine her feelings on such matters too closely. "Why don't we take a look at the outside of the place and see if there is something we can do to make it catch the eye a bit more."

Nate may have replied as Contessa walked towards the front door, but a high ringing overwhelmed her mind, blocking out any other noise. She was mere feet from the door when she whirled to face Nate, her heart pounding its way up into her throat. She didn't even get a word out before a pair of lethal knives sprang into Nate's hands from somewhere under his clothes.

Contessa lifted a foot to step towards him, but before it could land, there was the sound of wood banging against wood and an arm as thick as a tree branch wrapped around her neck. It yanked her back so hard her feet left the floor.

Blinking away tears from having her windpipe pressed on, Contessa's gaze landed on Nate, who had gone deathly still. His knives were still in his hands, and he had fallen into a low crouch, his muscles bunched to attack. He looked so tense Contessa felt like he should be quivering, but he stood stock still, as if waiting to pounce. Even as Contessa's toes scraped for purchase on the uneven wooden floorboards, she understood what it meant to face down the Beast.

Impatient with her struggling, the arm around her neck gave a sharp tug. Contessa went limp, focusing on taking shallow breaths and regaining her wits.

"Well, this is even better than we bargained for," rumbled the voice close to her ear. "Caleb sent me here to break a few bones and remind the Lions this block belongs to the Rattlesnakes. Instead, we find the Beast himself—and what's more, his pretty little wife."

The man shook Contessa as if they might have been unsure who he was talking about otherwise. Her brain rattled in her skull even as she tried to remember everything Rhosyn had ever said about escaping choke holds.

"Thomas, put her down," Nate said, not moving from his stance, his voice little more than a growl in the back of his throat. "Put her down, and we can figure something out."

Thomas's chest rumbled with laughter against Contessa's back. "Everybody says you're the best knife fighter in London because you've never lost a fight, but I know you better than that. I know you've never lost because, most of the time, you're too coward to fight at all."

By this point, several of the other Lions had come to back Nate up, blades and even a pistol or two in hand, but they waited for Nate to make the first move. They weren't fighting yet, but perhaps they could distract Thomas from his hold on Contessa just enough.

She swung a dangling leg around to try to trip up Thomas and take him to the ground. With the lack of leverage from hanging in the air, he kicked her leg out of the way easily, his boot connecting with a bone in her ankle in a way that made her eyes water.

"Well, if you don't want a fight, I'm more than happy to oblige. I'll just take this pretty little one to Caleb, and you can have her back once you get off Rattlesnake turf."

Nate didn't respond, not moving an inch. His nostrils flared and his gaze met hers briefly, holding an unholy glint that made her wonder how Thomas had the courage to back out the door with her still in his hold.

The cold drizzle hit Contessa as Thomas kicked the door to the gambling hall closed, and she found herself jostled and disoriented as there was a sudden onslaught of rough voices.

"We aren't fighting them after all?"

"Caleb won't be happy if we come back without spilling any blood."

"Who's the girl?"

Thomas brushed them off as he continued to walk into the street, Contessa hanging motionless in his hold to keep him from tightening his grip again.

"We've got something far better than a brawl today. Throw her in the wagon and get her back to Caleb, quick. It won't be long until the Beast comes after her."

Thomas turned her in his grasp, and if her reflexes had been faster, she might have been able to use the movement to escape from his hold, but before she could think, she was once again caged to his chest by arms like bands of steel.

"Now be a good little dove and get in the wagon. We won't hurt you if your dear husband does what he's told and backs down, so you should be fine. He always was a soft one," Thomas leered, giving Contessa a close view of his chipped yellow teeth.

Thomas began to push her backwards into the wagon, and Contessa squirmed, a single thought running to the forefront of her mind before she was shoved into captivity.

What would Rhosyn do?

In her best impression of a street brawler, Contessa reared her head back before slamming it forward with as much force as she could muster. There was a sickening crunch, and Thomas's hold loosened on Contessa for just an instant.

Unfortunately, the crunch seemed to have come from Contessa's own face as lightning bolts of pain exploded behind her eyes. She only managed to stumble into Thomas, her hands landing on his thick waist.

Before she could fully process the haze of pain, Thomas had caught her and was shoving her into the wagon, her knees hitting the edge and causing her to topple backwards. Her hands remained clenched in tight fists instead of breaking her fall. Thomas let out a ruthless chuckle as she tumbled to the floor with a thud, slamming the wagon door behind her.

"Oh dear, the Beast's poor little bride has gone and broken her face. I hope he doesn't mind too much."

Indeed, as the wagon lurched into motion, jumping and bobbing over the rough cobblestones of the street, Contessa brought a hand to her face to try to contain the blood dripping from her nose. Still, she brought up her other hand and opened her fist in front of her face to examine the prize she'd slid from Thomas's pocket.

Her heart fluttered in relief as her eyes focused on a switchblade, much plainer than Nate's but revealing a narrow blade when she pressed the mechanism. It would be thin enough to suit her purposes. She pinched her nose tighter and grimaced, even as she celebrated that she hadn't wrecked her nose to distract Thomas only to grab something useless like a handkerchief.

Contessa scooted across the rough floor of the wagon, glad she'd chosen to wear pants today as the material snagged on a few lose nails. As she crouched near the door, she let her hand drop from her face, giving up on staunching the bleeding and letting the blood drip onto her shirt. Getting out of this carriage was the priority.

She leaned in to examine the lock on the door, cursing for asking Julia to put her hair in a simple braid today instead of an elaborate style that would supply her with pins. Still, the blade she'd pilfered would work well enough for raking the lock. A more exacting form of lockpicking would've been difficult in a jolting carriage anyways.

As she examined the lock, Thomas's voice drifted in from the direction of the driver's seat, his rumble carrying over the clatter of the wheels.

"I wonder what Caleb will do with this one. He won't want to give up the leverage over the Lions, but I don't see him giving her back in one piece."

The muffled voice of the driver responded, followed by Thomas's raspy chuckle.

"True. Maybe he'll slit her throat and cut some slashes in her face. He could leave her on her father's doorstep so the Chief could have a matched set."

Contessa's heart jumped into her throat, and she ripped her attention away from eavesdropping, trying to focus on the task in front of her. Carefully, she slipped the blade into the keyhole and rotated it slightly until she felt the pins lift. She yanked the knife towards her and cursed when she only heard one pin knocked into place. Raking had never been her preferred method of lockpicking, being so imprecise, but there was nothing else to do. She slid the knife back into the lock to try again, only to freeze when the wagon shuddered to a halt.

Contessa braced for the ringing in her ears at the danger that surely awaited her inside the Rattlesnakes hideout, but the world remained quiet. Her breath stilled in her chest in the brief silence before a thud on the roof rattled the wagon, followed by a metallic *shick* and a wet gurgle that Contessa was sure she would be hearing in her nightmares for the rest of her days.

All hell broke loose with sudden shouting and the singing of metal against metal. Contessa swung back to her work with renewed fervor, drawing the blade out of the lock three more times as the sounds of a fight raged outside. She finally felt all the pins fall into place and the door swung open.

The sight that greeted her in the street was one of carnage, the type she'd always been taught to fear from the gangs of the lower city. At the center of the vortex of violence stood Nate, whirling and parrying with his knives in movements so much more graceful than what Contessa was used to from him, as if he was more himself with knives in his hands. The rain had matted his auburn hair down, making it several shades darker where it clung to his face and collar.

As she watched, a mountain of a man aimed a brutal swing of his knife at the side of Nate's head. Before Contessa could open her mouth to scream, Nate had caught the brute's blow on his forearm and sunk the dagger in his other hand into the man's flank. The thug toppled over as Nate yanked his blade free, blood splattering from the knife and falling to the ground where it mixed with the rainwater and ran into the gutters in a crimson river. Before the first fighter even hit the ground, a second charged up behind Nate, but Nate threw up a hand without even looking, slashing the man across the face as he tried to grapple Nate from behind.

Intimidated, the group of Rattlesnakes stepped back to regroup, circling Nate from a distance as he fell back into a crouch in preparation for their next assault. His mouth was pulled up in a silent snarl, and while Contessa had grown used to his appearance, she was suddenly reminded how frightening his scar could appear.

As the men faced off, it became apparent that Nate was severely outnumbered, and the Rattlesnakes glanced at each other out of the corners of their eyes. If they all charged at once, Nate's chances of victory would be slim.

Even if Contessa had thought to strap her own blades to herself that morning, she wasn't going to be much use against seasoned street brawlers. She glanced around desperately, when a distressed whiney behind her grabbed her attention. She spun around to find the wagon she'd just exited, attached to two horses, pawing the ground and whickering at the sudden death of their driver.

Without a further thought, Contessa clambered up into the front of the wagon, hands slipping on a combination of blood and rainwater. As she hoisted herself into the driver's seat, she was forced to shove the lifeless body of the driver aside to reach the reins, trying desperately not to think about the wide gash spanning his throat. Instead, she turned her attention to the horses, tugging them around as best she could. As the wagon slowly wheeled around to face the fight, the circle of thugs tightened around Nate like a noose. He'd managed to position his back towards the wall of a nearby building. She tugged at the reins one more time, trying to point the horses directly at the group of Rattlesnakes in the street.

Just before she snapped the reins, Nate's eyes jerked up to spot Contessa on her perch in the driver's seat. Then, the horses bucked, easily spurred to a charge in their frightened state. The Rattlesnakes looked up at the clatter of hooves, but it was too late. Where Nate managed to press himself into the wall just in time, the horses' hooves hit the first of the brawlers with a crunch, and the wagon jolted over a fallen body with a bump that rattled Contessa's teeth. The rest of the men scattered like pins in lawn bowling, running down the street away from the thundering wagon. Realizing their defeat, they split off into alleyways and ran in different directions, disappearing into the haze of rain. The street went quiet as the pounding of retreating footsteps disappeared. Pulling in the reins, Contessa soothed the frightening horses with some effort, and the cart ground to a halt.

Contessa slumped down in the driver's seat, exhaling. For the first time since stepping out of the wagon, she noticed the cold of the rain pattering against her face, the wet making her shirt cling unpleasantly to her skin and weighing her braid down against her back. The clamminess of her skin only served to make the hot pounding in her nose and the warmth of the blood still dripping onto her lips stand out even more. She ran her tongue over her teeth, gagging at the thought of how much more blood was currently running over the cobblestones of the street.

A thump to her left startled her, and she looked down to find Nate, standing on the ground next to the driver's seat. He looked up at her with wide eyes, his hand braced on the side of the wagon as if debating climbing up to the seat himself.

Without a thought, Contessa clambered to the edge of the wagon and slithered down the side. She barely held on at all as she descended, sliding down so fast she would have fallen to her knees in the street if Nate hadn't caught her under her arms.

He held her in front of him, scrutinizing her face. Contessa could only imagine the state she was in—blood crusted on her lip, her nose swollen and bruised. She might have raised her hands to cover her face if she hadn't been preoccupied making sure the blood splattered across Nate's shirt wasn't his.

"Which one of them… Who did that to your nose?" Nate demanded, his eyes taking on an almost feral cast in the flickering light from a nearby lamppost.

Contessa might have pointed out that whoever it was likely already got what they deserved, but instead, she said, "Oh, that's my fault. I can only blame myself."

Nate's brows drew together as his expression faded from hostility to confusion. "How?"

Contessa swallowed, then grimaced at the blood dripping down the back of her throat. "Well, I did my best to headbutt Thomas when he put me in the wagon. You all make it look so easy… I think I underestimated how much it would hurt."

Nate's face went blank, and he didn't say anything for a moment.

"It all worked out, though," Contessa prattled on, uncharacteristically nervous before Nate's expressionless stare. "It distracted him long enough that I picked his pocket so I could break the lock and escape."

The corner of Nate's mouth began to pull up, and for a moment, Contessa thought he was about to snarl in anger again. Instead, his face broke into a wide grin, his eyes softening in relief and something akin to wonder.

Before Contessa could gape at him for longer than a moment, she found herself crushed to his chest, his arms around her making her feel blessedly warm in the damp, her face buried in his neck. She would've fretted about getting blood on his jacket if that wasn't already a lost cause.

"I'm not sure why I expected anything less, honestly," Nate mused against her hair.

In response, Contessa wound her arms around his waist, pressing herself into his warmth and wishing she could smell the rain and his skin through her swollen nose.

Chapter Fifteen

The warmth in Contessa's chest began to spread, reaching down to the tips of her fingers, as she swirled the brown liquid in the cut crystal glass Nate had offered her.

As if in response to her thoughts, Nate asked from where he sat at the foot of her bed, "How do you feel?"

"Warm," Contessa answered honestly. "It's a nice change from the wet clothes. Rain can be lovely; it's a shame it is always so cold."

Nate exhaled sharply through his nose as she continued to examine the way the candlelight filtered through the sloshing amber liquid.

"Well, I think you're relaxed enough now. You think you're ready to let Gregor try and set that nose of yours?"

Contessa sighed and placed the glass down on the stand next to her with a clink.

"I'm not sure if ready is the word I would use, but now is as good a time as ever," she conceded as she rested her head back on the pillows and closed her eyes in preparation.

Gregor's voice came from somewhere near the head of her bed. "I'll try to be quick about this. Just hold still and do your best not to fight me."

The bedsheets crumpled in her hands as Contessa balled them into fists to brace herself, even as she tried as hard as she could to relax. She felt Gregor's fingers, surprisingly cool on her face, before he pushed at her nose in a way that made white shine behind her eyelids. Although she managed to stay still, a grunt escaped her lips. She would have been embarrassed by the noise if a warm hand hadn't come to rest on her shin over her dressing gown, a thumb soothing back and forth.

After a few more pushes and a painful click, Gregor declared her nose appeared to be back in place

"I've gotten much better at setting noses since I first started patching up the Lions," Gregor assured her as he stuffed some sort of awful cotton into her nostrils. Contessa tried not to squirm.

"Yours should heal much better than Kristoff's did. His was the first one I set, and I still feel guilty it healed so crooked."

Nate huffed in amusement. "I wouldn't feel too guilty if I were you. I know you think the crooked nose only accentuates his roguishness, and I'm sure Kristoff appreciates that."

"Yes, well..." Gregor cleared his throat and finished packing Contessa's nose in silence before putting some sort of rigid bandage on the outside.

Contessa felt Gregor shift away and she opened her eyes.

"I'll go get you a cold compress to help with the pain and swelling," said Gregor. "After that, all you should need is time and rest."

He slipped from the room to go fetch the compress, but Nate stayed seated at the foot of the bed. She glanced at him from what she knew to be bruised eyes, having caught sight of herself in the mirror on the way into her room.

"Well, how do I look?" she asked, happy that the liquor had gone to her system just enough to numb the embarrassment she felt at her nasal voice.

"Like somebody who just survived their first street brawl," said Nate. "As much as I'm impressed by your resourcefulness, maybe blindly headbutting thugs is ill-advised."

"No more ill-advised than coming after me without any backup," Contessa retorted, burrowing her head into the pillows behind her in an effort to get comfortable.

"I had sent the Lions from the hall to run for backup, but time was of the essence. If they had gotten you back to Caleb…" Nate didn't finish his thought right away. "Well, it was going to be easier to break you out of a wagon than it would have been to rescue you from the middle of a nest of Rattlesnakes. Besides, I knew I could climb over a building and cut them off."

Contessa wanted to press him on the matter, but at that moment, Gregor pushed back into the room, holding a compress as promised. She was untangling her hands from the sheets to reach for it, but Nate beat her to it, thanking Gregor before he slipped back out.

Nate slid up the bed until he was even with Contessa's hip, reaching up to gently press the compress to her bruised face. She hissed at the touch before relaxing into the feeling of cool, soothing the heartbeat echoing in her skull.

"You're going to go through a lot of these," Nate mused. "I remember the first time I broke my nose; the cold was pretty much the only thing that made it feel better. I didn't take anybody's advice about keeping the packing in, either. I hated not being able to breathe through my nose, so it took forever to heal."

"The first time you broke your nose?" Contessa prodded.

"I've broken it three times. My combat training was rather…learn as you go," Nate explained. "It's a good thing I gave up on vanity long ago, because I never seemed to get Gregor to set them in time."

Contessa narrowed her eyes, scrutinizing his nose. She supposed she could see a slight bend, but it was hard to discern under a rope of scar tissue that ran over the bridge of his nose. Seeing her looking, Nate ducked his head.

They sat in silence for a few moments, Nate still holding the cool compress to Contessa's face, and her making no move to take it from him. Instead, she continued to examine his face, comparing the soft expression she saw now to the snarl he had worn in the street.

"You killed a lot of people today," Contessa broke the silence without preamble.

Nate raised his eyes back to hers, his scar worn like a mask that kept his expression neutral.

"I did," was his only reply as he continued to examine Contessa's face.

She said nothing, offering him no reaction, even though she knew he could read her feelings, at least to some degree.

"You killed some people too," he commented.

Contessa inhaled, but still, she didn't say anything.

"How...how does that make you feel?" Nate asked, his voice as halting as his tone was inscrutable.

"How do you feel when you kill people?" Contessa asked in return.

Her eyes tracked the shadow that bobbed in the hollow of Nate's throat as he swallowed.

"Part of me feels like I could say I'm used to it," Nate conceded, "but I think it might be more accurate to say I've learned to keep going. I believe in what I do, and sometimes...sometimes I think how I feel about it isn't even relevant."

Contessa nodded, understanding it from Nate's point of view.

"I watched my father and his men come home wearing other people's blood all the time, and I still held them on a pedestal as heroes because they were making sacrifices to uphold the law," Contessa admitted, unsure if the words tumbling out of her mouth were prompted by the liquor or the pent-up demand of weeks, but knowing she had to say them all the same. "I tolerated murder in the name of the law because I was told the law was right—even though I hadn't evaluated it for myself. If I can live with death in the name of a code that was simply thrust upon me, I can learn to live with it in the name of a cause I chose for myself."

Contessa's gaze was steady over the compress, but there were still feelings crawling under her skin that made it difficult to rest despite her bone-deep exhaustion. Still, as Nate's eyes fixed on hers, she took comfort in the fact she didn't have to explain them to him, that he could feel. He may have even had them himself, which was why she was not entirely surprised when she closed her eyes and he made no move to leave. He stayed perched in his spot, a warm presence next to her hip as she released her mind to let it drift, freed by exhaustion, pain, and alcohol.

She was just about to slip out of consciousness, odd images from the day drifting through her mind, when one suddenly jumped to the forefront. Her eyes sprung open to find Nate was still watching her.

"When I was in the wagon, I overheard Thomas say something," Contessa said. "He said that maybe Caleb would cut my throat, slash my face, and leave me on my father's doorstep just like my mother."

Nate put a hand on her shin, misreading the distress rolling off her.

"We won't let that—"

"No," Contessa interrupted. "I think he killed my mother."

Nate's hand stilled where he had been gently stroking her leg. Contessa wished he would continue.

"The slashes." Nate's voice was deathly soft. "Caleb was the one who started them. The lieutenant that split with the Lions when I confronted him about being needlessly violent."

Cold washed through Contessa's veins, stifling the warmth of impending sleep.

"What do you want to do about it?" Nate questioned.

"I'm not sure," Contessa answered candidly, "but if there ever was somebody I wanted dead, it would be him."

The sunshine warming her face offered a nice contrast to the cool of the windowpane against Contessa's forehead. She opened her eyes and looked out at the street, watching people walk by and feeling envious of whatever it was they were doing. It seemed that, in the past week of training with Rhosyn, Contessa had become accustomed to a more active daily routine. Finding herself stuck in her room made her squirm.

She realized she was picking at her skirts again and settled them into stillness in her lap. Nate may have preferred she stay in bed today while her nose healed, but Contessa had insisted on getting up and getting dressed, loathe to rid herself of her routine entirely. She'd been tempted to insist she at least be able to go out for a walk as well, but after catching sight of herself in the mirror as Julia brushed her hair, she agreed to stay indoors. While the dark purple streaks outlining the underside of her eyes were unsightly, it wasn't vanity that kept Contessa indoors. She simply wasn't ready to face the questions her appearance would cause and didn't think it was wise to draw attention to herself.

Contessa pushed off the window seat and made to huff in frustration but found it rather difficult to do around the cotton in her nose. Just because she had to stay inside didn't mean she had to lie about in her room like an indisposed lady whose nerves had gotten the better of her. She traipsed down the stairs, unsure of her intentions but adamant she could locate something to occupy herself.

As usual, she found the lower level of the house silent, the dining room spotless as Contessa had been persuaded to take breakfast in her room today. Maybe if she could find Gregor, she could convince him to let her help with some tasks around the house.

As she headed to the back hallway, hoping to see Gregor in the garden, she was greeted by the unusual sight of the office door propped open. Padding up to it, she heard a distinctive scraping noise and peeked around the frame to find Nate sitting at the large desk and running one of his daggers methodically across a whetstone. She spotted the matching knife on the desk and cleared her throat to distract herself from thoughts of why he was cleaning and sharpening his weapons.

Nate's gaze shot up, and he hurried to his feet as soon as he saw her.

"Connie, what are you doing up? You should be resting."

Contessa waved him away, stepping fully into the office.

"It's a broken nose, not a broken leg. And even if I had broken my leg, my mind still works fine and doesn't do well with prolonged inactivity."

Nate settled back into his seat as Contessa perched herself in the spare chair across from his desk. He didn't look pleased with her explanation, but he didn't protest.

"Well," he said, pulling open a desk drawer, "I do have a gift for you while I have you here."

"A gift?"

"Don't get too eager," Nate cautioned. "I doubt it's anything to get excited over, but yesterday brought to my attention that teaching you how to fight with knives won't do you any good if you don't keep them with you."

He pulled a leather bundle out of the drawer and passed it over the desk to Contessa. She turned the items in her hand, finding them to be two sheathes with straps that could be used to attach them to her arms.

"They're just like mine," Nate explained. When Contessa glanced up, she found him shrugging out of his waistcoat. She blushed and looked down at her lap, berating herself for getting flustered at the sight of her husband in shirtsleeves when she'd seen him completely shirtless before. She composed herself and raised her gaze to find him rolling up one of his sleeves. Indeed, he had a long blade attached to his forearm in a similar fashion.

"See, there's a catch here," Nate pointed out a latch on the inner side of his wrist, "and if you press it—"

Contessa jumped as the hilt flew into his hand. Somehow, she doubted she would achieve such elegant results when she tried. Nate twirled the knife mindlessly in his hand a few times, and Contessa followed the blurred silver of the blade through its arcs before he slid it back into the straps on his arm, settling it into place with a muffled click.

Contessa held up the sheathes in her own hand, pressing the mechanism a few times and lifting it close to her eyes to puzzle out how it might work.

"These will go well under a shirt," she mused as she peered in the opening to watch the catch open to free the blade. "Although I won't be able to hide these under the sleeves of most dresses."

Nate blinked and looked her up and down. Today she was wearing a royal blue dress, blessedly free of bows and ruffles, as Julia determined such ornaments weren't necessary for sitting in the house.

"Right," Nate said, eyes settling on her skirts. "I'll have to ask Rhosyn to dig up some for your legs." Realizing he was staring, the tips of Nate's ears went pink, and he looked away to put his waistcoat back on. As he did, Contessa spotted the handles of two more knives in the sides where he could access them easily just by reaching under his coat.

They both settled back into their chairs in comfortable silence, and Contessa let her eyes roam around the room now that she was at leisure to do so without some emergency drawing her attention. It, like the rest of the house, was a rather bare space.

"What do you usually do in this office? You aren't home very much to use it," Contessa asked.

Nate looked around at the empty walls, as if noticing them for the first time.

"I suppose it's mostly a cover for the entrance to the passage. I use it for my comings and goings. I do meet with Kristoff in here, as well, but I think he only prefers to meet here so he gets a chance to see Gregor." Nate's smile was fond. "Otherwise, I'm only in here early in the morning or late at night to do some strategizing on our next job. I just stayed home for today because you were…"

Contessa let the silence stretch as she waited for Nate to finish his thought, but his gaze moved down to the desk where his fingers worried over the whetstone lying there.

"I guess that would explain why the house has no personal effects, if you don't spend that much time here," Contessa eventually mused. "Although, I will admit that the empty shelves in the library upstairs make my heart hurt."

THE TALENTED FAIRY TALES

"Yes, well," Nate tugged at his cravat. "I guess I've never really been one for books. I can send Julia out on an errand to fetch some if you like, though. What kind of books do you prefer?"

"Oh, I read everything. Philosophy, history, and I can read in French, too, although my accent is horrendous, so I rarely speak it," Contessa said. "I must admit my favorites are novels about adventures and fairy tales. Not very practical, I know, but they make me nostalgic."

Nate was looking at Contessa with wide eyes, fingers still rubbing over the surface of the whetstone.

"Let me guess, you prefer military strategy and politics?" Contessa prodded.

"Well, I don't..." Nate cleared his throat as his voice came out quiet. "I don't really read."

"Oh, that's a shame. Somebody as clever as— Oh..." Contessa's eyes widened.

Nate looked away again.

"Do you not know how to read? I could teach—"

"I can read," Nate interrupted, his shoulders pulling up towards his ears. "Just not very well. I didn't have the chance to learn as a child, so I started when I was a teenager. I get by, but I've always been too slow to enjoy novels."

Contessa swallowed to dispel the tightness in her chest.

"Considering by then you were on your way to running the biggest gang operation in London, I would say you get by more than well enough," Contessa said gently.

Nate looked up, and his embarrassment softened into a small smile. "Perhaps, but it left me ill-equipped to be married to someone who reads as much as you do."

"That's nothing that can't be easily remedied. Now I just get to build a collection specifically to my taste."

Nate exhaled sharply through his nose. "Good. Now, if I send Julia to get you adequate reading material, will that persuade you to stay in your room and rest at least for a few days while the swelling goes down?"

Contessa pursed her lips. "You are awfully keen on having me do nothing, considering you were the one who wanted me to be trained in self-defense in the first place."

"And embracing the strategic retreat is an essential part of all combat training," Nate pointed out.

Contessa pushed to her feet. "Well as long as you are willing to bribe me with proper reading material, then I suppose I will accept your lesson."

Contessa swept from the room with her head held high, catching the twinkle in Nate's eye before she rounded the corner.

Contessa stared at the dregs of her tea and debated with herself whether it was too early to go to bed out of sheer boredom when there was a knock at her bedroom door. Grateful for having something to do, she leapt to her feet and yanked the door open to find Nate blinking down at her.

"Oh, if you are already going to bed for the evening, I don't mean to intrude," he commented, finding her dressed in her nightgown and dressing gown.

"Nonsense," Contessa stepped back and ushered him into her room. "If I go to bed now, I'm likely to end up staring at the at the ceiling pondering how I've done nothing with my day."

"Well, good thing I brought something to distract you then." Nate produced an object from behind his back and offered it to her.

Her lips parted in a smile before she could even take the book from his hand, recognizing the embossed cover instantly.

"Julia has good taste," she commented as she ran her hand over the colorful dragon on the front.

"Well, you did say you like fairy tales. I have heard it's meant for children, but I—Julia thought you might like it."

Contessa perched herself on the edge of her bed, letting the book fall open in her lap, her fingers tracing over the words of familiar stories.

"I've always disliked people who say fairy tales are only for children. If the point of them is to escape into our imagination, then wouldn't adults who are so painfully aware of the weary ways of the world need them most?"

"A sound argument," Nate responded. "Although not one a person hears a lot."

Contessa flipped to a page and found herself looking at the title of one of her favorite stories about the girl who tricked a dragon out of its gold by winning in a game of riddles. A wave of nostalgia so painful it made her eyes water rolled over her, and before she consciously made the decision to speak, words were coming out of her mouth.

"You know, my mother used to read these exact stories to me before bed every night when I was small. She even turned the tales into songs to sing me to sleep sometimes. Even though my father said the stories were frivolous, he always stood in the doorway and listened to her read to me.

"When she died, he wanted to take all the fairy tales off the shelves in our library. He tried to get rid of everything that reminded him of her, saying it was too painful to see bits of her everywhere he went. I wouldn't let him get rid of this book, though, and I kept it in my own room. Even though I followed his advice and mostly studied politics and languages, I always had these stories to keep me company when I missed my mother the most."

When she finished, she looked up to find Nate leaning against the corner post of her bed thoughtfully.

"You seem to take after your mother in many ways."

"People say I look like her, with the blonde hair and pale skin and all. But everybody agrees that I have my father's cold disposition."

Nate shifted to face her more fully as he said, "Well, maybe that has more to do with your being around him for most of your life than anything else. I think you're more like your mother than many people might realize."

Contessa swallowed heavily but didn't respond, not trusting her voice to be steady.

"You probably even got your Talent from her," Nate mused.

Contessa started.

"I... My mother wasn't Talented."

Nate shrugged. "It may have been a small Talent, or something subtle like yours that she didn't even know about. Talent usually runs in families, though, and it would be highly unusual for yours to come from your father considering his position on the matter."

Contessa's eyes fell on the page in front of her, and she could practically hear her mother's voice, impossibly beautiful, spinning the words into a song. She remembered how everybody stopped what they were doing to listen when she sang, as if they were bewitched.

"It's possible," Contessa conceded.

There was a long silence, broken only by the clatter of wheels on pavement as a carriage rumbled past outside.

"Well, I'll leave you to your reading," Nate made as if to go.

"Wait." Contessa licked suddenly dry lips. "If you want to stay, I could maybe read out loud."

Nate's look was inscrutable as he paused.

"I mean, I know you said you don't read to enjoy stories, but I thought that maybe if somebody read them aloud to you, you might find them interesting," Contessa continued, uncharacteristically nervous.

"I would love that."

Contessa relaxed, situating herself more comfortably on her bed and flipping through the book to find an appropriate tale.

Nate settled himself onto the seat by the window, crossing one ankle lightly over his knee, looking much too large for the narrow bench. Contessa contemplated telling him that he could sit on the bed with her, but she turned back to the book in her lap.

"Oh, let's start with this one," Contessa said as she flipped the next page. "It's about a princess that must save a king from a curse that turns him into a serpent."

"Sounds delightful," Nate murmured, leaning his head back on the window and keeping his gaze fixed on Contessa.

Contessa tried to ignore the weight of his eyes on her as she began to read. She soon fell into a familiar rhythm, and she read until the candles had all but burned out.

Chapter Sixteen

"I brought you a visitor."

Contessa looked up from the book she was reading, using her thumb to hold her place in today's tome of mythology. She found Gregor peering around the door to her bedroom, a tentative smile on his round face. She raised her eyebrows and nodded for him to let them in, unsure who it might be. It wasn't like Nate to have his presence announced.

A head of curly red hair peeked through the doorway.

"Rhosyn! What are you doing here?"

The girl offered a cheeky grin.

"I thought you could use a little change of pace. The nose looks good, though."

Contessa touched her fingers lightly to the bridge of her nose, testing it since the bandages had been removed a few days prior. It was still bruised, but the deep purple marks had faded to a sallow yellow.

"I'm glad I'll be able to go outside soon without garnering unwanted attention. Why don't you come in and sit down." Contessa moved the pile of books off the window seat next to her and rearranged her skirts to make room. She gestured to the small table near her habitual perch. "Help yourself to some tea."

Rhosyn moved into the room, picking her way around the stack of books at Contessa's feet to take a place next to her on the bench. On the top of the pile was the book of children's tales she had been reading to Nate every night for the past week. He had continued to bring her all types of history and poetry, but he seemed to enjoy hearing the same stories that had lulled Contessa to sleep as a child, so she continued to read him those.

"You look so different dressed like this," Rhosyn's words brought Contessa back from her thoughts. "It was so easy to forget you were a proper lady when you were wearing trousers and sweating in the back room with me."

"I'm not sure this dress makes me a proper lady," Contessa commented drily, picking at the lace on her sleeve. "It makes me feel like a porcelain doll."

Rhosyn reached out a hand and tentatively ran a finger over a ruffle on today's periwinkle ensemble as she mused. "I suppose it would be different if I had to wear one every day, but your clothes are so beautiful. I can't even remember the last time I wore a dress myself. They get in the way of rolling around on the floor with children."

"Who's with the children right now if you're here with me?"

Rhosyn glanced up with the sly grin of a fox who had spotted a chicken coop.

"I talked Kristoff into watching them so I could have a day off, and he talked Nate into joining him. When I left, they had children climbing all over them like monkeys."

Contessa covered her smile as Rhosyn let out a devious chuckle.

"I swear, those two can face down an alley full of armed thugs without fear, but they are intimidated by a dozen little ones."

Contessa picked up her teacup and sipped delicately to hide the grin threatening to spill across her features at the memory of Nate playing with the children.

"Well," she put down her teacup with a light clink, "we better make sure you have a great day off so the men will not have subjected themselves to chaos for nothing. I think I might have an idea."

Half an hour later, the entirety of Contessa's wardrobe was spread across her bed, a garish heap in a cacophony of colors making Contessa wonder just what dressmaker Nate had asked to create her clothing. Still, Rhosyn stared at them all with wide eyes as Julia laced her into the ruffled number she'd selected. The pastel pink clashed violently with her copper curls, but she didn't seem to care as she admired herself in the mirror, executing a small twirl as soon as Julia had finished.

"Is this how it feels to be the delightful Mrs. Woodrow?" Rhosyn teased as she twisted to see herself from all angles.

Contessa's chest warmed as she watched the woman smooth her skirts, trying to make them lie gracefully. Watching the joy she took in trying on a dress reminded her just how young Rhosyn was to have the lives of so many depending on her all the time.

"It doesn't look quite right on me somehow, though," Rhosyn commented, tilting her head as she frowned at herself in the mirror.

"Well, of course it doesn't," Julia piped up. "We haven't even touched that lovely hair of yours yet."

Julia ushered her over to the seat in front of the vanity table, even as Rhosyn continued to look dubious.

"Good luck," she said as she helped Julia remove the leather band fighting valiantly to keep the stray curls from her face. "I doubt my hair is going to be as easily tamed as Contessa's over there. Hers is just so smooth."

Rhosyn looked wistful, but Julia wasted no time in waving away her concern.

"Yes, and it's so smooth it would lie flat on her head if I didn't tend to it every day. I know just how to deal with your hair too."

Indeed, it wasn't long before Julia had begun to coax Rhosyn's hair into a thick copper braid twining around her head like a crown. Rhosyn tried to twist and turn to catch a glimpse of the curls cascading artfully in the back, but Julia scolded her to sit still.

"Are you sure your ability to do hair isn't a Talent, Julia?" Rhosyn asked in wonder. "Perhaps a gift to bring beauty to those around you?"

Julia wrinkled her nose as her fingers continued to deftly weave the strands together.

"Oh, it's definitely not a Talent," Julia said around the hairpins she held in her mouth. "It took a lot of time to figure out how to do most of this. I subjected you and all the other girls to having your hair pinned and repinned several times a day to practice. I'm sure I made your scalps ache."

"You were amazing at it, even then. There was a reason we never complained about letting you style our hair." Rhosyn's eyes caught Contessa's over her shoulder in the mirror. "Speaking of Talents, how's testing yours going? I'm surprised Two-faced Timothy was able to grab you if you could sense him in advance."

Contessa grimaced.

"Apparently, I don't always get more than a few moments warning, and it's vague at best."

Rhosyn chewed on her bottom lip in contemplation.

"Have you and Nate tried anything to sharpen your sense? Like having him surprise you or anything? I know he said he had to practice to get his Talent as attuned as it is."

"You know," Contessa started, "I have been thinking about that while I've been stuck here for the past few days, and it occurs to me that it is still possible to surprise me. I don't think my Talent alerts me unless there is actual danger."

Rhosyn drummed her fingers on the dressing table in thought.

"That is certainly a good theory. Although that means it would be hard to test your Talent, considering I'm not willing to actually try to stab you in the name of experimentation."

"Pity," Contessa commented over the rim of her teacup.

"You know what this means, though?" Rhosyn asked as Julia put the finishing touches on her hairstyle. "We're going to have to bring you on real missions to develop your Talent more. Kristoff and I are planning a liberation mission for next weekend. The Lions could use a spare lookout."

Contessa set down her teacup carefully.

"I doubt Nate would be pleased with the idea of me being in a fight when the last one didn't go as well as we could have hoped."

"Nonsense," Rhosyn retorted, admiring the feather that Julia had worked into her braid. "We all heard about your stunt with the carriage. Winning in a street fight is more about resourcefulness than technique most of the time anyways."

Rhosyn stood from the seat, turned to face Contessa where she sat in the window seat, and put her fists on her hips in an exasperated manner that looked odd in her current clothing.

"Besides, you're Nate's wife. Tell him you'll make his life miserable if he doesn't let you come along."

"That's not exactly…" Contessa tried to come up with an adequate explanation for why she would not be doing that.

Rhosyn wasn't to be deterred and flounced over to where Contessa sat, flopping down next to her in a rustling pile of lace.

"We can plan it so you're not really in any danger, reassure Nate you'll be perfectly safe. I'll help. You have to admit that it sounds much more exciting than staying at home all day."

Contessa helped Rhosyn adjust her skirts properly on the bench to buy time in responding. Rhosyn had a direct way of attacking issues that caused Contessa to feel like she was mentally treading on very thin ice. Indeed, during her period of rest, she had plenty of time to reflect on what Rhosyn had asked her last time they were together. What did she really want? The answer had come to her in a single word.

Purpose.

Her former goal of bringing the Beast to justice had been shattered in the most unexpected of ways, but now she was granted the chance at a new purpose in giving factories full of children a better life. It may not have been the purpose she envisioned for her future, but it was the one she chose for herself.

"Alright," Contessa said. "But I'm going to enlist your help in working with Nate to create a suitable plan of attack."

Rhosyn sprang to her feet and whirled around the room a few times, and Julia chuckled at her antics even as she looked tempted to warn Rhosyn not to disturb her hair. Rhosyn stopped, her eyes bright in the orange light from the low sun coming in through the window, reminding her of the time of day.

"Do you want to stay for dinner?" Contessa asked abruptly. "It would be a shame for you to have gotten all dressed up and not have a chance to show it off."

The women descended the stairs to head to the dining room, and Contessa smiled at the way Rhosyn still managed to gallop down the stairs in a gown. Upon entering the dining room, they pulled up short at the unexpected sight of Nate, standing beside a table already laid with food.

"You two have certainly had a fun afternoon," he commented, looking Rhosyn up and down. She shamelessly twisted this way and that to show off her outfit.

"It was my turn to spend a day in the upper city while you got to play with the rascals for a change," Rhosyn retorted. "It seems you managed to survive unscathed."

Nate didn't appear to be the worse for wear, except for his hair, which stuck up at odd angles as though it had been pulled at by small hands.

"I like children." Nate shrugged one shoulder as he lifted the cover off a serving platter on the table to investigate what was beneath. "I only left because Gregor came to relieve me. Said he had prepared dinner and put it on the table for us and didn't want me to miss it."

Rhosyn snorted.

"You know that's just a cover for Gregor and Kristoff wanting to play with the children together," she pointed out.

"Naturally."

"It looks like Gregor made plenty for all of us," Contessa added, gesturing to the table. "Why don't we enjoy his offering while they have some fun."

The trio didn't get more than two bites into their soup before Rhosyn broke the companionable silence.

"Contessa's going to come with us on the next liberation mission."

Nate coughed on his mouthful of soup and hastily took a drink of water to clear his throat.

"And when was this decided?"

"Just this afternoon," Contessa jumped in, giving Rhosyn a look that indicated there might have been better ways to broach the subject. The woman just shrugged and turned back to her soup.

"We thought that, considering my Talent only displays itself when there is legitimate danger, there's little point in trying to hone it at home," Contessa explained. "My Talent can only really be developed on the job, as you put it."

Nate ran a hand through his hair, which somehow only managed to make the unruly tufts stand up further.

"I suppose you have a point," he admitted. "But can you at least promise me you will not try to use your face as a weapon against men twice your size again?"

Contessa nodded, taken aback by Nate's quick acceptance of their plan.

"We figured we would station her nearby, but out of harm's way where she wouldn't necessarily have to do any fighting if things go awry," Rhosyn said around a mouthful of bread.

"When do things not go awry, Rhosyn?"

Rhosyn glared at Nate. "Well, maybe now with Contessa standing watch they won't."

"What we need to figure out," Contessa interjected, "is how I should signal you if I sense a problem. I was thinking maybe flashing with a mirror, but that wouldn't work while you're inside."

Nate shook his head.

"That would take too much time to be useful. Last time, you only had a few seconds warning of danger. We'll have to rely on my ability to sense your fear as a warning."

Contessa frowned, but Rhosyn spoke before she could question Nate.

"That would make it hard to keep her out of any potential fight. She would have to stay close to us. You've admitted that you have a limited range on sensing people."

"Yes." Nate fussed with the napkin in his lap. "Although I can sense certain people from farther away than others. If I've become particularly…attuned to their emotional signature."

Rhosyn's brows shot up even as Contessa tilted her head in curiosity.

"You're saying you could possibly position me farther away if you were attuned to me?" Contessa clarified.

"We live in the same house," Nate hedged, abandoning his napkin in favor of twisting his fork over and over in his fingers. "I'm already quite accustomed to your presence."

"So how far away were you planning to put her?" Rhosyn interjected, as direct as always.

"I was thinking on the roof of the building next door."

Contessa blinked. Rhosyn let out a low whistle.

"And I thought your range on Kristoff was good." Rhosyn sounded impressed. "You're sure you'll be able to tell if she senses something from that far away?"

Nate's eyes briefly flicked to Contessa's, and he nodded.

Rhosyn immediately jumped into an animated discussion about how they should go about gaining access to the warehouse next to the factory. Contessa listened with half her attention, sighing in relief when she was reassured she would not have to climb up the outside of a building. The other half of her attention remained fixed on Nate, who kept glancing at Contessa out of the corner of his eye.

It wasn't until later, after Rhosyn had excused herself, saying she should get back to the children so Kristoff and Gregor could have some privacy tonight, that Contessa asked what she really wanted to know.

"How far away can you sense my feelings from?"

Nate sighed and leaned back in his chair, although from the expression on his face, it was clear he knew this question was inevitable.

"I start being able to feel you about a block away from home."

Contessa's spine straightened, but she didn't say anything.

"At that distance, it's still vague. I don't get distinct feelings until I'm much closer, but I can still tell you're there. It's part of how I was able to track the wagon so easily last week."

Contessa nodded slowly, even as she asked, "But while you are in the house?"

Nate flushed. "I try not to eavesdrop on your emotions, if that is what you mean, but yes, I could sense your moods clearly if I wanted to."

Contessa spent a moment neatly folding her napkin and placing it back on the table.

"Your Talent sounds like it might be difficult sometimes," she eventually responded. "Feeling my own feelings is quite enough for me without constantly having somebody else's moods in my head while I'm home."

Nate offered her a smile.

"I suppose it does get annoying, especially when I'm near somebody in a particularly foul mood. The worst is when I'm unprepared and I come across somebody drunk...but your feelings do not bother me." There was a long pause and Nate took a deep breath. "This house was so empty for so long, it's been a strange reassurance to feel you about. Having somebody here... Well, it finally feels like a home."

Contessa swallowed and found there wasn't much she could say in response to such a statement. Instead, she pushed back her chair and stood up, reaching out a hand to Nate across the table.

"Come on. Let's go upstairs and read," she invited. "If I'm not mistaken, tonight's story is one with a dragon."

Chapter Seventeen

Of the many things Contessa worried about during her first liberation mission, being hopelessly bored wasn't one of them. She'd spent the past hour and a half lying flat on her belly on an unforgiving rooftop, periodically peeking her head over the edge to watch the sparse traffic on the street below. Her bones creaked as she rolled her shoulders and ankles, trying to relieve her stiffness. While she ached to stand up and stretch her muscles, she didn't have it in herself to risk being spotted.

Contessa extended her neck over the side once more to check for traffic and found the streets in the industrial district almost completely empty in the darkness. Although she hated not being able to spot any threats on the street as easily, she breathed a sigh of relief now that the sun had set and taken the heat of day with it. She could still feel the sweat crusted on her neck and back from her time lying so uncomfortably with no shade. Honestly, she didn't think she had sweat as much in her entire life as she had in the past months.

Her attention was drawn from the itching sensation of dried sweat in the small of her back by the sight of faint shadows moving in the street. She risked edging forward to get a better view and relaxed when she determined that it was, in fact, the Lions. Not only were there five of them, as Nate had told her there would be, but they all had black fabric obscuring their faces. Contessa spotted Nate by the width of his shoulders and his stomping gait. It didn't help that a number of unruly curls had escaped one Lion's head covering and briefly shone a bright copper in the thin moonlight.

The group stole towards the back door where they paused for a moment while one of them worked the lock. Contessa took the opportunity to crawl on her belly to the edge of the roof that looked over the alley between the two buildings. Here she had a better view of all the entrances and exits, as opposed to the street. In a moment, the group slipped inside, and Contessa was left to wait in the oppressive silence. She tried to calm her breathing and watch carefully, both with her eyes and senses. With her mind on such high alert, she worried that she wouldn't be able to sense a change at all if her Talent was triggered. She focused on her heartbeat to distract her from that thought, choosing to trust that Nate would be able to sense the difference between tension and true panic.

Contessa began to wonder how long this operation would take, feeling like they had been gone too long. They already knew how to get the children out of the room where they were locked in to sleep without alerting the skeleton guard kept there at night. She was just reassuring herself that quietly corralling a group of children would be no quick feat when she felt it.

Even as the ringing in her ears grew so loud it nearly drown out her own frantic breathing, Contessa cast about wildly for the source of the threat. She spotted six large figures sneaking down the alley and the telltale glint of moonlight on sharpened steel. Contessa thought about projecting her panic as loudly and clearly as she could, unsure if that was even possible but hoping it was helpful. To her momentary relief, the figures stopped outside the door the Lions had entered through, flanking it, clearly setting up an ambush.

Contessa bit her bottom lip so hard she tasted blood, unable to do anything but wait and hope the warning she was able to pass to Nate was helpful even if wildly vague. Maybe if he knew there was a threat to look for, he would be able to locate and avoid it on his own. He had spent so many years surviving attacks without any warning at all.

A movement on the other side of the building caught Contessa's eye, and she squinted to get a better look. Her hand flew to her mouth as she stifled a sigh of relief. She spotted the Lions and a small herd of short figures creeping out the front door of the factory in the opposite direction of the ambush.

They had gotten her warning, so why was the ringing in her ears only intensifying? Contessa scanned the small group again and counted those present once, twice. Nate was missing. She could only see four hooded Lions among the smaller silhouettes, and she couldn't spot Nate's broad form among them. None of the enemies had gone inside the factory, so it seemed unlikely he had gotten caught or injured. It made no sense why he wouldn't be escaping with the rest of the group.

As if in direct answer to her thought, the back door opened with a crash, and Nate jumped into the ambush in a flurry of shining steel. In the noise of the resulting chaos, the Lions and the children bolted down the street away from the distraction that was Nate and his knives. Contessa couldn't see well in the darkness, but he seemed to be holding the enemies off admirably, although she knew six against one wasn't good odds even for someone as skilled as Nate.

Contessa reached for the catches that would release her own blades before immediately abandoning the idea of jumping into the fight herself. She would be more of a liability than an aid. Still, she cast about for a way to help Nate when her eyes fell on a coil of rope on the roof a few feet away. She sprang to her feet and snatched it up before darting over to the exit from the roof. Grabbing the handle, Contessa nearly dislocated her arm as she yanked, only to find the door would not budge. She shook the door violently and checked the handle to make sure it wasn't locked, but it appeared to simply be jammed. She threw her body into her efforts to open it, all while the backdrop of grunts and steel reminded her she had no time to lose.

Seeing no other option, Contessa strode to the edge of the roof and looked towards the ground. It was only a three-story building, and she reasoned that even if she fell from this height, she would probably survive, albeit with broken legs. Not giving herself a chance to consider it further, Contessa looped her rope over her shoulder, turned around, and lowered herself off the edge of the roof. She thanked every God that might be listening for the small, barred windows that gave her footholds as she scrambled down the side of the building with every bit of haste she could muster.

Contessa held her breath as she descended most of the way. The next time she looked down, she was a manageable drop from the ground. Contessa landed on her backside with a jaw-rattling thump. Still, she shot to her feet, fueled by adrenaline, and was grateful when a snarl from around the corner indicated Nate was still on his feet and in the fight.

With all the speed she could manage, Contessa unraveled the rope and used fumbling fingers to tie one end of it to a drainpipe running down the side of the factory. Then, she darted across the small alley between the factory and the warehouse, holding the end of the rope so it ran across the narrow passage.

Ducking around a corner still holding the rope, Contessa closed her eyes and tried to think. She needed Nate to lead the combatants over here to enact her trap, but she doubted he could infer that much from the odd mix of concern and determination he must feel coming from her direction. So instead, Contessa did the only thing she could think of to draw his attention. She panicked.

Her breathing grew fast even as Contessa imagined the ringing in her ears. She imagined the way she'd felt when Two-faced Thomas had grabbed her around the neck. Her mind even brushed up against the memory of her mother's blood running over her hands.

The response was instantaneous. A roar echoed through the alley from around the corner, followed by the thundering of multiple pairs of boots. Contessa managed the barest of looks around the corner, seeing Nate charging down the alley with four men hot on his heels. In seconds, he had crashed past her hiding spot.

Contessa pulled on her end of the rope, bringing it to knee height. It was ripped from her hands as Nate's pursuers careened into it, crashing to the ground in a heap. Nate skidded to a halt and looked around to find his attackers on the ground and Contessa unscathed apart from the rope burn on her palms.

Still, the heap of men started to move, one of them struggling to his feet. Nate wasted no time in leaping at him, executing a headbutt of the type that Contessa had been envisioning when she'd attempted the maneuver. The big man staggered, and Nate's fist, still closed around the handle of his knife, connected with his jaw. The man dropped as if he had been struck by lightning, but two of the others struggled to their feet. The fourth still lay on the ground, and Contessa was briefly distracted by the sight of jagged bone protruding through his skin.

The urge to vomit was pushed to the back of her mind as Nate took on one man while the other caught sight of Contessa. Blanching, she fumbled with the catches at her wrists, almost dropping her knives as they sprang free. She tried to settle into her stance as the man approached, and he grinned as they both caught sight of the end of her blade quivering as her hands trembled.

Then the man's head snapped back as Nate leaped on him from behind, wrapping his forearm around the thug's thick neck. Nate squeezed mercilessly until the man went limp against his arms and then lowered him to the ground.

The resulting stillness in the night air was unsettling after the chaos of the fight. Nate's head covering had been ripped off during the fight to reveal his face. He was panting and staring wide eyed at Contessa across the alley scattered with enemies.

Contessa swallowed heavily, trying to ease her pounding heart.

"The others..." she started.

Nate swore.

"We need to meet them at the rendezvous point, I told them to wait for me there." He stepped forward and grabbed Contessa's wrist, tugging gently as if he could sense she was rooted to the spot as her adrenaline faded. "Come on, we have to get out of here. The noise will have garnered unwanted attention."

Contessa let Nate pull her behind him as they darted along the streets of the industrial district. She was still out of breath from her fight and was grateful as Nate motioned her into a building after a few blocks, leading her to the hidden door Contessa recognized as connecting to the network of tunnels. Nate opened the passage to reveal Kristoff, pistols already drawn and ready to shoot, but he waved him off.

"Relax, it's just us," Nate reassured as he pulled Contessa into the passage and closed the door behind him. The space was lit dimly by a lantern held aloft by a Lion Contessa didn't know, and she could just make out Rhosyn trying to quiet and reassure seven harried-looking children.

"Come on," Nate ordered. "It's not far to the den. Let's get these children to safety and then we can talk."

Contessa wearily peeled herself off the door she hadn't even realized she was leaning against and followed the small crew down the passage. It only took a few minutes to reach the entrance to the den, as Contessa supposed she could have expected considering it was also in the industrial district.

As they stepped into the den, they were immediately greeted by the chatter of other excited children, as well as Gregor, waiting with a medical kit in hand in case there had been any injuries. Everybody's attention turned to the new influx of children, and Contessa slumped back against the wall with a sigh. She was feeling oddly light and ridiculously tired at the same time, the adrenaline still in her system causing her heart to thunder even as the world around her seemed bright and fuzzy.

A warm hand on her elbow steadied her.

"Are you alright?" Nate asked as Contessa leaned mindlessly into the strength of his arm. He put his other hand on her other elbow, no doubt sensing her need for support.

"Yes, I'm not injured," she reassured. "I'm just…" She looked around the scene vaguely as if that were an explanation for the chaos of the past half an hour.

Nate nodded and Contessa was once again glad she didn't need to come up with adequate words to express her feelings.

"You probably saved my life you know," he said quietly.

"You would have escaped somehow," Contessa commented, suddenly aware of how intensely Nate was looking at her, his eyes appearing golden in the candlelight.

"Maybe," he acquiesced. "But what you did was still incredibly brave, remarkably resourceful, and so...ridiculously you." Nate's voice was low, but Contessa could still hear him clearly.

"Well, I couldn't just stand by and watch while you got hurt," Contessa responded, her voice equally low. It occurred to her that Nate had gotten very close while they spoke, enough that her breath stirred the lose hairs around his face. He was near enough to kiss. With a jolt of surprise accompanied by a spreading warmth, she realized she would like very much for him to kiss her. His lips were just so close.

He took a sharp breath in, and Contessa knew he could sense the direction of her thoughts, and neither of them moved away. If he could sense what she wanted, then why wasn't he kissing her already? Would he just hurry up and—

Taking matters into her own hands, Contessa leaned forward and pressed her lips to his. He froze for a moment, before his fingers came up to cup her face and he kissed her in return.

His mouth moved slightly asymmetrically, and she could feel the hard ridges of his scar against her upper lip, but all she could think about was how warm and close and solid he was. His fingers tentatively brushed her hairline and Contessa inhaled his scent of sweat and woodsmoke. It drew her in, and she found her hands fisted in his shirt, holding him as close to her as possible. Nate didn't seem to mind, tilting her head back to kiss her more thoroughly, his fingers less tentative as they cupped her head, holding her still as he explored her mouth.

A sudden whoop of joy brought Contessa to the present, and she pulled back sharply, leaving Nate looking stunned. She glanced over his shoulder to find Rhosyn looking at them, practically jumping up and down and clapping her hands.

"Kristoff, Gregor, I told you!" she yelled, grinning.

"About damn time!" Kristoff swaggered up behind Rhosyn and clapped a hand to her shoulder.

"Pay up," Rhosyn demanded, and Kristoff dropped a few coins into her waiting hand.

Nate, coming to himself, closed his eyes, dropped his head to the wall over Contessa's shoulder with a thud and groaned. Contessa couldn't help herself. Maybe it was the adrenaline still fizzing in her bloodstream or the joy of the kiss, but she looked up to the ceiling and laughed.

Chapter Eighteen

The sweat at the nape of Contessa's neck had dried, and she scratched at it where it crusted a few loose locks of her hair to her skin. To be honest, the itching was a welcome distraction from the tense silence Contessa and Nate were sharing, standing at the bottom of the stairs. The giddiness of their earlier kiss had faded on the trip home, and now they both looked down at their shoes, seemingly unsure of where they stood with each other.

"Do you suppose it's too late for me to run myself a bath?" Contessa mused, trying to make conversation. She knew Julia would never complain about helping her at any hour, but it still felt rude to call for a bath in the middle of the night just because she was reluctant to go to bed still crusted in dust.

"I doubt Julia would mind being woken up if it meant she got to hear we had made it home safely," Nate responded.

Contessa nodded and looked down to contemplate the dirt on her boots, still reticent to ring for Julia at this hour.

"If you prefer..." Nate started. "If you prefer, you could use the tub in my chambers. It's much larger and more comfortable than the one in yours."

Contessa's gaze shot up.

"I didn't mean— I'm sorry," he stammered. "That must seem far too forward."

Contessa sighed and reached out, gently grasping Nate's wrist between her fingers. She could feel his pulse hammering even as he swallowed heavily.

"Nate, I would hardly worry about seeming too forward. We've been married for months."

Nate twitched in her grasp, but he didn't pull away.

"You know that's not what I mean," he said.

"I know, but a decadent bath sounds like just what I need right now. Lying on that roof was not kind to me," Contessa explained as she began to tug Nate up the stairs.

He followed her lead before turning the opposite way down the hall from her own room to lead her to the door at the end. Contessa let herself look around his bedroom as she walked, smiling at the slate painted walls and a wide painting of the sea above the bed. A dusty pair of boots lay haphazardly at the foot of the bed, and a black waistcoat draped over the back of the chair, indicating this room at least was more lived in than the rest of the house.

She only had a moment to appreciate it until Nate led her through another door to the bathroom. The color scheme from the bedroom was echoed here with creamy white and blue wallpaper, but Contessa's attention was drawn to the massive cast iron tub dominating the far wall of the room.

"And to think I've been making do with the small bath down the hall while you have a tub big enough to swim in right here," Contessa teased softly.

Nate had the decency to look abashed.

"I will admit that while I haven't given much thought to this house, the bath is one of the few comforts I've indulged in," he explained with a self-conscious shrug. "Nothing quite helps with bruises and aches like a warm soak."

Contessa walked up to the large basin and ran her fingers over the smooth white coating on the interior of the tub, feeling it cool against her hand.

"Well, then I'll have to give it a try."

Nate let out a noise halfway between a cough and clearing his throat behind her.

"I'll just go down the hall and fetch your nightclothes and dressing gown," he said, already beginning to back out of the room. "So you have something to put on when you are finished."

"Wait—" The word leaped from Contessa's mouth before she'd decided what she was going to ask for.

They both froze in place, and it was Contessa's turn to swallow thickly.

"Will you help me take my hair down?" Her voice was soft but clear. "I need to wash it after tonight's excitement."

Nate didn't respond but took a few measured steps forward, and Contessa turned around and closed her eyes. His fingers landed on her scalp gently at first, investigating just how to go about unwinding the braided twist Julia had concocted to keep her hair out of the way. Contessa didn't offer any instruction, just enjoyed the touch of his hands as he began slowly uncovering and removing pins. She let her eyes flutter closed, and her breath left her in a soft sigh. Eventually, the braid uncoiled itself, falling down her back, and Nate ran his fingers through it slowly, almost reverently, to unwind the strands. He continued to stroke her hair past when Contessa was sure the braid was untangled, but Contessa didn't say a word. She was sure her hair was plastered to her head oddly, with all sorts of strange bends and twists from its confinement, but Nate seemed fascinated by it, nonetheless.

After far too short a time, Nate removed his fingers and stepped back.

"There." His voice was bordering on hoarse. "You should be able to wash it now."

He made to back out of the room once more, and for the second time this evening, Contessa found herself saying, "Wait."

She licked her lips as Nate looked at her expectantly.

"Stay," she asked again. "It doesn't have to be— Just...stay."

Contessa wasn't sure what feelings Nate might have been sensing from her, but apparently, they convinced him. He hesitated for only a moment before nodding.

Contessa turned back to the tub and began fiddling with the knobs, testing the temperature until the water ran hot enough it would soothe her muscles. Without turning around, she stood and began methodically removing her shirt. Layer by layer, her clothing fell to the floor with soft swishes. When she moved to unlace her pants, Contessa chanced a glance over her shoulder to find Nate staring determinedly at his feet. The smallest smile curled her lips as she returned to undressing. By the time she was finished, the water in the tub had reached a level she was sure would cover her, and she stepped in, sinking into the warmth with a sigh.

She fanned her hair over the edge of the tub, sliding all the way down to her neck in the water, finding her toes still didn't reach the far end of the tub. Contessa giggled and wiggled her feet, causing little ripples to slosh against the side.

"You weren't exaggerating about how large this tub is. It almost feels like a waste to fill this thing up just to bathe somebody of my stature," she commented.

At this, Nate glanced up, finding her almost completely submerged in the water. He took one step forward, as if he didn't even realize he was doing it.

Contessa wet her lips one more time before continuing.

"You know, this tub is big enough for both of us." Her voice was steady even as her heart pounded. "No doubt you could use a bath, too, after today's scuffle."

Nate was so still Contessa was sure he wasn't even breathing.

"Connie," was the only word he managed in reply.

"Nate," she echoed, meeting his eyes.

His fingers creeped up to his neck, untying his cravat slow enough to give Contessa time to change her mind if she wished. Instead, she busied herself with a bar of soap she located on the side of the tub, beginning to clean herself. She heard the soft rustle of Nate removing his clothes, but she didn't look up, his self-consciousness seemingly mitigated by having her otherwise engaged.

She jumped when she heard a clang, making the water slosh over the side of the tub. Glancing up, she saw Nate looking sheepish as he placed another knife on the tile more carefully. He unstrapped several more from his upper arms. When he reached under his shirt to pull out two more knives, a laugh bubbled up in Contessa's throat. The sound echoed in the tiled room, chasing away any awkwardness. Nate chuckled, too, as he divested himself of the rest of his weapons and one small pistol tucked into the back of his pants.

When he was unclothed, Nate stepped towards the tub, hesitating at the edge. Contessa scooted forward, continuing to clean herself, giving Nate room to step into the water behind her. The only noise in the room was the water sloshing against the sides of the tub as Nate lowered himself down behind her. Without saying a word, Contessa shifted back so that Nate completely surrounded her.

He hissed when her back touched his chest, and his fingers gripped the edge of the tub so hard his knuckles turned white.

"It's all right, Nate," she soothed, putting one hand over his and relaxing his grip.

"Connie, you know you don't have to..." he started, trailing off as she brushed her fingertips over his knuckles.

"I know," she said. Contessa felt Nate's breath on the crown of her head, and the gentle press of what might have been lips. "Do you want to help me wash my hair?"

She offered him the bar of soap over her shoulder, and he plucked it from her fingers. She sighed as he used his cupped hands to pour water over her scalp. He went about washing her hair as methodically as he had unbraided it, and Contessa let herself drift in the sensation of warm water and firm fingers. She unconsciously pressed back into his chest, enjoying the slick heat of his torso against her and the way his arms surrounded her. The soap wasn't her usual soft and floral variety, but it smelled like Nate's skin had when he'd held her earlier, and that was enough.

When Contessa's hair was fully rinsed, she reached back to take the soap from him before announcing, "Your turn."

She maneuvered around to face him, such a dramatic move making water slosh over the sides and onto the floor, but neither of them was paying much attention to that. Being able to see each other's faces renewed the tension in the room as she began to work the soap through Nate's hair. He kept his eyes closed, and Contessa took the opportunity to examine him—the way the water droplets trailed across his lips and down his chest. She watched in fascination how the muscles of his abdomen tensed when she touched him, and her mouth went dry when her gaze drifted down past his waist to see what was partially obscured by soapy water.

Once Nate's hair was clean, Contessa dropped the soap and let her fingers trail from his hairline, down to his face, tracing her thumbs over his cheekbones. She leaned in close enough she knew he could feel her breath.

His hand shot out of the water and grabbed one of her wrists, halting her.

"Tell me you want this," he said hoarsely, his eyes snapping open.

Contessa blinked.

"I know you can feel how much I want this," she whispered, but he just shook his head.

"I need to hear you say it." His serious gaze allowed no room for argument. "Connie, I married you against your will. If I laid a hand on you without hearing you say in the clearest of terms that you wanted it, it would make me the monster that everybody already says I am."

Contessa nodded and began stroking her thumbs across his cheekbones once more.

"Nate, I've spent my whole life doing things because it was what other people told me I should want. But being around you has shown me how to decide how the world is for myself. You have allowed me to think about my own desires. And you might be the first thing I've let myself want, not because anybody else says I should, but because I want you. I want you more than anything."

Nate blinked at Contessa once, twice, then surged forward to kiss her for the second time that night.

Nate's lips traced over hers with enthusiasm. When he shifted to try to angle their lips more firmly together, his nose bumped hers, and there was a hiss of pain and a few giggles about how it was still healing. Then they were kissing again, and it was warm and slick and utterly perfect.

When Nate stood, he picked Contessa up and out of the tub before she had a chance to move, causing a veritable tidal wave of water to spill over the bathroom floor. Contessa didn't have time to assess the damage however, as her mouth became otherwise occupied with tracing the hollow of Nate's throat. She reveled in the noise he made when her teeth grazed his collarbone and repeated the motion just to hear it again.

Nate finally laid Contessa back on his bed, pausing for a moment as he looked down at her. Droplets of water still clung to their skin and hair, but Contessa was too consumed with the way Nate gazed at her to care. She had thought she might be shy, but instead, she basked in the fire glimmering in Nate's eyes, her skin burning just as hot. Then Nate was on her again, his fingers mapping every inch of her skin even as she tried to touch as much of him as she could in return.

He pulled back to look her in the eyes as his hands drifted lower, and a soft noise caught in her throat as his fingers trailed through the damp curls between her legs. He smiled as he found a spot that made Contessa squirm, and when she began making soft, desperate noises, he caught them in his own mouth, quieting her with kisses.

When Contessa thought she couldn't take it anymore and that she would dissolve into a puddle of joy and sensation, she retaliated. Her own hand brushed down Nate's stomach, through the trail of hair from his navel to grasp him. It was his turn to make a broken noise as his fingers stuttered where they worked between her legs.

"Now Nate," Contessa murmured into his neck. "Please."

Not being one to deny her, Nate propped himself on his elbows over Contessa, one hand cupping her cheek as he finally slid home. Tears pricked at the corner of Contessa's eyes at the sheer rightness of it—of being with somebody she wanted so desperately, even before she admitted it to herself. Of him being hers, and her being his.

Nate shuddered over her as her feelings washed over him, and he began to move. He was heartbreakingly gentle, stroking Contessa's face, her hip, her hair, until he found a spot that made Contessa squirm anew. As Nate's movement grew more sure, Contessa was delighted to find he made love the way he fought—powerful and raw around the edges in a way that did nothing to detract from his grace. Soon Contessa felt as if she might fly into a million pieces, bucking beneath Nate as she chased the feeling of tightness in her belly. She knew he could sense her desperation as he let out a strangled moan, ending in her name.

"*Connie...*"

It was all it took for her to tumble over the edge, pulling Nate with her with the intensity of her pleasure. It was long moments before Contessa came back to herself, cracking her eyes open to find Nate looking at her with pure adoration, undercut with a current of something more primal. Finding her looking, he smiled and rolled to his side, tucking her into his chest. Then it was just the two of them, with only the quiet night serving as a witness to their delighted explorations, contented sighs, and whispered promises.

The sun filtering red through Contessa's eyelids woke her, and she bit back a groan at how tired she felt, despite her habitual dawn awakenings. Her eyes fluttered open to find a pair of squinted hazel eyes reflecting the same sentiment. Still, she offered a smile, suddenly shy at the new experience of waking up next to somebody else. Nate reached up and traced her cheek with his fingertips in response, featherlight, as if he were unsure if he was still allowed to touch her now that the sun had risen.

Paradoxically emboldened by his hesitance, Contessa nuzzled into his hand and pressed a soft kiss to his palm.

"You're still here," Nate observed.

"Oh," Contessa said, wondering if she'd misread the situation. Now that she thought about it, she hadn't asked Nate if she could sleep in his bed. "I can go back to my room. Julia will probably be missing me—"

Nate effectively silenced her by throwing an arm over her waist and pulling her close.

"Don't go back," he reinforced. "You hate that room anyway."

"This one is more to my liking," Contessa pulled back from his chest so she could speak clearly. "No gaudy flowers, and a much more pleasing color palette." Contessa pushed on Nate's shoulder so he laid on his back and she rolled on top of him, propping up on her elbows so she could get a good look at him in the morning light. "Not to mention that you're here, and it turns out you are much better company than I ever could have hoped for."

Nate nodded and they fell silent, listening to the sounds of the city waking up as Contessa attempted to push strands of hair out of Nate's face only for them to stick out in every conceivable direction.

"Are you sure you're fine with my being here?" Contessa eventually whispered, focusing on the strand of hair she was twisting between her fingers instead of meeting Nate's eyes. "I know you can tell how I feel about you, but I know I'm not the only one of us that didn't exactly marry for love. I don't want to assume too much."

Nate grabbed the hand that toyed with his hair, stilling it, before bringing it to lay flat on his chest. His heart beat against her palm.

"Despite my ability to sense feelings, or maybe in part because of it, I've never been skilled at expressing my own emotions," Nate started. "I guess it's hard to put words to what I already intuitively know about other people. But I can say confidently that I want you here, actually being my wife and not just putting on a show of it.

"For so much of my life, I've felt damaged. I've been trying to tamp down my anger by helping others like me, but I still felt like shattered glass. Like if I let somebody try to pick up the pieces, they would cut their fingers on my jagged edges. But then we were getting married, and you looked at me, so lovely and so full of rage that you nearly knocked me off my feet. It was the first time I realized that maybe—maybe sharp things could be beautiful too."

Contessa blinked rapidly. Using the hand that wasn't pressed to Nate's chest, she reached up and traced the lines on the scarred side of his face. He shuddered slightly but didn't close his eyes.

"You are beautiful you know," Contessa admitted, as she let her fingers drag to Nate's eyelid, rough and permanently squinted. "Can you feel this?"

"No," Nate whispered. "Sometimes I can feel a light prickling, and occasionally, it burns, but most of the time...nothing."

Contessa craned her neck up and kissed the raised corner of his mouth, feeling its now familiar roughness against hers. She felt as if she should be sad her husband was once a broken boy who had suffered so much, but nothing could quell the happiness that he was here now, in her arms where she could make sure he knew he was loved.

In response, Nate wrapped his arms around her waist and buried his face in her hair.

"I'm glad you don't pity me," he said into the top of her head. "I don't need it when I have a beautiful wife, a worthy cause, and close friends."

Contessa smiled into his shoulder, and they lay in silence for a moment before Contessa felt a deep groan rip from Nate's chest.

"Speaking of close friends, I just remembered that Kristoff said he would be coming for breakfast. We have some things to discuss after last night's adventures."

Contessa attempted to sit up, saying, "Well, I better go get dressed. I can hardly entertain company as naked as the day I was born."

Nate hindered her efforts at escape with his firm grip on her waist. "We can let him wait a little bit. He's probably just flirting with Gregor, seeing if he can distract him into burning the bacon."

"Be that as it may," Contessa giggled, finally worming her way out of Nate's grasp, "I happen to want bacon this morning, and I would be quite put out if it did end up burned."

Nate gave a long-suffering sigh and reached over to ring for Julia, who bustled in mere moments later with today's dress in her arms. She didn't seem remotely surprised to find Contessa naked in Nate's bed. If she had any significant thoughts on the matter, she limited them to a cheerful comment about how she would have to teach Nate how to properly brush hair if Contessa didn't want to wake up with it so dreadfully out of sorts.

Chapter Nineteen

The bacon wasn't burned, but instead perfectly chewy, the way Contessa preferred it. She eyed the heaping plate of meat as she and Nate rounded the corner to the dining room, finding herself hungry from the eventful night behind her.

She was distracted from the mouthwatering smell of bacon by Kristoff jumping out of his seat and rounding the table to grab her in an embrace so tight it lifted her off her feet.

Kristoff ignored her undignified squeak, instead proclaiming, "At last the lovesick couple has come to their senses and Rhosyn, Gregor, and I can stop trying to discreetly hint that perhaps your being married isn't such a bad thing."

Contessa immediately tried to put her dress to rights upon being set down, hiding the heat on her cheeks.

"You are making a lot of assumptions considering you only saw us kiss last night," Nate grumbled with no real venom as he made his way to his seat.

"Well, I've never known you to be in bed past dawn, so there must be some explanation for you making your guest wait on your company," Kristoff retorted.

"I would apologize for the lack of courtesy, but it doesn't seem to have stopped you from enjoying your breakfast," Contessa remarked as she slid into her seat, nodding to the half-eaten plate of food already sitting in front of Kristoff's seat.

Nate huffed through his nose and passed Contessa the porridge.

"You know I can never resist Gregor's...cooking," Kristoff defended with a twinkle in his eye. As if on cue, the man in question rounded the corner carrying a pot of tea, with a few strands of his normally smooth hair notably out of place.

"Alright, we understand," Nate said as he scooped a hefty amount of marmalade onto his toast. "We're all hopelessly improper. Can we move past that and focus on what it is you are here to discuss?"

Kristoff clapped a hand to his chest in mock offense. "Can I not just be here to enjoy the company of my closest friends?"

"You could be," Contessa remarked, "but considering we were attacked last night and have yet to discuss it, that seems unlikely."

Kristoff's expression grew serious, but he pointed a finger at Contessa gravely. "That is indeed something we need to talk about, but don't think you are going to distract me from my celebratory mood forever."

"It was the Rattlesnakes," Nate jumped in without prelude. There was a long silence only broken by the clatter of Contessa's spoon as she set it down.

"How can you be sure?" Contessa asked.

"I saw their gang tattoos on their forearms."

Contessa furrowed her brows. "Well, that is convenient. It seems counterintuitive to ink your allegiance on your skin for everybody to see when you're in an industry that values secrecy."

"It is," Kristoff cut in with a wave of his fork. "That is why the Lions don't do it. I actually do have a Lion tattoo, though, but it is in a place I don't usually display to just anybody."

"Kristoff, focus," Nate cut in. "We need to figure out how they knew where and when to ambush us."

"Not to mention why," Kristoff offered. "They've tried to stop our operations from expanding into their territory before, but they've never tried to hit us on a liberation mission. It doesn't seem like Caleb would want to copy our recruiting tactics, either. He doesn't have the disposition to deal with children."

"They didn't seem too happy with the Lions the last time we encountered them," Contessa commented as she forked some bacon onto her plate. "At this point, they might be hitting us wherever they can to send a message."

"If they knew we would be there, they would attack us anywhere they could at this point," Nate said. "Which brings us back to the question of how they knew where we would be in the first place."

"Where did you get the tip on this warehouse?" Contessa asked.

"I eavesdropped on the owner of the business at the Standard Club," Nate said with a shrug. "He said he had just opened a new factory in the lower city and was having trouble hiring security with the current political climate. It made me think it would be a prime target."

"Is it possible Caleb has somebody who would be running in these same circles that could have heard this same information?" Contessa ventured.

Kristoff shook his head. "I doubt it. Caleb doesn't play the long game like that, but he would not be above cutting a deal with somebody powerful."

Contessa stirred her porridge as her mind skipped through the possibilities.

"You know, we never did figure out what gang was cooperating with Chief Cook at the executions," Kristoff pointed out. "He certainly wants us gone and already knows about our...recruiting practices."

Contessa opened and closed her mouth, then turned her attention back to her porridge. She felt naïve now for having lain the information about Nate stealing the children away from the factories at her father's feet, although her intentions had been good at the time.

Nate reached out and laid a hand on her knee, palm up, under the table. Contessa set her own hand in it and spoke.

"Be that as it may, I have a hard time believing the Rattlesnakes and my father could maintain any sort of alliance. They're the second most hated of the gangs in London, and the feeling seems to go both ways. I mean Caleb..." Contessa swallowed. "Caleb may have killed my mother."

"Your father likely still thinks it was me, though," Nate said, running his free hand through his hair. "Do you think if you talked to him, you could convince him otherwise?"

Contessa licked her lips and thought about how hard her father had grabbed her wrist the last time she'd seen him. She envisioned him calling her a cowering damsel.

She shook her head.

"I don't think he would trust me at all, not after I foiled his plan for framing you for the scene at the execution. He is angry beyond reason."

"Well, it was a thought," Kristoff sighed. "I suppose suspicion won't get us very far anyway. I'll have some men try and tail Caleb's lieutenants and see if they can spot any meetings with potential informants. Although I still have to figure out who replaced Two-faced Thomas after his unfortunate incident."

Contessa tried not to picture how she'd shoved Thomas's limp body out of the driver's seat of the carriage.

"For now," Kristoff continued, "we have slightly more important matters to attend to. I should go see the children we liberated last night and welcome them to the Lions, and I think you two have things you'd rather be doing."

Contessa thought about saying that of course they would be going with Kristoff to see the children, but she shut her mouth when she saw how Nate was looking at her. He obviously had plans for them upstairs, and she was of no mind to object.

Contessa shivered pleasantly as Nate traced nonsensical patterns over her back with calloused fingertips. She was lying on her stomach, chin propped on overlapping hands, contemplating the painting over the bed with no real focus. For a rare moment, she let her consciousness drift in the comfort of the solid presence of Nate, propped up on one elbow beside her, and the warmth of the afternoon sun drifting through the window.

"It seems decadent to be in bed in the middle of the afternoon," Contessa observed, her eyelids fluttering as Nate's fingers walked up and down her spine.

"Well, we don't usually live decadent lives, so I think we've earned an exception."

Contessa hummed in agreement and fell back into a comfortable silence, letting her eyes drift open again to land on the painting of the sea once more.

"I love the ocean," she commented with no real intent, reveling in the opportunity to talk for no other reason than the pleasure of each other's company.

"I've never been," Nate responded. "Although, the painting is nice."

Contessa flopped onto her back to look at Nate, squinting.

"You've never seen the ocean? It's not even a day's travel from here."

The sheets rustled as Nate shrugged. The movement pushed the blankets dangerously low on his hips, and Contessa let her eyes wander.

"I've never left the city really. There wasn't a good reason and always so much to do."

Contessa cocked her head.

"To be fair," she conceded, "I haven't been since I was a child. My mother used to take me for a few days every summer. My father never saw much point in it."

Nate was silent for a few moments, each absorbed in their own thoughts as the faint sound of a song over crashing waves drifted through Contessa's memories.

"We should go," Nate said abruptly.

"Go to the beach?" Contessa echoed as she was pulled back out of her contemplations.

"Yes. We never did go on a honeymoon you know. It would be a good chance to get to know each other better."

Contessa rolled onto her side to face Nate, resting a hand on his ribs and offering a smile.

"We already know the important things about each other," she pointed out.

"True." Nate reached up a hand to trail his fingers through Contessa's hair, which was now so hopelessly tangled that Julia would surely spend an hour getting it back in line. "I know you're brave and intelligent and wonderful. But I want to know all of the unimportant things too." Nate leaned in as he spoke, pressing a kiss to her cheekbone.

"I want to know your favorite season…"

He kissed her nose.

"What kind of soup you prefer when you're ill…"

The corner of her mouth.

"If you're secretly ticklish…"

Contessa felt herself grinning and acquiesced, nipping at Nate's own smiling lips.

"Well, when you explain it that way. When were you planning this trip?"

"Next week?"

Contessa blinked.

"That's certainly quick."

Nate shrugged again. "I've found that when I put the important things off, they never get done. Anything worth doing is worth doing now."

The bubble of lightness that had been forming in Contessa's chest for the past weeks grew, the new freedom making her positively effervescent. A feeling that she finally had a modicum of control over where she went and what she did—that she wasn't just a pawn in somebody else's game. Contessa could choose to go away with her husband next week, without having to justify herself to her father, to anybody.

"Next week it is."

Chapter Twenty

Contessa placed her queen on the chess board with a clink and smiled despite herself. Across the table, Nate growled at losing once again, but there was no menace to it. Contessa could see the amusement sparkling in his eyes.

"That was even quicker than usual," he commented, draining the last of his whiskey and wiping his mouth with the back of his hand.

They had taken to playing again each night, but the games were more enjoyable without thinly veiled threats being lobbed at each other. The games went slower now that they actually conversed, and Nate had managed to distract Contessa almost to the point of victory a few times, but she always scraped through in the end.

"Well, I decided not to toy with you tonight, since we should be getting to bed early. We're planning to leave for the cottage early tomorrow."

Contessa smiled at the thought of the cottage by the sea Nate had described. He had managed to persuade an acquaintance into letting them use his summer home for a few days, and Contessa pointedly didn't ask how Nate had managed this.

"Toy with me?" Nate demanded with false belligerence, "I don't let you toy with me."

Contessa stood, looking down and smoothing her skirts to hide the smile on her face as she replied.

"You can keep telling yourself that if that's what it takes for you to sleep at night."

Contessa only made it a few steps before there was a quick rustle behind her and Nate grabbed her by the waist and hoisted her into the air. Contessa let out an indignant squawk.

"Oh, I think you're the one who's not going to be sleeping tonight," Nate growled in a way that made Contessa's insides warm. He tried to toss her over his shoulder, but as he loosened his grasp to turn her around, Contessa managed to slip out of his grip using a trick Rhosyn had taught her.

"Using my own moves against me now, are we?" Nate asked, the good side of his mouth twisting up and giving away how pleased he was as he advanced on her. Contessa backed up against the railing of the stairs, offering her own coy smile.

She didn't resist as Nate caged her in with his hands resting on either side of the banister, leaning down to kiss one ear before playfully biting at it in a way that made Contessa yelp in surprise, even as her own hands flew up to grip his collar.

This had become part of their routine, too, and while Contessa thought it might be an adjustment to live like this after so long in her own world of relative isolation, she found she didn't miss going to bed alone in the rose room one bit.

Contessa was distracted from her fingers' work undoing Nate's necktie by an unmistakable clatter from down the hall. Nate obviously heard it, too, stilling immediately, shoulders hunched around Contessa to shield her from the hall.

"Nate!"

A familiar voice rang through the house, following the sound of pounding footsteps. Hearing Kristoff might have been reassuring if not for the uncharacteristic panic rising in his voice.

"Nate! Down by the port...the mob..." Kristoff seemed as if he was trying to start three sentences at the same time and failing at all of them as he skidded to a halt in front of Nate.

"A mob? What mob?" Nate's voice was steady but held none of the levity of just a few moments before.

"People are rioting in the lower city. Demanding that Prince Byron be put on the throne," Kristoff managed between pants, leaning to rest his hands on his knees. "The king—he died."

"Where was the mob at?"

"They were on Bennet's Hill headed down towards the docks, which—"

"Will lead them past the den." Nate swore colorfully, two strides already taking him halfway down the hall towards his study. Contessa and Kristoff rushed to follow, and she felt as if she were a dinghy foundering in the ginormous wake of Nate's frigate as he barked over his shoulder.

"Kristoff, take a horse and go to all the safehouses in the lower city. Warn everybody and make sure everyone is accounted for. Gregor can help too. I'll head to the den to help Rhosyn. I can bring everybody back here if worst comes to worst."

"Once everybody is warned, I'll bring help," Kristoff agreed before turning down the hall to the kitchen, presumably to find Gregor.

Nate had already braced his shoulder against his desk and was pushing it out from over the trap door when Contessa rushed to help.

"Hopefully, the children will be alright, but be ready for chaos when I get back if I need to get them out of there," Nate grunted as the desk finally gave way.

"Of course, I'll be ready for chaos, I'll be bringing the children back with you," Contessa pointed out, already working on pulling the trapdoor open.

There was a beat before Nate bent down to help her, and Contessa looked up at him to find him blinking and still for the first time since Kristoff had barreled into their home.

"You're coming with?"

"Why wouldn't I?"

There was only half a second pause before Nate was bending down to push the trapdoor the remainder of the way open.

"You have your knives on you?"

Contessa tilted her wrist, the cuff of her dress falling back to reveal the catch of her hidden sheathe.

"You've succeeded in teaching me a few things at least."

Nate gave a sharp nod before levering himself down into the tunnel, not bothering to climb down the ladder. Contessa peered over the edge, hearing the slap of Nate's boots hitting the stone floor. He rose from the crouch he'd landed in and reached up both arms, indicating for Contessa to jump down. She slid off the edge, although not nearly as gracefully as he had. She was surprised she didn't knock the wind out of Nate when he caught her, but there was just a sharp exhale before she was placed on her feet and then pulled down the now familiar passage in the direction of the den.

As they traversed the passage at breakneck speed, a prickling began creeping up the back of Contessa's neck that had nothing to do with the sweat breaking out at her hairline and under her arms. The heat creeped into her ears and transformed into a ringing, getting louder and louder with each passing step. She didn't need to say anything to be able to tell that Nate felt the danger rising in her senses. It was apparent he knew by the way his shoulders drew further and further up towards his ears as the ringing grew to a screaming in Contessa's skull.

By the time they reached the hidden entrance to the Den, Contessa was about to vibrate out of her skin with the force of the sensation. The roaring was no longer just in her head, but coming through the door, as well. Nate shouldered it open forcefully and swore loudly when a wave of heat hit them. Contessa caught a brief glimpse of the far wall drenched in fire, the flames beginning to lick across the bunk room before Nate's hand yanked on her shoulder. She was wrenched down to her knees where the air was clearer with a suddenness that shook her teeth. There was no time to recover before she began to crawl, following Nate into the blaze. He was crouched low, prowling through the wreckage. He called out for anybody in the warehouse but got no answer. He led them through the blaze to the front door, Contessa hot on his trail even as her dress snagged and ripped. Splinters dug into her knees as she crawled across the floor. Despite the suffocating heat of the inferno, it wasn't hard to pick a path to the already wide-open front door as the fire had yet to touch almost half of the building.

Contessa and Nate made it out the door into the marginally cooler air of the night, Contessa coughing the smoke from her lungs. The street was empty, but the brightness of the glow indicated that more than one building was suffering the same fate as the den. Shouting could be heard loud enough that the heart of the riot couldn't have been more than a few streets away.

Nate reached back to help Contessa to her feet and farther from the burning building. She waved him off, pointing into the street, trying to speak but not getting the words out around the hacking that was making her eyes water.

Nate's gaze traced to where she was pointing, to a crumpled figure on the cobblestones. In the shimmering light from the blaze, Contessa could just make out a flash of red hair spilled across the pavement. Nate was at Rhosyn's side in a flash, rolling her gently onto her back. Contessa's heart started again where it had stilled in her chest as the woman groaned in response.

"Nate, Nate..." Rhosyn gasped. The one eye Rhosyn had managed to open all the way was darting around in panic, the other limited to a squint by swelling and a fresh bruise blooming over her cheekbone.

"Rhos, what happened? Where are the children?"

"They took them, Nate. The fire started and I was trying to get everybody out and they just appeared," Rhosyn babbled, her breath coming in quick pants. "I tried, but there were too many of them, and they had the little ones. I couldn't..."

Rhosyn broke off in a choked gasp of pain and distress, a shudder wracking her body in a suppressed sob. Contessa reached to take her hand and found Rhosyn's brass knuckles still wrapped around her fingers. Blood smeared itself on Contessa's wrist as she eased them out of the girl's hand so she could hold it properly.

"Nate, I tried..." Rhosyn gasped out, her good eye squeezing shut, the faint glimmer of tears clinging to her lashes.

Contessa rubbed her thumb over Rhosyn's knuckles to soothe her.

"Who was it, Rhosyn? Who took them?" Contessa tried to ask gently but her voice came out rough after the smoke and the coughing. She paused as Nate shifted beside her, reaching over Rhosyn to grab a scrap of paper lying on the ground at her side.

"Men. Thugs. It all happened so fast—" Rhosyn struggled to answer but trailed off when she was interrupted by a growl low in Nate's throat.

"You were set up. Those bastards set the fire on purpose." The loose piece of paper trembled in Nate's hand, starting to crumple in his white-knuckled grip. Peering over Nate's shoulder, Contessa could just make out a short line of messy script and a crude drawing of a rattlesnake.

"We're going to get them back, Rhos." Nate's voice was as hard as stone. "We'll show them what it's like to fight the Lions when it's not an ambush, four on one."

"Actually, it was five on one." Rhosyn's hand still shook in Contessa's, but she managed a twitch of the corner of her mouth. "Stop trying to short me the credit I deserve."

Nate laid a hand on Rhosyn's shoulder.

"Kristoff and Gregor will be here soon. Then we can get you patched up so you can show them why they should fear you in a fair fight."

With Nate supporting her shoulders, Rhosyn managed to make it to a sitting position, hiding her wince admirably. Contessa looked over her shoulder in the direction of the shouting masses where more trails of smoke were rising, making the outline of the moon hazy and dim in the night sky.

"Do you think you can walk?" Contessa asked, turning back to Rhosyn. "I think we should try to move away from all these fires."

Indeed, the air was growing thicker with smoke by the minute, and Contessa's eyes were starting to burn and water.

Rhosyn nodded.

"My legs are fine. They mostly just did a number on my face and one side."

Contessa and Nate each took an arm and levered the girl upright. She did seem steady on her feet for somebody that had been nearly unconscious a few minutes ago, although she was hunched to one side, instinctively guarding her flank as Nate helped her stagger down the street. A clatter of hooves interrupted them as they made it to the end of the block. Gregor and Kristoff's horses skidded to a halt in front of them.

"We got here as fast as we could—" Kristoff started.

"We were too late," Nate said. Kristoff and Gregor looked like they were about to barrage them with questions, but Nate stopped them, holding up the hand that wasn't wrapped under Rhosyn's shoulders.

"Rhos is hurt, and that's what we need to worry about right now. Get her home and fix her up. We'll need everybody in fighting shape soon enough."

Kristoff scrambled down off his horse to help Nate lift Rhosyn up.

"Connie, you go with Gregor. The horses can't take all of us, so I'll meet you back at the house."

In a flurry of movement, Contessa found herself perched in front of Gregor on a horse, her position mirroring Rhosyn's with Kristoff. Contessa had just a moment to look back at Nate standing in the street before Gregor kicked their horse into a trot. The light of the fires behind him silhouetted his frame, and for just a moment, his eye's caught the light just right, glinting gold in his hard face. As they pulled around the corner and out of sight, Contessa thought there was still a reason her husband was called the Beast, and the Rattlesnakes were about to find that out.

※

While not usually uncomfortable with silence, the current quiet hung thick and heavy in Contessa's head, making her want to pace back and forth or pick at her fingernails—maybe even scream in frustration. Instead, she contented herself with squeezing her fists so tight her nails dug into her palms.

Across the room, Kristoff seemed to be faring similarly. His elbows were propped on his knees, and his head was in his hands. His face was obscured, but Contessa was sure his expression looked as lost as she felt.

The only noise came from the sharp intakes of breath coming from Rhosyn as Gregor prodded her bruised side, checking for broken ribs. It seemed she'd been right about most of the damage being restricted to her face. In the brighter light, it looked even worse. Dried blood from a split lip decorated her chin, and a bruise across her hairline joined her black eye.

The noise of the front door opening broke everybody from their reverie. Contessa recognized Nate's heavy footsteps coming down the hall, and she sprang to her feet, her need to move finally breaking free. She met him in the doorway to the sitting room, freezing, unsure of her intentions. There was a wildness in his eyes Contessa didn't see often, and the smell of smoke still clung to him. Contessa didn't know whether to embrace him or step away, but Nate made her choice for her. His hand cupped the back of her neck, and he bent his head to press his forehead to hers for a moment, inhaling deeply. Contessa closed her eyes, feeling his breath on her face, grateful at least to know he was safe and fighting. After a moment that felt far too short, Nate straightened and stepped around her into the sitting room.

"It was Caleb," he said without preamble, tossing the scrap of paper from the street onto the low table in the middle of the room. Kristoff jumped to his feet and snatched it up, only looking over it briefly before swearing and throwing it back down. Curious, Contessa stepped forward to see what it said.

Give up the Beast if you ever want to see the brats again.

Below was an address and the symbol of a snake.

"I'll go at first light," Nate declared, slumping heavily into a chair and smearing soot all over the upholstery in the process. At least it wasn't blood this time.

"You can't actually be planning on giving yourself up to Caleb," Kristoff protested.

Nate huffed in flat amusement.

"Of course, I'm not, but I have to at least pretend to get the children back," he pointed out.

"That's not exactly going to catch Caleb off guard," Rhosyn chimed in. "He'll expect you to pull a knife on him as soon as the rascals are safe."

"That doesn't mean I'm not going to do it," Nate pointed out. "We're both expecting a betrayal. There's no way around that in a hostage situation."

"You have a point," Kristoff conceded, "but I'm coming too."

"I know," Nate leaned his head against the back of his chair with a thump. "We need to take Caleb out. I've been trying to avoid an all—out war with him, but if he's going to resort to using actual children as pawns, then he needs to be stopped. Honestly, we can probably fight our way out of there even if they are expecting it."

Contessa slapped the note she was still holding down on the table in front of her, causing everybody in the room to jump.

"Probably isn't good enough," she snapped. "You think I win every game of chess I play by making moves that will *probably* work?"

"Connie," Nate's voice softened, "we don't really have a choice. Caleb is going to expect a fight no matter what, and what are our other options? We can't do nothing, and we can't give up."

"In chess, the best way to lure somebody's tile into a trap is by making them think they're escaping a different trap. Caleb won't suspect a betrayal if he thinks he's already succeeded in thwarting your plans for fighting back."

Kristoff let out a low whistle. "Where have you been while we've been planning strategies all these years? Your deception has *layers*."

"Do you really think we could trick Caleb like that?" Rhosyn asked.

"If anybody can sense that we've tricked him, it'll be Nate," Contessa pointed out.

Nate was beginning to nod along, leaning forward in his chair.

"We can lull him into a false sense of victory," Nate agreed. "Really make him think we've been beaten. And we have one thing up his sleeve that he will never see coming."

Chapter Twenty-One

Contessa looked between the spikes clutched in her sweaty hands and the tree before her with trepidation. She'd been so confident in this plan, keeping her out of any fighting as much as possible, playing to her strengths. Now, though, standing face to face with her tasks, Contessa mused that she perhaps had underestimated the difficulty of what she needed to do.

Forcing her uncharacteristically dry throat to swallow, Contessa hefted the spikes in her hands, feeling their solid weight and finding it comforting as she stepped up to the tree trunk in front of her. It was lucky that there was such a tree just outside of the fence surrounding Caleb's house in the middle city. Maybe it was hubris that led Caleb to not trim the branches that brushed up against a second story window, springy but still sturdy enough to hold the weight of someone as slight as Contessa. Or maybe he was expecting her.

Brushing those thoughts away, Contessa reached up to dig the spikes into the tree above her head before using her toes to scrabble for purchase along the rough bark. She would only need to pull herself up a few feet using the spikes before she could reach the lower branches. A better climber wouldn't have needed spikes at all, but Contessa wasn't about to turn down any possible advantage. It wasn't long before Contessa was able to loop her arm around the lowest branch and haul herself up, although she was already panting from the short exertion. She cursed the balmy night as she swung her foot onto the lowest branch and stood on it, balancing herself with a hand on the tree trunk and mapping out her path towards the second-story window of the house that Caleb used as a front for higher society

Rattlesnake business. Contessa's heart pounded against her sternum as she edged herself along the branch, and she tried to tell herself this wasn't any different than when she would climb trees by the seaside cottage as a child, while her mother kept watch from below. That felt impossibly long ago.

Now, Contessa was straddling a higher branch and edging closer to her anticipated point of entry. As slow as she tried to move, the rustling of leaves she caused seemed deafening. Still, a sudden noise from the front of the house told her Caleb's men would be distracted right now.

Unable to resist, Contessa peeked over the fence towards the street, catching the barest glimpse of Nate's figure approaching the house, trailed by two smaller figures she knew to be Rhosyn and Gregor. She wished just for a moment that he would look up at the tree he would know she was climbing, but he knew better than that. Contessa watched him disappear around the corner to where the front door was, hearing voices she couldn't make out. She knew they would search him for weapons, surely be gloating and taunting him, but she tried not to think about it. Instead, she thought about the nervous kiss she'd pressed to his lips, hurried with an uncoordinated bump of their noses as she wished him luck and asked for some of her own in return. She owed him a better kiss, and they both had to succeed in their parts of the plan if she was going to deliver it.

Contessa remained perched in her tree, crouched low among the leaves, as the noises at the front door faded. Her legs trembled as she held herself tightly to the branch below her, but she knew her timing had to be perfect. Contessa lost her sense of time as she tried to remain still and inconspicuous, but eventually, the sound of more activity from the front of the house drifted through the warm evening air. The indistinguishable chattering of children's voices made a knot release in Contessa's chest, and she spotted a small herd of figures, shepherded along by Rhosyn and Gregor, set off down the street. Even though Kristoff and Nate had assured her over and over that Caleb would have no use for a herd of children and he only wanted Nate, Contessa had worried he wouldn't let them go and that the poor little ones would be harmed, and coordinating this ridiculous operation would be for nothing.

Rhosyn's bright red hair disappeared at the end of the street, and Contessa breathed a sigh of relief, even as she wished Rhosyn were with her. Nate had been right that Rhosyn was too recognizable, and the Rattlesnakes would be suspicious if she weren't accounted for, but Contessa craved the comfort of somebody more experienced at her side.

However, the other more experienced member of their team was currently slinking through the back gardens. Kristoff darted from bush to bush, hiding himself in the shadows, although perhaps not as thoroughly as he could. Reaching the house, Contessa couldn't help but sigh with envy at the effortless way he grappled up the side of the house, clinging to the stones by the tips of his fingers. Kristoff reached a window on the second floor, down the side of the house from her own post. Holding himself precariously on the slim sill, Contessa assumed he was working the lock until the window sprang open and he levered himself inside.

She held her breath for a few moments in the silence she knew wouldn't last. The sound of several shots in quick succession split the air even sooner than Contessa expected, almost startling her out of the tree even though she'd known they were coming. She was too far away to be sure, but she thought she heard the thud of several bodies falling. Contessa tried to picture the chaos in the upstairs hallway in her head as pounding footsteps and yelling were punctuated by the pop of more gunfire. Kristoff had assured her that he had a flair for chaos, and he seemed to be delivering on his promise as the racket continued. Still, after several minutes, the sound of Kristoff's twin pistols was notably absent, and silence returned not long after. It seemed that Kristoff had been subdued, but if he had landed most of the shots Contessa had heard, he had gone a long way to making her job easier. Steadying her breathing, Contessa counted to one hundred as planned. Then, she picked up her inching towards the window where she'd left off. The bough bounced precariously with every shift of weight as she reached the end. Just as it dipped so dangerously that Contessa worried it would give out altogether, Contessa's fingers reached the windowsill. She clambered onto it, crouching awkwardly as she tried to find a way to balance without using her hands. She ended up halfway crouched and halfway kneeling with one shoulder braced painfully against the brick of the window casing. Still, she could reach the lock and her boot this way. Fishing out the lockpicks that had been stashed in her boot, she made quick work of the window latch, grateful to be using legitimate picks for once. When the window swung inward, Contessa immediately tumbled through, landing on her backside with a thump. She could only pray it hadn't been heard downstairs.

Looking up and down the hallway, it seemed Kristoff had done his work well. There was nobody in sight, and a series of dark splatters on the wall suggested exactly what had happened to the thugs who had been keeping watch upstairs. With Kristoff and Nate captured, all the main targets were accounted for, and replacing these guards wouldn't seem like an immediate priority. Contessa could have taught Caleb better, though. It's always the pieces you don't count as a threat that come back to steal your win from you.

Despite the apparent lack of life on the upper floor, Contessa pressed herself to the wall, peeking in every doorway and stepping as lightly as she could as she made her way down the hall. She wouldn't be able to fight anybody off if they surprised her from behind. Reaching the end of the corridor, she could just make out voices from the lower level. Knowing she'd reached the landing at the top of the stairs, Contessa crouched down, bracing her back against the wall. Reaching into the other boot this time, she fished out their secret weapon. In one hand, she held an object that looked like a pistol but with a gap behind the barrel where the chamber would be. She set it on the ground to work on the other object. As carefully as possible, she began to screw the cap off the syringe she held, not wanting to think of what would happen if she spilled any of the contents on her fingers. Contessa loaded the uncapped syringe into the chamber of the gun, cursing at how ridiculous this felt, although Kristoff had insisted this was something they had used before, if not quite in this capacity.

With her weapon ready, Contessa inched her head around the corner to peak onto the empty landing. Straining, she could just hear the low rumble of an angry voice that sounded like Nate's, giving her the impetus to creep out onto the landing. She crouched awkwardly as she inched forward, wanting to stay low while afraid of the noise her knees would make on the floor if she crawled. Contessa moved haltingly, stopping every time the floor squeaked beneath her, a hysterical giggle threatening to escape as she wondered how Nate managed to sneak so effortlessly when he must weigh twice as much as her. Pushing down her rising hysteria, Contessa reached the railing and hazarded a peek through the balusters down into the room below.

As Nate had predicted, he and Kristoff were being held in the large room. Nate was on his knees, flanked by uneasy looking thugs. Meanwhile, Kristoff seemed to have abandoned the discomfort of kneeling for reclining on one elbow, seeming for all the world as though he were sprawled on a chaise lounge in an elegant parlor and not in enemy territory. If the thugs on either side of Nate had looked ill at ease with their charge, the ones next to Kristoff appeared utterly disconcerted by his behavior.

Contessa's eyes roved away from her friends to the figure walking back and forth in the center of the room. Although she could only see the back of his head from this angle, his incessant pacing and expansive gesturing gave him the air of a mad king holding court. Kristoff had mentioned Caleb had a flair for the dramatic, always conducting his business in the grandest room of his house, as though he were an enigmatic nobleman and not an underworld gangster. However, it served their purposes well, Contessa mused, as she let her eyes drift up from his pacing figure to the gaudy chandelier dominating the space, hanging by a thick chain from the vaulted ceiling beams.

Taking a quiet breath to steady her hands, Contessa raised the gun contraption and aimed it at the top of the chain supporting the chandelier, barely two meters from where she crouched. She squeezed one eye shut as she tried to get a line through the makeshift sight, suppressing the voice in her head that sounded like her father saying that every good shot aimed with both eyes open. It felt strange to be lining up to essentially fire a squirt gun, but Kristoff had explained they had devised it to shoot the acid they used to melt through safe doors at a long enough distance that the user wouldn't risk being splashed. Contessa sent a brief prayer to any Gods that might be listening that it was as accurate as Kristoff had claimed. Then she pulled the trigger.

There was a click, then a grinding feeling in the trigger, which caught before Contessa could compress it all the way. Pulling back to inspect it, Contessa assumed it must be jammed. She turned it this way and that, trying to find the source of the stuck mechanism, but Contessa knew little about firearms and even less about retrofitted ones like this. She tried finessing the trigger back and forth slightly, but it wouldn't budge, and she stopped quickly, afraid of what would happen if she squirted the acid onto her pants.

Contessa snuck another desperate glance at the scene in the room below her, wracking her brains for what she could do before Caleb finished gloating over his victory. Her fingers ran over the catch to her knives at her wrist as Caleb paced near the edge of the landing where she perched. A skilled assassin might be able to jump down onto Caleb and take him out before he could throw them off, but Contessa dismissed that idea as quickly as it came. She was as likely to hurt herself in that endeavor as Caleb, and something about driving her knife into his throat made her shiver. As much as she burned to see him pay for the things he had done, the wet sound of blood splattering when Nate slit Thomas's throat haunted Contessa in quiet moments. A more hands-off approach was preferable, which is why they had made this plan in the first place.

Looking back down at the contraption in her hands, Contessa twisted the syringe free, pulling the cap from her pocket and screwing it back on. Contessa patted her thighs for a moment, forgetting these pants didn't have pockets, and cursed. Reluctantly, she placed the vial between her teeth after double checking she'd screwed the cap on tightly. She would need both hands free. Edging back towards the corner of the landing, Contessa straightened until she could reach the ceiling beam where it emerged from the wall. Before she could second guess herself, she hoisted herself up until she managed to swing one leg over the beam, trying not to bite down too hard on the metal cylinder in her mouth as she struggled awkwardly for a few moments.

This close to the wall with the ceiling dramatically pitched, Contessa had to press her stomach flat against the beam as she straddled it, and she remained wedged there as she caught her breath, the taste of metal strong on her tongue. As she began to edge forward, sliding on her belly, the ceiling pulled away from her back and she managed to gain more leverage. She looked down as she started to get the hang of the awkward sliding wiggle, only to immediately press herself flat against the beam again as she found she had passed the edge of the landing and was now in the open space above the hall. From this angle, Nate and Kristoff, as well as a few thugs, might be able to see her if they happened to look up, but Contessa kept herself from looking down in favor of focusing on the chandelier chain a meter or so in front of her. She wriggled forward. The rough wood of the beam scratched against Contessa's ribs through her shirt, but it wasn't long until she reached her goal.

Prying one hand away from its death grip on the wood supporting her, she plucked the syringe from between her teeth. Needing both hands to unscrew it, she awkwardly hugged the beam so as to not slide off as she worked. With the cap off, she aimed the syringe at the narrowest point of the chain, right where it screwed into the beam, her thumb braced on the plunger. She chanced a glance down. Caleb was directly below her. Just as she pushed the mechanism, Nate looked up as if he could sense Contessa and jerked in surprise.

Several things happened in quick succession, Contessa's mind seeming to slow time to absorb the mayhem, futilely trying to find a way to prevent catastrophe. Caleb, alerted by Nate's surprise, followed his gaze to find Contessa perched in his ceiling like some sort of overgrown squirrel. The chain holding the chandelier groaned as the acid immediately went to work, creating a fizzling, foul smoke, and a second later, an ear-splitting cracking rung through the hall. Looking up from the people below, Contessa's heart dropped when she saw the acid had splattered off the chain and was eating through the beam. There was a heart wrenching moment when the beam started to buckle and then stopped, as if it might hold. Then Contessa's stomach flew into her throat as the wood gave way completely and she hurtled towards the floor below.

A sickening crunch filled Contessa's head as she hit the ground, rolling to one side, multicolored lights dancing behind her eyelids. For a few stunned seconds, Contessa struggled to draw in the breath that had been knocked from her, her panicked brain trying to find which bone she had heard breaking. After a few seconds, pain set in, but it appeared to be nothing more than the dull ache of bruises.

She pushed herself to sitting among the ruins of crushed furniture and the shattered remains of the chandelier, looking around. Nate was on his feet, shaking out his hand and standing over the moaning forms of the men that had surrounded him and Kristoff. A sharper groan caught Contessa's attention, and she found she'd partially missed her target. Caleb was several feet away, apparently having to tried to jump out of the way, but not quite making it. Instead, his legs were caught under the heavy wooden beam, one of them sticking out at an odd angle from his knee. Seeing the back of his head had been one thing, but looking at the pointed face of the man who had killed her mother and framed her husband for it ignited something inside Contessa that had been quelled in the past weeks.

"Well, I suppose that is one way of cutting the chandelier and riding the rope down, but we need to work on your form," Contessa heard Kristoff comment, light as ever, but she was already scrambling to her feet. The hilt of her knife was cold against her palm, even though she didn't recall unsheathing it.

She'd clambered through the wreckage of the chandelier in the blink of an eye, her knife coming up to point at the hollow in Caleb's throat. He froze, ceasing his struggles to free his legs. Contessa's grip on her knife may not have been as sure as it could have been, and the tip may have involuntarily scratched along the lump of his throat, but her intent was clear.

Caleb was still, but despite his crushed legs and the knife at his throat, he only looked faintly amused. His eyebrows raised a millimeter, his face otherwise barely even betraying surprise.

"Why, if it isn't Mrs. Woodrow. What a pleasant surprise," Caleb commented.

"Be quiet," Contessa spat, pushing closer to her captive, the tip of the knife scratching a bit deeper into his neck. His eyebrows raised a tick higher, but instead of feeling pleased at getting a reaction, Contessa just felt like he was mocking her.

The silence stretched thickly through the room, and Contessa knew everybody was waiting for her to speak. Now that her mother's killer was at her mercy, though, nothing felt like the right thing to say.

"I don't know what you want with my husband, but you're not going to get it," she settled on, buying herself time.

"Ha!" Caleb's short exclamation of amusement was jarring, like an off-key note in the middle of a song. "I wanted him out of the way. For him to stop ruling the slums of the town quietly and make some noise. If I was running this town, nobody would have to slink around in the shadows anymore."

Caleb's thoughts seemed to come chaotically, his words spilling from his mouth in fits and starts, disorienting Contessa even further.

"Well, you're not killing him. Not today," Contessa announced as firmly as she could, trying to regain her footing.

"Perhaps not," Caleb raised one shoulder carelessly. "But maybe I got something better. The daughter of the police chief crashing down from my ceiling with a knife in her hand to participate in gang dealings is certainly a degree of chaos beyond what I'm usually able to achieve."

"Chaos? Is that all you want?"

"Chaos is the catalyst for change, my dear Mrs. Woodrow," Caleb explained grandly. "For new things to grow, everything old must come crashing down. And this city is ready for something new, wouldn't you say?"

"If you're so invested in causing chaos, then why did you agree to work with the Royal Police? Do you hate Nate that much?" Contessa hissed.

Caleb chuckled, and it sounded like the rasp of a match striking tinder. There was a rustle behind her, as if Nate were shifting his weight between his feet.

"Oh, I didn't agree to work with the Royal Police. *They* agreed to work with *me*." Caleb sounded giddy. "Your father may have tried to play it off as his idea to the rest of the police force, but he had to agree to help me when I threatened to reveal his little secret."

"You don't make any sense," Contessa hissed, "and I have no reason to trust a murderer like you. It's a shame that chandelier didn't finish you off so I wouldn't have to listen to your nonsense."

The venom in Contessa's statement was diluted by the fact that she hadn't moved to kill Caleb yet.

"It's hard to say who is a murderer and who is doling out proper justice sometimes," Caleb commented, as slippery as ever.

"You're the murderer!" Contessa finally snapped. "You murdered my mother, and there is no way you can call what you did justice! There was nothing *just* about me helplessly trying to stop the bleeding with my bare hands after you slit her throat and blamed it on somebody else! Was that just to cause chaos too?"

Contessa's chest was nearly heaving from the force of her outburst, but Caleb looked delighted.

"Oh my. You think I was the one who murdered your mother. What a delightful twist indeed!" Caleb let out a giggle that was borderline hysterical. "It was obvious you had figured out it wasn't your dear husband, but I thought you would have put the pieces together by now. Oh—and even better! This means you turned against your father without even knowing...chaos indeed!"

"Speak plainly or shut up!" Contessa shouted, feeling wobbly, as if she were tumbling down from the ceiling all over again.

"Oh, I'll speak plainly," Caleb's face spread into a gleeful grin. "I wasn't the one who slit your poor mother's throat. That was all your father's doing."

"Liar!"

Contessa barely heard herself shout over Caleb's words echoing in her head. Her father wouldn't. Couldn't.

"You're a liar, and I don't know why anybody has let you live so long." Contessa pushed the knife against Caleb's throat hard enough a drop of blood ran down to pool in the hollow of his collarbone.

"Contessa." Nate's soft voice behind her managed to cut through the clamoring in her head. "He's telling the truth. I don't know how but...he's not lying."

"Oh, I'll tell you," Caleb said with all the joy of a child being presented with a sweet. "When I heard that Nate here had killed the wife of the police chief, I knew it had to be a lie. It's the type of bold move I would have wanted him to make, but he was never daring enough for it. He should be called the Mouse, not the Beast." Caleb paused to chuckle at his own joke. "I was the only person I knew of who tried to pass murders off as Nate's at the time. Trying to sow fear and all of that. So, I decided to do some snooping of my own, steal some police records to see what new face on the scene would make a move like this. And as I went searching through the report on the murder, I found a lot of missing information and sloppy investigating. A report that Chief Cook never would have signed off on if he himself weren't trying to cover something up."

"That's shoddy evidence at best," Contessa argued, but her voice wavered on the last syllable. "Why would he murder his own wife? He loved her!"

"And what might make a man, who has made it his life's purpose to rid the city of the Talented, feel so betrayed that he would resort to murder? Maybe finding out that his dear wife was Talented herself?"

"My mother wasn't..." Contessa trailed off.

"Oh please. I guessed that one with barely any investigation."

"Oh, is that all this is? Guesses?"

"It may have started that way, but I was proven right by your father himself when I threatened to expose him." Caleb's grin was positively feral. "I just had to pretend to have evidence, and he rolled right over to show me his belly. Why would such a powerful man be afraid of being accused of murder by a criminal, unless he was guilty?"

Maybe Caleb was just cooking up this lie to cause more chaos. Maybe this was all just part of the massive, twisted game he played. Still, the icy shard of rage that had been driving Contessa forward had evaporated, and now she was left feeling an entirely new brand of rage, hot and trembling and directionless.

"Nate?" Contessa whispered, not entirely sure what she was asking him for, even though Nate seemed to be able to interpret her intentions just fine.

"It's true, Contessa. I'm so sorry but...he's not lying."

The hand holding the knife to Caleb's throat dropped to Contessa's side, as though she were a marionette that had a string cut. She took one step backwards, then another. She could sense the warmth of Nate standing just behind her now.

"You're not even worth the time it would take to clean your blood off my knife," Contessa stated before turning towards Nate. She couldn't stand to look at Caleb's pleased expression any longer.

Nate was there immediately, and she stepped into his already open arms to press her face to his chest. It was the type of comfort she might have ridiculed herself for wanting just weeks ago, thinking it made her weak, but she would have been wrong. She'd been wrong about so many things.

The sharp smell of the sweat on Nate's shirt had just started to clear Contessa's mind when it was filled with the shrieking of alarm bells. Nate felt it, too, his arms instantly tensing around her as there was a loud movement behind her. Before they could react further, the air was split by the loud crack of gunfire and the thud of a body falling to the floor.

Whirling around, Contessa was greeting by the sight of Kristoff holding the world's smallest pistol in the air, a satisfied look on his face and, for some reason, his pants entirely unbuttoned. The oddness of the sight alone was enough to drive some of the fog from Contessa's mind.

"Kristoff, why were you taking your pants off?" Nate asked exactly what Contessa had been wondering.

"Well, I had to get my gun out of course!" Kristoff waved his ridiculous weapon in the air as if this should have been obvious. "And for the first time in my life, I don't mean that as a euphemism."

"How on earth did you get that gun in here? Weren't you searched when you were caught?" Contessa asked. Her mind seemed to be rejecting the shock of the past minutes' revelation by grasping onto a more easily understood issue.

"Ah, thus why I was unbuttoning my pants," Kristoff explained conspiratorially. "You see, very few goons pat down the front of my trousers as thoroughly as they should, especially given my widespread reputation with men. It's as if they think it will catch or some such thing! Or maybe they just don't want to seem too eager."

"You snuck in a pistol in your underclothes," Nate commented as if he were disappointed in himself for not expecting this. "And why did you not mention to me that we had a contingency plan?"

Kristoff shrugged. "I know you expect me to say it would ruin the surprise or some nonsense, but it seems like one is much more likely to fall back on a contingency plan when you know it's there. I had hoped we would be able to avoid a standoff and it would never come up."

Kristoff's words had a sobering effect on Contessa, and she glanced over to Caleb's body where it was crumpled on the floor, limp finger still resting on the trigger of a pistol. She instantly regretted it. Nate stepped between her and the sight of Caleb's mangled head reflexively, and Contessa edged away from the spreading pool of blood that inched dangerously close to her boots.

"We should get out of here," Nate suggested. "No need to wait around for more trouble to find us." He quickly gathered his knives from the unconscious guards on the floor, sliding them each into their place with practiced efficiency.

Contessa nodded, grateful for the warm, rough fingers that wove between her own to lead her out of the ruined house. She'd thought when this mission was finished, she would have felt some sort of completion. A wholeness that made her feel as if she could move forward. Instead, as Nate led her out into the fresh air, her mind felt as splintered as the chandelier destroyed on the floor behind her.

Kristoff turned up the street, leading the way to the upper city and the house with the blue door. He was uncharacteristically silent, as if sensing it wouldn't be much use to distract Contessa from the whirling thoughts in her head. Her feelings were oscillating so wildly that she wasn't even sure what emotion was dominant, be it rage, sadness, or confusion. She had no idea how it must feel to be Nate. If he could sense each separate emotion tangling together like hopelessly knotted embroidery threads, or if it simply felt like an incomprehensible storm. Either way, he didn't comment, nor did he let go of her hand.

Contessa had been walking so blindly that if Kristoff had led her off a cliff, she might have followed over the edge without noticing, but she stopped suddenly as they passed a familiar street. Nate pulled to a stop beside her, Kristoff pausing when their footsteps went quiet.

"Connie," Nate said. She wasn't sure if it was a question or simply a statement.

"I have to know," Contessa answered.

Nate was silent for a beat, following her gaze down the dimly lit street.

"Alright," he said simply.

"Kristoff, go update Rhosyn and Gregor before they worry too much. We have some business to take care of."

Kristoff nodded and stepped forward hesitantly as if to say something to Contessa but settled for a comforting squeeze to her shoulder before turning and jogging towards home.

As his footsteps retreated, Nate took an audible breath beside Contessa before asking, "So, do we have a plan, or do you just want me to kick down your father's front door and stab anybody that has a problem with it?"

Chapter Twenty-Two

Contessa wondered why she hadn't thought to wear trousers when she snuck out of the house as a child. Crawling under the gap in the back hedge was easier without worrying about tearing cumbersome skirts. She emerged from the thicket, crouching behind a strategically placed bush of rhododendron as Nate wriggled through behind her with considerably more difficulty. The heavy smell of the flowers in full bloom was thick on Contessa's tongue, and while it once would have reminded her of her youth, now it just tasted bitter.

Nate came to crouch beside her and survey the side of the house, his eyes narrow and a few leaves from the hedge caught in his untamed hair. For a moment, she was reminded of the fearsome way he looked when they had first gotten married, and she was grateful to be beside him instead of against him.

"If we break into the cellar there, we can enter through a secret panel in my father's study," Contessa whispered. The shadow of the gray stone house before them weighed on her like a physical presence, and as she looked up at it, the architecture she'd once thought stately now seemed hostile.

They picked through the shadows of the garden, Contessa alert for any sign of her mental alarm bells even though she knew her father never had police patrolling inside the limits of his own property. He was adamant that having the force he commanded protect him too closely would project weakness. The lack of security had seemed overly proud to Contessa, especially after her mother's death, but it made sense now. No need to keep the criminals out of the house when they already lived inside.

Reaching the cellar door, Contessa slipped her lockpicks out of her boot and set to work. In the darkness, she had to go by feel alone, tumblers clicking into place slowly as the puzzle came undone in her hands. It took her longer than usual to work the lock, this one being a more sophisticated design. It would have proved a challenge for somebody less trained than Contessa, and the irony of that wasn't lost on her.

When the door was open, Contessa waved Nate inside and eased the hatch closed behind her as they descended into the cellar. She left it open just a crack so a sliver of moonlight lit their path. The cool air was refreshing after the humidity of the early dawn.

Contessa led the way through the cellar, letting her eyes adjust to the near blackness. It wasn't far to the secret door leading into her father's study, and they hadn't brought a lantern. Besides, a sliver of light coming from under the bookcase in her father's study might alert him of their presence, and she wasn't sure they would be able to corner him without drawing attention if they lost the element of surprise.

"Why isn't this passage protected if it goes straight to your father's study?" Nate breathed right behind Contessa's ear.

She paused to ease around a stack of crates, whispering over her shoulder. "It's an escape route for my father. He's paranoid, and so the only people who know of its existence are me and him. A secret passage stops being secret when you post guards outside of it."

Contessa put her hand on Nate's arm for silence as they took a few steps up to a panel set into the wall. She approached it, gingerly pressing her ear to the door to see if her father was inside. If she strained, she thought she heard the shuffle of papers, but it could have been her imagination. Her Talent wasn't alerting her to any danger, but she didn't think it would unless she'd been discovered.

She motioned Nate forward, and he slunk up next to her, a soft *shink* indicating his knives had slid into his hands. The noise made her shiver. Accosting her father in his own home didn't come without the risk of bloodshed, and she wasn't even sure she was trying to avoid it. She wasn't the one who had drawn first blood in this war after all.

Contessa braced her hands on the door, ready to swing it open into the room, mentally preparing herself. Nate nodded to her, indicating he was ready when she was.

The moment Contessa pushed the hinged bookshelf open, Nate was moving, faster than one of the bullets from Kristoff's guns. Contessa pushed into the room after him, finding her father sitting at the desk. His hand was already moving to grab the loaded gun in the drawer, and a sense of danger was screeching at the base of Contessa's skull. Nate was one step ahead, though, and already he was hurling one of his knives. The pommel hit her father squarely in the wrist, the pistol falling to the carpeted floor with a dull thud.

Her father wasn't stunned for long, grabbing the letter opener on his desk, but Nate was quicker. He leaped over the top with the power of a lion hunting down its prey and grabbed her father's wrist, digging his fingers in until he dropped the letter opener. Nate ducked under his arm, still holding his wrist so it was twisted up behind him. A matter of seconds after entering the room, Nate had her father immobilized, a knife pressed to his throat.

After such a rapid series of events, the room fell unnaturally still as two sets of eyes fell expectantly on Contessa, one trusting, one cold.

Contessa took a shaky breath, clenching and unclenching her fists a few times, suddenly wishing she had skirts to hide the action in. The odd, hot anger was washing over her again, making her tremble and her face flush.

"Well, I knew you'd been poisoned against me, but this is an unexpected gambit for you," her father said casually. Contessa knew he wanted to make her doubt herself, get her on uncertain footing—but she was here for a reason.

"Why did you kill mother?"

To his credit, Chief Cook barely blinked, but Contessa knew him well enough to know he was surprised.

"I'm impressed you figured it out. I knew I had given you the necessary skills, but it seems your investigative abilities surpassed even what I expected," he said smoothly.

"So, you admit it," Contessa said coldly. "Why?"

Chief Cook laughed humorlessly, and Nate tightened his grip, causing the chuckle to be cut off by a grimace.

"Considering you have your once sworn enemy holding a knife to your father's throat, I would think you would understand that sometimes the only way to respond to betrayal is with betrayal."

"You murdered your wife," Contessa's hands were shaking, but her voice came out hard. "There's no betrayal that could possibly be as great as that."

"She wasn't my wife when I killed her, not really. She had lied to me, tricked me. She wasn't the woman I thought I had fallen in love with," Chief Cook said emphatically, with all the conviction of a preacher at the pulpit.

"She loved you!" Contessa nearly shouted.

"She was a monster! She manipulated people with that Curse of hers, that singing voice. I don't know how I didn't see it at first, but for all I know, she could have used it to trick me into thinking I loved her, so she could take me down. Finish what the Talented had started when they assassinated King Royce and fully disgraced me. But I knew when I saw the way she could calm you with her singing, and I had to do something before she poisoned you too. Before the world found out I had been sleeping with the enemy."

Contessa had always thought her father to be the epitome of reason and cold logic, but that façade unraveled before her eyes.

"Is that what this has all been about? Have you been murdering innocent people because your pride was hurt when a Talented assassin got past you?" Contessa demanded.

"I had everything!" Chief Cook's gray eyes were unyielding, and for a moment, Contessa wondered if that's what her eyes had looked like when she first looked at Nate. "I hadn't been handed success and status; I had earned it by being the best at what I did. I was a good bodyguard, and the King trusted me, giving me status, power. Then one day, it was all taken from me by a perversion of nature. The world had to be rid of those who could gain an advantage through abominations, and I had the skills to do it."

"Mother was not an abomination," Contessa said, her voice hard.

"You were blinded to it," Chief Cook scoffed. "But you're lucky I dealt with her before you became like her and used tricks to get ahead. No, you're like me, and you get what you want by using the brains in your own head."

"I'm more like Mother than you might think," Contessa squared her shoulders and stared her father down with all the rage she could muster. "And I am nothing like you."

Chief Cook was unphased.

"You say you're nothing like me, but here you are, willing to slit your own father's throat in the name of justice. Go ahead, have the Beast kill me, then look in the mirror and tell yourself you aren't your father's daughter. At least I have a warrant when I have people killed."

Contessa looked over her father's shoulder at Nate, who had been notably silent the whole time. He met her eyes steadily, his eyes holding no judgement—just trust.

"You just admitted to murder," Contessa said. "I could have you hanged for that as well."

"I'm the Chief of the Royal Police, and you're holding me at knife point. I don't see this going in your favor," he commented.

Silence fell in the room, and Contessa's balled fists trembled. He was right. Nobody would believe her and Nate.

"Maybe not, but she has a witness."

Everybody jerked collectively as Joseph rounded the corner, holding a pistol aimed squarely at the men behind the desk. Contessa couldn't say whether he was aiming for her father or the Beast. From the wide-eyed expression on Joseph's face, she thought he might not be sure, either.

"Joseph," Contessa murmured, not sure what to say to the man who had once been her closest friend, now holding the justice for her mother's murder in the palm of his hand.

"Not now, Contessa," he snapped. "You're not innocent here, either."

"Joseph, seize her," Chief Cook commanded smugly. "She assaulted me in my own—"

"Not a word from you, either!" Joseph practically yelled before Chief Cook could finish giving orders, leaving him sputtering in disbelief. "I dedicated my life to upholding the law because of your mentorship, and now I find you've spit in its face?"

"I was doing what was right—what the law couldn't do. Sometimes you must go beyond what's legal and get your hands dirty to get the job done," Chief Cook explained, fanatical in his fervor. His eyes took on the unholy glint that Contessa had long thought was determination, but she saw now as being lust for power and vengeance.

"I have always followed the law to the letter." Some of the anger seeped from Joseph's voice, but still he held his gun steady. "I thought that would make me the only innocent one here. But I see now that following the law does not save me from guilt. Not after I heard you admit we've been killing Cursed—Talented—because you couldn't stand losing power. I've had people put to death because of the law, and now I'm finding out I might be just as guilty as everybody in this room."

"She's poisoned your mind too," Chief Cook insisted, a vein throbbing in his temple.

Joseph finally looked at Contessa after pointedly avoiding her gaze for the whole conversation. The expression on his face sent a crack rattling through her heart. It was the expression of somebody who was having the truths they held dear crumble around them and being forced to reassess everything in their reality. It was what Contessa had gone through, too, although over several months, with

Nate at her side. Now Joseph was watching it happen over a matter of seconds, and Contessa wouldn't let her friend go through it alone.

"Only you can decide for yourself what is right," was all she offered.

Joseph blinked and took a shuddering breath before turning back to the men.

"Chief Cook, you are under arrest for murder," Joseph said, his gaze flicking to Contessa and then back to her father's purpling face.

"How— They're...they're criminals! How could you betray me like this?" Her father's cool demeanor had evaporated, leaving no traces of the man Contessa had thought him to be.

"How could *I* betray *you*?" Joseph asked. "I looked up to you, and you just admitted I have been following the command of a murderer. At the end of the day, I trust Contessa because she is the one who told me to think for myself, while you always told me to follow you blindly."

Joseph pulled a set of cuffs from his belt and approached Chief Cook, Nate still pressing a knife to his throat. Nate shook the Chief, prompting him to hold out his wrists for Joseph to bind.

"I thought at least you might be smarter than Contessa," he spat as his wrists were fastened into the cuffs, "but it turns out you're no smarter than a girl who's had her head turned by a criminal."

"No," Joseph replied, finishing his work and yanking Chief Cook forward by his cuffs. "She's the smartest of us, seeing through your manipulations first. And me? I wasn't smart enough to listen to her the first time she told me to think twice."

Contessa let out a noise somewhere between a sigh and a sob, clapping her hand to her mouth. Nate, now no longer holding Chief Cook, strode over to her, pulling her to him as she shook with relief. Joseph glanced at her, an apology and regret mixed in his gaze.

"Now, Chief Cook, you will stand trial for what you've done."

Contessa gripped the bench she sat on so hard the wooden edge bit painfully into her palm. Nate reached down and pried her fingers from their death grip, instead clasping her hand in his and stroking it gently with his thumb. Still, Contessa felt so tense that she might snap as the new King Byron stepped up to the stand to pass down her father's sentence.

"I find the former Chief of the Royal Police, Emil Cook, guilty of murder. However, given his years of service to both London and my grandfather during his time as his bodyguard, I have chosen to be lenient. He is sentenced to life in prison."

Contessa trembled even as the knot in her chest released. Justice was served, but she wouldn't have to watch her father hang. Caleb had been right, and the records and police reports regarding her mother's murder had been sloppy, missing information. After that, Joseph's testimony alongside hers had been enough to convince the court of her father's guilt.

Contessa didn't even remember standing up and leaving the courtroom. She felt as if she were floating as Nate led her through the halls. She barely paid attention to where they were going, instead focusing on her intense relief. She was startled, almost colliding with the figure who stepped in front of them, forcing them to make an abrupt halt.

Contessa looked up to apologize to the man for almost running into him, only to choke on her words. Standing in front of them was King Byron himself. He had taken the throne several weeks ago, after his older brother, Prince Albert, had abdicated after only two days as king.

Contessa shook herself, curtsying awkwardly. She hadn't been prepared to greet royalty today. Nate was even worse, bowing so stiffly she thought he might topple over.

The King waved away his retinue, and they stepped back, giving them some space.

"I must thank you," he started.

Of all the things Contessa expected him to say, that hadn't been one of them.

"It's hard enough learning how to be a ruler, having the head of the Royal Police be corrupt would have only made things worse. I need people I can trust in positions of power."

Nate was opening and closing his mouth soundlessly, so Contessa jumped in.

"We are glad we could be of service, and I am thankful for your mercy towards my father."

King Byron nodded, making the golden crown on his head flash in the sunlight. He wore it well.

"I think London has seen enough executions in the past years. A lot of people would be happy to see them end." He shot a pointed look at Nate, who coughed.

"You know," Byron continued casually, as if it had just occurred to him, "I need people who care about this city—and all its people—to help me rule. I have some changes I would like to make, some policies I think are outdated, especially when it comes to the Talented. It would be great to have people who understand other sides of the issues to council me."

Byron looked between the two of them pointedly, and Nate finally found his voice.

"Connie here—Mrs. Woodrow, that is—has a good handle on many issues, given her history."

Contessa flushed but held King Byron's gaze as he nodded thoughtfully. "Then we shall have to meet sometime. See if we can come up with an arrangement." He turned his attention to Nate. "I also was thinking how I myself will need a personal bodyguard. Somebody skilled, who understands the concerns and moods of the public. Maybe somebody who would consider working inside the law to help the people, instead of outside of it."

Nate blanched and offered a stilted bow. Contessa took pity on him.

"Thank you for your kind considerations, King Byron. We will have to meet to iron out more arrangements some other time. For now, it has been a long trial, and we have some affairs to see to."

The King nodded understandingly as his retinue stepped up behind him once more.

"I will be in touch," he said as he began to walk away. "And do try to stay out of trouble until then."

Contessa could have sworn she saw a devious twinkle in his eye before he turned away.

As Contessa and Nate walked out of the palace to the carriage that Gregor had waiting to take them back to the upper city, Nate eventually spoke.

"Were we just offered jobs by the King?"

Contessa couldn't help but smile at the stricken look on Nate's face.

"Now everybody is going to know how great of a man you are, and there is nothing you are going to be able to do about it."

Nate helped her up into the carriage, offering her a smirk.

"Well then, I guess, when we get home, I am going to have to remind you just how bad I can be."

Standing in the dazzling sunlight next to the trickling fountain in the back garden, Contessa couldn't help but think how this was a much better wedding than her first one, despite the non-traditional setting and small number of guests. She smiled up at Nate instead of staring at his buttons, and now she wore her mother's veil out of pride instead of as a symbol of vengeance.

"I now pronounce you husband and wife...again," Kristoff declared grandly.

His statement was greeted by small applause and whoops from Gregor, Rhosyn, and Julia. Even Joseph offered a shy cheer, despite still seeming surprised that he was now friends with a haphazard crew of gangsters. He and Contessa had begun mending their friendship, working together through the confusion of feelings caused by her father's conviction. Having him here, among all the people who mattered the most to her, was one of the nicest wedding presents she could have asked for.

Contessa's heart swelled at the feeling of having friends here to witness this second wedding. The wedding they had planned to have to show they were choosing to love each other—that they weren't married for schemes or politics, but because they never wanted to be apart again.

"You may now kiss the bride!" Kristoff exclaimed.

Nate wasted no time in grabbing Contessa by the waist and kissing her so thoroughly that she bent backwards, supported completely by Nate's arms around her. The small group cheered again, this time accompanied by some whistles from Kristoff. Contessa laughed into Nate's lips with the sheer joy of it, and she felt him smile in return. This may not have been the official start of their marriage, but it was the start of a new life together, and Contessa couldn't wait.

Bonus Chapter

The Wedding: Nate's Perspective

The first rays of sunlight creeping through the single high window of the study marked the arrival of Nate's wedding day. He twisted the glass in his hand, watching the dawn light filter through the cut glass to turn the dark liquid within into a molten amber. The few sips he had taken burned his throat, and he considered downing the rest in a single swallow.

The groom getting drunk before the ceremony might be the only opportunity for a cliché today. After all, nothing about this wedding was real.

Only Nate's nerves.

Before he could throw back the rest of his whiskey, a tapping from the floor stole his attention. With a sigh, he pushed his chair back and reached for the trapdoor hidden below his desk. As soon as he cracked it open, a pair of sparkling blue eyes and a crooked grin greeted him.

"Good morning to the groom!" Kristoff exclaimed as he clambered out of the hidden tunnel.

Nate just grunted in response, slumping back in his chair.

His friend put his hands on his hips, taking in Nate's mussed hair and rumpled clothes—the same outfit Kristoff had seen him in just hours before during a scuffle with the Scorpions near the rail yard. Nate hadn't even bothered to wipe off the blood that had splattered his lapel—not his own, thankfully—but had just removed his coat and slung it over the back of a chair before pouring himself a drink.

"You didn't sleep at all?" Kristoff asked, although he clearly knew the answer. Nate shook his head and took another swallow of whiskey.

"I can't blame you for being nervous," Kristoff admitted. "I've heard Ms. Cook is very pretty."

"That's hardly material," Nate grumbled.

"No? Then why the nerves?" Kristoff prodded playfully. "She's a great enough beauty that you convinced all of London society that you asked her father for her hand in marriage before even speaking to her, just because you were so entranced."

Nate set his glass on the polished wood of his desk with a little more force than was necessary. "And I'm glad people believe that, although I'm interested to hear what explanation the gossips have made up for why she would accept the offer. I know it's just because she knows she needs to get out from under her father's roof as quickly as possible. And I wouldn't be surprised if the threat of having Chief Cook as a father-in-law scares away most suitors."

Kristoff shrugged, eyes twinkling mischievously. "Well, you are very rich."

"And I'm sure she can guess as well as anybody how I got all that money." Nate pointed out.

Propping one hip on Nate's desk, Kristoff crossed his arms and shook his head. "It doesn't change the fact that you're wealthy and about to be married to the woman that half of London society has been pining after despite how much they fear her father, yet one would think that you were being marched to the gallows. Stop feeling sorry for yourself and get dressed. Gregor has your wedding clothes ready and will be disappointed if he doesn't get to treat you like a proper gentleman for once."

Nate pushed to his feet with a heavy sigh. He tried to bring some lightness to his steps as he tromped from the office and to his bedroom to dress, telling himself that Kristoff was right. But it was no use.

All he could do was worry about how his bride would look at him, knowing that she had only agreed to this union to escape the execution that would surely follow her father discovering her Talent. Would she be tearful at giving up the chance to marry for love? Would she be disgusted by his scar, refusing to meet his eyes?

As Nate scrubbed his face, he resolved not to dwell on it. After the wedding, it would not matter. He would give Ms. Cook—Mrs. Woodrow, he supposed—the space to live her own life after today. This was just a formality.

A light knock came on the door, followed by Gregor entering, carrying a bundle of cloth. Nate stripped out of his dusty outfit from the night before, tossing it on the undisturbed coverlet of his bed. He reached for the fresh shirt his manservant had brought, only for Gregor to hesitate.

"Really?" Gregor asked, raising one brow so it disappeared beneath his sandy-colored bangs.

Nate looked down to see what he was asking about. He still had all his knives strapped to himself: Two on each arm, one on either side of his ribs, one on each leg, and a small one hidden at the base of his spine. He shook his head.

"Chief Cook isn't going to catch me off guard, even at my own wedding."

Gregor's mouth twitched, but he didn't say anything as he helped him into the fine clothes that had been ordered for his wedding. Nate had placed an order with the tailor for fashionable gowns for his new wife—he wasn't entirely sure why. Perhaps so he knew he could at least do one pleasing thing for his bride. Kristoff and Gregor had managed to slip in a special request for a new outfit for him beneath his notice.

As Gregor buttoned up his waistcoat, it was Nate's turn to ask "Really?"

Gregor smirked at the Lions emblazoned on the golden buttons.

"We had to taunt Chief Cook a little."

With a sigh, Nate grabbed his top hat and led the way from his room, marching downstairs to the front door. Gregor fetched the carriage quickly, and he and Kristoff climbed in for the short ride to the church.

Kristoff, normally vivacious and talkative, let Nate contemplate in silence as the wheels clattered over the cobblestones. When they lurched to a halt in front of the cathedral, Kristoff clapped him on his shoulder.

"Good luck. And don't forget to smile."

Nate snorted, sure the sight of his disfigured mouth twisting into a smile would be enough to send even the most stout-hearted of brides running. Still, he put his hand over Kristoff's and nodded once before exiting the carriage and entering the church.

Inside, the guests had already arrived, but a hush fell over the chattering crowd as he entered. He tried not to pay them any mind as he made his way to his position at the front. There would be very few familiar faces.

All of the guests would be friends and family of the Cooks—socialites he only knew in passing or from robbing with his Lions in the dead of night.

Instead, he took his appointed position, folding his hands in front of himself and staring at the double doors that his bride-to-be would be arriving through at any moment. The organ started to play, and he interlaced his fingers to keep from running them over the shape of the weapons beneath his sleeves. His knives might be a comfort in most situations, but this was not a challenge he would be able to stab his way out of.

As the organ music swelled, the doors to the cathedral swung open, silhouetting two figures in the bright light of the morning sun. Nate's gaze darted over the taller of the two—the familiar, austere figure of Chief Cook—to settle on the petite form at his side.

A delicate lace veil covered his bride's face, and he could barely make out the shape of her slim waist, so bedecked was her gown in bows and frills. While the dress and veil thoroughly obscured most of Ms. Cook, it left the tops of her breasts, pushed to inordinate heights by the squeeze of her corset, very exposed.

Nate swallowed and wrenched his gaze back to the sheet of lace where her face was hidden. At any other wedding, a groom might be encouraged to appreciate his bride's beauty, but this was not a typical celebration.

As he stared at the veil, Nate softened his mind, letting his sixth sense wash over him, hoping to glean some hint of how Ms. Cook felt. Was she as nervous as he was?

With his mind open, he gleaned polite interest, confusion, and even boredom pouring in from the crowd at all sides. A sharp sliver of shrewd indifference pierced Nate's conscious, straight from Chief Cook, setting his teeth on edge.

All those sensations were rapidly washed away by an iciness, so cold it burned, pouring from his bride to be.

As she stopped in front of him, he forced his hands to unclench, barely containing a slight tremor as he lifted the veil from her face. The moment he met her gray eyes, his knees nearly buckled at the strength of the emotion that washed over him.

Nate had considered that his bride might be sad or frightened or even the slightest bit relieved.

He had never considered that she might be angry. But here she was, so full of rage and staring at him with a chin raised in defiance—the most beautiful thing he had ever seen.

Even more unexpected than the realization that she was mad at him was his own reaction. He was relieved.

The ceremony passed with little fanfare, considering how dramatic Ms. Cook's entrance had been. Nate drowned out the priest's words, instead thinking of the rage he still sensed spilling from the woman next to him, disproportionate in intensity to her small stature. He had somewhat closed off his Talent, making the sensation far more manageable, but it was still noticeable.

Try as he might, though, he could not figure out why she might be so incensed. Sure, marrying him was not ideal, but if she should be mad at somebody, it should be her father. After all, the threat of being hanged by the Royal Police if her Talent should be discovered was Chief Cook's fault. Nate had given her a way to escape that threat, even if it was just the best solution he had been able to think of in the split second he had to act when he spotted her across a crowded room.

But Nate felt an odd knot release in his chest as Contessa bit out her vows next to him. The fears that had kept him from finding his bed last night were reduced to mist in the heat of her ire. He would not be bringing home a bride who feared him or was too disgusted to even look at him. Her anger was a balm, because it was a feeling he knew well. He carried it with him just as consistently as all nine of his knives.

Perhaps they would be able to come to an understanding.

That was the thought he carried in his head as he forced himself to move slowly and steadily as he gently and swiftly kissed his bride, trying to focus on anything—the weight of his knives at his wrists or the watchful eyes of Chief Cook—other than the delicate softness of her lips and her sharp intake of breath as he pulled away.

Before he could second guess himself, he took her hand and led her down the aisle into a night that still seemed awkward and bleak. But now, he carried the tiniest bit of hope.

Nate stared at the cake before him for a moment before darting a look at Ms. Cook—Mrs. Woodrow, he corrected—beside him out of the corner of his eye. She lifted her fork to her mouth and took a perfectly dainty bite of the immaculate white confection before dabbing her lips with a napkin.

He set down his fork, deciding it was better to not attempt eating in such company. Growing up on the streets of the Lower City, combined with his disfigurement giving him the tendency to spew crumbs as he ate, his table manners left something to be desired.

Instead, he sat and waited as patiently as possible as his bride and all her guests enjoyed the banquet. For long minutes, he wished for it to be over, until the musicians in the corner started to play, and he realized he would prefer awkward silence to what was about to come next.

The first dance.

With the heaviness of somebody marching to war, Nate pushed to his feet and offered his hand to his new bride. She started for a moment, as if she hadn't remembered that this would be happening, before carefully laying her gloved hand in his. When he closed his fingers, they completely enveloped her own.

Nate swallowed thickly and led her to the dance floor as the string quartet played the opening notes to a sedate waltz. He did not look forward to embarrassing himself in front of Mrs. Woodrow and her friends. His life had left him lacking even more dancing skills than table manners. He had asked for this wedding to aid her, though, and he would continue to play the part.

As they started to move, Nate's fears of being an inadequate partner to a proper lady were dashed and replaced by the dawning of a new horrific realization: She could not dance either.

While Nate at least had a sense of balance and rhythm from years of fighting, Mrs. Woodrow seemed to lack even that, and stumbled as they moved through the first steps—not that Nate could blame her for tripping in skirts that voluminous.

Nate tightened his arm around her waist so she wouldn't fall, pulling her closer to him. In response, her gaze snapped to his chest and her fingers tightened where they rested at his shoulders. Suddenly, Nate was forced to unstick his tongue from the roof of a very dry mouth.

For the next three minutes, he thought only of the pattern of steps, focusing painstakingly on where to place his feet and not of the warmth of Mrs. Woodrow's silhouette pressed against his front.

He never in his life thought he would be grateful for Chief Cook, but when he stepped in to take Mrs. Woodrow away for the next dance, an unprecedented wave of relief washed over him. As the next dance started, Nate beat a hasty retreat to the edge of the dance floor where he quickly located a drink and planned to camp out in solitude for the rest of the evening.

For the first time since he had seen her, Nate was alone with his wife—a word that held so much weight and yet did not feel real—and the silence in the carriage was deafening. He hadn't planned on saying much to the freshly minted Mrs. Woodrow, thinking that she would want little to do with him after getting out from under Chief Cook's watchful eye.

Still, she stared at him expectantly from across the carriage, which now seemed much smaller than with just him and Kristoff this morning. Nate's mouth went dry as he searched for something to say. Instead, he found himself looking out the window, trying to untangle the odd web of unease and determination seeping across the carriage from his wife.

He certainly did not want her to feel uneasy, so he crammed himself into the corner as thoroughly as possible, and let the silence persist.

"It was a lovely party."

Her voice nearly made him jump, and he tore his gaze from the window to look at her. Mrs. Woodrow's tone was painfully polite, but he sensed an edge to it as lethal as one of his knives.

"Do you generally enjoy parties?" he asked dumbly, unable to think of something clever to say.

She blinked as if surprised by the question. "No."

"Neither do I," he admitted. Another thing they seemed to have in common.

Afraid of staring and deepening her discomfort, Nate wrenched his gaze away from her mouth, her pink lips currently in a perfect little "o" of confusion, in favor of staring at the window again.

The rest of the short ride passed in silence, but Nate remained terribly aware of Mrs. Woodrow's presence—the light sigh of her breaths, and the rustle of silk every time she moved.

By the time they reached his home, Nate was ready to fly out of his skin. He jumped from the carriage before it had come to a full stop, leaving Mrs. Woodrow to climb down on her own. The front door swung outward as he approached it, flung open excitedly by Julia. He ducked around her quickly, knowing that she was bouncing with anticipation of meeting Mrs. Woodrow, and would be much more interested in her than him.

Likely Mrs. Woodrow would find Julia much better company than him as well. Behind him, Julia introduced herself and the women began to chatter. He ignored them in favor of shucking his coat and marching up the stairs.

He headed straight to his bedroom without pausing, as if putting as much distance between him and his wife might erase the feeling of her in his arms when they danced. With a huff, he kicked the bedroom door closed behind him and continued to the bathroom.

He did not spend much time at home, but he had to admit that he appreciated the luxury of his bath. After fiddling with the knobs, he began shucking his clothes and unstrapping his knives, stacking them in a teetering pile on the counter.

Wasting no time, he lowered himself into the water, embracing the scalding temperature against his skin. As soon as it was high enough, he dunked his head under the water, closing his eyes and lingering at the bottom of the tub.

He floated there, trying to let this moment of peace clear his mind. Instead, it kept drifting to the woman down the hall who would be getting ready for bed, taking off that ridiculous dress and only wearing a thin nightgown.

Even now, although he was not close enough to parse out her emotions, he could feel her presence. Normally, several rooms away would be too far for him to feel the mental weight—and the Talent—of a near stranger. But nothing about his new wife was as he expected.

Still underwater, Nate scrubbed his hands over his face.

This morning, he had worried about how his bride would feel about him—if she would be afraid or repulsed or even completely indifferent.

Somehow, he hadn't had the sense to worry that he might like her.

Little Red Shadow

Book Two

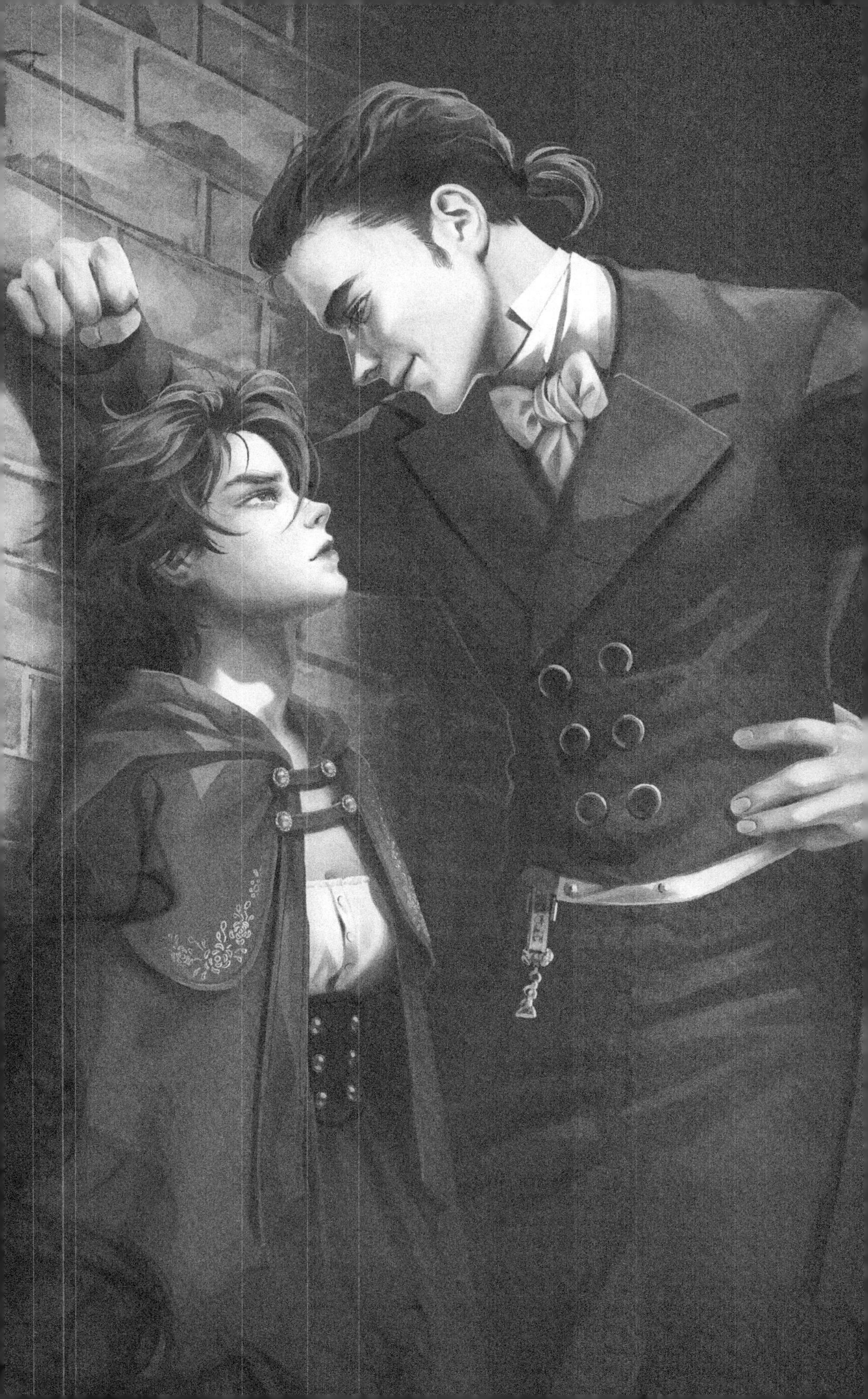

Chapter One

The ball would have been lovely if Scarlett wasn't expecting to be killed at any moment. Or rather, she anticipated somebody attempting to kill her, but she had no intention of letting them succeed.

Scarlett wove through the crowds of society's finest, gowns and jewels glimmering gaudily under crystal chandeliers that had been hung in the garden of all places. She shoved down the instinct bubbling up in her chest, telling her to cling to the edges of the party where she could listen to conversations unnoticed. Instead, Scarlett held her chin high, causing her feathered headdress to flounce above the socialites' heads despite her small stature. The blue silk of her voluminous skirts cut a wide swath through the crowds.

Heads turned as she walked, gossip tittering behind gloved hands. Scarlett fought to keep her shoulders square, reminding herself they weren't really looking at her. When she passed by, all they saw was the prize of the social season, with a dowry to match.

A bolt of energy shot up Scarlett's spine as she caught the assassin's attention, the back of her neck prickling as his gaze fell on her. A nervous shift and a hand sliding into a coat as if to grasp a weapon, and she knew she had found her mark. It took all of Scarlett's self-discipline to maintain her composure as she let her eyes drift up to the lower half of the man's face, not quite reaching his eyes. She offered what she hoped was a coy smile befitting a lady of her standing. If she hadn't known he was the would-be killer before, the tight twist of his mouth that passed for a smirk would have given him away.

Scarlett didn't linger, instead continuing to pick her way through the crowd. She loosened the reins on her instincts, letting them guide her to the edges of the revelry, where the light from the chandeliers was thin and the shadows could partially obscure her. A prickle on the back of her neck told her the man still followed, but at least now other partygoers were less likely to see her disappear with a man who turned up dead later. Scarlett ignored the sharp ache stabbing the base of her skull at that thought, instead slipping into the privacy of the hedge maze.

The dense shrubbery muted the sounds of the revelry, lending a distant feeling that helped her focus on the task at hand. Having space for something as frivolous as a hedge maze in the tight quarters of London struck Scarlett as ostentatious, even if it was lovely, but she was glad for the cover. She rounded a few corners, carefully listening for the sounds of couples stealing an illicit moment, breathing a sigh of relief when she heard none. Instead, boots tromped at the entrance to the maze, and she frowned at the would-be assassin's lack of stealth. Still, it would make her job easy.

Darkness curled around Scarlett as she stepped back into the shrubbery, urged on by her Talent, melding her midnight blue dress with her surroundings. Here in the shadows, she felt the most at ease she had all night, even as she slipped a knife from her lacy sleeve.

The tromping footsteps came closer, and her mark rounded the corner. He passed by her hiding spot, not looking in her direction, a small pistol raised in his hand. Scarlett coiled in on herself, ready to pounce, when the moonlight shimmered on the ornate barrel of the gun, illuminating the man's shaking hand.

Scarlett hesitated, taking a small step instead of leaping forward, knife first, as she had intended. That movement was enough to alert the man to her presence, and he spun to face her, gun inches from her face. They stood frozen like that for the barest of moments, although time seemed to stretch, looking into his wide dark eyes. Then Scarlett grabbed his wrist and twisted, digging her fingernails into the soft flesh between tendons. The pistol dropped from his grasp as he let out a breathy curse, and Scarlett snatched it from the air with her other hand before it could hit the ground.

The man's hands flew up in surrender as Scarlett leveled both weapons at him and got her first good look at his face. His full lips were parted in shock, but his eyes held something softer—something that looked strangely like relief, which was odd considering Scarlett could end his life at any moment. His nose lacked any of the tale-tale crookedness of repeated breaking, and the way he held his shoulders in his navy velvet waistcoat spoke of a comfort with fine clothing. This was no street brawler or undercover gang member before her. As she contemplated him, his dark brows drew together as he regarded her in return.

"You're not Georgette Ward." His voice was surprisingly steady.

Scarlett didn't attempt to deny it.

"You're not an assassin," she fired back, chancing a glance at the pistol in her hand. The flowery engravings along the barrel and the finely polished surface marked it as a dueling pistol, and not something to be hastily tucked into waistbands of lower city thugs.

"What gave me away?" he sighed, cocking his head as if he were bemoaning losing at a hand of cards and not attempted murder. If Scarlett had any doubts about her snap decision against slitting his throat, they were fading fast.

"Why do you want to kill Georgette Ward?" Scarlett demanded instead of answering his question.

"I have nothing against her, even if she is a little angelic for my taste," the man hedged, taking a shuffling step back. Scarlett matched his movement, not willing to let him forget about the gun pointed at his face.

"If you have no quarrel with her, then why follow me in here, thinking I'm Ms. Ward, with a gun drawn?" Scarlett's tone was icy, even as she was tempted to believe the man before her. The anger that boiled under her skin at the thought of a threat to Georgette's life cooled in the face of his manner. He didn't strike her as a killer, and Scarlett was far too familiar with the lifeless look of an assassin's gaze.

"I personally wish her no ill, but somebody else wants her dead, and they've made it my business," he said.

"The Wolves." It wasn't a question. The clawed pawprint on the bottom of the threatening letter Georgette had received made that part clear enough. It was why a ruthless street gang was after a socialite who had never even set foot in their territory that Scarlett couldn't puzzle out. The scribbled mess slipped through Georgette's open window as she slept hadn't even demanded money or favors.

"I'm not a Wolf," the man insisted, "I've just had some unpleasant run-ins with them. I'll even let you inspect my body to see I carry no gang tattoo, if you ask nicely."

The roguish wink he offered would have been enough to make Scarlett roll her eyes if his exaggerated manner hadn't made it clear he didn't ever take himself too seriously, even when flirting with a would-be murderer. Clearly not somebody well acquainted with the harsh realities of gang life.

"If you're not a Wolf, then who are you?"

"I could ask the same thing, considering you're clearly not Ms. Ward. But since I am polite, I'll have you know that I am Lord Benedict Pearce. Pleasure to make your acquaintance." He offered one of his hands to shake, but Scarlett's grip was full of weapons. Still, she let the gun and the knife drop to her sides. She was far less comfortable threatening the younger son of a duke than she was another piece of lower city scum. Now that she thought of it, alone with the son of a duke holding multiple weapons was not a position she wanted to be caught in.

"And you are?" he pressed.

"A friend of Georgette's," was all Scarlett offered. "And if you or any of your Wolf friends come after her again, I won't hesitate to start relieving you of body parts."

With that, Scarlett stepped back into the darkened passage in which she had hidden before. A flick of the wrist was all it took for shadows to leap into action, thickening until she was all but invisible.

Looking startled, Lord Pearce started after her, only to find the narrow row of hedges deserted except for darkness. He jogged down the pathway he thought she had escaped through, and Scarlett pressed against the leafy wall to let him pass, before doubling back to escape the maze.

As Lord Pearce passed, Scarlett thought she heard him mutter something under his breath sounding vaguely like "not friends with Wolves." Scarlett kept her shadows gathered around her as she ducked back into the garden, just enough to make her appear like a dark flicker to anybody that might look in her direction. She shoved her knife and the stolen pistol into her bodice as she picked across the lawn. Instead of heading back to the party in the main part of the garden, she darted to the back fence before launching herself upward to climb over it—a task that would have been much more difficult if she hadn't insisted on wearing her pants under the skirts. Still, she heard a rip as a loose piece of lace caught on a wrought iron pole, and she made a mental note to apologize to Georgette for damaging her dress.

It was only a handful of moments before Scarlett pushed through the doorway to a cellar a few blocks away and let out a sigh of relief as she threw the bolt behind her. As soon as she knew she was alone, she tore the elaborate wig off her head, dropping the mass of chestnut curls unceremoniously on a crate beside her. Shaking out her own mousey brown hair, ends just tickling her ears, restored a sense of normalcy to an evening full of surprises. Scarlett was no longer comfortable with the weight of headdresses and sculpted hairstyles, making the weight of her disguise a constant reminder of a life she had left behind.

She moved on to unlacing the dress, pushing the stiff fabric down her hips and pulling on the loose gray shirt she had stashed here earlier. Fabric that had once been white and crisp now draped against her skin, soft with years of daily wear. She glanced at the dueling pistol laying atop the heap of skirts, gleaming gently in the line of moonlight shining in through a gap in the doorframe. Scarlett considered for a moment before snatching it up and shoving it in her belt. It could fetch enough money to pay her rent at Granny's for a year.

Transformation complete, she shoved the discarded disguise into an empty barrel, making note of where it was so she could tell one of the Wards' manservants where to fetch it later. The weight of makeup still itched at her eyes and cheeks, and Scarlett scrubbed at it idly with her sleeve as she exited back onto the street, more in her element than she had been in hours.

The sound of a carriage clattering across the cobblestones approached. Scarlett darted through the dark patches between the flickering streetlamps so they wouldn't see her pass, making her way down the street as little more than a wraith.

"You know we have a front door," Georgette pointed out as Scarlett tumbled through the bedroom window, as she did every week when Scarlett made a late-night visit. It passed as a greeting between the two of them now, and Scarlett simply shrugged, as she always did.

"I'm assuming if you're here and whole, that the ball went as planned?" Georgette stood from her dressing table and pulled her silk robe more tightly around her, inspecting Scarlett with a worried gaze. Scarlett held out her arms, displaying her lack of injuries, and Georgette's round face relaxed.

"My mother and father still aren't home. I assume they're still at the ball trying to act as normal as possible to not give you away, although they will have to come up with some excuse as to why they came with a daughter and are leaving without one," Georgette fussed, pulling Scarlett farther into the warm bedroom, away from the chill drifting in from the still-open window.

"They'll just say you felt faint and went home to lie down," Scarlett assured Georgette. "It won't be hard to believe with how delicate you look and how tight you wear your corsets."

Georgette huffed in feigned exasperation. "I'm not as much of a princess and you and my parents seem to think I am, you know."

Georgette's appearance undercut her statement, with chestnut curls framing a face so pale and so fine-featured, it would be perfectly suited to a porcelain doll if not for her tendency to grin so wide you could count her teeth, or to scrunch up her nose when she was amused. The only reason Scarlett was able to successfully impersonate her was their similar heights and the fact Georgette hadn't been out in society for long enough for everybody to recognize her easily. She had only attended a few parties before the mysterious death threat confined her to her house. Still, it had taken a lot of powder to cover Scarlett's freckles enough for the disguise to be passable.

At the reminder, Scarlett rubbed at her itchy face with a sleeve, probably only making her face dirtier.

"Come here and I'll get that makeup off, now that you've already smeared it all over yourself. You can tell me what happened while I work, and I'll feel better if my hands are busy."

Scarlett did as she asked and sat down on the stool at the dressing table while Georgette dampened a cloth in the bowl on her washstand.

"Was there really an assassin?" Georgette murmured in a tremulous voice as she dabbed at the kohl around Scarlett's eyes.

"I wouldn't call it an assassin, but they did send somebody with orders to frighten you." Scarlett couldn't quite say he had been ordered to kill her, even though the threat to Georgette's life had been clear in the letter. Her life was just so soft and gentle, Scarlett couldn't bring herself to mar that any more than her presence already did.

"So, the Wolves did manage to infiltrate the ball." Georgette's voice was hardly more than a whisper.

"Not quite. They seem to have a man on the inside who they're having do their dirty work. Probably blackmailing him or having him rough you up as repayment for some corrupt business deal," Scarlett reflected, thinking about how adamant

Lord Pearce had been the Wolves were no friends of his. Still, he had pointed a gun at her.

"If he's not a Wolf, maybe he will tell you why they're after me. And if he's not actually a gangster, he could just be a good man caught in a bad situation," Georgette insisted.

Scarlett smiled at her optimism, even as she bit her tongue to keep herself from pointing out that "good people" were the reason she was a lower city gang member herself.

"I'm not sure how much they've told him, but I'll see what I can do."

Georgette beamed as if the whole issue had been resolved and those who wanted her dead weren't still at large. The sight of it made Scarlett's chest warm even as it ached. It was that optimism that kept her coming back to visit her oldest friend every week, even when she had sworn off high society. Georgette was the one bright spot keeping her from slinking into the shadows of the slums and embracing the future as a lower-city gangster she knew to be inevitable. Scarlett was aware it couldn't last though, as the amount of blood on her hands grew. Sometimes she thought she should climb out Georgette's window and never come back, but she wouldn't do it now, with her life in peril. If some of the scars on her conscience could come from protecting Georgette, then she would consider them more well-earned than the rest.

"Do you want me to ring for some tea while we wait for my parents to return?" Georgette offered as she wiped the last of the red paint from Scarlett's lips.

"I need to get home," Scarlett declined as she examined herself in the mirror to find the unassuming lower city girl returned. "I'll leave a note for your father about how it went and let him know I'm still working on uncovering the Wolves' motives."

"Of course." Georgette didn't seem the least bit surprised by Scarlett's refusal of tea. "With how hard you work, I'm sure you have to get up early. At least take this for your breakfast." She held out a packet of brown paper to Scarlett. "I had Cook make them up since I know they're your favorite."

Scarlett took the package even as she insisted, "You shouldn't have."

"I know, but I do anyway." Georgette smiled. This was one of their rituals too.

With that, Scarlett shoved the package in her shirt for safe keeping, finding it still warm against her skin and catching a whiff of the buttery scent of kippers. Her mouth watered, but she had places to be, so she would eat as she went.

With a final wave, Scarlett clambered back out the window, shimmying down a drainpipe before dropping the last few feet to the lawn. The guard on the ground jumped and whipped around but lowered his cudgel upon seeing Scarlett. Even if they were there to keep out thieves and would-be murderers, Scarlett creeping through the Wards' garden was a common sight. They knew she was a tame gangster.

Scarlett gave a mock salute to the familiar guard before ducking out through a gap in the hedges and turning her steps towards the lower city. After all, the night was young and the Talented of the lower city never slept.

The Roost was only a fifteen-minute walk from the Wards' mansion, but it might as well have been a world away. As Scarlett wolfed down her kippers, the neat brick homes with manicured hedges became more and more cramped, eventually giving way to wooden slat houses that looked as if they stayed upright only by virtue of leaning on each other. The horse-drawn carriages of socialites coming home from evening festivities were replaced by carts pulled by worn-down donkeys and thugs throwing dice on street corners. Even the air was different here, hazy with the smoke from the nearby factory district, cut with a sharp breeze from the docks.

Scarlett slipped into the Roost to be instantly accosted with the racket of gambling and fighting, while the light afforded by the oil lamps hanging from the ceiling was only slightly more than that in the street. Scarlett didn't mind the dark though, slipping into it like a well-worn coat that made her practically invisible, barely worth a second glance.

Of course, some people still spotted her.

"You're late," barked Jason from behind the bar, folding his arms in a way that made his biceps bulge, distorting the vulture inked on his upper arm—not that it was a very well-done tattoo to begin with.

"I had some family business I had to deal with," Scarlett defended, sliding up to the counter but not taking a seat on the empty bar stool.

"Ain't no family here besides the Raptors." He snorted, retrieving a sheaf of papers from underneath the bar and sliding it across to her. "Amos didn't want to wait for you. Left this here and told you that you better get it done by morning, no matter how much 'family business' you have."

Scarlett paid him no mind, flipping through the envelopes, seeing mostly names she didn't recognize, although a few names that rang a bell from the middle and even upper city.

"Just more messages tonight? Amos hasn't asked me to lift any jewels in a while," Scarlett mused.

"Lot of people haven't been paying up at the gambling tables recently." Jason commented with a shrug, grabbing a dusty glass to polish with an even dirtier rag. "These little messages normally do the trick. Nothing like waking up with a letter on the pillow next to them to scare a mark into coughing up."

Scarlett shoved the envelopes into her shirt, not one to turn down a reprieve from theft. After all, delivering threats to those who owed money without being seen was far less likely to turn violent than a burglary. Still, the letters sealed with the curled talon of the Raptors looked uncomfortably like the threat found at Georgette's window a few days earlier. Stealing and passing messages for the Raptors was what kept her safe in the lower city, and her Talent with the shadows made her perfect for the job.

"Mind if I take the back way?" Scarlett inclined her head towards the stairs leading up to the rooms where most of the Raptors lived. There was a window overlooking a roof there, useful for starting her night creeping above the city unseen.

"Course." Jason shrugged. "Although I don't know why you insist on renting at Granny's when you could just stay here. You've got the tattoo already."

Scarlett shrugged off his comment, even as it made her skin crawl, and started weaving her way through rowdy drinkers to the back steps. Moving into the Roost was another step in her inevitable descent into her lower city life, and Jason was right. Maybe once she could be sure Georgette was safe, she would stop digging in her heels.

The sun peeked over the pointed towers of the palace at the top of the hill by the time Scarlett slunk back to Granny's. She wasn't surprised to see Granny sweeping the floors when she slipped through the doorway, although the rambunctious urchins who tussled in the safehouse during the day were absent. She didn't know if Granny stayed up exceptionally late or woke up early, but Scarlett never seemed to catch her sleeping.

"Rent's due at the end of the week," the wizened woman barked, beady eyes flicking up briefly as Scarlett entered, before returning to her work. Her skin looked as rough as the wooden slats she swept, frown permanently etched on her face like a knot in a plank. Scarlett wasn't deterred by her sharp manner, finding it comforting in its familiarity.

"I'll have it to you this afternoon," Scarlett promised as she passed, heading for the steps in the back.

Granny just offered a grunt in response as Scarlett began trudging up the stairs, legs heavy from a long night of climbing up trellises and crouching on rooftops. As she unlocked her door, she hissed at the pulse in her fingertips where her nails had broken off as she clawed up a windowsill.

As she pushed into her room, barely big enough for a narrow bed and her trunk, Scarlett was tempted to collapse on her mattress face first and pass out just like that. Only habit carried her through her ritual.

She kicked open the chest at the foot of her bed, digging under her change of clothes to find the leather pouch hidden beneath. She fished it out, noting how light it had become in the past years, before dumping the contents on the threadbare mattress.

It didn't even take a minute to count the coins within. Enough for one last month at Granny's. A room in the Roost and a life running jobs for the Raptors now breathed down her neck. The money once intended for her dowry had allowed Scarlett to delay the inevitable, give her a choice for a time—but it was just an illusion. The Osprey tattooed on her shoulder blade gave her away as a member of the lower city gangs anyways.

Still, she was eternally grateful to Granny for letting her rent this room for as long as she had. It was a morning much like this when she had stumbled across Granny's threshold after wandering the streets for a night. Seeing the mud under her fingernails and the tear tracks on her face, a well-meaning urchin had pointed Scarlett towards Granny's, saying it was the safest place for runaway factory workers. She hadn't corrected him but staggered gratefully towards the promise of warmth and a place to sit down.

Granny had been about to snap at her to make herself useful the second she opened the door but stopped when she saw her. Scarlett's fine dress and pale skin had given her away as different from the normal urchins stopping in to scrub pots for a loaf of bread. Granny had taken pity on her, helping her blend with the other youth on the streets of London, even offering a few pointers on how to pick pockets. Allowing her to mix with the others until she found a gang that would make use of her Talent in exchange for protection from the Inquiries and even worse fates. Everybody in the lower city called her Granny almost ironically in reference to her harsh manners, unsure if she even had a name beyond that, but Scarlett knew the name fit.

Gathering up the handful of coins, Scarlett shoved them back into the pouch. Thoughtfully, she pulled the dueling pistol she still carried from her waistband, turning it over to examine it. She could still sell it. Maybe make enough to stay here for another year, although it wouldn't change much in the long run. Something about the thought of parting with it set her teeth on edge as well. Probably because it was the one clue she held to tracking down Georgette's would-be assassin.

Too tired to consider further, Scarlett hid the gun and the pouch back in the bottom of her trunk, catching a brief glint of the crimson fabric at the bottom——the one hidden treasure she allowed herself. Before she could think on that too long, she shed her clothes and finally collapsed onto the bed, letting sweet darkness overtake her mind.

Chapter Two

Scarlett dropped a handful of coins, the last of her dowry, on the counter as she left that afternoon. Granny snatched them up to count and pocket before the sharp-eyed children loitering about could filch any away. There were already several accomplished pickpockets among them, always happy to practice their skills. Scarlett kept the pistol well-hidden under her coat, where it was shoved into the back of her trousers.

Scarlett considered her path after pushing out the door into thready afternoon light, the sun obscured by smoke belching from the chimneys of nearby textile factories. She turned towards one of the shops where the Raptors pawned their stolen goods, and hesitated. Maybe Georgette was right about Lord Pearce being the key to uncovering the reason for the Wolves' threats. She didn't share the hope of him joining the cause from the goodness of his heart just because of his noble upbringing though. Perhaps the pistol could be used for leverage. There was always the possibility that he was wealthy enough to not be bothered by the loss of such a valuable weapon, but something this lovely might hold sentimental value.

Scarlett turned on her heel and trotted uphill towards the palace, around which the larger homes clustered. If the Pearces had not changed their London residence in the past few years, Scarlett remembered their street from her time living in the upper city.

Keeping her head down as she went, looking like a messenger boy or servant running an errand, she made her way into the wealthier neighborhoods with her hair tucked tightly into a cap. It wasn't the same invisibility afforded to her by her shadows at night, but the camouflage of anonymity was equally as familiar.

Reaching the ostentatious white stone house belonging to the Pearces, Scarlett paused to assess her strategy, bending down under the pretense of adjusting her bootlace. Before she could determine which window would best allow her to enter unseen, the clattering of carriage wheels forced her to leap out of the way.

A sleek black coach pulled up in front of the Pearce's house, and a man emerged through the house's front door. Scarlett quickly ducked her head, but not before catching sight of dimples and sparkling dark eyes. Lord Benedict Pearce.

Peeking up through lowered lashes, Scarlett saw him slide into the carriage before hearing a sharp wrap on the roof. The coach began trundling down the street. Scarlett only glanced at the house for a moment before trotting after. Thankfully the traffic at this time of afternoon was thick, forcing the large vehicle to maneuver slowly, while Scarlett could slip between pedestrians and carts. To her surprise, Lord Pearce's driver turned the horses towards the direction from which Scarlett had come. Around the point where the houses changed from stone to wood and there were no more window boxes to be seen, the carriage pulled to a stop.

Scarlett paused in the shadow of an open shop door, cap pulled low over her eyes, as Lord Pearce stepped down. He just offered his driver a jaunty wave before setting off on foot, continuing the way the carriage had been heading.

Trailing him down the street, casually weaving between the dense crush of people to remain unnoticed, Scarlett internally winced at Lord Pearce's manner. Even as he entered dodgier areas of the city, where hollow eyed urchins watched the silk trim on his top hat and his gold watchchain with open interest, he strolled as if he hadn't a care in the world. He turned towards Wolf territory, and Scarlett hesitated for only a moment. Trailing a mark in another gang's territory was dangerous, but it would only be a problem if Scarlett was seen.

Lord Pearce led her all the way to a large wooden building, the peeling paint on the door in the rough shape of a canine. As he opened the door to slip inside, the sound of dice being thrown and rowdy drinkers arguing, even at this time of day, drifted onto the street. Scarlett had never been here, but this must be the Wolves' Cave——just as the Roost was the center of the Raptor's operations.

As much as Lord Pearce had insisted he wasn't on good terms with the Wolves, all evidence now seemed to be to the contrary. If he was really working with them, the chances he knew of their motives—or their next move—were good.

Scarlett tugged on her sleeves, weighing her options, before pushing into the shop next door to the Cave. She pushed through the general store quickly, trailing the barest amount of shadows with her to avoid the shopkeeper's questioning, pleased she was distracted counting coins behind the counter. Finding the back door she sought, Scarlett pushed out into the alley and started climbing the wall of the Cave. If Lord Pearce was going to discuss a sensitive job with any of the Wolves lieutenants, they wouldn't chance doing it in the main gambling hall where they might be overheard. Scarlett would bet her dowry that Lord Pearce would be heading to one of the private offices on the top floors.

As her fingertips reached the third-floor windowsills, Scarlett paused to listen for sounds from within. Hearing none, she shimmied along the wall to the next windowsill, repeating the process. At the third windowsill, she paused as voices drifted to her ears.

"I'm surprised the headlines this morning weren't all about a murder at the Marquis's ball last night. Does that mean our little lordling didn't have the guts to do as he's told? Does he need a reminder of what's at stake?" The grating voice dipped low, rumbling in a way that set Scarlett's teeth on edge.

"No, I did as you asked, Gil." Lord Pearce's voice drifted through the window, conversational as it had been when Scarlett pointed a gun at his face in the garden. He was either uncommonly stupid or exceptionally brave. Scarlett hoped for his sake that it was the latter, because the longer she listened, the more the truth of his words regarding not being on friendly terms with the Wolves became apparent.

"Then she's dead?"

"Well, not technically, no."

"And what would you mean by 'not technically dead'?" The grating voice took on a growling tone.

"I guess I would mean that she's alive and well, but not for lack of trying. You see, there was some interference—"

A growl cut him off for a moment, and Benedict's words quickened.

"It would seem you warned Ms. Ward of her eminent demise. I would have thought announcing your intentions would be bad form as an assassin."

For all his bluster, a slight tremor permeated Lord Pearce's words. He was not as unperturbed as his flippant façade would imply. Scarlett's arms began to tremble as she hung onto the windowsill to listen, but she stayed frozen, straining to hear every word.

"You see, threats don't make somebody do what you want unless you...threaten them."

There was some scuffling followed by a grunt and the distinctive metallic sound of a blade being drawn.

"Would you like me to demonstrate how exactly we go about threatening somebody?" The grating voice was low enough that Scarlett could barely hear it.

"I think that won't be nec—" Lord Pearce cut out with a strangled gurgle.

Scarlett moved before she could think, hauling herself through the window and rolling across the floor. Before the men in the room could register her entrance, she swept one leg out, knocking the gangster's base from under him and bearing him down to the floor.

As she pinned him to the ground, there was a moment of silence where both men gawked at Scarlett, and she stared in horror at what she had done. Up in smoke were her plans for secrecy—for uncovering the gang's secrets without being seen. Instead, she had quite literally thrown herself into a den of Wolves.

As the tension of surprise faded from the room, the thug beneath her opened his mouth. In a flash, Scarlett unsheathed her knife and pressed the tip to his Adam's apple, raising her eyebrows in a clear intimation of *see what happens*.

Instead of shouting for help, the man licked his lips before asking, "And who the hell might you be?"

Scarlett opened her mouth, but no sound came out.

"Come, come. That's no way to greet a lad who clearly wants to make sure our business remains civil, Gil," Lord Pearce said from where he was still pressed to the wall before where she knelt above the man on the ground. The breathlessness of his voice betrayed the lightness of his words.

Scarlett looked up at him, meeting his gaze as her mind raced.

"So, who might I thank for volunteering to mediate our...disagreement?" Benedict prompted.

"Scarlett," she admitted, her cover already blown to bits by her dramatic entrance.

Lord Pearce blinked in surprise at the feminine tone of her voice before his lips parted in recognition.

"Ah, this would be the interference I mentioned." He gestured to her. "It seems this little bird has a vested interest in Ms. Ward staying alive. As you can see, she can be very persuasive when she wishes."

"What do you want with Georgette Ward?" The man beneath Scarlett growled.

"I need her alive," Scarlett said, grasping at straws. Searching for some explanation that would allow her and Lord Pearce to walk out alive.

"For what?" the man pressed.

"You know the Wards have an awful lot of money," Lord Pearce jumped in, saving Scarlett from her whirling thoughts.

"Killing Ms. Ward won't change how much money her father has," the man growled.

"Ah yes, but then nobody would get the young lady's dowry." Lord Pearce raised his eyebrows meaningfully at Scarlett, staring at her with his dark eyes as if trying to speak directly into her mind.

"And you plan to steal her dowry?" The man seemed dubious.

What Lord Pearce was suggesting finally hit Scarlett so hard she nearly gasped, but suppressed the noise in favor of saying, "If somebody were to marry her before she met an unfortunate end, the dowry would belong to them."

"And I have the advantage of being a highly eligible bachelor." Lord Pearce threw in a roguish wink for effect, even though the thug couldn't see him from where he lay on the ground.

Scarlett looked back down at the man beneath her, practically able to see the gears turning in his bald head.

"And the Wolves would get a cut of the dowry?"

"Even split," Scarlett chimed in, easing the knife from his throat and removing her weight from his torso as a sign of good will. Still, her fingertips itched with the shadows lurking behind her if things didn't go as planned.

Gil rubbed his jaw with a meaty hand as he considered.

"Could work..."

Scarlett surreptitiously leaned in to hear what he mumbled under his breath. Apparently the Wolves kept him around for his bulging biceps and not his brains, as he had to think out loud, even when the person who had just been threatening him with a knife could overhear.

"Add insult to injury..."

"She does have the largest dowry of any of the young ladies to come out this season, does she not?" Lord Pearce asked Scarlett conversationally, as if he were a gossiping matchmaker at a garden party.

"The Wolves are in," Gil announced grudgingly. "But if your little plot puts our plans in jeopardy, we won't hesitate to kill you along with the girl."

"Pleasure doing business with you, as always." Lord Pearce bent to pick up his top hat where it had fallen on the floor in the earlier commotion. Before he could dust it off and place it on his head, Scarlett grabbed his arm and towed him backwards towards the window.

"We'll be in touch," Scarlett said before toppling over the sill, dragging Lord Pearce with her.

He screeched for the brief moment they were airborne, but Scarlett could barely hear it over the ringing in her ears as she pulled shadows to her so thickly that they created a pillow of darkness around them. The shadows' physical forms dissipated as soon they were deposited on the ground, dusty but unharmed, although Scarlett kept enough darkness pulled close to keep them partially obscured in the hazy light of the back alley. She squeezed her eyes shut for just a moment against the incessant ringing that always accompanied the use of her shadows in a tangible form. It was sure to result in a headache tomorrow morning as well, but she would deal with that later.

"What was—"

"Stop talking and move, or that whole stunt will have been for nothing." Scarlett cut Lord Pearce off, hauling him to his feet and dragging them through the back door of the shop. To her surprise, since Lord Pearce hadn't seemed to shut his mouth even in the face of death threats before, he remained silent as Scarlett led them back onto the street and on a twisting path through several back alleys. She even cut through a gambling den run by the Scorpions to be safe. Scarlett only stopped when she reached a familiar warehouse with metal rungs running up the side.

She clambered up them quickly, hearing a curse behind her as Lord Pearce tried to follow, clearly less well dressed for pell-mell escapes from gangsters. Still, they would be safe on the roof of this abandoned mill, hidden in the shadow of the silo on top. Scarlett had laid low on this particular roof after dicey jobs a handful of times before.

Lord Pearce reached the top of the ladder long moments after Scarlett, giving her a moment to survey the surrounding streets from their vantage point for any signs of pursuit. Luckily, the pedestrians all seemed to be milling about doing their usual business. They were back in Raptor territory anyways.

"You're Talented," Lord Pearce remarked as he clambered onto the roof, resting his hands on his knees as he caught his breath.

"It's not illegal anymore," Scarlett snapped, hackles rising as she narrowed her eyes at Lord Pearce.

His fine coat was covered in a thin layer of dust, and his dark hair fell forward over his face, yet it didn't make him look disheveled. Somehow, Scarlett thought he would manage to look debonair in a potato sack, and it irked her.

"I know, it just explains how you were able to escape me in the garden last night so easily," Lord Pearce said.

Scarlett relaxed infinitesimally but remained on the balls of her feet, ready to run at a moment's notice if need be. Even if Talents had been legal for almost a year now, the habit of hiding her abilities ran deep. After years of the Inquiries—of hearing angry crowds yell *cursed* and *witch* as people hung—a new way of living was slow to take hold.

"While the display of your Talent just now was impressive," Lord Pearce continued on, seemingly oblivious to Scarlett's tension, "I do have to wonder at its purpose. Diving out a window is a wonderfully dramatic way to make an exit, but I think Gil would have let us use the door once we came to an agreement."

"I didn't want to be recognized walking through the Cave and have news of me being there get back—get to the wrong ears. Not to mention, they would have had us followed, and you and I need to have a private chat. Starting with why on earth you thought it was a good idea wandering into a gang hideout unarmed after failing on a job for them?"

Scarlett huffed and folded her arms, wondering why she was bothering to scold a near stranger for almost getting themselves killed. Probably because her reluctance to let him die forced her to give her game away to the Wolves.

"I wasn't unarmed. I had this." Lord Pearce dug around in his coat before producing a thin metal instrument. The duke's crest of a blossoming tree gleamed in brass on the handle.

"That's a letter opener," Scarlett pointed out.

"So it is. But I bet it could still cause quite a bit of pain if you jabbed it in someone's delicate bits." He pantomimed exactly where he planned to stab his assailants in dramatic fashion.

A laugh bubbled up unbidden in Scarlett's throat. She bit her lips to stifle the sound, but not before it rang through the air for a brief moment. He offered her another dashing grin with an eyebrow raised. His nose was too long and bent to be traditionally handsome, but it fit perfectly with his crooked smile.

"Besides, you relieved me of my much more effective weapon last night, Ms.... I'm sorry I don't think I caught your last name?"

"It's just Scarlett," she said, remembering the weight at the small of her back that was the dueling pistol.

"Well in that case, little bird, you may call me Benedict."

He sketched a polite bow as if Scarlett were a lady he was asking for a dance, even as she fished the pistol out of her waistband.

"I'm surprised you didn't sell it," he commented with raised brows upon seeing it.

"Me too," Scarlett admitted, offering the weapon to him handle first. Considering she had taken the liberty of unloading it earlier, it wouldn't do Benedict much more good than his letter opener at the moment. "That's two you owe me now."

"I think we're even on this most recent encounter actually," Benedict argued. "You may have tumbled in the window, weapons drawn like a ragamuffin savior, but my quick thinking got us the rest of the way out of that pinch."

"Well Benedict, your fast talking may have gotten us out of the Cave—"

"Thus proving that my mouth is more effective than any weapon I might have brought."

"—but it's only bought us time. The Wolves still want Georgette dead, and that is something I can't allow."

Benedict cocked his head to the side. "Who is Ms. Ward to you? Did her father hire you to protect her?"

Something inside Scarlett bristled at his casual assumption that she was no more than a paid bodyguard to Georgette, even though that was how she intended to appear. She purposefully made herself seem as distant as possible from the refined and intelligent Georgette.

"Something like that," she grumbled. "Either way, I don't trust the Wolves not to go behind our back and kill Georgette despite our agreement. She's in danger until I find out why they want her dead and foil whatever it is they're planning."

"Until *we* figure it out," Benedict corrected.

"*We?* I thought we just established that you are not prepared to take on these gangs when you thought a letter opener was an adequate weapon." Scarlett put her hands on her hips.

"Yes, but I did just promise the Wolves I'd seduce a woman into marrying me before disposing of her and keeping the dowry. I've just taken a very skillful swan dive from the frying pan into the fire, so I'm afraid whatever you're planning will have to include me to some degree," argued Benedict.

"Nobody is seducing Georgette!" Scarlett threw up her hands in frustration. "I don't think her father will even let her leave the house until her life is no longer in danger."

"Then I guess I'll have to seduce you."

Scarlett opened her mouth to retort and then choked as the full force of his words hit her. She had lost track of this conversation.

"You posed as Georgette before. I can pretend to court her when it's really you, just in case the Wolves decide to go back on their deal. If they do come after us, you can help us escape with your—" Benedict wiggled his fingers in an imitation of Scarlett's shadows. "And we can use the time together to uncover the Wolves' motives."

Scarlett blinked as she regained her composure and digested his words. She hated to admit that it was a good plan, or the beginnings of one at least.

"I'll have to talk to the Wards," Scarlett hedged. "They'll need to be aware to help with our ruse. I can meet with them tonight and form a plan." Her mind already whirring with thoughts, Scarlett began to back away.

"Wait." Benedict took a step forward after her. "How will I contact you?"

"You won't, I'll find you."

"You better, little bird. Ms. Ward's isn't the only life at stake here."

Georgette pulled her shadows around her like a cloak and jumped from the rooftop, but not before catching a flash of urgency in Benedict's usually teasing gaze.

Chapter Three

Georgette shoved a rumpled piece of paper under her pillow as Scarlett opened the window. She did her the courtesy of pretending not to notice. Instead, Scarlett busied herself closing the window and drawing the curtains behind her to keep out the chill of the evening.

"Did you talk to the man from the ball? I'm getting tired of being cooped up in here," Georgette said as soon as Scarlett was fully in the room.

"I did, but I'm afraid it'll be a little bit longer," Scarlett admitted, shaking her head as Georgette motioned towards her window seat. Scarlett's pants were filthy from her earlier adventure, and she didn't have it in her to soil the delicately embroidered pillow.

"It sounds like you made some progress then?" Georgette's round eyes held as much hope as ever. Scarlett's lips twitched at her unyielding optimism.

Before she could answer, a sharp rap sounded at the door.

"Georgette dear, is that Scarlett?" Mr. Ward's voice filtered through the wood. "The guards told me she just arrived."

Bouncing from the bed, Georgette opened her bedroom door.

"She was just telling me about the headway she made," she explained as her father stepped into the room. The stern look he perpetually wore under his bushy mustache stayed in place even as he gave Scarlett a polite nod.

"You would know when she was here more easily if she just used the front door," Georgette shot over her shoulder to where Scarlett still stood by the window. "Tell her she can use the front door, Father."

The firm set of Mr. Ward's lips softened just a touch, the way it only did when he talked to his daughter.

"She knows how to use the door," he said over the top of Georgette's dark curly head. As their gazes met, Scarlett nodded at their unspoken agreement. Mr. Ward knew that a public friendship with Scarlett would hurt Georgette's reputation, the only thing the sole daughter of a wealthy family really had. Even if his heart held too much kindness to send Scarlett away, Mr. Ward preferred their friendship to exist in the shadows. Scarlett preferred to remain an invisible companion as well.

"What intelligence have you been able to gather on the Wolves' motives?" Mr. Ward pressed, moving further into the room and shutting the door behind him. Of course, he saw the advantages of having a pet gangster as a family friend as well.

Scarlett launched into the tale of her afternoon, internally cringing at the part where she leaped into a dangerous situation with no plan at all. She tried to play it off as more calculated, as her not wanting to lose her only lead, but couldn't quite convince herself. Even as she talked, she tried to exude the sense that she had the situation under control, that the danger was minimal, to avoid frightening Georgette. As she gauged her reactions though, the girl simply listened with wide eyes, betraying nothing.

"And you and this Lord Pearce are prepared to pose as a courting couple while you continue to investigate? I'll not have Georgette endanger herself for a ruse," Mr. Ward said at the end of Scarlett's story. Georgette only chewed on her lip and stayed silent.

Scarlett nodded, even though it was the part of the plot she dreaded the most. Something about playing at being a society lady picked at an old wound in her chest the way running the streets of the lower city never could. Benedict didn't seem like the type to make it painless either, although wrangling his antics might serve as a distraction.

"In that case, I'll have some preparations to make," Mr. Ward said. "Why don't you two ladies work on picking out some dresses for Scarlett for her outings." With a kiss pressed to the top of Georgette's head, he swept from the room.

"I'm sorry this means missing more of the social season," Scarlett apologized as Georgette opened her wardrobe with a thoughtful expression. "And if it appears you're being courted by the younger son of a duke, it will probably scare away any other callers. I know your father wanted to see you married during your first season."

"Truth be told, I don't mind. I wasn't impressed by any of the men I danced with at the opening ball. Besides, I doubt Lord Pearce will scare other suitors away. He's known for leaving a trail of heartbroken ladies in his wake," Georgette commented, her tone light as she pulled out a moss green dress dripping with lace. The pink spots high on her cheeks gave her away though.

"Oh really?" Scarlett asked, her tone teasing.

"This would be perfect for a stroll in the park." Georgette held the dress up to admire, seemingly trying to change the subject. "Very public too, for any Wolves who might be watching."

"Are you sure your lack of disappointment about missing the season doesn't have anything to do with a certain art dealer's son?" Scarlett pressed, unable to help the smile playing at her lips.

"I haven't the slightest idea what you mean," Georgette said, although the appearance of dimples on her cheeks betrayed her amusement.

Scarlett, who had been edging towards the bed, quickly snagged the paper Georgette had stowed beneath the pillow. She held up the piece of paper triumphantly, yellowed and crinkled as if with repeated readings.

"My Georgie," she read in a sing-song voice.

Georgette squeaked indignantly and lunged across the bed, dress forgotten and falling to a heap on the floor. Even as she grabbed for the letter, Scarlett stepped back and held it aloft.

"I am travelling to Paris to ask my father for my share in the family business," Scarlett kept reading. "Once he does, hopefully I will return to you with a fortune more suitable to marry a lady—"

Georgette jumped, succeeding in wrenching the paper for Scarlett's grip.

"Ah, so you're waiting for dear Leon?"

Georgette smoothed her fingers over the ink on the page, as if checking the words were all still present, before folding it neatly on the well-worn creases.

"I'm not exactly in a hurry to rush to the altar with somebody else if that's what you mean," Georgette agreed.

"But he's been away for a while," Scarlett clarified, to which Georgette nodded. "That would explain why I haven't run into him sneaking down the trellis when I've come to visit recently."

"That was one time!" Georgette's voice was little more than a high-pitched squeak, and Scarlett chuckled. Seeing a pantsless Leon fall into the snow drift below the bedroom window in his hurry to escape notice had been the highlight of an otherwise dreary winter.

"Besides, I thought he'd be back by now." Georgette's voice dropped low. Scarlett leaned in and put a hand on her shoulder.

"That man is crazy about you," she said sincerely. She didn't know Leon well, but she had passed secret letters between the lovebirds enough to see what any blind person could: that Leon was smitten. "I'm sure he hasn't run off and abandoned you."

"Yes, but he has all these noble ideas. I'm afraid his father isn't going to agree to give him his rightful stake in the business, and he won't come back until he can make me a proper bride." Georgette's fingers fluttered anxiously as she tucked the paper back under the embroidered cushion.

"Paris is a long way," Scarlett said. "He's probably just traveling. Besides, maybe hearing that you're being courted by Lord Pearce will make him hurry home."

At that, Georgette's smile returned, wide enough to crinkle the corners of her eyes.

"Then we better get you dressed to impress."

Even with stopping to drop off a large bundle of dresses and cosmetics at Granny's, Scarlett still made it to the Roost earlier than she did the night before. The sight that greeted her when she entered made her glad of her punctuality.

"Ah, there you are!" Amos called from where he held court, sitting on the bar. "I hope you're ready for a bit more action than delivering unfriendly messages tonight."

Scarlett slid between two familiar brawlers who made room for her as she approached Amos. He leaned back, resting on his hands with his legs thrown wide in arrogance, the smile on his face as oily as his slicked-back hair.

"And here she is, the ace up our sleeve!"

In response to Amos's proclamation, the brawlers cracked their knuckles and flexed brawny biceps in anticipation. Scarlett resisted the urge to shift nervously in response to the crackling promise of violence in the air. You didn't survive as a Talented in the lower city by showing fear.

"What game are we cheating at tonight?" Scarlett asked, folding her arms.

"The Scorpions think they can carve out some of the Lions' old territory for themselves," Amos explained, his excited tone riling up the nearby Raptors even more. "The Wolves may have taken the majority of the territory left by the Lions, but we've claimed the factories down by the port. It's time to remind the Scorpions what's ours!"

"A fight?" Scarlett clarified, mentally checking for the weight of all her knives against her skin. One in her boot, two up her sleeves, two against her ribs, and a short blade against the small of her back.

"A negotiation." Amos's smile, wide enough to display several chipped teeth, held no reassurance. "Brandon has agreed to meet with me and three of my lieutenants at midnight in the alley off broad street to negotiate our territory. But if he doesn't agree to our terms, we're prepared to make him see things our way."

"Looks like you have your three lieutenants ready to go," Scarlett said, glancing at the men gathered around her. While they weren't Amos's most influential enforcers, they were certainly the largest. What they might lack in cunning they made up for in crushing strength.

"Oh Scarlett my darling, I don't intend on this being a fair fight." Amos chuckled in a way that indicated he thought he was being charming. Scarlett's top lip inadvertently pulled up into a snarl at the way he casually threw around pet names with her, and she willed her face into neutrality.

"You're going to work your magic and hide on the roof next door until the negotiations take a turn for the physical. Then you'll jump into the fray, and we have a one-man advantage." Scarlett nodded silently. She was used to this kind of task. The invisible lookout, the unseen reinforcement.

With that the small group set out of the tavern to hearty cheers and encouraging slaps on the back. Despite her apprehension, the encouraging whoops and pats on her shoulders relaxed some of the tension in her stance. The Raptors were as much of a family as she had these days.

The group made their way through the darkened streets towards the few blocks of warehouses and factories they would be fighting to claim tonight. The area had once been under the protection of the Lions, but since the end of the Inquiries and the pardon of the Lions' leader, Nathanial Woodrow, the gang had all but disappeared. Rumor had it that Mr. Woodrow and his wife were working to get all their former gang members legal work, or at least the appearance of it. As the only people to be officially pardoned for their actions during the Inquiries, Mr. and Mrs. Woodrow seemed determined to publicly distance themselves from criminal activity.

Now all the remaining gangs rushed to divvy up the abandoned territory. "Negotiations" like this were becoming weekly occurrences. The power vacuum left by the dissolution of the Lions and the death of the Rattlesnakes' leaders had lit the fuse on the powder keg that was the lower city.

The Royal Police, left in disarray after their former chief had been revealed as a murderer and sentenced to a life in prison, didn't have the manpower to suppress the infighting. As hard as the young Chief Joseph Thorne tried, much of the populace had lost faith in the police.

Approaching the alley where the meet-up was to take place, Amos motioned silently to Scarlett. With a nod, she broke off from the group, the cool whisper of her shadows brushing against her skin as she cloaked herself in darkness. Practically invisible, she darted over to the building bordering the alley. The climb up to the roof was quick thanks to an open window and the fact that it was only a single story high. Scarlett was grateful that the building was low enough that she likely wouldn't twist an ankle when she jumped down into the fray.

Once on the roof, Scarlett didn't straighten, instead sliding across the roof on her belly to peek over the edge. She kept the shadows pulled tight around her but left as much of herself hidden behind the ledge of the roof as possible. The darkness made her nearly impossible to spot, but the Scorpions would be expecting a betrayal, watching the surrounding areas closely. Scarlett scanned the surrounding rooftops in turn. The Raptors weren't the only ones known to be less than honorable. She only picked out four figures entering the alley from the far side to meet Amos and his enforcers.

Voices rumbled in the alley below, and Scarlett barely drew breath as she listened, alert for danger.

"—Wolves have taken most of the territory for themselves, even though our gambling dens are the closest," argued a voice that Scarlett didn't recognize. It must be Brendan, the leader of the Scorpions.

"Sounds like something you should take up with the Wolves." Amos's silky voice was unperturbed.

"We all know you're working with them, Amos, why else would you give up so much of this area to them without a fight?"

Scarlett's brows drew together. She hadn't heard about any agreement between the Raptors and the Wolves. Brendan must be desperate, grasping at straws.

"Please." Scarlett could practically hear the dismissive wave of Amos's hand. "They've started a new operation that's bringing in more money than the Wolves can spend. Even I know better than to challenge Fang when his pocket is newly bursting with unspent coin. That could buy him a lot of manpower."

"Which is why the rest of us need to split up the remaining territory fairly, to keep Fang's head from getting too big for his top hat," Brendan argued.

"How magnanimous of you to assume I'll play fair."

At that, Scarlett bunched her thighs under her, prepared to leap at the Scorpions from behind. What Brendan said next though gave her pause.

"And how stupid of you to assume I didn't know you were a double-crossing bastard."

Scarlett thinned her shadows enough to let her see out, just in time to catch a flash of silver from the roof across the way.

As the man on the opposite building aimed down the sights of his pistol, Scarlett's dagger flew into her palm. She barely took a moment to aim before flinging it across the gap of the alley. There came the wet thunk of the blade connecting with its mark, followed by the strangled gasp of surprising pain. The man made to turn and see where the knife had come from, but the leg with the handle sticking from it buckled under his weight. For a drawn-out moment, he teetered on the edge of the roof before tipping over the side. The sick crunch as he hit the dirt below raised bile in the back of Scarlett's throat. The world swam as she clambered off the rooftop. She'd done it again. She hadn't checked the surrounding rooftops well enough, and another man had died at her hands.

Barely registering the sounds of fists meeting flesh and grunts of aggression from the brawling lieutenants, Scarlett dropped from the roof and sprang across the courtyard to where her victim lay. Her heart stuttered back into rhythm again as his conscious gaze met hers and he moaned in pain. He was alive, although his ankle bent at an angle completely at odds with his leg. It was only a one-story drop, nothing that would kill a man.

Distracted in her relief, Scarlett didn't register the body encroaching behind her until it was too late. A massive weight crashed on top of her, pitching her forward and banging her head against the ground with a thud that echoed through her skull. The man resting on her back suffocated her even as he pinned her wrists to the ground, one in each meaty fist. Amos's brutal training kicked in without thought.

Scarlett shoved one of her arms forward, wrenching to the side as hard as she could. The sudden shift of weight forced her assailant to drop to his elbows. Pressing the advantage, Scarlett jammed her thigh up into his knee where he pinned her down, gaining the leverage to flip their positions. As she pinned him beneath her, Scarlett flung out a hand, curling tendrils of darkness leaping from her fingers to cling to his face. He instinctively clawed at the ethereal blindfold, but his fingers found no purchase. As he was distracted, Scarlett took the opportunity to ram her knee into his groin, leaving him incapacitated on the ground. Leaping to her feet, she whirled around to see how the rest of the Raptors fared.

Thomas, one of the Raptors' brawler twins, licked blood from a split lip as he faced off against the last Scorpion still on his feet. With the Scorpion's attention on Thomas, Scarlett unsheathed her blade. Just as the Scorpion swung for Thomas, fist whistling through the air with the force of his punch, Scarlett leaped on his back. With all the force she could muster, she clocked the bruiser on the temple with the hilt of her knife. He teetered for a moment, and Scarlett managed to jump clear before he crumpled to the ground.

The alley fell silent, and Scarlett glanced around to see all the Scorpions sprawled on the ground, blinking the sting of dust from their eyes. Timothy, Thomas's twin, pinched a bloody nose, but the Raptors all still stood. From how unrumpled Amos looked, Scarlett doubted he had even joined in the fray, his grin looking even slicker now than when they had left the roost.

Sauntering over to where Brendan lay on the ground, cradling a swollen wrist, he spoke down his nose at the fallen Scorpion. "This is our turf, and you better remember it. We have big plans, and you bugs will be stepped on if you don't get out of the way."

Chapter Four

As much powder as Scarlett patted on her face, she couldn't fully cover the bruise on her brow where it had met the cobblestones the night before. She winced at the press of the powder puff as she dabbed it against her brow, trying to pack on enough product to obscure the purpling blotch. Looking in the warped shaving mirror propped on her rickety bed, Scarlett sighed in defeat. Her attempts to beautify herself only succeeded in making her face look drawn and dirty.

Thankfully, Georgette had also lent Scarlett a feathered hat to add to her disguise. She would just pull it lower over her face than was fashionable to disguise her injury, as well as the fact that her features weren't quite as delicate as Georgette's.

For now, she tucked it under her arm, not wanting to don such a fine piece of clothing until she was closer to the park. As she tromped down the stairs, all the children milling about Granny's stopped what they were doing as they caught sight of her before dissolving into giggles. Scarlett tugged at the bodice of the lilac dress, overly conscious of how tight it nipped in at the waist where she usually hid herself in overly large shirts and bulky jackets. Her efforts only succeeded in pitching the already dangerous neckline of the dress even lower, exposing skin that rarely ever saw the light of day. As Scarlett huffed in defeat, Granny herself came around the corner, the sound of her cane rapping on the aged floorboards quieting the urchins back into their chores or games.

"It's nice to see you dressed up for once," Granny said, the corners of her already weathered eyes crinkling further in what was her version of a smile.

"Another day, another scheme." Scarlett shrugged.

Granny responded with a noncommittal grunt, but Scarlett could have sworn she saw the amused twinkle fade from Granny's eyes before she hobbled off to scold a ragamuffin for the way he wiped down a table.

Scarlett pushed out the door and into the bustle of the cobblestone street. Lifting her skirts, she picked carefully through the road so as not to damage Georgette's dress. Walking dressed as she was in the lower city drew lots of stares, and Scarlett's skin prickled in discomfort. She itched to cut through the side alleys and pick through the shadows where no one would spare her a second glance, but that only worked in her normal getup of a gang runner or messenger boy. Dressed as a fine lady, in all the regalia of the jewel of the season out for a stroll, there was no escaping curious eyes.

Luckily, she only had to walk a few blocks to the fringes of the middle city where Mr. Ward's carriage driver picked her up.

"Ms. Ward," he greeted with a knowing nod, hopping down from the driver's seat to give her a hand up into the carriage. Scarlett narrowly avoided catching and ripping the lace trim of the dress on the stair as she pulled them up into the box of the coach. She didn't wear so much fabric—or ride in carriages—very often anymore.

As the driver tapped the horses into motion and the wheels began clattering across the cobblestones, Scarlett spotted an envelope on the bench across from her. Upon examination, it had her name printed neatly across the back and carried Mr. Ward's seal. Breaking it open she read the contents, printed in Mr. Ward's impeccable cursive.

Lord Pearce has accepted Georgette's invitation to a promenade in the park today. She is sure to be the talk of the town after accepting his attentions in such a public manner.

Scarlett nodded and tucked the letter away in her skirts, pleased that Benedict was playing along with their ruse. Pushing aside the drape across the window, Scarlett watched the passing houses as the horses pulled the carriage into the upper city. Servants running errands for their distinguished families occupied most of the street here, bustling about with baskets of vegetables or wrapped parcels sure to contain the most fashionable dresses for upcoming parties. A few fine ladies strolled down the street, parasols shielding their delicate complexions from the reedy sunlight.

As Scarlett watched, a lone child with grubby hands slipped unnoticed through the busy street towards the pack of ladies. As he darted past the ladies and closer to the Wards' carriage, he tucked a scrap of fabric into his shirt. Seeing the pickpocket tuck away an embroidered handkerchief that would fetch enough coin for several meals niggled something nearly nostalgic in Scarlett's mind. The days of merely pickpocketing for the Raptors had been simpler, before the stakes were raised as Amos realized her Talent's usefulness.

The carriage turned off the road and into the drive of the sprawling park that occupied a large swath of the upper city. As it pulled to a halt, Scarlett spotted the man of the hour milling near the rosebushes at the edge of the path. He wore his dark hair loose, and it curled at the base of his neck beneath his top hat, a bit longer than was fashionable, but it suited him.

Scarlett shook herself and busied her hands with pinning the hat into her wig, pulling it forward while trying to push the feathers out of her face. When Mr. Ward's driver opened the door and sunlight pierced the darkness of the carriage, she could only hope she looked as elegant as Georgette would in her place.

Benedict turned from the rosebushes and greeted her with a smile that almost convinced her she could pass as one of the most desirable matches of the social season. He was a good actor, for all his bungled plans so far.

"Ah, Ms. Ward." He offered an arm to her with great ceremony, and Scarlett laid her hand in his elbow as delicately as she could manage. That part at least wasn't too difficult, as the one thing Scarlett did share with Georgette was a petite build. Where it made Georgette seem like a porcelain doll, it enhanced Scarlett's ability to slip under the radar. Now though, she felt multiple sets of eyes on her as Benedict led her onto the garden path.

"I'm glad to see you again so soon," Benedict continued conversationally. "You left me with a lot to consider after our last meeting, and I've thought of further questions."

"I'm sure those questions can wait." Scarlett surreptitiously dug her nails into his sleeve and glanced around at the others in the park. While they all gave her and Benedict a respectful berth, she wasn't convinced they couldn't eavesdrop if they wanted to. The gossips of the upper city were incorrigible. "After all, it's such a lovely day, and it would be a shame to distract ourselves from it."

Benedict chuckled, a free and musical sound like bells. It startled Scarlett enough from her inspection of their surroundings to look at him. He stared at her with open amusement.

"Of course. This outing is for pleasure, not business." The corners of Benedict's eyes crinkled in amusement.

Scarlett huffed. "Do you ever take anything seriously?"

"Not if I can help it." Benedict shrugged, his arm flexing under Scarlett's fingers.

"If you're not careful, it's going to get you into trouble one of these days," Scarlett said, a hint of very real caution underlying her generally light tone.

"Trouble seems to have a way of finding me whether I take things seriously or not. I refuse to give it the satisfaction of not seeing me enjoy everything to the fullest," Benedict argued.

"Is that how you came by your reputation of being a rake?"

"Oh no, I got that simply by being a rake."

Scarlett let out a short, surprised laugh for the second time in as many days at Benedict's antics. He looked down at her with a smile, seeming proud of her amusement. Seeing him for the first time in sunlight instead of a shadowy alley or hedge maze, she realized that his eyes weren't as dark as she had originally thought them, but instead a warm honeyed brown.

As she examined him, Benedict frowned.

"Let me help you with your hat," he offered. Scarlett moved to object, but Benedict was already adjusting the ornamental hat pin. "You know, you're supposed to show off the feathers, not pull them over your face like you're trying to mug somebody."

Scarlett bit her tongue to avoid shooting back that she didn't need to bother with a such a ridiculous hat to rob somebody.

As he repositioned the hat on Scarlett's wig, he pulled it off her brow, revealing the shadow of her injury under a thick layer of makeup. A frown creased his brow, and for a moment his hand drifted towards her face as if he planned to brush his fingers over it. Scarlett tensed, thinking that she should brush his hand away but standing as frozen as one of the statues scattered around the gardens instead.

A sudden wave of tittering passed through occupants of the path like a cat running through a flock of birds, and Benedict dropped his hand, Scarlett's injury apparently forgotten. Refocusing on their surroundings, Scarlett found the epicenter of the tittering to be a couple strolling down the path towards them. The wide brim of the man's hat partially obscured his face, but as he tilted his head to listen to something the lady was saying, Scarlett stiffened.

The thick scar running from his chin through his mouth and eye, distorting his face into a permanent snarl, marked him as Nathanial Woodrow. The former Beast himself, now the personal bodyguard to King Byron. The only other time Scarlett had encountered him, she hadn't seen much of his face, only his fearsome prowess with a knife as he quickly dispatched a mob of Rattlesnakes intent on taking more than money from a woman they were mugging. Even then, he couldn't be mistaken for anybody else with that scar and hulking build.

Scarlett didn't recognize the woman with him, but she would bet Benedict's purse it was his wife, Mrs. Contessa Woodrow. The lovely blonde on Mr. Woodrow's arm wasn't what Scarlett had expected for the woman who had discredited the police captain and was recognized for putting an end to Inquiries. Even now, she supposedly had the king's ear when it came to controlling violence in the lower city. From the way Mr. Woodrow's ruined face twisted into a smile as he listened to her talk, it was clear she was more than the delicate lady she seemed.

Everybody else on the garden path seemed equally curious about the couple, whispering shared rumors behind gloved hands.

"Advisor to the king—"

"—can read minds."

"Shouldn't be among decent society."

Benedict leaned in to murmur in her ear, close enough that Scarlett felt his breath on her skin. She shivered despite the warm sun warming the garden path. "Is Mr. Woodrow an...acquaintance of yours?"

Scarlett shook her head slightly, not taking her eyes off the couple, just as curious as everybody else. As she did, Mr. Woodrow's eyes darted to hers, and her breath froze in her chest for a second. His golden gaze met her own, and for a moment she wondered if he really could read her thoughts, so intense was his expression. His eyes narrowed and then darted between Mrs. Woodrow and Scarlett once before relaxing. Then they had walked past, the whole interaction only having lasted a second.

"I thought you might have run into him before in your...line of work?" Benedict murmured once more as he led them down a side path towards a trickling fountain.

"I only ever saw him in passing once," Scarlett admitted, keeping her voice hushed. "And he wouldn't have seen me."

They entered what was nearly a room made by hedges, deserted but for the statue of an angel standing at the center of the fountain, endlessly pouring its pot of water onto the tile flowers around its feet.

"Rumor has it the Lions were awash with Talented. I'm surprised you never worked for them."

"I wasn't so lucky," Scarlett admitted, the barest edge of bitterness creeping into her casual tone. The Lions had earned a reputation as a safe haven for Talented youths during the Inquiries, but Scarlett hadn't been wise to the ways of the lower city and ended up with a Raptors tattoo out of desperation. Other gangs would give you a haven from the Royal Police as long as you used your Talents to line their purses. If you refused, the reward for turning in a Talented to the police would be a fine consolation prize.

"Lucky?" Benedict echoed, bringing Scarlett's thoughts back to the garden path. "I'm not sure I would be able to consider working for Nathanial Woodrow as lucky. Most people still don't trust the Woodrows. I can't blame them either. He looks like he could rip you apart. Still, I don't suppose I envy them being the first openly Talented members of polite society, even if people don't actually know exactly what their Talents are."

Scarlett nodded thoughtfully. If the Woodrows couldn't integrate into the upper class with the king's explicit support, then there was no hope for anybody else.

"We should get back to the main path," Scarlett commented, tearing her mind from that grim train of thought. "If the whole point of this charade is to be seen, we aren't doing much good back here."

Benedict obligingly turned them back towards the hedges demarking the main concourse, lacy parasols just peeking over the top. Still, he chuckled. "True, but people wouldn't believe us having a proper courtship if I didn't try to sneak you away to steal a kiss. I do have a reputation to uphold after all."

Scarlett's cheeks felt warmer than was warranted by today's temperature at the mention of kissing, and she had to chide herself for reacting to Benedict's flirtatious manner. She wasn't some innocent noble woman, and he wasn't really flirting with her anyways.

"Be that as it may," she countered to distract herself, "I don't want to ruin Georgette's impeccable reputation."

"I suppose it is a challenge to balance my status as a known rogue and Ms. Ward's as an angelic flower. We will have to settle for fluttering eyelashes and gazes full of longing," Benedict concluded.

The laugh that tumbled from Scarlett's lips seemed a little more natural this time, if a bit truncated still, as if Benedict's presence somehow reminded her body it had the capability of making such a noise. On the other hand, Benedict's responding chuckle was warm and easy, as if joy just bubbled up naturally inside of him so often it had to spill out of his mouth.

"So, what do you do for amusement?" Benedict asked, so sharply changing the topic that Scarlett blinked in confusion for a moment.

"Are you really asking me that?" she asked. "I would think you wouldn't really want to know the answer."

"Well it's the type of question I would usually ask of a woman I'm courting, so it seemed appropriate."

"Why don't you ask me a question I'm less likely to answer with something…incriminating," Scarlett hedged. She was loathe to admit to both herself and Benedict that amusement hadn't been a part of her life for several years now.

"Alright." Benedict ran his fingers along the brim of his hat as he thought. "What is your favorite thing to eat?"

"Kipper."

A barking laugh tore from Benedict and several people strolling nearby turned to look at the sound. Scarlett ducked her head as if in amusement, letting the loose curls on the wig partially obscure her face in case anybody near was familiar with Georgette.

"All the wonderful foods out there, and you choose kipper?" Benedict asked in disbelief, "Not toffee, or petit fours, or even fine cheeses…but kipper? Seems rather mundane."

"I will not have my favorite breakfast besmirched." Scarlett turned up her nose as they strolled. "They're buttery and salty. When they're cooked just right with herbs they melt on your tongue and warm your bones perfectly on a chilly morning."

"I've never heard somebody wax poetic about kipper, but I guess when you put it that way..." Benedict shrugged.

They walked along for a few minutes in companionable silence, drawing interested glances from other couples and groups of ladies strolling around the park. If Scarlett's skin prickled under the scrutiny, Benedict seemed to bloom with it, offering easy smiles to those they passed. As aware as she was of the eyes of others, she was still more aware of the flex of Benedict's arm under her fingers as they walked. Even separated by his jacket and the lacy gloves Scarlett wore, her mind kept circling back to the casual touch.

Scarlett reminded herself that she touched people plenty for missions, whether she was punching them or bumping up against them to distract from her hands slipping their purse from their belt. Still, her mind insisted that this familiar touch was something else entirely.

As she stared at other couples to distract herself, Scarlett's gaze caught on a well-dressed woman standing on the edge of the path. On a gloved finger of an outstretched hand perched a sparrow, and the woman cooed to it softly. Scarlett frowned at the sight, wondering how the lady had coaxed the flighty creature. Perhaps it was a Talent with animals, one that she could risk people observing now that it wouldn't mean a march to the gallows. Still, it wasn't nearly as obvious as Scarlett's Talent, and people would take much more kindly to tame birds than curling darkness. Even if some were bold enough to subtly use their Talents in public, Scarlett was unlikely to ever be so lucky—not after using her shadows for so much harm. She tore her eyes away from the lady and the sparrow with gritted teeth.

With relief, Scarlett saw they had circled back to where the main path met the road, in view of where the Wards' man waited with the carriage. They stopped, and Scarlett wavered, but Benedict took the moment into his own hands.

"It was a privilege to accompany you on your turn around the park, Ms. Ward," he said, a little louder than the rest of their conversation had been but not loud enough to arouse suspicion that he was putting on a show. Then he lifted Scarlett's gloved hand from the crook of his arm before raising it to his lips.

Something about the mischievous twinkle in his eye and the way his breath warmed her fingers even through the gloves she wore locked Scarlett in place. His lips brushed across her knuckles, and Scarlett held her breath until he let go of her hand and stepped back. A stillness stretched between them before Scarlett finally inclined her head and turned to step into the carriage behind her.

As the Wards' manservant shut the door behind her, she reminded herself that Benedict was pretending to court her—not even her but Georgette. Still, if the way his gaze sent warmth skittering through her chest was any indication, he came by his reputation of being a rake honestly.

Chapter Five

Scarlett rested her chin on her knees and wondered about her decision-making skills. She sat with her legs tucked up, arms around her to hold herself in a tight ball as she sat in the rapidly lengthening shadow of a chimney.

When she had sent the note to Benedict via the Wards' servant, disguised as a letter from Georgette, this had seemed like a logical place to suggest a rendezvous. After all, the city square was easily found and not an area it would draw suspicion to be seen coming and going from.

Still, as Scarlett looked out over the open space below the roof she sat on, she regretted her choice. Despite how hard she tried to keep her gaze on the comings and goings of people from the square, colorful socialites and grime-crusted urchins alike, her focus kept darting to the dark patch in one corner. A stain marring the vibrancy of central London. The charred remains of the gallows.

For several decades, the gallows had stood tall, casting judgement over London during the Inquiries. The city would gather to watch the Talented hang, shouting at them that they were abominations—Cursed. It was in this very square where Scarlett had stood, clutching Georgette's hand tightly in her own, as her parents' lives were snuffed out before her eyes. She sometimes wished she had been able to squeeze her eyes shut like Georgette did as it happened, but she hadn't been able to bring herself to take her gaze from her parents even as their necks snapped.

She hadn't returned to this spot until just last year, the day King Byron declared an end to the Inquiries and made being Talented legal once more. Scarlett ran with the mob from the lower city that charged into the square with torches, setting the gallows ablaze. She cheered until she was hoarse as the flames reached high into the sky, covering the middle city in a blanket of smoke. Still, as the wooden beams broke and collapsed in on themselves, the crowd grew quieter as collective realization dawned on those of them who had lost loved ones—entire families—to the Inquiries.

Burning down the gallows couldn't bring anybody back from the dead. It couldn't undo things that had already been done. Just as the charred chunks of wood and soot stained the main square, the Inquiries had permanently stained lives, and the blackness couldn't be scrubbed clean. It seemed a little piece of that blackness had wormed its way into Scarlett's soul, living as the anger she constantly tamped down.

A panting from the edge of the roof behind her drew Scarlett from her reverie. She recognized the cadence as belonging to Benedict, despite having only encountered him a few times. Her time spying for the Raptors from her shadows honed her observation skills, and Benedict had somehow managed to permeate her awareness uncommonly fast. Probably because he had already caused her so much trouble.

"Do you simply fly up to these rooftops, little bird? Because you seem to have a habit of perching up high, and I'm not very accustomed to this much climbing."

Scarlett glanced over her shoulder and blinked at the sight that greeted her. Benedict had forgone his normal ensemble of velvet waistcoat and cravat, even leaving off his top hat. He had attempted to pull his hair back into a tail at the base of his neck, but the strands that weren't long enough to reach dangled in his face, and he swiped them out of the way. He was clearly sweating from the climb, and his light shirt clung to his chest and biceps.

Scarlett blinked and returned her gaze to the square. She saw plenty of Raptors strip their shirts entirely to fight or tend to scrapes and bruises. Still, for a gentleman like Benedict, it seemed borderline indecent to see him in such a state, perhaps because he was usually so meticulously dressed. Her mind seemed to catch on the flex of his arms as he wiped sweat from his brow, and she wrenched her thoughts free with great discipline.

"I've had a lot of practice," Scarlett said with a shrug as Benedict sat down beside her on the roof. Where she kept herself confined to as small a space as possible, he sprawled out next to her, legs extended and flung unnecessarily wide as he leaned back on his hands.

Scarlett sighed and with a jerk of her head extended the shadows of the chimney beside them to blur his silhouette. The ease with which she did so in another's presence after years of hiding her Talent surprised her, but Benedict had already seen much more impressive shows of her shadows. Besides, she didn't want anybody watching them if they happened to look up.

"So where are we going to start our investigations?" Benedict asked casually, swiping his fingers through the misty shadows that danced around him as if they were cobwebs. His manner was almost curious, not scared like many were by Scarlett's darkness. Then again, he had already proven his sense of self-preservation to be suspect.

"I was reminded the other day that the Wolves have recently gained a fair bit of territory, and coin to go with it." Scarlett quickly filled Benedict in on the situation of the turf disputes in the lower city, purposefully vague about her involvement in the brawls over coveted ground. Benedict nodded along as if he were listening to her assessment of which horses to bet on, seemingly unscandalized by the rough and tumble nature of gang life.

"So you think their newfound power has emboldened the Wolves to track down bigger prey?" Benedict asked.

"It seems plausible," Scarlett huffed. "But it doesn't tell me anything about why they've targeted Georgette in particular. Amos—I heard somebody mention something about a new operation though."

"What kind of operation?"

"If I knew, I wouldn't be sitting here picking the brain of somebody clearly better equipped for flirtation than criminal politics," Scarlett snapped, irritated by her lack of progress.

Benedict chuckled, seemingly unoffended. "Is that your way of telling me you want me to flirt with you instead of coming up with ideas? Because I was going to suggest that we start investigating the Wolves new territory to find this 'operation.'"

Something about Benedict's teasing eased the seed of frustration in the pit of Scarlett's stomach. She nodded.

"I'll comb the area and see if I can find anything. If I do, I'll send you another message via Georgette."

"*We* will comb the area you mean," Benedict insisted. "I didn't dress like this because it's the new fashion you know."

"You'll only slow me down," Scarlett argued, pushing to her feet, debating leaping over to the next roof and off into the twilight, knowing she could easily lose him. "I think we proved that last time when your grand plan was castrating enemies with a letter opener."

"Ah but I have this now, and I promise you I know how to use it." Benedict stood as well, producing his pistol from the waistband of his pants with a flourish. "And I'll be able to point out anybody that ah...recruited me...for the business with Georgette."

Scarlett hesitated, muscles bunched and ready to dart away and leave him to wait for her next message. Still, he could prove useful if he recognized any Wolves who were part of the scheme on Georgette's life. Her shadows could conceal both of them if he managed to keep that mouth of his in check.

"Alright," Scarlett agreed, "but you'll have to be quiet. And if you give us away, you'll find out exactly how much pain one can inflict with a letter opener."

Scarlett turned away to climb down the roof the way Benedict had come, suppressing the warmth in her stomach brought on by Benedict's triumphant smile. It had just been such a long time since anybody besides Georgette had seemed happy to be in her presence.

To his credit, Benedict behaved admirably as Scarlett led them through the streets towards the blocks of warehouses down by the wharves that had once been the purview of the Lions. They clung to the edges of the street, the thickening twilight especially dense around them. Benedict stayed silent, although he continuously dragged his fingers along the shadows subtly clinging to their silhouettes. He seemed mesmerized by the way they afforded the slightest resistance in this form, as if the air itself had congealed. Scarlett would have to summon much denser darkness to make it as solid as the mass that had cushioned their fall from the windows. She stuck to ephemeral darkness for times like this though, knowing this use of her Talent was less likely to leave her debilitated with a splitting headache the next day.

Scarlett internally debated telling him to stop touching them, but she didn't have it in her to tell Benedict that she could feel his fingertips as a phantom touch in the part of her mind that controlled her Talent. It seemed an oddly intimate thing to admit.

Soon enough, they crept into the blocks bordering the Port of London, newly claimed by the Wolves. Scarlett hadn't ventured down here often when it was under Lion control, mainly sticking to Raptor territory, but even she could tell that it seemed different. Before, it had been relatively quiet, a few urchins on the corners alert for anybody not keeping a keen eye on their purse. Now, it was quiet, but undercut with a dangerous vibration, as if the neighborhood waited with bated breath. The few pedestrians scurried quickly to their destinations, keeping their eyes on the ground. Nobody loitered on street corners.

Not wanting to stand out, Scarlett pulled Benedict briskly down the street and around a corner. They stood on a narrow stone ledge where the last building on the street backed up against the Thames. The murky waters ran sluggishly between the banks, the gurgling noise obscuring Scarlett's voice from anyone walking on the street.

"We'll climb up to that window." Scarlett gestured to an open sill on the third floor. "You go first and I'll keep a look out."

"What's wrong with front doors?" Benedict huffed, even as he began inspecting the uneven stone before him.

"When I'm spying on people, I generally don't like to announce my presence," Scarlett hissed.

With a resigned sigh, Benedict began to climb. His progress was slow, but Scarlett had to commend him for not complaining further, even as she was sure his well-manicured nails were shredded by grappling for purchase in the rough mortar. Just as he was an arm's reach from the open window, a loose stone broke from the wall where Benedict's foot had rested. Even as it fell to the ledge beside Scarlett with a dull clatter, Benedict began to slide down, toes scraping against the wall. Just as he looked as though he were about to lose his grip, pitching back into the murky waters at her feet, Scarlett grit her teeth and a patch of shadows formed a lip under his boot. His weight landed on it and the force of it jarred like a gong at the base of her skull. The sensation passed quickly as Benedict regained his footing and disappeared through the open window.

Not hearing any commotion from his entrance and seeing nobody watching on a quick study of her surroundings, Scarlett followed up the wall. In about half the time it took Benedict, she perched on the windowsill. She found him waiting for her in what appeared to be an uninhabited storage room and hopped down lightly to the wooden floor.

After ensuring that the room was deserted, she turned her attention towards the rest of the building. Creeping towards the door into the rest of the building, Scarlett strained her ears for sounds. Sure enough, rowdy voices filtered up from the floors below. She motioned for Benedict to stay put as she eased the door open, thanking luck for quiet hinges. Sneaking out into the hallway, she felt a presence behind her and suppressed a grunt of annoyance. She would have scolded Benedict for not doing as he was told if it wouldn't make so much noise.

Instead, she led the way down the hallway towards the stairs. There, they peeked over the rickety wooden railing to find a dozen men milling about below, laughing boisterously. Several empty bottles tipped over on the rickety table and a rather one-sided arm-wrestling match added to the impression of some Wolves enjoying their spoils. Getting the impression they wouldn't learn anything here from drunken brawlers clearly not thinking of business, Scarlett made to head back the way they had come and try a different building.

Before she could take a step, Benedict tapped frantically on her shoulder. When she looked over her shoulder, she found him gesturing emphatically between him and the men below, before pointing at his neck.

Turning back to the scene below, she squinted and found that one of the thugs had his tattoo of the howling wolf across the side of his throat. She jerked her head towards him and raised her eyebrows in question, to which Benedict nodded emphatically.

At his confirmation, she chanced sneaking closer, trying to get close enough to make out their words.

"—never had it better."

"Living like kings," the one with the neck tattoo agreed. "And it's only going to get better."

"The operation is already raking in the coin. How are we going to get better than that?"

Scarlett chanced stepping down another stair at that, not wanting to miss a word.

"Fang has some friends in high places. They're going to spread the word at the viscount's ball next week, see if we can't reel in some bigger purses."

"Even bigger fish? We better have some good fighters," the first commented, worry creeping into his tone.

"Don't you worry, we've got that part under control. Fang knows how to keep them under his heel," neck tattoo assured with an air of superiority, leaning back in his chair and folding his hands behind his head. "Now why don't you quit questioning Fang's plan and get us some more drink to celebrate another lucrative night. There's some whiskey in the storeroom upstairs."

With a grumble, the first thug pushed back from the table and Scarlett's heart accelerated in her chest. Not waiting to hear more, she turned around, nearly knocking over Benedict where he crouched on the stairs behind her. Grabbing his arm before he could fall, she yanked him back down the hallway the way they had come. Prioritizing haste over stealth, she dragged them back into the room they had entered, closing the door behind them.

By now, the Wolf's footsteps were audible on the stairs. Glancing at the climb down, she cursed, knowing they only had a matter of moments before they were discovered. Benedict couldn't climb down that fast. Still, the ledge three stories below them was narrow, dropping off into the turgid waters of the Thames.

"Phillip, you up here? Better not be stealing the drink," a voice called from the hallway. The Wolf must have heard the door shut.

Scarlett chanced a glance beside her at Benedict, finding him wide-eyed and reaching for the pistol in his belt. With a bolt of resignation, Scarlett knew she wasn't willing to risk his inexperience in a fight.

"Hold your breath," was all the warning she gave him before she grabbed his arm and jumped out the window, towing him behind her.

They hit the sludgy surface of the Thames with a slap, the pollution making it thicker than the usual consistency of water. As they surfaced, Benedict spluttered beside her. Scarlett couldn't hide her grimace either as she dashed mud from her eyes.

Thankfully, Benedict seemed able to swim. Not wanting to climb out of the river right next to the building they had just exited with so much gusto and arouse suspicion, Scarlett paddled in the direction of the sluggish flow towards a nearby dock. Reaching the outskirts of the port, she clambered up onto one of the rickety docks, Benedict heaving himself up behind her.

"That is—" he paused to spit out the remnants of a mouthful of river water "—the second time this week you have thrown me out of a window."

They both clambered to their feet on the wooden planks. Thankfully, at this edge of the port, nobody was watching them.

"The word is defenestrated." Scarlett gathered as much of her short cropped hair as she could to squeeze the water from it. Moments like this made her grateful she had taken to lopping it off with her dagger, knowing it would make it easier to wash the muck from it.

"I didn't know they taught lower city gangsters such big words," Benedict responded.

Scarlett opened her mouth the retort that she wasn't from the lower city, but snapped her mouth shut. That wasn't something she needed to share with Benedict. Instead she said, "I don't really think you can accuse me of throwing you out a window when I went with you both times. Besides, it was worth it."

"Your ears are sharper than mine, because I didn't quite catch anything. But as excited as I am to hear your revelations, I'm even more excited to get this river water off me." Benedict swiped at his muddy face with equally soiled hands, only succeeding in smearing the sludge around. A patch of mud clung to the prominent arch of his nose. "Why don't we go back to my home to regroup and get clean."

"I'm not sure—" Scarlett started.

"I refuse to think about you trying to get clean after that using a rag and a basin," Benedict insisted, already tromping up the dock towards the street, dripping a trail of brown water. Scarlett had to take a few steps at a jog to keep up with his longer strides. Her boots squelched with every step, punctuating how much she really could use a hot bath. They were hard to come by at Granny's.

"It'll draw attention for the two of us to come in like this," she argued anyways.

"You think that I, a younger son infamous for my improper behavior, don't know how to sneak in and out of my own house?"

"Your family—"

"Won't be home," Benedict cut her off, his tone curt. "Now spend your breath walking and not arguing. I want to get these clothes off and incinerated as fast as possible."

As Benedict led the way through the back carriage entrance and into the kitchens of the duke's grand estate, Scarlett blinked to find them completely empty. It seemed that not only was his family away, but all of their staff as well. Benedict didn't seem surprised by this, tramping up the stairs to the main house without a comment.

He continued through a richly appointed sitting room to a much grander staircase leading to the upper levels. Scarlett trailed him, blinking at the moonlight sparkling off the unlit chandelier, affording the main hall a haunted look.

"Pick any bathroom at the end of that hall you like." Benedict gestured vaguely to the left as they reached the top of the stairs. "They're all just wasted space right now."

Scarlett hesitated, but Benedict didn't even wait for her to turn away before he started shucking off his shirt. Catching the barest glimpse of dark curls leading down from his navel as he lifted the cloth, Scarlett whirled around to contemplate the row of doors at the end of the hall.

Walking past them, she reached out and opened one at random. She found it to be a bedroom, although rather bare. The mattress was stripped of any linens and the walls and mantlepiece devoid of any decoration.

Scarlett moved to the next door and almost moaned in relief when she found it to be a bathroom, most of the space dominated by a clawfoot tub. Although somebody as tall as Benedict might have to bend his knees to soak, Scarlett would be able to sink right to her chin. The image of Benedict in the bathtub jumped back into her mind, and she shook her head to be rid of it. His ceaseless flirting and comfort with undress was turning her mind.

Instead, she shut the door behind her, gratefully shucking off her clothes and removing the weapons beneath. Knives fell with a clatter to the tile at her feet. She tried to bathe as quickly as she could, scrubbing dirt from under her fingernails and rubbing at her face until it was positively raw. After all, she was only here because of her mission to keep Georgette safe. And she was only bathing here because she was sure Benedict didn't want her making his house smell like the Thames. Still, as she rubbed the bar of floral soap she found on the shelf through her hair and let the grime from her skin turn the water brown, she found herself involuntarily relaxing. A luxurious bath like this was almost like something from her life before...

Scarlett shook herself from that train of thought and finished cleaning with brutal efficiency. Stepping from the tub, she looked down at her pile of muddy clothes in disappointment. She didn't relish putting them back on, but her only other change of clothes was in her trunk back at Granny's. She washed them as best she could in the tub, even sacrificing some of the expensive soap to the cause. Wringing them out, she pulled the sodden clothes back on with a shiver. They may be cold, but at least they were cleaner. She ran fingers through her hair quickly, declaring it good enough as soon as it stopped sticking out from her head in every conceivable direction.

Trying not to think about how much mud she had left in the tub, Scarlett ventured from the bathroom. The door at the end of the hallway in the direction Benedict had gone was still closed, and she saw no trace of him.

It didn't do to linger outside his door while he bathed, so Scarlett picked her way downstairs, taking in her surroundings more thoroughly than she had on the way in. While the house itself was certainly grand, bedecked with carved woodwork and impressive fireplaces, it seemed rather sparse. There was very little art on the walls, and even the furniture seemed scarce. It was almost as if the

Pearces were moving out. Perhaps they had purchased a different house here in town.

As Scarlett wandered through the living room to the front parlor, her breath caught in her throat. Positioned under the window was a pianoforte, dimly illuminated by the light from the rising moon. Sheet music was strewn in haphazard piles on the bench, and the cover lay open, ivory keys gleaming as if invitation.

Ignoring the feeling that she was doing something forbidden, Scarlett approached the instrument. Reaching out, she let her fingers just brush over the keys, a featherlight touch, not even enough to make a sound. She itched to sit down on the bench but didn't want to leave a watermark on the satin cushion.

Holding her breath, she cautiously picked out the first few notes of a familiar melody, the memory hidden in the recesses of her memory coated in dust and cobwebs. As the opening tones of the song echoed through the empty room, a lump rose in Scarlett's throat. She swallowed thickly to dispel it, even as she found herself blinking rapidly. Her soul shuddered within her body as if trying to escape the confines of her skin, trying to force her to want things that were long gone.

Even as she willed herself to step away and not lose herself in the song from her past, her fingers continued to play unbidden, just a few more stilted bars. There were so few things Scarlett allowed herself to miss from before her parents were killed, focusing instead on surviving. But music—it awakened a part of her heart she had long considered dead.

"You play?"

Scarlett snatched her hand from the piano as if burned by it, whirling on her heel to find Benedict leaning on the doorframe. His still-damp hair clung to his neck in dark swirls. While he had put on pants, his top half was clad only in a burgundy dressing robe, the angle of his body causing it to drape open and reveal a triangle of chest dusted with dark hair.

Scarlett blinked, Benedict's single raised eyebrow reminding her he had asked a question.

"A little," she answered noncommittally, stepping away from the instrument.

"Well aren't you full of surprises." Benedict stepped closer. "I would say you should accompany me, since I haven't had anybody to play with my singing in quite a while."

"You sing?" Scarlett asked in disbelief.

"How else am I supposed to serenade my lovers on their balconies?"

"Then I guess you will have to recruit one of them to play for you, assuming they're not too busy swooning at your feet."

Benedict grinned wide, revealing a chipped bottom tooth. "Now you understand my struggles. Come on, let's get something to eat." Benedict led the way back down to the kitchen before rummaging through cupboards as if he did so all the time. He lit the stove and put the kettle on with practiced hands while Scarlett leaned against the wooden counter, looking on with her head cocked.

"The son of a duke makes his own tea?" she questioned.

"Younger son," Benedict clarified as he pulled out two cups. "We don't warrant quite the same bowing and scraping."

"I would have assumed that you would have been able to charm your servants into the same sort of service."

"Alas, my brother has a whole regiment under his command at his post in the army, and they seem to be immune to my charms. What is left of our bare-bones staff is in the country with my mother and younger sister. We have only a carriage driver here now, and he'll be out for the night." Benedict imitated Scarlett's posture, leaning on his hands behind him as they waited for the water to boil.

"And your father?"

"He'll stumble in sometime well after dawn, most likely after getting kicked out of several gambling halls. I got my roguish ways from somewhere after all." Benedict offered Scarlett another crooked smile, but this one lacked the dazzling effects of his usual grins. His eyes weren't in it.

"Is...is that how you got entangled with the Wolves?" Scarlett asked haltingly. She had told herself it didn't matter why Benedict was entrapped with lower city scum, only that he could help her save Georgette. Still, the empty cavern of a house combined with emptiness of Benedict's perpetually dancing gaze pushed her to ask.

"Like me, Father doesn't know how to quit," Benedict said with a lopsided shrug, staring at the ground. "While I tend to be tenacious in pursuing beautiful women though, Father is likely to double-down in games of chance whenever he's losing. First we had to sell off some paintings, and then let go of some staff. Eventually though, the Wolves demanded he pay his debts in full, and when he didn't have the money…well…" Benedict shrugged.

"What about your brother?"

"He's been stationed abroad for so long, being a responsible heir by serving king and country. I had hoped to be able to handle things without bothering him, be more than the middle sibling only good for throwing parties and telling jokes. Alas, I don't seem to be having much luck being the child who can solve problems, only make them." Benedict seemed to be attempting to plaster his rakish demeanor back in place, but it was slow to adhere after his moment of vulnerability.

Scarlett searched for something to say to his admission, looking for kind words to soothe Benedict's guilt and finding them difficult to grasp. As if she had spent so long being a shadow for the Raptors she couldn't remember how to offer words of comfort. The whistling of the kettle saved her from her ineptitude as Benedict turned away and busied himself with the tea. By the time he faced her again, offering her a teacup, his confident demeanor was back.

"As much as our most recent escapades might have ended in trouble, we are also making steps to solving our shared problem it seems," Scarlett commented as she took it from him. She lifted the cup to her lips and let the steam warm her face, combating the chill from where her damp clothes clung to her skin.

"I was too busy trying not to breathe so as not to draw attention to hear what was being said below," Benedict admitted sheepishly.

"They mentioned the viscount's ball. Something about hunting down bigger purses there. It appears that they're targeting more socialites than just the Wards."

"Well then it would seem to me that our next stop should be the viscount's ball. I can't say I'm disappointed that our next expedition should not involve a swim in the Thames. And it can serve a dual purpose if you attend as Georgette. I can put on an excellent show of wooing you on the dance floor." Benedict sipped his own tea.

"Just make sure you aren't so busy waltzing me into a stupor that we don't keep our eyes peeled for a stray Wolf."

"So you admit I could waltz you into a stupor? Don't worry, I shall be prepared to catch you if you swoon," Benedict teased.

Scarlett hid her smile in her teacup. As much as she dreaded the heat of a wig and the stress of pretending to be Georgette, spying on the Wolves at a ball didn't seem to be the worst turn this investigation had taken.

Chapter Six

Amos was in the type of dark mood that made Scarlett itch to wrap herself in shadows until she could disappear, slipping from the Roost and the violent atmosphere brewing within. Instead, she planted her feet and crossed her arms as she stood before where Amos sprawled across his wooden bar stool as if it were a throne.

"Tonight is going to be a good haul for the Raptors," Amos declared with his signature oily grin. Scarlett ground her heels into the rough wooden floorboards to avoid shifting her weight in discomfort. Still, she longed for another night of slipping threatening notes onto people's pillows. After all, she preferred delivering threats to actual violence.

"In fact, tonight, we will be paying a house call to Mr. Davies."

Scarlett's stomach twisted into a knot at the name. She had slid a note onto Mr. Davies' pillow, between him and his sleeping wife, not three nights prior. A repeat visit could only mean the debt remained unpaid. From the bruisers surrounding Scarlett, it appeared that Amos planned to extract his payment in other ways.

Scarlett furrowed her brow.

"Mr. Davies has the ear of the king. Are you sure roughing him up wouldn't cause more trouble than it's worth? I could always tack on some interest in the valuables I steal, to drive home our message." Scarlett added the last bit on with a shrug.

"Oh, he won't call the Royal Police on the Raptors if he knows what's good for him." Amos waved a dismissive hand. "After all, he would have to tell them why we were paying him a visit in the first place."

Scarlett nodded, keeping her face blank. A warning bell rang in the back of her mind though. After all, Mr. Davies likely owed the Raptors money after a few unlucky hands of cards. While gambling was generally the purview of the gangs, it wasn't technically illegal. The worst the Royal Police would do to Mr. Davies for gambling would be to give him a disapproving look.

"Timothy and Thomas will be coming with for security. The three of us will pay a visit to the upstairs bedroom while Scarlett combs the downstairs for appropriate offerings to resolve his debts," Amos ordered, drawing Scarlett from her thoughts.

"How much does this man owe? If it's not that much, I could always slip in and relieve Mrs. Davies of her jewelry without risking the Raptors being implicated." Scarlett aimed for nonchalance.

"I'm starting to think you don't want the Raptors to get their due. Are you saying we should let our marks just skip out on their payment?"

Scarlett shrugged one shoulder, resisting the urge to squirm under Amos's stare. He contemplated her with one eyebrow raised, head cocked to the side like a predator. Shadows coalesced at Scarlett's fingertips, just bare traces of smoke that took significant willpower to disperse.

"You spend a few days running around the upper city and you think you're one of them now? That you're better than us?"

The blood froze in Scarlett's veins. Did the Wolves mention her and Benedict's deal with them to Amos? He would not be pleased with her making promises to other gangs behind his back—especially ones she didn't intend to keep.

"Oh yes, we've seen you leaving Granny's in those fancy dresses, probably trying to charm some man out of their purse, thinking you could pass as a lady."

Scarlett's heart stuttered to a hesitant start in her chest again. Amos didn't seem to know about her arrangement with the Benedict. Still, he pressed on.

"You know, you've always acted like you're better than the rest of us—renting a room at Granny's instead of living at the Roost. But putting on a fancy dress doesn't change anything. You're a killer like the rest of us. Your neck would have been stretched with the rest of the Talented in the Inquiries if you weren't under the protection of the Raptors."

Scarlett reared back as if she had been slapped in the face. She only managed to avoid sneering at Amos by gritting her teeth so hard they creaked in her skull. His words burrowed under her skin like knives heading straight for her heart, because she knew they were true.

Her room at Granny's was the one shred of separation Scarlett had left between herself and her life with the Raptors. Going home to her own space, no matter how tiny, allowed her to compartmentalize her nocturnal crimes. It didn't change the facts though. She had too much blood on her hands to ever be anything other than what she was now. It didn't make a difference how many strolls through the park she took or balls she attended with Benedict.

Amos seemed to sense his victory in her silence, offering a slimy smirk. "Now be a good shadow and help us take our due."

Scarlett nodded, mentally tallying the weight of her knives strapped against her skin and offering up a silent prayer that they wouldn't be spilling blood tonight.

Scarlett's lungs screamed for air as she held her breath, waiting for the night watch to pass her hiding spot where she crouched under a hedge. Her shadows coalesced around her in a cool mist, dense enough in the dark of night that they wouldn't see if they happened to glance this way. Still, Scarlett had learned the hard way that her ability to avoid being seen didn't help if her enemies could hear her panicked breathing.

The polished standard boots of the Royal Police tromped by before disappearing around the corner. Scarlett inched out from beneath the brambles, thoroughly dusty and covered in tiny scratches. She waited a moment for the officers to get far enough away that they wouldn't hear her boots scrape along the cast iron before launching herself at the fence surrounding the Davies' garden. She made quick work of the climb, her wiry muscles long since having developed the strength to lift her slight frame.

Dropping lightly to her feet inside the fence, she unlocked the gate from the inside so the rest of the Raptors could follow her without having to replicate the climb. Thomas and Timothy might be strong, but their muscles were more useful for punching than climbing. Darting past the sterile hedges towards the house, she fell into a crouch just in front of the main door and pulled her shadows tight to her back. Even if Scarlett wasn't the quickest lock pick in the Raptors, she had the advantage of being able to avoid detection while she worked, making her a valuable advance guard for the gang.

Several attempts later, and a bitten tongue to avoid cursing audibly, the pins clicked into place under her picks and the knob turned. In place of an exclamation of victory, Scarlett let out a low trill like that of a nightingale to signal the Raptors that the way was clear. Even as she glanced back towards the gate to shield the bruiser's passage, she winced at her own birdcall. It felt on the nose for the Raptors to imitate the calls of birds to signal each other, and Scarlett struggled to master the sounds.

As the thugs and Amos did their best to sneak across the lawn, Scarlett slipped inside, finding herself in a marble entrance hall. Although the impressive chandelier wasn't lit, the moonlight streaming in through the tall windows reflected off the marble, bouncing of the crystals in the light fixture, casting a strangely ethereal glow considering that she was breaking and entering.

Amos and the thugs ruined the stillness of the house as they pushed in the door, tramping where Scarlett had tiptoed. Now that they were away from the potentially prying eyes on the street, Scarlett let the shadows drip away from all of them, the darkness slipping away back into hidden corners.

With a jerk of his chin, Amos indicated that Scarlett should begin raiding the ground floor.

"We're going to greet our unknowing host and his lovely wife," Amos growled. The violent grins Timothy and Thomas gave in response sent shivers down Scarlett's spine. She turned away to focus on her task as the men headed up the stairs.

The first room off the hall was a parlor. An enameled clock shimmering with inlaid crystals glimmered on an end table, and Scarlett snatched it up to shove in the satchel slung across her back. She picked her way through the richly appointed room, stepping past silk upholstered chairs and velvet curtains in her search. She nabbed an engraved silver plate off the mantle and a snuffbox inlaid with what appeared to be jade.

She was about to search for an office, hoping for a safe she could crack, when movement at the window caught her eye. Scarlett ducked behind the heavy velvet drape. She poked her head around just in time to see five men walk through the still-open gate, the shape of their helmets giving them away as Royal Policemen. Scarlett stood frozen for half a second before turning and bolting. Forgoing any illusions of secrecy, the soles of her boots slapped the ground as she crossed back through the marble foyer and bounded up the stairs. Seeing light at the end of the upstairs hall, she sprinted towards it.

"Police!" she shouted as she rounded the corner.

The sight that met her in the bedroom was a grim one, Mr. Davies sprawled on the ground, pitiful groans escaping from behind his hands where he clutched his nose. Timothy held Mrs. Davies by the hair, keeping her pinned and unable to help her husband.

Amos froze, his foot already pulled back as if to kick Mr. Davies in the spleen. "You're sure?"

"They're here! We need to make ourselves scarce," Scarlett panted. She thought she could hear the front door slamming open downstairs.

Instead of running, Amos snarled, focus turning back to the man cowering at his feet. "You thought you could get the Royal Police to protect you? As if you're innocent yourself?"

"Had to stop you..." Mr. Davies mumbled, voice clogged as if he were speaking through a broken nose.

"Nobody crosses the Raptors," Amos declared, voice as sharp as the blade that sprang into his hand. A wet *shink* filled the room as Amos dragged the blade across Mr. Davies' throat before his wife's ear-piercing scream split the air.

Scarlett stood frozen in horror as his body slumped to the floor, the floral design of the rug darkening as it was soaked with blood. Then time picked up again double speed as a battalion of police officers crashed through the door.

The leader shouted, but Scarlett couldn't make out his words through Mrs. Davies' screaming. Timothy lost hold of her as she thrashed, throwing herself to the ground on top of her dying husband as she wrenched herself free.

As the police officers charged forward into the mayhem, Amos grabbed Timothy and Thomas by their collars, shoving them towards the officers like human shields. Scarlett's shadows sprung up around her without a thought, instinctually shielding her from the violent scene. The police grappled with the bruisers, struggling to subdue them with their clubs. One officer pulled out a pistol and waved it around helplessly, seemingly hesitant to fire in such close quarters. Another threw himself down next to Mr. Davies, using his hands to try and staunch the blood streaming from his neck. His efforts were hindered by Mrs. Davies clinging to him desperately, leaving crimson handprints on his crisp uniform.

Scarlett shoved herself back into a corner, seemingly unnoticed in her thick patch of shadows that the two lit oil lamps were unable to disperse. In the mayhem, she almost missed the flutter of Amos's coat as he launched himself from the window to escape the scene, unsurprisingly indifferent to the fate of Timothy and Thomas.

Scarlett looked around for her own escape route, desperate to get away before she was noticed. Thomas grappled with the officers between her and the windows, fists and clubs flying in a violent whirlwind. Scarlett fingered the blades at her wrists but knew joining the fight would mean getting arrested. She couldn't go to prison—not when Georgette was still counting on her.

Her gaze snagged on the empty fireplace on the wall next to her. Only ashes lay in the grate, no fire necessary in the warm spring weather. Scarlett glanced towards the chaos of the room one final time, the sight of Mr. Davies limp on the carpet searing into her mind before she ducked below the mantle and crouched in the fireplace.

Reaching up, rough bricks scraped her fingertips as she traced the edges of the chimney. It would be a tight fit, and she would have to leave the bag of stolen trinkets behind, but she could make it. She dropped the satchel and braced her palms on opposite walls. Levering herself up, she wedged the back of her shoulders against one wall, arms bent tightly against herself to brace her palms on the brick in front of her. She squirmed determinedly, worming her way up until she could find purchase with the toes of her boots on the edge of the chimney.

The passage was too tight for her to climb properly. Instead, she had to shimmy, pushing herself up with her hands and feet as the majority of her weight was supported by her back pressed flush against the wall behind her.

Scarlett bit her lip to suppress a yelp as a sharp brick raked across her shoulder blade, not wanting to ruin her escape by making too much noise. Still, her shirt loosened around her indicating that it had ripped, and a warm trickle down her back told her she was bleeding. Still, she wriggled onward, gaining ground by inches. Her movement knocked loose soot and ash, making it fall onto her face and into her eyes. She desperately tried to blink it from her burning eyes even as the smokey air and compression on her ribs made it hard to breath.

Scarlett looked up, the hint of stars in the hazy sky peeking through the top of the chimney seeming impossibly far away. Even as she tried to calm herself and get her muscles to cooperate, panic rose in the back of her throat. Shoving it down,

Scarlett clawed at the brick before her, ignoring broken nails and scraped skin as she gained another foot.

Long moments passed, and Scarlett had the hysterical thought that she would die in here, her body only to be found when the smell attracted crows or somebody lit a fire and noticed the smoke wasn't escaping properly. Just before she burst into a horrible combination of laughter and tears, fresh air brushed Scarlett's face. The top of the chimney was just inches away.

Redoubling her efforts, Scarlett managed to reach up and grab the lip of the chimney, levering herself up and out. Her arms trembled with the effort as she slumped over the edge, shoulders hanging out as she gulped down fresh air, legs still dangling in the chimney. She rested there a moment, the hysterical sobs of Mrs. Davies still filtering up from the room below. Scarlett needed to get away—as far away as possible from the corpse below.

She kicked her legs to get herself the rest of the way out of the tight passage, only to find her arms too unsteady to hold her weight after the climb. With a yelp, she tumbled from the chimney stack to the slate tiled roof below. Scarlett twisted in the air, and bright pain flashed behind her eyes as her left ankle landed under her, wrenching at an unnatural angle.

She lay on her back for a moment, panting through the sharp sensation until it faded to a manageable throbbing. Gingerly she sat up before using the chimney to haul herself up, keeping her weight on her uninjured side. She slowly tested her left foot and let out a sigh of relief as she found that it held her weight. Still, it throbbed angrily enough that it would keep her from running or jumping.

Weighing her options, Scarlett searched around from her vantage point on the roof. There was no trace of Amos, indicating he had fled the scene while leaving the rest of the Raptors to fend for themselves—not that she expected anything more from him. However she did spot figures moving on the street, the gleam of moonlight off helmets indicating that more Royal Police were coming. Her chances of getting out of the upper city unnoticed dwindled before her eyes. Shadows could conceal her somewhat, but injured as she was, Scarlett would move too slowly to go completely unnoticed. She wasn't in good shape for a fight either.

She cast about the roof frantically. It wouldn't be ideal to hide here until the police left the area, but she might be able to wait them out. As she searched for a place to hunker down, her gaze caught on familiar gables a few houses over—the duke's house.

Scarlett chewed her lips as she considered and then immediately stopped as she choked on a mouthful of ash that still dusted her face. Benedict had seemed sure that his family and servants wouldn't be home last night, so it was likely the same was true tonight. If Benedict was the only one in the house, she could sneak in the window and hide out there until morning without him even noticing. And if he did notice her—well then she would solve one problem at a time.

Hobbling across the tiled roof, Scarlett searched for an easy climb down and was lucky enough to find a trellis facing away from the street. With some hopping and slipping, she managed to climb down mostly using one foot. The pain when she did step on her left side nearly scattered her shadows, leaving her completely exposed, but she managed to keep herself cloaked enough to avoid notice from anybody not staring directly at the house.

Once her feet landed on the manicured lawn, Scarlett hobbled through the garden to the back fence. Another torturous climb later, she found herself in the adjacent gardens with a straight shot to the back of the duke's house.

When Scarlett reached the familiar home and picked a window, she was surprised at the quality of the locks securing them. It hadn't looked as if the Pearces had much valuable left to steal, but she remembered Gil's threatening words, and Benedict's mother and younger sister. She didn't blame the Pearces for increasing their security when the Wolves were out for their blood. Scarlett plucked the right picks from her boot and got to work.

A few minutes of concentration later, the window swung open on blessedly silent hinges. Carefully, Scarlett lifted herself into the library at the back of the house, feet landing softly on a rug that had once been soft and rich but had clearly seen better days. Turning back to the window she eased it shut behind her.

As the latch clicked, tension faded from Scarlett's shoulders, leaving her feeling heavy and limp. She leaned her head against the cool glass of the window pane and closed her eyes, only to immediately snap them open again. The image of Mr. Davies bleeding on the carpet as his wife desperately tried to keep his life force from spilling out seemed etched into the back of her eyelids. Nights like this were why she craved evenings of creeping around in the darkness alone, her only job to deliver letters, when she could feign ignorance to the violence of their contents. These missions with the Raptors, though, reminded her how far into the life of the lower city she had fallen. Amos was right: She was no better than the rest of the Raptors, whether she slept at the Roost or not. After all, she had the same blood stains on her hands.

"Little bird?"

Scarlett jolted so hard she knocked her forehead against the window pane. Her knives flew into her hands before she could think, spinning around and falling into a crouch as her ankle screamed in protest.

Benedict stood in the doorway, clad in his nightclothes. His hair was rumpled as if from restless sleep, but he clutched a cut crystal glass of brown liquid in one hand, indicating he hadn't been in bed. If Scarlett's heart hadn't hammered in apprehension from being found, she might have been breathless from how undone he appeared.

As it was, she hissed in pain as her ankle nearly gave out under her. She clutched at the embroidered footstool beside her as Benedict took a step towards her, setting his glass down on a nearby end table.

"You look terrible." His tone was concerned, surprisingly devoid of any anger from finding her trespassing in his home.

"You would too if you just climbed up a chimney," Scarlett shot back through gritted teeth. Before she could react, Benedict slid under her armpit, slinging her arm around his shoulders to act as a crutch on her weakened side.

"Silly Scarlett, that's not how St. Nicholas works," he chided. "He's supposed to come down the chimney and give you gifts, not take your things before climbing out the window. Let's go get you cleaned up."

Scarlett tried to pull away once she had her footing, cringing at the soot smears appearing on Benedict's thin nightshirt, but he stayed with her.

"How do you know I was stealing?" she retorted, distracting herself from the way Benedict's muscles bunched under her arm.

"Because I'm the one of us more likely to be sneaking in to visit a lover," Benedict countered easily.

Scarlett's snort of laughter came out as a grunt of pain when the cut on her back brushed against the edge of the doorframe they squeezed through side by side.

"Did you decide jumping out of windows lacked flair or something?" Benedict continued, carrying the conversation for her.

"There were...complications."

Now they stood at the bottom of the stairs. Scarlett stared up them with a look of dismay. Before she could grit her teeth for the trek up, gravity shifted and her feet swept out from under her.

She squawked inelegantly and flung her arms out, nearly punching Benedict in the nose as he swept her into his arms. He jostled her bumps and scrapes, even bumping her sore leg against the banister as he maneuvered up the grand staircase, but Scarlett was stunned into silence.

Her brain searched through memories for the last time she had been held and came up blank. Even when Granny had patched up her injuries when she first started running for the Raptors and ended up tumbling from roofs more often than not, she had treated her clinically. Granny's affection was practical and gruff. Benedict held her to his chest as if she were a bride he was sweeping over the threshold on their wedding night. Although his breath came faster as they trudged up to the bathrooms, he didn't utter a word of complaint.

In her shock, Scarlett's hand had come to rest on his chest, fingertips brushing bare skin at the edge of his loose neckline. She snatched it back and rubbed her fingers on the filthy cloth of her trousers to banish the feeling of his heart fluttering beneath her touch.

"I'm getting your shirt filthy," Scarlett protested. Indeed, his shirt, which had been fine and white when he found her, now was streaked with grime. Scarlett swallowed heavily at the sight of a crimson smear on one of his shoulders. She hoped the blood was hers.

"I don't get a chance to sweep ladies off their feet very often. I'm not going to pass up the opportunity when one tumbles through my window," Benedict huffed. Scarlett was glad she didn't weigh much more because Benedict was clearly unused to this much physical labor.

"I'm not a lady," she shot back.

"Clearly, or you wouldn't be letting me hold you like this." Benedict leaned in conspiratorially as he spoke, his breath tickling across her neck.

Scarlett shook her head. The delirium of her narrow escape and Benedict's incorrigible flirting were a combination headier than the Roost's strongest brandy.

They'd made it to the top of the stairs, and Benedict turned down the hall towards the bathroom he had disappeared into a few days earlier. He still didn't put her down until he could deposit her gently on the sink. Once he was sure she wasn't going to slip off, he turned to light a lamp, revealing pale blue tile and a massive clawfoot tub taking up one half of the room.

"So can I ask why you broke into my house looking like you were on the business end of a flock of angry hummingbirds, or should I just enjoy the midnight visit and not ask questions?" Benedict questioned as he rummaged around in the cabinet behind the mirror.

Scarlett bit her lip. She had managed to distract herself with finding a place to hide and tending her injuries, and Benedict's question reminded her why she had visited this part of town in the first place. Why it was a very bad idea to be sitting on a nobleman's sink when she had just been engaged in very un-noble things.

Benedict turned back to her with a brown glass bottle and a roll of bandages in hand. He cocked his head to the side, still waiting on her answer.

"I had to pay a visit to one of your neighbors," Scarlett hedged.

"I take it this wasn't a social call?"

"I wish it were, but my acquaintances get very finicky when people lose money at the gambling tables and don't pay up." Scarlett sighed.

Benedict unstoppered the brown bottle, pouring some of the contents onto a clean cloth. As he approached Scarlett, the sharp tang of rubbing alcohol assaulted her nose.

"It seems that my father isn't the only one on this street who wagers more than he has then," Benedict commented as he picked up Scarlett's hand where it lay on the counter and began dabbing at the ripped skin with the cloth.

Scarlett's wince wasn't just from the sting of the alcohol as it touched open wounds. Benedict's current predicament was caused by lower city gangs' intimidation tactics when it came to collecting debts. Mr. Davies' death would only prove that he was right to be scared and comply with the Wolves' demands.

Scarlett should pull her hand from his and tend to herself. It seemed wrong to let Benedict care for her when people like her were the reason his life was in danger. He held her hand gently though, wiping at it with a level of care that Scarlett hadn't experienced in a long time—that she likely didn't deserve. In the aftermath of the night's chaos, Scarlett didn't have it in herself to deny herself the moment of comfort.

"I didn't mean to wake you," Scarlett admitted. "I was hoping I could hide here until the Royal Police had gone. I thought you might not even notice."

"I was awake anyways," Benedict commented.

"You keep later hours than I thought."

Benedict shook his head, loose hairs brushing against his neck. "I don't sleep much these days. Too busy worrying about my mother and sister...my father. Wishing I was better equipped to help them. Alas, dancing and flirting don't do much to get us out of the mess we've found ourselves in."

"I'm sorry," Scarlett murmured as Benedict finished with her hands.

"For what?" He motioned to her ankle, and Scarlett held out her leg for him to inspect.

Scarlett shrugged, unable to articulate exactly what she was apologizing for. For breaking in through his window in the middle of the night? For further entangling him in the violence of the lower city? For being a murderer?

"You know, I knew you were in the gangs when I agreed to work with you," Benedict said, beginning to wrap a bandage around her ankle, tight enough to stabilize the weak joint. "It's not like it comes as a shock to me that you're involved in some...unsavory happenings. Although to be fair, many members of polite society are involved in unsavory dealings too, although they're just less open about it, but that's beside the point. My point is, the first time I met you, you were risking your life to save Georgette's. The next time I saw you, you put your head on the chopping block to save mine. So even if you do make a habit of breaking into people's homes in the dead of night, I have no reason to hold it against you. Besides, I was willing to kill to save my family. I can't blame you for the same."

Scarlett swallowed thickly, glad that Benedict's gaze was cast down at where her foot rested against his chest as he tied off the wrap. She didn't think she could handle meeting his eyes right now. He might be wrong, but Scarlett didn't have it in her to shatter this image he had built of her. She couldn't bear to mar this view of her as somebody kind and virtuous with the smear of her guilt.

"How's that feel?" Benedict asked, gesturing to her ankle.

Scarlett gave it an experimental wiggle and found the bandages did a good job at keeping it immobile. The makeshift splint would offer enough support for her to limp back to Granny's.

As she let her foot dangle again, Benedict stepped forward, thighs nearly brushing her knees where they hung off the edge of the sink. Scarlett had to tilt her head back to see his expression. Shadows under his eyes marred his handsome face, betraying an exhaustion which echoed in Scarlett's bones. Where she hid her weariness with shadows in the dark of night, Benedict disguised his with jokes and dazzling smiles. Now though, in the quiet of the bathroom, his face serious, the worries that weighed on him were as clear as day.

His hand drifted up to brush her temples, pushing stray hairs away from an abrasion she sustained during the climb.

"I'm glad you weren't seriously injured," he said. His voice was quiet but echoed loudly in the tiled bathroom.

"It would certainly have put a damper on our plans," Scarlett agreed.

"That's not what I meant." Benedict braced on hand on the counter next to Scarlett's hip, the other still lingering on her hairline, near the cut on her forehead.

Without her telling them to, Scarlett's legs opened so he could step into the gap between her thighs. He encroached on her space, near enough now that his chest brushed against her tattered shirt as he inhaled. Scarlett breathed in as well, Benedict's scent of citrus and earth and the whiskey clinging to his breath enveloping her as he stood so close.

Scarlett's breath stuttered. Benedict's gaze drifted from her forehead her mouth at the sound. She should push him away—he wasn't even supposed to know she was in his house, let alone treat her injuries. Let alone look at her mouth with something warm and intangible in his gaze.

Unable to meet those eyes that held something far too close to softness, Scarlett's gaze drifted down to where his shirt lay open across his chest. The red smear of blood across one shoulder snapped her back to reality so forcefully she nearly heard the crack in her mind. She jerked back, bumping against the wall behind her.

As her injured shoulder blade made contact with the tile behind her, she hissed at the stinging cold, shattering the charged moment. The tension had probably only been in Scarlett's head anyways, a product of fading adrenaline and Benedict's relentlessly flirtatious nature. While she was no stranger to brief romantic liaisons, she shouldn't encourage Benedict. After all, he couldn't possibly be interested in Scarlett as more than a useful ally. She was a criminal covered in soot, smearing her grime all over his home and his life. As soon as they disentangled themselves from the Wolves, Scarlett would slip back into the shadows of the lower city, never to see him again. She shouldn't leave any stains on Benedict's life, or any loose ends her mind would cling to.

"Where else are you hurt?" Benedict asked, focus returning to the task at hand. Scarlett drew her gaze from the lines of concern knitting his brows to display her back to him.

"I think I cut my back," Scarlett explained.

"You really did a number on it." Benedict inspected the wound through the rip in her shirt before moving in with his cleaning solution and bandages. Scarlett had a brief moment of gratitude that the cut was on the opposite side of her Raptors tattoo, so she wouldn't have to reveal that tonight too. If Benedict's fingers lingered on the nape of her neck as he wrapped the bandage around her shoulder, it was probably just Scarlett's imagination searching for comfort after such a chaotic night.

Chapter Seven

The bright light of midday assaulted Scarlett's eyes, even as it filtered in through the tiny window facing the shadowed alley in her room. She felt like she had been run through a mill, muscles filled with a heavy ache and tiny cuts stinging her skin from head to toe. Something familiar but unexpected pulled at the back of her mind, and she peeled her eyes open further to see shadows dancing around her form where she huddled under a threadbare blanket. She gasped, and they dispersed like mice frightened by a cat, skittering away to meld back in with the darkened corners of the room.

Scarlett took several deep breaths, carefully walling off the part of her mind that controlled her Talent. It had been years since she had lost control of her shadows in her sleep, having carefully tamped down her Talent during the years of the Inquiries. Not since she had first come to Granny's had she summoned shadows in her sleep, emotion overcoming her in her dreams as her unconscious mind replayed the image of her mother and father being dragged from their home on repeat.

Her dream last night had been very different. The ephemeral image of her sitting at the piano in the Duke of Pearce's house, playing a familiar melody as Benedict watched, smiling, slipped farther from her mind as she thought about it.

With a groan, she pulled the threadbare blanket over her head and took a few deep breaths. As she did, she noticed her hands were still carefully bandaged, evidence that her midnight visit to the Duke of Pearce's house had not been a dream, although it had been far less pleasant than her imaginings. In the bright light of day, it seemed hard to believe that the younger son of a duke had tended injuries she sustained while breaking into his neighbor's house. Perhaps the night had seemed like a dream to him too.

Thinking of Benedict, Scarlett shoved the sheets down with a huff. They had an appointment today, and Scarlett needed to get to work if she was going to transform herself into a lady that could pass as Georgette by the time she was supposed to meet him in the market.

It ended up taking Scarlett the better part of an hour to scrub off the remainder of the soot from the night before, and even then black crescents lingered under her torn nails. Scarlett hid them under long white gloves, covering the rest of her injuries with a powder blue dress featuring long lacy sleeves. A flowered hat completed the ensemble, and by the time she looked in the warped mirror propped on top of her trunk, Scarlett could almost convince herself that she hadn't spent the night before sneaking around covered in ash and blood. Almost. The rage and revulsion at Amos's careless spilling of blood was harder to disguise.

As she tromped down the stairs, heavy footfalls at odds with her ladylike ensemble, Granny met her at the bottom of the stairs.

"Bad dream?" the wizened woman asked as a good morning.

Scarlett shook her head, but Granny looked her up and down appraisingly.

"It's just been a while since I woke up to darkness curling under my door," Granny said, voice heavy with meaning.

Scarlett swallowed thickly, nodding. Granny had risked the wrath of the Inquiries by helping Scarlett hide her Talent years ago. Even if it wasn't illegal anymore, she would do well to keep it under control.

Granny hobbled away without another word, and Scarlett hurried out the door. Thankfully, the square where she planned to meet Benedict wasn't more than a ten-minute walk from Granny's, although it took her almost double that with her sore ankle. Still, Benedict's wrap from last night held, and it seemed not to be broken.

When she arrived in the square, Benedict stood next to the sleek black carriage, leaning against it casually.

"I have a treat," he announced as Scarlett approached, dipping his head and sweeping off his hat in greeting.

"A treat?" Scarlett inquired, glad that their rhythm didn't seem any different than it had before last night. The intimacy of the quiet moments in the bathroom stayed hidden in the dark of night, where it belonged, away from the harsh scrutiny of daylight.

"I figured that you might not be in the mood to walk today, and so I prepared a bit of a diversion for us." Benedict opened the door of the carriage for her and pulled down the step. He held out a hand to help her inside, and when Scarlett leaned on it more heavily as she put her weight on her tender ankle, he didn't comment.

Once Benedict stepped up after her, he took the bench opposite and rapped sharply on the roof to tell the driver to set off.

"You know, hiding us in a carriage won't get the word out that you're courting Georgette," Scarlett pointed out.

"That's true, but there's a bit of an outing planned at a nearby estate. It'll be the talk of the town that I brought you with. I even set up a bit of a picnic for us," Benedict responded with a self-satisfied smile.

Scarlett had to admit it was a good idea. Not to mention, people would give them a wide enough berth that they could speak without being overheard.

The carriage left London behind them, trundling out into the countryside. It surprised Scarlett how quickly the dense shuffle of the city gave way to gentle hills, covered with grass the pale green of early spring. She couldn't remember the last time she had left town, escaping from its constant noise and pollution. The air seemed lighter out here, and Scarlett's soul lifted as she pushed back the curtain to let in more fresh air. Benedict smiled at her antics, the sun warming his dark eyes to a honey color.

It didn't take long to reach the estate in question. Scarlett spotted fine ladies playing lawn bowling and couples sitting at tables set for tea scattered around. The carriage dropped them off at the edge of the festivities, where the manicured lawn gave way to a sparse wood.

"So I have another surprise," Benedict admitted as he helped her down from the carriage. Scarlett only teetered a bit on her unsteady ankle as she balanced on the stair. "My friend who owns this estate said I could use his hunting dogs for the day. He knows I like to impress ladies with my aim."

Scarlett glanced over at the picnic table set up nearby, and her heart sank as she spotted two fine hunting rifles propped up against the table.

"I hope you are ready to be thoroughly disappointed by my skills," Scarlett admitted as they approached the table.

Benedict hefted the weapons in practiced hands, handing one to Scarlett with a raised eyebrow.

"I would have thought you would be comfortable with guns," he said, not pointing out where he would have gotten that impression. Scarlett swallowed.

"Guns don't lend themselves to secrecy very well. Too loud," she admitted. Knives were more befitting of a silent assassin.

"I guess that explains why I prefer guns. I tend to make a lot of noise," Benedict said with a grin.

A short while later, it became clear that Scarlett's assessment of the situation had been right. As the dogs chased the birds from the brush, Benedict landed shot after shot with casual ease. Dogs cheerfully deposited a growing pile of pheasants at his feet, and he gave them affectionate scratches behind the ears.

He nodded at Scarlett to take her turn, and while she leveled the sights and pulled the trigger, she couldn't even be sure she fired in the direction of the bird as it flapped off into the woods. She propped the gun at her side with a sigh.

"I told you I wasn't any good," she said.

"I suppose at some point I had to be better than you at something," Benedict commented lightly.

Scarlett cocked her head at him.

"I must admit, this is good for my wounded pride after following you around the city feeling rather useless the past week," Benedict admitted sheepishly.

"I suppose you're a good shot with a pistol too then." Scarlett considered him, thinking of the dueling pistol she had snatched from him the night they first met.

"Well I wouldn't like to brag, but I can do a few neat party tricks with one. I generally avoid shooting at people though."

Scarlett appraised him thoughtfully. Perhaps he wasn't as helpless in the lower city as she would have liked to believe him to be, if his skill with the rifle was any indication. He could be a threat with the pistol he carried if worst came to worst. She was grateful he hadn't fired when he first encountered her in the hedge maze.

"I could show you?" Benedict offered, jerking Scarlett from her thoughts.

"Excuse me?"

"Here. You're coordinated enough that I'm sure you could be a good shot too with a little practice." Benedict approached, stepping up behind her.

He motioned for her to raise her rifle, which she did. He laid his hands over hers, helping her position it against her shoulder. Stepping up close, he put his head in the gap between her cheek and his shoulder. At the feeling of his solid chest at her back, Scarlett closed her eyes, steadying herself. A stolen moment like this would do wonders to convince anybody who saw them that Benedict and Georgette's courtship was progressing.

"Look down the sights, little bird," Benedict instructed, and Scarlett peeled open her eyes to do as he asked.

As the dogs darted through the underbrush, the birds took to the air, flapping and squawking. Benedict guided her hands, tracking their movements with the barrel of the gun. As his breath caressed the skin beneath her ear, Scarlett's hands shook so hard she barely managed to pull the trigger.

Her ears rang with the crack of the bullet, even as the birds fluttered away unscathed. Benedict dropped his hands and stepped away, letting Scarlett breathe again.

"Ah well, maybe I'm a good shot but not a good teacher," Benedict said with a shrug. "Why don't we stop terrorizing pheasants and have some refreshment?" he asked, gesturing to the low table set up on a nearby patch of grass.

Scarlett nodded her agreement, glad for the reprieve. As Benedict busied himself with the picnic basket, Scarlett took a deep breath to steady herself. This was all an act.

"I said I had a treat," Benedict turned around with a covered dish in his hands.

"Hunting and a picnic with your fine self isn't treat enough?" Scarlett found herself teasing, immediately biting her lip. Put her in a fine dress and apparently she was about to turn into an insufferable flirt, fluttering eyelashes and all.

"Well, it is, but I brought something especially for you." With a flourish, Benedict whipped the cover off the plate to reveal a kipper, topped with herbs and melting butter.

Scarlett's heart fluttered in her chest like a hummingbird even as her mouth watered at the delicious scent wafting off the plate. It was easy to pretend that a picnic like this was meant for Georgette and that Scarlett was just playing a part. But the kipper—Benedict had brought those for *her*.

"They aren't a particularly romantic picnic food, I'll admit. But you said they were your favorite, so I figured, why not? I think I did a good job with a wine pairing for such an unconventional dish too." Benedict passed the plate to Scarlett and turned to the basket to dig out a bottle, completely oblivious to the odd warmth blooming in Scarlett's chest and radiating up to her face. She took the reprieve to compose herself.

In a matter of moments, they each had a plate of kipper with a piece of fluffy white bread and a full glass of wine.

"Cheers." Benedict lifted his glass to Scarlett before taking a healthy sip. "I have to say, this is quite lovely. I feel bad that Georgette is missing her opportunities to have this for real."

Scarlett glanced around, but the only people she could see were several ladies playing croquet across the lawn. Even though they shot curious glances at the couple, as was the plan, they were well out of earshot.

"I would think so too," Scarlett admitted. "But she's glad to escape from the matchmaking of the social season."

"She isn't interested in making a good match? Isn't she Mr. Ward's only daughter?"

"It's more that she's already set her sights on somebody," Scarlett hedged. These weren't her secrets to tell.

"Well then, she's still missing a proper courtship with him. What's an engagement without being preceded by secluded picnics and wild rides through the countryside?" Benedict argued.

Scarlett avoided saying that was unlikely to be the case, given that Leon came from significantly less money than Benedict. Still, something in the pit of her stomach grew heavy at the reminder that he and Georgette weren't engaged yet. Leon had not returned from his trip to collect his family's blessings.

"Do you know Leon Blayford?" Scarlett blurted before she could think better of it.

"The art dealer?" Benedict asked, taken aback by what must seem to be an abrupt change of subject. "He's purchased some of the paintings my family had to...liquidate."

"When was the last time he bought a painting from you?"

"Probably several months ago. Why? Is he about to receive a visit of an unsavory sort?"

Scarlett shot him a look. "No, but he's traveling and has been gone quite a bit longer than was expected."

Understanding dawned on Benedict's face. Scarlett was unsure whether or not she was relieved that Benedict had figured out the purpose of her questioning without her having to explain it.

"And you and Georgette are interested in seeing him return safely I take it," Benedict clarified, to which Scarlett responded with a nod.

"There is a statue in the house that I've been trying to hold onto but may need to sell. I might put in an inquiry with his assistant and see when Mr. Blayford might be available to take a look at it."

Scarlett nodded her gratitude. As much as it twisted her gut to be relying on Benedict both to help her find Leon and to protect Georgette, she was glad she'd have some good news for her friend next time she visited.

Chapter Eight

A groan bubbled up in Scarlett's throat as Georgette held up a tiara in the mirror. The wig of chestnut curls was heavy enough without an additional headpiece.

"How do you stand having your hair pinned up and bejeweled all the time without getting a headache?" Scarlett bemoaned as Georgette worked the shimmering accessory into the wig.

"You've just gotten so accustomed to short hair that your scalp isn't used to it anymore," Georgette commented. "Honestly, I'm a little jealous of how pretty you look with hair that barely covers your ears. I don't think I'd look good if I lopped mine off."

Scarlett bit her tongue. Her hair had been waist length before she hacked it all off with a dull knife. Without a lady's maid to help her manage it—or even a hairbrush for that matter—it had become a veritable rat's nest, unable to be salvaged. Only weeks after her parents' deaths, she knelt in a back alley and hacked at her hair viciously, gritting her teeth to suppress her anger. It had been about survival.

Now she smiled at Georgette in the mirror as she admired her handiwork. Something about Georgette's sweetness was a balm to the anger that bubbled under her skin, making it easier to shove down in her presence.

"This tiara is my favorite," Georgette explained as she fetched her box of cosmetics from her drawer. "It was Mother's, and it's what I would wear if I were trying to catch the attention of a duke's son."

"Younger son," Scarlett said as she closed her eyes so Georgette could apply paint to her lids.

"So all the money with none of the responsibility," Georgette teased.

Scarlett kept her mouth shut, loath to admit to anybody that the Pearces currently flirted with bankruptcy. Benedict's admission of vulnerability was something she felt the need to keep to herself.

"I've heard he's the more handsome one too."

Scarlett opened her eyes to find Georgette staring at her with mischief in her gaze.

"Not as handsome as a certain art dealer, I would say," Scarlett deflected, not wanting to think about how handsome Benedict may or may not be right now. She regretted changing the subject when Georgette's shoulders slumped.

"I still haven't heard from him," she admitted.

"Benedict is going to help me inquire after him. I'll let you know as soon as I hear anything." Scarlett patted Georgette's shoulder in comfort.

Georgette smiled softly but remained deflated.

"You're doing so much for me. I hate sitting here doing nothing. Like I'm just waiting on other people to fix my problems or something," Georgette admitted.

"You're being my friend. That's something."

"Yes, but that's hardly work."

Scarlett bit down the urge to disagree—to say that these visits with Georgette were sometimes the only thing that calmed the ball of anger that lived locked in her chest, even if it was only temporary. And Georgette risked her future by associating with Scarlett, seemingly uncaring of the scandal that would arise if the world knew that she had tea with a gangster most nights.

Now Georgette moved onto her lips, painting them a deep crimson that would generally be too eye catching for Scarlett's taste, but was perfectly in character for Georgette.

"There you go," Georgette declared with a satisfied smile. "Now he won't stop being able to think about how much he wants to kiss your lips all night."

"You mean your lips," Scarlett corrected. She was going to be pretending to be Georgette after all.

"No, I mean yours," Georgette said matter-of-factly as she stowed her cosmetics back in her vanity drawer.

"This is all an act," Scarlett reminded even as something akin to excitement fluttered in her chest.

"Yes, but that doesn't mean you can't have a little fun with it."

Scarlett busied herself with collecting a fan and handkerchief from Georgette to avoid thinking about what Georgette was implying.

While the first ball where Scarlett met Benedict had been out in a garden, open to the cool night air, the dance floor at the viscount's ball was indoors. The grand space was large enough to hold the Roost twice over, and it was packed with every member of polite society, their gossiping filling the hall with a deafening buzz. As Mr. Ward led her into the room, taking care to avoid those who would recognize her as an imposter, Scarlett couldn't help but mentally mark all the exit points. It would be a challenge to find the Wolves' agents among the glittering masses. At least having less darkened corners to hide in and observe would mean the Wolves had fewer places to hide as well.

"Ms. Ward, may I request the pleasure of having the first dance of the evening?"

A familiar voice pulled Scarlett from her contemplation of the surroundings. Benedict stood in the path of her and Mr. Ward, holding out his hand in offering.

Scarlett had seen Benedict covered in mud and in his nightclothes in the past week, but now seeing him in all his finery, she had a visceral appreciation for how he managed to leave many a heartbroken lady in his wake. His emerald green cravat matched his waistcoat, golden buttons gleaming almost as brightly as his eyes. He had kept his hair loose, letting it curl at the nape of his neck and frame his angular face. His nose, which might be considered too large by common standards, seemed to fit perfectly with his lopsided smile and eyes that danced with amusement even in the direst situations.

"She would love to," Mr. Ward answered, nudging Scarlett and giving her a stern look, probably worried about why she had been standing there motionless for several long moments.

"Of course," she demurred, doing her best impression of a flattered young lady. Benedict tucked her hand into the crook of his elbow and led her across the room to the dance floor where a string quartet played a lively tune.

Letting the volume of the music cover her words, Scarlett leaned in to murmur to Benedict, "I don't think the dance floor is going to be the best vantage point for spotting any funny business from the Wolves."

"Yes, but it would look suspicious if I didn't take several turns around the floor with you. I am known for being on the dance floor all night you know." Benedict leaned in conspiratorially. "Unless I've convinced the lady who has my attentions to duck out with me for a different sort of escape that requires far more privacy, that is."

He spoke the last words directly into the shell of Scarlett's ear, sending a subtle tremor down her spine. She brushed it off by shooting him a glare that she hoped conveyed the need to focus. He smirked back before his face fell.

"The dances, you don't know them—"

"I know enough to get by," Scarlett interjected. "I'm just...out of practice."

Benedict raised an eyebrow at her, but she didn't elaborate. He huffed in amusement.

"Dancing, playing the piano...you could pass as a proper lady if you didn't toss me out of windows so often."

"I told you, if I'm jumping out too then it hardly counts as throwing you," Scarlett argued.

At that moment the music drew to a close and the couples currently dancing on the floor parted ways with polite bows and curtsies. Benedict led Scarlett onto the floor, leading them to a place where they couldn't be missed.

As the violinist began the new song, Benedict swept Scarlett into his arms. She gulped as she recognized the opening notes of a dramatic waltz, and they were off.

Even if it had been years since Scarlett last danced, nights of running over rooftops and dodging punches had honed her coordination and balance. While Scarlett could outpace Benedict in the back alleys, he blew her away on the dance floor, just as he had while hunting. With a firm arm around her waist, Benedict swept them around in a graceful arc. Perhaps it had been too long since Scarlett had danced with a man, her parents having died before her first season out in society, but the feel of Benedict's fingers splayed across her ribcage stole her attention. As her focus zeroed in on their warm pressure, her faced warmed in a way that almost drove away the awareness of a ballroom full of gazes fixed on them.

As the musicians built to a dramatic crescendo, Benedict took the opportunity to brace both hands around her waist and lift her around him, making Scarlett's stomach swoop in a way not altogether unpleasant. She might tease him about his upper body strength compared to her when they climbed through windows, but he clearly knew what he was down on his home turf.

Placing her on her feet again, Benedict maneuvered Scarlett in a small dip, his face dropping dangerously close to her throat, near enough that his breath tickled her hammering pulse.

"Remember, you're supposed to be falling madly in love with me," he murmured low enough that nobody else could hear.

Scarlett blinked in confusion to dispel the odd feeling of drunkenness working its way through her mind.

"You look so stricken, I'm afraid people watching might think I'm stomping on your toes," Benedict continued.

Right, this was part of their elaborate show, proving to the guests—and any Wolves who might be spying—that Benedict was seducing the hapless Ms. Ward out of her sizeable dowry.

"I'm afraid you're the one having to deal with bruised feet," Scarlett countered as Benedict saved her from stumbling through a turn she hadn't practiced in quite a while.

"An injury I'm more than willing to bear for uninterrupted time with a beautiful woman," Benedict responded easily. He certainly knew how to act the part of a charmer when the job demanded. It was no wonder he was starting to turn Scarlett's head.

With that, the waltz drew to a close, and Scarlett offered a wobbly curtsy. The strings began to strike up a lively quadrille, and Benedict inclined his head in question. Scarlett shook her head forcefully enough that she felt her wig shift ever so slightly. If a sedate waltz tested her muscle memory, then anything involving more coordination was sure to end in disaster. Not to mention, dancing with Benedict didn't seem conducive to keeping her wits about her.

"I could use a glass of punch," Scarlett admitted.

"Of course. You need fuel to have a properly good time at any of these balls." Benedict tucked Scarlett's gloved hand into his elbow once more. As he led her through the crowds to the adjacent parlor, Scarlett could feel the weighty gazes of dozens of London socialites trailing them. She tightened her fingers around Benedict's biceps to resist the call of her shadows, wanting to shield her from the eyes of those long considered to be unfriendly. They might not look kindly on those they considered lower city dirt, but right now she was Georgette Ward, jewel of the social season and a lady Benedict would be proud to have seen on his arm. The fashionable dress she wore, plunging low at the neckline and adorned with silvery ribbons, served as both armor and disguise.

As if hearing her thoughts, Benedict's other hand came up in a proprietary gesture to cover where she clutched his arm. Even if it was for the benefit of their audience, it helped Scarlett relax her grip and push down the beacon of safety offered by the shadows at the edge of her mind.

Once they each had a glass of punch in hand, Scarlett situated them in the alcove of a bay window where they could observe the room as a whole while also being seen by any gossip who might look their way.

As Scarlett settled herself into the window seat, she took a moment to glance out the window. Through the glass, the darkened city looked peaceful and quiet. From the top of the hill, the viscount's house had a view of a vast swath of London, twinkling street lights leading down to the middle city until they trailed off into the darkness of the lower city. Shadows covered the streets until they reached the Thames, where moonlight glittered off the sluggish water. Even though Scarlett could see the lower city from here, imagining the brawls and thefts that would occur on a night like this, it seemed a world away from the glittering spectacle of this ball. It felt impossible that bloody-knuckled gangsters could exist on the same streets as these refined socialites, living such different lives in the same space. It gave Scarlett whiplash to run jobs with the Raptors one night and then dance in the arms of a duke's son the next.

"Where do you think the Wolves would plant their agents at a party like this?" Benedict murmured, pulling Scarlett's attention away from the window and back to the party where it belonged.

"It's hard to say," Scarlett admitted. "As far as I knew, Nathanial Woodrow was the only gangster ever to frequent society balls. I doubt the Wolves have an undercover agent like that on the guest list. My guess is that this is a surreptitious backroom rendezvous situation."

"We could always pretend to sneak off for a rendezvous of our own and see if we find anything," Benedict suggested.

"And risk missing our lead because we were wandering around the house? I think not," Scarlett retorted. "Besides, I'm here to make it seem like you're courting Georgette, not to ruin her status."

"You think a man of my reputation hasn't learned how to be discreet?" Benedict clapped a hand to his chest in exaggerated offense.

"If you were discreet, then you wouldn't have the reputation." Scarlett took a delicate sip of her champagne.

Benedict's responding chuckle was low and warm. "Can't get anything past you, can I?"

Scarlett grabbed his arm to indicate he should be quiet as she spotted movement across the hall. While most of the crowd churned aimlessly, flowing and eddying into pockets of conversation only to break up and regroup in new arrangements, a few figures cut through the crowd in a direct path. The dark silhouettes of three men in suits trailed from the ballroom towards a door leading off to what appeared to be a study.

Scarlett jerked her head towards the figures. Benedict's gaze scanned the crowd, brow creased in confusion a moment before it settled. With a quick nod, he sprang to his feet, Scarlett right behind him.

She took the lead as they began weaving through the partygoers. Although her height caused her to lose sight of their targets as soon as she entered a throng of tittering ladies, she managed to slip through the clusters of partygoers relatively easily, used to going unnoticed and hindered only by the voluminous skirts she wasn't accustomed to. Benedict wasn't quite as agile, but his stature allowed him to keep sight of their quarry, and he directed Scarlett with a soft hand on her shoulder.

Soon they were across the room, standing before the door the men had disappeared through. Benedict blocked Scarlett's form with his frame as she leaned in close. The door had been left ajar, but the room beyond seemed to be empty. If there were voices, they could not be heard over the general hubbub of the party.

Cautiously, Scarlett inched the door open further, revealing a darkened library. Seeing it was empty, she opened it just wide enough to slip inside before yanking Benedict in after her.

"What are—"

Scarlett moved to press a hand to Benedict's mouth to silence him and ended up flopping her hand against his jaw in the darkness. Still, he got the message and fell silent. With the door closed behind them, muffling the music and din of conversation, the low cadence of several voices became audible. Creeping across the room, Scarlett could just make out the shape of another door, outlined in light seeping through the cracks near the floor and at the hinges.

Benedict trailed her towards the source of the voices, and Scarlett unconsciously wreathed them in even deeper shadows, despite the darkness of the room. Reaching the door, Scarlett nearly pressed herself against the wall, straining to hear the voices within.

"—hear you like games of chance," came a grating voice that plucked at something in the back of Scarlett's memory.

Benedict wedged himself between Scarlett and the bookshelf next to the door to listen as well. The warmth of his breath tickled the nape of her neck as he pressed behind her to eavesdrop.

"You're not wrong, but why go to the lower city when there are plenty of good hands of cards to be played at parties with far more creature comforts?" asked a voice with the polished accent of a society gentleman, followed by another chuckle of agreement.

"I don't think the hands of whist you play at balls have quite the same stakes the Wolves can offer you," the first voice responded, sounding like his best approximation of a posh businessman despite the natural gruffness of his tone.

"I attended two weeks ago, and I can assure you that games of dice in polite society don't hold the same...entertainment value as what the Wolves offer at their new establishment," another voice cut in.

General rumbles of agreement drifted through the door, but Scarlett couldn't manage to catch any words as multiple conversations occurred at the same time.

"So what do you say?" the Wolf asked. "Can I tell Fang to save the best seats in the house for you lovely gentlemen on Friday?"

Murmurs of ascent ran through the room.

"I better go squeeze in several dances with my wife then. Help placate her before I excuse myself from her sister-in-law's party on Friday."

Before Scarlett had time to retreat from the door, footsteps approached and it began to swing open. Benedict seemed to realize they were about to be discovered at the same moment she did, and he yanked her back into him, pulling them both behind the narrow bookshelf by the door.

Instinctually, shadows coalesced around them, making the darkness of their hiding spot denser than the gloom of the rest of the room. Several figures filed out of the back room, but Scarlett couldn't focus on identifying them. Instead, she found her mind fixated on the press of Benedict's body against hers. He had her pinned against the bookshelf, his hands braced on the shelf on either side of her hips. The wooden edge dug into the small of her back, giving her no room to retreat. Even as she took quiet, shallow breaths in an effort to remain silent, the movement caused her breasts to brush against the buttons of Benedict's waistcoat, and an unfamiliar warmth rushed from the crown of her head to the base of her spine. She had the fleeting thought that this dress was daringly lowcut compared to her usual attire.

Even as she battled for control over her racing heartbeat, Scarlett found herself enveloped by Benedict's scent as her nose lingered mere inches from his neatly tied cravat. Fresh citrus undercut by deep earthiness invaded her senses, making it impossible to focus on the murmured words of the men now pushing back into the party.

Alone in the study once more, Benedict didn't move away immediately. Scarlett peeled her hand away from where it gripped the edge of the shelf behind her, finding that she had dug her fingernails into the wood, to push Benedict away from her. She hesitated as his head dipped. As his face came closer to the space behind her ear, she could swear his breath sounded as ragged as hers had suddenly become. He seemed to shudder, shaking himself free of the moment before quickly stepping back.

With a snap, the spell was over and the sounds of revelry from the next room over rushed back in as if Scarlett had just surfaced from underwater. The light filtering in from the cracked door silhouetted Benedict's profile as he ran a hand through his hair, seemingly uncaring if he disturbed its careful styling.

"So the Wolves have started some sort of gambling operation," he remarked, for once his tone empty of its usual levity. Perhaps it was the harsh shadows cast by the backlighting, but Benedict looked uncharacteristically tired. Scarlett frowned.

"The gangs have always run gambling operations though. It's not even illegal—although the amount the house cheats is usually not above board," she reasoned. "So why all the secrecy? And what does it have to do with Georgette?"

Doubt weighed heavy in Scarlett's stomach, turning the punch there into acid. Perhaps she had gotten off track and whatever the Wolves were doing in the Lions' old territory had nothing to do with their threats towards Georgette. Maybe she and Benedict were just wasting precious time unraveling this mystery when her friend's life was still in danger. Soon enough, the Wolves would grow impatient, waiting to hear that Benedict had acquired the dowry and Georgette could be disposed of.

The soft brush of fingers on her wrist drew Scarlett from her spiraling worries.

"Knowing what the Wolves are up to can only help us keep Georgette safe," Benedict assured, as if he could read Scarlett's thoughts. He must have been able to feel her pulse hammering in her wrist, both from frustration and the lingering effects of their close proximity.

Scarlett nodded, pulling her wrist from his grasp and subtly scrubbing it on her skirt to dispel the odd sensations still surging through her. She wasn't going to be able to help anybody if she couldn't stay focused.

"I guess we will need to find this...event on Friday then," she mused.

"I think I might be able to help with that," Benedict commented. "I recognized Baxter's voice in that room. We've hunted together often, so if I play my cards right, I'm sure I can persuade him to bring me along. Especially if I play on how a love for gambling runs in my family. For all I know, this *operation* is what landed my father in such deep debt with the Wolves anyways."

In the dim light, Scarlett could just make out a muscle in Benedict's jaw tick. Her hand twitched as if to comfort him in turn, but she kept it at her side.

"We'll get both of our problems solved." *And then we'll go our separate ways.* Scarlett added to herself as a reminder. This partnership with Benedict was only temporary, and when it was over, she would be moving into the Roost to live out her life as a Raptor until she was either killed or thrown in jail. The thought filled her with a heavier sadness than usual.

"I'll go catch him before I lose him, and regroup with you in a minute," Benedict said before slipping back out into the party. Scarlett took a few moments alone in the dark to regroup as well, making sure her wig was still firmly affixed and her wits were gathered.

When she slipped back out into the ballroom, she quickly found Mr. Ward. He smiled warm and broad as she approached, as he would if she were Georgette. Slipping into his radius, Scarlett positioned herself between Mr. Ward and the wall, so any other of Georgette's admirers would have to get past a scowling father to ask her to dance.

They stood in companionable silence for a moment, not uncommon for the two of them on the rare occasions they were left alone. Most of their understandings were better left unspoken.

"You do only seem to have eyes for Lord Pearce." Mr. Ward broke the silence.

"I'm glad to find out that acting lies among my talents."

"That's the odd part. I got the distinct impression you weren't doing much acting, despite being fully costumed," Mr. Ward observed, his voice even.

Scarlett froze, glancing around them, but by now everybody in attendance seemed to be deep in the punch and paying them no mind.

"I wouldn't know what you mean," Scarlett deflected.

Mr. Ward sighed heavily, the expression on his face drawing attention to the streaks of gray in his sideburns and the lines around his frown.

"I know I haven't exactly...protected you well since—" Mr. Ward cleared his throat looking more uncomfortable than Scarlett had seen him before. "But maybe I can change that just this once. I recognized the expression on your face when you danced with Lord Pearce, and it wasn't just for the benefit of the onlookers. I have no doubt you can dodge a knife, but the kind of hurt you're setting yourself up for here isn't as easily avoided."

Scarlett swallowed, not moving to deny his claims. She was all too aware of the battle with her attraction to Benedict, but Mr. Ward's comment made it clear that she was denying the severity of her predicament. Even as her heart wrenched with the realization, it warmed in her chest.

Any resentment she held towards Mr. Ward for not taking her in when her parents were killed was buried deep with all her other hurts. After all, she hadn't given him the chance to offer, disappearing into the shadowed alleys of the lower city at the realization that her Talent would put anybody who tried to shield her in danger, and unwilling to pile any more burdens onto her conscience. But Mr. Ward's concern for her soothed a wound inside her even as it made her realize it still festered.

"The son of a duke is expected to marry well, and you've long since discarded your own good name," he pressed on, echoing the thoughts that ran through Scarlett's subconscious but she had avoided thinking because they would mean acknowledging that Benedict had become more than an inconvenient partner.

At that moment the gentleman in question appeared in the crowd, cutting through the throngs to where they stood. His hopeful expression and the way Scarlett's own frown involuntarily softened in response confirmed what she already suspected—she had inadvertently thrown her own feelings into the line of fire.

"I'll tell you what I learned while we dance. After all, the night is young and we must make the most of it." Benedict swept Scarlett towards the dance floor, and she went without protest. She spared a glance over her shoulder at Mr. Ward's grim expression before they were engulfed by a cluster of partygoers. Even if he was right to be concerned, Scarlett suspected that she was in too deep now to disentangle herself from Benedict easily.

Chapter Nine

"Message for you," Granny said by way of greeting as Scarlett stumbled bleary eyed down the stairs the next morning.

She barely managed to grab the folded piece of parchment Granny shoved at her, clutching it to her chest in surprise. Not even Georgette sent notes to Scarlett, Mr. Ward hesitant to send a man to the lower city on a regular basis on the off chance somebody connected Georgette with the gangs and besmirched her reputation.

"You got an admirer?" Granny asked in her typical blunt fashion. She didn't even look up from the counter she rubbed with a cloth ragged enough that it looked as if it might disintegrate in her hands.

"You know I don't," Scarlett said, turning the paper in her hand to find it sealed in blue wax, emblazoned with a sparrow.

Granny's responding hum was unconvinced, and she fixed Scarlett in her beady gaze. "That lip paint smeared on your face tells me otherwise. Besides, you could use somebody to show you a good time. You've been wearing that scowl more and more for years now."

"You're one to talk," Scarlett snorted, racking her brain for a memory of Granny smiling and coming up blank. "Maybe you should get an admirer."

"You don't know what I get up to at night," Granny argued, giving up on scrubbing the counter and bracing her hands on her hips. "Now go upstairs and read your little love letter and get me my rent money while you're at it. Due on Friday."

Scarlett froze. She had emptied the last of her dowry onto Granny's counter a few weeks back. With as busy as she had been dashing around the city on the Wolves' tail, she had nearly forgotten about her decision to move into the Roost. She thought she had come to terms with the inevitable, but facing it down, Scarlett felt the world shift under her feet like sand. She was about to take the final step into being a lower city gangster. As many stairs as she'd descended to get to this point, this last leap had a foreboding sense of finality to it.

Somehow, her time with Benedict in the upper city had approximated her old life—even if she was living it as somebody else—and thrown into sharp relief how far she had fallen. It was one of the reasons she relegated her time with Georgette to stolen midnight visits. Being reminded of all she had lost only made her angry, the feeling a luxury that Scarlett couldn't afford in the lower city where the constant objective was survival.

"See, now I know you've taken a lover. I've never seen you stand and daydream like that before," Granny cut in with a shake of her head, drawing Scarlett from her contemplation.

Scarlett shot a glare at her before bounding up the stairs to open her note in the privacy of her room, another luxury she wouldn't have for much longer.

Once the door closed behind her, she pulled a dagger from the sheathe under her sleeve to use as a letter opener. Without consciously deciding too, she slid the edge under the wax seal and popped it off without cutting through it. The sparrow embossed in Emerald sparked the memory of Benedict calling her *little bird.* Putting the seal in her pocket she unfolded the letter and read the elegantly looping script.

Scarlett,

While I managed to secure an invite to tonight's festivities, Mr. Baxter has informed me that it's not the type of event I should bring a lady friend too. I can lead you to the location, but you may have to use your own unique charms to invite yourself inside.

I also made the inquiry you asked about for selling the marble bust. It seems that Mr. Blayford has been back in town for several weeks and is happy to come by and appraise the statue at my earliest convenience. Shall I schedule a meeting with him, or do you wish to make your own arrangements?

Yours,

Benedict

Scarlett twirled her still-unsheathed dagger in her hand as she frowned down at the letter. It was a habit she often made fun of brawlers for but had picked up when she found it kept people away from her, where they couldn't cause her trouble. Now it was a subconscious distraction as she mulled through Benedict's letter.

The first part wasn't an issue. As long as she knew where to go, she should be able to sneak inside. After all, she had gotten used to creeping into enemy territory over the last few weeks. What caused her brows to crease was the second paragraph. She couldn't think why Leon wouldn't contact Georgette if he were back in town. It seemed as farfetched as Amos throwing a tea party to imagine that he wasn't interested in her anymore. Even if Leon hadn't been successful at securing the money for their marriage, he had to know Georgette would want to be assured he got home safely.

Scarlett chewed her cheek hard enough to taste blood as she considered the information before her. It wasn't her place to tell Georgette about Leon, but it rubbed at her nerves to leave her in the dark when she knew he was back. Scarlett could lie to a lot of people, but not Georgette. Either way, Scarlett wouldn't have to decide right away because she wouldn't be seeing Georgette until tomorrow. Tonight, she had a date with the Wolves.

Benedict's warm chuckle echoed down the sidewalk to where Scarlett hid in the shadow of a doorway. He was all charm and easy smiles as he and Mr. Baxter climbed out of their cab in front of an unassuming building in Wolf territory. The only sign that anything unusual was happening inside was the bruisers flanking the entrance and the excited chattering that spilled out into the darkened street whenever the door briefly swung open.

As Benedict approached the men at the entrance, she could have sworn his eyes darted to the patch of shadows where she crouched, as if to ensure she hadn't had issue following them here. His gaze flickered over her briefly before returning to his companion, who retrieved a piece of paper from the inner pocket of his waistcoat. After inspecting the document briefly, one of the thugs opened the door and beckoned them inside.

The carriage clattered away, the driver no doubt searching for a place to have a drink of his own before coming back to pick up his charges. As it rounded the corner out of sight, Scarlett eyed the task before her. There weren't many points of entry, the building almost intentionally windowless as it hid the illicit activities within. Given that she didn't know what kind of situation she'd be entering, Scarlett decided on the front door.

Keeping herself shrouded in a swirling miasma of darkness, Scarlett crept as close as she dared to the entrance, pausing just outside the pool of light cast by a streetlight. From here, she could hear the bouncers conversing in low grunts.

"Shame we don't get to watch the fun."

"True, but if we watch the entrance, then we get a cut of the winnings."

Looking at the size of the first one's bicep as he crossed his arms with a disappointed huff, Scarlett decided against fighting them. Steeling herself, she focused on the patch of darkness on the far side of the streetlamp. With a deep breath she focused on the shadows there until they began to shimmer, coalescing until they morphed into the shape of a woman. Scarlett grimaced against the high-pitched ringing in her ears that always came when she forced the shadows to do something so dramatic.

"Who goes there?" one of the bouncers barked, only for the other to jab him in the ribs with an elbow.

"May we help you?" the second one added on, clearly trying to prove his manners to the darkened lady.

Screwing up her face, Scarlett forced the silhouette of the woman to fall to the ground as if in a dead swoon. Instantaneously, the thugs jumped into action, rushing towards her figure. It was all the opening Scarlett needed to dash towards the unattended door and slip inside.

The sight that greeted Scarlett inside took her off guard. As soon as she slid through the door, she plastered herself against the wall, unsure if she would be confronted as she entered. Instead, nobody paid her much mind, only sparing her a glance as they milled about a large open space, some with drinks in hand.

Scarlett cautiously drifted further into the room and away from the exit, in case the bouncers came to check if anybody had entered uninvited. She slid through clusters of people, predominantly men, more well-dressed than she would expect for most lower city haunts. The general atmosphere buzzed with excitement, so thick it hovered in the air like mist, as palpable as Scarlett's shadows. She craned her neck, trying to find Benedict, when she caught sight of what was to be the evenings attraction.

In the center of the large open room was a roped off ring, surrounded by low benches, with plenty more room for spectators to stand behind them. A small cordoned off area held more comfortable-looking seats in one corner. As she watched, a man with a Wolf inked on his forearm beckoned Benedict and Mr. Baxter inside to where several other finely dressed gentlemen already sat.

Scarlett frowned at the arrangement. Boxing matches were a common entertainment, even in the upper city. They might be lucrative for the Wolves—indeed, stacks of cash were already changing hands as Wolves prowling through the crowds collected bets—but they certainly didn't warrant this level of clandestine security.

"Gentlemen, please get your drinks and place your final bets!" Scarlett recognized the Wolf with the neck tattoo, standing in the middle of the ring, arms raised as he grandly announced, "The first match of the evening will start soon, and tonight we have a great lineup, but if you blink, you might miss it!"

Scarlett frowned even as the buzz in the room hit a crescendo. The Wolves meandering through the room hollered for final odds, thick stacks of cash being shoved into their already overflowing hands. Who did they have fighting that could raise this sort of ruckus?

As the crowds clamored to get a good view of the arena, Scarlett glanced around for a good vantage point. A roped-off staircase in the corner led to a landing that would afford a good view of the ring. It was child's play to avoid the notice of the Wolves collecting bets and slip up to the second floor, barely having to use the aid of her shadows.

No sooner had Scarlett hidden herself in the corner of the landing so as not to be immediately noticeable from below but still have a good view of the proceedings, that the familiar Wolf stepped into the ring once more.

"Ladies and gentlemen!" he pontificated as if announcing for a traveling circus, "tonight, we have a special warm-up match between a returning champion and a new challenger. Stepping into the ring for the first time, let's hear it for Bartholomew, the bladed wonder!"

The man who stepped into the ring was everything Scarlett would expect from a boxer. Clothed only in a pair of trousers, every one of the ropy muscles of his torso was on display, leading up to a neck as thick as Scarlett's thigh. The mean glint in his eye and the stern set of his brow signaled a tough fight for his competitor. The crowd cheered as he stepped into the ring, but Scarlett frowned at the tattoo of a scorpion, poised to strike, inked across his chest. Perhaps he had defected from the Scorpions to join the Wolves when they expanded their territory, although a second inspection revealed no marking of the Wolves. If he really was a Scorpion, this boxing ring involved more of the lower city than just the Wolves.

The furrow between Scarlett's brow only deepened as the Wolf announced the second fighter. "And our returning winner from last week's opening match, let's hear it for the Jumper, Jim!"

Despite Scarlett's wonder at what kind of name that could possibly be, the crowd went wild as a twig of a boy stepped into the arena. He held up his hands to bask in their whoops and applause as if unconcerned by the man twice his size clearly about to beat him to a pulp.

The opponents squared off against each other, Bartholomew falling into a defensive crouch, fists up before his face. Jim stood up straight, not even adopting a fighting posture. Scarlett's teeth creaked in her skull as she ground them. She had more experience than she cared for fighting somebody bigger than her, and normally the trick was taking them unawares.

The announcer stepped up to the bell just outside of the arena, his hand hovering on the rope. An anticipatory hush swept through the room as every gaze fixated on the pair in the arena.

Clang!

The echoes of the bell still rang through the hall when the bigger man lunged. He charged forward, flinging his arms out as if to tackle Jim to the ground, but Jim wasn't there. Scarlett blinked at Jim standing on the far side of the arena. She was quick in a fight, but not even she could move that fast.

Bartholomew growled, whipping around to find his opponent standing casually by the wall of the ring. With a snarl, he lunged again. This time, Scarlett was watching for it. Right before Bartholomew reached him, Jim evaporated from existence, blinking back into being a few feet to the left.

Scarlett's stomach dropped all the way through the bottom of her boots and into the jeering crowd below. These competitors weren't boxers. They were Talented.

Obviously growing frustrated with the game of cat and mouse, Bartholomew rounded on his evasive opponent. At first, Scarlett thought he was shaking with rage, until she realized it was just his skin shifting. The crowd roared as spikes emerged from his knuckles, his elbows, even the backs of his shoulders. They were pale like bone but came to lethal points, turning the competitor from an intimidating brawler into a fighter bred for destruction.

His powers unleashed, Bartholomew began swinging in earnest, and the pace of the fight picked up. Jim continued to flash step out of the way of every blow, not making any swings of his own, clearly trying to tire his opponent out. While Bartholomew's chest began to heave, and even Scarlett could see the sweat dripping down his back from this distance, he came closer to connecting with Jim every time. The manic gleam growing in his eyes made bile rise in the back of Scarlett's throat. She had inched forward out of her hiding spot as she watched, her fingers gripping the railing on the edge of the landing with blanched knuckles.

The crowd gasped as Bartholomew's next blow skimmed against Jim's shirt, tearing the fabric before he disappeared. Jim seemed to have been thrown off his rhythm by the contact, stuttering in his next dodge. As Bartholomew threw his next bladed punch, he threw his other arm behind him. As Jim blinked back into existence behind his opponent, he froze. The room grew quiet, as if collectively holding their breath. In the resulting stillness, a haunting gurgle slipped from Jim's lips.

He staggered backward, revealing that he had impaled himself on the elbow spike of Bartholomew's opposite arm. His hand came to his stomach, blood already dripping onto the floor. As Scarlett watched him collapse, she realized that the entire floor of the ring was littered with rusty stains. This wasn't the first puddle of blood to be seen in this arena.

The ringing in Scarlett's ears at the realization was nearly loud enough to drown out the screams of the crowd. With growing horror, she realized that they weren't screeching in horror at the violence before them, but cheering on the victor who now wore a look of triumph on his face. Rivulets of crimson dripped from the bone blade still protruding from his elbow, running down his arm, but he didn't seem to care.

The Wolf who served as an announcer jumped into the ring, grabbing his fist and hoisting it into the air in victory.

"We have a first-time winner!" he shouted, the announcement met with stomping feet and applause.

In the crowd, Scarlett saw more money changing hands as some celebrated their winnings and others bemoaned their losses. Either way, the house always won.

Without orders, several figures emerged from the crowd. Two picked up the now limp form of Jim and hauled him into a back room—to get him medical treatment or let him die in private, Scarlett didn't dare to hazard a guess. Another Wolf jumped forward with a rag to attend to the blood stain, mopping up most of it even while rubbing the red stain into the rough-hewn floorboards, a permanent mark of the carnage wrought there.

Scarlett stared dumbfounded over the scene before her, something she hadn't imagined in her nightmares. As if drawn by gravity, her gaze traveled to Benedict. He was already looking at her, the horror she felt at what they had just witnessed mirrored in his expression. These were gladiator matches, pitting the Talented of the lower city against each other for the amusement of well-paying spectators. No longer were the Talented just the muscle of the lower city, they were its entertainment.

Heat built under Scarlett's skin, bubbling in her veins as if an angry bird were trying to claw its way out from under her skin. She screwed her eyes shut, blocking out the sight of Benedict's wide eyes that somehow only made her angrier. She counted measured breaths through her nose, trying to get the sensation under control. They had to get out of here, and causing a scene wasn't going to do her any favors. She could retreat to the shadows and find a way to fix this. For now, she just had to endure, just as she had when her parents died. Thinking kept you alive; anger got you killed.

Opening her eyes, Scarlett found Benedict still staring at her. She jerked her head towards the exit, and he offered her the smallest nod before turning to his friend. Scarlett couldn't help but be impressed by the unbothered façade he put on, as if he too were enjoying the evening and was sorry to duck out.

"Ladies and gentlemen, it's time for the main event!" The announcer stepped into the now empty ring once more. "It's time for the match you've all been waiting for. We have our undefeated champion, the king of ice himself, Ivor!"

Scarlett watched in morbid curiosity as she edged towards the stairs, another musclebound man stepping into the arena as if drinking in the enthusiasm of the crowd around him.

"Facing off against recent fan favorite, the boulder who can take a beating, Leon!"

Scarlett turned to stone where she stood as a familiar figure stepped into the ring. Last time Scarlett had seen Leon Blayford, his sandy hair was shiny and his face lit with a smile as he handed her a love letter to deliver to Georgette. Now his hair hung in dirty strands around his face, framing gritted teeth and a bruise across one cheekbone.

"No one has been able to stand up to Ivor's icy punches yet, but Leon here has shown himself capable of hanging in there even when things get rough."

Scarlett was pressed against the railing once more, paying no heed to if she could be seen from the floor below.

Ivor's face split in a wicked grin and breath puffed from his nose in a visible cloud, as if he were outside in winter. Leon remained stoic, but the briefest flicker of fear in his eyes combined with the lingering fire under Scarlett's skin spurred her to action.

Bracing her palms on the banister before her, she leaped over it. She sailed through the air for a fleeting moment before landing in the center of the fighting ring, breaking her fall with a roll that made the rough floorboards scrape along her still-healing shoulder blade. She ignored the sensation, letting the momentum of her tumble carry her to a crouch among a cacophony of shouts and gasps.

The Wolf who served as the announcer jumped back into the ring, advancing on Scarlett. She straightened and backed up, putting herself between him and Leon.

"Just who do you think you are? You don't look like you came with an invitation," he asked, his tone holding none of the bravado it had when announcing the fights, instead going low and cold.

"I'm—" Scarlett stammered, her gaze flickering to Benedict over the Wolf's shoulder. He would know how to fast-talk his way out of this situation. "I've come to challenge him." Scarlett jerked her chin at Ivor, who watched the proceedings with a scowl and folded arms.

"Scarlett?" Leon asked from behind. She didn't spare a glance over her shoulder. It wouldn't help to have the Wolves know that she had jumped in to protect him.

"You know her?" the Wolf asked.

"We've run into each other before," Scarlett cut in before Leon could answer. "What matters now is the fight at hand."

"The fights are only for Talented girl, as much as I might enjoy seeing Ivor beat you to a pulp," the Wolf snorted.

With a smile that she wore like a snarl, Scarlett unleashed her shadows, letting them drip from her fingers and crawl up her arms until she wore them like shadowed talons. The angry beast within her seemed to crow in approval, but she snapped it to heel. This was a precarious situation, and she didn't need to jeopardize it with clouded judgement.

The Wolf hesitated, clearly intrigued with the display. Scarlett's gaze flickered to Benedict over his shoulder once more. His complexion was pale, and his dark eyes wide and conflicted. Scarlett raised her eyebrows at him infinitesimally, mentally begging for his help. He seemed to deliberate for a split second before his features smoothed themselves.

"After an entrance that dramatic, I'm curious to see what she can do!" he commented loudly to his neighbors, clear enough to be heard by the announcer. His comment was met with a rumble of agreement.

"Everybody came to watch stone skin though," he argued, seemingly disgruntled by this upheaval.

Scarlett stowed that comment away to ask Leon about later. For now, she racked her brains for what she might say to tip the scales in her favor.

"Let the girl fight, Zed."

A hush fell over the room as an imposing figure emerged from a back room. Although Scarlett had seen Fang from afar in a street fight, back when he had only been a lieutenant in the Wolves, she barely recognized him now. His black trousers and bloodred waistcoat gave him the look of somebody who had recently acquired a large amount of money but not the taste to accompany it. His rested his hands before him on a walking stick topped with a silver snarling wolf's head and smiled at Scarlett in a way that showed far too many teeth. It didn't reach his narrow, black eyes.

"After all, everybody loves to cheer for an underdog, and she looks like she'd just be a snack for Ivor." The appraising way he looked Scarlett up and down made her shadows thicken subconsciously. It wasn't the lecherous way men sometimes stared, but the look of a man looking at a business venture—at a means to an end.

"You have a name, girl?" Fang asked when Scarlett continued to glare at him, unmoving.

"Scarlett."

"Well then ladies and gentlemen, we have a surprise match for you this evening! Scarlett, the girl with the shadows steps up to challenge Ivor, the reigning champion. Just give us a few minutes to get the competitors set and then you're in for more action than you bargained for," Fang announced, the crowd erupting into titters. "Everybody place your bets! It's sure to be good odds for Ivor, but you could make a killing if you're willing to gamble on a newcomer."

As everybody scrambled to find Wolves to take their money, no longer paying attention to the ring, Scarlett finally turned to look at Leon behind her. Up close, he looked even more haggard.

"Go find Georgette," she snapped. "Let her know you're safe."

"I can't let you do this for me," he argued, paying her order no mind.

"It's a little late for that now."

"You don't know what you're signing up for," Leon insisted.

"I saw the last match. I think I have a pretty good idea." Scarlett walked to her corner of the ring, not looking at Leon. "Besides, I've been living in this world far longer than you have. I think I know how to take care of myself."

Scarlett may have been exaggerating on that last bit. Clearly, if she knew how to take care of herself, she wouldn't keep dramatically hurling herself into situations she had no business in the first time somebody was in danger, although she didn't have time to unpack that now.

"I'll at least wait until the fight is over," Leon insisted.

"I'm here with a friend. He's over there with the blue cravat." Scarlett jerked her head to the cordoned off area, finding that Benedict continued to stare at her with an expression that looked too close to abject terror for her comfort. Another thing to push aside and unpack later.

Leon opened his mouth to speak again but Scarlett cut him off.

"Go."

With a jerky nod, he stepped out of the ring and the crowd engulfed him. Scarlett didn't watch where he went, trying to return her focus to the fight at hand. That was the only way to survive: Take things one fight at a time and worry about the rest when she could, if ever.

The announcer, Zed, stepped up beside her and gave her a quick once over.

"I'll need you to turn in your weapons. And don't try pretending you have less than four blades on you. I'm smarter than I look."

Scarlett nodded, expecting as much. She reached up her sleeves and into her boots as she asked, "What are the rules?"

"Rules?" He sneered. "You've come to the wrong place if you want rules. The only thing we care about is that you make it entertaining. You'll get your cut of the house pot if you win. We skim some off if you kill your opponent, to make up for the fact that they won't be able to fight again. Don't let that stop you though, because more people will come to watch you next time if you make it bloody, and the pot will be even bigger."

A tingle of fear shot up Scarlett's spine as she removed the last dagger from the small of her back and handed it over. It might have been because she was so rarely unarmed, or because the size of the crowd indicated that Ivor generally didn't shy away from a brutal showing.

Once Scarlett had divested herself of all her knives, the announcer moved away. She rolled up her sleeves, bouncing on her toes to get her blood flowing, and sizing up her opponent. She'd fought men Ivor's size before, but rarely did they have Talents—or at least ones they were willing to use openly. Then again, Scarlett tended to conceal her Talent out of habit as well. Now she could let her shadows run free.As she observed, Ivor took a jug of water and proceeded to pour it over his hands. Vapor clouded the air as it froze around his fingers, turning his meaty fists into icy clubs the size of a mace. One direct hit from those could lay her out flat.

Benedict's gaze burned into her like a brand from across the room, but Scarlett refused to look over to where she knew he stood. She didn't want to think about him watching whatever was to come.

"Place your final bets. The fight is about to begin!" Zed stepped up to the bell, resting his hand on the rope connected to the clapper.

Scarlett lifted her fists, wisps of shadows gathering around them like curls of dark smoke. She drew in a breath through her nose and blew it out slowly through her mouth as the room tensed in anticipation.

The bell clanged.

Chapter Ten

The echoes of the bell still rang through the room when Ivor rushed her. Scarlett sidestepped and ducked under the icy club of his fist easily. She bounced backwards on her toes, taking the measure of how he moved. As he spun around to face her once more, he snarled, cold breath clouding his face.

Another swing whistled by Scarlett's face as she spun out of the way, turning her momentum into a sweeping kick. Ivor countered faster than she expected, grabbing her leg as it lashed out at his side. He yanked her forward by her ankle so hard that Scarlett's head snapped back. Even as he dragged her towards his oncoming fist, Scarlett dropped to the ground, falling out of his grasp and rolling out of the way.

Coming to her feet in a crouch, she took a sweeping kick at Ivor's ankles, knocking his legs out from under him. The thud of his back against the wooden floor was drowned out by the gasps and cheers of the crowd.

Pressing her advantage, Scarlett sent a wave of shadows to cover his eyes with a flick of her wrist. As he was blinded, Scarlett aimed a kick at his flank, causing him to grunt in pain as her foot connected with his kidneys.

Before she could rear back to land another blow, Scarlett gasped as pain penetrated the base of her skull, the feeling an icy shock as if she had just jumped into the Thames in the dead of winter. A coat of frost encased the shadow clinging to Ivor's face before it shattered apart.

He took advantage of her surprise by grabbing her ankle, pulling her to the ground next to him. The impact stole the breath from her, and he moved to pin her as her vision swam before her eyes. Still gasping for air, Scarlett pulled her knees to her chest, pushing her feet out as he rolled on top of her, forcing him backwards. As her feet connected with his chest, she pushed against him to roll backwards over her shoulder and put distance between them.

In a matter of moments, they were both on their feet again, circling each other warily once more. Her ankle still protested from its injury last week, but Scarlett ignored it in favor of tracking her opponent's every move. With a jerk of his arm, Ivor sent a shard of ice like a dart hurtling at Scarlett's face. She threw up her arms, creating a shield of shadows. The ringing in her ears from the effort of making the darkness solid nearly distracted her from the tooth-aching cold as the ice shattered against her shadows.

Scarlett let the shadows dissipate just in time to see Ivor charging. She dodged out of the way, not quite fast enough as the frozen club of his fist clipped her ribs. Her back slammed into the ground as heat bloomed in her side. She escaped the paralyzing grip of pain just in time to wriggle out of the way of Ivor's oncoming fist. It crashed into the floor next to her head, the encasing ice shattering like thrown glass, razor shards scattering across her face. She blinked blood from her eyes, metallic copper coating her tongue.

Unable to see, she couldn't block the kick that Ivor aimed at her knee, throwing her arm up just in time to take the punch aimed for her face on her forearm. The next kick to her already bruised ribs had black spots dancing across her bloodied vision.

As Scarlett blinked to regain her sight, she found Ivor pacing around the ring, arms up as in an act of showmanship. The jeers of the crowd pressed in around Scarlett, drowning out the feeling of blood on her face and the pain beating at her consciousness. This audience reveled and cheered at her pain. As she lay there the hoots and shouts of encouragement telling Ivor to finish her off changed. They morphed into a sound that haunted her dreams, the jeers of the crowd waiting for her parents to hang. The end of the Inquiries might have meant the end of the hangings in the square, but people still showed up in force to watch the Talented bleed.

Heat boiled Scarlett's blood, burning away the pain of her injuries in a rush of adrenaline. The wild animal under her skin reared its head, and this time she didn't call it to heel. She had compressed her rage into a ball of molten rock in her heart when it meant survival, but she hadn't endured this long to be beaten for entertainment.

Ivor approached Scarlett where she still lay on the ground, the ice still encasing his one fist lengthening into a lethal dagger. He drew it back, ready to plunge it into her throat. As he swung it down, Scarlett's hands shot out, catching him by the wrist at the same moment she kicked up with her legs, throwing Ivor over her head. By the time he hit the floor, she was on her feet again.

As soon as he stood, Scarlett was on him, fists flying and teeth bared. She hit him everywhere she could reach. He tried to return her blows, but Scarlett blocked them with walls of shadow, barely feeling the pain of his ice in her head as adrenaline raged through her system.

Before she could think on it, darkness curled around her fingers, hardening into an obsidian set of brass knuckles. She could no longer hear the cheers of the crowd over the ringing in her ears, but she didn't care. Even as her fists pummeled at Ivor, he met her blows, so much larger than her that her inferior strength couldn't drive him to his knees. She took a step back, reevaluating her target, determined to bring him down.

The beast inside Scarlett screeched in frustration, and she answered with a matching snarl. Charging at her opponent, she threw out a solid step of shadow using it to launch herself into the air. As Scarlett flew over Ivor's head, she twisted, grabbing him around his thick neck and driving her knee between his shoulder blades. She bore him down into the ground, landing atop him. At some point, her shadows had formed into dagger in her hand, which she now pressed to the back of Ivor's neck, right in the hollow at the base of his skull.

The world fell still. Ivor tapped at the ground with his free hand, indicating his surrender. For a moment, Scarlett's eyes lingered on the point of her dagger of darkness, pressing against Ivor's skin just hard enough to draw a single drop of blood, bright red against the black of her blade. She looked up, her gaze instantly meeting a set of wide brown eyes. She had almost forgotten Benedict was watching this fight, so consumed was she by the heat of her anger.

Without a thought, Scarlett's shadows dissolved into nothing, the ringing in her ears disappearing with them to leave a painful silence in its wake.

"—have a new champion!"

Scarlett shoved away from the prone body pinned beneath her. She didn't quite make it to her feet, instead falling to her knees in the middle of the arena. As the anger within her retreated to the recesses of her mind, Scarlett began to feel cold. Pain rushed to the forefront of her consciousness, and she swayed, beginning to pitch forward.

Before she could topple over, arms came around her, and the smell of citrus and earth engulfed her as she was hugged to a familiar chest. She squeezed her eyes shut against the onslaught of emotions that rushed in on the heels of her retreating anger. Her mind was too fuzzy to form a protest, even as she squirmed against Benedict, knowing he shouldn't be holding her after what she had just done.

He paid her no mind, shifting her in his arms so he could carry her properly.

"You can't— People will think..." she started, not able to put together a coherent sentence but knowing she should object to what was happening.

"They'll think that I've fallen for a lower city brawler? Let them." His perpetually laughing tone was gravelly. Scarlett shook her head in confusion even as the world quieted around them. Benedict had carried her out onto the street, the silence of the night deafening compared to the cacophony of the ring they had left behind.

Benedict shifted Scarlett's weight, and she let out an involuntary gasp of pain as his forearm pressed into her ribs. The stabbing sensation that radiated through her chest spoke of bone deep bruises.

"Apologies." Benedict winced as he looked down to regard her. "Would it make you feel any better to know you look beautiful like this? All bloody teeth and bruised knuckles?"

"I didn't take you for a sadist," Scarlett gasped through the pain, scrabbling for their normal joking cadence. Anything to distract her from the fact that Benedict had just seen her at her most feral—fully possessed by the dark part of her mind that she had walled off in the months after her parents' deaths.

"It's not that." Benedict shook his head, gazing at her with something much too close to care. Scarlett squeezed her eyes shut to block out his expression. "From the moment you held me at gunpoint, I knew there was so much you kept hidden. Back in the ring...it was one of the first times I got to see more than a glimpse of what lives under your skin. Even as I feared for your life, I couldn't look away."

The world tipped around Scarlett. She struggled to remain conscious as Benedict's words penetrated her mind. Had she taken a blow to the head? She didn't remember.

Her thoughts were interrupted by the familiar clatter of hooves and carriage wheels. She clung to the familiarity of the noise, which was the only thing that seemed real in this fever dream of pain and confusing words. Using her shadows more than she ever had before left her feeling drunk and unbalanced, barely clinging to awareness.

Benedict lifted her into the carriage, placing her gently on the velvet-upholstered bench before sitting across from her. As the carriage jerked into motion, the jolting of the wheels over the cobblestones jostled Scarlett's injuries. Benedict's worried face swam in her vision as she tried and failed to hold onto consciousness. As her eyes slid shut and she began to tip sideways onto the bench, arms came around her once more.

"Rest little bird, I've got you."

Chapter Eleven

Scarlett couldn't remember the last time she had felt this comfortable, or this hungover. Her brain pounded against her skull as if it were trying to beat itself to death, and aches and pains scattered over her body competed for attention. Still, she couldn't bring herself to spare them much attention as she luxuriated the cloud-soft mattress cradling her aching bones. She inhaled deeply to revel in the scent of citrus and earth permeating her soft surroundings, regretting her actions immediately as her bruised ribs made their displeasure known.

Her eyelids snapped open at the sensation before squinting in protest to the bright light streaming in a window much too large to be the one in her room at Granny's. As she puzzled out her surroundings through slitted eyes, the reason for her current sorry state came back to her. Using her shadows as much as she had the night before always made her feel as if she had downed an entire bottle of whiskey—one of the many reasons she tended to use them subtly.

She took stock of her body from top to bottom, wiggling her fingers and toes. At her movement, a figure stood from the window seat and rushed over. Scarlett froze, not having realized she wasn't alone. Benedict's face swam into focus as he leaned over where she lay, and she relaxed again.

"Did you take me to your home?" she asked. Or rather, she attempted to ask, but it came out as more of a croak as she tried to maneuver her tongue, which was currently as useful as and similar in texture to a lump of wool.

"I wasn't just going to push your unconscious body out of my carriage on some random street, and I don't exactly know where you live." Benedict poured a glass of water from a pitcher on the stand next to the bed.

As he did, Scarlett pushed herself to a seated position, the process not as painful as she feared it might be. A bandage covered her battered forearm, and even her perpetually bruised and split knuckles were meticulously dressed, something she rarely bothered with anymore.

Benedict handed her the glass of water and scrutinized her as she took a few grateful gulps. In her eagerness to parch her aching throat, she spilled a few drops, dripping down her chin to her neck.

Before she could move to mop them up, Benedict's hand darted out to capture the rogue droplets, brushing against the tendons of her neck and lingering in the hollow of her throat.

Scarlett blinked at him, her sluggish brain still catching up to what was happening, and Benedict snatched his hand back before she could process his touch.

"You didn't sleep for as long as I was afraid you might," Benedict commented as he took the glass from her. "You were in a pretty sorry state, but I was afraid of the type of attention calling a doctor would draw."

"I don't need a doctor. I've had worse," Scarlett objected. Benedict raised a single eyebrow at her, and she conceded, "Well not much worse."

As her eyes continued to adjust to the sunlight, she took in her surroundings. The bed she was in took up one half of a large room, not nearly as sparse as the rest of the Pearces' house she had seen. A painting of a horse dominated the wall over the mantel, and several books were stacked haphazardly on an end table, boots kicked off underneath the legs.

"Is this your room?" Scarlett blurted out.

"Well...yes." Benedict scratched the back of his head. "None of the other rooms had sheets on the bed and well..."

As he trailed off, the warm look in his eyes brought her back to the night before as he cradled her to his chest and told her she looked lovely. Something soft stirred beneath her ribs—something she didn't want to examine too closely until she sorted through this mess. Still, she couldn't shove it aside completely, as if loosening the reigns on her anger last night in the fighting ring had broken the dam keeping all her other feelings at bay.

"This situation with the Wolves. It's…" Scarlett buried her face in her hands, finding the cuts on her face had been treated with some sort of salve as it smeared on her bandaged fingers.

"A mess bigger than a brisk gavotte at a holiday ball where the punch was far too heavily spiked?" Benedict filled in.

"I suppose that's a polite way of saying it," Scarlett admitted.

The more they dug into the Wolves business, the deeper it seemed the conspiracies went. She needed the truth, or at least some version of it, if they were going to untangle this web of violence.

"I need to talk to Leon. And Georgette for that matter," Scarlett thought out loud, already swinging her legs out of bed. It was then that she realized her legs were bare, her pants and shirt from the last night removed. All she wore was an oversized nightshirt, large enough to come to her knees. Her time in the lower city had seared away most of her modesty, but something about Benedict undressing her made her uncomfortably warm. Benedict took advantage of her stillness to argue.

"You're not going anywhere before you've eaten something."

Scarlett chewed her lip, anxious to get to the bottom of things while still wholly unbalanced by the image of Benedict running his hands over her skin to check for injuries.

"How about you write them each a note, and I'll have a courier deliver them while you eat?" Benedict suggested, pushing further. "Suggest Leon meet us here. It's the least he can do after you took a thrashing for him last night."

As if to agree with Benedict, Scarlett's stomach rumbled audibly.

"Alright."

Benedict showed her to a writing desk against one wall, producing pen and paper from the drawers before disappearing downstairs to see about some breakfast. Before leaving, he grabbed a dressing gown off the hook and draped it over the back of the desk chair. Scarlett slid it on, tempted to sniff at the citrus sent that clung to the collar, but forcing herself to focus on the issue at hand.

Scarlett quickly scrawled out a note for Leon, asking that he meet them at the Pearces' house at his earliest convenience. Over the letter to Georgette, Scarlett hesitated. Her friend had known they were going to investigate a lead last night and probably anxiously awaited any news. Still, Scarlett wasn't sure what this meant for Georgette, only that it couldn't be good. In the end, she wrote a brief note saying that they had made progress but there had been a complication, and she was recovering at Benedict's home while they made their next plan.

Folding the letters up, Scarlett shoved them in the pocket of the dressing gown. Looking around, her clothes were nowhere to be found. Considering Benedict had undressed her the night before, it seemed superfluous to worry about him seeing her in a dressing gown now. With that, she pushed out of room and padded down the stairs, having to hike up the fabric of the gown so as not to trip over it as she walked.

Her nose twitched, and she used it to follow the scent of butter and herbs to the dining room. Benedict finished setting a plate on the table as she entered and motioned to it with a smile as she entered.

"Kipper," he explained brightly.

The softness in her chest stirred again, and she tried to smile, only for it to turn into a wince as the expression pulled at the still-healing cuts on her face. She handed Benedict the letters and he passed them to his coachman waiting in the doorway. As the coachman left, Benedict pulled out a chair for her, and she almost giggled at the ridiculousness of sweeping his dressing gown around her to take a seat. It seemed an oddly domestic vignette considering she was there recovering from injuries obtained in an underground fighting ring. The thought sobered her as she tucked into her breakfast with gusto, Benedict sitting down across from her. She moaned appreciatively at the buttery taste on her tongue, and Benedict's gaze darted over to her.

Something about the way he looked at her made her shift in her seat. She itched to break the silence.

"About last night...I'm sorry."

"Sorry for what?" Benedict asked, fork pausing midair on its way to his mouth. "The worst you did was get blood on my shirt, and that's hardly worth mentioning."

"I exposed us by quite literally jumping in from the rafters."

"And it was the dramatic entrance dreams are made of," Benedict pointed out, to which Scarlett scowled. He went on with a sigh, "It's not like I would have expected anything different. The first time I met you, you were impersonating your friend to find out why she was receiving death threats, and the second time I saw you, you dove in a window to get me, a stranger, out of a dire situation. It's not like I didn't know dramatic interference was in your nature, little bird."

Scarlett scowled deeper, shoveling food into her mouth. Something in her rankled that Benedict described her like a hero when she could only think of the depths she had sunk to survive. In favor of pursuing that line of thinking, she asked, "Why do you call me that?"

"Little bird?" Benedict gazed at her pensively. "Well besides the fact that I didn't know your name at first, it seemed like you were so ready to fly away at the slightest movement. But I saw something in your eyes when you pointed that gun at me. I had the feeling I would find something special if I could get close enough—if I could just get a good look at you."

Scarlett blinked, an unexpected lump in her throat making her words tight as she responded, "You might have seen something special from me last night, but not in the way you'd hoped."

Benedict shook his head, putting down his fork, meal forgotten. "I don't think you're as dark as you want people to think you are. Maybe pretending you've fallen too far to climb back up is easier than trying to claw your way back."

"What would you know of it?" Scarlett snapped, unsure where the sudden harshness in her tone came from. The feelings she had unleashed last night continued to tumble forward, and as successful as she had been in suppressing them this morning, Benedict's words caused them to stampede in her chest, beating against her heart like the hoofbeats of racing horses.

"It's clear you weren't always a gang member in the lower city, you know." Benedict took her anger in stride. "Who were you before the gangs?"

"It doesn't matter. That girl is dead. I killed her long ago." It was true. Scarlett had plunged the dagger into the chest of the girl she used to be again and again. The first time she picked a pocket, the first time she ran a job with the Raptors, the first street fight where she broke a man's arm. The time she killed somebody.

"You might surprise yourself," Benedict said softly. "I saw you let out the anger you so clearly carry last night. Who knows what else you might find if you let it out?"

The legs of the chair scrapped against the floor as Scarlett shot to her feet. She didn't remember deciding to stand, but now stood, fists shaking at her sides and teeth bared. It took a deep breath to shove her unexpected anger back into its cage in her chest, the beast under her skin screeching and clawing.

"I need a moment," was all she managed before she turned and pushed from the room. She found herself in the drawing room where she paced across the rug a few times, her knee twinging from a kick the night before. Scarlett welcomed the pain, letting it ground her. She had lived for so long by thinking only of survival, not pulling out her emotions to examine too closely. If she stopped to do so, she surely would never be able to pull herself out of the pit she found herself in. But Benedict had a way of *seeing* her, of looking through the shadows she gathered around herself, without fear.

Deflating, Scarlett slumped down on a bench, finding herself seated before the pianoforte. Hesitantly, she reached out a finger and stroked a key, a single clear note echoing through the room. She did it again, the sound drowning out the clamoring in her head, a welcome change. With slow fingers, she began to tap out a melody.

Her other hand drifted up to join the first, picking out the countermelody slowly at first before building in confidence. There were some things one never forgot, no matter how deeply one buried the memory. No matter how hard you tried to pretend they were gone.

The music filled the room, melody rising and falling like the breaths in her chest, coming faster now. That newfound softness beneath her breastbone seemed to grow in response. There were many things Scarlett missed about her life before the Raptors, but this was one of the most acute. The need to lose herself in a song, to let the music rise until it drowned out all other thoughts in her mind.

After a dramatic crescendo, the song drew to a close, the last notes lingering in the air like one of Scarlett's shadows, almost dense enough to touch. In the growing quiet, Scarlett heard a shuffle behind her. She turned to find Benedict paused in the doorway.

"That was breathtaking," he whispered, almost as if he didn't want to break the spell of the song by speaking too loudly. He took measured steps into the room, then stopped to stand next to where Scarlett sat at the piano bench. She craned her neck to look up at him.

"Why do you care about who I was so much?" Scarlett whispered. She needed to know why he insisted on trying to crack her ribcage open and pull out all her secrets hidden behind layers of shadows and years of pain. After all, they were only temporary allies, on two separate roads running parallel.

"You have to know little bird," he murmured.

His lips crashed into hers in a way that was both unexpected and also inevitable since her gaze met his over the barrel of a gun. Scarlett only hesitated a moment before throwing her arms around his neck, pulling him down to kiss him more thoroughly. With her emotions as raw as they were, throbbing like an exposed nerve, Scarlett didn't have it in her to deny herself this. Even if it was only temporary, right now, she could have this.

Having to bend over to kiss her like this, Benedict's hands came around Scarlett's waist, lifting her until she sat on the keys of the piano. They let out a cacophony of sounds, a chaotic melody of their own making that echoed the fluttering of Scarlett's heart as she tilted her head to kiss Benedict more thoroughly. Her tongue slicked into his mouth, and his greeted it greedily. He ran his hands from her hips to her neck to cup the back of her head, snagging on the belt of the dressing gown in the process. It fell open, exposing more of her body to the cool air, still not relieving the building heat under her skin.

Scarlett's hands ran through Benedict's thick hair, reveling in its softness. As she let the silky strands twist between her fingers, his lips traveled away from her mouth to the hollow beneath her ear and down to her throat. His tongue darted out to mark her pounding pulse, and he groaned.

"You taste as good as I imagined," he groaned with a nip at the junction of her shoulder.

"You imagined this?" Scarlett asked, her voice breathless as she dared to hope, her heart fluttering against her ribcage like the little bird Benedict always called her.

"Ever since I saw you for the first time." Benedict pushed at the neck of the nightshirt to expose more of Scarlett's collarbones.

"I was dressed as somebody else when we first met," Scarlett said, sinking inside.

Benedict shook his head, nuzzling into the crook of her neck as he did so.

"The more I saw of you, the more I craved you." He punctuated his point by slipping the dressing gown off her shoulders, letting it pool around her on the piano keys.

Scarlett pulled his lips back to hers, needing to silence his words. Words that would make her think of what they were to each other—and what they could never be. For now, she just wanted to let herself feel, a luxury she had denied herself for so long.

As Scarlett kissed him with all the ferocity she contained, Benedict's fingers trailed up her thighs, pushing up the nightshirt inch by inch.

"I want to see you," Benedict murmured into her mouth.

Scarlett hesitated. She certainly wasn't naïve. With the loss of Scarlett's social status, there had been no need to maintain an innocent reputation, and so she had indulged in rushed trysts and excited fumbling with other Raptors on occasion. In the cramped quarters of the lower city though, there was little privacy, and they only undressed as much as necessary.

Now Scarlett nodded jerkily against Benedict, and he pulled back far enough to pull the nightshirt off over her head. Her upper half was left completely bare, only the smallest scrap of fabric around her hips keeping her from being completely exposed.

Not waiting a moment, Benedict dipped his head, instantly dispelling any insecurities in the onslaught of sensations that came with his tongue tracing over her breasts. Her back arched involuntarily, and she braced her hands on the keys next to her, drowning out her stuttering breath in another chorus of disconnected notes. His lips migrated back up to her neck before nipping at her earlobes, hands moving to cover the aching nipples his mouth had just left. Velvety warmth spread from the points of contact, dripping down her body to gather low in her belly. Benedict's fingers followed the heat, tracing down her sides in light strokes that made her shudder even as he took care to avoid the spreading purple bruise over her ribs. They came to land on her hips, toying with the waistband of her underthings.

"Tell me I can take these off. Please," Benedict murmured directly into the shell of her ear, punctuating the request with a light stroke of his tongue.

Scarlett nodded again. If her mind hadn't already been fraying at the edges from the sparks dancing under her skin, she would have taken time to process the ragged huskiness in Benedict's voice.

Now he slid her last piece of clothing down her legs, tossing it forgotten onto the piano bench behind him. He rested his forehead on Scarlett's collarbone to watch his fingers trail over her belly towards the apex of her thighs.

"You're exquisite," he breathed, sending a puff of warm air over her breasts, feeling like a caress.

Her knees drifted inwards subconsciously as he watched his fingers pet through her thatch of curls. They were so close to the where she wanted them, but nobody had ever looked at her like this—watching her as if she were the only thing in the world in that moment as he slowly shredded her composure with gentle touches. Benedict stepped between her legs, keeping them from closing with his hips. He pressed a soft kiss to her shoulder before running his fingers across her center. Her fingers curled at the sensation, and she found shadows springing up around her without being consciously called. They curled around her in dark mist, shielding her skin, littered as it was with cuts and bruises, from Benedict's reverent gaze.

"Don't hide from me, little bird," Benedict chided with a shake of his head, making the ends of his hair brush over her sensitized skin.

With an ounce of hard-won concentration, Scarlett pushed the shadows away, but they still lingered, swirling and pulsing around her hands and at her sides as if barely leashed.

"If you must do something with them, let them touch me instead."

Scarlett hadn't even had time to fully process Benedict's request when he found her most sensitive spot and circled it. Her shadows seemed to have understood without her brain getting involved, leaping forward to coat Benedict's shoulders. They caressed his other hand where it cupped her breast, winding through his hair, even trailing down his shirt to stroke the dark thatch of hair on his chest.

"You want this just as much as I do." Benedict's words sounded almost surprised and a bit questioning, as if the wetness coating his fingers left any room for doubt. While, as usual, Benedict seemed to be able to talk himself through anything, words were beyond Scarlett at this moment, so she settled for another stilted nod.

"I'm going to make you come apart, right here on this piano."

Scarlett didn't doubt his promises in the slightest as he teased her entrance with a single finger. She swallowed, finally finding her voice again, although it came out breathy. "Are you just going to talk about it or are you going to do it?"

Benedict huffed in amusement, fingers still exploring tortuously. "If you thought I was going to be quiet, then you don't know me very well." He looked up with a playful glint in his eye. "Maybe I can find a better use for my mouth."

Benedict's lips trailed over her chest to her stomach, and he sat on the piano bench in front of her. At this angle, his face was level with Scarlett's core, currently throbbing with unrelieved heat. Scarlett desperately wanted to close her eyes, to not exist beyond the feeling of his fingers dragging lightly over her thighs, but those honeyed eyes kept her pinned. He saw Scarlett as she was, and she could not be unseen.

"I want to hear you sing, little bird."

With no more warning, he leaned forward and drew his tongue up her seam in one long stroke. Her shadows jerked with an intent of their own, renewing their caresses of his chest and shoulders.

Scarlett gasped at the onslaught of sensations, biting her lip to stifle the sound as she was overwhelmed by Benedict's mouth, hot and slick against her center along with the odd caress at the back of her mind that came from the touch of her shadows. Emboldened by her reaction, Benedict lifted her knees over his shoulders, licking into her as if ravenous. Scarlett panted through gritted teeth, any sense of composure rapidly slipping.

With another skillful flick of his tongue, he succeeded in pulling a ragged moan from her. Scarlett's fingers scrabbled at the piano behind her, adding to the symphony of desperate sounds now clawing their way from her throat. Benedict only devoured her more enthusiastically, Scarlett's shadows fluttering over every inch they could reach, pushing him away and pulling him closer in equal measure. After the incessant teasing of his fingers and his words, Scarlett's pleasure was already baring down on her, hot and undeniable. There was no stopping the way Benedict undid her.

With a cry, Scarlett shuddered through her release, shaking so hard she nearly fell off the piano, but Benedict's firm hands on her thighs kept her pinned, continuing his onslaught until the only sounds he could pull from her were desperate whimpers.

With one last kiss to the seam of her thigh, he pulled back to look at her with a smile that would have been smug if he didn't look positively dazed.

"I knew you'd be a lovely songbird," he remarked softly.

Scarlett let out a huff that might have been a laugh if she had any breath in her, surprised at how easily he seemed to pull amusement from her, even after such intense feelings.

As she gazed down at where Benedict still sat between her splayed thighs, her shadows lingered around him, tracing his neck and shoulders in lazy circles. He reached up as if to pet one, finding that it wasn't quite solid in this state, fingers drifting through it like water.

"These are lovely too," he commented, admiring them as if he really meant it. Scarlett shuddered. To have somebody touch her shadows and admire them not for what they could do, but simply for their existence was utterly foreign. It felt almost as good as Benedict's mouth on her—almost.

Coming back to herself slightly, Scarlett realized that Benedict was still fully clothed. He could expose her so easily, in more ways than one—even things that she had hid from herself. As the thought dispelled some of the languid haze in her mind, she reached for Benedict, intent on distracting herself from such thoughts by returning his explorations.

The clang of a bell echoing through the house froze her in place, hand outstretched.

Benedict swore under his breath. "That must be Leon."

Scarlett scrabbled for her clothing, the lingering warmth in her veins chased away by cold reality setting back in.

"Your clothes are on the chair by the fireplace in my room. I got them as clean as I could," Benedict said, helping her pull his dressing gown back around her shoulders.

She pushed off the piano and came to her feet, legs a bit wobbly beneath her. At least the morning's...diversion had chased away most of the lingering headache from the night before. Scarlett quickly darted towards the staircase to get herself decent. She spared a backward glance before she left the room though to see Benedict trying to set his own clothes to rights, rumpled as they were by the touch of Scarlett's shadows. Despite her mind already racing with questions for Leon, the image of Benedict's tousled hair played at the softness in her heart as she bounded up the stairs.

Chapter Twelve

When Scarlett made her way back downstairs, she was much more decent, although it was still a relative statement. Her clothes bore several small tears from the night before, and Benedict clearly wasn't as good at getting blood out of clothes as Scarlett was, judging by the dull coppery stains dotting her shirt. Still, she was glad for her short hair, which was easily tamed with a quick finger comb. As she glanced in the mirror above Benedict's washstand, she pronounced herself good enough, knowing there was nothing to be done about the cuts littering her face or the hollows under her eyes from too many nights spent prowling rooftops instead of sleeping.

Scarlett followed voices back into the dining room, where Benedict had somehow embroiled Leon in a discussion on the recent rise of romanticism in paintings. Despite the direness of the situation, it seemed Benedict had an easy time conversing with people, even in the most intimate of situations. Scarlett's cheeks warmed at the thought of the things he murmured to her not ten minutes earlier and reminded herself to focus on the matter at hand.

As she rounded the corner into the room, Leon sprang to his feet. Taking two large steps forward, he stopped abruptly, as if he wasn't sure whether to hug her or keep his distance, looking her over from head to toe.

"That was incredibly stupid," he settled for saying.

"Bold words for somebody I once watched fall out of Georgette's window with his pants around his ankles."

Benedict coughed violently into his teacup.

Leon shook his head. "You shouldn't have done that for me. I would have been fine."

"You can thank me for taking that thrashing for you by explaining to me what exactly you were doing there, and why on earth you haven't contacted Georgette yet. If you've gone off of her, I might just throw you back into that pit and let Ivor have his way with you after all." Scarlett slid into a chair and propped her chin in her hands, looking at Leon expectantly.

Leon looked back and forth between Benedict and Scarlett before resuming his seat with a heavy exhale.

"I assume Georgette told you I had gone to Paris to get my father's blessing to propose?"

Scarlett nodded, and Benedict leaned in with interest.

"When I got there and saw my father, he told me he had no intention of sending me back to London. He wanted to send me to America to expand his art trade. When I refused, saying I planned to return to London for Georgette, well…" Leon ran his hands through his hair, showing that he too bore bruised knuckles. "He disowned me."

Scarlett grimaced. She knew all too well the struggles of being forced to fend for oneself overnight.

"What about your art trade?" Benedict chimed in.

"I'm trying to set off on my own with it," Leon explained, spreading his hands on the table in front of him. "But all our pieces legally belong to my father, and I don't have the capital to acquire many works on my own."

"So how did you become embroiled with the Wolves?" Scarlett asked.

"I was in a pub in the lower city, trying to plan my next move, when I overheard some men talking about how the Wolves were looking for Talented, saying they could make a killing. And well—I've never told anybody about my Talent, and it hasn't been hard to hide, but if there was ever a time to use it, I figured this was it.

"When I asked, they told me about the fighting rings and that any fighters get a healthy cut of the purse. I figured I could do it to get just enough money to get the art business up and running, and then I would propose to Georgette as a successful man. What could it hurt?"

Scarlett huffed. "You could get killed is what it could hurt."

Leon shook his head. "Watch." He reached across the table and grabbed a knife that still lay there from breakfast. Before Scarlett could react, he plunged it into the hand that still lay spread on the table.

Benedict let out a grunt of surprise, but it didn't quite drown out the metallic clang as the knife bounced harmlessly off Leon's skin.

"You're invulnerable?" Scarlett asked once she managed to stop staring with her mouth agape. Some Talents were more powerful than others, but she had rarely heard of any so dramatic.

"Not quite," Leon explained, holding up the knife and finding the tip bent from the impact. "I have to focus on it, and it only affects parts of my body when I'm actively concentrating on them. See?"

Leon now dragged the edge of the knife along the back of his hand, drawing a few drops of blood from flesh that a few moments ago had been as hard as steel.

"That would come in handy in a fight," Scarlett admitted.

Leon laughed humorlessly. "It does, although it doesn't mean I knew how to fight. At first, I mostly just took a beating and watched people break their hands when they tried to punch me. It turns out the crowds enjoyed it though, and I've made a killing."

"Then why haven't you proposed to Georgette?" Benedict interjected.

"I was going to, but it turns out I was making the Wolves too much money."

Scarlett's heart sank as she guessed where this story was going. Greed ran the lower city, and somebody like Fang didn't let go of a valuable asset.

"When I told the Wolves I wouldn't fight anymore, they threatened me. Of course, I told them their weapons were no good on me. That's when Fang played his trump card." Leon's tone was utterly defeated. "The whole time I had been fighting for them, he had been learning all he could about me. He told me he knew about Georgette, and if I stopped fighting, he would kill her. I didn't know if he could do it, but I wasn't willing to risk it. Then I heard Georgette was being courted by the son of a duke—" Leon inclined his head towards Benedict, "and I knew it was over. There was no point in trying to get out anymore."

"Ah you see, that's where your wrong," Benedict piped up.

"Georgette still very much wants to marry you. She's been worried sick," Scarlett agreed.

"Then you're not..." Leon looked between the two with a bewildered expression.

"The Wolves delivered a death threat to Georgette, and Mr. Ward asked me to try and figure out why. I've been disguising myself as Georgette in public to keep her safe while we get to the bottom of this," Scarlett explained. "That's why we were at the fight last night in the first place."

Leon furrowed his brow, clearly trying to process this chain of events. "How did you get involved?" he asked Benedict.

"They were trying to blackmail me into killing Georgette, and I suggested that I seduce her out of her dowry first," Benedict replied cheerily.

When Leon's eyed widened into perfect circles, Scarlett jumped in, shooting Benedict an exasperated look. "It was all a ruse to buy us more time to figure things out."

"Well, I've told the Wolves that I'm in to stay if they leave Georgette alone," Leon said.

"Although they might still expect me to marry her and then dispose of her," Benedict pointed out completely unhelpfully.

"We might have made this even more of a mess," Scarlett admitted, brain churning uselessly through possible solutions. Before she could come up with one, the bell chimed again.

Benedict looked up in confusion. "I wasn't expecting any other callers today."

He pushed up from the table and headed to the front door, and there came some muffled voices before two sets of footsteps approached the dining room once more. Benedict rounded the corner followed by a rather petite footman. Before Scarlett could get a good look at him, there was a shriek, and the figure threw itself at Leon, nearly toppling him out of his chair. In the commotion, the cap fell from his head, letting a cascade of silky brown curls spill out.

"Georgette!" Leon gasped as she leaped into his lap, throwing her arms around him and burying her face in his neck.

"You're here! You're really here." Georgette cupped Leon's face in her hands and stared at him intently, as if verifying his identity. Seeing the bruise on his cheekbone, her eyes widened. "What happened? And why didn't you tell me he was here?" She rounded on Scarlett.

"He wasn't when I sent the letter," Scarlett said. "What are you doing here?"

Georgette squirmed so she sat across Leon's lap more comfortably, apparently having sworn off propriety entirely when she forewent her normal lady's attire. "When you said you were recovering, I knew something awful had happened. I felt so guilty about you taking all these risks by traipsing around as me, especially if you were hurt. Then it occurred to me that if you could masquerade as me, then I could leave the house safely if I pretended to be you. I'm not quite as good at climbing out the window though."

Scarlett blinked in surprise.

"I have to say, I've never worn pants before, and I can see why you do it," Georgette added.

"They are rather freeing," Benedict agreed when nobody answered.

Leon stared at Georgette as if she was an angel who had materialized in their presence, a mix of awe and adoration. Benedict only seemed amused by her appearance. Scarlett's mind whirred, half still occupied by the delicate situation they found themselves in while the other dealt with Georgette's sudden appearance.

"So what happened to you, and how did you find Leon?" Georgette asked, taking a moment to stroke Leon's cheek again and give him a soft smile.

"It's a long story, and I'm afraid we have a bit of a situation," Scarlett hedged, not entirely sure where to begin. How could she tell Georgette that Leon was trapped in an underground fighting ring to keep her alive? Leon didn't seem to be piping up.

"Tell me," Georgette urged. "I might be able to help."

Scarlett chewed her lip. This was exactly the type of situation she didn't want Georgette embroiled in, even if it was too late at this point.

"Oh stop it," Georgette snapped. "I'm optimistic, not naïve. Stop trying to shelter me like I'm some porcelain doll."

The words hit Scarlett like a slap across the face. She had always tried to protect Georgette from the realities of her life in the lower city. It was part of the reason Scarlett kept her distance. Georgette was so kind and so positive—it seemed like wiping muddy hands on a white dress to draw her into the dire politics of the gangs. But here Georgette was calling Scarlett out on it and reminding her that she was the one friend who hadn't cut all ties with Scarlett after her parents had been exposed as Talented.

"Ok, I'll tell you. But first, I want you to know that even though we don't have a plan yet, we *will* find a way out of this," Scarlett urged.

Before Scarlett could embark on the tale of the prior night, the doorbell echoed through the house once more.

"I don't think I've ever had this many callers, and that's saying something," Benedict grumbled as he left the room once more. He was gone for a moment, but when his footsteps approached down the hallway once more, they were followed by another set punctuated by the sharp rap of a cane against the floorboards.

Benedict rounded the corner stiffly, eyes wide. The sight of the figure following him twisted Scarlett's stomach uncomfortably and she lurched to her feet. Out of the corner of her eye, she saw Leon's grasp tighten on Georgette's waist, stony fear etched into the lines of his face.

Fang himself strode through the doorway, once again in an ostentatious waistcoat and a silk top hat, broadcasting just how much cash the Wolves were drawing in these days. He stopped a few steps into the doorway, propping both hands onto the snarling wolf head on the top of his cane. The gesture would have been construed as gentlemanly if Scarlett hadn't been willing to bet the crown jewels that the cane concealed a sword. His eyes darted over the scene before him appraisingly, a spark of interest lighting in their steel gray depths.

"How considerate of you to gather everybody I have business with in the same place," he remarked conversationally.

Scarlett took a step in front of Georgette and Leon, shadows already dancing at her fingertips.

"Come now, I'm not here to fight. Why would I have come alone if I planned to kill you all?" Fang said.

"Then why are you here?" Scarlett bit out, not believing for one moment that Fang was truly unprotected. Surely Wolves were stationed around the house, waiting to crash in and overwhelm them if whatever was about to transpire wasn't working out in Fang's favor. While Scarlett could certainly hold her own in a fight, and Leon might be helpful as well, they wouldn't be able to protect Georgette and Benedict from superior numbers.

"I've come to deliver your cut of the house's winnings last night of course," Fang explained, pulling out a purse. He set it down on the table with a metallic thud that spoke of a hefty amount of money within.

"While that's considerate of you, you're not welcome here. You can take your money and leave," Scarlett protested.

"Come now, you haven't even heard the offer I've come with."

"And what could you offer us?" Scarlett asked, still firmly planted between Georgette and Leon, while Benedict stood with his back to the sideboard a few steps away.

"I would actually call it a...firm request," Fang said with a smile that looked more like bared teeth than an expression of friendship. "You see, the spectators last night loved you. Something about a little scrap like you taking on a behemoth of a man...and with such ferocity!"

Scarlett shifted her weight slightly at the reminder of last night's loss of control but stayed silent.

"As I'm sure Leon has made you aware, I don't like it when fan favorites say they won't fight anymore. I tend to come up with terms that make staying more agreeable." Fangs eyes darted over Scarlett's shoulder to where Leon and Georgette still sat. "Then again, why did you jump in for Leon in the fights last night? Is it just that he's attached to the honorable Ms. Ward, who you are most clearly trying to protect?"

Benedict shifted by the sideboard, and Fang's eyes darted to him.

"Your involvement is curious as well. It took me longer than I care to admit to see that you were never actually courting Ms. Ward but working with Scarlett here to deceive us. I puzzled out that you were double-crossing us when you jumped so eagerly to Scarlett's rescue last night. I suppose thinking I could get a fighter and a handsome dowry out of this arrangement was a little optimistic of me."

For once, Benedict kept his mouth shut, eyes darting between Fang and Scarlett, still facing off against each other across the dining room.

"So what do you say Scarlett? Keep fighting in the rings, or I'll put a mark on anybody in this room, because you've clearly taken a vested interest in all of them," Fang suggested, as if he were simply haggling over the price of salt cod at the market.

"I'm already with the Raptors. Amos won't take too kindly to me fighting for the Wolves," Scarlett argued.

Fang huffed in amusement. "Amos is already in on it. He's been helping deliver messages to…persuade Talented to volunteer to fight and collecting some debts for a cut of the winnings." Fang tilted his head in thought as he stared Scarlett down. "In fact, I would think you had been helping him with it. Nobody ever seemed to know how the messages were delivered, and I see now that you could be quite the asset when it comes to stealth."

Scarlett swallowed heavily. Is that what she had been doing for Amos? The letters she had been laying on pillows throughout the city in the dead of night—she was just delivering the Wolves their prey. Even Mr. Davies just last week...his debts may have been from the fighting rings, explaining why Amos assumed he would be hesitant to alert the police and admit that he regularly spectated at death matches for entertainment.

"You're saying Amos would be fine with me leaving the Raptors? You clearly don't know him like I do," Scarlett argued.

"He may not like it, but he knows better than to mess with the Wolves. With all the territory and resources we've gained, it's best to let us have our way." His eyes flashed in a dangerous way that reminded Scarlett of the Wolves likely stationed outside the windows and doors. He had Scarlett cornered, but he had also handed her a very valuable card. He wanted Scarlett to fight for the Wolves in the rings.

"I'll fight, but you have to let Leon stop," Scarlett stated.

Benedict made a distressed noise in his throat, but Scarlett didn't spare him a glance.

"Why would I do that?" Fang asked, "when I could have both of you? I'm still willing to dispatch Ms. Ward over there if either of you don't do as you're told. Besides, it turns out I won't actually being getting a cut of Ms. Ward's sizeable dowry that I was promised, and I think I deserve some compensation."

It was Georgette's turn to let out a distressed squeak, followed by some low murmurs from Leon trying to comfort her.

"You said it yourself. The crowd loves a scrappy underdog, and I put on a better show." Scarlett's shadows pooled down her fingers and crawled up her arms, creating black gloves tipped with glimmering talons for effect. The base of Scarlett's skull throbbed once at her use of solid shadows so soon after overextending herself the night before, but she grit her teeth through the sensation.

Fang tilted his head, as if considering. Scarlett kept pushing.

"And if I leave the Raptors, I'll be able to secretly deliver your threats for you, without you paying Amos a cut. That should make us even for your cut of Georgette's dowry."

THE TALENTED FAIRY TALES

She saw in Fang's face that he was softening in his conviction, and Scarlett knew that appealing to his greed was the way to get what she wanted. Her eyes drifted to the bag of coins on the table between them as Fang nodded.

"How much is the normal fighter's cut of the winnings?" she asked.

"Fifteen percent."

Scarlett's eyes darted over to Benedict at the sideboard. "I'll only take five percent if you forgive the Duke of Pearce's debt."

Benedict took a step forward, mouth opening as if to interrupt. Scarlett's heart throbbed as she threw up a shadow to cover his mouth where Fang couldn't see. She could end this all in one fell swoop. Just one shrewd deal and everybody would get what they wanted—everybody except Scarlett of course. The things she desired were impossible anyways.

"You drive a hard bargain," Fang commented, but Scarlett could tell he was tempted to accept. His fingers tapped on his cane as if doing mental calculations.

"You were using Benedict to threaten Georgette's life, but if you let Leon leave the fights, you won't need that anymore. If you take this deal, you'll be repaid the money you are owed over time, as opposed to getting nothing at all," Scarlett pressed.

Fang hesitated only a moment longer. "It's a deal."

He held out his hand and Scarlett grasped it to seal her fate. She kept her gaze on Fang's smug smile, once again revealing too many teeth. If she looked at Benedict over his shoulder, standing frozen, she wasn't sure she would have the composure to shake Fang's hand with a decisive nod.

"I'll be expecting you to fight the night after tomorrow," he announced as he released Scarlett's hand, straightening his waistcoat, "As for the rest of you, I suppose our business is concluded, as long as Scarlett here upholds her end of the agreement."

With one last meaningful look in her direction, he turned on his heel and strode from the room. His confidence in turning his back on Scarlett rankled. He now had her on a tighter leash than Amos ever had, and he seemed to know that he held all the cards. The sound of the front door closing behind him echoed through the house with a sense of finality.

"Scarlett," Benedict breathed, a hitch in his voice. Scarlett couldn't look at him quite yet, not knowing what she would find in his eyes and not sure she wanted to know. Instead, she looked at the purse on the table. She picked it up and weighed it in her hand. This would at least pay her rent at Granny's for another few months. Low words drew her gaze over to Georgette and Leon.

"They were threatening me to get to you?" Georgette asked Leon, eyes wide and bright.

He nodded solemnly.

"What did they want from you? Were you...a Wolf?" The hesitant way Georgette asked it, as if being a Wolf were the highest crime, made the beast beneath Scarlett's skin raise its hackles. She was one of them now, but she had chosen that. She would pay the price for her friends' freedom.

Still, she found she couldn't bear to watch as Leon began explaining to Georgette what he had told Scarlett and Benedict, stroking her hair reassuringly. Scarlett turned and strode from the room, into the front hallway. She could leave if she wanted to. Disappear into the lower city as she had when her parents died, this time cutting all ties completely, not holding onto Georgette like a child to a favorite blanket, pretending it was a connection that could be sustained as Scarlett continued to scrabble for survival.

"Scarlett!" Benedict's footsteps echoed across the marble foyer behind her. She stopped but didn't turn.

"Scarlett, look at me," he pleaded.

Finally, she did. When she met his gaze, his eyes were dark, holding none of their characteristic amusement that had endured through many crises. A tenderness in her chest tried to push forth, but she shoved it down. This was why she had kept her feelings on a tight leash for so long. Because wanting was so often at odds with what was needed for survival.

"Why did you do that?" he asked, his voice, barely above a whisper, amplified in the empty vastness of the space.

"It was the obvious solution. One deal, and everybody wins." Scarlett shrugged. "Georgette is safe, and Leon is free to propose, having gotten the money he needs. Your family is free of debt, and you can go find a bride with a healthy dowry to restore your family's wealth." The acidity of the words burned her throat, but she fought to keep her tone smooth.

"You don't win." Benedict shook his head.

"I was already a gang member, what does changing allegiances matter?" she reasoned.

"Is this really the life you want for yourself?" Benedict half pleaded, half demanded, "Fighting and stealing for somebody else just to make ends meet? It's not who you are."

"You don't know that," Scarlett snapped.

"But I do. You wouldn't have gone to such lengths to keep us all safe if you didn't care."

"Better I pay the price than you," Scarlett shot back.

"But why?" Benedict insisted.

"Because its already too late for me," she admitted, voice rising in pitch.

Benedict cocked his head at her. "You clearly belonged to high society once, and being Talented isn't illegal anymore. You don't need to hide away from society. Is it a matter of money? Or connections? I could—"

"It's not that." Scarlett cut him off. She braced herself with a deep breath, needing to explain to him why her life had to be what it was. She needed him to understand, so he wouldn't make this any harder than it already was. "It used to be my Talent, but it's so much more than that now. I joined the Raptors to survive the Inquiries, working for them so they would protect me from the police. But now I'm a criminal in other ways. It doesn't matter if being Talented isn't a crime because my other crimes are numerous. I've stolen, lied, cheated. The end of the Inquiries...it doesn't undo all of that. I'm already a monster, and I'll gladly become more of one if it's for you."

Scarlett swallowed thickly. She hadn't meant that last sentence to sound like it had, but she didn't have it in herself to take it back. Benedict deserved to know that he had made her want more for herself, even if she knew she could never have it.

He shook his head, for once seeming at a loss for words.

"Everything can go back to normal now," Scarlett said. "Your mother and sister can come home, and you can go back to being the most notorious rake at every ball. This can be a fun story you tell at parties."

"What about us?" he asked.

His question shattered something in Scarlett's soul, loud enough she thought everybody in the house could hear the sound of breaking glass. As if "us" was a concept that had existed for a moment and now lay in pieces at Scarlett's feet.

"There never was an us, just a dream," she said. Then she turned and walked out the front door into the afternoon light, but despite the bright sun cutting through the eternal haze from the factories, Scarlett couldn't feel the warmth on her skin.

Chapter Thirteen

Scarlett stumbled back into her room, bruised and battered from her second fight in the Wolves' rings. She had been more prepared this time, not taking nearly as much of a beating. Still, the use of her shadows in such dramatic displays left her with a head full of sodden rags. If she were any more alert, she might have noticed the dark silhouette beside her doorframe. As it was, she was taken by surprise when the door slammed behind her and she found herself pressed up against it, forearm against her throat.

A dagger flew to her fingers from the cache on her wrist, having been returned to her by Zed after she collected her winnings for the evening. A quick hand grabbed her forearm, keeping her from stabbing her assailant.

"Did you think to make me look like a fool?" An oily voice cut through the darkness.

"Amos." Scarlett relaxed a fraction. He knew better than to kill her at Granny's. Even he wouldn't violate the neutral ground.

"Working with the Wolves behind my back? Running a scam for them with your upper city friends when you were supposed to be working for me?" Amos was close enough that drops of spit sprayed across Scarlett's face. She would have been disgusted if she weren't already coated in grime and blood.

"I cut a deal with Fang, and you wouldn't cross him." Scarlett's tone held the whisper of a threat. "You can't compete with him when it comes to manpower."

"It's not him I have an issue with, it's you." Amos shook her to punctuate his point, her head knocking against the door at her back. "You were doing a job with the Wolves, targeting Ms. Ward with them, when you were supposed to be working for me."

Somehow Scarlett didn't think it would help the situation if she reminded Amos she had been double-crossing the Wolves in that arrangement as well.

"And what do you want me to do about it? Fang won't take kindly to you putting his new prize fighter out of commission."

"You owe me a job," he sneered.

"A job?"

"You worked for the Wolves when you and your Talent still belonged to the Raptors. Now you need to do one more job for me to make things even."

"And why should I do that?" Scarlett asked, debating driving her knee up between Amos's legs. She steadied herself, not wanting Amos's howling to wake Granny at this hour.

"I know you bargained to pay off a certain duke's debt with the Wolves. Makes me think you would be upset if something bad happened to him or his family." Even in the near darkness, Scarlett could make out Amos's feral grin.

"Fine. What's the job?" Scarlett asked. She was already making a spectacle of her Talent, letting people bet on her and jeer at her injuries to keep Benedict and his family out of trouble. One more job for the Raptors was a simple price to pay.

Amos released her and stepped away at her agreement. "You always were too fond of your upper-city friends. What have they ever done for the likes of us?"

"What do you want me to do?" Scarlett asked again, ignoring his question.

"Oh, just something that will make good use of your particular skills."

Scarlett supposed it was fitting that the last job Amos demanded of her was likely to be the most dramatic robbery of her career, and the most likely to go terribly wrong. If she hadn't recently sold herself into a lifetime of Talented gladiator fights, she would have a hard time believing she even agreed to it.

The newly unfurled leaves on the tree branch Scarlett crouched on rustled as she inched along it. She took caution to move lightly enough that the sound was easily mistakeable for the night breeze sweeping through the garden. With an ephemeral coating of shadows, Scarlett dropped to the ground on the far side of the wrought iron fence.

Taking her bearings, Scarlett didn't see any guards or servants about. She didn't expect to, with the bribes Amos had made, but she had been on too many missions where somebody double-crossed them to take that security for granted.

As she glanced around the well-manicured garden, her gaze caught on a hedge maze to the left. It hadn't been lost on Scarlett when Amos told her who the mark was that this was the same manor she had pretended to be Georgette at the month before. An uninvited guest once more, she tore her eyes away from where she met Benedict for the first time and turned back to the mission at hand.

To the right, the carriage house lay partially hidden behind the main manor. Scarlett kept to the walls, crouched below the level of the windowsills as she rounded to where her target lay. She crept closer to the door, finding the latch sealed with a large padlock. She grimaced at the size of the metal she would have to cut through and the noise it was likely to make as she pulled out the bolt cutter stuffed down the front of her jacket. While she was sure she could pick the lock with some patience, it might not leave evidence that the lock was forced, and she hated to implicate the coachman, even if he had taken a bribe from the Raptors.

She worked the bolt cutters around the padlock and waited until the clop of hooves on the street outside could be heard. As the passing horse was at its loudest, she snapped through the metal, hoping to disguise the sound. Still, she winced at the metallic screech as the lock gave and listened with bated breath for a few minutes to see if anybody in the house had heard.

When there was no movement from the direction of the manor, she opened the door and slipped inside, leaving an opening through which a slat of moonlight could illuminate the interior. She sucked in a breath through her teeth at the sight that greeted her. As promised, the coachman had left a horse harnessed to Lord Worthington's stylish new phaeton. The animal stamped and whickered as Scarlett drew closer. Quickly, she slipped an apple out of her pocket and held it forward, hoping to silence him. He eyed her suspiciously for another moment before leaning forward to accept her gift. His warm breath tickled her wrist as he chomped down on the fruit, and she took the moment to inspect the carriage he drew.

The four wheels stood nearly as tall as Scarlett, their royal blue paint job just visible in the dim light. She swallowed thickly as she examined the minimal body, room for just a driver and a jump seat in the back, perched high on the frame. Built for speed, Amos insisted that this carriage was sure to win the Raptors many street races, but she didn't envy the driver. Races in the lower city were rarely clean, and one ram from a competitor's vehicle could easily unseat somebody from a seat so precarious and lightly sprung. Then again, it would be just like Amos to insist on such a flashy vehicle, clearly stolen from a high-profile mark.

The horse butted his head against the middle of Scarlett's chest, nearly knocking her back a step as he searched for more treats. She petted his nose with a light shushing noise, enjoying the velvety softness under her hand and the soft whicker he offered in response. This next part would be easier if she had the animal's trust.

With her focus split between the horse before her and thoughts of driving this deathtrap of a carriage, Scarlett's mind was slow to register the footsteps outside the door. By the time she realized she was about to be discovered, the door was already inching open. Scarlett fell into a crouch, shadows coalescing around her, making the horse snort in discomfort.

The door opened to reveal a figure dressed all in black, scarf pulled over his face just like Scarlett. With the moonlight reflected in his eyes, Scarlett could just make out his gaze take in the carriage behind her before flicking to her. This wasn't a cop or a coachman.

Before Scarlett could think any further than that, he lunged. She rolled out of the way, the silver flash of a knife slicing through empty air where she had been just a moment earlier. Her own knife sprang to her hand even as she backed away with a muttered curse. Of course the time they successfully bribed guards and footmen, another would-be-burglar would set fire to her carefully laid plans.

He lunged again, swiping his knife at Scarlett's face, clearly intent on eliminating his competition. Scarlett sidestepped and grabbed his wrist, twisting in a way she hoped would make him drop his weapon. Instead, he twisted with her and used her momentum to throw her over his hip onto the ground. Dust rose around her in a cloud as the breath escaped from her lungs.

A neigh split the air, shrill with distress. Her assailant, lifting his foot to pin Scarlett in place, stumbled back as the horse reared, striking out at the air. She took the opportunity to roll away, narrowly avoiding hooves slamming back into the ground as she put the horse between her and her attacker. Springing to her feet, she leaped for the phaeton, clambering onto the seat without finesse. With the noise of the confrontation, the residents of the house would soon come to investigate, and she would rather be gone when they did.

As spooked as the horse was, she had barely grabbed the reigns when he charged forward, nearly flinging Scarlett from her perch. She hung on as they crashed through the doors, a shouted curse echoing behind her. She only prayed that Amos had delivered on his promise to have the back gate left open for her. Rounding the curve of the drive to find her way clear, the wave of relief that crashed over Scarlett was quickly washed away by the pounding of hoofbeats behind her. A glance over her shoulder revealed the thief, leaning low on the neck of another of Lord Worthington's horses as they galloped in hot pursuit.

Scarlett urged her horse faster as they barreled through the front gates. Her teeth rattled against each other with the bumping of the wheels over the cobblestones at this speed. Sparing another glance behind her, she found the other horse gaining on them, albeit slowly. A carriage was slower than a rider, but the thief was limited by lack of proper tack.

At the last second, Scarlett pulled her horse into a sudden turn, the phaeton tilting dangerously, skidding around the corner on two wheels. As it slammed back down on all four wheels, she looked behind her again. The rider managed to turn his mount without the direction of a bridle but slipped dangerously to the side as it changed direction. Scarlett cursed as he succeeded in pulling himself back into a proper seat.

Rounding back onto the main road, the few people out at this time of night jumped to the side, pressing themselves against buildings as the chase crashed by. The wind from their speed stung Scarlett's eyes until they watered, tear tracks streaking her temples as she looked for another way to lose her tail. By the time they were in the middle city, the thief was just a carriage length behind her.

Pulling into another sudden turn, Scarlett directed her carriage down a narrower side street. Just wide enough for the phaeton, the thief wouldn't have enough room to pull up next to her. She grit her teeth as she maneuvered through a series of side streets, brick walls coming close enough to touch as she crashed around progressively narrower corners.

She soon ran out of side streets, re-emerging back onto a main thoroughfare in the lower city. More people were out and about at this time of night here, making them harder to avoid.

"Move!" Scarlett shouted repetitively at the top of her lungs, barely able to hear herself over the rumble of the carriage like thunder in her head. Still, she was forced to pull on the reigns, slowing somewhat to not crush those who couldn't jump out of the way fast enough.

The thief, on the other hand, continued at a breakneck pace, more easily able to maneuver his mount. Soon, his horse's head drew level with the back wheels of the carriage. A thud rocked the precarious vehicle as he leaped from his mount onto the jump seat behind her. Before Scarlett could react, an arm wrapped around her neck, forearm pressed brutally against her windpipe. She brought one hand up to claw at it but left the other on the reigns. If they crashed, then they were all dead. Still, her broken nails were ineffectual, and his grip tightened.

The adrenaline coursing through her system and the lack of oxygen reduced her thoughts to a panicked buzz. Still she fought against them, mustering all her concentration to summon a shadow where she thought her attacker's face would be. The slight loosening of his grip told her she had succeeded. She used the ability to move her head to bend forward before snapping it back. The crown of her head connected with something hard. She didn't have time to dwell on the crunch of bone and the grunt of pain. As the arm around her neck slackened enough for her to slip free, she ducked under it at the same time she wrenched the horse into another turn. As they tilted, the man toppled off the jump seat. Scarlett slid to the side of the bench, teetering precariously on the edge. One hand grabbed at the lip, while the other clutched the reigns in a grip so hard, she knew the stitching would be embedded on her palm. For a heart-stopping moment, Scarlett was sure she was going to crash to the cobblestones with the thief. Then the carriage righted itself and she sucked in a breath. Glancing behind her she saw the crumpled form of her pursuer roll over on the cobblestones, but he didn't get up.

Scarlett slowed the horse to a safer pace but continued to trot towards the drop-off point in Raptor territory. She was ready to be off this carriage and done with Amos. Even in the intermittent light of the streetlamps, a sheen of sweat was visible on the horse's flanks and foam from its mouth streaked his neck. Scarlett panted nearly as hard from the fading terror of the chase and lingering feeling of being choked. Her throat throbbed where his forearm had restricted her airflow.

Finally she directed the carriage into an alley in Raptor territory and pulled to a halt. The horse let its head sag in a weary way Scarlett commiserated with. As the echo of hooves faded from the alley where they stopped, it made the clambering in her mind feel louder.

A door opened at the end of the alley, and Scarlett straightened. Amos strode out, beady eyes flicking appraisingly over carriage before rising up to where Scarlett sat.

"I wasn't expecting you so soon, but I thought I heard wheels."

"I wasn't originally planning on galloping the whole way here, but we had some competition," Scarlett explained as she slithered down from her perch. Her legs felt like water beneath her, and she laid a hand on the horse's flank to steady herself, hiding from Amos how shaken she was.

He hummed casually in response, striding up to the horse and lifting its head to look in its eyes. The animal wrenched its head away, and Amos huffed, "I thought the Rattlesnakes might have had eyes on the same prize."

"And you didn't think to tell me?" Scarlett forced out from behind gritted teeth.

"I assumed you'd handle it. Besides, I thought killing a Rattlesnake might be a fitting sendoff from the Raptors. Didn't you kill one in a turf war right when you joined us?" He asked it casually without looking at her. As if the image of a crumpled form at the bottom of a steep drop wasn't etched into the back of Scarlett's eyelids, only fading with years of continued violence. As if the crunch of bones hitting pavement didn't echo in her ears, punctuating the moment Scarlett knew her old life was gone forever.

"All that matters is that we're even now." Scarlett nearly spat, but she contained herself with a slow breath in through her nose. Amos couldn't control her anymore, which was a comforting thought, despite knowing she had traded his assignments in for an even worse job.

"Careful, you might make me think you didn't like us," he responded, finally looking at her.

Scarlett considered him for a moment. While there was no doubt in her mind that she despised Amos with his oily smiles and cavalier attitude towards violence, she couldn't pin down her emotions regarding her time with the Raptors. They were the reason she had survived the Inquiries, and Scarlett wasn't one to discount the value of simply enduring.

With a shrug, Scarlett turned and strode away without another word. Her time with the Raptors was over, but it left more marks on her than the osprey inked on her shoulder blade. She had little hope that her time with Wolves would mar her any less.

Scarlett quietly let herself into Granny's, easing the door open on noisy hinges, only to see that she shouldn't have bothered. The wizened woman herself sat hunched over the counter, the light of the single lamp filtering through the brown liquid in the glass before her. With the flickering shadows dancing across her lined face, Granny looked even more weathered than usual, and Scarlett was struck by the thought that she might actually be aging. Granny always seemed more figurehead than person, an indelible fixture in the lower city with a sense of permanence amongst the constantly shifting borders and alliances within the gangs. So many lieutenants and bruisers had received a meal or shelter from a cold day at one point or another that she had indisputable immunity from the sporadic violence in the streets.

"Back before dawn I see," she commented, downing another sip of the liquor before her.

"Just had one job tonight, but it was more than enough trouble to last me a week."

"Need something to take the edge off?" Granny gestured to the bottle, still open on the counter next to her.

As much as Scarlett had been dreaming about collapsing into her lumpy mattress, she found herself nodding. She slid onto the stool next to Granny, grabbing the bottle and taking a swig straight from the neck, not bothering to dig up a glass. She grimaced as the liquor burned her throat where it was tender from being choked.

"Looks like it." Granny nodded to her neck. "Got a nice purple set of gems for a collar there."

Scarlett took another swallow by way of answer, and Granny pushed off her stool, hobbling to the ice box in the corner.

"You're lucky ice delivery was this afternoon, or you'd be shit outta luck," Granny explained, using a pick to hack off a chunk of ice. She handed it to Scarlett.

Her breath escaped her mouth in a hiss as she pressed it against her bruised skin, the cold a jarring contrast to the warmth of the alcohol. Still, they both served to numb the ache. Granny climbed back onto her stool and took another sip. They sat like that in companionable silence for a few minutes, drinking and letting the ice go to work.

"I thought you were gonna tell me you were done running jobs," Granny commented eventually.

"What gave you that impression?" Scarlett swirled the bottle in her hand.

"You were leaving in nice dresses, getting fancy letters. I thought you might be leaving us to go back to the upper city."

Scarlett eyed Granny out of the side of her eye. The older woman was staring ahead at the dimly lit common room. Besides Georgette, Granny was one of the only people to know who Scarlett was before she joined the Raptors, although they never talked about it.

"It was just another job," Scarlett murmured, as if she could convince herself.

"Someday you're going to have to stop picking pockets and running cons, you know. You've got a life to live."

"Do I?" Scarlett mused, to herself more than Granny.

"When you stumbled in here and I gave you a place to stay, I was hoping you planned to do more than just survive." Granny shrugged, downing the last of her drink before setting it down with a thunk that felt jarringly loud in the quiet of the night. Then she stood and shuffled towards the stairs. "Rent's due," she shot over her shoulder before disappearing around the corner.

Scarlett dug out her purse and laid it on the counter before grabbing the bottle and carrying it up to her room with her, downing another mouthful along the way. At least what little she won from the fighting rings could pay her rent at Granny's. For now, she didn't have to move into the Wolves' Cave, and that was enough.

Chapter Fourteen

The rickety door on the small room where Scarlett waited did little to block out the noise of fists pummeling flesh filtering in from the next room. She stared down at the floor only to find a rust-colored stain where a puddle of blood had been the night before after another Talented found themselves on the business end of Ivor's icy fists.

Over the past few nights, Scarlett had come to realize that waiting to fight in the ring was the worst part of her new arrangement. When facing down an enemy—usually one much larger than herself—the adrenaline of the fight took over. She could drown out the sounds of the crowd around her and focus on staying alive. But as she waited, the jeers of the spectators pushed in close around her, reminding her that she was no more than a spectacle. It made the angry beast in her chest snarl and snap, although she hadn't unleashed it again the way she had when facing down Ivor. She beat her opponents dispassionately, took her tiny cut of the winnings, and went home.

"There's everybody's favorite underdog." Fang's raspy voice cut through the noise from outside as he came into the room.

Scarlett nodded, not enthusiastic to engage. Fang didn't seem to care.

"I have to say, seeing somebody of your stature taking down my normal bruisers has certainly been a change of pace," he continued, sitting on the bench beside her. Scarlett resisted the urge to inch away from him, even as he took up most of the room on the seat, spreading his thighs and bracing both hands on his infamous cane between them. He leaned in conspiratorially as he continued to talk, unbothered by her lack of response. "Although it occurs to me that the quick way you take them down might be too much of a change of pace. The crowds here have come to expect something a little more...brutal."

Scarlett's eyes darted over to her opponent for the night in the far corner of the room. He currently faced away, wrapping his knuckles, likely unable to hear Fang over the din in the main room.

"You wanted me to fight, and I fight to win," she said with a shrug.

"I have no problem with you winning dear—"

Scarlett ground her teeth so hard she was sure Fang could hear it.

"—but it's more about the way you win. If people wanted to see a polite surrender, they'd go to a regular boxing match and not bother the trek to the lower city."

Scarlett didn't respond, chewing his words.

"I gave you an easy opponent tonight," Fang pressed on quietly, nodding his head towards the man in the corner who had just finished wrapping his hands. "Consider this your chance to put on a bit of a show. Really unleash, and I won't lower your cut of the pot when you kill him."

The urge to punch Fang in the face and the need to vomit warred within Scarlett at the thought that this man was being handed to her like a sacrifice. He was a lamb, and she was the Wolf they expected to tear him apart.

"That's not part of the deal," Scarlett bit out with a sharp shake of her head.

"Deals can be altered."

Scarlett's stomach turned leaden.

"You wouldn't go back on our arrangement. If word got out you didn't hold up your bargains, you'd have a hard time getting the manpower you need to run this place." Even as the words sounded weak to Scarlett, she knew they were true. In a world where cutting deals got you ahead, loss of reputation could be death.

"I won't go back on our agreement," Fang agreed. "But I'm not above adding terms. There are other ways to get you in line."

Scarlett nearly snorted. She knew he wouldn't kill her. It would only put him down a fighter. With her friends protected by their original deal, there was nothing left to take from her. She remained quiet, eyes fixed on her bruised knuckles. Fang pushed to his feet with a heavy sigh.

"Think on it, my dear. I wouldn't want you to have regrets about your performance tonight."

As he pushed from the room, a roar from the crowd signaled an end to the prior match. Scarlett pushed to her feet as well, glad to finally be done waiting. Her adversary stood as well, and she sized him up. He was smaller than some of her prior opponents, and despite him being clad in nothing but a pair of pants rolled up to his knees, she didn't spy a tattoo. He didn't belong to a gang at all, making it seem likely that he was another victim of Fang's blackmailing.

Seeing her looking, he eyed her back warily. Scarlett didn't miss the flicker of fear in his eyes, and bile rose in the back of her throat. Fang really expected her to slaughter a man—barely more than a boy really—who looked like he had never seen a real fight before. Scarlett set her shoulders and pushed out into the main room.

She barely listened as Zed announced her arrival when she stepped over the ropes into the ring. The noise rolled off her shoulders like rain, and she bounced from foot to foot.

"Tonight we have a newcomer, let's hear it for Darius!"

Her opponent stepped up next, and she looked him over for any indication of what his Talent might be. He likely knew hers, having had it on full display in previous fights over the last week. Still, even as Scarlett pulled her shadows close to her hands as they squared off against each other, he gave no indication.

Zed rang the bell, and Darius vanished.

Scarlett blinked once in confusion. Then the air shifted before her and she saw it. Darius was still there but camouflaged against the wall behind him. As he made to dart to the side though, the image warped, and Scarlett could clearly see his outline.

With a grimace, Scarlett swung her fist, connecting with Darius's forearm as he tried to block. Fang was right, her opponent's Talent wasn't hard to overcome in a fight. It would be useful for remaining unseen when one wasn't expecting it, but with Scarlett knowing what to look for, his movement was easily tracked throughout the ring.

Scarlett drew up her knee and threw a sweeping kick at him from the side, sending him stumbling back. He clearly wasn't a trained fighter. Scarlett swung her fist again, putting considerably less force behind the attack than she usually would. Continuing to advance, she let her shadows dance around her to hide her movements even as she drove him back with light attacks. She could put on a show without brutalizing an opponent who was clearly outmatched.

Darius backed into a corner of the ring, trapped by ropes on either side. Scarlett spun around and jumped as she flung her leg out in a maneuver that was impractical against a more experienced enemy but would hopefully entertain the crowd enough for Fang's liking. Just before her kick landed, she froze as her eyes locked on a familiar face among the spectators behind Darius. She tripped on the landing and her opponent took advantage of her momentary shock. Lashing out, his fist connected with her face hard enough to cut her cheek against her teeth.

Scarlett tore her eyes away from Benedict as the taste of copper flooded her mouth. Questions about what he was doing there swirled through her brain even as she fought to focus on the task at hand. In a flash, she swept her leg out, knocking Darius's legs out from under him. She didn't have the focus to put on a show anymore. Not when she could feel Benedict's gaze on her like a brand.

As Darius crashed to the ground, she leaped on top of him, planting a knee in his gut and summoning a shadow in her hand with enough solidity to approximate a blade. Scarlett only held it to Darius's throat for a moment before he tapped the ground in surrender. Scarlett looked up to find Fang standing at the edge of the ring, raising his eyebrows at her. He gave her a small nod as if in permission, but Scarlett's gaze slid away to where Benedict still stood.

The steady gaze he leveled at her calmed her as much as it made her want to leap out of her skin. She pushed off Darius forcefully. Turning away from him, she left him lying there on the ground as she stalked away. The bell rang to signal her victory, but the cheers that followed seemed subdued.

Scarlett didn't bother to look at Fang's reaction as she stepped over the ropes blocking off the platform. Instead, she stalked through the spectators towards the front door. The space felt too small with both Fang and Benedict watching her. She itched to disappear into the night, unseen among her shadows where she could shove all the feelings bubbling up inside her back into their cage. She didn't even stop to collect her cut of the purse. Fang could keep the money if it made him feel better about her not brutalizing her opponents.

She didn't make it two steps out the door before footsteps sounded behind her. She quickened her pace striding purposefully towards a side street where she could disappear.

"Scarlett!"

Benedict's tone made her pause before continuing even faster. She turned around the corner, out of sight of the bouncers outside the Wolves hideout, before stopping. Benedict jogged around the corner, nearly crashing into her when he realized she halted.

"Scarlett," he sighed.

She looked up at him, finding it felt like months since she had last seen him, even though it had only been a week or two. He somehow looked lighter than he had when she had left him before, the circles under his eyes faded, his eyes brighter.

"What are you doing here?" she asked.

"I came to see you." Benedict took a step forward. Scarlett backed away, hitting up against the stone of the wall behind her. Silence stretched between them, a tenuous, uncomfortable thing. Part of her wanted to ask why he wanted to see her, while the other part screamed that it wouldn't change anything.

"Did your mother and sister make it back from the country?" Scarlett asked instead, to remind herself why she had chosen to give herself over to the Wolves.

Benedict nodded. "It's good to have them home again. I sleep better at night knowing they're no longer under threat."

Scarlett nodded this time.

"I wish I couldn't sleep though," Benedict pressed on, his voice pitching low. "It would be easier if I sat up every night again, because every time I drift off, I dream of you."

A choked sound escaped the back of Scarlett's throat. Benedict's eyes were so intensely fixed on her that she felt shadows curling around her fingers, itching to hide her from his penetrating gaze.

"You shouldn't have come." Scarlett's voice was on the edge of cracking.

"Why not?" Benedict stepped forward again, near enough now that the warmth of his body so close to hers contrasted against the rapidly cooling sweat on her chest.

"You make me want things I can't have."

"You already have me," Benedict argued.

Scarlett opened her mouth to say that she couldn't—not in the way that she wanted, but the words were silenced by Benedict's mouth against hers. He pinned her to the wall behind her, trapping her like a bird in a cage. She had no desire to escape. Not when he kissed her rabidly, savagely, tongue slicking into her mouth hot and unapologetic.

For somebody who managed to seem suave when faced with mortal danger, the abandon with which Benedict kissed her now was all the more shocking. Gone was the polished rake of high society, replaced by a man possessed, as if he could right every wrong if he just owned her mouth completely.

The fizzling adrenaline from the fight roared back to life in Scarlett's bloodstream and she gave as good as she got. As Benedict's fingers tangled into the short strands of her hair, she dragged him closer to her by the lapels of his waistcoat, yanking his cravat free in the process. She wanted, *needed* to make him feel the same ache she did and take some comfort in the fact that she didn't suffer alone.

The warm taste of Benedict mixed with the lingering tang of copper on her tongue, a heady combination that made shadows curl around her in anticipation. She sent them skittering over Benedict's skin, stroking the back of his neck, winding through his hair and even skating down his trim thighs. He shuddered against her and broke the kiss with a gasp.

"I realized something last night when I woke from a dream with the taste of you on my tongue," Benedict panted against her lips raggedly.

Scarlett redoubled the efforts of her shadows, forming them into semisolid hands to stroke Benedict all over. If he couldn't concentrate enough to talk, then he couldn't break her with whatever he was about to say.

"I set out to save my family and prove I wasn't the useless party boy everybody thought I was. With my older brother a war hero and my perfect younger sister an angel, this could have been my chance to finally prove myself worth something. Instead, I just lived up to my reputation as a rake by tricking a beautiful woman into taking the fall for me." Benedict dropped his head to her neck, breathing the words against the sensitive skin there. "Now though, I intend to fight for you."

"With a letter opener?"

"With whatever it takes."

Scarlett purposefully ran the most solid of her shadows over the front of Benedict's pants, determined to either silence him with pleasure or drown out his words with the ringing in her ears from such a use of her Talent. The touch in the base of her skull jolted and preened at the hard length her shadows encountered.

"Scarlett, let me fight for you," Benedict nearly begged as he bucked just slightly against her at the ephemeral touches she tortured him with. His teeth dug into her neck, sure to leave a fresh purple mark among the yellow band of bruises around her throat.

"There's nothing to fight for," she murmured.

With what seemed to be a great effort, Benedict lifted his face from her neck and took a step back. It only put inches between their heaving chests but felt like he had created a great chasm between them.

"Stop hiding from me," Benedict grit out, equal parts desperate and angry.

"I'm not. This is who I am," Scarlett insisted.

"I won't have you like this," Benedict argued with a jerky shake of his head. "I won't let you slip away into your shadows, denying that you're anything more than a dog on the leash for the Wolves. I want all of you, that soft heart you've hidden away again, the anger you wear as a shield around it, whatever it is you're still hiding. I won't be satisfied with back-alley fumbling. I want you in my bed, in my home—in my *heart*."

Scarlett's eyes burned. She blinked rapidly, dispelling tears that she hadn't spilled since the fateful night she caused a Rattlesnake to fall to his death. The sudden swell of her emotions at odds with the words that escaped her. "That part of me is gone."

Even as she said it, the tender ache in her heart told her it was a lie. Still, it was easier to believe that the soft parts of her were gone when she had to fight for the Wolves. She still had to work for Fang to keep her friends safe, and peeling back the armor around her heart would make it impossible. She had to keep her feelings hidden behind a wall of shadows if she was going to uphold her end of the bargain to protect those she loved.

"I couldn't save my family, and now I can't save you." Benedict's face crumpled as he looked at Scarlett.

She tried to argue with him, but the words wouldn't come. She wanted to tell him that he had already saved her by showing her that there were things worth fighting for besides survival, and those things were him and Georgette and Leon. The words balled up in her throat, choking her.

Without a word, Benedict turned on his heel and walked off into the night. Scarlett could do nothing but watch as the London smog swallowed the silhouette of his receding figure.

Chapter Fifteen

Hesitant beams of sun crept over the peaked rooftops of the London skyline, barely strong enough to penetrate the thick clouds of smoke belching from the factory chimneys even at dawn. They told Scarlett she had been sitting on her perch for hours, legs stiff from being hugged to her chest as she huddled on the steeply tilted roof. She looked out at the main square, eyes fixed on the blackened scorch marks where the gallows used to stand. For the first time in years, she let her mind wander to the day the girl in her died.

She stood in that very square, Georgette's hand grasped tightly in hers, as her parents were marched up to the gallows. Part of her had hoped until the last moment that somebody would run in, say there had been a mistake. Instead, the crowd watched without protest as proof of her parents' Talents had been read out. Her mother could manipulate light in the way that Scarlett could shadows, and a neighbor had spied her playing with shining balls for Scarlett's amusement and reported her to Chief Cook. Her father had tried to use his Talent of persuasion to get the Royal Police to leave, but when they had realized what he was doing, Chief Cook had ordered his officers to drag him away too.

Scarlett sobbed silently as her parents died, not even able to draw enough breath to scream out her grief. As Georgette held her tightly, Scarlett could feel the weight of hundreds of gazes fixed on her. She could still feel the phantom pain of her nails biting into her palms as she desperately tried to keep her shadows from lashing out in her sorrow and anger. As Georgette and Mr. Ward led her back to their carriage, Scarlett saw it. Not only did the crowd eye her warily, knowing that

Talents tended to run in families, but now they eyed Georgette with suspicion as well.

Scarlett clenched her fists again now, the sharp pain in her palms reminding her that she had disappeared into her shadows to protect her friends, so she would never have to watch anybody hang because of her again. Now Benedict's words swirled in her head too, mingling with the memories of her parents in a dizzying mix.

As the sun grew brighter, Scarlett pushed to her feet, every joint in her body snapping and cracking in protest. Whatever decision she was trying to come to in her head, she knew she would never get there without at least a few hours' sleep.

She hopped over rooftops until she reached the lower city, ready to collapse face first onto her lumpy mattress. After a few minutes, she jumped down to the street level, walking the last few blocks to Granny's. As she turned onto the narrow street that served as the neutral territory around the safe haven, her ears pricked. The ever-present sounds of squabbling children roughhousing and collecting messages to run for various gangs were absent. The street was unnaturally still and devoid of life.

Hairs pricking up on the back of Scarlett's neck, she quietly unsheathed two daggers, padding quietly over the cobblestones towards the door to Granny's. Approaching, she found it hanging askew off its hinges and partly open.

As Scarlett peaked into main room, the sight that greeted her was carnage. Tables were upended, with splintered legs scattered throughout the room. Chairs were smashed to bits, gouges taken out of the paneled walls as if somebody had swung the furniture up against it to break it.

Seeing and hearing nobody, Scarlett carefully stepped inside, shattered glass crunching underfoot. She walked through the room, gaping in horror at the wreckage that used to be the only safe haven in the lower city—the one block that no gang claimed for themselves and weapons were rarely seen drawn.

As she stepped on another broken bottle with a loud crunch, a moan from behind the counter responded. Scarlett hurried over to find Granny's crumpled form. Falling to her knees beside her prone figure, Scarlett sighed in relief as Granny groaned again.

"Granny?" Scarlett carefully rolled her onto her back before blind rage coursed through her at the sight that greeted her. One of Granny's eyes was swollen shut with a purple bruise, and blood dribbled from a split lip.

"Of course you didn't come home until dawn today," Granny scolded, her voice pained but strong even as she clutched her hands to her chest. "They left a note for you." She nodded towards a scrap of paper pinned to the wood of the bar with a knife.

"Who did?" Scarlett demanded even as she reached for the note.

"The Wolves." Finally, Granny let her hands drop, revealing the wound she had been covering on her chest. Burned into Granny's flesh, bubbled and blistered but still recognizable, was a pawprint.

Scarlett saw red as she yanked the knife from the paper, holding it up to read the messy scrawl written there.

These are the new terms. Put on a better show or we'll come up with new ways to make you pay.

The paper crumpled in Scarlett's shaking fist, shadows curling around it as if she could undo all of this by making the note disappear.

"Very intimidating, but I'd rather you help me off the floor than storm off in a blind rage." Granny's voice cut through the boiling anger drowning Scarlett and brought her back to the present.

"I'm going to fix this," Scarlett promised, even as she put her arms around Granny's shoulders to help her up and to her bedroom.

Several hours later, Scarlett crept through the neat rosebushes behind the Pearces' house towards the parlor window. She had left after helping Granny into bed. Scarlett had set to set the frame right side up and shove a considerable amount of stuffing back into the mattress before it could be used. Scarlett had managed to clean and bandage Granny's wounds before the prickly old lady banished her from the room, insisting she'd survived worse.

Scarlett walked straight down the stairs and out the door, letting her feet carry her towards the one person she needed to see more than anybody right now. This time when she approached the window, she found it already unlocked, easily slid open. She vaulted inside before turning to slide the window shut behind her.

A delicate cough sounded behind her, nearly drowned out by the thud of the window against the sill. Scarlett turned, expecting to see Benedict, perhaps in in dressing gown with a glass of whiskey in hand again. She froze at the sight that greeted her.

In the doorway stood a young blonde in a simple white dress that she managed to make look like a priceless gown with her effortless elegance. Her wide dark eyes held something strikingly familiar.

"May I help you?" she asked.

Scarlett looked around her, making sure she had climbed in the window of the right house in her distraught state. Her eyes landed on a piano in the corner forever burnt into her mind, reassuring her she had.

"I'm not sure," Scarlett admitted. "I'm looking for Benedict…"

"Lottie, who are you talking too?" A familiar voice filtered from the hallway as footsteps approached.

Neither of them could answer before Benedict rounded the corner, freezing as he took in the sight before him.

"Scarlett, what's wrong?" he asked, clearly able to tell something was amiss from her harried appearance.

The blonde opened her mouth in recognition before crinkling her eyes in a smile that made her look suddenly much younger. She couldn't be much more than a girl, despite her willowy height.

"Oh you're Scarlett! I've heard so much about you," she exclaimed, striding towards Scarlett purposefully, as if to embrace her, but pulling up short.

"This is my little sister, Charlotte," Benedict introduced, sounding hesitant.

"You can hardly call me little when I'm nearly as tall as you," Charlotte argued.

Scarlett blinked. She hadn't considered that Benedict's sister and mother would be home now, back to being a proper socialite family with their debt forgiven. And here she was tumbling through their window with blood still crusted on her knuckles from the night before.

She shrank back, feeling small.

"Come, I'll ring for tea," Charlotte announced as if this situation were completely normal.

Scarlett glanced between the siblings apprehensively.

"Actually, could you distract mother and father for me?" Benedict interjected. "Scarlett and I need to have a private word. I'll take her up to my room."

It was Charlotte's turn to look between them knowingly. "I knew it!"

"There's nothing to know," Benedict insisted with a cough, beginning to herd his sister from the room. "We just have some things to figure out."

"It's good to meet you!" Charlotte shot over her shoulder as Benedict shooed her from the room. "We should still have that tea sometime!"

"Come on, let's get you upstairs before my parents see you and start asking so many questions that we never get to what it is you're here to talk about." Benedict took a step towards Scarlett and took her hand before leading her into the hall. She almost protested that she knew where his bedroom was already, but the feel of his smooth palm against her calluses was too pleasant. They darted up the stairs to his bedroom, and Scarlett slumped as soon as the door shut behind them.

"Sorry about my sister. Her inquisitiveness is charming, but discretion isn't part of her vocabulary," he commented once they were alone.

"She's lovely," Scarlett said honestly. In the few moments she had met her, it was already apparent the girl could charm the lid off a teakettle.

Silence fell between them, Scarlett suddenly feeling awkward in his presence. When they had parted last night, he had stormed away with sadness in his eyes, the taste of him still lingering on her lips. It had felt so distant after a sleepless night and the shock of Granny's injuries, but now it came crashing back as she shifted her weight from foot to foot, back pressed against his bedroom door.

Benedict didn't look angry though, eyes roving over her with concern instead. "What's wrong?"

Scarlett shook her head, unsure where to begin. She came with a plan to ask for his help, but first she needed him to understand the reasons behind her actions. Even if it made him think the worst of her, she desperately wanted him to comprehend why she pushed him away.

"My last name is Forster," she blurted out.

He stared in confusion, clearly caught off guard. After opening and closing his mouth a few times, realization dawned on his face. "As in the former Viscount Forster?"

Scarlett nodded with a heavy swallow.

Benedict swore colorfully and collapsed in a chair situated at the foot of his bed. "I had forgotten he had a daughter. Everybody assumed she had died."

"I wanted it that way," Scarlett murmured.

"But why? Didn't you have any relatives to stay with?"

Scarlett shook her head, thinking back to the memories she had dredged up this morning, trying to find the words. "I didn't know them anyways, and I couldn't do that to them."

Benedict watched her intently, waiting for her to continue. She licked her lips.

"Everybody was already suspicious of me, knowing Talented parents normally have Talented children. At that age, I didn't have great control of my shadows. Whoever I lived with would inevitably know about them. Their choices would either be to turn me into the Royal Police to hang like my parents or cover for me and die alongside me when the truth came out. I didn't want to stick around to find out what they would choose.

"So I disappeared. I took my dowry and ran to the lower city. Eventually I took up with the Raptors, knowing a gang was the best way to be protected from the Inquiries. They had enough officers in their pockets to keep the Royal Police from looking at me too closely. With everybody eventually assuming me dead, they wouldn't hunt me down."

Benedict scrubbed his hand over his face, looking weary with realization. "Why didn't you claim your title when the Inquiries were ended?"

Scarlett blinked, knowing she had come to the hardest part, but the part Benedict deserved to know.

"I killed somebody."

The words came out quietly, barely above a whisper. Scarlett didn't think she had ever said it out loud before.

"Who?" Benedict asked.

Scarlett shook her head. "I don't even know. It was one of the first fights with the Raptors. I saw one of the Rattlesnakes stationed on a nearby building, aiming a gun down into the fray, and I panicked. I used a shadow to blind him, and he slipped and fell off the roof."

"It was an accident," Benedict murmured. The sympathy in his tone, as if she were the victim, shot like an arrow into Scarlett's heart. She squeezed her eyes shut.

"He's still dead. And the other Raptors saw it happen. If I ever tried to leave them, I knew they would turn me into the Royal Police. And with the bribes in their pockets, they wouldn't give me a chance to defend myself, not that I could have. It wasn't just the murder either. I've stolen, intimidated, cheated...all of it."

When Benedict didn't respond, she peeled her eyes open, finding him staring at her as if crestfallen. This was the moment, she knew. The moment he realized he was better off letting her slip into the lower city, never to be seen again. She needed one more thing from him first.

"I figured I'm already a criminal, and I would rather be doing it to keep my friends safe than just for my own survival. But the Wolves—no matter how much I sacrifice, it's never enough to keep everybody I care about safe."

The admission tugged at Scarlett's guts. Tears pricked at her eyes for the second time in as many days, and she squeezed them shut again. The air shifted as Benedict pushed to his feet and approached, and Scarlett knew he stood right before her. She let out a shuddering breath to brace herself.

Then arms wrapped around her, pulling her into a solid chest warm with the masculine scent of citrus and earth. Scarlett stiffened in Benedict's embrace, unprepared to be the one comforted after all she had confessed too. He held firm though, and after several long moments she melted, tears finally slipping from her eyes to leave salty tracks down her cheeks. She was glad her face was buried in Benedict's shirt, her pain hidden from his gaze.

"Do you know how I know you're not a murderer?" Benedict asked, his voice stirring the hair on the crown of Scarlett's head.

She responded with a noncommittal noise of question and protest, followed by a muffled sniffle.

"Every interaction I've had with you has revolved around you putting your life on the line to save somebody else. When you impersonated Georgette, taking Leon's place in the fight, jumping in to save me even when I had tried to kill you just the night before—"

"You wouldn't have done it," Scarlett mumbled into his shirt.

"I know that now, but I still had a gun pulled with violent intentions. Even the man you claim you killed, you did it defending others. You're so single-minded in your protection of those around you, that you'll sell your own soul to keep them safe."

Now Scarlett pulled back to look up at Benedict. He loosened his hold so she could, but his arms remained looped loosely around her waist.

"My soul wasn't enough this time," she confessed.

"Tell me," Benedict prompted, walking backwards towards the chair he sat in before, tugging Scarlett with him. He sat, pulling Scarlett into his lap. She stiffened again, not sure she had sat in anybody's lap since she was a child. Benedict remained patient, settling her comfortably across his thighs and holding her to his chest.

Once Scarlett got over the shock of their current position and relaxed, she told Benedict what happened with Granny. Not one to have thought herself a lap-sitter, she found herself grateful for the comfort the position offered when she envisioned the blistered brand on Granny's chest. Benedict's thumb rubbed small circles between her shoulder blades, keeping the worst of the bubbling anger at bay.

"The Wolves need to be stopped," Benedict said with a shake of his head.

"I'm not sure I could kill Fang, and even if I did, one of his lieutenants would just take his place." Scarlett kept her gaze downcast.

"I might have an idea," Benedict started.

Scarlett looked up and tilted her head in question.

"When I realized all you had sacrificed for us, I knew I couldn't just leave you to be killed or beaten in the fighting pits. In my time with you, I certainly proved that I wouldn't be able to get you out by force in any way. It occurred to me though, if I'm going to be labelled a high society scoundrel, I might as well use my charisma and my connections to my advantage. Maybe I could recruit the help of people that *could* stop the Wolves."

"What did you do?"

"I'm going to Mr. and Mrs. Woodrows for dinner tonight."

Scarlett blinked. "The Beast?"

"I wouldn't call him that to his face," Benedict said. "He's one of the king's bodyguards now after all, officially pardoned for his work with the Lions. And his wife is advisor to the king now, helping him dismantle the remnants of the Inquiries. They are the only openly Talented people in his inner circle. If anybody would care about what's happening to the Talented and have the power to do something, it's them."

"Do you know them?" Scarlett asked.

"We haven't been officially introduced, but I mentioned my father, and his name has a lot of sway," Benedict admitted. "Besides, I doubt they get many social invitations with everybody giving them a wide berth. They probably see this as a way to start integrating the Talented back into polite society."

"It seems like a stretch," Scarlett conceded, even as her mind whirled with possibilities. The Woodrows might very well want to leave the violence of the lower city in their past, given that their pardons had made it possible. Even so, Scarlett couldn't pin down her feelings towards the couple. Mrs. Woodrow, formerly Ms. Cook, had stood at the front of the crowd next to her father, the Chief of Royal Police responsible for the executions of so many, as her parents hung. Still, she was credited with the end of the Inquiries and the conviction of Chief Cook for the murder of his wife a year ago.

"It would be less of a stretch if you came with."

"Me?" Scarlett's eyebrows shot up.

"You have an intimate awareness of the Wolves' operation that I don't. And your name…it would hold weight to have a member of a prominent family entangled in this asking for help."

Scarlett swallowed. Using her real name and presenting herself to prominent members of society in the open went against everything her instincts wanted. Her shadows tugged at her consciousness, wanting to cover her in darkness where she could survive safe and unseen. Hiding had only gotten the people she cared about hurt. Maybe it was time to try things Benedict's way.

She nodded. "Alright."

"We'll need to find you something a bit more befitting of your status to wear," Benedict mused, looking her up and down.

"Former status," Scarlett clarified, even as she cringed at the state of herself. She still wore the loose shirt and trousers she had fought in last night, crusted in sweat and grime.

"I'm sure my sister wouldn't mind lending you a dress, but you'd trip over her hem. She shot up a few years back and we had to get a whole new set of dresses or risk her exposing her entire calf every time she took a step."

"How scandalous," Scarlett remarked drily with a glance down at her trousers, fitted in a way that showed off a lot more than her ankles. "Georgette's dresses always fit me well, and I owe her a visit anyways."

Scarlett shifted her weight, but Benedict's arms tightened around her waist, as if he weren't entirely ready to let her go yet.

"Are you sure you don't want to stay for breakfast? I could scrounge up some kipper," he offered, resting his chin on her shoulder. Even if the way he kissed her last night lit a fire in her veins, the way he held her now made the softness in her chest melt like a pool of butter on warm toast, simultaneously soothing and uncomfortable in its intimacy.

"Then I might have to risk meeting your mother, and I think your sister and the Woodrows will be enough socialites to deal with in one day. My manners are still a bit rusty. Besides, I need at least a few hours' sleep if I'm going to be fit for company tonight." Scarlett slid from his grip to stand, acutely feeling the loss of his arms, even as she stepped away. His hands hung in the air for a moment before letting them drop to his lap. Scarlett was grateful for the distance, allowing her to think straight. Even if she itched to let him hold her in reassurance, there was still work to be done.

"Should I fetch you from the Wards' for dinner tonight?"

Scarlett nodded.

"Then I'll make sure my parents are distracted and you can slip out." Benedict pushed to his feet and walked to the bedroom door.

Scarlett stopped him with a shake of her head.

"I may have told you who I am, but you haven't yet convinced me that doors are superior to windows for entering and exiting unseen."

"As long as you don't throw me out with you, you're allowed to climb in and out of my window any time you like," Benedict responded with a crooked grin.

Despite herself, Scarlett smiled back.

"One more thing before you go." Benedict stopped her, stepping forward until he was mere inches away. "Don't disappear on me again."

He leaned forward and pressed his lips to hers in a whisper of a kiss, somehow still enough to send sparks skittering down to Scarlett's toes. It was a promise that he hadn't forgotten where they left things the night before. Neither had Scarlett, not when the feeling of his body trapping hers against the alley wall was burned indelibly into her brain.

"I'll try not to," she said, voice not rising above a whisper. Then she turned and hopped onto the windowsill, already open to let in the warm summer breeze, before swinging down to the trellis below.

As used to fragmented sleep as Scarlett had become over the past years, her body had been pushed to its limits. After checking on Granny and finding her sleeping soundly as she had left her, Scarlett pushed into her room to find that it hadn't escaped the destruction either. Her bedframe had been smashed against the wall, splinters of broken wood scattered across the floor. Her ripped mattress lay on the floor, stuffing strewn about, tiny bits floating in the air like snowflakes as they were stirred by the breeze blowing in through the open window. She didn't have the energy to deal with the carnage now, just making sure there were no sharp fragments of wood or her smashed basin in her way before collapsing onto the remains of her mattress and falling immediately into unconsciousness.

When she woke, bright afternoon sun high enough to peek over the surrounding rooftops told her she had only been asleep for a handful of hours, but even that amount of rest left her much more prepared to deal with the mess of her situation.

Rising from the thin cushion on the floor, she glanced around her. In the corner, she spotted her chest, tipped on its side as if somebody had thrown it against the wall. Crouching down, she was relieved to find it hadn't been opened despite the apparent efforts to smash it. The lock she invested a month's worth of rent in to protect her dowry held fast, despite the fact that it only protected a handful of coins and a change of clothes at this point.

Tipping it flat again with a dull thud, Scarlett fished into her pocket for the key, ready to put on clean clothes now that she was awake enough to feel the way her shirt clung to her skin, stiff and pungent. Clothes in hand, she hesitated before closing the lid once more. Her gaze snagged on the crimson shadowed in the bottom, where she rarely looked.

Her hand drifted into the chest, fingers stroking against the velvet fabric and finding it as plush as the day she hid it away. She didn't even know why she had brought her mother's cape with her when she fled her old home with nothing but a fat purse of coins and the clothes on her back.

It had been lying across the back of a chair in the entry, right where her mother had left it after coming in from a carriage ride the day she was arrested. It had been a cold day, snow on the ground. Wet spots dotted the hem of the velvet from splatters of snow when her father had playfully lobbed a snowball at her in the park. Despite mother being one of the most elegant ladies in London society, she had giggled like a young flirt at Father's antics, retaliating with her own snowball, which hit Father full in the face, knocking off his top hat and leaving him spluttering.

It was with that image in her head that Scarlett had tucked the velvet cape under her arm before dashing out the door and slipping down to the lower city. If she ever found the strength in her heart to remember her parents without melting into a nonfunctional heap of emotions, that day in the park was how she wished to remember them. It was the only piece of her parents she had left.

Now she pulled out the cloak, shaking it out. Creases marked the fabric where it had remained folded and untouched for years. It wasn't something Scarlett would have considered wearing herself, loath to wear anything but browns and greys. She preferred colors in which she could readily blend in and escape from unfriendly eyes. Tonight though, she was walking into a dinner with the intent of being seen just as she was. For so long, remaining invisible had been her best tool in keeping herself and her friends alive. Tonight, maybe she could use some of her parents' strength.

After changing into her clean clothes, she bundled the weighty velvet under her arm and headed down the stairs. Hopefully Georgette had a dress that went with red.

Scarlett swallowed a lump in her throat with difficulty and gazed up at the tall doors before her, painted emerald green to offset the intricate brass knocker. It seemed odd that she had been less nervous to participate in a fight to the death than she was to knock on her best friend's door. She considered circling back around to climb directly into Georgette's window but shook the idea out of her head.

Georgette wouldn't be expecting her at this time of the afternoon and likely wouldn't be in her room. Besides, today she was visiting as Scarlett Forster, not the shadow of the lower city. She wouldn't be able to enter dinner with the Woodrow's via the window, she might as well practice using the front door at Georgette's home.

The sharp rap of the knocker felt jarringly loud. Scarlett cringed as she looked up and down the street, but nobody seemed to be paying her any mind. After a few moments where Scarlett considered shrouding herself in shadows and darting away before anybody answered, the door swung open.

The Wards' butler looked down at Scarlett and blinked in surprise. The last time he had seen her, she had been leaving for a ball with Mr. Ward dressed as Georgette. Without the wig and dress, she doubted she was recognizable.

"I'm here to see Ms. Ward," Scarlett said, suppressing the urge to shift her weight from foot to foot.

Recognition dawned on the butler's face. "Of course you are," he said as he stepped aside and beckoned Scarlett in. "She's in the parlor."

As he led her around the corner, Scarlett barely had time to take in the delicately appointed room before she was nearly tackled by a missile of chiffon and lace.

"You're alright!" Georgette exclaimed, voice so shrill in her excitement that Scarlett winced against the volume so close to her ear. Still, she embraced her friend. She couldn't remember the last time she had been hugged this much in one day.

"And so are you," Scarlett commented as they separated. She bent to pick up the embroidery that had been tossed aside when Georgette flew to her feet.

"Thanks to you." Georgette blinked watery eyes, tears clinging like crystals to her unfairly long lashes. "You left before I even knew what was happening. I wanted to find you, but then I realized that I didn't know where you lived. I couldn't even thank you for what you did to keep me and Leon safe, let alone tell you how much of an idiot you were."

"An idiot?" Scarlett asked.

Georgette shoved her in the middle of the chest with frustration but no force. "Yes, an absolute wooden spoon." She huffed and returned to the settee, collapsing on it in a rustle of fabric.

"I don't see how thinking on my feet to get everybody out of trouble makes me an idiot," Scarlett settled onto the cushion next to Georgette, moving her gunmetal skirt out of the way to make room.

"Because you had to have known that I wouldn't want you to do that for me." Georgette slumped back, her voice losing some of its enthusiasm.

"It wouldn't have changed my decision." Scarlett toyed with the silk tassels trimming the decorative cushions of the seat.

Georgette considered Scarlett for a moment, her normally expressive eyes unreadable.

"I don't think I've been a very good friend," she murmured eventually.

Scarlett stared. It wasn't what she expected from somebody who was the literal embodiment of goodness.

Georgette sighed and smoothed her hands down the front of her dress. "You just did what you've always done, sacrificing to protect me. It's what you did after your parents died. When you ran away and refused to let me be seen with you, it didn't take a genius to figure out that you were trying to protect my reputation.

"I couldn't begin to figure out how to help you, so I did the only thing I could think of. I tried to be positive. To be the best friend I knew how to be. You never told me about what you were doing, and I assumed it was because you didn't want to talk about it. I hoped I could make your life a bit brighter by giving you a place to escape. But now…Now I think I might have made a mistake by making you feel like I had to be protected from the realities of the world. I tried to focus on the good, and I made you think you had to shelter me from all the evil in this city."

Scarlett shook her head before Georgette even finished talking.

"No." Scarlett spat the word out with vehemence. "You were the best friend I ever could have asked for. Your light—the way you always had a smile for me, even when you must have guessed what I'd become—it was the reason I kept coming back to see you, even when I knew I should stay away. It was the reason I would give anything to protect you. Your optimism is what kept me going for so long."

Georgette tilted sideways to rest her head on Scarlett's shoulder. Her silky curls tickled the crook of Scarlett's neck.

"And now you've thrown your life to the Wolves for me. Leon told me what it was you agreed to." Georgette's tone brimmed with sorrow.

"How are things with you and Leon?"

The edge of a smile chased some of the sadness from Georgette's expression. "He's used the money from the Wolves to restart his art business, and we came clean to Father about our feelings for each other. He's decided to let Leon properly court me. It turns out that after having my life threatened, a less than advantageous marriage doesn't seem quite as much of a catastrophe."

"I'm glad," Scarlett said earnestly. If Georgette could get her happy ending, then perhaps what Scarlett had done wasn't completely in vain,

"And it's all because of you." Some of the sadness returned to Georgette's eyes.

"I'd happily sell my soul to keep yours bright," Scarlett murmured.

"I know, but I wish you wouldn't." Georgette paused, and they sat in silence for a moment. "You know, I had never seen your Talent before the other day. I had assumed you had one, but you never used it in front of me."

"I didn't want you to have to lie if the police ever asked you about it, or to implicate yourself by keeping my secret." Scarlett lifted one hand before them and let the thinnest of shadows weave between her fingers. "Keeping it secret is a hard habit to break."

"And now you're using it to entertain bloodthirsty crowds," Georgette said, a bitterness Scarlett had never heard from her before creeping into her tone.

"That's actually why I'm here." Scarlett quickly recounted the details of the past day. As she spoke, Georgette turned to face her. Even though Scarlett had never mentioned her living situation to her friend, Georgette seemed appropriately horrified that the Wolves would violate the neutral territory and brand an old woman who, while not helpless, definitely couldn't put up much of a fight.

"Benedict and I are going to tell the Woodrow's what the Wolves are doing, since they seem like the ones with the power to do something about it who might be the most sympathetic. I don't exactly have anything to wear to dinner with the king's bodyguard and advisor." Scarlett looked down at her threadbare clothes and the canvas bag now in her lap. "Well, I have one thing to wear, but it would hardly be decent to wear it alone."

"Lord Pearce might like it if you showed up indecent," Georgette commented.

Scarlett spluttered and Georgette politely covered a giggle with her hand.

"I'll find you something fitting to wear," Georgette assured. "I'm glad I can finally be the one helping you for once."

Scarlett blinked at her image in the mirror and was surprised to find her own face looking back. The only times she had been made up in past years, she had been trying to make herself look as much like Georgette as possible. Now though, no heavy powder obscured the freckles scattered across her nose, and the only hair on her head was her own cropped locks. Still, Georgette had made the few inches of hair she had look better than she had seen it, several sprigs of small white flowers pinned in as decoration. Something about it even made the color that Scarlett would usually describe as 'mousy' look richer.

Standing from the vanity, she fidgeted, trying to get her skirts to fall right. Georgette had found a forest green dress that had few enough ruffles to meet Scarlett's approval, even as she looked at the amount of fabric cascading around her and wondered if she could put her pants back on.

"We can't forget the finishing touch!" Georgette grabbed the canvas satchel where it sat on her bed and took out the red velvet cloak within. With a graceful movement, she swept it around Scarlett's shoulders, fastening it at the neck with the brooch in her parents' symbol—a crown made out of a combined *M* and *W* for their initials.

When Scarlett looked at herself in the mirror once more, her mother looked back at her for a moment. Then she blinked, and she was gone, replaced by her and Georgette, who looked proud of her handiwork. Still, even though it was likely too warm out for a cloak to be strictly necessary, it felt like armor around her. In it, she could use her own name and be proud of it.

A knock snapped the pair out of their admiration of Scarlett's appearance.

"A Lord Pearce is here with a carriage for Ms. Scarlett," the Wards' butler announced through the door.

"If they aren't impressed with you, then they're blind," Georgette declared with an encouraging pat on her shoulder before Scarlett left the room and headed down to meet Benedict.

When she stepped out into the mild spring night, Scarlett couldn't tell if the rush of heat that ran over her skin was from the thick cloak around her or Benedict's gaze as he spotted her from where he leaned against his carriage.

She stopped just steps away from him, but he hadn't moved, just staring at her with his mouth slightly agape. Scarlett shifted awkwardly in the silence and Benedict shook himself from his stillness.

"You certainly are a sight in a dress," he complimented as he helped her up into the carriage. His hand on the small of her back as she made her way up the step made her insides twitch in a pleasant way.

"You've seen me in a dress before," she argued as she settled onto the velveteen seat.

"I've seen you as Georgette in a dress," Benedict corrected as he settled in across from her. "The effect is different when you aren't pretending to be anybody but yourself."

Scarlett looked down with a hot face, finding that her hands were already worrying at the lace on her skirt. Something about the compliment pierced the softness in her chest, and now it bled warmth into the rest of her body.

"So what's our strategy with the Woodrows tonight?" she asked to distract herself.

"The strategy is that I act like my charming self, and you tell them what you know about the Wolves' operation."

"You make it sound so simple," Scarlett worried out loud.

"I think simple is best here," Benedict commented. "We tell the truth and let the chips fall where they may. We're more likely to get their help if we show our hand."

"I'm not sure I'm comfortable with the amount of gambling analogies used in this plan." Scarlett bounced her leg.

"Unlike my father, I tend to be rather lucky," Benedict promised, giving her a smile that almost reassured her.

It didn't take long to reach the Woodrow's house, which sat central amongst the upper city. As Benedict helped Scarlett down from the carriage, she blinked at the sight that greeted them. Instead of an austere show of wealth that seemed to be the way of most houses in this area, the front of the Woodrows' house seemed almost quaint. A sky-blue front door made for a welcoming entranceway, surrounded by flower bushes blooming impressively for early spring. She pulled her cape around herself despite not being cold, the feeling of safety it provided combined with the hospitable entranceway almost enough to assuage Scarlett's apprehension.

Benedict used the knocker, wrought in the shape of a rearing lion, to rap sharply on the door. Silence greeted them, and they shared an uneasy glance. As the quiet stretched on, Benedict raised his hand to knock again, and Scarlett opened her mouth to advise him not to be rude when they were about to ask for aid.

The door swung open to reveal a sandy-haired man, his round face reddened as he panted lightly.

"Lord Pearce, I presume," he greeted, to which Benedict nodded. "I apologize for the delay. We're not accustomed to having guests who don't take the liberty of letting themselves in." His eyes landed on Scarlett. "And who might you be?"

Scarlett had to pry her suddenly dry tongue from the roof of her mouth to respond. "Ms. Forster," she murmured with a slight incline of her head. Her family's name still tasted odd on her lips, but it was becoming easier to admit every time she said it, like a stuck garden gate swinging open more smoothly with each use.

"Mr. Topps at your service, but you can call me Gregor." The young man stepped aside and gestured them into the hall. Once inside, Gregor took Benedict's coat and cane. He hesitated, as if to take Scarlett's cloak as well, but when she made no move to remove it, he didn't mention it.

"Why don't you meet Contessa and Nate in the parlor while I set an extra place at the dinner table?" He gestured them towards an open door before rushing off towards the back of the house. It struck Contessa as odd that Gregor had referred to his employers by their first names, but he also seemed to manage the entire house by himself.

Benedict took Scarlett's elbow and led her into the room Gregor had indicated. The petite blonde they had seen in the garden what seemed like years ago but had actually only been a just over a month stood before a hulking man, straightening his cravat while he wore what must have been an expression of great forbearance. It was hard to tell on his mangled face, a rope of scar tissue twisting his mouth into a snarl and narrowing one eye to a squint. The sight reminded Scarlett of the violence she had seen the Beast commit the one time she had been unlucky enough to encounter him in action, and shadows tickled at her fingertips as if ready to jump to her defense.

"Lord Pearce," Mrs. Woodrow greeted upon seeing them. She swept her voluminous gray skirts behind her and approached Benedict with a hand outstretched in greeting. The elegance of the movement made Scarlett feel more like an imposter in her dress. Even Contessa's gray eyes made her stomach turn. She could still see the same gray eyes of the police chief who had dragged her parents from her home to hang for something they couldn't control. Scarlett took a deep breath, reminding herself this woman was the reason the Inquiries were over. Still,

Scarlett's feelings swirled as they tried and failed to decide their stance on Mrs. Woodrow.

A sharp exhale of breath from the Beast drew Scarlett's attention, and she looked up to find him staring at her with an intense, unreadable expression.

"I see you brought a companion," Mrs. Woodrow commented, turning her steely gaze to Scarlett. Despite the pale gray of her eyes, almost unnerving in their colorlessness, they held a warmth that Scarlett didn't recall in the former Royal Police chief's.

"I'm sorry I didn't think to ask if you would be bringing anybody," Mrs. Woodrow continued on. "I'm afraid we're rather unaccustomed to having company. Social calls are few and far between."

"Something tells me this isn't really a social call," Mr. Woodrow cut in, stepping up next to his wife and placing a proprietary hand on her lower back. His voice was not the harsh growl Scarlett had expected, but a smooth tenor that made him seem much younger than his grisly appearance suggested.

"Well now you've deprived me of the opportunity to soften our purpose with my substantial charisma. You've really done yourself a disservice there, I've been told I can be quite charming," Benedict cut in with a crooked smile, and Scarlett didn't know if she wanted to laugh or be swallowed by the carpet at her feet.

Mrs. Woodrow huffed a breath through her nose by way of laugh. "Nate here has a way with reading people," she said with a wry smile. Scarlett wondered if the rumors of the Beast's Talent being the ability to read minds were true.

"Now that we're not bothering with pretenses, allow me to introduce Ms. Scarlett Forster." Benedict gestured to Scarlett. Contessa's brow furrowed for a moment before her eyes widened in recognition. To her credit, she schooled her features quickly, shaking Scarlett's hand politely.

"And what business did you hope to discuss?" Mrs. Woodrow asked, seemingly wary now that she knew who Scarlett was.

Benedict hesitated for a moment, clearly seeking a place to begin.

"We need your help," Scarlett blurted out, shocking herself with her candor. Apparently now that she had come this far, admitting her family name and making herself vulnerable to those she had always hidden from, she was determined to plunge forth with abandon.

Everybody in the room stared, and she gripped the edge of her mother's cape, letting the soft texture of the velvet in her hands ground her.

"It's the Wolves. They have to be stopped," she plunged forwards.

"I know they've taken over our—the Lions'—old territory, but it's inevitable that one of the gangs would move in," Mr. Woodrow pointed out.

"It's not that." Scarlett shook her head. "They've started a fighting ring. Now that people in the lower city are no longer hiding their Talents, the Wolves are tracking them down and coercing them into fighting each other for entertainment." Scarlett swallowed heavily, forcing the last words from her throat, "Sometimes to the death."

Benedict's warm hand wrapped around her wrist, thumb rubbing circles while her pulse fluttered erratically with nerves.

It was Mrs. Woodrow who swore colorfully, surprising Scarlett "Are you sure?" she asked, oddly enough looking at her husband and not Scarlett.

Mr. Woodrow stared at her with piercing golden eyes, and Scarlett was struck once more with how accurately the name the Beast described him. He nodded sharply, not breaking eye contact.

"Come sit." Contessa gestured them towards a settee in the middle of the room. "Tell us what you know."

Scarlett settled onto the seat, maneuvering to spread her skirts around her and not managing it quite as elegantly as Mrs. Woodrow did across from her. Benedict sat next to her, hand coming back to rest on her forearm. Scarlett opened her mouth to start, but now that she had gotten over the first hurdle of stating her purpose, she didn't quite know where to go.

Benedict spoke first instead, giving her a chance to collect her thoughts.

"They've set up in one of the warehouses in the lower city, but many socialites come to bet on the fights," he explained, starting to describe everything he could tell from being in the audience.

Mr. and Mrs. Woodrow chimed in with questions as he went.

"Are all the fighters' members of the Wolves?" Mr. Woodrow eventually asked. This time Scarlett answered.

"No, although many are. They have managed to make agreements with other gangs, at least the Scorpions and the Raptors, to have more fighters if they get a cut of the house's earnings. And some of the fighters aren't even gang members," Scarlett explained, remaining deliberately vague about how she knew this. Still, Contessa pinned her with a discerning gaze. "They're making so much money on this that everybody wants in on the action."

"Which means getting rid of Fang wouldn't be enough to stop it." Mr. Woodrow ran a hand through his shaggy auburn hair, already tousled enough to show that this was a habit of his. For a moment, Scarlett was distracted by how odd it was to be familiar with such a human mannerism on a man that she had considered more a legend than anything else for so long.

"We'll need Joseph and the Royal Police's help to take down the whole operation," Mrs. Woodrow said as if thinking out loud.

Scarlett stiffened, heart skipping a beat in her chest. Benedict's hand on her arm tightened, but it was Mr. Woodrow whose gaze met hers.

"You needn't worry about the police chief. He works with us, after all," he commented with what might have been a wry smile, although it was hard to tell with one side of his face frozen by scar tissue.

"Easy for you to say when you've been personally pardoned by the king. We haven't all been so fortunate," Scarlett snapped before she could think better of it, surprising herself once more. Despite having spent her whole life trying to stay hidden and prioritize survival, she certainly wasn't shying away from antagonizing some of the most powerful people in London now that she had their attention.

The room was silent for a moment that stretched painfully, broken when Mrs. Woodrow cleared her throat. "Nate, why don't you go fetch Joseph, and probably Kristoff too so we can strategize. Ms. Forster and I will take a moment to find Gregor to tell him about the change in dinner plans."

Mrs. Woodrow stood and shot Scarlett a pointed, but not unkind look. Scarlett hesitated, but Benedict subtly nudged her forward with the hand on her arm.

"My man should still be around. I'll have him help Mr. Woodrow here fetch his associates," he suggested. He offered Scarlett a hint of a smile.

With that she followed Mrs. Woodrow from the room. She led her towards the back of the house into a dining room that was cozier than the large halls fit for formal dinners Scarlett expected to see in the Upper City. Gregor bustled about the table, rearranging plates.

"There's some unforeseen business, Gregor," Mrs. Woodrow announced as she entered. "Nate and Lord Pearce have gone to fetch Kristoff and Joseph to join us. I hope we can stretch dinner to feed everyone and that you don't mind keeping it warm."

Instead of seeming disgruntled by the continuing changes, Gregor smiled at the mention of more guests.

"You know I always make enough for guests," he responded. "Let me go get more silverware."

As he bustled from the room, Scarlett hovered awkwardly in the doorway, at a loss for what to say after her brief outburst. Mrs. Woodrow didn't address her right away, instead walking to the sideboard and grabbing a decanter and two crystal glasses. After pouring a finger of amber liquid in each, she offered one to Scarlett.

"I'd offer you tea, but I have a feeling something stronger is warranted with the type of conversation we're having this evening," she explained.

Scarlett took the glass from her outstretched hand but didn't drink.

"Mrs. Woodrow, I—"

"Call me Contessa, and you can call my husband Nate," she cut in. "As much as I'm anxious for Nate and I to integrate into society more thoroughly, I find I don't have the stomach for too many formalities anymore."

"Contessa," Scarlett amended, "I didn't mean to imply anything about you and your husband."

"You did more than imply," Contessa pointed out as she took a sip of her drink, but her tone lacked venom. Still, the steely eyes that pinned Scarlett unnerved her with their cutting intelligence and their resemblance to the late Chief Cook's.

"I suppose it's fair for me to be an object of your ire though, considering my father hung your parents," Contessa continued on when Scarlett remained silent. "You are that Ms. Forster aren't you? The one everybody assumed dead or gone?"

Scarlett nodded, surprised by how openly Contessa discussed the tension between them, but unexpectedly glad to have her cards on the table. Contessa blew out a breath through pursed lips.

"I guess we both lost our parents to the Inquiries then, albeit in different ways. If it's taught me one thing, it's that forgiveness is a fickle thing," Contessa mused.

"I don't blame you," Scarlett responded, shocked to find that she meant it. Seeing Contessa and her husband had ignited some of the anger that still simmered inside her when she thought of the Inquiries, but Scarlett found she didn't have it in her to be angry at somebody who had been as much of a girl as she had at the time.

Contessa shook her head, the elegant blond curl that fell artfully from her twisted hair brushing against the skin of her neck.

"I've found the hardest person to forgive is myself, both for things I did do and for the times I failed to act when I should have. There are days I feel like I've moved on, and there are days when I can think of nothing but the times I should have intervened when innocents were dying for things they couldn't change. The most important thing I've found though, is that without forgiving myself I don't have the power to set things right again. And that atonement is the most important part of forgiveness after all."

Scarlett digested Contessa's words, remembering they came from a woman who put her own father behind bars. As different as Scarlett thought she might be from somebody who had become an invaluable advisor to the king, guilt was something she understood all too well. The damage dealt by the Inquiries echoed through both their lives, but Contessa had made it her work to undo the damage they had done. The growing softness behind Scarlett's ribcage yearned for a purpose beyond survival as well.

"I'm sure I have more to be forgiven for than you," Scarlett said, even as she wondered at their similarities.

"Don't judge a book by its cover," Contessa countered.

"That's silly. I always choose my books based on their covers," Scarlett shot back.

"Me too."

The women shared a tentative smile, and Scarlett found a spark of hope flickering within her. Meeting Contessa's steely gaze, Scarlett saw an ounce of recognition there, acknowledgment from another woman forced to live in the gray areas by the horrors of the Inquiries.

Boisterous laughter from the hall interrupted the moment. A darkhaired man rounded the corner with a winning smile on his face, similar to Benedict's flirtatious grin but overflowing with even more mischief. Upon spotting Contessa, he swept into the room and kissed her hand in a dramatic fashion with which she seemed familiar.

Mr. Woodrow trailed after him, his stomping gait in caricaturish contrast to the other's easy manner. Benedict followed with a tired-looking man in uniform bringing up the rear.

"Scarlett, this is Joseph Thorne, Chief of the Royal Police. And this is Kristoff Mainsworth, Nate's...associate."

A myriad of rings glittered on Kristoff's fingers as he sketched an elaborate bow. Joseph merely inclined his head in greeting. Before Contessa could introduce

Scarlett, another figure tumbled through the door, almost running into Joseph in her haste.

"And Rhosyn, apparently," Contessa added on.

The young woman blew an unruly red curl out of her face and grinned.

"You know she's impossible to keep away when she knows a plan is afoot," Mr. Woodrow grumbled as he threw himself into a chair at the table, although Scarlett got the sense he wasn't really angry.

"Even when her Chief tells her that cadets aren't usually involved in important strategy meetings," Joseph added.

Rhosyn, for her part, seemed unapologetic, folding her lanky limbs into the seat beside Nate. Scarlett recognized the easy grace with which she moved as belonging to somebody accustomed to fighting.

"If you're asking for Kristoff's help, then I already know we aren't exactly doing things by the book," Rhosyn said, her voice heavily accented with a Northern brogue, as everybody else took their seats at the dinner table. Benedict maneuvered so they sat next to each other, for which Scarlett was grateful. The dinner party had doubled in size, and Scarlett acutely felt every pair of eyes.

"I've never been one for playing by the rules anyways," Benedict agreed as he settled in.

"I knew I liked you already," Kristoff shot across the table, only to look away quickly as Gregor entered the room carrying a roast, blue eyes fixing intently on the manservant.

"And you need somebody to actually pay attention, since Kristoff tends to be distracted whenever Gregor is the one serving dinner." Rhosyn shifted, and Kristoff jerked as if kicked in the shin under the table. Redness creeped up from Gregor's collar to his cheeks, but he didn't comment as he set down the roast and moved a terrine of potatoes from the sideboard to the table.

Scarlett shrank down in her seat in response to the easy familiarity of the group. After years of constantly looking over her shoulder in the Raptors, it was the sort of thing she had liked to imagine didn't exist. It made it easier to live with the fact that she would never have this kind of camaraderie.

Now Benedict put his hand on her arm and pulled her in headfirst, joking, "I get the impression that Gregor distracting Kristoff is the only reason anything can get done around here."

Mr. Woodrow laughed, and Scarlett jumped, not having considered that the former Beast would ever make such a sound. "Then we should get everybody up to speed before Kristoff gets tired of staring at Gregor's backside, although that seems unlikely."

Contessa jumped in and caught the newcomers up on the fighting pits. Occasionally she glanced over at Scarlett to fill in some detail, which Scarlett supplied despite suppressing the urge to squirm in her seat and shooting glances out of the corner of her eye at Chief Thorne. If he had any significant thoughts about her comments, he didn't show any signs beyond a deepening crease between his brows.

"You're right that we need to pull this operation out by the roots," Chief Thorne commented when Contessa finished, rubbing a hand over his face. "It's not going to help the public's trust in the Royal Police or the relationship with the Talented when it gets out that we let this spring up right under our noses. Things are already contentious enough as it is. If we could bring down Fang and his operation in one fell swoop though, it might help prove that the Royal Police have turned over in a new leaf."

"Are you thinking a raid?" Kristoff asked. Despite all their joking, he had listened intently to Contessa and Scarlett, although Gregor had ended up perched on the arm of his chair while they talked, Kristoff's arm draped familiarly around his waist. "That way you could arrest Fang, his lieutenants, and even some patrons in one move."

"That location is terrible for a raid," Nate said. "They would see you coming from a mile away from the front, but having it backed up to the Thames limits your options for surrounding them."

"It could also limit their escapes," Contessa mused.

"People are more than willing to jump out of a window into the river in a pinch," Benedict chimed in, with a pointed look at Scarlett.

"If we got them to move their operation to a specific warehouse though, we might be able to get the drop on them. Use an entrance they don't even know exists," Nate mused. Despite Scarlett's confusion at his statement, Contessa and Joseph were already nodding.

"We'd need somebody on the inside to get them to move their location though."

Every set of eyes at the table swung in Scarlett's direction, and she tensed, shadows tugging at her mind, wisps dancing where she gripped the arms of her chair.

"I—" she hesitated, shooting a glance at Chief Thorne, who met her gaze calmly.

"Would be doing a service the Royal Police," he said.

Scarlett sucked on her teeth for a moment before speaking again. "I'm willing to do what I can, but I'm not sure Fang trusts me as it is right now."

"Why not? Do you think he knows you've come to us?" Mr. Woodrow asked.

With a shake of her head, she haltingly relayed the abridged story of her last fight. As she told them of Fang's suggestion that she kill her opponent, Nate's fingernails gouged into the edge of the table, and Contessa twisted her skirt into knots in her lap.

"So he doesn't think you're violent enough in the ring?" Rhosyn piped up.

"And I'm not sure what Fang will do if I don't do what he wants in my next fight tomorrow night." Despite her best efforts, a hint of desperation tinged with rage laced her voice.

In contrast, Rhosyn's eyes glittered with mischief, a slow smile spreading across her face. "I think I have an idea."

Chapter Sixteen

Scarlett took a deep breath of the night air, more comfortable outside than she had been in the crowded dining room, considering she still wore her heavy cape. The sun had set as she and Benedict sat in the Woodrow's house, planning the Wolves' downfall, and now she glanced up, unable to see the stars beyond the low hanging clouds.

The still of the night was broken by the trundle of wheels as Benedict's carriage pulled up in front of the house.

"I can walk back to Granny's," Scarlett offered. "I know the Lower City is in the completely opposite direction." As uncomfortable as the fashionable shoes she wore were, she could stop by Georgette's to get her own clothes and boots.

Benedict cleared his throat, stance filled with an uncharacteristic awkwardness. "Why don't you come back to my house?"

"I wouldn't want you to have to choose between sneaking me past your parents again or having to try to explain to them who I am," Scarlett said, even as her heart fluttered faster. Benedict had been a grounding presence next to her all evening, but now his proximity had a different effect. Standing in the empty street beside his carriage reminded her of the look on his face when she first emerged from Georgette's house this afternoon.

"My family won't be home," he said with a shake of his head. "They took my sister to a ball this evening. Trying to make up for the fact that she missed the first half of her first season hiding out in the country."

Scarlett should say no. She should tell Benedict that just because he had helped her get the Woodrow's aid in shutting down the fighting rings, nothing had changed when it came to them. He was still the son of a duke, needing to marry for a large dowry. Even if Scarlett was free of the Wolves, she'd still be a criminal.

When Scarlett looked into his hopeful brown eyes though, she thought about how she was about to double-cross one of the most dangerous men in the lower city, and recklessness surged through her. Before the rational, cautious part of her mind took over, she nodded.

Silently, Benedict helped her up into the carriage. As he banged on the roof to signal the driver, Scarlett's stomach did a flip, unsure of the sudden thrill running through her. They rode in silence for a moment before Benedict sighed heavily.

"That didn't go quite as I planned it," he admitted.

Some of the blood pounding in Scarlett's ears calmed as she processed his statement and frowned. "What are you talking about? We have a plan to stop the Wolves now."

Benedict shook his head with a rueful smile. "This is just another time where I tried to help you, to do what I could to save you from a bad situation. Instead, you're going to be the one putting yourself in danger. If Fang suspects you or the raid goes wrong... You're the one who pays the price, while I do nothing once again."

Now it was Scarlett's turn to shake her head. "No, it's more than that. You've done something more important than save me." She swallowed, feeling like she was peeling back her own skin to show herself raw and exposed to Benedict. Uncomfortable as it was to reveal her feelings to Benedict after so long, keeping everything closely guarded in a cage in her chest, she forced herself to say the words. "You convinced me to save myself. You showed me that there are things worth fighting for besides just survival. As much that I hate that you made me want things I have no right to, it's given me a reason to push back. To hope against hope that I can claw my way back from this life I've fallen into." Scarlett's voice threatened to shake, but she tamped down.

"And what do I make you want?" Benedict's eyes glimmered in the light of a passing streetlamp.

"You." This time her voice did break.

"You have me. Everything that I am." Benedict's voice was low but didn't hesitate.

Scarlett let out a shuddering breath that had remained caught in her chest, hope igniting in its wake, although a new and fragile thing.

"Why me?" she asked, barely above a whisper.

Now Benedict smiled. "Because I saw your anger, snarling and savage, but you still cared for and protected those around you. You held all that rage inside you for so long, but never let it harden your heart. Those contradictions are what poetry are made of."

Scarlett could hear her ribs cracking as Benedict pried open her chest to clutch at her beating heart. Still, he continued.

"And the first time I made you laugh, you looked like you were surprised that you still knew how. But I knew nobody with a laugh that beautiful was meant to live a life of pain. Even if I can't save you all the time, if I can pry out some of that light you've held within yourself for so long, I'll feel lucky."

Before Scarlett could fling herself across the small space at him, unable to listen to any more of his speech without bursting into flames, the carriage jerked to a stop. Scarlett blinked in surprise, nearly having forgotten where they were.

Benedict wasted no time throwing open the carriage door and jumping out, pulling her after him. With his words still swirling in her head, he tugged her up the few steps to the front door. By the time the latch clicked shut behind them, Scarlett had regained her senses enough to execute her original plan.

She tugged Benedict back to her and he came willingly. His lips crashed against hers with the force of a thunderclap, and the electricity of a lightning strike surged through her body as she rose on her toes to meet him. This time, Scarlett wasted no time opening her mouth to him, pouring herself into him as he hoisted her up, letting her wrap her legs around his waist despite the hindrance of her dress. If she was going to risk everything to fight back against the Wolves and the situation she had backed herself into, she was going to let herself have this first.

Benedict carried her over to the stairs, breaking the kiss to navigate up them. While she was in a more convenient position than she had been the last time he carried her up these stairs, he now had to contend with the distraction of her tongue and teeth against the soft skin behind his ear.

He swore lightly and chuckled breathlessly at her antics as he kicked open the door to his now-familiar room. Benedict sat down on the foot of his bed, and Scarlett found herself straddling his lap, a position she took to with great enthusiasm. She busied her hands untying his cravat to expose his throat to her ministrations. He helped her by shrugging out of his overcoat and ripping his shirt off over his head. Feeling drunk on the sight of him, Scarlett ran her tongue hungrily over his Adam's apple. Her fingers wound into his hair even as she attempted to grind against him through the many layers of her dress.

Benedict halted her with a firm hand in her hair, pulling her back to meet his eyes. Even as Scarlett nearly panted, she was gratified to see the color high in his cheeks as his own breaths came rapidly.

"As much as I love you in this dress, I need to get you out of it, little bird," he said, dark eyes alight.

Scarlett nodded emphatically, unhooking the brooch at her neck and carefully laying the cloak across the corner of the bed. Benedict stood, setting her on her feet and switching their places so her back was to him. As he unlaced her dress, he leaned down to whisper in her ear.

"If I've convinced you to fight for yourself, now I'm going to convince you to be careful. I'm going to leave no inch of you untouched, ruin you so thoroughly that I know you'll keep fighting to get back to this—back to me." His voice was velvet against her skin as he pressed his lips behind her ear. Even as her bodice loosened, Scarlett found it hard to breath.

She wanted to tell him she would return to him, that she would fight to get back here in his arms. But she couldn't promise that, not when this was likely all they would have even if they did stop the Wolves. Instead, she responded with a soft moan, letting him know how good his fingers dancing across the bared skin of her back felt.

As the dress fell to a puddle at her feet, Benedict's fingertips grazed over her shoulder blade where an osprey was inked into her skin.

"You really are my little bird," he murmured, pressing a kiss to the nape of her neck. Scarlett leaned back into him, sighing with relief that Benedict saw the mark as her own and not a sign of her shadowed past. His hands snaked around to her front, tracing up her now-bare stomach before cupping her breasts. He sucked a mark into the juncture of her neck and shoulder as his thumbs stroked over her nipples, torturing her with waves of pleasure. She retaliated by grinding against the hardness she felt behind her, and Benedict let out a sound between a growl and a groan. He pushed forward to bend Scarlett over the bed. She went willingly.

He walked his fingers down her spine, and Scarlett sighed at how exposed she felt, although he had seen it all before. By the time his hand reached its destination between her legs, her nipples were so hard they rubbed against the coverlet beneath her, flirting with the border between pain and pleasure.

"You're incredible." Benedict's tone was hushed as he ran his fingers through Scarlett's wetness before wandering down to play with the bundle of nerves that throbbed for attention. She let out a choked sound as he rolled it between his fingers, her back bowing into the sensation.

Then his fingers disappeared, and a whine escaped her. She would have been embarrassed at the noise if she hadn't been so busy reaching tendrils of shadows back towards Benedict. Tracing them over his hands, she found that he was untying his pants.

"I like you like this, finally letting yourself want." Benedict's voice was accompanied by the sound of fabric as he slid his pants off. Scarlett crawled onto the bed the rest of the way to give him room to climb up behind her.

"I've wanted you for so long," she admitted, eyes fluttering shut against the admission and the heat of Benedict coming to kneel behind her.

"Open your eyes," he said, voice gentle but persuasive.

She did as he asked, wondering how he had known she had shut them in the first place. Looking up from where she had let her head hang between her forearms planted on the bed, she found that she faced a large mirror against one wall. Her gaze instantly found Benedict's burning into her. She might have shied away from the sensation if his hands smoothing over her ass to rest on her hips hadn't soothed her.

"I want you to see what I see when I look at you."

Scarlett nearly choked with desire as she felt him slide his member back and forth, slicking them both up with her wetness. Then he slotted into her entrance and pushed in achingly slowly, making Scarlett feel every inch. Her eyelids fluttered, but she managed to keep them open, pinned by the intensity of Benedict's gaze on her in the mirror.

"I want you to see how beautiful you are. How strong. How incredible." Benedict punctuated each sentence with a small thrust, pushing deeper until he was fully seated within her.

"Benedict," Scarlett breathed, other words failing her where they always came easily to Benedict. Still, she knew he could feel the tremor running through her body and see the slack-jawed expression of pleasure on her face that spoke volumes.

Then he began to move, and it was all Scarlett could do to keep her eyes on his in the mirror. She didn't want to miss a single expression that passed over his beautiful face, from his eyes half-lidded with pleasure to the clench of his jaw as he pounded into her harder. She pushed back against him, wanting more, greedy for all of him she could have in this moment and knowing it would still never be enough.

Seeming to feel her desperation, Benedict pulled her up so her back was flush with his chest, thighs spread obscenely over his as he continued to drive up into her. His hand at her throat, not tight but possessive, kept her face towards the mirror.

"I want this image burned into your brain, the way you look when you take me." Benedict's voice was broken with pleasure. "Because I'm never going to forget how good you feel, and I'll never stop wanting you."

Scarlett whimpered as his hand that wasn't on her neck trailed down her body to where they were joined, tracing the point where he entered her.

"And I want you to feel me here for a week, so every time you move, you're reminded that you have somebody who will fight for you, who wants you."

All rational thought flew from her brain at his words. The part of Scarlett that knew there were still so many reasons she couldn't have Benedict the way she wanted to dissolved into the bliss his words pulled out of her. She pushed back into him, wanting everything he could give her. He responded by rubbing fast circles over her most sensitive point with the fingers that danced between their legs.

The sensations threatened to overwhelm her, and she was eager to let them. Her head fell back against him, lolling against his shoulder as her pleasure built.

"Look at me," he urged hoarsely, squeezing the fingers on her throat gently.

Scarlett pulled her head forward and met his gaze in the mirror again the moment before she shattered, the adoring, hungry look in his eyes pushing her over the edge as much as the friction of his fingers. She tensed and shuddered on top of him, mouth open in a silent scream as he drank in her release. He pounded into her, extending her pleasure until he too tensed beneath her, shattering bliss written all over his face.

Only once both of their breathing returned to normal did Scarlett lean her head back against Benedict's shoulder again. Now she let her eyes flutter closed and drank in the citrus and earth scent of Benedict's skin that clung to her as well. As she went pliant in Benedict's arms, he tipped them sideways, laying them down while keeping her firmly pressed against the lines of his body.

Slick sweat coated both their skin, but Scarlett couldn't be bothered by the stickiness, not when the beast in her chest that so often prowled behind her ribcage with raised hackles now crowed in satisfaction. It would not get to rest long, but for now, Scarlett let herself drift.

Footsteps in the hall jerked Scarlett from her half-asleep haze. As she started, the back of her head slammed into Benedict, who had nuzzled into the back of her neck. He let out a soft *oof* and rubbed at his bleary eyes.

She could barely see in in the room, the thin moonlight coming in through the window indicating they hadn't dozed for that long. Even the intimacy of a short rest, bare legs tangled together, was a far cry from Scarlett's past experiences, which rarely even occurred in a bed.

She blushed as she detangled herself from Benedict, her heart squeezing at the sweet domesticity of falling asleep together. It made it even more difficult to tear herself away from Benedict's warm embrace, knowing what faced her as she entered the Wolves' den once more. This one night, the memory of it would have to be enough to carry her through the tests to come. Even if the Woodrows' plan to bring down the Wolves did work, and Scarlett was free of them, this stolen moment would likely be all she and Benedict would ever have.

Knowing how it felt to really be with Benedict—how all-consuming it felt to let herself feel and want—Scarlett knew that intermittent tastes would only be torture. She could endure a pummeling in the fighting ring, but stealing moments with Benedict when he would eventually marry somebody else would break her.

Benedict himself seemed unaware of Scarlett's turmoil as she rose from the bed, clutching a sheet to her chest.

"Lottie and my parents must have just gotten home from the ball," he whispered, sitting up. Scarlett's mouth went dry at the way the blanket he had draped over them pooled low around his hips, and she tore her gaze away.

Looking around, she cringed at the sight of Georgette's dress crumpled on the floor at the foot of the bed. She would prefer to exit through the window to escape the Pearces' notice, but she didn't look forward to climbing down in a gown.

"Do you have to leave right now?" Benedict asked, crawling to the edge of the bed and pressing a kiss to her bare shoulder. She shivered at the combination of casual intimacy and warm breath on her skin.

"I need to check on Granny and be back in my routine before the Wolves suspect anything," she explained, only slightly exaggerating how quickly she needed to depart. She picked up the dress and held it up, dreading lacing herself back into a corset.

"You could borrow some of my clothes, although I know they're too big," Benedict offered. "I can have my man bring Ms. Ward's dress back to her."

When she nodded, Benedict stood and rifled around in his dresser, producing a gray shirt and basic trousers, probably the most plain clothes he owned. Scarlett tugged them on, making do with rolling up the sleeves and cinching in the waistband. Fully dressed, she looked down at the cape draped across the foot of the bed, a splash of crimson in a room leached of color by the darkness.

"You could leave it here for safekeeping," Benedict said, gaze tracking where she was looking. "Then I would be sure that you would come back to me."

Despite her better judgement, Scarlett nodded. "Alright."

She stepped towards the window and Benedict followed, catching her by the wrist and pressing a brief kiss to her lips. She closed her eyes, savoring the fleeting contact as she thought it might be a kiss goodbye, even when the new-but-stubborn hope flickering within her whispered that maybe it wouldn't.

"Keep my cape safe," she murmured. Even if she didn't manage to come back for it, Scarlett could think of no place she would rather it stay. It seemed fitting to leave the strongest link to her identity with the person she had let see all the hidden pieces of herself.

"I will," Benedict promised.

Scarlett launched herself out the window, plunging back into the night and her waiting shadows.

Chapter Seventeen

Scarlett kept her eyes on the boots she was currently lacing up as the door to the backroom at the fighting pits swung open.

"No funny business until you're out in the rings where the audience can appreciate it, alright?" Zed said as he ushered the newcomer into to room.

"Of course. A show is what I promised and a show is what you'll get," came the answer in a familiar Northern brogue.

An odd mixture of relief and dread churned in Scarlett's gut, turgid as the water of the Thames, as the door swung shut behind Rhosyn. Other fighters lingered in the room, preparing and posturing for their own brawls, and Scarlett only made the briefest eye contact with the young woman as she strode across the room to a bench on the opposite wall. Rhosyn responded with an infinitesimal nod before taking her seat in the corner and pulling out a strip of fabric to wrap methodically around her knuckles.

As always, Scarlett ground her teeth until she was surprised they were more than useless nubs as pairs of fighters filed out of the room to be pummeled to a bloody pulp before a riotous crowd. The numbers in the room dwindled until only Rhosyn and Scarlett were left. Alone, they finally looked at each other.

"I'm honestly surprised that Fang let you enter the headliner fight at such short notice," Scarlett observed. Even as she didn't relish brutalizing the girl, Scarlett knew she would have to display a penchant for violence with whoever she fought tonight to get back in the Wolves' good graces. At least Rhosyn had volunteered for the thrashing.

"It wasn't hard to convince him of how lucrative two pretty women fighting might be once I put the idea in his head," Rhosyn admitted with a shrug.

"And you were even able to convince him you have a Talent?" Scarlett asked, keeping her voice low in case of unfriendly ears outside the door.

"Not everybody's Talent is as flashy as yours. I just told him I have Nate's Talent, so I can read people's intentions to know what moves they will make in advance," Rhosyn said. "It shouldn't be difficult to fake if you telegraph your moves like we discussed."

Scarlett nodded before wincing as the sound of a thud and a crunch filtered through the door, followed by a large cheer.

"You sure about this?" Scarlett asked, even though it was likely too late for Rhosyn to back out. "Even with us making it look worse than it is, I'm going to have to rough you up pretty badly."

Rhosyn smiled ruefully. "I've been done down for less noble causes. Besides, police training doesn't get your blood pumping like a good old-fashioned brawl."

Scarlett winced at the reminder that she was about to thrash a new member of the Royal Police, even if the cadet did volunteer for it. Then again, Rhosyn had a very different background than most officers.

Before they could say anything else, the door banged open to reveal Zed, wearing an impatient expression.

"Last fight was way too quick. Hope you ladies are ready to put on more of a show," he barked, shooting a pointed look at Scarlett as he waved them out of the room. They approached the ring just in time to see a limp form pulled from the raised platform and into the crowd. The spectators obscured the figure before Scarlett could discern if he was breathing or not.

True to Rhosyn's estimation, the hall shook with stamping feet and enthusiastic hollers as Zed announced the matchup. The redhead took the part of the showman, using her long legs to step over the ropes of the ring as she grinned and waved.

"She might not be very showy, but something tells me our resident shadow is going to have a hard time landing a punch on this one here!" Zed riled up the spectators.

As Rhosyn didn't have a visible Talent to show off, she settled for flexing her slim arms, leading to cheers and laughter from the crowd. Scarlett didn't bother with seeming enthusiastic as she stepped in behind Rhosyn, opting for her normal angry demeanor. Still, she let shadows drip from her fingers more than strictly necessary as she squared up, putting on the show the Wolves desired in her own way.

As they faced off, Scarlett met Rhosyn's eyes one more time. The redhead's eyelid twitched in the barest of winks as the bell clanged, and then she leaped.

As Rhosyn moved first, Scarlett danced out of the way, a fist just brushing across her shoulder as she spun clear. As she did, she swung out a leg to trip Rhosyn, making the movement a touch larger and slower than she might with another opponent. Seeing it coming, although with her eyes instead of a Talent, Rhosyn neatly leaped over the limb with her crooked grin still in place.

They continued like that for a few minutes, Scarlett lashing out with fists and shadows, albeit relatively slowly, and Rhosyn dodging out of the way. Scarlett's fists missed her by a hairbreadth several times, close enough to brush the wild red curls coming free of their tie. The crowd gasped at Rhosyn's seemingly uncanny ability to dodge, as Scarlett mentally patted herself on the back for purposefully missing so narrowly. A few times Scarlett's shadows connected with Rhosyn, and if they weren't completely solid when they snapped her head to the side, only Rhosyn and the lack of ringing in Scarlett's ears were any the wiser.

As the fight dragged on and both women were coated in a sheen of sweat, Rhosyn shot Scarlett a meaningful look. This time, when Scarlett swung for her, Rhosyn didn't dodge as quickly, allowing the punch to hit her in the flank. While Scarlett used only half her strength, Rhosyn let out a dramatic *oof*, sounding convincingly like the wind had been knocked out of her. Doubling over with an arm across her abdomen, she looked up at Scarlett and cocked her head in challenge.

Scarlett lashed out, kicking Rhosyn in the shin, although purposefully avoiding her knee joint and trying to hit to the side of the bone so as not to break it. The redhead stumbled but didn't fall, instead stepping forward. With a movement so fast it was lost to Scarlett's eyes, Rhosyn lashed out, elbow catching her square in the windpipe.

Scarlett sputtered and coughed, tears in her eyes blurring the lamplight to white smudges as the crowd roared. Somehow, the shock of pain and breathlessness spurred Scarlett into action. Before she could think on what she did, shadows sprang forward, attacking Rhosyn from every angle. This time the woman didn't, or couldn't, dodge, letting out several pained grunts that Scarlett had the wherewithal to hope were exaggerated as the darkness pummeled her.

Taking advantage of Rhosyn's distraction, Scarlett dove forward, taking the woman to the ground with the weight of an elbow to her gut, even as she surreptitiously caught most of her momentum on her knees. Rhosyn flailed like a feral animal, spurring on some of Scarlett's more violent instincts. Rhosyn managed to flip them over, pinning Scarlett for a split second before she lifted her feet and drove them into her abdomen, driving the redhead back once more.

Scarlett fell on her with a detached ferocity, feeling as if she gave her anger more slack on its leash while still watching it from a distance. This time, her fist connected with Rhosyn's jaw with a solid thud, loud enough to be audible over the now-uproarious noise of the crowd. The snap of Rhosyn's head to the side was no longer completely exaggerated. Still, she fought back, squirming and wrestling until they were both short a few chunks of hair and the familiar tang of blood coated Scarlett's tongue.

Only then did she land a blow solid enough for Rhosyn to cease fighting back. Thinking this was the end of their fight, Scarlett pushed back to her feet. To her horror, Rhosyn turned her head and spat out a gob of blood containing a few teeth. Scarlett took a step back, thinking Rhosyn was tapping out, but the woman struggled as if to get to her feet again. Even as she pushed to sitting, she used her other hand to beckon to Scarlett in a universal taunt.

The spectators shouted and hollered with renewed fervor, and Scarlett took a moment to wonder, not for the first time, if Rhosyn was actually insane. Before she could think better of it, she took a kick aimed at Rhosyn's side, sending her falling back and rolling away again.

Still, Rhosyn pushed to try and stand. This time, Scarlett's foot connected with her shoulder, then her thigh. Rhosyn refused to tap out though, and Scarlett decided to take the matter into her own hands. She fell on the woman, grappling her into a choke hold, straddling her back to pin her down. As Rhosyn squirmed against her, Scarlett watched her hands like a hawk, but the woman only used them to weakly try and dislodge Scarlett until she slumped to the floor.

Scarlett lowered her down and stood up, trying to not let her horror at knocking the redhead out show on her face even as she raised an arm in triumph. A wave a nausea crashed over Scarlett as stamping and clapping deafened her, but she forced a victorious smile onto her face.

"An incredible showing by our reigning champion!" Zed leaped into the ring and lifted her other arm in the air, shaking it enthusiastically. As spectators excitedly moved to cash out their bets, he leaned down to murmur in Scarlett's ear so only she could hear, "I see you learned Fang's lesson. You'd be making a killing fighting like this if you weren't taking such a small cut of the purse."

Scarlett shoved down the urge to punch Zed that overwhelmed her as violence worked its way out of her blood stream, instead plastering on a grin that was more a baring of teeth than a smile. "I guess I'll just have to draw in enough people to make five percent of the earnings more than enough."

"That's more like it." Zed clapped her on the shoulder before meandering off into the crowd.

As they spoke, Scarlett watched out of the corner of her eye as a familiar sandy-haired figure darted into the ring to kneel by Rhosyn. She desperately wanted to join Gregor and make sure she hadn't seriously injured the other woman, but she didn't dare give herself away now. With some difficulty given Rhosyn's height, Gregor hoisted her onto his shoulder and made to carry her from the ring.

For a split second, as Rhosyn's face lolled towards Scarlett, her eye cracked open. She raised her eyebrow so slightly Scarlett might have imagined it before her eye slipped closed again and Gregor bore her out of sight.

With a heavy sigh, Scarlett made her way to the edge of the ring on the far side, ready to collect her winnings and collapse onto her under stuffed mattress at Granny's to catch a few hours of rest before starting on the next part of their plan. As she ducked under the ropes, she caught sight of Fang in the corner of the room. Seeing her looking, he tipped his hat at her with a slight nod. At least she hadn't knocked Rhosyn's teeth out for nothing.

Georgette giggled so hard, she snorted as Scarlett shied away from the crates on the stable floor.

"Ladylike," Scarlett teased, even as she avoided thinking about what inside the crate was making the persistent scratching and squeaking noises.

"I think in this situation, you're the one acting like the fainting lady while I'm just being reasonable." Georgette continued to laugh, hiding her smile behind her palm.

"I'm being reasonable! Rats bite, and they carry diseases." Scarlett took another step away from the crates on the ground.

"Don't you have to deal with rats in the lower city all the time?"

"There are a lot of them, but usually not in such high concentrations. And I don't voluntarily make contact with them because of the biting."

"These ones don't bite," Georgette proclaimed confidently. "I caught them all myself."

"If they don't bite, then how will they be enough to drive off all the Wolves' gamblers?" Scarlett worried out loud.

"They are quite large," Georgette explained, cracking the lid on one of the crates to peek inside. Scarlett chanced a glance in at the writhing mass of brown fur and tails and recoiled instantly when she found that Georgette was telling the truth.

"Those are easily three times the size of any rats I see in the lower city," Scarlett admitted with a cringe. She had certainly run into her fair amount of vermin running in the gutters and scavenging for discarded food, but normally they ran from her footsteps and had thin patchy fur. The four large crates before her now were filled to bursting with rats nearly the size of a housecat.

"That's because they're well fed. It's also how I was able to catch them so quickly. They're used to me feeding them when I come to ride my horse, so they let me approach them and pick them up," Georgette explained lightly.

Scarlett gaped. "Your groomsmen have to hate that." Georgette shrugged, a blush coloring her pale cheeks. "They think it's sweet, if a bit silly."

Scarlett had to agree, but she found herself smiling, despite the fact that she was about to take possession of several large crates of vermin. It was so incredibly unexpected, yet in character for Georgette to have tamed a veritable army of rodents through kindheartedness and general goodness.

"You do have a way with strays," Scarlett admitted.

"I just like to think I see creatures for what they are, and not just how other people perceive them," Georgette argued with a pointed look in Scarlett's direction. Scarlett tore her gaze away from the earnestness in Georgette's eyes.

"It's going to be a job and a half to get these all into the fighting hall without being seen," Scarlett admitted, thinking that perhaps Kristoff's cheery suggestion that they force the Wolves to move their operation by burning the current location down hadn't been that bad of an idea after all. Arson seemed like a good option compared to the writhing mass of rodents she currently faced down.

Still, it was true that Scarlett was likely to burn down the whole block if she tried to light the building on fire, with how densely packed the structures were in the lower city. The goal was to protect as many innocents as possible, so she had to resort to more subtle means.

With a sigh she began loading the crates onto the cart behind her, pointedly ignoring the scrabbling of tiny claws against wood and the way that the weight inside them shifted as small creatures crawled their way over one another.

"Thank you so much for this Georgette," Scarlett said as she placed the last crate on the top of the stack.

Georgette smiled softly. "I just wish I could help you more. What I've done...I know it's not nearly enough with all you've risked."

Scarlett smiled wryly. "It's more than you know."

It wasn't just about the rats either. Georgette was in no small part what had helped Scarlett protect that softness in her heart that Benedict saw when he looked at her. Even if what Scarlett had shared with him couldn't last, she owed Georgette's unwavering friendship for the endurance of the girl she had once been.

"I suppose it's too much to ask that you don't let them hurt the rats, but do try to keep yourself safe at least." Georgette stepped back to allow Scarlett to maneuver the overloaded cart through the door.

"Oh wait!" Georgette fished into the pockets of her skirts. "I forgot that the Woodrows' man came by and left this for you this morning."

Scarlett took the folded paper from her outstretched hand, unfolding it easily, as it hadn't been sealed. As she read the writing scrawled across it in messy script, the warmth of hope that was growing stronger by the day blossomed even further.

Scarlett,

Thanks for the best fight I've had in a while.

Rhosyn

P.S. The teeth were fake.

Scarlett looked down to keep her cap low on her face, even thickening the shadows there to keep herself guarded as she pushed her cart down the street. She carefully maneuvered around the myriad divots and bumps in the cobbles, not wanting to jostle her cargo. She could easily pass herself off as a delivery boy bringing wares to one of the businesses in the area, as long as the rodents didn't give themselves away with too much squeaking and scratching. Luckily in the light of day, the street was busy enough that the occasional scuffling in her cargo was drowned out by voices and wagon wheels.

Stopping beneath an overhang, Scarlett leaned against the door as if resting for a moment. It wasn't truly an act, as her breath came in quick spurts from pushing her burden such a long way. Still, as she folded her arms and bent her head, her gaze darted up and down the street appraisingly. As it wasn't business hours, bouncers didn't stand outside the door to the fighting hall, but it still wouldn't do to have her seen entering. Besides, there were still probably a handful of Wolves inside to avoid.

Scarlett had only waited a minute when a carriage far nicer than any of the other carts trundling around rounded the corner. It made it halfway down the block, just a few doors away from the entrance to the fighting hall, when a loud crack spilt the air, making everybody on the street jump.

Wood splintered onto the street as one of the large wheels broke, the carriage listing to the side dangerously before the driver pulled the spooked horses to a stop. Benedict sprang from the coach in fighting form, door swinging open to display him in opulent dress. Scarlett nearly smiled at the visible gold chain and pocket watch, even as he wore entirely too much velvet for her taste.

"Goodness me, I could have died!" He looked over the damage with his hands on his hips. "How will we get this home?"

Others on the street began inching towards him as if they could smell his wealth and an opportunity. Benedict encouraged them, looking at one of the young men approaching him.

"You wouldn't know how to fix this would you? I promise to reward you handsomely if you help me get my coach home in one piece," Benedict offered magnanimously.

A few more onlookers jumped into the fray, offering their expertise or to drive Benedict home in their own cart. Scarlett didn't miss the handful of street urchins creeping up, eyes on Benedict's purse and pocket watch. A few of the bolder ones inched towards the carriage instead, obviously curious what valuables they could find inside such a lavish vehicle.

As the racket in the street grew, the door to the fighting hall banged open, and Scarlett ducked her head more determinedly. A handful of the Wolves' enforcers barged into the street to see what all the fuss was about. Catching sight of Benedict, gesticulating and waving madly at his broken carriage, the eyes of the lead thug twinkled at the sight of such a rich mark dropped directly in his lap.

They took a few steps into the street, ready to rob Benedict blind under the guise of helping him with his broken wheel, but Scarlett didn't stick around to watch. As they cleared the doorway, Scarlett pushed her cart over to the entrance. With a quick glance behind her she made sure nobody was looking before ducking inside.

Once inside, she worked quickly, prying the lids off the crates. Scarlett recoiled as the rats scurried out through the shadowy room, finding plenty of nooks to hide in and chair legs to chew on. As she turned to leave, the sounds of scuffling and squeaking were audible even over the commotion on the street.

She just hoped the rodent infestation would bother the other patrons as much as it bothered her.

Scarlett hugged her legs to her chest on the little stool where she perched, setting her chin on her knees as she tried to avoid touching the floor at all costs. She wasn't the only fighter in the backroom to take such a posture, although some tried to show their toughness by continuing to stand around. Their efforts to seem unphased were undermined when they would let out a undignified squeal as a large rat darted across the room and over their boots.

They scurried across the room every few seconds, and even when they weren't visible, the quiet *scritch* of their tiny claws against the wooden walls was ubiquitous. Georgette had been right about their size being truly intimidating, especially for lower city dwellers used to malnourished vermin. What was more, they weren't nearly as afraid of people as normal pests, Georgette's kind handling of them emboldening them to dart over feet and even attempt to crawl up pant legs.

A bang caused Scarlett to jerk, almost losing her balance on her stool and tumbling to the rat-infested floor. The door slammed open on its hinges so hard, Scarlett was surprised the shoddy thing didn't fall right off.

"We have no spectators," Fang snarled as he burst into the room. "These vermin have driven them all off."

Zed trailed behind him, looking nervous. "Should I call the rat catcher?"

"Do you think the rat catcher will be able to get rid of an infestation of this size? Besides, I already heard some gentlemen saying this building is clearly full of disease. How else could the pests get so big?" As if to punctuate Fang's question, a rat sidled up to the base of his cane, sniffing around it curiously. He smacked it away in annoyance, and Scarlett winced at its squeal of distress, remembering how much Georgette liked the creatures.

"What should we do then?" Zed wiped his hands on his pants, visibly perspiring.

When Fang paused in thought, Scarlett seized her opportunity.

"We could always move the fights to another building," she offered with what she hoped was a nonchalant shrug. Benedict was better at persuasion than she was, and she hoped for a bit of his way with people right now.

"Where would we go?" Fang spat.

"There has to be some vacant buildings here in the Lion's old territory, so you could stick to the same area." Scarlett cocked her head in thought. "Has anybody taken over the Lion's old Den?"

Fang's eyes narrowed, and Scarlett hoped it was in thought and not suspicion.

"It is a few blocks from here," he admitted. "Everybody has stayed away though."

Scarlett shrugged again. "It was just a thought. It certainly does make a statement about who's the new boss in town to take over the Beast's old lair."

Fang's eyes flared, and she knew she caught him. Greed and pride were his twin downfalls, and Scarlett had learned that playing into them could get her what she needed.

"Zed," Fang snapped over his shoulder, "grab the boys and see how fast you can get a new ring built. Everybody else, your fights have been rescheduled for tomorrow night."

Scarlett's stomach performed a somersault of victory and nerves as she thought about what tomorrow might bring.

Scarlett was so distracted staring at the riot of blooms in the Woodrow's garden that she didn't hear Nate until the tip of a knife touched her throat.

"It's just me, Scarlett." She put up her hands in surrender, showing she held no weapon.

With a soft *shink*, the lethal blade disappeared back under his sleeve. Some of the hardness in his golden eyes softened in relief. Still, Scarlett's heart pounded from the moment of adrenaline. Thanks to her shadows, she was used to being the one sneaking up on people and not the other way around. Despite cloaking herself in darkness as she snuck into the Woodrow's garden to deliver her message, Nate had been able to sense her. No wonder he had earned a reputation as the deadliest man in London.

"It's done?" Nate asked, as if greeting somebody with a knife to their throat was common practice despite his perfectly polished clothes and immaculate garden. Something in his attitude made Scarlett want to smile despite the desperateness of the situation. Nate was a man who straddled the lines between lower city gangster and prominent socialite more thoroughly than most, giving Scarlett evidence that it was possible.

Scarlett nodded. "They'll be at the Lion's old Den tonight." She passed off all the details she had on the coming fights, anything that might give the Royal Police an edge during the raid.

Nate nodded. "We'll get this information to Joseph. You just need to make sure that the secret entrance is clear."

It was Scarlett's turn to nod, nerves about tomorrow night's operation returning in full force. Nate tilted his head as he considered her, scarred face unreadable.

"Do you want to stay for tea?" Nate offered. "It might calm your nerves, and I know Benedict would be happy to see you, as well as Contessa."

Scarlett blinked in confusion. "Benedict?"

"He's been over for tea most evenings, and to get updates on our plan." Nate shrugged. "He wants to help however he can."

Scarlett swallowed thickly but shook her head. "I need to get some sleep before tonight."

Nate continued to consider her with piercing eyes, and the full force of how disconcerting it was to have somebody know what she felt hit her.

"He would go with you tonight if you asked." Nate's voice was low. "Against my better judgement I probably would too. I shouldn't be seen near anything like this, but I still wish I could do more to help too. Sometimes things like this were easier when it was just me and the Lions."

"That's why I won't," Scarlett admitted. Truly, she itched to see Benedict, but Scarlett feared what she would say if she did. She couldn't let Benedict risk himself by joining the raid tonight, and so she wouldn't even give herself the chance to ask. "Tell him—tell Benedict I'll come get my cloak tomorrow."

"I will." Nate paused. In the quiet, a breeze ruffled through the leaves of the beautiful garden, and the sound of a trickling fountain drifted through the air. Scarlett turned to go.

"I noticed you on the garden path that afternoon," Nate started.

Scarlett turned back to him, puzzled.

"I was walking with Contessa, and I felt how angry you were. Out of all the people in the park, your emotions grabbed my attention immediately."

Scarlett recalled the way his eyes had snapped to her that day with Benedict, freezing her in place. She opened her mouth to defend herself, to say that she hadn't been angry at him, but Nate cut her off.

"I myself met an angry woman not all that long ago, and she also tends to want to carry the weight of the world on her shoulders. I don't mind sharing it with her sometimes." Nate's perpetual scowl softened a little as he spoke of his wife.

Scarlett's chest squeezed and she looked away. "Tell Contessa and Benedict I say hello." With that, she vaulted herself over the back fence to head back to Granny's. Tonight, Scarlett would face the Wolves, and she would be damned if anybody besides her got hurt.

Chapter Eighteen

The Wolves hadn't set up a back room for the competitors yet at the new fighting hall, making Scarlett's job increasingly difficult. Nothing blocked her pacing along the back wall from the view of the spectators, and worst of all, the other Wolves. She tried to play her walking back and forth off as nervous energy, which wasn't too hard considering what the night had in store.

When not glancing up to see if anybody was watching, Scarlett kept her eyes on the lower edge of the back wall, searching for the crack indicating the entrance to Nate and the Lions' secret tunnel. He had been reluctant to let the Royal Police know of the tunnels in an official capacity, as now they were no longer his secret, but just this once it would give the Royal Police the edge they needed to pin down and surround the Wolves.

Scarlett paused under the pretense of tying her boot as she saw a promising-looking seam in the panels of wood. She chanced a run of her fingers along the gap, shoving her fingernails into the groove and finding it to be the opening she was looking for. Luckily, nobody seemed to notice her odd behavior, as the first fight of the night was starting and everybody was busy finalizing their bets and vying for the best view.

Turning back to her task, Scarlett frowned as she saw a crate and a large sack partially blocking the other side of the door. She would have to move them to give the police a clear path when they came charging in.

Standing from her crouch, she leaned her back against the panel of wall holding the hidden door and crossed her arms. Scowling at the fight getting going before her, she leaned to the side slightly, using her thigh to push the barriers out of the way. The racket of the nearby fighters offering their own opinions on the current match drowned out the scraping of wood against the floor. Satisfied that the tunnel entrance was clear of obstacles, Scarlett pushed her weight off the wall but didn't go far.

She took the opportunity to scan the crowd, mentally cataloguing where all the Wolves stationed themselves. Many mixed with the spectators, collecting bets and jangling their bags of coins. That would cause difficulties for the police trying to arrest them without hurting civilians. Then again, many of the spectators would find themselves arrested for participating in such illicit activities, but their well-stocked coffers would have them walking free in the morning.

Scarlett's gaze strayed to where the most important cogs in the machine of the Wolves lingered. Fang himself sat in a heavy chair, one leg thrown over the other casually while a hand caressed the head of his cane, his posture holding all the arrogance of a king holding court while waving his scepter. Scarlett fought to keep her facial expression blank as her lip threatened to curl in distaste.

Stationed around Fang were several lieutenants and enforcers, some lounging comfortably as well while others stood with beefy arms folded, making sure nobody approached Fang uninvited. Zed flitted back and forth between Fang's corner and the ring, alternating between riling the crowd up for the coming matchups and whispering gossip in his boss's ear.

Scarlett was mapping out the quickest path to Fang's corner, so she could engage his protection immediately when the Royal Police arrived, when her gaze snagged on a familiar head of dark hair, pulled into a low tail. Her stomach plummeted to the splintered floorboards when the figure turned, displaying Benedict's familiar face.

Scarlett opened her mouth before she tamped down the urge to scream in frustration, or perhaps march up to him and shake him as she demanded to know what he thought we was doing. Benedict saw her staring and met her eyes calmly, which did little to reassure her. He did maintain eye contact as he patted absently at his coat though, where a slight bulge might be concealing a weapon. Hopefully it wasn't just a letter opener.

Scarlett's eyes narrowed in irritation laced with fear. He wasn't supposed to be here. She had told Nate as much in the garden earlier. Only the Royal Police would be doing the raid, and Scarlett was here as the inside agent, especially as her absence would arouse suspicion. Even Contessa and Nate, who had been instrumental at coming up with the plan, were sitting this one out as they tried to stay out of visible trouble to boost the reputation of the Talented in polite society. Not to mention, the Royal Police needed a victory to patch up their own image as well.

Her feet were taking steps before she decided to move, taking her towards Benedict. Even if she gave herself away, she needed to make sure he got out before the raid started. She couldn't let him get caught in the crossfire.

She didn't make it two steps before a flash of light in the window stopped her in her tracks. It was too late. If she didn't give the officers at the back entrance the signal, the whole raid would be botched. They had already given too much to back down now. With another cry of frustration clawing at the back of her throat, Scarlett darted back to the wall with the hidden panel. She rapped on it sharply three times and then jumped aside just in time for the panel to swing open to admit a swarm of officers. At the same moment, the front door crashed open, revealing Chief Joseph himself armed with a baton and determination.

Chaos erupted immediately, tables and chairs knocked to the floor as people scattered. Wolves and patrons alike ran for windows, but the Royal Police would have the place surrounded already. Seemingly realizing their predicaments, gangsters started jumping into the fray, hoping to fight their way out.

Scarlett didn't spend any time watching to see who had the upper hand, leaping back towards where Fang and his crew were stationed. Already, the enforcers were pushing a path towards the back where there might be another exit. Scarlett couldn't let them escape. Still, as she dodged fists and batons to get to Fang, her gaze darted away from her target to find Benedict.

To her dismay, he was pushing through the crowd to intercept her instead of away from the danger. Scarlett would just have to make the fight quick so he didn't get hurt. Using her smaller size and years of stealth, Scarlett slipped through the chaos quickly, jumping free to leap onto one of the enforcers. Catching him by surprise, she dropped him quickly with a knee to the gut and a grip that left the bones of his wrist cracking beneath her fingers.

Seeing her attack, several lieutenants pulled guns, aiming them into the crowd. Scarlett dropped and rolled as the gunfire split the air, the Wolves seemingly not caring if the bullets embedded themselves in friend or foe. None of them hit her as she sprang to her feet and tried not to think about the agonized scream somewhere behind her. She leaped forward once more, taking on two Wolves. She managed to kick the gun out of one hand and punch another in the flank before a third joined the fray and grabbed her around the neck from behind.

The feral beast inside Scarlett ripped free from its leash as she kicked out and bit down hard enough on the forearm before her to draw blood. It loosened just enough for Scarlett to squirm out of the grasp, stomping on her assailant's foot as she did.

Her shadows began dripping from her hands with abandon, blinding some attackers while shielding her movements from others. The ringing in her ears grew so loud that she almost didn't hear the bloodcurdling shout from her left, but Benedict's voice was enough to draw her attention. She looked over just in time to see Benedict launch himself onto Fang's back, yanking up the arm holding the gun pointed directly at her. Fang fired just as Benedict landed, the bullet whizzing by Scarlett's side so closely she felt the heat of it. Her opponent collapsed to the ground as the shot hit him in the shoulder instead.

Before she could recover from the shock of her brush with death, she was shouting again. Fang grappled Benedict easily, hitting him in the shin with his cane before twisting around to get the gun to his temple. Scarlett screeched in fury, leaping towards Fang wearing shadows like talons, letting them ripple in her wake like wings, but the few remaining Wolves stopped her. She forced herself to look away to deal with her opponents quickly, even as Fang marched Benedict out the door, the officers unwilling to stop him with a civilian in his grasp.

Scarlett barely thought about how she dealt with the next few opponents, feeling nothing but the insistent tug in her chest dragging her towards the exit where Benedict had just disappeared. Still, it took too long for her to extricate herself from the fight, dashing out into the night. By the time her boots hit the cobblestones of the street, Benedict and Fang were nowhere to be seen. She looked around frantically, searching her surroundings for any inkling of where they might have gone, when she heard receding hoofbeats at the end of the street.

Scarlett ran faster than she ever had, wind whipping against her face and tugging at her clothes. As the carriage turned a corner, she vaulted over a fruit stand onto an awning before pulling herself up onto a roof where she could track their progress better.

Sprinting across the roofs, shadows trailing behind her in angry wisps, Scarlett momentarily imagined she could fly. She could be that little bird, that fierce osprey, just to get to Benedict. The horses pulled the carriage faster than Scarlett could run, but she managed to keep sight of them from her higher vantage point.

The carriage stopped in front of a rundown chapel near the town square. From this distance, through watering eyes, Scarlett could barely make out two shapes heading into the building, the one in front holding his arms up as if a gun were pressed between his shoulder blades. At least Benedict appeared uninjured.

Instead of bursting through the front doors after them, when Scarlett approached the building she let a flying leap carry her to the roof. Looking up, the clock tower sported several broken windows she could use to enter. Fang might not expect an attack from above.

Scrabbling up the uneven stones, Scarlett tried to stay as silent as possible, hoping to maintain the element of surprise. As she edged through a broken window, the lingering shards of sharp glass scraped across her arm, cutting her shirt and the skin underneath. She bit her lips to avoid grunting in pain, but when she turned her intention to the inside of the clock tower, she saw she shouldn't have bothered.

Fang stood in the opposite window, gun aimed directly at Scarlett's head. What caused her squeak of distress though, was his grip on Benedict's throat, keeping him balanced just at the edge of the window, cantilevered out over the sill just enough that if he were to loosen his grip, Benedict would go plummeting to the ground below. Up several stories as they were, with unforgiving cobbles lining the street, Benedict would be lucky to survive.

Scarlett put her hands up and stepped around the large bell in the middle of the room.

"Let him go, Fang," she said, trying to keep her voice calm but unable to avoid the slight quaver in her tone.

"Funny, I thought you would be begging me to hold on tighter." To illustrate his point, Fang tightened the fingers at Benedict's throat, who let out a slight choking noise, toes scrabbling at the stone windowsill. Scarlett's gaze darted to him briefly before focusing on Fang once again. She had to stay calm, and she had to stay focused, but the panicked look on Benedict's face threatened her grip on the remaining threads of her composure.

"A hostage like him, the younger son of a duke, he's definitely worth more to you alive than dead," Scarlett reasoned. "You could use him to bargain your way into an escape."

"I came to this safehouse with the plans of using him to negotiate my escape, but now that you're here, I'm tempted to drop him. The look on your face would be priceless," Fang snarled. "And you would deserve it, you traitor. It was you who sold us out to the Royal Police wasn't it? And why? Just to impress your little lover here even though you're still lower city garbage."

A more insistent choking sound from Benedict distracted Scarlett from the sting of Fang's words. She glanced at him to find him looking at her and then down several times in quick succession. The moment she saw his fingers inching towards the bulge in his jacket, her eyes snapped back to Fang. If she stared, she might give him away, although if he attacked Fang, he would surely fall. Still, it's not like they hadn't gone out a window before. She would just have to buy him enough time to get the shot off. She knew he wouldn't miss.

"Traitor?" Scarlett shot back. "That's bold coming from somebody who forces the Talented to kill each other when the Inquiries were supposed to be the end of our deaths serving as the public's entertainment."

At the edge of her vision, Benedict edged a familiar pistol out of his waistcoat and leveled it at Fang, holding it low. The safety clicked softly, and Fang frowned, making to look at Benedict.

Scarlett leaped into action as time warped around her. With an exaggerated cry, she launched herself at Fang, drawing his attention back to her. She drew thin shadows around herself, making it harder for him to aim. Two gunshots echoed in quick succession, followed by the deafening ring as one of them hit the bell behind her. Or maybe that noise was just the ringing in her ears as her momentum carried her into Fang and the trio all tumbled out the window. Screwing her eyes shut, Scarlett summoned a soft cushion of shadows to break their fall, the effort causing searing pain to shoot across her skull as the screaming in her head became deafening.

The shadows were solid enough to slow their fall, but not as pillowy as Scarlett hoped, and they hit the ground hard enough to knock the wind out of her. She felt, more than heard something crunch beneath her.

She lay there, stunned, unable to form any thoughts around the unwieldy pounding in her head. The tangle of limbs around her had other ideas, pushing her off and rolling her over.

"Scarlett!" Benedict's warped voice echoed in her head, distant and strange as if he were speaking underwater.

She lay on her back now, and he appeared over her, face haloed by the backlighting of a flickering streetlamp. She was drowning, staring up at an angel leaning down to save her. Even in her oddly dazed state, she was happy to see him well, although he held one arm to his chest with his wrist bent at an odd angle. What concerned her more was the look of abject terror on his face.

"Fang," she mumbled, knowing that she couldn't let Benedict be threatened again. She flopped her head to the side to see a crumpled form beside her.

"Is he…"

"He isn't going to hurt anybody else," Benedict assured, even as he cupped her face and turned to look at her once more. She yelped as the touch felt like a hot wire pressed against the side of her head. The sound was somehow lopsided.

"Oh god, what happened," Benedict pleaded, looking panicked. He took his hand away and Scarlett was shocked to see it covered in blood as he dug a handkerchief out of his pocket. He pressed the lacy cloth to the side of her head once more, and Scarlett hissed in pain, although it was feeling oddly distant.

"I think you were shot," he murmured.

"In the head?" Scarlett mumbled, thinking she would definitely not be talking if that were the case. Still, she remembered two gunshots and a searing pain before she tumbled out the window. Bencdict said some more words, but Scarlett couldn't make them out. Sound didn't seem to process right on the side of her head with the injury.

"Why did you come?" Scarlett asked instead, feeling that she urgently needed to know before she lost consciousness. She already felt the familiar fuzziness creeping up in the back of her mind.

"Because you were definitely going to do something like this," Benedict admitted. "I knew you'd jump in front of a bullet to save us all, and I wanted to make sure there was somebody there who would do the same for you."

Scarlett blinked, and she wasn't sure if her vision was hazy from blood loss or emotion. With her one good ear, she just made out the last words Benedict uttered before her eyes fluttered shut.

"I couldn't live without you."

Chapter Nineteen

The idea of Hell as a fiery pit had never really resonated with Scarlett, but as she peeled her eyes open to burning crimson light, she was forced to re-evaluate her conception of the afterlife. As her blurry vision focused more, she saw that the fiery color above her was ostentatious red velvet drapes on a four-poster bed. That didn't explain why everything seemed to be glowing crimson though.

Turning her head to the right, she snapped it forward again with a hiss. The pillow, soft as it was, felt like a dagger against that side of her head. Raising her hand to investigate, she found bandages wrapped around her forehead and coating the entirety of the right side of her scalp and some of her face. Still, it was shocking to wake up at all considering she was pretty sure she had been shot in the head.

"Little bird," came a relieved voice from her side, muffled through the bandages.

Benedict appeared in her line of vision, the bed dipping with his weight as he sat by her side.

"Where are we?" Scarlett asked, her voice scratchy.

"We're in the Woodrow's house, in one of their spare rooms. Their sense of style leaves something to be desired."

Scarlett lifted her head to look around, this time more careful of her sore side. Indeed, the wallpaper sported gaudy splotches she could just make out to be roses, while the red light came from the sun filtering through the sheer crimson drapes on the windows. The effect was generally hideous.

"Still, it was generous of them to let you stay here while Gregor patched us up," Benedict said.

Scarlett noticed Benedict's own wrist in a splint, and the concern on his face as he knelt over her in the street came back to her. She worked to sit up, and even though her head pounded slightly, she was able to do so easily with Benedict's helping hand on her shoulder

"What happened?" She gestured to her own bandages.

Benedict grimaced. "The bullet barely missed your head, but it managed to take off most of your ear and burned a bit of the side of your face. An inch over and you'd be dead." Benedict's voice was very quiet.

"Good thing I gave up on vanity long ago," Scarlett murmured.

"I'm so sorry." Benedict's voice was mournful. He reached out to trail his fingers over her unbandaged cheek.

"For what? We made it out alive."

Benedict nodded as his fingers worried at the blankets over Scarlett's legs. She reached out and interlaced her hand with his. He squeezed it in thanks.

"Fang?" she murmured quietly.

"Dead."

Scarlett opened and closed her mouth, not knowing how to ask the question that weighed on her.

"I don't know if the fall killed him or the bullet, and I didn't check," Benedict offered, voice above a whisper.

Scarlett nodded, lump in her throat. Somehow, Benedict volunteering to share in the weight of a man's death, even a man so horrible as Fang, meant more to her than words could express. She squeezed his hand, eyes stinging.

Benedict smiled sadly. "But you shouldn't have had to take a bullet for me."

Scarlett swallowed, remembering Benedict's last words before she lost consciousness.

I couldn't live without you.

She wouldn't want to live in a world without Benedict either.

"I would jump in front of it for you again, even if the bullet got me properly in the head next time," she murmured truthfully. "And besides, you saved me from Fang first. You're the reason any of this was able to happen."

Benedict shook his head. "You need to stop keeping score. Whether you saved my life a million times or not at all, or even if you spent the rest of your life flinging me out of windows, which at this rate seems likely, I would still love you the same."

Scarlett blinked, sure that she must have understood Benedict wrong, given that she didn't seem to have any hearing in her right ear.

"You love me?"

"You've stolen my heart, little bird."

Scarlett harbored no doubts that the heart hammering away in her chest right now belonged to him in return.

"You have to know I love you too, but—"

"There are no 'buts' to the way I feel about you," Benedict declared determinedly. "It's not something that will be stopped by logic. I know firsthand now what it's like to look at a life without you, and it's not something I'm willing to do again. If I have to sing for coins on the streetcorner or become a pickpocket to stay at your side, I will."

Scarlett's mouth hung open. There was nothing she could think to say to a declaration like that. Only two words came to mind.

"Kiss me."

Benedict obliged, using his uninjured hand to pull her close by the waist. Her head may have been aching earlier, but all of that dissolved into the feeling of floating. Kissing Benedict before had been overwhelming, but mixed with the incandescent joy of knowing this might be the first of many embraces, his touch was intoxicating.

Soon she was gasping into his kiss, tugging at his waistcoat with grasping fists. Benedict pulled back slightly with a chuckle.

"I don't think it would be very gentlemanly to take advantage of a lady with a headwound, in somebody else's bed no less," he teased, nose still nuzzled against hers.

Scarlett grinned back. "Who said I was a lady?"

"You are a lady to me," he explained with a nip to her lower lip that drew a very unladylike noise from Scarlett.

He drew back, much to Scarlett's dismay, even as she knew he was right. Even their kissing had made her woozy in her current state.

"I should let the others know you're awake. They'll be pleased," he said with a pat to her shin.

He left for a few moments and returned with Gregor, who smiled upon seeing her sitting up. He proceeded to check her bandages and ask her how she was feeling, to which she responded honestly that she felt surprisingly well.

Gregor nodded understandingly. "Honestly, the bullet mostly took off cartilage, which people poke holes in for jewelry anyways. You probably passed out from pain and blood loss, more than anything, combined with your use of your Talent. It should heal quickly as long as you keep it clear of infection, although I'm sad to admit that there is nothing I can do about the appearance. Your ear is pretty much gone."

"I guess I'm in good company when it comes to scars," she mused, thinking of Gregor's employer. "If I grow my hair out, I can probably come up with some styles that cover it well."

"Mrs. Woodrow's lady's maid would have fun helping you. She's obsessed with trying out new hairstyles on anybody she can get her hands on," Gregor commented.

As if summoned, Contessa herself peaked her head around the doorframe.

"Scarlett! So glad you are alright." She smiled, and Scarlett found herself happy to see the other woman, despite their brief acquaintance. "Joseph is downstairs to collect official statements for the police reports."

Benedict glanced at Scarlett, who glanced down at herself in turn, dressed only in what she assumed was one of Contessa's nightdresses and still feeling rather discombobulated.

"I'll go down and tell him my perspective first while you take a moment," Benedict suggested. He leaned in and pressed a kiss to her cheek, making Scarlett's heart stutter that he would show such affection in front of others. Contessa and Gregor seemed unphased as Benedict stepped from the room.

"I'll get you some tea and some breakfast as well," Gregor offered.

"I'll keep her company," Contessa offered as Gregor exited and left them alone.

Contessa perched herself in the chair at the bedside Scarlett assumed Benedict had been stationed in before she woke. Scarlett awkwardly fiddled with the blankets over her lap, feeling odd about entertaining a proper lady in a borrowed nightdress, looking like…well she wasn't sure what she looked like at the moment, but she was sure it wasn't good.

"This used to be my room," Contessa mused, breaking the silence.

"Oh." Scarlett hedged, finding it unusual that Contessa had once slept anywhere besides her shared room with her husband. "It's lovely."

Contessa huffed in a ladylike version of a snort. "No, it's not. I always hated it, but I forgot that I wanted to redecorate it after I moved down the hall. I've just been so busy."

"I'm sure being an advisor to the king keeps you occupied," Scarlett agreed.

"It does." Contessa sighed. "And dealing with the aftermath of the Inquiries… The damage they did runs deeper than even I imagined, and I despised them to begin with. What happened with the Wolves, it really emphasized to me how far my work is from over, and how much I need more help from people who understand."

Scarlett cocked her head but stayed quiet, unsure what Contessa was getting at.

"You know, it would do wonders to have more people helping the Lions with our work."

"I thought the Lions were gone?" Scarlett asked, eyebrows shooting up in question before she winced at the pull they caused in her scalp.

"The gang may be gone, but Kristoff, Rhosyn, and Nate will always see themselves as the Lions. So will I, in all honesty," Contessa explained. "They fought the Inquiries from the beginning, and now that they're over, our purpose has shifted. Rhosyn is becoming a police officer, and Nate and I work with the king, while Kristoff works odd jobs that are better off the record. We could use somebody like you though, familiar with the ins and outs of the lower city as well as society."

Scarlett swallowed thickly. This morning seemed determined to dangle in front of her everything she wanted most but had been sure she could never have, making it seem so close in the light of dawn. She had brought down the Wolves, maybe she could have Benedict and a purpose beyond survival too.

"I'd love that," Scarlett admitted. "But I would have to work some things out first."

"I'm sure you'll be able to make arrangements," Contessa nodded, smoothing her elegant silver skirts as she stood. "I've already asked the king to approve my starting an official task force for helping Talented after the Inquiries, and I mentioned that I want you on it. After hearing about your involvement with our latest activities, he requests an audience with you next week."

Scarlett tugged at the clasp at the throat of her crimson cape. She had insisted on wearing it to her audience with the King, but the bright color combined with the bandages still wound around her head drew many eyes. After years in the habit of staying invisible, it was an odd sensation. Benedict held her hand as they walked through the palace though, not caring about the heavy gazes on them. Scarlett found she didn't mind their weight as much either when she focused on his fingers intertwined with hers.

Her nerves returned anew as a footman ushered her into a room with a long table, announcing her presence.

"Lord Benedict Pearce and Ms. Scarlett Forster, Your Majesty."

King Byron sat behind a large desk while Contessa sat at one corner, papers strewn before them. Nate stood at alert a few feet away, hands clasped behind his back.

"Lord Pearce, Ms. Forster, thank you for joining me," the king said kindly, gesturing for them to come closer.

Scarlett fought not to slump her shoulders in an attempt to take up less space as she approached the desk,. She wasn't sure what she had expected of the King, especially one whose father had been partially responsible for the Inquiries, but his easy manner took her off guard. As she drew closer, lines around his eyes and a stray silver hair around his temple became visible, which Scarlett wouldn't have expected from his age.

Stopping before his desk, Scarlett offered a wobbly curtsy while Benedict executed a more elegant bow.

"Mr. and Mrs. Woodrow here have filled me in on your...situation," the king started. Scarlett stiffened, but he continued lightly, "They also told me of your significant role in bringing the Talented fighting rings to the law's attention and subsequently helping with their dismantling. You have done the Crown tremendous service."

Scarlett nodded dumbly, unsure what to say. Her tongue seemed glued to the roof of her mouth.

"What's more, you have done this despite the monarchy having wronged your family in the past. This being said, I would like to officially honor you for services to the Crown. Of course, this comes with a full pardon for any gang involvement you may have had, as it was part of an undercover mission to aid the Royal Police."

Scarlett looked back and forth between the king and Contessa, who was smiling knowingly, although she didn't meet her eyes.

"Thank you, Your Majesty," Scarlett managed to squeeze out of vocal cords that were frozen in shock and relief.

"You should know that this honor comes with a significant sum of money as well. It would make a sizeable dowry," the king mused. "Certainly enough to make a good match with the younger son of a duke."

Benedict coughed beside Scarlett.

"Of course, this does all come with one stipulation," the king continued.

Scarlett froze, not that she had been doing much but staring with wide eyes as her life was irrevocably changed.

"Mrs. Woodrow here insists you join her new task force, or I can't give you this recognition."

Scarlett almost laughed. "Nothing would make me happier."

It was partially a lie. Being able to marry Benedict would make her the happiest of all.

***

Scarlett elbowed Benedict in the side to prompt him to flip the page on the sheet music before her. He tore his eyes away from her face to do as she requested, allowing her to continue the song she had been playing on their piano. It was the first thing they moved into their new home, a few blocks down from the Woodrows'. The Duke of Pearce had let them take theirs from the parlor as a wedding gift, even though Scarlett nearly choked every time he mentioned it. These keys had seen a lot.

Now she picked out a new melody she had learned as their dinner guests relaxed in their sitting room. Contessa and Nate sat in one corner, heads bent over a chess board, while Leon and Georgette shared the settee, inching closer to each other by the second. Though their wedding in a few weeks was sure to be the celebration of the season, they didn't seem inclined to keep their hands off each other until then.

Despite the relative modesty of their new home compared to Benedict's former residence, he insisted on having guests over often. Scarlett found she loved the life and laughter it gave the house after years in a stark bedroom at Granny's. Of course, that was part of why they had chosen to buy a cozier home. Scarlett insisted on sending money to Granny every month to make up for the loss of rent. Benedict had offered to buy her a new home closer to theirs, but Granny had waved them off, stating that she would stay right where she was as long as there were hungry urchins on the streets of the lower city.

Benedict leaned in closer as Scarlett continued to play, and she missed a few notes as he pressed his lips lightly to the juncture of her neck and shoulder.

"You play so lovely, little bird," he murmured.

"I would play even better if I didn't have somebody distracting me with their breath on my neck," she countered.

"Maybe you just need more practice," he whispered into her good ear. Gregor had been right that most of her right ear was now gone. A hint of Scarlett's vanity had reared its head as she looked at the patch of scar tissue on the side of her head for the first time. Rhosyn had stopped by to visit that day though and promptly declared that she and Nate now matched. Just like him, nobody would cross her if they could avoid it.

Benedict certainly didn't mind, if how often he distracted her with hands up her skirts and lips on her jaw were any indication. He only ever joked that he could spoil her with jewelry twice as much, as he would only ever need to purchase one earring. Now as she finished the song, she turned to look at him in mock reproachment.

"Whatever am I going to do with you?" she scolded.

"Whatever you want," Benedict teased with a lopsided grin. "But I do have several suggestions."

Scarlett tipped her head back and laughed, heart soaring like a bird.

The Hood and his Thief
BOOK THREE

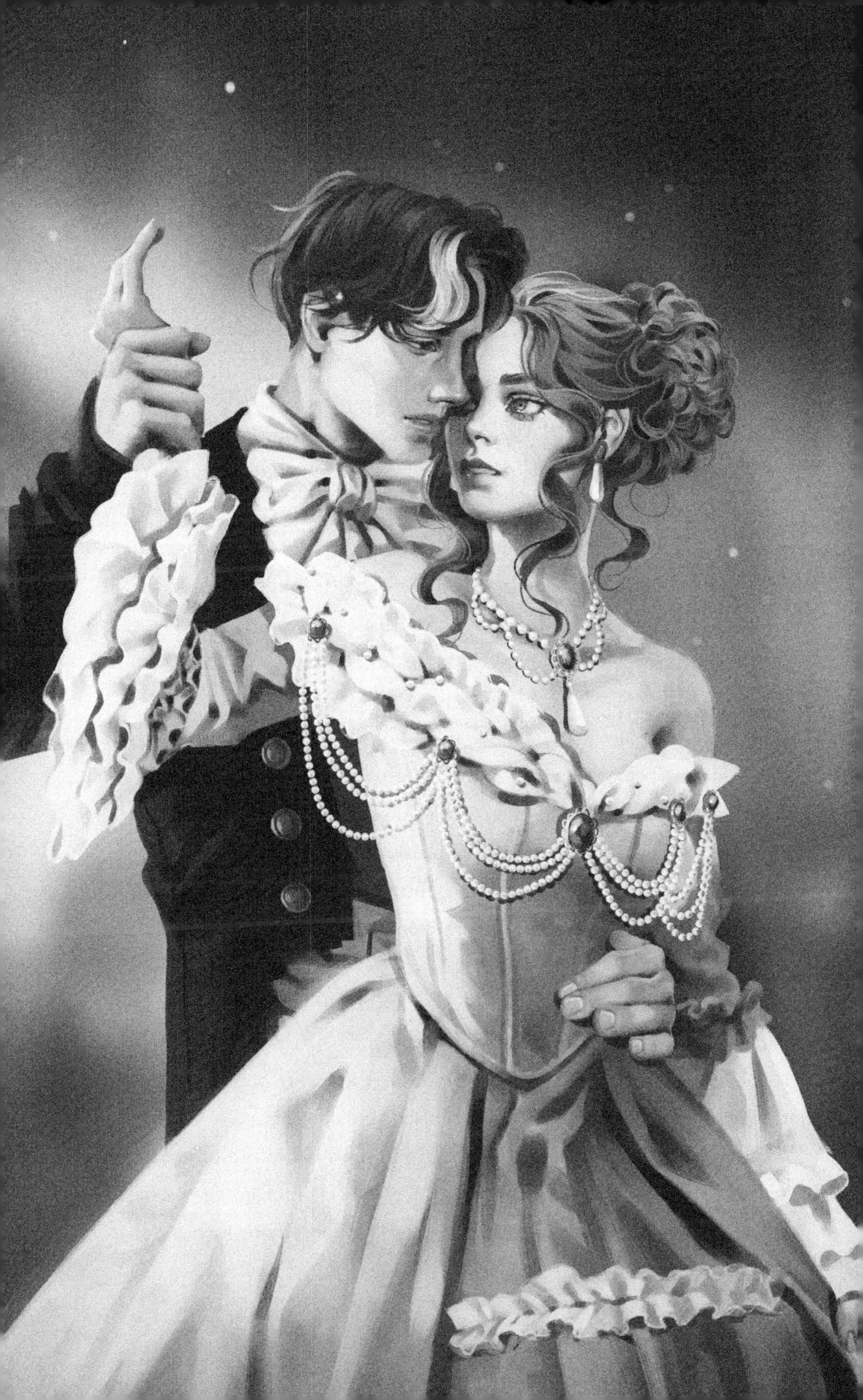

Chapter One

Being one of the best pickpockets in London came with certain advantages. For one, Rhosyn was able to easily spot those less practiced at their craft. As her deft eyes swept the street on her normal patrol, they zeroed in on a skinny child bumping into a well-dressed gentleman with a little too much intention. She pulled her standard-issue police baton from her belt and swung it casually in her hand as she veered towards the side of the narrow, cobbled street. Her gaze trained on the urchin darting off toward a shadowed alley, with a prize clutched to his chest.

She intercepted him just before he turned off the main drag, thrusting her baton in his path before he could scamper off into the darkness. He froze in place, gaze trailing up Rhosyn's torso and eyes widening in his dirt-smudged face as he took in the golden buttons and badge emblazoned on her Royal Police uniform.

Before he could turn to run, Rhosyn grabbed him by the kerchief around his neck, not hard enough to jar him, but firmly enough that he couldn't escape. She held out her hand expectantly.

With a degree of wide-eyed innocence that could only be coaxed from a guilty child, he shook his head. "What have I done, ma'am?"

"I'll warrant that watch in your pocket wasn't there when you left home this morning," Rhosyn prodded, propping her free hand on her hip.

With a thick swallow, the urchin reached into his jacket and produced an engraved pocket watch, swinging on a thick golden chain. Rhosyn had half a mind to let him keep the thing, to punish the owner for carrying such an ostentatious accessory through a part of town where every streetcorner was occupied by pickpockets and gangsters, all searching for their next mark.

Instead, she plucked it from his grip and let go. The boy hesitated, clearly wanting to run away, but unsure if it would get him into any more trouble. After all, Rhosyn towered above him, with legs even longer than most of the male police officers, making catching a running youngster all too easy.

"If you look around like you're wondering if you've been spotted, you give yourself away," Rhosyn told the child against her better judgment. "Don't let me catch you again."

He smiled tentatively, the hint of a sparkle in his eyes before turning and disappearing among the shuffle of people in the street. Rhosyn sighed, knowing he was likely to be trouble again, but she didn't have it in her to arrest every person who committed petty theft in the lower city. After all, that would probably be half the populace of the streets she patrolled. She was interested in the more sinister criminals who prowled these blocks, knives up their sleeves and revolvers tucked into their jackets.

A judgmental voice in the back of her mind nagged that she was letting the thieves go because she was one of them. She shoved that voice aside with a practiced hand, and it retreated to the shadowy recesses of her mind with a grumble.

She returned her focus to the task at hand. Rhosyn cut across their street, people giving way for her when they caught sight of her uniform. She stopped before a man smoking a pipe outside of one of the nicer gambling dens in the area.

"I believe you dropped this." She held up the watch, letting it swing on its chain in front of his surprised expression.

Patting his pockets, he found that she was right. "My goodness, I don't know how I could have been so clumsy. Thank you, ma'am."

"Just doing my job." Rhosyn deposited the watch in his outstretched palm. "And keep a wary eye on your purse."

With a brisk nod, she turned and strode up off the street. She swept the area with her gaze constantly as she walked, alert for the trouble that never seemed far away. Many eyes caught hers as she observed, greeting her with a brief nod of familiarity. After several years as a Royal Police officer, the residents of the lower city were familiar with her presence. Many new officers left the lower city beats as soon as they had paid their dues, but Rhosyn had asked Chief Thorne if she could stay on this patrol. As harried as he was in the years since the end of the Inquiries, he hadn't been of a mind to object.

Rhosyn preferred to keep an eye on her old stomping grounds, and if anybody remembered her as the young rascal who ran jobs with the Lions, they had the sense not to say anything. Not to mention, she still felt more at home among the crooked flats and smoky air of the streets here than in the middle city where she now lived. Maybe she always would.

As the sun lowered behind crooked chimneys in the bruised sky, Rhosyn turned her steps uphill, toward the police station at the border of the middle and lower city. The night watch would be heading out and it was time to turn in her report for the day before heading back to her rented room. Her mouth watered at the thought of the scones waiting for her there, carefully wrapped in paper by Gregor and handed to her with a smile when she left the Woodrow's house early that morning.

Before she could contemplate whether she might be able to borrow some jam from the couple she rented from, shouting grabbed her attention. Rhosyn immediately broke into a run, darting into an alley, trying to cut over to the next block where the racket came from.

No sooner had she turned the corner than a solid frame crashed into her, knocking her down with a bone-rattling *thump*. Glaring up, she found a shape dressed in all black, a hood pulled low and obscuring his eyes, another piece of cloth covering his lower face.

"Sorry, ma'am. I'm afraid I have to run," the man said in a light tone, only sounding a little out of breath, despite having been running full tilt just seconds earlier. Before Rhosyn could think to order him to halt, he threw himself at the wall to the right, scaling the uneven bricks with all the ease of a bird taking flight.

Rhosyn sprang to her feet, just in time for two other officers of the Royal Police to materialize at the other end of the alley. Their batons swung in their hands as they huffed and puffed.

"Where'd he go?" one officer wheezed.

"The roof." Rhosyn pointed.

The officers looked up just in time to see the man's coat flaps disappear over the eaves, faces falling in dismay. They turned and retreated back down the alley, apparently planning on pursuing him from the street. Granted, with how fast the man climbed, the two men would likely lose him faster than a gambler could throw a hand of dice if they tried to follow him across the buildings.

Rhosyn, on the other hand, was far more comfortable among the chimneys and gables of the lower city.

She flung herself up the wall in hot pursuit, using an obliging drainpipe to help her shimmy up the building. She crested the edge, jumping to her feet and looking around. The dark silhouette was already on the next building over, about to leap to a third.

Rhosyn wasted no time in breaking into a sprint. The gap between the first two roofs was narrow enough that she leaped it without having to break her stride. Her long legs carried her swiftly enough that she should gain ground on her quarry.

However, the gap between the next two buildings was larger, almost twice as broad as Rhosyn was tall. The man ran at it full tilt, launching himself into the air and even performing a flip as he arced over the distance, hovering for what seemed to be a moment too long—or maybe that was just the way time stretched in a chase. He landed lightly on the balls of his feet, as if his joints were spring loaded.

Rhosyn didn't have time to gawk as she grit her teeth for her own jump. If she were being judged on style, she certainly would have lost to the pursuant, but she managed to make it over safely, tucking her head in and rolling to absorb the impact as she landed.

Coming to her feet again, she dashed across the slanted rooftop, boots clacking against the chipped shingles. She gained a few meters on the man, but he was deceptively fast for all that he appeared to be a few inches shorter than Rhosyn and much more densely built. Still, he couldn't run forever, and a drop between buildings loomed just ahead.

The hooded man leaped over the edge without hesitation, and without second thought, Rhosyn barreled after him. Her heart stuttered through a moment of free fall before relief restarted it at the top of the adjacent building just a story below.

She landed heavily in a crouch, ready to pounce forward and tackle her target. Instead, her head snapped back, as if somebody grabbed her by her collar.

The hooded man stood a few meters away on the edge of the roof, one arm raised to reveal a small crossbow mounted to his forearm and pointed directly at Rhosyn. He had fired so fast and so sure that she had barely registered the bolt whizzing past her face, piercing through the jacket of her uniform, before embedding in the wood paneling behind her. She yanked on it to no avail, the arrowhead clearly buried deep in the side of the building.

"It's been a while since any of the Royal Police gave me such a good chase, but I'm afraid this is where we part ways." The man lowered his arm.

Rhosyn strained to see under his hood, but he had fastened it well around his face and his features were fully obscured by the shadows of rapidly descending twilight. Instead, she let her eyes rove over his physique, trying to generate as thorough a description of him as she could without seeing his face.

He was clearly athletic, which she could tell from his speed and agility, but the notion was only driven home by his thick, shapely thighs and broad shoulders that tapered to narrower hips. Rhosyn blinked. She would not be writing *shapely thighs* on the report she filed with Chief Thorne under any circumstances.

The hooded man turned away from her as she continued to tug fruitlessly at the bolt pinning her in place. The thin sunlight peaked through the clouds long enough for her to tell that his clothing was actually a dark forest green, instead of the black she had originally thought.

"There's nowhere for you to run," Rhosyn insisted.

Indeed, they had reached the corner of the block, and all the nearest rooftops were far too distant to consider jumping. Crashing and shouting told Rhosyn that the other officers in pursuit had arrived in the street below, blocking him in if he were to climb down.

"Come quietly and I'll put in a good word," Rhosyn offered reasonably, even as she surreptitiously began unbuttoning her jacket under the guise of continuing to struggle. If she could slip out of the garment that kept her trapped, she could tackle the man before he tried to run again.

Instead, he looked over his shoulder, posture casual, as if there were nothing dire about his situation.

"Although this has been fun, I have no interest in being on good terms with the Royal Police."

Pulling free of the jacket, Rhosyn lunged, but her arms closed around open air. The hooded man had leaped into the open space between buildings, arms spread wide as if diving off a cliff into the ocean.

Rhosyn teetered on the ledge, watching in disbelief as he made it a surprising distance into the street, but still nowhere near the building on the far side. As he started to fall, he twisted, grabbing onto a clothesline hung between buildings. With all the skill of an acrobat, he swung around it once, twice—building up momentum before launching himself at the height of his swing. With a light *thunk*, he landed neatly on the far roof.

Rhosyn stared slack-jawed as he had the audacity to look back and offer her a mock salute, before darting off into the rapidly thickening shadows of evening. Jerking herself from her shock, she turned and scrabbled down to the ground as quickly as possible. Dropping from a little too high, her heels hit the cobbles with enough force to rattle her teeth in her skull. Still, she knew the moment she turned to dart across the crowded street that the hooded man would be long gone by the time she managed to scale the next building.

The two officers she had encountered earlier were waiting for her, still staring up at the clothesline above them where moments earlier a man had flown.

"What were you trying to bring him in for?" Rhosyn asked, bringing their attention back to the present. As they lowered their faces to look at her, she cocked her head in curiosity. While their faces were vaguely familiar, she couldn't recall names, and she thought she knew everybody that patrolled the lower city.

"Officer Rhosyn Walsh," she offered.

"Officers Fletcher and Davies," the taller of the two introduced himself and his partner. "Why don't we get back to the station and we can fill you in while you help us file our reports." He looked around pointedly at the crowded streets. Whatever had happened, it wasn't something he wished to be overheard.

Chief Joseph Thorne shuffled through endless stacks of paper, trying to clear enough space on his desk for him to write on and failing. While Rhosyn could tell there was a system to the stacks of reports, the cramped desk in the corner was not nearly large enough to accommodate the amount of work Chief Thorne was burdening it with.

For that matter, Chief Thorne himself didn't seem able to accommodate the amount of work he was trying to complete, if the pallor of his skin and the shadow of a beard that had not been shaved in several days were any indication. Still, he pushed on doggedly, gesturing Rhosyn and the two officers with her to take a seat in the wooden chairs across from him.

The whole setup was rather cramped, shoved into a cordoned-off corner of the Royal Police's headquarters. While there was a perfectly good office down the hall, with more space and a bigger desk, Rhosyn didn't have to wonder why he didn't use it.

The weathered brass plaque on the door to that room still read *Chief Cook,* despite the man's imprisonment years ago. Chief Thorne could easily have his former mentor's name changed out for his own, but Rhosyn got the impression that it was left there as a sort of reminder for all who passed through. After all, the echoes of the corruption bred by Chief Cook's leadership still cropped up every once in a while. The aftereffects of the Inquiries still ruled the city's underworld, and too many of the rich and influential still disagreed with their sudden end, despite the passage of years.

"Officers," Chief Joseph Thorne greeted. "I take it your sitting here means you were unable to apprehend the thief."

"I'm assuming the man you were chasing was the thief?" Rhosyn asked as the other two officers nodded dismally.

"There have been a series of jewel thefts from some of the wealthiest households of the city. We've had shockingly little intel on them, even from our ears in the black market. We finally got an anonymous tip from somebody implicating the man in the hood," Officer Fletcher explained.

"Seems to be causing a lot of trouble for a simple jewel thief. Who is he?" Rhosyn asked. It struck her as odd that such a case would be reported directly to Chief Thorne, but he did have a rather hands-on approach. Rhosyn got the impression he liked to have his fingers in every investigation, to prevent something like the sloppy case that allowed Chief Cook to get away with the murder of his wife.

Chief Thorne scrubbed a hand over his face. "He certainly has picked targets that have made my life difficult. Several of the houses that were broken into belong to those who have sponsored Talented. Given that they have spent a substantial amount of money helping us give the Talented of the lower city another chance, I would prefer not to seem incompetent at catching a petty thief."

"Which is why it is unfortunate that we still don't know who he is. Our informant only gave us a tip on his location," Officer Davies commiserated.

"Perhaps your encounter with him today can help us identify him. With a detailed description, you could use your connections in the lower city to see if anybody has noticed him around," Chief Thorne gestured to Rhosyn, who shook her head.

"He wore a hood and mask over his face. I can give you a general description, but not enough to get a solid identification on him," Rhosyn explained.

The expression on Chief Thorne's face seemed to indicate that he would be banging his head against the solid wooden surface of his desk if it wouldn't be deemed unprofessional. "Well, write up everything you saw and add it to Fletcher and Davies' report. Every little bit of information helps."

"Do you want me to join them in the search?" Rhosyn offered. "I might be able to recognize his voice or movements if we encounter him."

The man had displayed a certain grace in his movements that Rhosyn wasn't sure she would be able to put into words for an official description. She had the distinct impression she would recognize it if she encountered it again, though.

"No." Chief Thorne waved Rhosyn's offer away. "I have a different job I need you to focus on. Fletcher, Davies, go start your report while I finish here with Walsh."

The other officers shuffled from the corner and off to their desks. Rhosyn furrowed her brow at Chief Thorne, wondering what could be so important. To her knowledge, the lower city had been as peaceful as it ever was. Her regular watches kept her fingers on the pulse of the lower city, and she had not noticed the undercurrents of impending trouble. While turf wars between gangs were inevitable, and every so often skirmishes and crooked dealings ignited into full-fledged violence, there had been nothing as sinister as the Wolves' illicit fighting rings in several years.

"I need your help gathering intel on a gang," Chief Thorne admitted. He pulled out a thin stack of papers from a pile and held them out to you. "The Foxes."

"The Foxes?" Rhosyn frowned at the few sheets of paper in front of her, a handful of very sparse reports. "They must be new. Or at least they weren't around when—before I joined the Royal Police."

Rhosyn corrected herself out of habit. Chief Thorne certainly knew Rhosyn had formerly been a member of the Lions, and a key member at that. After all, he had met and recruited her after his best friend married the leader of the Lions and the gang formally dissolved. Rhosyn had jumped on the opportunity for a new purpose, with her role as the Lions' den mother ripped out from under her. Still, Chief Thorne and Rhosyn had an unspoken rule about keeping police business official, and only mentioning the murkier aspects of her past when in the Woodrow's home.

"They've only just started cropping up, but for several weeks there have been skirmishes and thefts that we haven't been able to track back to any known gangs. If they are responsible for even half of those, then they are worryingly active for a new organization," Chief Thorne explained.

"There's not much to go off of," Rhosyn pointed out as she skimmed the reports in her hand. A few overheard conversations from their moles in the Raptors and Rattlesnakes comprised most of the information before her.

"That's why I'm asking you." Chief Thorne lowered his chin, looking at her meaningfully. "The people of the lower city have been oddly quiet about this new group, when normally gossip isn't hard to come by. They trust you though, and you might be able to find something others can't. I trust you can take advantage of...discreet sources."

Rhosyn raised a single brow. That was as close as Chief Thorne came to suggesting Rhosyn use her connections to former Lions to gather information. He must know that he himself could ask Kristoff for help if he ever wanted to do some investigating in a less than official capacity. In this delicate dance, though, he preferred to have a degree of separation—even if Chief Thorne often brushed shoulders with Kristoff with friendly familiarity at the Woodrow's dinner parties.

Paper crinkled as Rhosyn's fingers tightened around the reports. Try as she might to help London in the best way she could think of—protecting the lower city on the right side of the law—Chief Thorne still saw her as the officer to turn to when he needed somebody to brush elbows with residents of London's underbelly.

She forced her grip to relax. This is what she had signed up for, and she had done her job well for years now.

"I'll see what I can do," Rhosyn assured him, tucking the reports into the front of her jacket, retrieved from the roof where it had been pinned before she returned to headquarters. The bolt in the pocket would go with Davies and Fletcher's report to help them track down the hooded jewel thief.

"First, fill out your report and then get some rest. We have a social obligation tomorrow." Chief Thorne made a face of distaste at the reminder.

Rhosyn nearly chuckled at his reaction to the thought of leisure. He was almost as bad as Nate, burning the candle at both ends. Then again, Rhosyn wasn't really in a position to judge.

"You're coming with the Woodrows to the ball at the palace tomorrow?" she asked.

"Unfortunately, making sure the public sees the crown and the Royal Police as a united front is as much a part of the job as actually policing the streets," Chief Thorne sighed. "I guess I'll just have to get as much of tomorrow's work done tonight as I can."

As Rhosyn headed to join Davies and Fletcher, Chief Thorne was already absorbed in reading a paper on his desk, chewing his bottom lip as he frowned at it. She did not envy him.

The creak of Rhosyn's boots on the stairs echoed deafeningly through the quiet house, no matter how lightly she tried to creep. The home in the middle city belonged to two former Lions who had gotten married after the Inquiries, acquiring jobs as a butcher and a seamstress. Not having children of their own yet, they were more than happy to rent a spare room to Rhosyn, having spent their youth running jobs with her.

As Rhosyn passed their bedroom, she paused for a moment, only hearing the deep, measured breathing of people resting peacefully. Sometimes, as she passed them on the stairs in the morning, she considered asking them how they slept so soundly in the quiet, after years of living in crowded safehouses with constant comings and goings—Lions gambling and laughing through all hours of the night.

Shutting the door to her own bedroom, Rhosyn looked around the small space with a sigh. The bed was nicer than any she had slept on in the Lions' Den, the mattress plush and an embroidered quilt to keep her warm even on the coldest of winter nights. As she toed off her boots, she frowned at the empty space.

After years with the Royal Police, she had hoped she'd adjust to the luxuries of a comfortable bed and a room with a door she could lock. Instead, she looked forward to another night of awakening every hour to a phantom cry of a child having a nightmare, only to realize she was no longer responsible for a pack of youngsters. It was still odd to awaken alone in her bed every morning instead of finding a child, usually one freshly rescued from the cruelty of a factory, tucked into her arms, having climbed in to join her as she slept.

As she changed into her sleeping clothes, she chuckled at the irony. For years, she sat on the rooftop of the reclaimed warehouse she and the youngest Lions called home, wondering what it would look like to be free of the responsibility of being a universal big sister to all those Nate and his associates tried to give a better life.

Instead of freedom, the lifting of that burden only made her feel untethered.

Rhosyn splashed water from the bowl on the washstand onto her face, chiding herself for being dramatic. She just wasn't used to the quiet of the middle city at night and was restless after too many weeks of poor sleep.

Maybe she would ask Chief Thorne to let her switch back to nighttime patrols, so she could sleep during the day, soothed by the backdrop of city traffic. After she gathered the information she needed on the Foxes, she would do just that.

Chapter Two

Rhosyn grappled with the urge to twirl continuously just to watch her skirts swirl around her. Instead, she settled for a playful sway as she waited, just for the joy of feeling their fullness swish back and forth.

As much as Contessa sometimes grumbled about the impracticality of her wardrobe when trying to get something done, she still held herself elegantly, as if she were born to it. Rhosyn on the other hand, felt rather like she was wearing a costume every time she ventured into polite society, but she let herself enjoy the frivolous novelty.

"You look colorful," Contessa greeted as she walked down the stairs of her home to the front hall where Rhosyn waited.

Rhosyn held up her arms and twisted this way and that, so her friend might fully admire the vivid orchid of her dress. "My hair makes me bright enough anyway, there's no point in trying to blend in."

While Contessa's lady's maid, Julia, had tamed Rhosyn's coppery red hair admirably before scurrying upstairs to help her mistress, it still had an air of wildness about it that could not be smoothed. Julia, thankfully, had practiced doing Rhosyn's hair many times, when she was dreaming of a life as a lady's maid as a young Lion living in the Den. She knew it was better to work with Rhosyn's riotous ringlets, letting the stray curls frame her face instead of pinning them into oblivion and ending up like a rat's nest.

"I have to admit, I like the bright colors better when every available inch isn't covered in frills and bows. The dress suits you well," Contessa complimented as she reached Rhosyn.

She herself was in her customary gunmetal gray silk, and while Rhosyn would have felt silly in something with an air of such understated elegance, it suited Contessa perfectly. Instead of washing her out, the sedate color complimented her pale complexion and silvery hair, the exact opposite of Rhosyn's, as it easily smoothed into a silken twist. Her icy eyes matched the dress nearly perfectly. If Rhosyn hadn't spent several months years ago dumping Contessa on her ass and watching her reddened, sweaty face twist in frustration, she might even find her beauty cold.

Now, Rhosyn grinned wryly, and her friend smiled back.

A familiar stomping interrupted them as Nate marched into the hall. "Ready, ladies?"

"Watch who you're calling a lady," Rhosyn shot back, even as Nate behaved like a perfect gentleman and offered his elbow to his wife, who grasped it delicately with her gloved hand.

Nate shot Rhosyn a look as he donned his top hat, indicating he would ruffle her hair if it wasn't clear how much effort had gone into it, and the trio headed out to the carriage. The Woodrow's manservant, Gregor, already had it out front, waiting to take them to the palace for the night's festivities.

"What about the others?" Rhosyn asked as the carriage began trundling across the cobbled streets, slowly climbing towards the palace at the top of the hill.

"The Pearces are taking their own carriage, and Joseph sent a runner to tell me he would be making his own way to the palace tonight, since he was coming directly from headquarters," Contessa explained.

Rhosyn nodded. Even though the Lions were not what they once were, back when the name and membership in the gang alone was enough to grant you a modicum of protection in the lower city, they existed in a different capacity now. The Woodrows, along with Kristoff, Gregor, and Rhosyn, stayed true to the purpose of helping the Talented in London, albeit in somewhat less illicit capacities. The Pearces, Benedict and Scarlett, had joined their band a few years ago after helping dismantle the underground Talented fighting rings. As much as Chief Thorne—Joseph—was part of their group too, he was unlikely to admit it out loud.

"Well, thank you for bringing me along," Rhosyn said earnestly. "I know this is a bigger imposition than bringing me to the odd party and implying that I'm one of Nate's distant relatives."

"It's not an imposition if you're here on business," Nate pointed out. "Contessa and King Byron want to put a good face on both sponsorships for the Talented and the Royal Police's continued loyalty to the Crown. It's why, on nights like tonight, he has his other security relieve me of my bodyguarding duties, so I can be paraded around like a rehabilitation success story."

Nate's tone held wry amusement, as if the thought of the former Beast being an exemplar of anything for the crown was an amusing joke, but he took it in stride.

When they arrived at the palace, Rhosyn had to focus to keep her mouth from hanging open as she took in the sights. Servants led them into the garden where the soiree was to be held, decorated with enough lanterns to send the Woodrow's sizable house up in flames. It gave the whole thing a dreamlike quality, enhancing the elegance of the socialites already milling about in pools and eddies of luxurious fabrics. The moment they entered the crowd, Contessa and Nate were whisked away into the conniving grasps of those who wished to gain an advantage by ingratiating themselves with the King's bodyguard and trusted advisor.

In a matter of moments, Rhosyn found herself alone at the fringes of the party, spending most of her effort on appearing like she belonged, and most likely only drawing attention to her lack of proper poise in the process.

Rhosyn tugged at her dress, suddenly conscious of the way it hung on her and the tightness where it clung to her waist and dipped low at the neck. As much as she loved it, she almost regretted her bold color choice as she found herself dressed in the most eye-catching shade in the vicinity. She attempted to brush off the thought, squaring her shoulders and not thinking about the way it caused her bodice to pull dangerously low. It always amused Rhosyn that Contessa continued to wear an expression like she was doing something forbidden every time she donned pants when she showed this much of her décolleté on a daily basis.

A playful elbow in her side distracted Rhosyn from her worries about her presence among such elegant company. Rhosyn looked down to see Scarlett Pearce at her side. At this point, it didn't surprise her that the woman could sneak up on her, as Rhosyn was convinced Scarlett was half a shadow herself.

Scarlett looked pointedly at Rhosyn's hands, which were fisted in the fabric of her skirt, sure to leave wrinkles. She uncurled her fingers with effort, intentionally pressing them flat on her lower bodice so they wouldn't misbehave.

"I still feel a little out of place at functions like this, as much as I work with the King these days," Scarlett confided quietly, clearly having sensed Rhosyn's moment of discomfort.

"At least you have a suitable dance partner to make sure you don't end up standing in a corner completely out of place," Rhosyn pointed out, just as the man in question, Scarlett's husband Benedict, stepped up behind them.

"And what a wonderful dancer he is," Benedict joined into the conversation seamlessly. Scarlett smiled up at him fondly, and he smoothed her chin length hair back, as if he would tuck it behind her ear if it weren't on the side where the side of Scarlett's head bore nothing but scar tissue after a run in with a stray bullet.

"If a dance partner is what you need, I might just be able to help," an unfamiliar voice joined the conversation.

Rhosyn turned to find an unknown man, although she didn't know how her eyes hadn't jumped to him the moment she entered the party. After all, how could one consider looking away from someone so ostentatiously dressed, yet disarmingly handsome?

A jade-green waistcoat, nipped in tightly around his waist, accentuated his athletic figure as much as the matching color of his mischievous eyes. A metallic gold vest and cravat, along with canary-yellow pants should have clashed, but the casual pose and crooked smile he wore transformed the look from obnoxious to endearingly eccentric.

Rhosyn blinked. The whole effect was remarkably charming, but it struck her that was exactly what the man was aiming for—like he had modeled himself after a character in one of Contessa's books and not a real person.

"I don't believe we've been introduced," the man prompted, drawing Rhosyn from what she realized had been an embarrassingly long perusal.

"Allow me," Benedict chimed in. "Mr. Ansel Blakely, this is Ms. Rhosyn Walsh. Rhosyn, I had the pleasure of making Mr. Blakely's acquaintance on my unsuccessful quest to fetch my wife some lemonade."

Mr. Blakely inclined his head politely, although his gaze remained trained on Rhosyn's face. The lantern-light flickered over his hair with the movement, revealing a single streak of silver running through his otherwise dark hair near his temple, although he couldn't be much older than her.

Rhosyn gave a small bow in return, before realizing a curtsy would be more appropriate for the occasion and her dress. She smiled ruefully at her new acquaintance and tried not to think about how bending over probably afforded him a view straight down her bodice. To his credit, his polished smile did not slip an inch.

"Well then, Ms. Walsh, I'd be happy to save you from...how did you put it? Ah—standing in the corner completely out of place." Mr. Blakely offered his hand.

Rhosyn took it without hesitation, although she looked over her shoulder as her new partner led her onto the dance floor. Benedict waved her on encouragingly, while Scarlett bit her lips in contained amusement.

Mr. Blakely swept her into his arms as the musicians started a new song, and Rhosyn's hands automatically rose to the appropriate position at his shoulders, thanks to the begrudging afternoons of dance lessons with Contessa on the days when Rhosyn could see that knife fighting practice would frustrate her more than it would help. While Contessa argued that she was not coordinated enough on the dance floor to be a good teacher, those afternoons had led to a surprising amount of giggling as they both attempted to follow, neither familiar with leading. Rhosyn picked up dancing faster than Contessa had picked up fighting, finding that they weren't really that different.

However, afternoons stumbling around the parlor with her friend had not prepared her fully for the intricacies of dancing as a social pursuit. Rhosyn had no idea if she should talk or smile or simply school her expression into one of pleasant vacancy. She didn't have nearly the skill for vapid beauty as those raised in high society, taught to keep their opinions hidden behind bland smiles.

As Mr. Blakely's fingers curled around her waist and the heat of his touch seeped through the delicate material of her gown, Rhosyn decided conversation was a must—something to distract from the unfamiliar fluttering beneath her sternum.

"I have to thank you for saving me from my evening of standing in the corner," she ventured. "My height tends to scare away many men."

"Well, that's foolish. A skilled partner can handle any amount of woman." Mr. Blakely demonstrated the truth of his statement by guiding Rhosyn into a slight dip, despite the top of his head being level with Rhosyn's eyeline.

His hand spread across her lower back as he did so, pressing her to him.

Rhosyn swallowed to combat the sudden dryness in her mouth. "Even if the woman is a woefully inexperienced dancer herself? I must admit, I don't come to these parties often."

"And what could possibly be keeping a lovely lady like yourself at home when there is revelry to be had?" Mr. Blakely asked.

"I'm not really a lady," Rhosyn admitted. "I'm an officer for the Royal Police, but I'm fortunate in my friends."

Something sparked in Mr. Blakely's eyes. It wasn't the disapproval that Rhosyn had come to expect from the admission, but she couldn't place the expression.

"I'm glad you chose to come out tonight, then, because I hear the entertainment is supposed to be incredible." Mr. Blakely's smile was mischievous as he nodded to a stage erected at the far end of the garden. Currently, scarlet drapes hid it from view.

"What is the entertainment?"

Just as Rhosyn asked, the song ended. Mr. Blakely stepped back. "You'll have to wait and see."

The sparkle in his eye as he bowed caught Rhosyn's attention, as the glimmer seemed to come from behind the poreless mask of proper manners. She wondered what else he might keep behind the glass.

Before Rhosyn could think of an argument to persuade him to tell her about the expected show, for she was not known for her patience in waiting for surprises, Mr. Blakely had turned away and melted into the crowd of dispersing dancers. Rhosyn's gaze tracked his receding back, but he was swallowed by the milling partygoers despite the vibrancy of his attire.

Rhosyn blew one of the curls that had fallen into her face aside with a disappointed huff, turning toward the edge of the dance floor where she was sure to wait for the rest of the evening. The three men she knew in attendance who were taller than her were unlikely to take to the floor with her. Benedict liked to dance, but threw propriety to the wind and insisted on stepping out with Scarlett for every single song at most balls. Nate refused to dance on principle and would spend the entire evening hovering over Contessa's shoulder as she constantly elbowed him to stop glaring.

Chief Thorne wouldn't be seen dancing with one of his own officers, determined to keep his professional reputation as spotless as could be. However, Rhosyn had noted with interest that he had taken Benedict's sister, Lottie, for several turns at the last few parties they attended. She hoped he would do so again tonight, as he always seemed a little less exhausted after a dance with the statuesque blonde.

Rhosyn edged her way to the table of lemonade, determined to at least enjoy some refreshments when Joseph intercepted her, apparently not dancing yet, taking her by the elbow.

"I have somebody for you to meet," he said, guiding her away from the lemonade. Rhosyn looked longingly after it as she followed, already sweating in the layers of her dress and her mouth watering at the thought of the cold liquid. Still, she dutifully followed her Chief.

"Who would you have me charm with my less-than-ideal manners?" Rhosyn asked.

"Mr. Gower. He's one of the biggest supporters of the Talented in society at the moment. He's already sponsored about a dozen of them, including Paul and Olivia."

Rhosyn's eyebrows rose in interest. After Scarlett had brought to the crown's attention the difficulties of Talented criminals reintegrating into society, Contessa had the inspired idea to encourage noble households to sponsor them. The socialites would pay the expenses of their pardon with the crown and give them a position in their household where their Talents might be put to use doing honest work.

Very few socialites had taken the bait in the first few years, but after Contessa mentioned that the Woodrow's famously beautiful rose bushes were the result of their gardener, Gregor's Talent, a few wealthy citizens had chanced to sponsor one or two Talented. After all, there was certainly no harm in hiring a coachman who was so uncannily good with the horses it was as if he could talk to them, or a seamstress who could tailor a dress perfectly without even looking at a measuring tape.

It was an imperfect system, leaving out those with more intimidating Talents, like Scarlett, but it was a start. One household sponsoring a dozen Talented was unheard of, though, and a costly proposition.

Joseph stopped in front of a large man with the most impressive mustache Rhosyn had ever laid eyes on. Bowing beside her, Joseph surreptitiously stepped on Rhosyn's toes, startling her into a less-than graceful curtsy of her own. Still, it was with great effort that Rhosyn ripped her eyes away from the silver facial hair, polished and shaped so long that it nearly stuck out past the man's ears.

"Mr. Gower, allow me to introduce Officer Rhosyn Walsh of the Royal Police," Joseph introduced as they both stood up straight once more. "As one of our most experienced officers in the lower city, she sees the benefits of your generosity firsthand."

Rhosyn smiled politely as Mr. Gower's eye swept up and down her form. The smug superiority of his gaze rubbed icily against her skin, and Rhosyn had the sudden urge to point out that it would take more than offering better lives to twelve Talented to undo the harms of the Inquiries to the lower city. She swallowed down the barb, surprised at the sudden ferocity of the thought, and smiled wider instead. After all, Mr. Gower was setting an example, which they hoped more socialites at this ball would follow.

"I hear you've sponsored young Paul and Olivia," Rhosyn said. "They're wonderful children. I doubt you'll regret it."

"You know them well?" Mr. Gower's eyes narrowed and Rhosyn swallowed, sensing it was unwise to admit that they had lived under her care as young Lions at the Den. It was there that Paul's Talent for lulling people into deep sleep with his voice, and Olivia's for lighting fires with a clap of her hands, sprung to life—back when an obvious Talent like that could easily lead to a short drop from the end of a noose.

"I met them when they were quite young," Rhosyn hedged. "I'm glad to hear they are doing well."

Mr. Gower nodded. "Having so many Talented working in one houschold can be challenging, but I manage to keep them in line. I'm sure my newest additions' abilities will be a valuable asset."

Rhosyn bit her lip to keep from frowning, hiding the expression by looking down and smoothing her skirts—a gesture she had learned from Contessa. She couldn't let the way the man's words rankled show. For him, the Talented sponsorships were an investment—one that the lower city sorely needed.

"I do hope they turn out to be trustworthy," Mr. Gower barreled on, seemingly oblivious to Rhosyn biting the inside of her cheek. "I'm afraid I don't know who to trust in my own household these days."

Joseph made a face that spoke to holding back a long-suffering sigh. "I assure you, Mr. Gower, the Royal Police are doing all we can to apprehend the thief of your wife's jewels and return them to you. It is unlikely to be a member of your staff, considering there have been a rash of these thefts across the upper city."

"You better be right, Chief Thorne." Mr. Gower's mustache bristled. "I'm supporting the Royal Police's efforts by sponsoring these Talented, and it disappoints me to hear that you are still struggling to do your job."

Joseph reddened, and not for the first time, Rhosyn offered silent thanks for being a patrolling officer and not the Chief. After all, it wouldn't be very fitting for the figurehead of the Royal Police to punch an innocent citizen in the gut for being an arrogant prick.

Thankfully, Rhosyn was distracted from the itching in her fists and the strange urge to unearth her trusty brass knuckles by a ripple of excited chattering through the crowd.

"Ladies and gentlemen!" A familiar voice boomed through the garden from the direction of the stage. Rhosyn turned to find a green and gold clad figure standing on the edge of the stage, just in front of the crimson drapes.

"Allow me to introduce myself. I am Mr. Blakely, and it is my absolute privilege to have been invited here alongside my little troupe by His Royal Highness, King Byron, for your entertainment."

A tittering ran through the crowd at the promise in Mr. Blakely's voice, and Rhosyn found herself drifting forward, away from her interrupted conversation, to get a better view of the stage. No wonder her dance partner had been so complimentary of the night's festivities. He had supplied them.

"Tonight, I have the pleasure of introducing the acrobats from Archer's Traveling Circus. Please give a warm welcome to the Merry Men!" With an exaggerated flourish, Mr. Blakely stepped aside as the curtain split in the middle to reveal the scene on the stage.

A gasp escaped Rhosyn at the sight of platforms elevated at a dizzying height above the stage, connected by a series of tightropes and swinging trapeze bars. Six men perched on the elevated platforms, and one of them raised a hand in a confident wave.

Then, he jumped.

Rhosyn's heart hammered in borrowed fear, but he easily caught one of the trapezes, using his momentum to swing, then letting go and performing an elegant flip before grabbing onto the next one.

One by one, each of the men jumped into the fray, weaving between each other in a dizzying choreography of gravity-defying daring. One man levered himself until he was hanging from the swaying bar by his knees and reached downwards so another performer could grab his hands as he flew through the air.

A third stepped onto the tightrope as Rhosyn looked on in awe. Before she could reason that perhaps she, too, might be able to walk on a rope—how different could it be from running across a peaked rooftop?—the acrobat dashed the thought by kicking up into a perfect handstand, still balanced on the rope, but now upside down.

At that point, Rhosyn gave up on making sense of how such a performance was possible and just enjoyed the spectacle. The acrobats flipped and flew, streaks of green swooping across the stage and launching themselves into inconceivable flips. Every time they plummeted towards the earth, Rhosyn's breath caught, sure that this time they would fall, but they caught the next bar in the nick of time.

Rhosyn clapped her hands in delight as they soared higher and higher. One of the performers launched himself off a swinging rope, executing a neat flip before sticking the landing on the elevated platform where he had started. As he did, the vision of the hooded man, whom Fletcher and Davies had dubbed "The Hood", swinging from the clothesline flashed through her mind.

She narrowed her eyes at the performers, but none of them were the right build. Most were long and lithe, slim legs and wiry muscles affording them the mobility to twist quickly in midair. None had the broad shoulders and powerful thighs she remembered all too distinctly on the criminal. Not to mention they were missing…something—the odd hovering in midair before gravity took hold. She shook her head, chiding herself for dramatizing the Hood's skills just because he had managed to slip away.

As the performers landed on their platforms and took a bow, Rhosyn was so busy joining in with the thunderous applause that she almost missed a sudden flurry of movement from the side of the garden. Her hands froze mid clap as her eyes zeroed in on a member of the King's guard pushing through the crowd to where Contessa and Nate mingled. No sooner had he leaned in to whisper something in Nate's ear than the trio began all but sprinting towards the palace.

Rhosyn turned away from the stage and pushed through the crowd, shoulder bumping into Mr. Gower's and making him splash brandy onto his expensive looking waistcoat. He sputtered in indignation, but Rhosyn paid him no mind, hurrying to intercept her friends. If there was trouble afoot, then that's where Rhosyn belonged.

She reached them as they entered the palace, turning to head into the bowels where the walls were adorned with less decoration and the corridors seemed slightly narrower. Rhosyn quickly overtook Contessa, who made slower progress with her shorter legs, to jog alongside Nate.

Before she could ask what had happened, Nate and the other King's guard turned abruptly off the main hall. They stopped suddenly in a doorway, faced with the carnage of what appeared to be an office. Papers lay strewn everywhere, drawers pulled from the desk and cast on the floor, cabinets on the walls left hanging open as if somebody dug through them unceremoniously and emptied their contents on the ground.

A sharp gasp behind Rhosyn signaled Contessa's arrival.

"My office!"

Contessa pushed between the trio standing motionless in the entry, but Nate's hand shot out to grab her wrist before Contessa could make it to the desk. She looked up at him and furrowed her brow at her husband, but she shook her head gently.

"We're not in any danger," she assured.

At this, Nate nodded and let go of her wrist. Her skirts puddled around her as she crouched to the ground to look at the papers littering the floor, gathering them up into a stack.

Rhosyn stepped further into the room, eyes darting around to carefully catalogue anything that might be evidence of how somebody had gotten into the office of the King's advisor, and who it might have been. However, she breathed easier at Contessa's assurance that they weren't in danger, and if Nate agreed with her, then it must be true.

After all, Contessa's Talent for sensing peril had only become more precise over the years, and with Nate's Talent being so attuned to Contessa's feelings, he would know if his wife's mental alarm bells were ringing in the slightest.

As Contessa continued to shuffle through papers, Nate grumbled orders to Rhosyn and the King's guard to watch over her before hurrying out the door. While he technically wasn't on duty bodyguarding the King tonight, the office might not be the only target if somebody broke into the palace.

Rhosyn nodded, reaching into the front of her dress to produce a short, but still quite sharp, knife. The King's Guard frowned at it, clearly concerned that a guest had been able to bring such a weapon to a celebration when His Royal Highness was in attendance. Rhosyn resisted the urge to roll her eyes. She knew as well as anybody that one didn't need a weapon if they were intent on doing some serious damage.

"It's fine, I'm an officer of the Royal Police," Rhosyn offered by way of explanation instead, which seemed to placate the guard. "Contessa, keep track of anything you think might be missing."

Contessa nodded, eyes already narrowed in on each report she rifled through, her steel trap of a mind likely cataloging each and every one. Stepping around the desk, Rhosyn headed toward the window on the far wall to inspect it for any sign of forced entry. Before she could reach it, she paused with a frown. While all the cabinets lining the walls of the office hung open, contents in some degree of disarray, the one in the far corner remained tightly closed, seemingly untouched. Rhosyn edged closer to it, seeing that no lock kept the handles closed.

She looked back at Contessa as she approached it, but the woman remained on the ground, seemingly unperturbed by any mental signs of danger. The King's Guard had stationed himself in the doorway.

Tightening her grip on her knife, Rhosyn reached for the handle of the closed cabinet, curious why this one had escaped the intruder's ire.

The door nearly smacked Rhosyn in the face as it smashed open, a slight figure springing forth from the enclosed space. In her effort to avoid having her nose broken by the swinging wood panel, Rhosyn jumped aside, giving the hidden occupant just enough room to slip past her.

With a crash, the thief leaped through the window, shards of glass exploding outward as they avoided the guard in the doorway. Shouting erupted behind Rhosyn, but she had already leaped into pursuit. She threw her arms up to protect her face from any errant glass as she followed her quarry out the window.

A tearing sound and a tug at her waist told Rhosyn her skirts had caught at the jagged edges clinging to the window frame, but she paid them no mind as she pounded through the courtyard. The shadowed figure had gained the slightest lead in Rhosyn's moment of frozen surprise. Now, they turned out toward the gardens and the surrounding buildings.

Rhosyn's long strides ate up the ground between them, but her legs tangled up in her now tattered skirts. With a huff of annoyance, she hoisted them out of her way as much as she could without slowing her pace.

In the moment it took her to slow, the thief turned abruptly, crashing through the doors to one of the outbuildings. Rhosyn hurtled through after them and nearly pulled up short at the cacophony of color that greeted her within.

"Stop them!" Rhosyn shouted into the crowded room, the words nearly swallowed by the hubbub.

The thief was already bobbing and weaving between brightly dressed figures in all manner of curious ensembles. Rhosyn tried to follow, but found herself slowed considerably by trunks and boxes, as well as the crowded nature of the room. She frowned at the people around her as glimpses of her quarry in the distance became less frequent.

Finally, breaking free of the crowd, she dashed out the back exit the thief must have taken, only to barrel headfirst into a familiar figure.

"Rhosyn," Chief Thorne exclaimed as he righted himself.

"Did you see where they went?" Rhosyn panted without preamble.

He frowned at her. "Nobody came out this door. I was just coming in to sweep the outbuildings after Nate told me what happened."

Rhosyn spun on her heel, staring back into the crowded room and blinking in confusion at the sight that greeted her. Now that she wasn't running, she recognized the strange outfits as costumes of performers. A nearby woman in a short, frilled skirt held the type of clubs used for juggling while a man wore the outfit she remembered on the acrobats, what seemed like hours ago.

This was where the circus was preparing for their performances.

"I was chasing the thief. They disappeared when I followed them in here," Rhosyn explained.

"Then we better start searching," Joseph ordered grimly.

Together, they swept through the open space, Rhosyn keeping a keen eye out for anybody in plain, dark clothing. To her dismay, everywhere she looked was a performer dressed more flamboyantly than the last. They all moved aside easily, letting her search, even opening the larger trunks for her, in case the burglar had attempted to hide again.

A few King's Guards joined them after several minutes, but by then Rhosyn knew the trail was lost. The thief must have doubled back and slipped out the front entrance when she ran into Joseph. She asked the circus performers if they had seen where they went, but they all shook their heads earnestly, citing that it had all happened so fast.

The guards moved on to continue sweeping the area, but the thief would likely be long gone by now. Rhosyn trudged back to Contessa's office, this time with Joseph, failure weighing heavy on her heart.

"I could have caught them if not for this damn dress," she grumbled, only for it to turn into a grimace as she looked down at the now ruined garment. With the way the skirts were torn, she was showing a near indecent amount of ankle and calf, but Joseph had the civility not to comment on that.

"You weren't expecting to be in a chase tonight," Joseph offered, his tone clearly attempting to be reassuring, but coming out more tired than anything.

Rhosyn's upper lip curled in a snarl of frustration. This was the second criminal in as many days she had failed to apprehend, this one caught sneaking around the palace, no less. Some credit to the Royal Police she was.

They entered Contessa's office to find her deep in muttered conversation with Nate. They both looked up hopefully when Rhosyn and Joseph entered, only to frown at their clear expressions of disappointment.

"Do you know what they took?" Joseph asked.

"From what I can tell, there is just one stack of papers missing," Contessa admitted with a grim look. "I can't seem to find any of my records on the sponsored Talented."

A muscle in Joseph's jaw ticked and he scrubbed a hand over his face. "Why would somebody want those?"

"I don't know, but I doubt it will be good," Nate grumbled.

"Will the King's Guard need help investigating?" Rhosyn asked. "I could—"

"You already have a case that I need you to focus on," Joseph reminded her sharply but not unkindly. "You can just give me your description of the thief and then rejoin the festivities."

Rhosyn sighed, looking down at the wrinkled tatters of her dress. She wasn't likely to get the good kind of attention dressed like this, and certainly wouldn't be putting forth a good face for the Royal Police.

It was too bad, really. She would have enjoyed seeing the rest of the Circus's performance. She wouldn't have minded another dance with Mr. Blakely either.

Chapter Three

Rhosyn was never more grateful for pants than when she had spent the prior night traipsing around in a skirt. She bounced down the cobblestone street of the lower city feeling herself again and ready for a more successful day. The Foxes wouldn't escape her like her last two targets.

The warm, spiced scent of roast meat filled the air and Rhosyn paused, nose turned up. Looking around, she located the source of the smell as Mrs. Landon's cart, selling meat pies just across the street. Rhosyn bobbed among the busy traffic to reach it, hand already digging into her purse, her mouth watering at the prospect of a heartier breakfast than the sip of tea and stolen bit of toast she had grabbed from the kitchen as she ran out the door.

Mrs. Landon's pies were a fixture of the lower city and a favorite of Rhosyn's, although when she was younger, she could only stare at them longingly. Instead, she had pinched her pennies, saving every spare coin for secondhand clothing and toys for the young Lions in her charge.

Now, very occasionally, she would treat herself to a Cornish pasty when she passed by. Today, she had an extra incentive to part with the small amount of coins she carried with her.

Once Mrs. Landon had deposited two pies into Rhosyn's waiting hands, she turned and strolled towards the street where Granny's haunt was located. Given that Granny's was a safe haven for many lower city children, she was sure to find what she was looking for there.

THE TALENTED FAIRY TALES

Warmth seeped through the paper wrappings to Rhosyn's hands as she walked, and she resisted ripping into it to get the meal beneath. Finally, she found what she was looking for. Outside of one of the dingy shops on the street stood a familiar urchin, sweeping the front stoop with a ragged broom. She didn't know his name, but she walked these streets often enough to recognize his round face and the too long bangs that fell into his eyes.

Rhosyn approached slowly, twisting her baton to the back of her belt so she didn't approach the child weapon first. He looked up as she approached, but when he started to draw back into the shop, Rhosyn gave her friendliest smile—the one she had reserved for the most skittish of Lion cubs in her care.

He paused.

"What are you up to?" she asked.

"Not stealing," the boy answered automatically.

Rhosyn chuckled easily. "I wouldn't think so, unless you're stealing that broom."

That coaxed a smile from the boy.

"I've seen you around here before haven't I...."

"Bruce," he offered.

"Bruce," Rhosyn repeated with a genuine smile.

"You might've," Bruce admitted. "I help Mr. Corvey at his shop for some extra coin." He jerked his head towards the shop behind him.

"You look like you're working hard," Rhosyn observed. "You must be hungry. Mrs. Landon gave me an extra meat pie. Do you want to sit with me for a minute and eat it?"

Bruce's gaze darted back and forth from the brown paper packets in Rhosyn's hands to the shop door, clearly fighting a losing battle between hunger and responsibility.

"I won't let Mr. Corvey get you in trouble," Rhosyn assured. "It'll just be a minute."

As soon as they were both seated on the stoop, Bruce tore into the offered pasty, biting into it with the ferocity of a rabid dog. Rhosyn set to hers at a more restrained pace, but not by much.

Rhosyn swallowed as Bruce chewed a particularly large mouthful. She used the opportunity to ask, "So I hear there's a new big gang in town?"

Bruce's gaze narrowed in suspicion, but Rhosyn just took another bite of her pasty. She used the back of her hand to wipe the flaky bits of pastry from her lips, making a point not to use her better manners.

Bruce shrugged. "Maybe, but I don't know much."

"Really?" Rhosyn snorted. "Even I've heard about the Foxes. The others at Granny's must be talking."

"I don't know any runners for them or anything, honest." Bruce talked around a large mouthful of spiced meat. "But some of my friends did just get work with Mr. Barrett. Seems he's got more to sell these days."

Rhosyn nodded to herself. Mr. Barrett was a well-known fence in the lower city. If the Foxes were supplying him, then he would be able to give her more intel. He would be a tough nut to crack, as his reputation in the gangs as a safe merchant to sell to kept him in business. Mr. Barrett had given Rhosyn reliable information on a few occasions when the situation was serious. She would just have to convince him that this was one of those situations and assure him nobody would ever find out he turned nose.

"Thanks, Bruce." Rhosyn rewrapped the remaining half of her pie and handed it to him. He snatched it up eagerly despite not having finished his own yet.

"Thanks, ma'am."

Rhosyn stood and turned back down the street, pleased with herself even as her heart sunk. It pained her how easy it was to get the children of the lower city talking just by distracting them with the promise of a full belly. She could only hope more Talented children secured a place in a home with regular meals through a sponsorship.

The walk to Mr. Barrett's shop took her across the lower city, right to the border between the poorest neighborhoods populated by the gangs and the neater but still cramped houses of the middle city. Here, Mr. Barrett could still be easily accessed by his "suppliers" while catering to a slightly wealthier clientele.

The light tinkle of a bell on the door signaled Rhosyn's entrance, causing Mr. Barrett to look up and instantly scowl at her uniform. Then again, Rhosyn got the feeling that Mr. Barrett scowled at everybody.

"I don't have time for you to be breathing down my neck today." He turned his back to her and stomped away to the far end of the counter.

"Is that any way to treat an old friend?" Rhosyn's tone was easy as she walked further into the shop. She stopped casually before the counter, pausing for a moment as if to peruse the cases filled with the more valuable trinkets.

Mr. Barrett folded his arms, lines around his eyes and mouth deepening. "Ain't friends with no Royal Police officers."

It was Rhosyn's turn to frown. "What are friends if not people who help each other out once in a while?"

Mr. Barrett glanced around his shop as if to make sure they were alone. Only the two of them stood among the shelves of odds and ends.

"What are you looking for?" he asked, tone furtive.

"The Foxes...have you heard anything about them?" Rhosyn leaned over the counter as she spoke, keeping her voice low in case any prying ears paused at the doorway or open windows.

It also gave her the advantage of being able to closely observe Mr. Barrett's body language—the way his knuckles whitened where they gripped the edge of the counter and the slight irregularity in his breathing as the name of the Foxes left her lips.

"Haven't heard of them." Mr. Barrett shrugged. "Are you sure your intel is good?"

Rhsoyn's eyes narrowed. "Come now, if I've heard the whispers of a new gang in town, you must have too."

Mr. Barrett turned away to fuss with some merchandise, as if he needed to do something with his hands. "Listen, if you want to waste your time investigating a gang that doesn't exist, then be my guest."

Rhosyn sighed internally. She had worked with Mr. Barrett enough times to know that he wouldn't change his mind if it was made up, and badgering him would only make him less inclined to cooperate on her next case.

"Maybe it's just people telling tales," she suggested, also turning away. As she did, the thin sunlight flashed on something silver in the glass case below the counter. She hesitated, leaning in to get a closer look.

The sparkle that had caught her attention came from a dramatic hat pin, the ornamental end wrought in the shape of a silver flower with a large green gemstone in the middle. She didn't spend much time around people who would wear such a decoration, but something about it rung familiar.

"Where'd you get this?"

"You don't strike me as the type for such a shiny thing," Mr. Barrett deflected. "Although the green might look good with your hair."

"How long have you had it?" Rhosyn ignored his comments. She did enjoy wearing green, but no matter how much she pinned it, a hat never sat nicely on her unruly hair.

Mr. Barrett shrugged. "Quite a while. It's hard to sell such a pricey piece."

Rhosyn nodded; it would be expensive. Likely stolen by one of his suppliers from a wealthy family.

She grinned in triumph as it hit her. The stolen jewels.

When helping Officers Fletcher and Davies fill out their report on the hooded man, she had flipped through the description of the stolen jewels, including one jeweled hat pin. She might not be making progress on her own investigation, but she had made a discovery on another by happy accident.

"That's interesting," Rhosyn said with feigned casualness. "You can't have had it that long, because it was just stolen a few weeks ago."

Mr. Barrett looked at her with tired eyes, but Rhosyn couldn't help the wolfish grin that crossed her face.

Chapter Four

"Your second high society event in a week. Contessa might turn you into a proper lady yet," Joseph mused as their carriage trundled up the hill to the wide streets where the wealthiest residents of London lived.

"If I'm proper, then Contessa is meek and demure," Rhosyn scoffed.

Joseph laughed and the smile made him look younger, softening the constant creases of consternation he wore from frowning at paperwork so often.

"I hope you can at least put on the act for another night," Joseph commented. "Mr. Gower specifically requested that I bring the officer responsible for the return of his jewels, so he could thank them personally."

At this, Rhosyn frowned. "We still haven't caught the Hood yet though."

Indeed, when Fletcher and Davies showed up to retrieve the stolen jewels and question Mr. Barrett on who sold them to him, he had described the same man Rhosyn had chased across the rooftops earlier: a piece of fabric hiding his lower face with a hood pulled low over his eyes. They had gained no further hints to his identity, and so could still only refer to him as the Hood.

"That might be true," Joseph admitted, "but hopefully he won't try to steal the same jewels twice. As long as Mr. Gower is happy and will keep sponsoring Talented, then it will at least take that worry off my plate."

Rhosyn didn't respond, playing through her chase with the Hood in her mind again. She told herself she was searching for some hidden clue in her memories she had overlooked earlier. In reality, the picture of him performing a perfect flip in the air, quads flexing as he landed and threatening to split the seams of his pants, came to her mind at all sorts of odd times. When she was taking a pause to eat lunch. When she was lying in her bed at night waiting for sleep to come.

Rhosyn was infuriated that he had gotten away.

She was also curious.

The cease of rumbling around her drew her from her musings, and she realized the carriage had come to a halt. They had arrived at the Gowers'.

Joseph helped her down from the carriage as Rhosyn suppressed the odd urge to giggle as she lifted her canary-yellow skirts out of the way of her satin slippers. The whole production felt similar to the first time she played dress up with Contessa's gowns years ago.

Still, she did her best to seem like she belonged there as she took Joseph's elbow and let him lead her into the grand house. The crystal chandelier and ornate wood railings on the sweeping staircase did nothing to make her feel more at ease.

However, the sight that greeted her just inside the parlor lifted her heart. A familiar young man hovered in the corner, a tray of crudites balanced in his white-gloved hands.

"Paul." Rhosyn made a beeline across the room to her former charge, although she knew she should probably greet the more distinguished guests first. He must not have heard her the first time, not reacting at all. "Paul!"

When Rhosyn stepped in front of him, he blinked several times as if not processing what he was seeing. It was probably since Rhosyn was dressed far more formally than she ever had been while minding the young Lions in the den. She took his moment of recognition to look him over.

It struck her immediately that he was still so young, barely more than just a boy. It seemed impossible that he could already have a job in a fine house. Then again, Rhosyn had been the same age when she put herself in charge of all the Lion's rescued children.

"Rhosyn?" Paul said slowly.

"I'm so glad to see you here," Rhosyn gushed. "I was so happy to hear that Mr. Gower sponsored you, but I wanted to check on you."

Paul's lips turned up in a smile, but something in his eyes seemed vacant, a strange flatness Rhosyn hadn't remembered in his expression. "I was glad to be sponsored, too."

"Are you feeling alright?" Rhosyn resisted the urge to press the back of her hand to his forehead and check for a fever. He seemed glassy-eyed, and taking care of him was a habit that died hard.

"Yes," Paul assured. "Just tired from learning how to be a proper footman."

"They're not working you too hard, are they?"

Paul shook his head. "I mostly use my Talent to help Mrs. Gower sleep—she suffers from insomnia—and lend a hand at parties like this."

Rhosyn opened her mouth to tell Paul to reach out to her if he was mistreated, but a hand on her elbow interrupted her.

"I think some of the other guests might be offended you prefer the footman's company over theirs," Joseph murmured in her ear.

The heat of annoyance flared in Rhosyn's chest, but she knew Joseph was right, and her irritation was further soothed by the apologetic look Joseph gave Paul. As Rhosyn let Joseph guide her into the thick of the party, Paul resumed his initial posture against the wall, looking like a decorative statue.

They picked their way through the assembled guests, looking for their host, the only person Rhosyn expected to recognize in there. The thick aroma of expensive perfumes mixing in the air threatened to overwhelm Rhosyn more than the cacophony of smells down at the ports ever did. Some women had already congregated near the piano where a lady much more well-bred than herself was picking out a cheerful melody. Rhosyn couldn't help but think that Scarlett played much better.

Joseph spotted Mr. Gower in a knot of gentlemen at the far end of the room and jerked his chin, indicating they should head in that direction. Just as they stepped into the circle surrounding Mr. Gower, a familiar voice sounded from Rhosyn's right.

"Why, if it isn't Ms. Walsh."

Rhosyn's eyebrows rose at the sight of Mr. Blakely, this time dressed in eggplant purple silk, a silver cane with some sort of animal head at the top balanced loosely in his hand.

"I see you are familiar with my guests of honor, Officer Walsh and Police Chief Thorne." Mr. Gower puffed up as he spoke, as if having such a collection of people in his drawing room was a momentous accomplishment. "I invited them after they returned some of my wife's most valuable jewels to her."

"Did they now?" Mr. Blakely asked, his tone impressed even as something inscrutable passed over his face.

"They did, although I wish they would apprehend the scoundrel that stole them in the first place."

Joseph stiffened beside Rhosyn, but Mr. Gower plowed ahead as if oblivious to the sore spot he obviously struck.

"And after the ball at the palace, I simply had to have Mr. Blakely to one of our soirees. Mrs. Gower was so taken with his contortionists that she insisted I invite him over at once."

"I'm afraid I missed the contortionists," Rhosyn admitted to Mr. Gower, although her eyes kept darting to Mr. Blakely.

"I heard you were drawn away by a commotion," Mr. Blakely commented. "It's a shame, I would have liked another dance."

Rhosyn usually tried to avoid blushing at all costs, as the flush clashed terribly with her flame-red hair, but she felt heat climbing up her chest to her neck. For the first time, she understood ladies' urges to carry a fan.

"I'm afraid there won't be any dancing tonight to remedy the situation," Mr. Gower said apologetically, "but maybe a game of cards would suffice?"

"I certainly wouldn't mind a hand of Whist," Rhosyn offered, a sly smile inching across her face. "Chief Thorne and I will be a team."

"Then, Mr. Blakely and I will play against you," Mr. Gower offered as he ushered them over towards one of the tables set up around the edges of the room for just such a purpose.

As they walked, Joseph grumbled in Rhosyn's ear, "You know I'm terrible at Whist."

Indeed, every time a deck of cards came out at the Woodrow's occasional dinner party, it became a tight race between Rhosyn and Benedict to see who would win the most hands, with Joseph losing trick after trick.

"It doesn't matter, I'm good enough for the both of us," Rhosyn murmured back.

"I don't think fine society takes kindly to cheating." Joseph spoke low enough that only Rhosyn could hear.

She grinned.

"Then they won't find out."

And so, Rhosyn found herself seated at a small square table with Joseph directly across from her and Mr. Gower and Mr. Blakely to her left and right. Before anybody could offer, Rhosyn snapped up the deck of cards and began shuffling.

Out of habit, she showed off a bit, making the cards flutter down in a perfect bridge before tossing them back and forth from hand to hand. Joseph cleared his throat and Rhosyn looked up, finding Mr. Gower glaring at her with undisguised disapproval. She might have expected as much, as the ladies of breeding he was used to would not have spent their youths among sharps in gambling dens.

More disappointing, though, was the scowl Mr. Blakely shot towards her hands as her fingers deftly controlled the cards through their acrobatics. Rhosyn resisted the urge to duck her head and dealt four even hands. After all, who was Mr. Blakely to judge her for knowing her way around a deck of cards, when he owned a circus?

The match began with Mr. Gower, as he sat to Rhosyn's right, and Mr. Blakely promptly took the trick with the queen of spades. Joseph lost the next trick by playing the ten of diamonds, but it was worth it to find out that Mr. Gower did not have any of the correct suit. On the next trick, Mr. Gower played the queen of hearts, already confidently reaching out to sweep the cards onto his side of the table when Rhosyn stopped him by slapping down the ace of hearts.

"Don't get too confident," she teased as she swept the cards away, using Mr. Gower's moment of consternation to flick a card up her sleeve. Now the queen of hearts replaced the three of spades in her hand.

Honestly, maybe she should have worn gowns with these wide, lacy sleeves in the gambling dens of the lower city. They made it incredibly easy to palm a card.

"Maybe you're the one that's too confident," Mr. Blakely quipped. "What if we made this more interesting?"

"I wouldn't have taken you for a gambling man," Rhosyn shot back.

"Well, I'm certainly not," Joseph grumbled.

"Me neither," Mr. Gower agreed.

"Then what about a bet between just me and Ms. Walsh," Mr. Blakely suggested. His voice took on a low timbre that made Rhosyn sit up straighter in her chair.

"And what would we be betting?" she asked.

"If I win, you have to be a special guest at one of my circus's performances," Mr. Blakely said firmly.

"That hardly seems like an imposition," Rhosyn pointed out.

"Imposing isn't my goal. And what would you like if you win?"

Rhosyn narrowed her eyes at him thoughtfully. "I want you to tell me what act you performed in the circus."

Mr. Blakely's eyes flashed. "How do you know I ever performed? Maybe I just run the shows."

Rhosyn snorted, nodding to his outfit. "I know a showman when I see one."

"Alright, if you win, I'll tell you about my act in the circus, if I performed at all."

They reached across the table to shake on it. As Mr. Blakely's hand grasped hers, rough calluses at the base of his fingers scraped her palm. She raised her eyebrows. Maybe he was a juggler.

Then they returned to the game. They went around the table playing the first card, both teams being evenly matched. Coming into the last trick, both teams were tied, and Mr. Blakely smiled at Rhosyn triumphantly.

"I'm afraid you'll never know my hidden performance skills," he said in mock disappointment.

It was Rhosyn's turn to set down the opening card—her last one—and she grinned. "You're so confident you can best the queen of hearts?"

Mr. Blakely blinked down at the red silhouette staring up at him from the table. Slowly, he laid down his own card, the jack of clubs.

"Oh ho!" Mr. Gower clapped his hands in delight, even though his team had lost. "Now, Mr. Blakely, you must tell us of your hidden talent."

Mr. Blakely stiffened.

"Oh, I didn't mean Talent as in..." Mr. Gower hurried to rectify himself.

"Of course not," Mr. Blakely waved a hand of dismissal, as if Rhosyn hadn't felt the air quiver as the muscles in his body went rigid a moment earlier. "But maybe a demonstration of my skills would be a better explanation."

"Some entertainment!" Mr. Gower exclaimed, clearly pleased to have a similar show to the King at his party.

"I'll need a few things though," Mr. Blakely said, "A knife, an apple, and of course a lovely volunteer."

"I think you have your volunteer right here," Joseph chimed in, gesturing to Rhosyn.

"As long as you promise not to be scared," Mr. Blakely said, something hard and challenging in his gaze.

"Oh, so this is going to be dangerous? I'm growing more excited by the second," Rhosyn quipped.

"I'll see if I can't get a servant to fetch the other things." Mr. Gower pushed to his feet, meandering off to find one of the footmen doing their best to blend into the walls.

An anticipatory silence fell over the table, broken by Joseph. "So how does a young man like yourself come to be running a circus?"

"It belonged to my father." Mr. Blakely folded his hands carefully on the table in front of him. "When he passed five years ago, I knew he would want me to keep it running."

"Ah, a family business," Joseph nodded. "I'm sorry to hear of your father, though."

A crash sounded from above them before Mr. Blakely could speak. Rhosyn's gaze snapped to the ceiling above her, the chandelier quivering with the force of the noise. A hush fell over the assembled partygoers. Another crash, this time accompanied by the sound of shattering glass, and Rhosyn was on her feet.

Joseph was hot on her heels, as she darted through the crowded parlor towards the grand stairs in the entrance, cards forgotten on the table behind them. Hindered as she was by her dress, Joseph overtook her as they bounded up the stairs. They turned right at the top, in the direction of the noise.

Mr. Gower stood red-faced with a stricken expression on his face, the carnage of what appeared to have been a library around him. "There—When I... I came in and there was somebody here... They tried to attack me!"

"Which way did they go?" Joseph demanded, his commanding officer persona surfacing in the moment of chaos.

Mr. Gower pointed to the hallway behind them. As one, they turned and looked down the series of doors on the upper level.

"We didn't pass them on the way up the stairs, so they must still be here," Joseph thought out loud.

"I'll sweep the rooms on the right, you get the ones on the left," Rhosyn suggested. She took two steps down the hallway, before Joseph's hand on her arm stopped her.

She turned and found him holding out a knife, handle first. She took it, observing it to be the flat kind that Nate wore no fewer than nine of beneath his clothes.

Rhosyn raised her brows at Joseph.

"I've picked up a thing or two," he grumbled.

With that, they set off down the hallway. Rhosyn peeked into every darkened room she passed, looking for any wardrobes that could hide a thief or open windows that could serve as an escape route. The hilt of the knife was smooth and heavy in her palm as she held it in a reverse grip.

Looking into the third room, a guest bedroom by the looks of it, she was glad for the weapon in her grasp, although part of her itched for her trusty brass knuckles. She wasn't as good with a knife as Nate, and it had been too long since she wielded anything but her police baton.

Every room Rhosyn glanced in appeared completely undisturbed, although the amount and opulence made Rhosyn's head spin. All the children who had crammed into narrow bunks in the Lion's Den could nearly have their own bedrooms here.

When she reached the last door on the right side, she paused. The modest-sized sitting room appeared deserted, but something about the stillness of the air drew Rhosyn further into the room. Her eye caught on a large fireplace along the far wall and her brow furrowed.

Scarlett had relayed a horrifying story about escaping up a chimney one time, and it flickered through Rhosyn's mind now.

Maybe—

The open door slammed into Rhosyn, catching her in the temple and nearly knocking her to the ground. As she took a step to regain her balance, she tripped over her skirt and had to grab onto a nearby settee with her free hand to remain upright.

Her assailant took the moment to jump out from behind the door where he had been hiding. As he stepped into the beam of light coming in from the hallway, Rhosyn gasped.

"You!"

THE TALENTED FAIRY TALES

Standing in Mr. Gower's sitting room was the Hood, complete with fabric covering nearly all of his face and a miniature crossbow strapped to his forearm. He pressed the advantage in Rhosyn's moment of surprise, lashing out with a madcap right hook.

Rhosyn ducked, the blow barely missing her and wind from it ruffling her rapidly deteriorating hairstyle. As she sidestepped, she threw out an elbow, catching the Hood square in his stomach.

He let out a soft *oomph* but was not deterred, taking advantage of Rhosyn's proximity to throw an upper cut. Rhosyn tried to dodge, but her skirts caught on the table behind her, and she couldn't get completely out of the way in time. The blow glanced off her cheekbone, skittering across her temple.

A familiar ringing filled her ears from the impact. Rhosyn's lips pulled back in an expression halfway between a grin and a snarl. She leaped forward as best she could, given the constraints of her current attire. Her fists flew in a series of rapid blows to Hood's face and torso.

He blocked most of them with his forearms, but Rhosyn was too vicious a brawler and pummeled through his defenses, landing a solid blow to his shoulder.

The Hood staggered back, the grace with which he had scampered over rooftops disappearing in the face of Rhosyn's assault. She prepared to leap, hoping to pin him to the ground and rip the covering from his face.

Before she could act, Joseph burst through the still open door, clearly drawn by the commotion. His appearance distracted Rhosyn just enough that she didn't notice the Hood fish his hand into his pocket until it was too late.

Glass shattered as Hood threw a small vial to the ground, and immediately a thick smoke with an odd bluish tint filled the air. It nearly blocked the silhouettes of the two men from view as it billowed up from the ground.

Rhosyn jumped forward into it with an annoyed growl. She was not going to lose her mark a second time, letting him disappear in a puff of smoke like some half-rate magician.

As she stepped into the fumes, they filled her nose and she coughed around the strangely sweet scent. The smoke swam around her. Or maybe it was her vision. Rhosyn continued to push forward, but her equilibrium was nowhere to be found. Her silky slippers, so different from the thick soled boots of her uniform, caught on the carpet.

Her knees hit the ground before she knew she was falling, the world continuing to spin around her. The Hood emerged from the smoke, looking down at her with his head cocked. Rhosyn tried to curse at him but her tongue was too large and thick against her teeth.

Instead of responding, the Hood bent down. An odd shiver ran up Rhosyn's spine as he appeared to reach for her, only to pick up something on the ground at her side.

He held up a playing card—the three of spades, Rhosyn knew—that must have fallen out of her sleeve during their altercation. Without a word he tucked it into his pocket, offered a tiny, mocking bow, and disappeared.

Rarely had Rhosyn been so happy to collapse onto the too-soft bed in her too-quiet bedroom. She flopped onto her coverlet, burying her face in the pillows. Lying perfectly still, she hoped sleep would take the last of her wooziness away.

Whatever had been in the smoke bomb the Hood had used hadn't ever knocked her completely unconscious, but it had left her and Joseph disoriented enough to do nothing but lay on the ground while he made an escape. The cloth across Hood's face, likely combined with him knowing to hold his breath, had given him a chance to slip away into the night.

By the time Mr. Gower came and opened a window to let the fresh air in, their culprit was nowhere to be found. Unfortunately, the night had not ended there.

While the rest of the party guests had left quickly, scared off by the commotion and threat of an intruder, Rhosyn and Joseph stayed as Mr. Gower went through his documents and valuables to ascertain if anything was taken.

As their host did, Rhosyn ventured through the house looking for signs of forced entry. By the time Mr. Gower announced that nothing had been taken, she had found no signs of how the Hood may have entered, although with so many comings and goings for the evening's revelries, and not knowing what he looked like under the mask, it was possible he may have slipped in unnoticed without even picking a lock.

Rhosyn and Joseph had shared a carriage back to the middle city, Joseph resting his face in his hands.

"Why would they try to rob him after we just managed to return his wife's jewels to him?" he asked in a tone of utmost despair.

Rarely one for quiet, Rhosyn had just shaken her head and looked out the window. In two weeks, she had gone to two parties that ended in ruined dresses and failed chases. Even before she was an officer of the Royal Police, Rhosyn had tasked herself with protecting the people of London in whatever way she could. Recently, she had failed at every turn.

Now she rolled onto her back with a sigh, closing her eyes and letting her mind drift. Despite the unusual heaviness of her limbs from the remnant of the drugs in her system, Rhosyn's blood rushed through her body with unnerving speed. She would not be able to sleep soon. It had been too long since she had been in a proper brawl, and even just the taste of a fight with the Hood today had been enough to reactivate old instincts. Hell, the last time she had been able to let her reflexes take over like that was when she fought Scarlett in the Wolves' fighting pits. She missed it—the adrenaline and freedom that came from throwing herself at a problem with everything she had.

Rhosyn rubbed a hand over her eyes. She was now an officer for the Royal Police, and that was the best way for her to protect the city she had called home all her life—where she had chosen to stay to be with her adoptive family even when adventure and the sea had tugged at her blood. It didn't do to dwell on such things, though, and she forced her mind to focus on something else.

The memory of trading blows with the Hood morphed into exchanging easy jabs with Mr. Blakely over cards. Disappointment flooded her that he, along with the rest of the guests, had been gone by the time she and Joseph recovered from the drugged smoke. It was probably for the best though. As much as she enjoyed Mr. Blakely's charms, it was clear she should keep him at arm's length.

With the way he had stiffened when Mr. Gower spoke of being Talented, and how determined he seemed to be to climb the social ladder by brushing elbows with the elite and wealthy, she doubted Mr. Blakely's casual flirtations would continue if he were to find out about her checkered past.

Still, if she wasn't going to be able to sleep anyways, it didn't hurt to imagine. She and Mr. Blakely might meet again, but instead of leading her towards a dance floor, they would break out into a shadowed corner of the garden—perhaps an ostentatious hedge maze like the Worthingtons had.

But then what would he do? Mr. Blakely was a gentleman, but Rhosyn was far from a lady. She knew how things would go in the darkened alley of the lower city, but proper romantic trysts were not in her repertoire.

In line with these thoughts, the vision morphed, so it wasn't Mr. Blakely she pressed herself against in some darkened corner, but a masked figure with a hood pulled low over his face. With those powerful thighs and broad shoulders, Rhosyn didn't doubt that the Hood could easily hoist her in his arms.

She shook herself, snapping her eyes open and tracing her gaze over the spiderweb cracks in the plaster ceiling. She really wasn't fit for society if her mind preferred to ponder romantic entanglements with the man who had just punched her before leaving her fighting for consciousness on the floor. Maybe she just hadn't been in a proper brawl in too long.

Rhosyn's fingers drifted up to her face, tracing over her battered cheekbone, the ache of something deeper bothering her more than the pain of the bruise. She missed running with the Lions.

Joseph intercepted Rhosyn the moment she walked in the door, pouncing on her as if he had been waiting. She blinked at him groggily, having tossed and turned most of the night. The deep furrow between his brows chased the sleepiness from her mind though.

"Mr. Gower sent a message early this morning." Joseph began without preamble. "He found that something was missing."

"What?"

"His household staff, the Talented ones," Joseph admitted grimly.

They had been walking through the mess of desks towards Joseph's station in the corner, but Rhosyn froze.

"Paul..."

"He and Olivia are missing," Joseph explained.

Rhosyn turned on her heel, ready to storm out and march through the city until she found her former charges, but Joseph's hand on her shoulder stopped her. Her head snapped toward him and at the very last second she schooled her face out of the snarl that threatened the corners of her mouth.

It wasn't Joseph's fault.

"I already have Davies and Fletcher on it. They've been investigating the Hood for months now."

"And do they have any leads?" Rhosyn snapped.

"I need you in the lower city," Joseph side stepped the question, giving her all the answers she needed.

Rhosyn pulled her arm from his grip, but his beseeching expression kept her from storming away.

"There was another turf war in the lower city last night, by the train yards," Joseph admitted in a low tone. "They dispersed by the time we got there, but my gut tells me it was the Foxes. This is escalating too quickly. With so much happening with the Hood in the upper city, I need to know I have somebody I can trust keeping an eye on things."

The heaviness in Joseph's eyes said the words he left unspoken. He knew she would take care of the lower city, because those were her people. While many of the Royal Police were from the middle city, with the higher-ranking officers consorting with those in the upper city like Chief Cook had, the dirty back alleys and dice houses were Rhosyn's London.

"Alright," she acquiesced. "But don't keep me in the dark."

Or I may not be able to stop myself from performing my own investigation.

"That's why I told you. I'm not a Chief that keeps secrets."

"I know," Rhosyn nodded. In that moment, she was sure he was comparing himself to his former mentor.

And so, Rhosyn found herself walking a familiar beat among her usual streets, eyes darting around for signs of violence. She had roamed these neighborhoods on many days where furtive glances and a certain tenor in the voices of those out and about had made the city seem like a powder keg about to blow—usually when turf wars and skirmishes reached a peak.

Today wasn't one of those days. The sun was strong enough to pierce the perpetual smog, and voices echoed loudly off the cobblestones as people shouted their greetings and went about their business. Rhosyn frowned. Perhaps this area was too far from the rail yards to be affected by last night's bloodshed.

She directed her steps away from the shops and factories and in the direction of the mess of intersecting rails where goods from the factories and those received from the port would begin their journey to the rest of the country. It wasn't an area she spent much time in as a youth, being firmly ensconced in Scorpion territory, but she knew it was a prime area for violence and crooked deals. The rail workers cleared out at night, and there were plenty of heavy shadows and abandoned train cars where people could conduct business best done in the dark.

So, as she stepped out from behind a spare train car languishing on the track, she started in surprise at the brightly colored sight that greeted her. Workers scurried about, loading bundles and boxes into carts that then trundled out to the surrounding streets. At the epicenter of the activity stood a train, brightly colored in green and yellow, a far cry from the dark steam engines that dominated the area.

Rhosyn drifted closer, gaze catching on words printed on the side of one car in dramatic, curling script.

Archer's Circus

No sooner had her brain fired in recognition, than a familiar voice greeted her.

"You certainly don't take any time off."

Rhosyn spun on her heel, little pebbles crunching underfoot as she turned to see Mr. Blakely. Today, the trappings of a man trying to wheedle his way into society were gone, replaced with a workman's garb. A light shirt was tucked into plain trousers, his sleeves rolled up to nearly his elbows. A sheen of sweat made his hair cling to forehead, dark aside from the contrasting streak of silver at his right temple.

"Neither do you, it seems," Rhosyn said, trying to keep her gaze from lingering on his bare forearms. Perhaps there was something to exposed ankles being indecent, if such an innocuous thing could be so thoroughly distracting.

"Ah, but I didn't end up working last night," he responded, crossing his arms across a surprisingly broad chest for one of his stature.

"I'm afraid I might become an unpopular party guest, if every event I attend continues to end in a police investigation," she griped.

Mr. Blakely's eyes twinkled. "Or maybe it will just give you an air of mystique."

"That doesn't get you as far in law enforcement as it might in the circus," Rhosyn pointed out.

Mr. Blakely laughed, the sound light and easy. Rhosyn had found him charming in all his finery, but she found her smile coming more freely with him like this.

"And what brings you down to the railyard the morning after such an eventful celebration, Mr. Blakely?" Rhosyn prodded.

He waved a dismissive hand. "Call me Ansel, please. Nobody else in this traveling pack of fools calls me Mr. Blakely, so I save the airs for when I'm trying to impress."

"Well, Ansel," Rhosyn started, a strange amount of bite working its way into her tone as she processed that she was not somebody he was intent on impressing—although she had presumed as much in the quiet of her bedroom the night before. "What brings you to such a part of town?"

"The rest of my show has arrived," he explained, gesturing to the train behind her. "I came to London a few weeks ago with just a handful of my best acts, trying to drum up interest. After performing at the King's party, the Merry Men have gained enough notoriety for me to bring my entire circus for an extended stay. They just arrived."

Rhosyn's eyes narrowed. "Did your train have any trouble upon arriving?"

"No," Mr. Blakely—Ansel—cocked his head. "Other than the ungodly early hour it arrived this morning."

Rhosyn considered him. Her mental hackles rose at the thought that he might be lying. His train had arrived at the spot of a dangerous turf war just hours after it occurred. What's more, he had been at the last two events that had ended in thefts or kidnapping. Then again, so had she.

Ansel observed her as she thought, expression guileless.

"I guess it's for the best that yesterday's festivities ended early then, if you had to be up before the sun," Rhosyn commented.

Ansel shrugged. "Despite the fact that I lost our bet, I found myself disappointed that I didn't get to show off my skills for you. After all, your slight of hand was very good, and I don't like to be upstaged."

A fire in Rhosyn's chest sparked at his accusation—despite the fact that she had cheated—but settled into the heat of a challenge, instead of rage, when he saw that his expression was more amused than angry.

"Only a sore loser confuses luck for cheating," she quipped.

"Oh, I'm no stranger to luck," Ansel answered cryptically, "but I do have a knack for remembering what cards have been played. I'm pretty sure you played the Queen of Hearts twice."

"Well, there's no proof of that."

Ansel's eyes flashed, green catching in the sun like the emerald at the center of Mr. Gower's stolen hat pin. "Then I guess I still owe you a demonstration."

"Technically, you only have to tell me about your circus act."

"And deny a performer a chance for dramatic effect?" Ansel asked. It struck Rhosyn as an odd comment somehow, in the broad daylight where he seemed to be just another man working to unload a train of its cargo, in plainclothes with a smudge of something like grease along his jaw. Last night, in all his finery, he had certainly seemed the consummate showman, but now it seemed as if he was missing something. It left Rhosyn unbalanced, wondering which man was the real one—the suave Mr. Blakely she played cards with last night, or Ansel who she bantered with in a trainyard.

"Maybe we can still find time for you to show off," Rhosyn suggested.

"My circus will be performing its opening show next weekend. Why don't you come and see for yourself. Front row seats are hard to come by, but I know the owner," Ansel joked.

"Now you're just cashing in your side of the bet."

"I have very little incentive to play fair against you." He grinned, expression sly.

Rhosyn's rational mind told her to refuse his offer—steer clear of a social climber who likely wouldn't take kindly to her background. After all, she had a thief to catch, the Foxes to bring down, and missing Talented to find.

But Ansel wore his smile like a challenge, and Rhosyn never backed down.

"I expect tickets on opening night."

"So it shall be." Ansel opened his mouth as if to say something more, but his gaze caught on something over her shoulder. "Careful with the trapezes! You'll get them all tangled doing that."

In a second, he strode away, commanding the workers who were loading bundles of ropes into a wheelbarrow. Rhosyn stood watching for a moment in the middle of the mayhem, a rock in the center of a hive of worker bees. Then she turned from the Archer's Circus train and began weaving her way through the much bleaker and less lively engines.

She wasn't sure what she expected to find. The gangs of the lower city were skilled at hit and run tactics, striking each other swiftly and melting back into the shadows before the authorities arrived. Such guerrilla tactics were how the Lions had thrived for nearly a decade.

It was doubtful the Foxes left any more evidence around than boot prints in gravel, already worn away by the stomping of the rail workers this morning. Maybe the trains themselves would give her a clue as to what they might be smuggling that was worth spilling blood over.

A quick perusal of the manifest in the small office at the side of the rail office showed nothing of note, besides the arrival of the Archer's Circus train, which she already knew about. The only things coming in and out yesterday and today were steel and coal, as well as a large shipment of textiles. The last would be very valuable—prices had been driven up enormously since Contessa advised the King to enact a policy demanding fair wages for the factory workers—but not something any gang would try to steal.

Rhosyn left the rail yard behind her with lead in her usually bouncy gate. Perhaps Chief Thorne's faith in her was misplaced, thinking she could protect the lower city from whatever trouble was brewing.

A comforting weight like a blanket settled over Rhosyn's shoulders as she opened the sky-blue front door of the Woodrow's house. The only thing that would make it feel more like coming home would be climbing up from the secret passage beneath Nate's desk in the study. However, it had been filled with stones and boarded up after the Royal Police were alerted to the secret passageways' presence a few years ago. Nate was unwilling to give those that might want revenge such easy access to his home—and his wife—now that the secret of tunnels was no longer owned only by the Lions.

Still, Rhosyn was no more inclined to knock on the front door than she was when entering through a trap door, and she strode into the foyer and past the sweeping staircase casually. Nate and Contessa wouldn't mind. After all, two of their most frequent visitors were Kristoff and Scarlett, who Rhosyn knew through experience preferred windows to doors.

Rhosyn meandered through the parlor, listening for signs that the Woodrows were home. It looked much the same as it had since Nate first moved into the mansion, elegant but plain furniture and nondescript still-life paintings adorning the walls. The most prominent sign of life was the overflowing vases on every surface, immaculate flowers kept blooming by Gregor's presence. As much as Rhosyn had hoped the place would be more lively after Contessa moved in, she had proved disinterested in decorating, most of her time spent either helping the King or working with the Lions on projects of more questionable legality.

Still, certain details spoke of the home's inhabitants. An ornate marble chessboard sat prominently on the table in the middle of the room, a birthday present for Contessa that Nate had agonized over several years back. Dozens of books, a mix of poetry, fairy tales, and politics, lay stacked on the surfaces not occupied by flowers. On top of one of the teetering piles, a silvery blade gleamed, apparently unable to have been packed onto Nate's relatively well armed form.

It appeared they weren't home.

Rhosyn sighed, turning towards the rear of the house where the kitchens would be, along with the possibility of hot tea and Gregor's round smile. She should probably go try to get a good night's sleep, but she wasn't willing to leave just yet. This house brought her more of a feeling of home than the barren bedroom in the middle city.

Hand reaching for the doorknob that would lead her into the kitchen, Rhosyn froze, ears pricked at a sudden noise. It had sounded like a groan, and Rhosyn hesitated to burst into the kitchen. While it wouldn't be the first time she had accidentally barged in on the Woodrows in a compromising position, Contessa was still enough of a lady to be mortified every time.

It came again—a breathy moan in a voice Rhosyn recognized. She smiled and grabbed the doorknob.

"Kristoff, stop defiling Gregor," she shouted.

From the other side of the door came a scuffling and a deep chuckle, along with a quieter, more embarrassed-sounding groan, then the door sprung open.

"How do you know *he* wasn't defiling *me*?" Kristoff asked by way of greeting.

Rhosyn raised a brow as she stepped past him into the kitchen.

"Maybe nobody was defiling anybody," Gregor remarked in a deceptively even tone from where he stood at the wooden table, chopping potatoes as if he had always been doing so, but a blooming bruise just below his ear gave him away.

"Sorry to interrupt," Rhosyn teased, bumping Gregor with her hip on her way past him.

"Would you like some tea?" he deflected.

Rhosyn nodded as she perched on the wide windowsill at the back of the room swinging her legs. "Thank you. I'd be glad to have the walk over not be for nothing, since it appears Contessa and Nate aren't home."

"I'm afraid they haven't made it home for dinner yet this week," Gregor admitted as he lifted the kettle onto the stove. "If you need something though, I can give them a message."

Rhosyn shook her head. "I don't need to worry them if they're already that busy. The Royal Police are working on it after all."

"But?" Kristoff folded his arms as he leaned one hip against the table in the center of the room, his deep blue eyes sharp.

Rhosyn cocked her head. "But, what?"

"But obviously you're still worried if you came."

Rhosyn's boot heels thumped against the wall behind her as she considered Kristoff. His dark hair managed to look perfectly disheveled from Gregor's hands, and whirls of black ink covered his forearms where he had pushed his shirtsleeves up. Every inch of him still screamed rogue, despite the fact that most of the jobs he ran these days were on behalf of the crown. After all, Nate and Contessa worried about the specifics of how Kristoff executed his missions, while King Byron remained glad to benefit from having an inside source in the underbelly of the city.

A lick of envy flared in Rhosyn's heart, and she moved to quash it quickly.

When the Lions had ceased to be a street gang and Rhosyn had considered her future, Kristoff had been the first to encourage her to train for the Royal Police. He knew she craved a purpose and action, and he convinced her this was her chance to go straight—to live the life she might have had if not for the Inquiries. When she asked him why he didn't join the Police too, he ruffled her already messy hair and told him he was far too much of a troublemaker to ever wear a uniform.

Now she wondered if the same couldn't be said about her.

"It's Paul and Olivia," Rhosyn admitted. "They're missing."

"And you're investigating it with the Royal Police?"

Rhosyn shook her head. "There are officers on it, and Joseph wants me to stay in on a case in the lower city. But…"

"But Lions protect their pack." It was Gregor who finished for Rhosyn in a decisive tone.

"I just worry about doing off-the-books investigating when Joseph is trying so hard to keep the Royal Police spotless," Rhosyn pointed out.

"Isn't blindly following orders what got the force into such a mess in the first place?" Kristoff asked.

Rhosyn folded her arms. "Only because the Chief was the one doing illegal things."

"Still, I think that's enough evidence that the spirit of the law is more important than the letter of it."

"I'm not sure it would be above board for a Royal Police officer to concede that point." Rhosyn frowned.

"And yet you came to some of the most notorious criminals in London for advice."

Rhosyn resisted the very immature urge to stick her tongue out at Kristoff for verbally backing her into a corner. He had a way of pulling argumentative urges out of her like Rhosyn imagined a sibling would, if she had been lucky enough to have one.

"You have good instincts," Gregor chimed in more gently. "Chief Thorne knows it, I'm sure."

Rhosyn jumped as the teakettle started whistling, and Gregor turned away to remove it from the heat. Kristoff kept observing Rhosyn pensively, the corner of his usual devilish smirk slipping slightly.

"I'll keep my ear to the ground for any news about Paul and Olivia," he promised quietly, "But I don't think you should be hard on yourself for wanting to make sure they're safe."

Rhosyn nodded her thanks as Gregor bustled over with a cup of tea. Like a brother, Kristoff had a way of knowing what she needed to hear, just like he knew how best to tease her.

"Maybe you just need a man in your life to distract you," Kristoff prodded. "Contessa said something about you dancing with a gentleman at the King's ball."

"I hardly see how who I dance with has anything to do with my job as a police officer," Rhosyn shot back.

Gregor grinned. "He's just trying to play matchmaker with everybody since he's tired of waiting for Contessa and Nate to have a baby he can slowly corrupt to his villainous ways."

"They say they're trying, but I hardly see how that's happening when they spend every night working into the small hours of the morning." Kristoff threw his hands up in defeat.

Rhosyn snorted into her tea. "Well, I'm sorry but I don't think I'll be supplying you with a child to dote on any time soon, either. I'm more concerned, at the moment, with finding the ones who have gone missing."

Rhosyn jumped up and down, wiggling inelegantly to pull the too small pants over her hips and thighs. Finally, she managed to button them, blowing a stray curl off her sweaty forehead. For years, she had worn only the navy uniform and gold buttons of the Royal Police, or an occasional gown gifted to her by Contessa and altered to fit, but tonight's task required discretion. So, she had dug to the very bottom of her small chest of clothes and fished out the black shirt and trousers she used to wear when the Lion's went on liberation missions.

Fortunately, Rhosyn had filled in since the lanky days of her teenage years, but she had failed to update her espionage wardrobe. She would just have to deal with tight pants during tonight's creeping about, and avoid thinking about how

Contessa would blush at the way the trousers showed every curve of her ass and thighs.

Rhosyn wasn't exactly a lady, after all.

Shoving a black scarf into her shirt, to conceal her hair once she reached her destination, Rhosyn slipped out of her middle city residence and turned her steps uphill. Where Rhosyn normally strode confidently down the middle of the street where all could see her uniform, tonight, she stuck to the edges where the shadows of buildings might obscure her face. As the houses changed from wood to stone, becoming more widely spaced with blooming flowerbeds out front, a thrill ran up Rhosyn's spine.

Something wild in her lifted its head in interest at this new development, as if it had missed illicit midnight missions. She mentally wagged a finger at it. This was a one-time thing, to make sure Paul and Olivia were found. Still, she shivered as she paused to pull out her scarf and wrap it around her hair and lower face.

Soon, the silhouette of Mr. Gower's house shadowed the cobblestones in front of Rhosyn. Surveying the front of the house, the windows remained dark and impenetrable, concealing anything that might be happening within. No matter. Rhosyn was more interested in the back of the house where the servants' quarters resided.

She darted between shadows, creeping around towards the back of the mansion. Her brows drew together as the rear windows remained darkened, but the flickering of a lantern off to the side caught her eye. She crept towards it, finding the light seeping out the cracks around a large door, leading to what must be the carriage house and stables.

Rhosyn inched forward, pressing her palms to the wooden panels and aligning her eye with the seam between the double doors. With her narrow frame of vision, she could just make out a sleek black coach occupying the center of the stable, backlit in shadowy lighting that appeared to be spilling from one of the stalls.

She stiffened as voices drifted through the still night air. Straining forward, nearly pressing her nose into the door, she tried to distinguish words, but only succeeded in making out a faint murmur.

Perhaps it was only the groom, indulging in a little late night...conversation. But nobody knew more about the goings on in a great house than the help, so often treated as invisible but carrying secrets that could ruin many socialites if they so chose. Mr. Gower's household staff may have some inkling of what happened to Paul and Olivia.

As slowly as she could muster, Rhosyn unlatched the stable doors—still unlocked as if the groom hadn't yet closed up for the night—and pressed the door open. She sent up a silent thank you for the wealth that kept Mr. Gower's stable hinges well-oiled, as the wood silently swung forward just wide enough for her to slip inside and ease it shut behind her.

She placed her feet gingerly on the hay-strewn floor, soft boots padding gently as she inched towards the source of the voices. The voices became clearer, and she paused next to the coach, which took up the majority of the open space, crouching partially behind it near one of the large, spoked wheels to listen.

"—need them back as soon as possible."

Rhosyn frowned at the familiar voice. She hadn't expected to hear—

"They might still come back of their own accord, Mr. Gower."

She inhaled sharply through her nose, air full of the warm smell of hay and sleepy horses. What would Mr. Gower himself be doing in the stable in the middle of the night?

"If they wanted to come back, they wouldn't have left, Hamish." The voice was definitely Mr. Gower's, but gone was polish of civility that coated his tone in ballrooms and parties. He sounded frustrated.

"We don't know that. The Royal Police might still bring them back."

"The Royal Police wouldn't know a lead if it bit them on the nose."

Rhosyn bristled and tried not to think about how she herself was working outside of the Police's jurisdiction at the moment.

"I expect them back soon." Mr. Gower spoke again. "I refuse to change my plans."

"They weren't here for long enough for me to—"

"I don't take kindly to excuses, especially from you, Hamish." Mr. Gower interrupted the groom's attempts to explain. "Remember what will happen if you fail to help me."

A rustling came from the stall where the two men spoke, and Rhosyn's heart leapt into her throat as she realized Mr. Gower was about to step around the corner, with her only partially obscured by the shadow of his carriage. She had been so preoccupied by his conversation that she had failed to devise her plan of escape.

She sprang from her crouch, preparing to make a break for it, hoping she wouldn't be recognized even if she was seen. Before she could run, the door of the coach at her back slid open and an arm wrapped around her neck. She tipped backwards into the interior of the coach, another hand clamping over her mouth, muffling the instinctual scream that threatened to break free.

The carriage door closed before her with quiet *snick* as she squirmed in her assailant's hold, one arm firm across her chest as they hunched over her on the lushly upholstered seat.

"Quiet," a male voice hissed in her ear. "I don't want to get caught any more than you do."

Rhosyn froze, still but for the frantic pounding of her heart and the rushing beneath her skin. She knew that voice. Her eyes darted down, and sure enough, a wrist bow decorated the forearm banded across her heaving chest.

The pair stilled, listening for any sounds indicating their scuffle had been noticed. A shadowed silhouette drifted past the small glass window set into the door, but it didn't pause or give any indication they had been found.

Still, they didn't move yet, the only sound in the space their carefully schooled breathing. If Rhosyn's was a bit ragged, it was from the sudden jolt of adrenaline. It certainly wasn't the sudden wash of awareness coursing through her body as she strained to remain perfectly still, despite the press of the Hood against her back, his muscular thighs bracketing hers. His chest against her was certainly as solid as the width of his shoulders suggested it might be.

Rhosyn opened her mouth, quickly deciding to bite the Hood's palm. She needed him to let go of her, and certainly the immediate danger had passed. Before her teeth could close around the meat of his hand, he snatched it out of the way, as if he had sensed her intentions. Her teeth snapped on thin air.

"That wasn't very nice, considering how I just helped you." The Hood didn't release her, his fingers instead drifting up to where a coppery curl had slipped out of her scarf. He plucked at it gently, rubbing it between his thumb and pointer finger. The red of her hair was stark against the dark gloves he wore. Rhosyn swallowed.

"Ah, I thought I recognized you," the Hood murmured as if to himself. "I shouldn't have expected you to play fair."

"I'm not the one who has to drug my opponents to escape," Rhosyn hissed.

He huffed in what might have been a chuckle, the breath filtering through his mask warm and ticklish on her neck. Rhosyn squirmed.

The Hood tightened his grip. Rhosyn prepared to throw her head back and break his nose, but she hesitated. Even if it seemed they were now alone in the stables, she wasn't willing to risk a full-on brawl on the Gower's property—especially when she wasn't supposed to be there.

As if reading her thoughts, the Hood spoke. "And I'm not the Royal Police officer who appears to make a hobby of breaking and entering."

Rhosyn flushed, seriously considering breaking his nose anyways just for the satisfying crunch. "You were here the night of the party," she deflected. "What do you know?"

Maybe he was the one responsible for Olivia and Paul's disappearance. Perhaps an associate stole them away while the Hood distracted Rhosyn and Joseph. After all, Mr. Gower's description of his attacker didn't match the Hood...but then why would he be here now?

"Are you here to steal more Talented from their new lives?" she hissed accusingly.

The Hood's arm stiffened around her, but he didn't answer her question. "I'm going to let you go, and you're not going to tell anybody you saw me here, or you'll have to explain why you were here too."

"I'm investigating a crime scene. There's nothing hard to explain about that." Rhosyn hoped her words would distract him as she shifted surreptitiously in his grasp, searching for a way to slip free without things descending into a full out brawl. Then again, maybe throwing a few punches would clear her head.

"Something about the way you slipped in under cover of darkness makes me think that you don't exactly have a warrant."

He was right, but Rhosyn wasn't inclined to confirm that. Instead, she hooked her foot around his calf where she kneeled between his legs. She simultaneously threw her weight sideways, grabbing at the arm around her neck and grappling with her leg to take him down with her. The pair rolled on the floor of the carriage, the Hood falling on his back with a heavy *ooph* as Rhosyn landed on top of him.

The momentum of the fall from the seat was more than Rhosyn expected, and her shoulder crashed into the carriage door with a bone-rattling thump, slamming it open. She tipped out of the black box and hurtled to the ground below. The Hood held fast to her shoulders, following her down.

Rhosyn flung out her arms and bent her knees, trying to tuck into a roll that would bring her to her feet. A ripping sound filled the still air of the stable as Rhosyn failed to break her fall. Her forehead smacked the straw strewn floor, and her ears rang.

When awareness of her body beyond the sharp pain in her head returned, the Hood's weight was no longer on top of her, and the strange sensation of a cool breeze caressed her ass.

"I thought those pants might be a little tight for crime fighting," a familiar voice chuckled just above her. "If you were trying to distract me, it very nearly worked."

Then light, quick footsteps began retreating.

Rhosyn regained control of her limbs a second after realizing Hood was escaping. Hastily, she scrambled to her feet, grateful that the stable now appeared to be empty of both Mr. Gower and the groom, Hamish. She raced to the door, left slightly ajar, just in time to see a dark silhouette leap from the top of the garden fence, performing a flip in the air before landing lightly on his feet and darting off into the night.

With a sigh, Rhosyn let him go. The Hood seemed to be made of smoke, and the harder she tried to grasp him, the more he slipped through her fingers with surprising agility. She couldn't risk being caught chasing him through the streets at night and being forced to explain herself to Chief Thorne.

Rhosyn twisted and looked over her shoulder to assess the damage to her pants, finding the entire back middle seam torn open and amended her thoughts. She definitely couldn't be caught racing through the streets at night with her entire *bahookie* on display.

She slipped back into the stable and made sure to set the carriage to rights before exiting and shutting the door behind her. Once she had snuck back around to the front of the grand house and onto the street, she unwrapped the black scarf from her head and used it to tie around her waist. It would be enough to keep her halfway decent on the walk home, if any late-night drinkers were still wandering the streets.

Not that it seemed to matter too terribly much anymore. Hood had quite literally caught her with her pants down tonight before slipping away, and she still didn't know where to find Paul and Olivia.

Chapter Five

The flags at the zenith of each large tent flapped lazily in the thin breeze that gained energy this short distance from the concentrated buildings of the city. Rhosyn craned her neck to look up at the green banners emblazoned with the golden bow and arrow of Archer's Circus.

She picked her way through the main thoroughfare, boots sinking gently into the well-trodden ground of mud and hay. Even though the Circus had only been open for a day, word seemed to have spread quickly. What appeared to be half of London had turned out at the end of the workday to see the spectacle.

The air swirled with excitement and the rich, buttery aroma of popcorn, working to dispel the frustration that clung to Rhosyn's consciousness throughout her day patrolling the lower city. Even now, Mr. Gower's whispered conversation with Hamish replayed in her head as she tried to make sense of it and decide where she might look for Paul and Olivia next. Maybe she should turn around and spend the night scouring the rooftops for the Hood.

Instead, she trekked towards the tallest tent, standing proudly at the center of the festivities. That was where Ansel had indicated he would be when he sent her ticket with a messenger, and Rhosyn could certainly do with the distraction of some entertainment right now.

As she walked, she peeked through the entrances of some of the surrounding structures, revealing small stages occupied by brightly dressed jugglers or gaudily painted contortionists. At one point she jumped at the roar of a mighty beast somewhere nearby. She had seen posters for a lion tamer, and she hoped he was skilled enough to keep the animal in check.

Finally, she reached the grandest of the quickly erected structures, marveling that such a cathedral of green and white striped canvas could be constructed overnight. This tent seemed to be drawing the bulk of the crowds, and Rhosyn let herself drift inside with the milling tide.

The setup looked familiar: tightropes and trapezes towered above the stands, already filling with spectators. It seemed the acrobats were considered the crowning jewel of Archer's Circus—the Merry Men, as Ansel had introduced them.

As if summoned by her thoughts, a touch at her elbow drew Rhosyn from her thoughts, where she gaped at the network of ropes above her.

"I was hoping you'd come," Ansel said by way of greeting. He smiled magnanimously, just the barest peek of the silver stripe in his hair visible below the silk top hat he wore.

"Why wouldn't I?" Rhosyn followed in the direction he nudged her elbow, out of the thickest of the entering crowds.

"I know you're busy." Ansel shrugged. "Clearly you've been working."

Rhosyn glanced down at her pressed, navy-blue uniform, looking dusty after a full day's wear, and inwardly shrank. She might have changed, but she wasn't inclined to ruin one of the dresses Contessa gifted her in the muck of the grounds, and it had become clear last night that her older clothes were no longer a safe option.

"Crime never sleeps," Rhosyn grumbled.

And neither do I, she added silently.

"Then we'll have to make the most of your time off. I saved the best seat in the house for you." Ansel led them through the spectators, milling this way and that as they found their seats, and back behind a flap that appeared to separate the backstage area.

He turned right up a narrow set of wooden stairs, only slightly too deep to be called a ladder. Rhosyn took her first step upward only to find this angle gave her an extremely close view of Ansel's backside. Immediately, she paused, letting him get a few extra steps in front of her and looking determinedly at her feet as she followed. She should be behaving professionally, especially while in uniform, Rhosyn reminded herself, not gawking crassly like the lower city street urchin she was.

Such thoughts were forgotten when Ansel pulled back the curtain at the top of the steps and revealed a small box overlooking the stage from above. From this height, she was nearly level with some of the tightropes. As Ansel beckoned her into the space, she approached the edge and looked over the railing at the other spectators below.

What would it be like to be one of the acrobats, to dangle from this height with only your balance and wits to protect you? Even as the idea made her dizzy, a thrill ran up her spine.

"I take it you like the accommodations?" Ansel asked, a brow raised.

"I think a private box might be a little grand for just me," Rhosyn said, turning to the small number of comfortable-looking chairs crowded into the tight space.

"You did best me," Ansel argued.

"Don't think this will get you out of showing me your circus act." Rhosyn jabbed a finger into his chest. It was surprisingly firm, indicating more muscle than his size would suggest. "Were you an acrobat? The strong man?"

"You don't have much patience, do you?" Ansel deflected. "Even when you're given entertainment fit for a king to occupy you while you wait."

"Why is patience always the virtue people espouse?" Rhosyn grumbled. "Why can't getting things done be the virtue?"

Ansel chuckled. "I guarantee I'll give you the promised demonstration. For now, I must leave you to your own devices to go and get the show started."

With a small bow, he backed out of the space, leaving Rhosyn to take her seat. She didn't have to wait very long until Ansel appeared on the stage below, raising his arms. The voices of the spectators fell to hushed whispers, the air practically quivering with the barely contained tension of anticipation. It captured Rhosyn in its threads, pulling her to perch on the edge of her seat, leaning forward so she wouldn't miss anything.

As Ansel spoke, thanking the audience for coming and welcoming them to Archer's Circus, the Merry Men slipped quietly onto the platforms across from her, from which they would leap. They wore the same green outfits as before, and Rhosyn's heart rate accelerated in excitement. Sitting level with them, imagining diving off the edge in a freefall before catching the trapeze at the last moment, added a thrill she hadn't anticipated.

The crowd erupted in applause as Ansel finished his introduction, gesturing upwards to direct the rest of the audience's attention to the acrobats, moments before they began the dizzying dance of falling and flying.

Seeing the Merry Men for the second time did nothing to lessen the heart-pounding effect. Gravity seemed to have lifted its spell temporarily, letting the performers achieve feats that Rhosyn wouldn't have even dreamed of attempting.

As one of the men flipped off a platform before easily grabbing a swinging trapeze at the peak of its arc, the image of the Hood performing a perfect front flip from the fence last night flickered through her mind. She had entertained the thought he was one of the circus performers before, but dismissed it when she didn't spot anybody fitting his build at the King's ball. Maybe he hadn't been performing that night though. Or perhaps she had missed something.

Rhosyn's eyes narrowed as she began consuming the performance with a clinical eye. One by one, she appraised the men flying through the air. A good number of them she ruled out quickly for being too tall. A few were too thin, while several were bulkier than the wiry strength of the arm banded across her chest last night would suggest.

What's more, something in their posture was off. As awe inspiring as the Merry Men were, none of them quite carried themselves with the effortless confidence she remembered on the Hood as he repetitively slipped from her grasp.

Rhosyn shook herself. She was just exaggerating the Hood's prowess for being the most challenging and intriguing criminal she had encountered in years. These men were her best suspects. After all, she had encountered the Hood for the first time just the day before they performed at the King's ball.

She just needed evidence.

Rhosyn tore her attention from the spectacle before her, instead inspecting the rest of her surroundings. For now, she was unattended, and everybody in the vicinity was preoccupied with the performance. If there was any evidence to be found backstage, now was the time for an unapproved investigation.

With one last look to confirm Ansel's position at the corner of the stage, eyes darting between the forms flipping above him, Rhosyn slipped from the private booth. She descended the ladder to the ground level quickly and quietly. When she turned and looked around the backstage area, she found it deserted, as she had hoped.

Finding what she was looking for, though, might be another challenge entirely. The area wasn't exactly organized—or if it was, it was sensible only to the people who had done it. Cracked open crates with swathes of colored fabric spilling out the top dotted the area. Rhosyn had to slip past a large spinning wheel and a stack of painted wood slats as she perused the area.

Finally, in the back, against a wall that had green curtains hung against it, folded over as if for storage, lay a series of bundles. They looked like discarded clothes and personal effects—likely where the performers kept their things after changing into their less practical costumes.

Rhosyn knelt and began rifling through the bags and bundles with deft fingers. As she went, she carefully catalogued exactly how clothes were draped and packs stacked. It was a habit from years of lifting little trinkets and emptying purses to feed her young charges—and thankfully one that returned quickly when she wanted to investigate without giving herself away.

As she reached the third pile of belongings, she asked herself exactly what she was looking for. Maybe the familiar hood itself, or the wrist bow that the

Hood seemed to favor, although he might not carry those everywhere. She had already uncovered several small blades, but carrying a knife didn't necessarily mean one was a criminal. For those who walked alone at night, Rhosyn would nearly consider it reckless not too.

Although, as the fourth bundle revealed yet another set of knives—clearly well cared for and stored in sheathes that could easily be strapped to ankles or forearms—she did have to wonder at how well armed this performing troupe was.

So focused was Rhosyn on looking through the remaining contents of the satchel, intent on sussing out any hidden pockets that could contain incriminating evidence, that she didn't hear the footsteps coming up behind her. A hand reached over her shoulder and deftly pulled free one of the knives, forgotten in her hand as she continued her search.

She spun in place, already swinging her leg out in her crouch to catch her potential attacker in the ankles. Rhosyn stopped her kick just short, as she found Ansel staring down at her with a bemused expression.

He tossed the knife up, where it flipped twice before he plucked it out of the air easily by the handle. Rhosyn blinked, nearly forgetting that he had caught her looking through his performers' belongings. He hadn't even been looking at the knife as he tossed it. The only person who she had ever seen handle a blade so confidently before was Nate.

"You don't seem concerned with waiting for a warrant," he commented. He twirled the knife absent-mindedly and Rhosyn suddenly became all too aware of her position kneeling at his feet. She shot upright and scowled.

"What's that supposed to mean?" she demanded.

"An officer of the Royal Police rifling through my circus unattended? One would think you suspected us of something," he shrugged. His tone was casual, but his eyes were sharp.

"Maybe it was personal curiosity," Rhosyn deflected, knowing it was a weak argument.

"I thought you made it clear this wasn't personal when you showed up for a night of revelry in uniform," Ansel said, and although his tone remained teasing, for some reason the observation rang of sadness to Rhosyn.

She shrugged. "Well, it hardly matters, because I didn't find what I was looking for anyways."

"Oh, and what was that?"

"Clues to what your circus act was, since you seem intent on keeping that information under wraps." Rhosyn knew Ansel was too sharp to let her meddling drop, but was surprised when he rose to the bait, eyes twinkling as a smirk curled his lips.

"Oh, but you did." Ansel tossed the knife in the air again, and Rhosyn's gaze tracked the swirling silver as it rose and fell.

She raised her brows in question.

"Call a target," Ansel instructed, gesturing to the empty backstage.

Rhosyn's eyes swept over the cluttered area and landed on the stairs up to the box she had occupied before her ill-fated exploration.

She pointed. "The steps. Fourth one up, dead center."

Without windup or preamble, Ansel's arm whipped past Rhosyn's face, wrist snapping forward a moment before the knife embedded itself in the wooden stair with a solid *thwack*—exactly where Rhosyn had specified.

She blinked in surprise, but quickly schooled her features.

"*Psh*. That's hardly worth selling tickets to see. I could do that."

On a good day, with a healthy amount of practice, she amended in her head. She had once been proficient with throwing knives, but they hadn't been in her repertoire for a while now.

"You're a tough sell." Ansel reached for Rhosyn's hand and pulled the second knife out of the sheath, which dangled forgotten at her side. "How about something a little tougher then."

He bent and rustled through the packs at their feet, making no effort to leave them looking undisturbed, as Rhosyn had. He emerged with an apple and handed it to Rhosyn.

"I'm not really in the mood for a snack," she commented drily.

Ansel fixed her with an impatient look. "Go on. Throw it."

Rhosyn gave him a look of question. When his expression remained sincere, she shrugged and gave the fruit a solid toss. It arced through the air away from them.

At the zenith of its flight, Ansel threw the second knife. It embedded itself in the far wall a moment before the apple fell to the ground, split neatly in two.

Now, Rhosyn didn't hide her surprise. Comparing knife tricks was a classic pastime among the gangs, but she had never seen somebody perform such a feat.

"I'll admit, I don't have any tricks quite that good."

"Come now, I'm sure we could find a place for you in the circus if you got tired of police work. Maybe some sleight of hand?"

Rhosyn sighed dramatically. "Well, I do know one trick." She turned to face Ansel and stepped close. He blinked at her sudden proximity. Rhosyn took advantage of the moment, leaning in and widening her eyes at him pleadingly. "It's silly though, so you have to promise not to laugh."

Ansel swallowed thickly and nodded, clearly so thrown by her sudden invasion of his space that he paid little attention to anything besides her face, inches from his. It was far closer than people tended to get in proper society, but she wasn't above using her lack of her propriety to her advantage.

A smile split Rhosyn's face and she stepped back. As Ansel frowned, Rhosyn lifted her hand, which had subtly slid into his pocket as he was distracted.

"I'm quite a good pickpocket. Let's see what we have here."

Ansel lunged forward as if to steal her prize from her grasp, but Rhosyn danced back to examine what had felt like a slip of paper. Perhaps it was a secret note or an embarrassing letter.

To her confusion, upon examination, it seemed to be a single playing card. She turned it over in her fingers, wondering why he might be carrying such a thing in his pocket. The three of spades stared up at her and her eyebrows knit together.

An image flashed in her head—the Hood, hunching over her and picking up a fallen playing card from the ground as she gasped for air. He had tucked it into his jacket before slipping away into the poisoned smoke.

Rhosyn had swapped this card for the queen of hearts in her hand the night of the Gower's party.

Her head snapped up to stare at Ansel, but he had already realized his mistake by the time her mind fit the pieces together.

His fist flew towards her face, but she had just enough time to turn away. The blow brushed past her nose by the breadth of a hair.

Rhosyn let the momentum of her dodge carry her into a full spin. As she came back around, she threw her elbow out. It caught Ansel square in the chest and he stumbled back. With him on the back foot, she advanced.

She lashed out with fists and feet, her standard issue police baton remaining forgotten at her belt. Sure, she was attempting to apprehend a criminal, but the Hood's crimes remained in the back of her mind.

This brawl was personal.

Ansel had flirted with her and tricked her—he had been right under her nose the whole time, smiling and dancing. He would answer to her fists. Rhosyn was a daughter of the Lions, after all.

With a kick to his knee, Rhosyn sent Ansel sprawling to the packed dirt ground. She fell on top of him, pinning his torso to the ground beneath her thighs. As frighteningly competent as he was with a knife, both blades were now on the opposite side of the room, and he was no match for Rhosyn in an all-out brawl. She was used to inelegant fights and had the crooked nose to prove it.

However, even as Rhosyn bore Ansel into the ground, his hands remained free. He managed to get one on Rhosyn's face, shoving it to the side. This time, she didn't refrain from biting him, closing her teeth savagely around his finger.

His howl of pain split the air as Rhosyn tasted copper. His shout was loud enough to risk being heard in the main tent, even over the roar of the still-cheering crowd.

He wrenched his hand away, trying to hook Rhosyn's legs to flip them over. Rhosyn countered by grabbing his wrist, trying to pin him to the ground. She nearly lost focus as pounding footsteps sounded behind her. Ansel's shout must have drawn an audience to their tussle.

"You. Are under...arrest." Rhosyn grunted as she continued to wrestle Ansel into the ground despite his struggles. She was suddenly glad she was wearing her uniform.

"John," Ansel gasped. "John!"

Rhosyn only had a moment to frown before thick arms wrapped around her torso, hauling her up and back. She kicked and hissed but it was no use.

The form behind her was easily twice as broad as Ansel. Her efforts to dislodge his grip were as fruitless as attempting to push a steam engine by hand. Still, Rhosyn kicked out, nearly catching Ansel in the head as he pushed to his feet. She bared her teeth, prepared to call him a set of creative names, but a cloth pressed over her nose and mouth just as she inhaled.

It smelled and tasted just like the smoke from Hood's bomb, but so concentrated it made her eyes water and throat burn. She coughed as her lungs tried to reject the vapors, but it was too late. Her vision began to swim, her efforts to escape weakening quickly.

Ansel's mouth moved as if he was saying something, but his voice reached her muffled and quiet, as if she were listening to him from under water. Just before the darkness at the edges of her vision closed in, Rhosyn met Ansel's eyes, but instead of triumph, she could have sworn they held regret.

Chapter Six

Rhosyn sank luxuriously into the mattress beneath her. Even though it was lumpy and thin, she couldn't bring herself to open her eyes. She couldn't remember the last time she felt so relaxed. Usually, she jerked awake before dawn out of habit, ready to don her uniform and head out on patrol. Even now, she often shot up, imagining she heard a child's cry, even though she hadn't had any in her charge for several years.

Today, though, she lounged, embracing the heaviness in her limbs that seemed to keep her bound to the bed. It was that feeling of immobilization in her limbs that planted a seed of doubt in Rhosyn's mind. Questions slowly wormed themselves into her sluggish brain: what time was it? Where was she? Why wasn't she jumping up to prepare for a day of work?

Voices, somewhat muffled as if passing through a door, interrupted her thoughts.

"—can't keep her here. Somebody is sure to come looking."

"You know I wouldn't consider the alternative."

Rhosyn's eyes snapped open at that voice. Ansel—the Hood—the tone belonged to both of them, yet neither of them. It didn't have the flirting cadence of Mr. Blakely and wasn't pitched quite as low as the Hood's. Instead, Ansel sounded resigned, but his voice brought memories rushing back all the same.

Rhosyn's gaze focused on an unfamiliar ceiling, after a few slow blinks to clear the blurriness from her vision. Battered gray slats, looking weathered enough

Rhosyn was surprised she couldn't see the room above, told her she was no longer in the tent where she had been knocked unconscious.

She made to sit up, only to find that the heaviness of her limbs was not just from her exhaustion, but from a set of ropes binding her wrists and ankles to the bedposts. With a grunt, she struggled against them and succeeded only in rattling the rickety bedframe.

"*Shhh.*" Ansel's voice filtered through the door again. "I think she's awake."

Rhosyn exhaled heavily through her nose in frustration. In her anxiousness to get free, she had given up any chance to inspect her surroundings unnoticed. She stilled, listening for any snippets of the conversation outside that could give her an idea where she was, or how to escape.

"Well...what are you going to do?" the unfamiliar voice asked, low but still just audible.

Silence stretched.

"You can't just leave her in there," it pressed.

"I'm going to...talk to her."

Ansel's companion responded with a snort. "Oh, she definitely seemed like she would respond well to a reasonable conversation."

"I can hear you, you know!" Rhosyn shouted at the ceiling, losing patience. She may as well make something happen if her captors were intent on waffling in the hall.

After a moment of extended stillness, a creak indicated the opening of a door. Rhosyn lifted her head, the crane of her neck an uncomfortable strain with her arms stretched above her. Ansel stood in the doorway, an unmistakable combination of the two men who had haunted her life of late. He was dressed like the Hood, in dark green, practical gear that contrasted greatly with the pageantry of his circus-owner garb. He had forgone the hood though, leaving his expression visible. Although his green eyes and the silver streak in his hair were familiar, his welcoming smile was replaced by a hard look. He stared at Rhosyn like she was a problem he couldn't solve. From his frown, she would have thought he was the one who had woken up tied to a bed.

After a moment of staring, Rhosyn raised her brows in silent question.

"I didn't mean for this to happen," Ansel started.

"Funny, these knots seem rather intentional." Rhosyn tugged on her wrists for emphasis.

A furrow formed between Ansel's brows. "You know that isn't what I meant."

"I wouldn't have thought you would need to resort to drugging and kidnapping to lure a woman into your bed." The words popped out before Rhosyn could think better of them or realize that she wasn't in the best situation to be taunting her captor.

Ansel pursed his lips. "It's not my bed."

"Well, if this isn't a social call, would you care to enlighten me on where I am?"

"You know who I am," Ansel pointed out. "You were going to arrest me."

Rhosyn huffed. "Assaulting and kidnapping an officer of the Royal Police is a criminal offense too, in case you didn't know."

With a tired sigh, Ansel took a few steps further into the room, coming up next to the bed. At this angle, Rhosyn could finally relax her neck against the pillow and just turn her head to keep him in her line of sight.

"I am aware, but I couldn't let you stop me. I have some important things to take care of." Ansel didn't meet Rhosyn's eyes, instead reaching out to run a finger along the rope binding her. She watched as he slid one finger between the loop and her wrist, as if testing to see how tight it was. The callused pad of his finger rasped against the sensitive skin of her inner wrist. She thought of the dexterous way he twirled a knife and swallowed thickly.

"If you keep me for more than a few hours, people will realize I'm missing." Rhosyn commented to distract herself from Ansel's touch as he repeated the same movement on the other wrist. She tried to curl her fingers to claw at the back of his hand, but he withdrew quickly. "Chief Thorne will notice if I don't show up for my patrol in the morning."

"I'm afraid that ship has left the harbor." Ansel grimaced.

Rhosyn furrowed her brow. "What do you mean? How long have I been here?"

"You've been out for almost twenty-four hours. I was afraid Little John accidentally killed you, although I shouldn't be surprised that you needed the sleep—"

"It's been a whole *day?*" Rhosyn cut off his conjecture and began squirming anew.

"Honestly, it seems like you should be thanking me for helping you catch up on your rest." Ansel snorted. "With you patrolling the streets during the day and prowling on your own by dark, it's no wonder you haven't been sleeping."

Rhosyn drew back her lips in a snarl at the mention of her private investigations. She certainly wasn't going to be able to find Paul and Olivia while tied up goodness-knows where.

Ansel cocked his head at her. "You clearly don't trust the Police's methods if you are doing your own investigations off the books. I had hoped we would be able to come to some sort of...understanding."

An audible growl worked its way up from the back of Rhosyn's throat. "Don't you *dare* think I'm a thief and a kidnapper like you. I am a good officer of the Royal Police, because I care about this city, and I will do whatever it takes to protect it from people like you."

Ansel's boots *thunked* heavily against the floor, a juxtaposition to his normally graceful gait, as he stumbled back like Rhosyn's words hard been physical blows.

Rhosyn settled back on her pillows, partially satisfied that she had managed to verbally wound Ansel. Under the thin layer of vindication lay a hollowness, though. The city's criminals looked at her and saw not somebody who was there to protect her home, but an ally. Sure, she had started life on the wrong side of the law, back when the Royal Police were rife with corruption, but now things were different. Still, a thief—and potentially a kidnapper—looked at her and saw somebody who could be corrupted.

Her glare hardened further and Ansel's expression turned stricken.

"I see you aren't ready to talk. Maybe you'll change your mind after another day or two." With that he backed out of the room. Part of Rhosyn wanted to scream and snarl and tear apart her bonds through strength of will, but she remained quiet as he left the room, not trusting her words. Her lack of judgment had gotten her into this situation, and now she needed to think.

The door thudded closed, signaling that Rhosyn was alone once more. Murmured voices told Rhosyn that Ansel's friend had been waiting for him, but the conversation drifted away before she could catch any more words.

She turned her attention to her bonds and anything in the room that might help her, but came up blank. The grayish wooden slats of the walls stared back at her bleakly, looking like every room for rent in the lower city, and giving her no indication where she might be. Straining her ears, she thought she heard some boisterous laughter and the sounds of general merriment from the floors below.

Perhaps the ground floor held a tavern. It almost reminded her of the sounds one would hear in one of the Lion's communal safehouses, above their gambling parlors—the ones where young Lions who outgrew the Den lived, while Rhosyn lingered behind to keep the next wave safe and fed.

It seemed counterintuitive that Ansel and his partners in crime would want to keep her in a tavern though, where it would be difficult to keep her presence a secret. Rhosyn's brain sparked. Perhaps she *was* in a gang hideout, and the Hood had already made some dodgy friends who were willing to hold her hostage in exchange for a cut of whatever plot he was undertaking.

She winced as the rough ropes of her bonds chafed her skin, pulling tight in her struggles, even after Ansel had checked that they wouldn't do her permanent harm.

Escaping would be no easy task. If she had been in shackles, she might have been able to use some of her Contessa's lockpicking tricks, but they wouldn't be any use on the expertly tied knots. She wished for Scarlett's shadowy Talent to help her slip free, but she remained Talentless—something she had fervently thanked luck for during the Inquiries.

Rhosyn was left only with herself and her unfortunate tendency to punch first and ask questions after.

She tried to ask herself what Nate or Kristoff would do, but her brain unhelpfully refused to offer anything outside of an amusing image of Kristoff trying to flirt his way out of his predicament. It might not have been such a bad idea if Rhosyn hadn't just spat a slew of insults at her captor.

Despite her best efforts, Rhosyn's attention soon drifted to the soft pillow under her head. It sucked her in with unusual gravity, lulling her into abandoning her plans of escape for the time being. Sleep sang its siren song, more alluring than ever, even after a full day of unconsciousness.

Maybe the drugs Ansel's ally had used on her were inordinately strong. Or maybe, tied down with nobody to punch and no fight to pick, Rhosyn gave into rest.

A door slamming jerked Rhosyn awake hard enough that she nearly gave herself whiplash trying to jump to her feet, before remembering her bonds. As it was, her head snapped forward to see the figure who had made the sudden noise.

A man, so wide and muscular Rhosyn was surprised he fit through the door, stood at the foot of the bed frowning at her. Every thought she had of clever things to say to her captors flew from her mind as she took in the sheer mass of him.

"Where'd the H—Ansel—dig up a lower city bruiser like you?" The words tumbled out of her mouth without a thought.

The man's wide-set features crumpled into a frown. "I'm not from London."

Rhosyn blinked, but her visitor didn't offer any more information. She looked him up and down curiously once more, when her gaze snagged on a cup of water, dwarfed in his meaty paws. Automatically, she tried to swallow around the incredible dryness in her throat, after so much rest and nothing to drink. The sight of water drew unavoidable awareness to the feeling in her mouth of having swallowed a fistful of sand.

"Is that for me?" Rhosyn asked, trying and failing to nod at the water with her neck crooked at such a tight angle.

The man nodded, but stepped forward hesitantly, as if Rhosyn were the one that looked like she crushed boulders with her biceps to pass the time.

Impatient, Rhosyn snapped, "I don't bite."

"The teeth marks on Ansel's hand say otherwise."

Rhosyn grimaced. "I try not to bite the hands that feed me," she corrected.

He resumed his approach, still slowly, and Rhosyn watched him carefully. While the bulk of his frame was clearly composed of muscle, he didn't carry himself with the grace of a fighter. Not to mention, size wasn't everything in a scrap. The hardest fight Rhosyn had ever had was against Scarlett, who didn't even make it to her chin.

Maybe Rhosyn shouldn't try to emulate Contessa or Scarlett's skills to escape. Maybe she should just be Rhosyn, and let the chips fall where they may.

She kept her eyes trained on the liquid sloshing in the cup as her captor leaned in, trying to appear completely distracted by her thirst. He put his hand behind her head to help her tip forward to drink, the move so polite that Rhosyn nearly felt bad for what she was about to do.

The moment he bent over to tip the water into her mouth, she snapped forward, slamming her forehead into his nose.

The world went white as the man let out a loud curse. A shattering crash split the air as the cup of water fell to the floor, but Rhosyn couldn't feel any satisfaction at landing a solid blow. She was too busy blinking stars from her vision and wondering if it was possible to scramble your brains in your skull.

As her sight cleared, she was incredulous to find that the man looked relatively unfazed, thick fingers wiping the tiniest dribble of blood from his nose and upper lip. Rhosyn had used her face as a weapon more than was strictly advisable in her life, and in her experience that should have shattered her opponent's nose. Instead, she was left reeling, while he only seemed mildly annoyed.

She would have to stop teasing Contessa about breaking her own nose in an ill-advised headbutt after this.

Before Rhosyn or her visitor could do more than take a quick stock of her injuries, the door slammed open once more.

"I see you've taken the liberty of introducing yourself to Little John, Rhosyn," Ansel observed as he took in the chaotic scene before him.

"... don't know why you're insisting on keeping her," the man, who must be Little John, grumbled under his breath.

Ansel ignored his comment and Rhosyn tried to wrap her head around him referring to this giant as "little".

"Go wash your face. I'll handle this," Ansel instructed. A few heavy footsteps and a creak of the door on its hinges, and they were alone in the room.

Rhosyn tried to scowl but was pretty sure she ruined it with eyes still crossed from the blow to her head. She didn't regret it though. If Ansel insisted on holding an officer of the Royal Police captive, she wasn't inclined to make it easy for him.

"I was trying to convince Little John that we could at least untie your feet, but you seem determined to undermine me at every turn." He crossed his arms over his chest as he stared down at her with the look of a man assessing the broken wheel on his carriage.

"Being tied down doesn't induce me to act quiet and polite," Rhosyn countered.

Ansel snorted. "You would have more of a point if you hadn't been asleep for the better part of a day."

"Which is concerning for you, because the longer you hold me here, the worse it will be for you when Chief Throne tracks you down."

"He won't be finding you here."

Ansel's tone held so much surety that a thrill ran up Rhosyn's spine. Maybe she was trapped here, immobilized at the mercy of a man who had become a notorious criminal nearly as fast as Nate had been dubbed "the Beast". Perhaps she should have been more concerned by her predicament, but an oddly familiar fire burned in her gut, the threat of danger igniting in her blood.

"I wouldn't be so sure," Rhosyn threatened with a too-wide grin.

Ansel's brows rose at the challenge in her words. "Oh, because your Royal Police were doing so well at tracking us down before now. And the one officer who came close to discovering us is no longer on the board." Ansel inclined his head towards her. "If they can't track down the missing Talented, they won't be able to find you."

Rhosyn jerked, the excitement in her veins sizzling into anger at Ansel's implication. He didn't just know what had happened to Olivia and Paul—he had them.

"Where are they? Where are Olivia and Paul?" The words came out a hiss between her gritted teeth.

Ansel's posture straightened, as if he wanted to back up a step against the force of Rhosyn's anger, but had trained himself too well to retreat in the face of danger. "I'll tell you, but I need you to show me that I can trust you first."

"And why would I do that?" Rhosyn asked, voice like stone.

"Because I have a feeling you might see things my way, but I need to know you're not going to ruin our plans before I tell you anything."

Her curiosity piqued, but her hands still involuntarily curled into fists, tight enough that nails she had bitten down to the quick still dug into her palms. "If you've hurt one hair on Paul's and Olivia's heads, you'll have more to worry about then spending the rest of your life rotting away in prison."

Ansel's solemn nod indicated that he took her threat seriously. Rhosyn wasn't wholly satisfied, but her inner Lion purred in pride.

"I'm going to untie your legs. If you can prove to me that you won't immediately try to break all my associates' noses, I'll let you see Paul and Olivia."

After a moment's hesitation, Rhosyn nodded. Ansel bent over to untie her feet, although he watched her warily, as if he half expected her to kick him in the face. She didn't blame him, but remained relaxed against the mattress.

As the bonds immobilizing her lower body went slack, Rhosyn flexed her legs and circled her ankles, grimacing at the stiffness in her hips after staying in one position for so long.

To her surprise, Ansel put a hand on her calf, rubbing it to restore any lost circulation. Once again, she noted calluses rasping gently on the sensitive skin just below the inside of her ankle bone. It almost tickled, and Rhosyn had a sudden urge to squirm, despite his touch being focused on such an innocuous area—no, she would not admit to Contessa that there was anything remotely scandalous about ankles, thank you very much. Instead, she thought about the roughness of Ansel's palm, which made more sense now that she had seen his practiced ability with a knife. She snorted quietly at the thought.

Ansel looked at her curiously.

"When I felt your hand the first time, I guessed you were a juggler because of the calluses. I don't know how I didn't recognize the hands of a knife-fighter," she explained. In fact, Ansel's hands felt similarly rough to her own, although missing the hardened skin across the fingers that came from Rhosyn's brass knuckles.

"Who says I can't juggle knives?" Ansel asked, a hint of the charismatic circus performer leaking into his voice. Now though, it didn't seem as exaggerated, less the purposeful airs of a performer than a teasing twinkle in his eyes. Rhosyn wondered if it was genuine.

Realizing his hand had stilled on her calf, Rhosyn yanked it out of his grip. He had dazzled her into overlooking his guilt before, and it wouldn't happen again.

Ignoring the weight of Ansel's gaze, she twisted her legs this way and that to relieve any stiffness. She stretched her spine too, frowning. She felt...great. Certainly not how she would expect to feel after being knocked unconscious and kidnapped.

Her muscles felt pliant but strong, responding quickly to her commands, a far cry from the sluggishness she often battled against at the end of her patrols. She was still thirsty though, and her stomach grumbled in hunger. Although she had ruined her chance at a glass of water a few minutes earlier, she couldn't completely bring herself to regret it.

She continued to work out her stiffness, surreptitiously testing the bonds on her wrists. They remained immovable, clearly expertly tied—perhaps assembling the trapezes and tightropes that held the weight of multiple performers every night conferred you with impressive knot tying skills—but the rickety bedframe creaked with her movements.

Rhosyn smiled sheepishly at Ansel, trying with difficulty to summon the more docile side of her nature. "If I promise not to break your nose, can we try again with a glass of water."

Ansel nodded. "If it's any consolation, I doubt you did any permanent damage to Little John's nose."

"It makes it sound even crueler when you call him 'Little'," Rhosyn grumped.

"When he was younger, his friends thought it was a clever name for the circus's strong man. They realized it wasn't, but the name had already stuck." Ansel smiled wryly.

Rhosyn blinked at the realization that Ansel hadn't hired John from a gang for intimidation. He was actually a member of the circus.

Ansel took a few steps back in her silence. "I'll be back with water."

As the door hinges creaked, Rhosyn lay still, waiting for the click of the lock to tell her she was alone. The moment Ansel was gone, Rhosyn heaved with her abs, folding her body in half.

She wasn't as flexible as she once was, when she spent so many hours teaching youngsters self-defense and how to stay limber, but she still managed to swing her legs over her head until her feet planted on the wall above the headboard.

Her face twisted into a combination of a grimace and a chuckle, thinking how she had only ever found herself in this position in very different circumstances.

Ansel would be greeted by a remarkable view of her ass if he were to open the door at that moment, but she needed the leverage.

She pushed against the wall, thighs straining next to her ears. The ropes around her wrists creaked at the pressure but showed no sign of breaking. Rhosyn paid them no mind—it wasn't them she was trying to break.

As she had hoped, the bed, which had already been squeaky and rickety, gave an almighty groan. Rhosyn gritted her teeth and redoubled her efforts, veins beginning to pop in her neck. Splintering gave way to cracking as the bedframe surrendered to her strength.

The entire headboard ripped free so suddenly that Rhosyn almost hit herself on the head with the heavy plank of wood. Before the bed could collapse completely, she rolled sideways, letting her legs fall so she could land on her feet.

Her boots hit the floor so hard the entire downstairs would have heard, but secrecy had flown out the window with the earsplitting groan of wood giving way. She straightened, head whipping back and forth as she absorbed her predicament. Her hands were still bound to the heavy board she had ripped free, but it would be useful as a makeshift club to use against those who would resist her escape.

The hazy light of the lower city filtered in through one grimy window. Rhosyn hurried over to it and grimaced when she saw a several story drop. Scarlett might have made the jump, but Rhosyn didn't have shadows to break her fall. She wouldn't be able to climb down with her hands hindered.

No matter. Fighting her way out the front door was more her style anyway.

Feet pounded on the stairs outside and Rhosyn turned towards the entrance, ready for the onslaught. The door swung open, but Rhosyn was already charging, lowering her shoulder to bowl over anyone in her way. Ansel jumped out of the way, but Rhosyn barreled past, straight into an unfamiliar man behind him.

They teetered for a moment before tumbling down a narrow flight of stairs. Lightning lanced up Rhosyn's limbs as she banged knees and elbows against the walls and steps. She shoved the sensations aside as they rolled to a stop on a landing, springing to her feet.

The man who fell with her tried to do the same, but a kick from Rhosyn left him howling in pain. She spun, finding the next flight of stairs and bounding down them two at a time.

"Rhosyn!" Ansel shouted behind her, but Rhosyn didn't hesitate.

She leaped down the last few stairs and skidded around a corner, only to be brought up short by the sight before her. A crowded room, filled with young men and women sitting around tables scattered with dice and tankards, stood between her and the exit.

Grimacing, she had the fleeting thought that she regretted being right about being kept in a gang hideout. She didn't have time to consider what gang it might be before the sound of Ansel pounding down the stairs behind her told her she was out of time.

In the few feet of open space between her and the nearest cluster of people, she took a running start before leaping. She landed on the surface of the first table in a crouch. Shouting broke out as she stood, traversing the length of the table in a few long strides.

She jumped to the next table as people leaped into action. A burly man tried to reach for her ankle, but she kicked a tankard as she passed. It caught him full in the face, and he reared back, spluttering.

By the time her long legs carried her to the next table, a hardened-looking woman stood in her path, fists raised in challenge. Her opponent swung, and Rhosyn lifted her arms, headboard still bound between them. She caught the blow on the wood like a shield, and the woman swore as her knuckles met a surface far more solid than flesh.

Rhosyn pressed the advantage, driving her knee up into the woman's lower stomach. She doubled over with a gasp as the breath was punched from her. Rhosyn rolled over her back, kicking out as she did so at another grasping hand.

Another jump and she was just a few tables from the door. Her balance slipped as the sole of her boot landed on a deck of cards. She threw her hands out, but the unfamiliar weight of the headboard overbalanced her.

Her knees hit the tabletop with an eye-watering crack. Another man wasted no time jumping on her. She lashed out, smacking him in the face with her plank of wood. He grunted, but the blow had been off center, and he continued to try to pin her down.

With a cry, Rhosyn raised her hands before bringing the board down over the crown of his head so hard, the already-splintered wood cracked in two. At this, the man stilled, dazed from the impact.

"Rhosyn, wait!" Ansel's voice cut through the crowd, but the blood pounded too intensely in Rhosyn's ears for her to make sense of his words.

Rhosyn wrapped her calf around her opponent's, flipping them over and continuing the roll until she landed with her knee at his neck. She pressed down with enough weight to keep him subdued without strangling him.

Her head whipped left and right, hair falling in sweaty tendrils across her face as she looked for her next opponent—her snarl dared them to approach.

"Rhosyn." Another familiar voice cut through the cacophony of the hideout, but it wasn't Ansel.

"You have to let him go, Rhosyn."

She searched the faces around her for the source of the voice, the fury of the fight rushing from her as if somebody had thrown a bucket of cold water over her. The anxious expressions of those surrounding her swam, blurring together until she found him near the entrance—a child that had somehow grown into a man without her noticing.

"Paul?" Rhosyn asked, her chokehold on the man beneath her slackening. "Paul, I have to..."

She had to save him and Olivia. She had to protect her Lion cubs as she always had, even though they had left the Den.

"Just let him go and we can work it all out," Paul soothed. Rhosyn recognized the rhythmic cadence in his voice that always emerged when he used his Talent. While it had been a godsend when other children in the Den suffered from nightmares, Rhosyn bristled at the realization of what he was doing.

She shook herself, renewing her pressure on her opponent's neck.

"No, please. It's alright." Paul insisted, the Talent overtaking his voice entirely. Try as she might to ignore him, his voice wormed into her skull and laid a warm blanket over her thoughts.

Even as her eyelids grew heavy and she couldn't make out what Paul was saying, only the lulling cadence of his words, she tried to make sense of what was happening.

Paul must be working with Ansel. Maybe he had left his sponsored position with the Gower's for a life of crime after all.

The sting of betrayal cut through the exhaustion now weighing down every limb. She fought against it, trying to blink rapidly and shake her head. A wave of anger rolled over her as her sluggish brain processed the thoughts, almost breaking her free of Paul's mental grasp.

She had given her youth to protecting the Lions and fighting the Inquiries, so children like Paul and Olivia could have the life she had given up by choosing to stay with Nate and Kristoff. All that sacrifice, and here Paul was, throwing in with a criminal despite it all. Maybe being a lower-city urchin wasn't something you could outgrow, no matter how much Rhosyn fought.

With that thought, despair washed away the tide of Rhosyn's rage, leaving her empty and vulnerable to Paul's Talent. The thug beneath her slipped out of her slackening grip, leaving her off balance. She tipped forward, too tired to even put out her hands to break her fall.

Before she could pitch off the table and slam face first into the parquet floor, arms closed around her. Her face pressed into a well-sculpted chest, as the one who had caught her pulled her to him. Rhosyn's nose filled with a smell that was both sweet and spicy, like burnt sugar, undercut with a musk of masculinity.

She was too tired to muster up frustration at Ansel having the audacity to smell so good while ripping her life to shreds. Instead, she used the magically-induced exhaustion as an excuse to take a deep lung-full as she fell into a dreamless sleep.

Chapter Seven

Rhosyn's position this time she woke from an artificially induced slumber was much less comfortable. The wooden slats of a chair dug into her arms, wrenched back and tied firmly behind her. Still, her eyes opened sluggishly, despite the sharpness of the discomfort dragging her towards consciousness.

As she blinked away the bleariness in her vision, the reason for her placidity became apparent. Paul sat in a chair across from her, expression wary as he muttered soothing nonsense. It left her too tired to struggle against her bonds, but he wasn't keeping her fully asleep.

Instead of trying to tug free, she took inventory of her situation, looking down to find her ankles and calves roped to the legs of the chair.

"I see my accommodations have been downgraded." Her voice came out more drowsy than scathing, but Paul still grimaced when she looked back at him.

"It was the one piece of furniture around here we thought you might not be able to break," he admitted.

"You're stronger than you look, but we already knew that," a female voice chimed in.

Rhosyn turned her head, the movement feeling slow, as if she were underwater, and was greeted by a familiar round face.

"Olivia!" A mix of relief and disappointment washed over her. She was glad to see the girl safe, even if she had hoped Paul's sister hadn't also fallen in with Ansel.

"I would say it was good to see you again but..." Olivia twisted her hands fitfully in the apron she wore.

"Tying me to the chair wasn't the greeting I had hoped for. And after I had been so worried about you!" Rhosyn's words came out with more bite now that Paul was no longer talking, his Talent only working with his voice.

"I couldn't let you hurt any more people," Paul admitted ruefully, his tone devoid of any persuasive hypnotism.

"You can't blame me for roughing up the people who I thought had kidnapped you," Rhosyn argued.

"But now you know we're not here against our will—" Olivia started.

"Which doesn't make me any less inclined to punch something," Rhosyn shot before biting her tongue. Olivia's eyes widened and Rhosyn shoved down the guilt she felt at causing such an expression. Even though that doe-eyed look made her look like the child who had been plagued by nightmares until her brother's Talent awoke, she was a teenager now, and old enough to know wrong from right.

"Nate and Contessa, they—we have fought too hard to give you the chance for a life where you don't have to run from the law. And then you throw it all away...for what?" Rhosyn fumed. "You've thrown in with thieves. After all we've gone through."

Rhosyn swallowed thickly, the acid taste of hurt clawing up her throat. How could Paul and Olivia be siding against her? Not when they had been in that group of children captured by Caleb and the Rattlesnakes, who Contessa and Nate had risked life and limb to get back.

But the real bitterness came from the fact that a small part of her understood. After all, hadn't she just slipped into the haze of a street brawler so easily when faced with a challenge? Her police training had flown out the window in a mere second, leaving her throwing punches in a gambling den like she had never left.

"It's not like that," Paul chimed in softly. "You've—I'd hoped you'd understand, if you'd just give us a chance to explain."

Olivia's wide eyes continued to fix her with a beseeching stare. Rhosyn slumped, the awkward angle pulling at her shoulders as they bent around the chair behind her.

"You have until my arms go numb to convince me that I wouldn't be a corrupt police officer for not arresting you alongside Ansel."

The siblings exchanged a glance before both started speaking at once.

"We couldn't stay at the Gower's—"

"We heard the Foxes—"

They both cut off until Olivia nodded at Paul to continue. He took a deep breath, before beginning again more calmly.

"When we were first offered the positions with the Gowers, we thought it was the best thing we could ever hope for. A chance that we only ever dreamed of as Talented children." Paul shifted in his seat. "We barely read the sponsorship papers and jumped in. But after years in the factories as children, it didn't take us long to after we started to realize what it actually was—indentured servitude."

Rhosyn frowned. Contessa wouldn't support something like that—not after fighting so hard to free so many orphans from the horrendous working conditions in the factories—and sponsorships had been her idea. She opened her mouth to chime in before snapping it shut. Chief Thorne had impressed upon her, with great difficulty, that interrupting witnesses was not a good way to go about gathering information.

"In the factories, they paid us, but they forced us to live in their rooms and charged us more than we made. After a few weeks, we were in such deep debt that they basically owned us, while acting like they were saints for taking in children who lost parents to the Inquiries." Paul's face twisted at the memory, the movement pulling on the scar in his forehead and hairline. It had healed to a shiny white, not nearly as gruesome as Nate's, but Rhosyn still remembered how he got it. He had arrived into her care, head wrapped in bandages after being injured in his escape from factory service.

"The Gower's house was the same. After he paid our pardons, took us in, and dressed us for his house, we owed him so much that it would take decades of work to ever be free of him," Paul explained.

"Did he mistreat you?" This time, Rhosyn couldn't stop herself from interrupting.

Paul hesitated.

"The whole time we were there is such a blur," Olivia chimed in. "We were so busy, I could barely keep up with my work and think straight at the same time."

Rhosyn had to take a deep breath in and out through her nose to stay composed. Olivia's voice was so small, still so terribly young. Her childhood had been stolen from her by the textile factory she worked in, and the job that was supposed to be her salvation had apparently worked her so hard that her mind became addled from lack of sleep.

"Why didn't you come to me?" Rhosyn asked, her voice low. Only through an effort of will did she restrain the growl that threatened to creep in, both in anger that Mr. Gower would treat them so badly they felt the need to run away and that they would choose a random thug to help them over her.

"I...I don't know." Paul seemed genuinely baffled as he tried to dig up an answer. "I just—I went on an errand for the Gowers, and at the market I heard a rumor that a new gang was helping Talented people leave London. It felt like the first time my head had been clear in months when I heard that. So, I followed the man who had been gossiping.

"I had to use some of the...skills...you taught me," Paul looked sheepish, "but I eventually tracked the rumors back here. I met Ansel and the Foxes, and they told me he could help. He would even steal our sponsorship papers from the palace so they couldn't hunt us down and force us back. And then...well, I guess you can fill in the rest."

For a moment, Rhosyn thought Paul was infusing his words with his Talent again, as her mind couldn't seem to keep up with what he was saying. In the long pause when he finished, staring at her with a mix of expectancy and apprehension, her mind hummed with all the force of the factories in the industrial district.

"The Foxes?" she asked, her police brain homing in on that detail first. Her investigation into Foxes left her thinking that they were more myth than reality, and Paul had stumbled on them by accident.

"That would be us." Ansel stood in the doorframe, leaning casually against it with his arms folded, one leg crossed in front of the other. It would have been a relaxed pose, but something in his posture told Rhosyn he was ready to jump into action in a moment's notice. To be fair, she hadn't given him a reason to believe that any given conversation with her wouldn't end in a fight. He must have appeared there sometime during their talk, with his uncanny knack for stealth.

"You?" Rhosyn echoed. She had surmised Ansel had gang help, but he seemed to be suggesting that he led the gang.

"Well, my associates and I," he clarified with a shrug.

"...The circus?" Rhosyn asked.

"We are a group of many skills," Ansel said, the hint of a wry smile tugging at his lips, even though the rest of his expression remained serious. Rhosyn stared for a second, taking in the lines creasing his forehead that seemed too deep for his age and the hollows under his eyes. They looked like hers.

"I wouldn't have thought clowning and crime had much overlap," Rhosyn admitted.

"Little John is our strong man, and he seems to do just fine at standing in as the muscle."

Rhosyn blinked dumbly. "So, Archer's Circus...is the Foxes?"

Ansel bowed his head in affirmation.

With this admission, more pieces of the puzzle started falling into place. Contessa's office had been robbed of the sponsorship papers the night Archer's Circus had performed there, and the thief had disappeared into the hubbub of the dressing room. The supposed turf fight with the Foxes had occurred in the rail yard the night the circus train had arrived. And the gang had supposedly sprung into life out of thin air a few weeks before, when Ansel and his advance guard of performers arrived in London.

Rhosyn slumped. She swung her head to look at Paul and Olivia again. Grown as they were now, something in their expression still made them look like children waiting to be scolded for some mischief or another—although truth be told, they were some of the less devious children she had minded at the Den over the years.

"So, you were just trying to run away, and the Foxes were your way out." It wasn't exactly a question, but the siblings nodded in affirmation. A few pieces of the puzzle were still missing though.

"Why are you stealing Talented away from their sponsorships?" She directed the question at Ansel.

He signed heavily and pushed off the doorframe, taking a few steps further into the room. "That is a question with a lot of history behind it."

Rhosyn looked pointedly down at her ankles where they were bound to the chair. "It doesn't look like I'm going anywhere."

Paul, Olivia, and Ansel all grimaced in unison.

"Sorry," Paul mumbled under his breath.

"I would prefer not to have you bound at all times," Ansel admitted. "But your fists have already cost me my juggler for tonight's show. If my performers keep getting mysteriously injured, people might start asking questions."

"I suppose promising to be on my best behavior doesn't mean much at this point." Rhosyn tried to look contrite, but it wasn't an expression that came to her naturally.

Ansel shook his head. "How do I know you won't run off and tell your Chief all you just learned about our little operation?"

Rhosyn chewed her lip to keep herself from spitting back that he didn't. After all, she should do just as he said. The Foxes had done more than break the Talented siblings free. They had broken into the palace—Contessa's own office—and stolen a small fortune in jewelry from several upper city families.

A good police officer wouldn't hesitate to put the entirety of Archer's Circus behind bars. But the fear that Rhosyn had pushed aside for too long reared its head and couldn't be pushed down this time.

Maybe she wasn't a good police officer.

She desperately wanted to be—wanted to claim that she lived fully on the right side of the law and had reclaimed the life she might have had if she hadn't chosen to throw her lot in with the Lion's after she aged out of the Den. After all, Chief Thorne worked tirelessly to turn the police around and make them the protectors they were always meant to be. Rhosyn had never wanted to do anything but help the people of London, and joining his new force had seemed like the best way.

But the dirt of the lower city had rubbed its way under her skin.

Rhosyn closed her eyes, steeling herself. She picked her next words carefully. "If I'm being held hostage, I can't very well tell the Royal Police where Olivia and Paul were. It would be a shame if I weren't to escape until after they had left London. Then, they'd be outside our jurisdiction and the Royal Police would be unable to see that they were returned home safely."

Ansel cocked his head, his green eyes inscrutable. Paul and Olivia, on the other hand, slumped in relief.

"Thank you," Olivia breathed emphatically.

Their gratitude twisted her gut with guilt even as it lightened her heart.

The Lions protected their own.

A knife sprang into Ansel's hand, having been hidden somewhere beneath his sleeves. The thin lamplight in the small room reflected off a blade sharp enough to make Nate proud. Ansel knelt before Rhosyn's chair and gave her a long look.

Her throat felt tight as she swallowed with difficulty and nodded. She would not run. She told herself that this was a compromise—a necessary evil. Rhosyn hadn't promised Ansel that she wouldn't get the Foxes arrested for their crimes. She had only suggested that she wouldn't be doing so until after Paul and Olivia were far away.

A dull *snick* and the ropes around Rhosyn's calves loosened, sliced cleanly through by Ansel's blade. She flexed her legs and rolled her ankles as he stood and rounded her chair.

The heat from his body soaked through her uniform as he bent over her to cut away the binds on her arms. As he leaned in, his breath disturbed the curls at the nape of her neck, long since escaped from the knot she tied them in for patrol. She tried not to focus on the goosebumps it raised as her wrists sprang free and she was able to move her arms into a more comfortable position.

As she stretched, pulling her arms alternately across her chest to regain her mobility, Ansel rounded the chair and looked at her appraisingly.

"If you're going to be the Foxes' guest, you'll need something else to wear. Olivia, Paul, can you see if you can dig your friend up some clothes?"

Rhosyn looked down at her uniform and grimaced. It was rumpled and dusty after three days of wear, a stain on one thigh from a spilled drink as she jumped over tables. She had even managed to lose one of the golden buttons that dotted the navy fabric. Not to mention, it wouldn't do to have her walking freely in a gang hideout wearing the outfit of an officer of the law.

Paul nodded. "Something of mine might work, even if the pants are a little short."

With that, he and Olivia scurried off to do Ansel's bidding. The door banged against the frame as they left, and they found themselves alone. Ansel stood before Rhosyn, close enough his thighs nearly brushed her knees. She tilted her head up to look at him.

"So, what now?" he asked.

She stared at him, lifting a quizzical brow. "Aren't you the one in charge here? You don't seem to have mastered the art of holding someone hostage."

"And you have?"

Rhosyn shrugged, "Maybe not holding a hostage. But I have put lots of people behind bars, and I'm certainly better at conducting interrogations."

"This wasn't an interrogation." Ansel let out a frustrated huff through his nose. "It was a...persuasion."

"Well, now that I've been *persuaded*, I'd like to stretch my legs if you're leaving the plan up to me." Rhosyn stood, forcing Ansel to take a step back.

He immediately stepped forward again as Rhosyn's knees buckled, an odd mix of wobbly and stiff after being tied for so long. Ansel caught her with one arm under hers and the other around her waist. Rhosyn threw her arms around his neck on reflex.

They stood like that, perfectly still. Rhosyn's nose was a few inches from Ansel's, close enough that she could make out the shimmering lamplight reflected in his eyes. The way they held each other, it was almost like the time they first met, dancing at the King's ball. But that wasn't the first time they had met—that had been a chase over steep roofs, ending in Rhosyn's humiliation.

That thought gave Rhosyn the impetus she needed to wrench away, legs much more prepared to hold her weight this time. The man who had flirted with her—who had made her hope she had successfully left her past behind her, while making her wonder if she were broken for wanting to shatter the layer of veneer that coated his manner—that man was a lie.

This man was the Hood. More a representation of the past that she was trying to leave behind than her present. And while the Hood's manner was also naturally flirtatious, she chafed at the way she had jumped to his challenges.

"I did untie you, but I'm not sure giving you a tour of the premises is wise," Ansel admitted, drawing Rhosyn from her thoughts, apparently completely unfazed by their recent proximity.

She jutted out one hip and rested a fist on it. "You have your insurance for my cooperation."

For now, she added silently.

Ansel bit the inside of his cheek as if considering. It was a more human gesture, speaking of indecision and doubt, than Rhosyn had ever seen on him as Mr. Blakely. She found herself softening her posture.

"You don't even have to let me see where we are, just let me walk the hallways," she compromised. After all, she could learn plenty about the Foxes from inside their hole, even if she didn't know its precise location.

"Alright," Ansel conceded. "But I'm not letting you wander anywhere alone."

"Of course not. You need to tell me the story of how you found yourself stealing Talented away from their jobs."

Ansel gave her a long-suffering look as he led her from the small room into a narrow hallway. It was dingy and cramped, with doors lining it all the way down. He didn't speak as he led the way down past the doorways, some stood open to reveal tiny bedrooms and others closed, voices coming from within. It looked so much like the safehouses where her friends in the Lions lived that if she closed her eyes, she could pretend she was seventeen again, visiting the teenagers who had aged out of the Den and her care.

"It started when Mr. Archer still owned the circus actually," Ansel started without any preamble as they turned the corner at the end of the corridor towards the stairs.

"Mr. Archer?"

"The one whom the circus is named after. He was my...mentor."

Rhosyn considered the back of Ansel's head as he led them down the stairs. He didn't elaborate for a minute as they squeezed past others, many of whom nodded courteously at Ansel before catching sight of her and paling. Their shock at seeing her walking free told her that most of them witnessed the scene in the common room earlier. She grinned.

Finally, they arrived on what Rhosyn surmised was the ground floor, where a familiar room full of tables and chairs greeted them.

"Will, get our friend here something to eat and drink. She'll be staying for a while." Ansel shouted toward a group of men gathered around a table with their heads bent together. One of them looked up, staring for a moment before hurrying to do Ansel's bidding.

Rhosyn watched him go, wondering why he seemed familiar until it hit her. "Your acrobats."

Ansel nodded as he took a seat at an uninhabited table, gesturing for Rhosyn to take another. "The Merry Men. The act that made the circus famous."

"I originally thought that one of them was the Hood," Rhosyn admitted.

"The Hood?"

Rhosyn cleared her suddenly stuck throat. "It's what I—we—the police started calling you, since we didn't know who you were. You always wore a hood though."

"I don't know if I should be flattered that I'm notorious enough to have a nickname with law enforcement." Ansel grimaced.

"The best criminals do." People still called Nate "the Beast" behind his back, but nobody would do it where the king or his intimidating bodyguard might overhear.

"If I were good at doing my job, I wouldn't be drawing enough attention to be infamous," Ansel admitted.

"Your acrobatics aren't exactly subtle." Rhosyn shot Ansel a meaningful look. "Now that I know who you are, I'm honestly surprised your act in the circus was knife throwing."

Ansel reclined, leaning the chair he was sitting in back on two legs and balancing there. "It wasn't at first. When Mr. Archer took me in, when I was just a boy, I was one of the first Merry Men."

"Then why did you take up knife throwing?" Rhosyn asked, as Will put a plate of bread and drippings in front of her and scurried away. She didn't hesitate digging in, saying around a mouth full of bread, "You clearly didn't leave acrobatics for a lack of skill."

"That's just it. I was too good at it."

Rhosyn wanted to say something scathing in response but was too busy chewing, so she settled for rolling her eyes, only to freeze when Ansel continued.

"Mr. Archer was afraid I was going to give away my Talent."

She forced her mouthful down her throat with difficulty. "You're Talented?"

Ansel smiled, the expression simultaneously mischievous and wistful. "You asked me how I started stealing the Talented away from the sponsorships, but in truth, it isn't anything new. It's what we've always done, since long before I was in charge.

"That's the beauty of the circus, you see. People come to see things that shouldn't be possible—things that are extraordinary. The spectators expect things to be inexplicably magical. So, when a lion seems to truly understand what his tamer is telling him, or a fire breather can shape flames like a sculptor...well, that's just the magic of show business."

Rhosyn stared. "You're *all* Talented?"

"Not all." Ansel shook his head. The silver strand of hair that Rhosyn had only seen neatly coiffed into his pushed back hairstyle, fell forward with the motion. "It was...a passion of Mr. Archer's. You see, he had a son who was Talented. Had a way of predicting the weather down to the second that was almost scary—as if he controlled the rain. They hid it easily when they lived in the country, but when Mr. Archer started the circus, he moved them to London for the bigger crowds.

"They learned too late that the cramped quarters of the city, combined with the bloodthirstiness of the Royal Police, made it nearly impossible to conceal a Talent for long."

Rhosyn's stomach dropped to the soles of her boots, the bread she had hastily swallowed turning leaden. "He..." She trailed off, not wanting to ask the question and fearing she already knew the answer.

Ansel nodded solemnly. "I think that Mr. Archer thought that if he could just smuggle enough Talented out of London, it would wash away the guilt he felt for his son's death. And so, he sent out word through whispers in the lower city that he was searching for incredible acts to go on tour. People were skeptical at first, but when they realized it wasn't a trap, the Talented flocked to him with all sorts of interesting displays, which he played off as clever tricks and sleight of hand. Then, he bought the train and headed out to the country.

"Acts would drop off at every remote stop where we put on a show, and Mr. Archer never said a word. Just gave them their coin and let them set out to start a new life. Every year, we would come back to London and fill up with a fresh set of performers."

A question built in the back of Rhosyn's mind and spilled off her tongue when he paused. "But you, you never left to start a life in the country where you could hide your Talent?"

Ansel let his chair fall back onto four legs and rested his elbows on the table. "Some of us—I—fell in love with performing. After being petrified to use my Talent for so long, it was liberating. It felt like cheating the system to flex that muscle in front of unsuspecting audiences and be praised for it, even if they never knew. After a while, the circus train became more of a home for some of us than London ever had been. So, a group of us stayed for the long haul."

Rhosyn looked around the room they were in, with plenty of young men and women both milling about and sitting at tables with drinks or dice. The sight, the warmth of casual laughter, even the smell of cheap alcohol and tobacco—it would be enough to make Rhosyn nostalgic if not for the feeling that she was watching the scene through a pane of glass. These weren't the Lions, and the wary glances and wide berths everybody but Ansel gave her told her they still noticed her uniform, however rumpled. After so long trying to cover the blemish of her history with a spotless police record, she should have been proud that Ansel's compatriots saw her as the enemy. Instead, bitterness rose up in her throat to choke her.

"So, once you inherited the circus from Mr. Archer, you turned it into a band of thieves and kidnappers?"

A splintering thud, and the tip of a dagger buried itself in the table millimeters from where Rhosyn's hand rested. To her credit, she didn't flinch away, but the suddenly hard look in Ansel's eyes made her wish she had.

"Mr. Archer died for this circus, and those of us who stayed honor him by continuing what he started." Ansel's voice carried a flinty edge that gave Rhosyn pause. So far, as both the Hood and Mr. Blakely, she had delighted in teasing him, rising to the challenge of a suave attitude that promised to never take itself too seriously. The steel in his green gaze now, though, was something else.

It flashed away as quickly as it had come when Ansel pulled the knife from the table and leaned back in his chair. He tossed the blade with one hand and flipped it, catching it by the handle without looking, in an action that was as much soothing habit as it was intimidation tactic. It was the same way Rhosyn used to twirl her brass knuckles around her index finger.

"The Foxes were born out of necessity, but we're still Archer's Circus at heart."

Rhosyn sat back in her own seat, taking a deep breath to keep up with Ansel's changing posture as he slipped back into his curated demeanor. "The Inquiries are over. I wouldn't think you'd have much business smuggling them out of the city anymore."

"Do you have the life you would have if the Inquiries never happened?"

The question hit Rhosyn like a slap to the face. The dreams of being a sailor like her father—of visiting distant lands and never staying in one place for too long—had dissipated like smog from a smokestack the day she had decided to stay with the Lions. She knew she would never forgive herself if she turned away when she could give the children living in the Den a better childhood than she had. But the Lions had slipped away too, like so much smoke at the end of the Inquiries, and Rhosyn had grasped at the straws of yet another life, helping people in the best way she knew how.

"I have the life I need," Rhosyn bit out.

"Not everybody was so lucky," Ansel observed. "It seems to me that the Talented have two choices: continue to make a living as a criminal or sell themselves into a lifetime of servitude with a sponsorship. The Foxes wanted to give them another choice. A fresh start."

"And so, you steal them away from their sponsors."

Ansel inclined his head in his acknowledgment.

Rhosyn cracked her knuckles to distract herself from the desire to argue further. She wanted to tell Ansel that robbing the residents of the upper city who were trying to use their power to aid the Talented wasn't a long-term solution.

But wasn't that what she and the Lions had done, stealing orphans away from brutal factory jobs?

It wasn't news to her that the law and what was right were not always aligned, but things were supposed to be different now. Chief Thorne was a good man. Contessa and King Byron worked tirelessly to right the injustices of the past.

Rhosyn was saved from having to answer by the appearance of Paul, a small bundle of fabric carried in his arms.

"These will have to do, although you might have to show an indecent amount of ankle," he admitted, putting the stack of clothes on the table.

"It would hardly be the first time somebody accused me of indecency."

"I doubt it will be the last," Ansel added, seemingly under his breath but still loud enough that Rhosyn shot him an exasperated look.

She pushed back from the table, picking up the pile of fabric. Maybe once she got changed, the Foxes would be more comfortable with her, and she would be able to glean more specifics of their activities to report back to Chief Thorne. And maybe she wouldn't feel like such a traitor to the uniform for walking freely among thieves.

Either way, it was time to live with the Foxes.

Chapter Eight

"You can't be serious."

"Why not?" Ansel asked.

Rhosyn stared suspiciously at the single, rickety bedframe before her. "Aren't you worried about your reputation?"

"I'm a young man who is apparently wanted by the Royal Police and owns a circus. I wouldn't think I had much of a reputation to maintain." Ansel shrugged, sitting down on the bed and beginning to pull off his boots as if the matter had been decided. "Besides, aren't you worried about *your* reputation?"

"That ship has left the harbor," Rhosyn admitted. "But why can't you just tie me to the bed again?"

"You've already proven that isn't enough to hold you, unless we immobilize you completely, and that hardly seems humane. Besides, we only had one free bed, and you have left it unfit to sleep in," Ansel pointed out.

Rhosyn grimaced.

"There are no more beds, and besides, wouldn't you be more comfortable if I only had to bind one hand? I'm a light sleeper, so if you try to escape, I'll wake. None of my performers will have to lose a full night's sleep keeping an eye on you and need the next day off," Ansel explained. "You sharing a bed with me should be the most agreeable solution for everybody."

"I slept just fine when I was tied down," Rhosyn grumbled.

Ansel moved on to removing his waistcoat and unbuttoning his vest. "I noticed, and honestly, I'm mildly concerned. But if you could sleep like that, then certainly my presence shouldn't bother you. I'm told I don't even snore."

Rhosyn swallowed. Truth be told, it shouldn't be an imposition to sleep in the same bed as Ansel. These days, she so rarely got an opportunity to shut her eyes for multiple hours together, and any offer of sleep wasn't one she should turn her nose up at. After years of multiple small, squirmy orphans pushing their way onto her narrow cot with her, she could likely share a bed with the circus's lion without issue.

It was the fact that the bedmate in question was Ansel that gave her pause. He had already wormed his way past her defenses as Mr. Blakely, and Rhosyn had paid the price for her lapse in vigilance. Now, letting her guard down around him, even in the unconsciousness of sleep, seemed unwise.

For the rest of the afternoon, as she spoke with Paul and Olivia under Little John's always watchful eye, Ansel's tale had seeped into her brain. He made it sound so sympathetic—so like something Nate and the Lion's would have done. As the Foxes joked and conversed around her, she had to remind herself on occasion that these were criminals, wanted by the Royal Police, who were no longer corrupt.

She would wait until Olivia and Paul were safely away. Then she would do her duty as an officer of the Royal Police, escape, and turn in Ansel and his whole operation. A few nights in the same bed wouldn't change that.

With determined steps, she walked to the opposite side of the bed and sat.

"That's a shame for you," Rhosyn commented, "as I snore terribly."

She pulled her own boots off, keeping her back to Ansel but still hyper aware of the sounds of rustling cloth as he undressed. Her shoes hit the ground with a startling thump as she dropped them, and Rhosyn paused in the resulting stillness, staring down at her clothes. She would normally undress further for bed, but that level of familiarity seemed ill-advised.

When she and Mr. Blakely had danced, blood had rushed to her cheeks—and much less ladylike places—at the firm grip of his fingers on her waist, despite having engaged in more than polite dancing in her life. In the moments Rhosyn had spent with him as the Hood, his hard chest pressed tightly against her back as they hid in the confines of a carriage, her heart had pounded with a cocktail of adrenaline and something wild, which awakened at the feel of his hand muffling her mouth.

Now, she was about to let her guard down almost completely around Ansel, who was the amalgamation of two men who had led her thoughts down the path of impropriety. Staying anything but fully clothed seemed almost comically unwise.

"It's nothing I haven't seen before, you know."

Ansel's voice came from close behind her, startling Rhosyn out of her thoughts where she had been staring at her boots, haphazardly toppled on the floor. They were filthy, she noticed dispassionately.

"Excuse me?" Rhosyn asked as the meaning of his words hit her.

"If you keep yourself under the blankets, I'll see far less than I did that night in the Gower's stables."

Rhosyn turned to glare over her shoulder, finding Ansel staring at her with a single brow arched. The expression, casual as it was, hit her like a challenge.

Rhosyn didn't back down from a challenge. Not from a rival gang in her youth—as evidenced by the slight bend in her nose and her callused knuckles—or from a difficult case facing her as a police officer.

Her fingers drifted towards the button of her pants, slowly but deliberately. Refusing to undress now, when Ansel had already reminded her of her former indecent exposure, would be admitting that she had something to be embarrassed about.

To his credit, Ansel didn't watch her undress, the rustling of the bedding indicating that he was busy sliding under the covers as Rhosyn slid her pants down her legs, kicking them off on top of her boots. The shirt Paul had dug up for her was long enough to cover her hips and the very top of her thighs, but plenty of skin was still on display.

She made a point not to hurry her movements as she turned to slide her bare legs beneath the sheets, despite the goosebumps rising on her thighs. Rhosyn hoped Ansel couldn't see them.

When she settled beneath the covers, she chanced a glance at him, finding him determinedly staring at his own fingernails. Part of her relaxed at the thought of him not trying to disarm her further with his proximity. Another smaller and more rebellious part in the back of her mind—the part of Rhosyn she had been determined to shove into a tiny drawer since she left the Lions—was disappointed that he hadn't looked. After all, how could you win the challenge if your opponent didn't show up to the fight?

The rough sheets rubbed against her bare skin as she slid down, pulling the blankets up to her chest. She tried to focus on getting comfortable, and not the warmth radiating from beside her, when a sudden shift made her freeze.

Rhosyn's breath stole from her lungs and Ansel rolled towards her, propping up on one elbow to lean over her. His unlaced shirt gaped open, giving her an unobstructed view of a broad chest dusted with dark hair, just inches from her nose.

"Wrist," Ansel prompted expectantly.

Rhosyn didn't move, her suddenly addled brain struggling to catch up with his request. When she simply stared, Ansel dangled a looped rope before her face, snapping her back to reality.

She resumed breathing and rolled her eyes all at once.

"You lock me in a room with you and still insist on tying me to the bed? One might think you expect me to cause trouble." Still, she held out her arm.

The scrape of rope against the soft skin of her inner wrist was enough to keep her cognizant of why it was imperative to keep her guard up around Ansel. Sympathetic as his story might be, he was a criminal, and she was a police officer.

Besides, resuming breathing meant being engulfed by his sweet and sharp burnt sugar scent again, and the sooner he leaned away, the sooner she could get back to building a mental wall between them.

When the knot was tied to his satisfaction, he rolled back to his side of the bed, and Rhosyn looked up to survey his handiwork. Once again, the knot was expertly tied, but not so tight as to be dangerous. The other end was affixed to the headboard.

"Aren't you concerned I'll untie myself?" she asked against her better judgment.

"I'd be more concerned with you picking a lock if I had cuffed you, but my trapeze artists' lives depend on me being able to tie a knot that can't be undone with just one hand. And I should wake up if you try to rip another bed in half."

Rhosyn slumped back against her pillow. It wasn't like she would run anyways—not with Paul and Olivia still at risk of being returned to the servitude they ran from so fervently.

"Good night, Rhosyn." Ansel snuffed out the lantern at the side of the bed, and they were plunged into darkness.

As his breathing slowed to a deep, even rhythm, Rhosyn urged herself to stay alert. Tied in the bed of a wanted criminal, she should be a sleepless mess, especially after so much rest in the preceding day. Maybe if she tossed and turned enough, she could keep Ansel awake too, and he would slip up in his resulting exhaustion.

She stared at the ceiling, trying to run over the events of the day with an analytical mind—to find a weakness of Ansel's she could exploit without putting Olivia and Paul in harm's way.

Her bedmate shifted in his sleep, reducing the distance between them to mere inches, the warmth of him seeping through the sheets and the minimal layers of clothing between them. Even now, the faintest burnt sugar scent still permeated her brain, likely worn into the pillow beneath her head.

Her eyelids grew impossibly heavy, and as she closed her eyes, she tried to justify to herself that there wasn't much to be done right now anyway. The last thought that flickered through her brain before sleep took her was that escaping might not be the issue—maybe it would be remembering that she was a hostage at all.

The sheets chilled Rhosyn's bare skin as she woke. She moved to pull the blankets more closely around her and tugged at the forgotten bind around her wrist. The chafe of rope snapped her back to reality and her eyes sprang open. But when she turned her head, the pillow beside her was empty, barely a dent left where Ansel's head had been, making it seem as if she had imagined his presence. It might have been a comforting thought, given how well rested she felt, when she should have spent a sleepless night in the bed of her enemy.

A clearing of a throat drew her attention and her eyes snapped to the corner the noise came from. Scrunched onto a small stool sat Little John, knees nearly coming to his chest as he folded himself onto furniture clearly not built for someone of his stature.

"Do you make a habit of watching people sleep?" she grumbled, voice scratchy.

"I do when Ansel tells me to." Little John seemed to be fixedly staring at some point beside her shoulder as he spoke.

Curious, Rhosyn glanced down and found the cause for his reticence. She had managed to tangle her legs with the blankets, leaving the entirety of their length visible. Even more, her long shirt had ridden up with her unconscious movement, a generous curve of hip on display. She quickly yanked down her clothes to keep herself decent.

Perhaps she should have felt embarrassed at the strong man having had such a view, but she was only mildly amused by his embarrassment.

"You're fine with holding me hostage and leaving me tied to your boss's bed, but a little thigh is where you draw the line?" Rhosyn teased.

"Don't drag me into it. This was all Ansel's idea." Little John folded his arms, meaty biceps threatening the seams of his shirt at the motion.

At that, Rhosyn pictured Ansel getting up before she woke and wondered if she had been in this state when he did. That thought did make her neck and chest prickle with heat, but she grit her teeth against the feeling. This situation was on him. Of course he was trying to goad her.

"Where is Ansel?" Rhosyn asked, feigning casualness as she stretched.

"Busy."

"A man of few words," she observed. "That bodes for a very long day of silent staring as I'm stuck tied to this bed."

"I can untie you, but I'll be keeping an eye on you." Little John stood and shuffled over to the head of the bed where her bonds were anchored. She waited as it took him a surprisingly long time to untie her and grimaced. Ansel hadn't been bluffing about her being well bound.

Finally free, Rhosyn sat and reached to grope around for her pants, still haphazardly tossed over her boots on the floor.

"So, what's on the agenda for today?" she asked as she pulled on her clothes and boots.

Little John looked off at the corner as she did, clearly not wanting to openly watch her dress but unwilling to turn his back. He learned quickly.

"It's not my job to entertain you, just make sure you don't escape."

"Great," Rhosyn said cheerily, "then you can just follow as I look around."

With that, she traipsed towards the door, finding it unlocked. Apparently, Ansel considered Little John enough of a guard given his leverage over her.

Stepping into the hallway, she picked a direction at random and began to walk the halls. John followed after like a large, lumbering shadow, but she paid him no mind, poking her head into open doorways as she passed.

As she suspected, nothing noteworthy jumped out at her. Ansel would have kept her locked in the room if there were anything potentially useful for her to find. Still, she started constructing a map of the building in her mind, making mental marks for windows that might make potential exits for when it eventually came time for her to escape.

It would also be useful to know the layout to relay to Chief Thorne when he conducted the inevitable raid, to upend this criminal operation.

Eventually, her search brought her down to the common room where she had fought and later listened to Ansel's tale. It was sparsely populated now though, only a few figures seated at tables bent over in quiet conversation. Two of the inhabitants were familiar.

"Olivia, Paul," she greeted, weaving through tables to where they sat.

They looked up, smiling with something that looked like relief. Perhaps they hadn't trusted that she would keep her word and cooperate as a captive until they were out of Mr. Gower's reach. The thought reached into Rhosyn's chest and twisted her heart.

She avoided grappling with those thoughts by looking at the piles of brightly colored fabric strewn across the table before them.

"What's all this?"

"Costumes," Olivia explained brightly. "I'm doing my best to make myself useful to the circus, to help Ansel."

Indeed, Olivia held a needle in her hand, poking at the eye with bright green thread that matched the cloth in her lap.

"You're sewing?" Rhosyn asked. If Olivia was any good with a needle and a thread, it wasn't due to her time in the Den. Rhosyn was only good at educating youngsters in less ladylike arts.

"I taught myself so I could pick up odd mending jobs for extra money…before the Gower's sponsored us of course." With the needle successfully threaded, Olivia turned to the garment in her lap, which turned out to be some sort of unitard onto which she was appliqueing a dizzying pattern of stars.

To Rhosyn's surprise, Paul picked up the next in the pile of garments—an obscenely fluffy layered skirt—and started using a small knife to pick apart a seam near the waist.

"You too?"

"I learned to be pretty good at undoing and redoing stitches while Olivia was teaching herself," Paul explained. Olivia shot him a look that was half annoyed, half fond at his teasing.

Rhosyn glanced around the room, a thought occurring to her. Little John had sat himself at the adjacent table, arms folded over his chest as he observed Rhosyn's conversation. She wasn't likely to get much investigating done with John hovering over her shoulder every waking moment. Maybe, the investigating could come to her.

"Why don't you teach me?" Rhosyn suggested, slipping into a chair and gesturing to the gaudy assortment of textiles. "It looks like there is plenty of work to go around."

They both blinked at her, as if she had suggested jumping off the top of the clock tower—which she had done before, although they wouldn't know that—and not helping with some mending.

"You...want to sew?" Olivia clarified.

Rhosyn shrugged. "It's not like I'd be allowed to do much else around here, and you know how hard it is for me to sit still. Besides, it's not as if I can really do much harm with a needle and thread."

Several hours later, it turned out Rhosyn had been very wrong. She could do serious damage with the most ladylike of instruments, although mostly to her own fingers. It seemed that years of calluses on her knuckles still didn't protect her from pricking her fingers and nearly bleeding all over Archer's Circus's wonderful wardrobe.

She managed to gouge the needle into her finger savagely and grimaced, using the motion to sneak a glance at where Little John still sat, watching over her. She ducked her head to hide a smile, seeing that a comrade had joined him. They bent together in conversation, John only glancing over at her every thirty seconds or so to make sure she hadn't gotten up to any mischief.

Contessa would be proud, she thought. After all, her friend had been the first one to lament how easily an embroidering lady blended in to the background, making it the perfect cover for eavesdropping—a strategy Contessa had never been able to employ because she couldn't put two stitches together without ripping out her shiny blonde hair.

Despite Rhosyn's personal lack of skill, the strategy did seem to have merit.

"You're stabbing it too hard." Olivia glanced over her shoulder. "It's muslin, it doesn't fight back you know."

"Old habits die hard," Rhosyn grumbled, staring at the plain shirt in her hand. She had been relegated to fixing ripped undergarments, where her sloppy work could be hidden under costumes. "Never mind that though. It's nice of you to help Ansel."

"We like to earn our keep if we can," Paul said.

"I was hoping to get through all of these, but I don't think we will be able to get it done by the end of the week," Olivia huffed in disappointment.

"The end of the week?" Rhosyn prodded, glancing up at John and finding him engaged in conversation still. She surreptitiously scooted around the table under the pretext of having more room to straighten out the garment in her grasp, trying to get into earshot.

"We'll be leaving for the country on Sunday," Olivia explained. "Originally, we were supposed to leave town with the circus on the train at the end of their visit, but given...current circumstances...Ansel found a way to smuggle us out with a contact earlier. He told us first thing this morning."

That drew Rhosyn's focus back to Olivia, her straining ears pausing in their efforts to overhear John and his companion. "Sunday. That's five days from now."

Olivia nodded before her eyes widened, seeming to understand what she'd just conveyed. Rhosyn only had to cooperate with Ansel and the Foxes for five days...and she only had five more days to gather all the information necessary to take them down, once Olivia and Paul were safe from the threat of being returned to the Gower's service.

Olivia opened her mouth as if to say something, but Rhosyn cut her off.

"I'm sure you'll be happy to start a new life in the country." Rhosyn kept her voice as casual as possible, trying to convince Olivia and Paul not to worry about what happened once they were out of the way.

"I am! We're planning on going to Sussex where..."

Olivia's words faded into the background of Rhosyn's thoughts as she described how she was looking forward to living somewhere where the air wasn't always heavy with factory smoke and she might have room to start a small garden.

Rhosyn also tried not to dwell on her plans for escape in five days time either. Instead, she let her senses of the room broaden as Olivia and Paul planned excitedly for the future. More Foxes had entered the safehouse as the day wore on, and conversations grew in volume as they seemed to forget Rhosyn was there.

"... Worthingtons should be the next mark."

A snippet from the table at which Little John sat grabbed her attention. She cocked her head but kept her eyes down on the needle and thread in her lap.

"His investment in the mines made out well recently. He doesn't need all that wealth," John grumbled.

"And if we do hit the Gowers again, we'll need the cash."

Rhosyn frowned at her stitches, and not just because she had managed to stab herself hard enough to get a drop of blood on her project. Her concern was twofold—not only were the Foxes planning another robbery, but they were planning to hit the Gowers house again. Try as she might, she couldn't puzzle out why they might risk returning to terrorize the same family again and again, even if they did overwork their servants.

"Ansel went to—"

A loud cheering from the far side of the room cut off Little John's companion. Rhosyn suppressed an internal groan as she looked up towards the source of the commotion.

Standing on the table was a young woman, about the same age Rhosyn had been when she left the Lions, grinning as she juggled a no fewer than seven shining objects. Rhosyn's eyes widened as she focused her gaze enough to recognize the objects as glass beer mugs. The juggler didn't seem concerned, barely looking at the flying mugs as her fingers scarcely touched the twirling handles before spinning the glasses into the air once more.

The volume of the crowd crescendoed as a spectator tossed another glass into the fray. The juggler's grin only widened as she caught it without hesitation, seaming it into her rhythm without faltering.

"Ey, knock it off, Tory," Little John shouted without menace. "I know you won't break anything, but it's not kind to our host's nerves."

Indeed, the barkeep grabbed the counter he stood behind with white knuckles, eyes wide with nervous incredulity. He had likely expected brawls when he let a gang overrun his bar—probably for a healthy cut of their scores—but very little could prepare him or Rhosyn for the sights of Archer's Circus.

The juggler stopped her rhythmic tosses, instead catching the glasses one by one and stacking them neatly in her hands. She shot a sheepish glance at the bartender and hopped down off the table as the crowd dispersed.

Unfortunately, her performance had decidedly ended Little John's conversation as his companion stood and went to speak with somebody else.

"I'm not sure I'll ever get used to the way these performers use their Talents so freely," Olivia sighed, her tone wistful.

"I don't know, you might be able to put on an impressive fire breathing show with your Talent," Rhosyn pointed out.

"Maybe." Olivia shrugged. "But even at the Gower's, I felt like I had to look over my shoulder every time I lit a fire in the hearth. I suppose it would be different if I had learned to hide my Talent in plain sight like they have, though."

Rhosyn considered as Paul and Olivia continued to discuss the Talents they had seen in the Circus—the lion tamer who could understand the creature's roars as if they were words and the magician whose tricks nobody had ever figured out, likely because he could actually make small objects pop in and out of existence.

The thoughts of a youth so similar, yet so different from her own in the gangs, where Talents were both a death sentence and a source of power, twirled in her head for the remainder of the day. While she mulled things over, she kept a sharp ear out for any gossip that drifted within ear shot, but she learned nothing more interesting than the rumor that the contortionist had been found in the sword swallower's bed—apparently both showing off their skills.

Contrary to most gang haunts, the crowds of Foxes thinned as the day wore into evening, likely headed off for a night of entertaining revelers. By the time a familiar figure wearing a top hat graced the doorway, Olivia was dozing lightly in her seat and Rhosyn was feigning heaviness in her own eyelids, seeing if Little John would take it as an opportunity to lift his watchful eye.

Ansel sighed as he entered the room, sweeping off his hat and running his hand through his hair. The stiff, pushed back style he wore during the day came undone, falling across his forehead, nearly brushing his eyes.

"You can head off, Little John." He nodded to his friend as he took in the room. "I'll watch things around here while you go to the Circus."

John nodded, pushing to his feet and stretching, several joints popping audibly as he coaxed movement back into his bones.

"He shouldn't be too tired. I went easy on him today," Rhosyn quipped.

"That doesn't mean I won't keep just as close of an eye on you tomorrow." John pointed a meaty finger at her as he tromped past. Rhosyn shot him her most winning smile in return.

"It looks like I'm the tired one today then," Ansel admitted. "And that means it's time for bed for both of us, even if you're still full of energy."

Olivia, who had woken at some point during the conversation, looked momentarily shocked by his phrasing, but Rhosyn waved off her concern.

"Mr. Blakely here is a perfect gentlemen. Aside from being a lying, cheating gangster, that is," Rhosyn assured brightly.

With that, she stood and walked towards the stairs, leaving Ansel to trail behind her. It wasn't until they were back in the room they had shared last night that Ansel spoke.

"I distinctly remember that *you* are the one who cheats. In fact, I'm pretty sure that is how we found ourselves in this predicament."

Rhosyn flopped down on the bed, preparing to take her boots off. In a roundabout sort of way, Ansel was right. If she hadn't found the playing card in his pocket, it might have taken her an embarrassingly long time to put together who the Hood was.

"I don't have many opportunities to hustle people anymore. I have to practice when I have the chance, or I might get rusty," Rhosyn explained through a yawn.

Ansel paused in undoing his cufflinks. He cocked his head. "You used to cheat at cards a lot? Not a pastime I would expect of an upstanding officer of the Royal Police."

Rhosyn's fingers stuttered over the laces of her boots, somehow knotting them tighter when she meant to untangle them. The reference to her past had tumbled out of her unbidden. A day in a gang haunt, and it slipped off her tongue like second nature—like it had only taken one day to forget that her past was behind her and she now stood firmly on the right side of the law. Or at least tried to.

"Who doesn't have a few dalliances in their youth?" Rhosyn grasped her composure back, shrugging off his question.

Ansel let out a *hmph* that didn't sound satisfied with her answer, but didn't push her further on it.

"The circus business is harder work than I expected," Rhosyn said, changing the subject. "You were gone by the time the sun rose and back after dark. It certainly keeps you busy."

"You know I do more than own a circus," Ansel pointed out. "But if you think I'm going to tell you what else I was doing today, then I'm afraid you'll be disappointed."

As he spoke, he had rolled up his sleeves and his forearms flexed as he reached up to tug at his cravat. In the dim lamplight of the room, the shadows cast by the veins there deepened, and Rhosyn had to force her gaze away, mouth traitorously dry.

"Asking about each other's day seems to be the bare minimum of polite for two people about to share a bed," Rhosyn retorted. As she did, she moved to unbutton her pants. She shouldn't be flustered by Ansel undressing after last night, but if she was, she wouldn't pass up the opportunity to disarm him in return.

As she stood to push the trousers down her thighs, she peeked out of the corner of her eye at him, and found him not looking, busy with the buttons on his shirt. She couldn't decide whether to be impressed or frustrated that a gang leader boasted such a robust sense of honor.

With a stifled sigh, Rhosyn slid into the bed, staring up at the ceiling. She tried not to listen to the rustle of fabric as Ansel continued to undress. The bed dipped as he slid into his side, and she contained a jump as bare skin brushed her shoulder. She turned her head to find that he had chosen to forgo a shirt tonight.

Quickly, she snapped her gaze back to the ceiling above her, but it was no good. Ansel's chest dominated her vision again as he leaned over her to grab the rope attached to the headboard.

Rhosyn pushed her head back into the pillow as he bound her wrist to the bedpost, as if the millimeters of distance it put between her nose and his sternum could stop her from seeing the thatch of hair dusted there and wondering if it would be soft to rub her face on. The little space the motion afforded her certainly did nothing to dampen the sweet and spicy smell of burnt sugar that clung to his skin. At this proximity, the scent permeating her senses, it struck Rhosyn as familiar—it was the aroma of toasted nuts and spun sugar at the circus. As if Ansel had spent so much time among the traveling performers, that the essence of Archer's Circus had gotten under his skin.

Ansel paused in tying his knot, glancing down at Rhosyn's face, attention ostensibly grabbed by her rigid posture.

Seeing her staring fixedly at the divot between his pecs, he chuckled, the noise rumbling from his chest so close that Rhosyn felt the vibrations.

"Sorry, I'll be quick so as not to offend your ladylike sensibilities."

Rhosyn held perfectly still as Ansel finished binding her wrist for the night. Then, he rolled back to his side and snuffed the single lamp on his side of the bed. The incomplete darkness of the lower city fell—the darkest it could get in the neighborhood where the streets never slept and the light of the tavern perpetually creeped under the door as patrons were served until the wee hours of the morning.

It was a soft sort of quiet, and the familiarity of it combined with the sugary spice still lingering on the back of Rhosyn's tongue stirred something in her.

"I'm not a lady. Never was and never will be." The words spilled out of her without permission. She paused, wondering if she should stop but finding that she didn't want to. "I'm just like you."

"A police officer like a gangster?" Ansel didn't sound derisive, but instead curious. As if he were really trying to understand Rhosyn. For some reason it hurt her chest.

"I wasn't always with the Royal Police. Before the..." Rhosyn hesitated but the words banged against her ribs, begging to be let out of where they were caged in her chest. In the quiet of the night, she was surprised Ansel couldn't hear them, even though she hadn't spoken yet. "During the Inquiries, I ran with the Lions. And not just that, I was one of their leaders."

Ansel shifted slightly, the rustling of sheets loud as a gunshot in the pregnant silence.

"That's quite a change of heart," he eventually said, but his tone didn't hold judgment.

"It didn't feel like it at the time." Rhosyn admitted—and it wasn't a lie. The decision to help Chief Thorne, when he so desperately needed officers he could trust, was a familiar one. She turned her back on her criminal past in an instant, just as she had turned away from her hopes of a simpler future when she stayed with the Lions to help Nate and Kristoff. She had joined a gang to protect those with Talents when she had none herself, and she had given up the life she had built with the Lions to protect the city in the aftermath of the Inquiries.

"It hasn't been hard...not until now," Rhosyn murmured at the ceiling. "Not until I spent time among you and the Foxes."

"And what is it now?" Ansel prompted, his voice a little more than a whisper.

"Like being homesick."

The admission hung in the air, soft and palpable. It felt like a peace offering.

Fabric rustled again, and so lightly that Rhosyn might have imagined it if she hadn't been conscious of every slight movement, knuckles brushed against the bare skin of Rhosyn's thigh. The touch was both intimate and innocent, and Rhosyn allowed it. It seemed that Ansel had accepted her offering, but didn't push for more, knowing this could only be a temporary truce. They may understand each other, but it didn't change the truth of their situation.

Hair tickled Rhosyn's nose, consciousness slowly filling her, just as air filled her lungs. But she was so comfortable, and she wasn't ready to wake yet. Pushing away awareness, she instead burrowed deeper into the solid warmth beneath her, filling her lungs with another deep sigh that tasted of spicy sweetness.

As she nuzzled her nose further into the ticklish hair, she realized that for once it was not her own rebellious curls having fallen into her face at night, but much smoother and shorter. Her eyelashes fluttered, but she forced herself to keep them closed, as the realization that she cuddled into a decidedly masculine body took hold. She didn't move as she took stock of the situation.

Somehow, she had ended up burrowed into the crook of Ansel's neck, the hair at his nape stirring with her every breath. He lay on his back, one of her legs slung across his hips, her front molded tightly to his side.

What stole her attention more than the muscular press of his side into her chest, or the way her angle positioned one of his thighs between hers, was the heavy arm laid across her own shoulders. The hand belonging to the arm came to rest on her head, fingers burrowed into her hair at the crown of her head. In response to her small movements, the fingers began to move, infinitesimally massaging into her scalp.

A breath stuttered out of Rhosyn at the tingles the touch sent down her spine. Unconsciously, she arched back into the touch, and the fingers moved again, rubbing in the tiniest of circles and pulling lightly at the hair at the nape of her neck. Her lashes fluttered as her eyes rolled back in her head.

Having Ansel play with her hair shouldn't feel absolutely sinful, but here she was one breath away from moaning.

A rustle of sheets broke the quiet of early morning as Ansel turned his head on the pillow, and a small part of Rhosyn cringed to know that he was awake and aware, not just unconsciously responding to her proximity. A much larger part of her reveled in the feel of his lips moving against the crown of her head as he murmured her name.

"Rhosyn." His voice was rough from sleep, rumbling in his chest far more than his normal smooth tone. The word was both a question and a warning—and just as delicious as the fingers that hadn't quite stopped moving in her hair.

Her only response was to nuzzle deeper into the crook of his neck. If she responded, she would have to face some semblance of reality, instead of enjoying the toe-curling feel of his nails now lightly raking against her scalp. The slight scratch sent warmth dripping down her spine to pool in her core.

She shifted her hips unconsciously at the sensation, and she discovered the delicious friction of Ansel's thigh pressed between her own. Rhosyn shifted her hips again, more purposefully this time. Now, her core was pressed firmly to him, growing so warm that she was sure he could feel the heat of it through her long shirt.

Ansel let out a strangled grunt as she circled her hips infinitesimally once more. His fingers tightened in her hair, and the response drew attention to a growing hardness against her thigh.

She moved again, this time letting her thigh move as she ground against him.

"Rhosyn." He only said the same single word as earlier, but this time it was a command—to stop or keep going, she couldn't be sure.

She shivered in response to his tone. In this haze of early morning pleasure, still laced with the sense of unreality from last night, she could think of little beyond wanting this feeling to continue—to deepen.

Rhosyn wanted to touch him.

She reached for him, only to have her shoulder jerked back as rope grew taught around her wrist. Her bonds did more than hold her back from Ansel. They snapped her back to reality, and immediately she tensed.

She wrenched herself away from his gentle grasp, rolling onto her back on the side of the bed where she was tied. Ansel blinked at her in surprise before his gaze trailed to her wrist. The openness of early awakening in his eyes shuttered at the sight. The tangible evidence of their animosity sobered them both.

While at a temporary truce, in five days Rhosyn would break free of these bonds and be his enemy once more.

Without a word, Ansel stood from the bed and pulled on his clothes with hurried efficiency. He walked out the door with boots in hand, not even bothering to put them on before leaving.

If Rhosyn's mind hadn't been reeling at their sudden sobriety, she might have tried to untie herself. As it was, Little John entered before she could make any moves towards freedom. She exhaled heavily, facing down another day captured in the Foxes's den.

Rhosyn repositioned herself in her chair for the tenth time in the last five minutes, and Olivia eyed her sympathetically.

"If I have to sit still for another hour, I'll rip my hair out." Rhosyn set down her pitiful attempt at sewing and admitted defeat.

After spending the morning and the first part of the afternoon revisiting her eavesdropping strategy from earlier to no avail, she was ready to throw in the towel. Rhosyn had never been suited for long stakeouts, preferring to face her enemies out in the open.

"I think that might be challenging, based on how thick it seems."

Rhosyn twisted in her seat to find Ansel standing at the bottom of the stairs. She wasn't entirely sure how he got there, given that she hadn't seen him come back to the Foxes's haunt after leaving this morning, even though it seemed that you had to cross through the common area to get from the main entrance to the stairs in the back.

"At least it would give me something to do besides sewing," Rhosyn griped at him as he strolled over to look over their handiwork.

He picked up one of her poorly darned undershirts and inspected it. "You might be better at it too."

Rhosyn wrinkled her nose at the jab, but didn't deny it.

"Are you sure this isn't your underhanded way of trying to put Archer's Circus out of business—to have everybody's costumes fall apart on stage until we are shut down for indecency?"

"It's not my fault you left me with nothing else to do," Rhosyn pointed out.

"And what exactly would you like to be doing?"

Rhosyn shrugged. "Punching something, probably."

"I don't think any of my men who were on the receiving end of your fists would be lining up to do it again."

Rhosyn cocked her head at him, considering. Her eyes caught on the biceps she had pillowed her head on just hours ago and her face heated. Now she really wanted to punch something.

"What about you?" she goaded.

"Me?"

"Yes. How do you feel about being on the receiving end of my fists?" She raised an eyebrow in challenge. If she couldn't work out her frustrations with Ansel on his thigh in the quiet of his bedroom, then her fists would have to do the job.

"Oh, I'm not too scared of them." Ansel shrugged. "Every time I've faced off against you, I seemed to get the upper hand."

Rhosyn bristled. "You think you won those fights? You cheated!"

"Once again, it's you who proved to be the cheater."

Rhosyn stood and her nostrils flared. In reaction to her movement, Little John rose from his table, as if he expected to have to restrain her from leaping across the table at Ansel.

"All I'm hearing is that you're afraid to fight me without all your tricks."

"Nothing is against the rules in a lower city brawl," Ansel retorted.

She bared her teeth at the words and the conflict that rose in her mind at his statement. After her time with the Lions, she knew there was no such thing as fighting dirty if it meant you could best your opponent. The conditioning of the police force continually urged her to pull her punches. In one sentence, Ansel had prodded at the divide in her soul that became wider with every passing moment with the Foxes.

"If I stopped fighting by the rules, you wouldn't be able to get the upper hand," Rhosyn challenged.

"Why don't we test that out?"

Little John stepped closer, the look of consternation on his face echoed by Olivia and Paul. "I don't think that's a good idea, boss."

Ansel shrugged off his concern. "I'm the one who goaded her. If it's inevitable Rhosyn is going to punch something, then I'd prefer to have myself being on the receiving end of her fists than you."

Rhosyn raised her brows. "Nothing like a little sparring to combat the monotony of being held hostage." Her palms itched.

Ansel jerked his head towards the bar. "We have a storeroom we cleared out to use for training. It should do nicely."

He led the way behind the bar and Little John moved to follow. Ansel stopped him with an outstretched arm. "We'll be fine."

John opened his mouth as if to argue, but clearly thought better of it from the firmness in Ansel's tone.

An edge of curiosity broke through the simmering anticipation of a fight under Rhosyn's skin. She trailed him through a small door into a blank room. He closed it behind them as she took in the space.

A pang of something bittersweet echoed beneath Rhosyn's breastbone. The middle of the room was clear, with barrels and crates pushed haphazardly against the walls to make the most room for all manner of activities.

It looked just like the back room at the old Den where Rhosyn had trained young Lions in self-defense.

Rhosyn turned to consider Ansel as he barred the door behind him.

"I wanted some privacy," he admitted. "And if you do manage to knock me out, anything I can do to slow down the mayhem you might cause is a good thing."

She cracked her knuckles, the sound loud in the empty room. "I should probably ask you why you agreed to this, but I don't want to talk you out of it."

"I'm glad you're not asking."

Before Rhosyn could ponder the meaning of his words, he lunged.

Reflexes that remained quiet, yet awake, grabbed at her muscles, letting her sidestep his attack just in time. As he swung past her, she threw out her elbow, catching him in the flank.

He let out a pained grunt but didn't falter, swinging around and trying to take her feet out from under her with a swing of his leg. With a jump, she managed to avoid the blow to her ankles, but it threw her off balance.

Ansel pushed the advantage, coming at her with a flurry of blows. Rhosyn stumbled back for only a second before catching his punches on her forearms. The dull pain of what she knew would be bruises grounded her. At the same time, adrenaline surged in her veins.

It was a heady feeling. Like the one of drinking too much whiskey without the loss of clarity. Like the giddy sensation of Ansel's hand in her hair.

The thought of their morning encounter threw fuel on the fire in her chest. Ansel had no right to make her feel such things, yet part of her yearned for more.

With a snarl, she ducked under his next right hook and drove her shoulder up into his stomach. The momentum knocked him back.

For a moment, the pair toppled through the air, seemingly weightless. Then, Rhosyn's teeth rattled in her skull as they hit the ground.

Ansel brought his knees up as he went down, driving them into Rhosyn's stomach and trying to kick her off. Her vision swam as her breath exploded out of her, but she bore down. She wasn't much taller than him, but it was enough to allow her to pin him.

He struggled for a moment longer before giving in. With a tap on her forearm, currently braced across his throat, he signaled his defeat. For a second, Rhosyn considered taking advantage of the situation and knocking him out with a swift blow to the jaw.

He might have deserved it, for the brewing torment within her that he kept prodding into a more fervent simmer.

Instead, she backed off, sitting back on her heels.

After landing a few good blows, her tender pride at being held hostage was placated. Still, it didn't feel completely satisfied, as if she were craving some other sort of release.

"Just as fierce as I remembered," Ansel said, seemingly to himself as he sat up. The comment drew Rhosyn from her thoughts. His hand went to his ribs as he moved, likely bruised from the force of Rhosyn's ramming shoulder.

"Fierce, eh?" Rhosyn prompted.

Ansel held up his other hand to reveal a bandage around his ring finger she hadn't noticed before. "You have tried to bite me twice. Once you succeeded, and nearly took my finger off."

"Just be happy I didn't manage to get my teeth around you in the Gower's carriage too."

"Oh, I am." Ansel admitted. "I'm all for a bit of biting between friends, but that wasn't the time or place for it."

Rhosyn swallowed thickly, unsure whether Ansel's return to flirting was a sign that the tension from their early morning encounter was dissipating, or if he was trying to use it as a weapon against her.

"Why were you there that night?" Rhosyn asked to change the subject. "You had already done your job to get Olivia and Paul away."

He considered her, both still sprawled on the dusty floor, slightly sweaty and panting. It wasn't the posture of a hostage and her captor—or a police officer and a gang leader, for that matter. But something about it made such questions feel less like a game for information and more like a real conversation.

Ansel must have felt the same, because he answered, despite having no obligation to.

"Something…didn't seem right," he admitted. "When we got Olivia and Paul back to the safehouse that night, they were so tired they seemed almost ill. They've been adamant that they weren't physically mistreated, but the way they seemed positively dazed put my hair on end."

Rhosyn grit her teeth. It ached in her bones to know that young Lions had come to be in such a state—even after everything Nate had done for them. She had been there that very night and thought Paul seemed off, but it wasn't her who had been able to help him and his sister.

"I'm not sure what I expected to find," Ansel continued. "Maybe I was looking for evidence that they mistreated their staff, to explain why Olivia and Paul barely seemed to be able to talk about their time there, other than to be glad they were out. But that conversation we overheard between Mr. Gower and that other man, Hamish..."

Rhosyn pondered, remembering the cryptic words of the stolen conversation she had barely had time to process, given that she and Ansel found themselves in a tussle moments later.

"He seemed desperate to have Paul and Olivia return," she remembered.

"I still haven't been able to figure out his urgency. But I know that it doesn't feel right in my stomach. Something about the way he collects Talented servants doesn't sit right with me."

Rhosyn frowned. Mr. Gower's tone when he had demanded Paul and Olivia be returned—and seemingly to the groom of all people—was certainly sinister. It didn't give her any compelling evidence as to his intentions. Perhaps he was just a rich, pompous prick who was unused to being denied anything.

"One overheard conversation is hardly evidence of wrongdoing," she pointed out.

"I'll leave the evidence gathering to the police." Ansel inclined his head towards her. "I know when to trust my gut, and it was right."

Rhosyn grimaced. Perhaps she should be more ashamed that she had broken into the Gower's property without a warrant that night, only to come away without evidence, but more of an instinctual notion that they were up to no good. Instead of focusing on that, she asked, "You were right?"

"I've spent the few days arranging chance meetings with most of the Gower's Talented staff out in the city and casually offering the Foxes's...*ahem*...services. None of them have said anything outright against the Gowers, but they've all accepted our help."

"That's why you're planning to hit them again." Rhosyn thought out loud about her overheard conversation with Little John and his associate yesterday.

Ansel's eyebrows shot up his forehead. "And how would you have known what we've been planning?"

"Don't blame Little John." Rhosyn smiled wryly. "He thought I was too busy stabbing myself with a needle to eavesdrop."

He ran a hand tiredly through his hair. "We might call ourselves the Foxes, but I had a feeling keeping you here would be like letting a fox into the hen house. May I ask what else you overheard?"

"You may, but I don't have to answer."

"You're my hostage right now. Is it wise to deny me?" Ansel asked.

Rhosyn gestured between them. "Do you normally talk to your hostages like this? I don't think you're very good at it then."

In truth, trying to beat the sense out of each other had gone a long way to level the playing field between them. As if the fight had temporarily funneled the animosity out of them and given them the ability to speak rationally for once.

"Maybe I don't want you to be my hostage anymore," Ansel murmured, looking down at his hands, which had come to lay in his lap during the conversation.

"That doesn't seem very wise. If you let me go, I might just tell Chief Thorne about your plans to rob the Worthingtons."

Ansel glanced up through his lashes. "You know they don't need all that wealth."

"And you do?"

"Not me." Ansel shook his head. "But getting all the Talented out of the city is expensive. They need funds to help them start new lives, and getting the Gower's servants out will take a substantial bribe."

Rhosyn's interest piqued. "A bribe? Why would you ever admit that to me."

"Because…" Ansel paused, leaning back on his hands. "Because last night you gave me hope that you might understand after all. You might be an officer of the Royal Police, but what you told me makes me think it isn't because you believe in the letter of the law."

Rhosyn's voice stuck in her throat. She had no good retort to that, even as she might wish to deny it—to insist she was loyal to Chief Thorne when the police had already suffered so much corruption.

"I might understand," she eventually choked out instead.

Ansel nodded, as if he saw how difficult of a concession she had made. "To help the Talented truly be free of their sponsorships, we need to destroy the documents binding them to their sponsors. If we don't, their sponsors have the legal right to find them and force them back into service. Without that evidence, though, they have no legal hold over their Talented servants."

"Which is why you raided Contessa's office," Rhosyn said.

"Contessa? You're on a first name basis with the King's advisor?" Ansel seemed taken aback.

"She *is* married to Nathanial Woodrow." Rhosyn shot him a pointed look, hoping not to have to spell out her connection.

Realization dawned. "The Beast." He nodded.

"Don't call him that, but yes."

Ansel snorted. "I saw him at that party. He's no less a Beast now than his reputation painted him as when he was the leader of the Lions. It's what makes him such an effective bodyguard. He just has the backing of a king now."

Rhosyn frowned and tucked that line of thought away to examine later—that Nate was both the King's protector and the same headstrong fighter she had always looked up to as a brother.

"So, you got the sponsorship papers from Contessa's office?" Rhosyn prompted.

Ansel sighed heavily. "Yes and no. We got the batch that had already been completed, but after that, the next set was put in a safe. Unfortunately, many of the Gowers' current staff's papers are in that set. We tried to steal them too, but we haven't been able to crack the safe. Thus, we need the money to bribe a guard to take them for us. It will be a hefty sum."

At the mention of cracking a safe, a thought dawned on Rhosyn, accompanied by a memory. For an instant she was back on a liberation mission with Nate and Kristoff. A small girl tugged against her hand, refusing to leave and pointing a dirt smudged hand at a safe in the corner of the office they slept in, laying on the floor and locked in by the factory foreman. Even now, Rhosyn could feel the light thuds of tumblers falling into place under her fingers as she cracked the safe, the subtle clicking in her ear signaling her success as she pressed the side of her face to the cold metal. Inside she had found a delicate gold necklace—the only memento the girl had of her executed mother, taken from her by the factory's foreman.

From that day until she grew out of the Den, the girl had never taken that necklace off.

Stealing sponsorship papers so more Talented could be free wouldn't be that different.

"What if you didn't have to bribe the guards?" Rhosyn asked.

"We don't have anybody good enough at lock picking to get into that safe. And unfortunately, our magician's Talent doesn't work unless he's seen the object in question, so he can't blink the papers of the safe."

Ansel's words nearly distracted Rhosyn from what she was about to offer—against her better judgment—but she stayed with the task at hand.

"But if you did, you wouldn't have to rob the Worthingtons?"

Ansel looked at her curiously. "We'd have to stretch the circus's earnings between the Gowers' servants to give them a fresh start, but it could be done."

Rhosyn took a deep breath, stealing herself.

"I can crack the safe."

Ansel blinked once. Twice.

Silence stretched through the room, broken only by the noises from the common room outside.

"You can?"

Rhosyn released a stolen breath, somehow relieved that his question wasn't why she would do such a thing. "I'm not just the best pickpocket in London. I happen to also be the second best lockpick."

"And who would the first be?" Ansel asked.

"Wouldn't you like to know." Rhosyn's own past was hers to divulge to Ansel, even if it was ill advised. But she wasn't about to admit to Ansel that she had picked up her best safe-cracking tips from the King's closest advisor.

To his credit, Ansel didn't push her. Apparently, he was wise enough not to ask imprudent questions when somebody who was supposed to be his enemy offered their aid.

"Let's say I take you up on this. I'm not just going to let you waltz out of here and up to the palace. I have no guarantee you wouldn't just announce yourself and tell them of our plans."

"Well, that's good, because you know I'm terrible at waltzing." The quip was out of Rhosyn's mouth before she could remind herself this was a serious negotiation. Planning like this felt far too familiar. Despite being sprawled across a dusty floor, she could almost imagine she was sitting at Nate's desk, her boots up on the polished surface no matter how much he frowned, planning another liberation mission.

To her relief, Ansel chuckled, and Rhosyn found a smile toying with the corners of her mouth.

"I'm not going to let you walk out of here alone either."

"You have to let me out if I'm going to crack the safe. And I'm not doing it while Little John looks on." Rhosyn searched for the right words, wishing for Contessa's skill with a diplomatic turn of phrase. "I'm sure you'll understand that I'd appreciate discretion with the Foxes on this."

She shied away from the thought of betraying Chief Thorne in a way that had to be hidden, but she couldn't risk one of the Foxes having a loose tongue and telling somebody that an officer of the Royal Police had helped them burgle the palace. After all, once Paul and Olivia were gone, she would have to go back to strictly legal activities.

Thankfully, Ansel understood her meaning without further explanation. "Then I'll come with you."

Rhosyn hesitated. Perhaps she should worry about what Ansel would do with the knowledge of the crime she was offering to commit for him. After all, it would make good blackmail material. But his words from when he first confronted her, tied to the bed upstairs, came back to her.

Perhaps we can come to some sort of understanding.

Maybe they would after all.

"Alright. We'll do it together," she agreed.

Ansel stood and stretched out a hand to help her up as well. She took it, and he hauled her to her feet, leaving her standing nearly chest to chest with him. Maybe she should back away, but he didn't let go of her hand immediately, leaving them standing mere inches apart in the middle of the room.

Rhosyn's breath stuttered as he smiled crookedly, simultaneously wearing the charm of Mr. Blakely and the promise of mischief of the Hood.

"Well," he said, "this should be fun."

Chapter Nine

The floorboards creaked incessantly as Rhosyn paced back and forth across the small room. It was nearly annoying enough to make her stop, but she had too much energy to work out, despite her little brawl with Ansel earlier.

The past hours were the first Rhosyn had spent alone with her thoughts since being captured by the Foxes. Now that Rhosyn had offered her aid, Ansel had deemed it safe to leave her alone in his room, although he had locked the door. She supposed she should welcome the opportunity to regroup, but instead she only fretted.

After their conversation, Ansel had left again, saying he needed to make arrangements for their mission to the palace. Rhosyn knew that it would happen rather quickly, but when he said they would head out when he got back, her heart rate doubled. In just a matter of hours, she would be helping a criminal steal documents from the crown.

The thought shouldn't make her palms sweat, but still, she ended up repetitively wiping her hands on her pants. It was hardly the first time in her life that she'd be breaking the law—not even the most serious infraction in her ledger. If things went well, they wouldn't be spilling any blood.

She clung to that thought with a vice grip. By volunteering to crack the safe for Ansel, she was preventing the Foxes from robbing a family of their wealth and potentially being less scrupulous with their violence in the process. With her on the job, she could make sure the operation was as quiet and peaceful as possible.

After all, wasn't saving lives and preventing crimes her job as an officer of the Royal Police?

At that thought she stopped pacing in favor of flopping back on the bed in the center of the room, her hair spreading out around her in a chaotic splash of crimson. Since joining the Royal Police, she had been able to protect her city by following the law and ensuring others did too.

The end of the Inquiries had marked a profound shift, where Rhosyn went from seeing the police and the Crown as her enemy to her allies. When Contessa's father, Chief Cook, had been leading corrupt law enforcement, breaking the law had clearly been in the name of justice, and Rhosyn had done it happily to be what the people of London needed.

When Chief Thorne took over, and the new King started taking steps to protect the Talented, the Royal Police were now on the side of righteousness, and Rhosyn had once again shifted to be what was needed—as close to a model police officer as she could be with her shadowed past. But if the law was no longer corrupt, why did she now feel like she had to break it to do the right thing?

With a groan, she dug the heels of her hands into her eyes so hard that lights exploded in her vision. Ever since meeting the Hood—Ansel—everything that had once seemed clear had become muddied.

A rustling at the window grabbed her attention. In a second, Rhosyn rolled off the bed, landing on the balls of her feet in a defensive crouch. After days on edge, her reflexes were primed to respond quickly to any unusual sounds.

The rustling turned into scratching, and she inched towards the window, staying low so as to be out of the line of sight of anybody at the sill—an impressive feat given that Ansel's room was on the fourth floor.

A clicking and then a metallic scrape indicated that the lock had broken—forced open instead of finessed—and the window swung open on loudly protesting hinges. The muscles in Rhosyn's thighs tightened like coiled springs, prepared to leap forward and dislodge the intruder as they clambered onto the sill.

Instead, a familiar silhouette, dark against the hazy evening sky swung up effortlessly, perching in the window frame with all the ease of a sparrow in flight.

Rhosyn blinked at the maneuver as Ansel paused, seemingly spotting her defensive posture. Even Scarlett, who for some reason insisted on entering through Rhosyn's bedroom window even though she was perfectly welcome to use the door, didn't boast such gravity-defying maneuvers.

This was also Ansel's own room, which begged the question, "And you chose to risk me punching you out of a fourth story window frame instead of using the door to your own room because…?"

Ansel dropped into the room, his boots barely making a noise despite the creakiness of the old building's floors. "I wasn't particularly worried about falling. I am rarely a victim of gravity," he admitted.

Rhosyn put her hands on her hips, but he just shrugged.

"After years on a trapeze, falling from a window doesn't seem like an immediate threat."

Realization dawned. "Your Talent."

She had been so concerned with learning of the dual role of Archer's Circus as the up-and-coming Foxes that she had barely registered Ansel's admission that he had a Talent—and that he had stopped performing as an acrobat because it had become obvious.

He smiled wryly. "Don't ask me what exactly it is, because I've never really had a satisfactory answer. The closest I've come is enhanced balance, but that doesn't seem to capture it. Whenever I climb or do acrobatics though, I can almost see in advance how things are going to work out. Like…"

"Like a sixth sense," Rhosyn finished for him. It was something Nate had said about his Talent, which also seemed to defy definition, especially to someone like Rhosyn who had no Talent at all.

"It makes running over rooftops easy, and can even come in handy in a fight, but unfortunately does not give me an advantage at many other things," Ansel admitted. "For example, I forgot that I locked the window in case you decided to make an ill-advised escape attempt, and now I have a broken latch."

"Which once again prompts me to ask, what do you have against doors?"

Ansel considered her, saying after a moment, "You wanted discretion. I left this evening and none of the Foxes saw me return. If we leave and return for the palace the same way, nobody has to know that I alone wasn't responsible for stealing the sponsorship documents."

Silence stretched, as Rhosyn drew a blank on any appropriate response. She and Ansel had pushed against each other at so many junctions, but here he had gone out of his way to honor her preference for secrecy. It was an acknowledgment of the concession she was making by doing this for them, and calculated as it was, it tugged at a string under Rhosyn's sternum she hadn't known was there.

"We better get going then," she eventually said, and the moment dissipated.

Ansel nodded, stepping around her to the foot of the bed. He opened the trunk there and rustled inside for a moment before emerging with a familiar garment: a jacket with a deep hood. He pulled it on and lowered the hood over his head, before tossing a similar article to Rhosyn.

She followed suit, glad to have something to cover her hair. The garment was too broad across the shoulders, and too short at the wrists, but it would do the job.

Next, he reached into his pocket and produced a bland-looking bundle. He handed it to Rhosyn, who unrolled it curiously, only for her heart to stutter at the shine of a full set of lock picks.

"I got them especially for you," he admitted.

She chuckled as she rerolled the packet and tucked it into her boot. "You really know how to charm a woman."

When she stood, the police officer was gone, replaced by a gangster with a shadowed face and hidden lockpicks. He was the Hood, and she was his thief.

Ansel looked at her and nodded in satisfaction before stepping towards the still-open window. He hesitated when he reached it. Then he reached for his sleeve, rolling it up to reveal a hidden sheath much like the ones that Nate—and now Contessa—had always used to conceal his numerous knives.

Ansel unstrapped it hurriedly and thrust it at Rhosyn's chest, as if doing it quickly before he had a chance to change his mind. "Don't make me regret this."

"I make no promises about regret," Rhosyn said as she took the outstretched offering and began strapping it to her own forearm. "But I do promise not to stab you when your back is turned."

"I guess that's the best I could hope for." Ansel's tone was rueful, but he smiled, nonetheless.

Rhosyn found herself smiling at him too. At the feeling of the leather straps against the skin of her forearm—the familiar yet foreign weight of a blade—the sleepy Lion in her mind perked up in interest. She had grown comfortable with the weight of a baton at her hip in the past years, but this awakened something in her that she had been denying to herself that she missed.

In the dark of night, she was about to climb out a lower city window in secrecy, a hidden knife at her wrist, to steal people's freedom back from their captors. Her heart fluttered, and a strange lightness took hold at the base of her skull. Rhosyn was *excited*.

She clamped down on the realization by scowling. "Well, we better get moving. I may be better than you at picking locks, but I am not as good at climbing down a wall from the fourth story."

"Then I'll be a gentleman, and not propose we race." Without further prelude, Ansel turned back to the window and levered himself over the sill. Rhosyn darted forward, knowing he wouldn't fall but heart rate skyrocketing, nonetheless. She leaned out into the night air just in time to watch him catch a hold of a clothesline in the back alley the window faced. He swung from it, putting the excess momentum into a somersault before landing on the ground.

It was so much like the first time they met, and Rhosyn suppressed a sigh at the realization that, just like that day, she would be following at a much slower pace. She turned and lowered herself down over the sill backwards, muscles in her arms straining as her toes scrambled for purchase on the wall. She picked her way down carefully, trying not to let the fact that Ansel was staring up at her rush her movements. Given the choice between having him enjoy a rather suggestive view of her backside from below or witnessing her falling, she would take the former. As he had so annoyingly pointed out, it was nothing he hadn't seen before.

By the time Rhosyn's boots hit the packed dirt of the alleyway, she was beginning to perspire, her shirt clinging to the small of her back and curls tightening in the humidity.

"I hope you can scale a wall faster than that," Ansel said, quietly enough that she could barely make out his words over the din of the street at the front of the building. While the middle and upper city would be quieting down at this point in the night, action in the lower city was just picking up.

"We'll need to be quick if we are to make it over the back wall to the palace between rounds of the King's Guard," Ansel worried out loud.

Rhosyn paused. She should have thought about how Ansel planned to get into the palace grounds, but she had spent her time worrying about her choice to go with him instead.

There was a way to get into the palace grounds without risking getting caught climbing the wall, though. Using it would require putting even more trust in Ansel.

They had come this far.

"Lucky for you, we don't have to scale the back wall."

Ansel raised a brow.

"Follow me." It was all the further instruction she gave him before trotting off down the alley to towards the slightly better lit main streets. As she emerged, she looked both ways, taking stock of where they were, although trying not to be too obvious in plotting out the exact location of the Foxes hideout in their mind.

"Graham Street," Ansel supplied.

When she looked at him curiously, he just shrugged.

"You were going to figure it out anyways. No point in forcing you to struggle to get your bearings at this point."

Rhosyn nodded sharply, turning left and weaving deftly through the milling crowds of dirty urchins and rowdy gamblers. She walked these streets every day on her assigned beat, but tonight, it felt different. While the residents of the lower city recognized her—even trusted her, as much as they could an officer of the Royal Police after the terrifying reign of the Inquiries—Rhosyn hadn't realized how *other* the navy wool and gold buttons of her uniform made her. When she patrolled, she rarely brushed shoulders with pedestrians or had to jump out of the way of an ambling cart. Everybody gave her a respectful berth.

Now though, she weaved and dodged like the Lion's runners, whom she had trained to carry messages quickly and secretly between safehouses. Nobody spared her a glance or averted their eyes, as if afraid of being accused of causing trouble.

Tonight, she was one of them. Just another citizen going about their business—perhaps legal, perhaps not.

Rhosyn quickly steered them towards the Lion's old territory. Now it was split between a few gangs, the worst of the skirmishes over the territory in the past with the fall of the Wolves. The particular building she was looking for was currently in Rattlesnake territory, but she didn't fear them anymore.

In a matter of minutes, Rhosyn led Ansel to the front of a butcher shop. She paused outside, plotting her strategy.

"Are we in need of meat for whatever your secret plan is?" Ansel asked as she considered.

"It's not what's in the store. It's what's underneath," Rhosyn explained. She headed for a gap between buildings, planning on entering through the side door. She gestured for Ansel to follow, but paused when she realized he was no longer right behind her.

He hesitated, hovering under the darkened shop's awning. His right hand gripped his opposite forearm, a gesture Rhosyn recognized as him palming a hidden weapon through his clothes, as if considering drawing it.

"You could be leading me into a trap," he pointed out.

Rhosyn stepped back towards him, propping one had on her him. "And when would I have had time to set up a trap? You've had me watched nearly every minute, day and night."

His mouth twisted ruefully. "It's turning out that you have many skills I don't know about."

"Well, telepathy is not one of them. No hidden Talents here," Rhosyn assured.

Ansel took a single step forward. "And how will a butcher shop help us get into the palace? Unless you prefer a meat cleaver to a proper dagger."

"Do you trust me?" Rhosyn asked.

"I shouldn't."

Rhosyn shook her head. "That wasn't an answer."

Ansel sighed heavily, a sound that held more meaning and feeling than a spoken answer might have. "Lead the way."

She turned back towards the door, popping the cheap lock easily. The screech of breaking metal couldn't even be heard against the din of the tavern across the street. Rhosyn said a silent apology and made a mental note to replace it for the shop owners. This was no longer a Lions' safe house, but the shop owners were former gang members.

Once inside, she navigated to the back of the shop, where meat hung from the rafters. Careful not to bump any, she located what she was looking for.

"Help me move these." Rhosyn gestured to a few salt barrels on top of her goal.

Ansel's expression was curious, but to his credit, he did as she asked without question. However, the crease between his brows smoothed into realization as Rhosyn bent to dust off a hidden handle.

"A trapdoor? You really are a woman of many secrets."

Too many.

Rhosyn ignored that thought in favor of heaving the door open, a small puff of dust following the motion, indicating that the tunnel below had not been used in quite a long time. For the most part, they were no longer used, as the Lions had been the only ones to know of their existence for many years, and their need for them had passed.

A few trusted police officers knew of their existence as well, after the raid on the Wolves several years back. However, what most officers, not even Chief Thorne, knew, was that they were aware of a small fraction of the tunnels. Only a few people had ever fully explored the labyrinthian network over the span of many years: Nate, Kristoff, and Rhosyn herself.

"This tunnel can get us into the palace?" Ansel drew Rhosyn back from memories of using chalk to mark the walls below, spending years memorizing the best routes between the Den and various safe houses.

"Yes and no," Rhosyn said as she swept a few cobwebs from the open hatch with her hand. "It will get us onto the grounds, but not inside the palace proper. The exit is in one of the outbuildings, and we can go from there."

Nate had seen to it that most of the entrances that could be used to threaten the King had been closed off, just as the entrance in his own study had been. However, he left just one, a tiny passage not even many of the Lions had ever used, just in case he ever needed to be able to smuggle the King to safety.

"It'll be dark, but I know the way," Rhosyn said, before levering herself down feet first into the passage below.

The air was cool and stale down here, the dank smell tugging at memories in the back of her mind. She let them surface, knowing they would bring with them the muscle memory necessary to navigate the maze ahead after all these years.

A light thud marked Ansel's arrival next to her, the sound of boots hitting stone echoing in the empty passage. At that, Rhosyn reached up, stretching on the tips of her toes to grab the trap door and shut it behind them. With a *thunk* laced with a remarkable amount of finality, it fell back into place, punching them into impenetrable darkness.

With their sense of sight nearly completely gone, sounds became louder. The even cadence of Ansel's breathing, so close next to her in the tight space, lifted the hairs on the nape of Rhosyn's neck. She was going to have to guide him.

"Here, take my hand." She reached out, fumbling in the darkness. After a moment, his hand met hers. She didn't need to interlace their fingers, but she found herself doing so anyways.

"Let's go."

Rhosyn placed the hand not holding Ansel's on the wall and set off down the passageway. At first, they walked in silence. Rhosyn tried to focus on the rasp of rough-hewn stone under her palm as she used her left hand to navigate in the darkness. However, her awareness kept slipping back to her right hand and the feeling of strong, callused fingers between her own.

It wasn't the soft touch of the society men Contessa had occasionally encouraged her to dance with at social events—the kind that would draw away with polite disgust as they felt the roughness of Rhosyn's own skin. Neither was it the unwelcome grab of a lower city thug that Rhosyn had no scruples responding to with a sharp knee to the groin.

Ansel's grip was firm, but not aggressive, as he let her lead the way through the pitch black in a remarkable show of trust. For a fleeting moment, Rhosyn wished she deserved that trust and wasn't going to shatter it by arresting him the moment the temporary truce she had agreed to for Paul and Olivia was over.

If she still planned to have him arrested, that was.

That thought prompted a queasy feeling to take hold beneath her ribs. Thankfully, Ansel seemed to be unnerved by the silence and distracted her from her thoughts with a question.

"So, do the Royal Police use these tunnels?"

"They have, but not this particular one," Rhosyn hedged.

"So, you know of this one because..."

"The Lions used them." She bit the words out with a bit more defiance than necessary, as she tried to stop dancing around a truth she had already admitted.

Ansel hummed noncommittally and they walked in silence for a few more minutes. Rhosyn occupied herself by drawing up the mental map of the intertwining passages in her mind, referencing it every time she had to make a choice at a fork in the path. The only words she spoke for a while were "watch your step" at the patches of uneven ground or "mind your head" when the ceiling dipped down for short stretches. Ansel exhaled through his nose in an aborted chuckle as she was forced to duck more often than him.

It wasn't until they were a few turns away from the exit Rhosyn sought when Ansel spoke again.

"Why did you join the Royal Police?"

Rhosyn's steps nearly stuttered, but she forced herself to put one foot in front of the other at an even pace. It was something that seemed obvious in her own mind, but having it asked so plainly—and by somebody who clearly saw it as a disconnect from her path—made it seem confusing. When she had told Nate and Contessa of her wishes to join the force, they had only nodded. Their understanding of what she desired went unspoken, given that they had transitioned from leaders of the most powerful street gang in London to the King's closest advisors.

Silence stretched too long, the sound of their boots scraping against the uneven floors and a quiet dripping somewhere in the distance nearly deafening. Rhosyn thought she might not answer at all when the words tumbled out of her of her own accord.

"I've always been what people needed. For years, the young Lions needed a big sister. Then, London needed protectors it could trust."

And now, I'm not so sure what is needed.

The last part echoed unspoken in her mind.

They reached the end of the corridor they were in, a tiny space opening up where both she and Ansel could crowd behind the hidden door at the rear of the servants' quarters. In the small opening, they stood so close that Rhosyn's chest brushed Ansel's as she breathed. It was still too dark to see, but the space stirred around her as they inhaled the same air. It was both painfully intimate, and blissfully anonymous, being this close but not being able to see him after what she had just admitted.

She thought Ansel might drop the subject, but instead he asked, "So who does that make you, if you've only ever tried to be what everybody else needed? Are you a gangster or a police officer?"

Rhosyn tried to swallow, but her throat stuck. "I could ask you the same thing." Her voice was hoarse but loud in the blackness. "Are you Mr. Blakely or the Hood?"

"I have a feeling we might answer that question the same."

Neither.

"Neither." Ansel echoed her answer, although she hadn't said it out loud.

Rhosyn's heart stuttered, pain lancing through her chest at knowing her enemy and captor was the one who had been able to so succinctly cut to the core of her psyche.

"Don't we have a palace to rob?" she asked, voice scratchier than she would ever like to admit.

"Of course. Heists are hardly the best time for philosophical debates about one's identity."

And like that, Ansel diffused the tension with just one quip. Air that had been sucked out of Rhosyn's lungs rushed back in as she breathed in relief. Teasing banter sat much more comfortably with her.

Turning away, Rhosyn put her ear to the wooden panel that served as a hidden door. The movement gave her a few moments of separation from Ansel, and her mind was able to latch onto the task at hand once more. It was the middle of the night, but the servants that lived in this outbuilding would work at all hours to keep the palace running smoothly.

Greeted only by silence, Rhosyn inched the door open, thanking the powers for quiet hinges. Perhaps Nate kept them oiled, just as he kept this passage open and secret.

They stepped out into a quiet corridor. It, too, was dark, but the blackness was less thick than it had been in the passage. From one end of the hallway came the dim silver light of the moon, seeping in around a doorframe.

Rhosyn gestured towards the exit and led the way on soft feet. In a matter of moments, they emerged into the soft evening air of the palace grounds. The main building towered in the distance, a fortress of stone that would not be easily penetrated. As they crept through the shadows, towards the high stone walls, she frowned at it.

Guards would be stationed at all the doors, as well as rounding the gardens at regular intervals. She would have to shimmy open the lock of one of the windows quickly. Unfortunately, the palace would not have the cheap locks that were easily persuaded to give way with correctly applied leverage. It would be a challenge to break it quickly enough to avoid notice. At least once they were inside the offices, Rhosyn wouldn't have to worry about the patrols of the ground interrupting her work on the safe.

They reached the shadow of the walls and Rhosyn crept towards the nearest window, keeping to the side in case somebody was up working late. She bent to the lock and cursed quietly under her breath.

Ansel leaned over his shoulder, close enough that his heat seeped through his clothes onto his breath tickled her neck. "What's wrong?"

"This is going to take a while to finesse. Breaking it would make too much noise." Rhosyn explained, pulling the lock picks from her boot.

Ansel huffed. "We don't have a while. Guards round every five minutes."

Her stomach turned to stone. Who knew how long it had already been? "Then I better get started."

Ansel rested a hand on her forearm, halting her. "Look."

Rhosyn tracked where he pointed with her gaze. Several floors up was a window, swung wide open as if in invitation. She shook her head. The palace walls would not be rough hewn with uneven mortar—not easily climbed.

"I can get you up," Ansel assured.

Before she could ask how, Ansel darted away across the lawn to a blossoming tree. Rhosyn hissed, suppressing the urge to shout at him for being stupid and drawing attention. He started up the tree, and frustrated as she was, Rhosyn's eyebrows shot up at the speed with which he reached the upper branches.

The tree was well pruned by the castle gardeners, leaving no low hanging boughs for him to use as handholds, but Ansel didn't seem to need them. He scurried upwards with the swiftness of a squirrel that spent all its life among the trees.

As he reached the branches level with the open window, he stepped onto one. Rhosyn's mouth opened, but she kept herself from shouting. Still, her heart froze in her chest as he picked his way along the branch. It was too thin and too far from the open window. He couldn't possibly make it.

But Ansel didn't seem to be informed about the laws of gravity. He ran along the branch as if it were a tightrope, not even attempting to use his hands to balance himself on adjacent limbs. As the branch got thinner, he only gained speed. Just as the branch began to dip dangerously under his weight, he leaped.

The tiniest squeak of fear escaped Rhosyn's still open mouth. He soared, stretching out towards the window sill, the distance impossibly far. Before he could plummet to the ground, bones crunching against the well-groomed grass, Ansel's earlier words echoed in her mind.

I am rarely a victim of gravity.

Ansel caught the windowsill by just the tips of his fingers, but stopping his fall still seemed effortless. His feet hit the stone wall below the open window and pushed back instantly, launching him through the open window.

The whole thing had taken a matter of seconds.

The only issue was that it left Rhosyn crouched on the ground, and the guards would be coming by any minute. She certainly wouldn't be replicating his stunt—not without breaking her neck.

Her heart hammered. After she had put her trust in him, had Ansel betrayed her, leaving her to get arrested for treason? Because that was what she was doing. Committing treason against the King who had ended all her friends' suffering.

Rhosyn was jerked away from the panic clawing at her throat by a knock on her head. Her chin jerked up to see a rope, dangling from the open window Ansel had just entered.

A gust of breath escaped her lips, which were quirked by a surprised smile. She grabbed at the rope, hauling herself up. She might not be the acrobat Ansel was, but she could scale a rope easily enough. She wrapped the end around her foot, using it as a step to pull herself up towards Ansel.

Just as she crested half the distance between the ground and her entrance point, a dull crunching from below drew Rhosyn's attention. Panic gripped her chest anew, squeezing her heart in an iron grasp as she fumbled, trying to climb faster.

The quiet noise shaped into footsteps, at least two guards by the sounds of it, about to round the corner at any moment. She wouldn't be inside by the time they did, leaving her open to their watchful eyes.

In her hands the rope jerked. All of a sudden, she was rising faster, the rope being hauled in even as she climbed. Ansel was pulling her up.

She scrambled, heat stinging her palms as her skin chafed against the rope. Her toes banged against the wall as she shoved upwards.

The footsteps were nearly beneath her when Rhosyn's shoulder crested the windowsill, and she pitched forward. The momentum of her climb combined with Ansel's pulling was enough to carry her through the empty frame. With a bone-rattling thud, she tumbled head over heels into the palace. The sound of the wind being knocked out of lungs didn't only come from her, but from the firm chest she landed on.

Ansel lay on the ground, Rhosyn sprawled across his torso. They both froze, ears pricked for signs of their detection, from both inside and outside the palace. The only noise was their own ragging breathing, close enough to be sharing the same air.

When no shouting of intruders began, Rhosyn slumped forward with relief. Her forehead landed on Ansel's collarbone. A sigh rustled her hair, and one of Ansel's arms came up, a hand resting between her shoulder blades. His thumb rubbed the smallest of circles there.

Rhosyn's skin prickled with overwhelming awareness, adrenaline still rushing through her at the near miss. Now that the immediate threat had passed, all that shivering anticipation turned towards the hammering of Ansel's heart, beating a tattoo through his clothes, so insistent she could feel it. Her own heart responded in kind.

His body was warm and solid beneath hers, and her thighs squeezed where they bracketed his narrow hips. At the motion, his abs tensed beneath hers. Rhosyn shivered at all the power and agility packed into Ansel's compact body. He had to be incredibly strong to pull her up like he did.

Ansel's hand rubbed more insistently at her back, and the movement focused the strange heat running through her body, forcing her to move. She rolled sideways, hitting the floor next to him inelegantly, but effectively separating them.

"Thank you," she murmured at the ceiling.

"It's the least I can do, considering you have to do the hard part later."

Rhosyn scrubbed at her forehead. "We should get moving. The quicker we get this over with, the less chance we get caught."

And the quicker we can go back to being on opposite sides.

She pushed to her feet and took stock of their surroundings.

The space was tight, the walls taken up by racks of worn-looking weapons and ammunition. It must be a supply room for the King's Guard, and a stack of miscellaneous supplies near the window explained how Ansel had been able to find a rope so fast. The musty smell of worn uniforms also gave Rhosyn a hint as to why the window had been left open.

"The safe is on the first floor," Ansel whispered.

Listening carefully every step of the way, they cracked open the door and exited into the hallway, once they assured themselves nobody was coming. Rhosyn didn't know the architecture of the palace perfectly, but it wasn't difficult to find stairs, as this section of the palace was a basic grid of offices and halls, stacked on top of each other.

Once they reached the ground floor, Ansel stepped around her, leading the way to the safe. It was in an office near Contessa's, but not in hers. Rhosyn was grateful not to be stealing from her friend directly, even if it still panged of betrayal in her heart.

The room Ansel led her to was nondescript, aside from the imposing safe in the corner. A standard desk and chair took up most of the space, and a large fireplace along one wall lay empty, no need for its heat in the warmth of late spring. Rhosyn approached the safe appraisingly. A brief tap to the side confirmed that the blackened metal was inches thick. The special devices some used to cut into vaults, or the acids that ate through sheets of metal, wouldn't do much good against walls this thick. Thankfully, Rhosyn was not a demolitions expert. She was a proper thief.

"Keep watch," she instructed Ansel over her shoulder, bending to her boot and picking out the tools she appraised would be the most useful.

"Don't want me stealing your secrets?" he whispered, although he had already turned towards the door.

"As if you could," she murmured under her breath, her mind already more on the task before her than the conversation.

The small door bore the crown jewel of locks for a lock pick: a Chubb lock. It wouldn't be able to be raked open, all the pins simply knocked into place. It would take finesse and subtle patience.

With that, Rhosyn got to work. She carefully selected each instrument in turn, inserting them delicately into the lock and feeling carefully for the pins' movement with a hand laid on the cool metal.

Her mind blocked out Ansel's presence, for the first time in hours forgetting the potential consequences of her actions. Where "patient" had never been a word Rhosyn would use to describe herself, she somehow managed it with the puzzle of a difficult lock before her. She had once asked Nate if it might be a Talent, but he told her he sensed no air of the supernatural around her. So, she practiced and practiced until the only person with a better knack for espionage was Contessa herself.

In the near trance that Rhosyn fell into when picking a lock, blind to all but the subtle changes in resistance under her fingers, she wasn't sure if it was five minutes or fifty before the last pin slid into place and her tools twisted easily in the keyhole.

The door fell open, revealing a thick sheaf of papers. At the sound of shuffling, Ansel left his post at the door, barely cracked to allow him to peer into the hallway.

"Are they there?" he whispered over her shoulder.

She quickly leafed through them, hissing when she gave herself a papercut in her haste.

"These look like sponsorship contracts to me," she said. Although not familiar with fancy legal documents, Rhosyn caught the words "Talented", "pardon", and "owed service" among the text. "What are the names on the documents we need?"

She bit her tongue around the word *we,* but Ansel answered before she could correct herself.

"Just take the whole stack."

"Have you ever robbed anybody before?" Rhosyn asked incredulously. "The less you take, the longer it takes people to realize something is missing—and the colder your trail will be when they try to find you."

"Well, you couldn't find me, so obviously my way works."

He grabbed for the papers in her hands, but she twisted away quickly, and his fingers closed around thin air. She narrowed her eyes at the concentrated jumble of words, seeking to find where the names of the Talented to be pardoned and employed were.

She located the names at the bottom of the page.

Name: Thomas Pemberton

Talent: Combustion

"Explosions?" Rhosyn mouthed in confusion. She couldn't fathom what service that might do to a fine family of the upper city, although maybe they didn't mean to use it at all and instead to have him be a footman. She spied Mr. Gower's signature at the bottom of the page.

Ansel peered over her shoulder, breathing down her neck impatiently. "We don't have much time."

Rhosyn ignored him in favor of flipping to the next page, also signed by Mr. Gower.

Name: Theo Hamilton
Talent: Walking through walls

Another odd Talent to pursue for a sponsorship, when there were others who could cook a perfect pie every time without a recipe. The third page was just as confusing.

Talent: Control over lightning

"Look at these Talents." She shoved the stack of papers into Ansel's hands. "And they're all for Mr. Gower."

Ansel flipped through pages, his eyebrows raising as he shuffled through faster and faster. There were dozens of documents.

"Doesn't it seem like..." she started.

"He's building an army," Ansel finished grimly. "Looking at the crimes these pardons are for, many of these are not just petty thieves, but violent criminals—murderers and rapists."

"What on earth for?" Rhosyn asked.

Ansel shook his head, and his expression was stony as her stomach felt. This, combined with the odd state of all Mr. Gower's servants, came together to paint an incomplete but sinister picture.

The silence stretched as they both considered.

That's when she heard it.

Distracted as they had been by their discovery, neither of them had noticed the growing sound of footsteps in the hallway.

Ansel's gaze snapped up, meeting hers with wide, urgent eyes.

Let's go, he mouthed silently.

Rhosyn grabbed the contracts from him and shoved them unceremoniously into the front of her jacket.

They turned toward the door, but by the time they reached it, it was too late. The footsteps were nearly right outside the door, their escape cut off. Rhosyn held her breath, lungs burning as she tried to control her hammering heart, as if it might be heard by whoever patrolled the halls at this time of night.

Right as the stomp of boots on stone—likely signaling a guard—reached its loudest, the steps stuttered. Then paused. Rhosyn's heart stopped. Where every door in the hallway they had entered through had been closed, the door to the room they occupied was ajar from Ansel's watch.

Rhosyn whipped her head back and forth. The room had no window, leaving no escape. Their only two options were to hide, or to fight their way out. For possibly the first time in her life, Rhosyn chose to hide.

She dove under the desk in the middle of the room. Ansel seemed to have a similar thought process. He darted towards the fireplace, ducking inside and reaching up into the chimney. Rhosyn grimaced as he disappeared, remembering a harrowing story of Scarlett's involving climbing through a chimney.

Ansel's toes disappeared behind the mantle just as a quiet squeak signaled the door opening.

Rhosyn counted every heavy step of boots against flagstones as the guard walked into the room. Some instinct told her to squeeze her eyes shut, as if that might make her invisible. Instead, she forced herself to keep them open, tracking the movement of his shadow as he strode across the room. Her knees brushed against her chin as she shoved herself as tightly as possible into the corner of the desk, trying to conceal every inch of herself in the shadows there.

The footsteps paused, and Rhosyn imagined the guard swinging his gaze back and forth like a lamp in the night. She thanked luck she had closed the safe after removing the papers, habit kicking in to always leave everything as she found it.

After long, breathless seconds, the guard's shadow retreated towards the door, seemingly satisfied that it had only been left open by accident. Just as his silhouette moved out of her line of sight, it happened.

A quiet sneeze from the fireplace.

Now Rhosyn did squeeze her eyes shut in despair. A metallic *shink* marked a weapon being drawn, and the guard's feet rounded the desk as he marched towards the open hearth. If he turned around and looked down, he would spot Rhosyn there, but his attention was on the fireplace, leaving his back turned to her.

He bent down to look in the hearth and Rhosyn's mind raced. With him distracted by Ansel, the route between her and the door was clear. She could make a break for it—leave Ansel to be discovered while she escaped. She could run straight to Chief Thorne and put an end to this whole thing.

The guard angled his sword ready to stab up the chimney to where Ansel hid, and Rhosyn knew that wasn't an option.

With a strangled shout, Rhosyn sprang from her hiding spot. Nate would have rolled his eyes, telling her a battle cry defeated the point of a surprise attack, but it served its purpose in bringing the guard up short before he could stab Ansel. She landed on his back, forearms coming around his throat.

He grunted at the impact, swinging his sword wildly as he tried to slash her over his shoulders. Before he could, Ansel tumbled from the chimney, so covered in soot that he looked like nothing more than a shadow. His roll from his hiding spot carried him seamlessly to his feet and he kicked the weapon from their assailant's hand.

It clattered to the ground, but the guard stayed intent on dislodging Rhosyn. She pressed down on his windpipe, trying to squeeze consciousness from him. His fingers grappled at her wrists, and her biceps screamed as she fought to keep him from pulling her loose.

With a muffled roar, he turned and lunged back, slamming Rhosyn into wall. Her skull cracked against stone, white spots dancing across her vision, but still she held tight. More often than not, brawls were won by the ability to take a hit, and Rhosyn was the best brawler of them all.

She *would* outlast this guard, who was not a scrappy boxer, but a polished fighter, much less threatening without his weapon in hand. Rhosyn gritted her teeth as she squeezed even tighter, and his struggles began to weaken.

His knees hit the ground with a thud, and Rhosyn landed on her feet, still keeping her arms around his neck. As he lost consciousness, she lowered him to the ground, not letting his head hit the stone as she released the pressure on his neck. By the time his face lolled back to an angle where he could have seen her, his eyes were closed. He had never seen her face.

Ansel stood frozen at the guard's feet. He and Rhosyn panted as they stared at each other. He opened his mouth like he was about to say something, expression unreadable under the layer of soot on his face.

Before he could speak, distant noises drifted down the hallway. The commotion of the brief fight would not have gone unnoticed.

"Run," Rhosyn ordered.

Ansel didn't need to be told twice, and together they sprinted from the room. Their footsteps echoed as they pounded down the hall, but it hardly mattered now. The time for stealth had passed and now their priority was speed.

A few doors down on their left, moonlight streamed in through a window leaving a silvery splash on the ground.

"Here!" Ansel panted.

That was all the warning she got before he veered off, covering his head with his arms as he crashed through the glass. Rhosyn followed suit, rolling as she hit the grass outside and thankful that they were on the first floor. She sprang to her feet, grateful for the lack of injury from the fall, only to be proven wrong by a stabbing pain in her calf.

She looked down to see a shard of glass as long as her finger sticking out of the bulge of muscle there. There was no time to process the sight, as Ansel grabbed her forearm and started dragging her towards the palace outbuildings.

Her thoughts turned to nothing more than a loud buzzing as her body took over, lurching her forward in stumbling, running steps beside him.

Thankfully, Ansel remembered where the passage entrance was, guiding them while Rhosyn focused on keeping moving. Shouting behind them in the distance signaled that the whole palace had been alerted to their incursion, but it was too late.

They stumbled into the servants' quarters and dove into the secret tunnel, shutting the hidden panel behind them just as the noise caused doors in the corridor to swing open in curiosity. Still, Ansel didn't stop urging Rhosyn forward.

She didn't know how far she made it, stumbling in the dark, before she tripped, tipping forward into Ansel's back. He broke her fall with a grunt, twisting and maneuvering her arm over his shoulders.

"We need to get you help," he said, hoarse voice echoing in the relative quiet. It seemed strange, given that Rhosyn's ears seemed to be ringing, pulsating in time with the hammering of her heart from lingering adrenaline.

"It's not anything I can't patch up myself," Rhosyn assured. Now that they slowed down, giving her a moment to take stock of her injuries, she knew she was right. She probably could even walk on her own if she had a moment to catch her breath, but for some reason, she was loathe to lean away from Ansel's supportive warmth. Maybe it was that the solidity of his muscles shifting under her arm grounded her after the pell-mell sprint of their escape.

Either way, she just needed to remove the glass and clean the cut. She had patched up worse scrapes on young Lions who had tumbled down the stairs or gotten in ill-advised scraps over the years.

Ansel shook his head, the movement making his hair brush Rhosyn's forearm where it draped over his neck. The touch was surprisingly soft and ticklish after the harshness of their encounter.

"It's still too far from the tunnel entrance to the Foxes' safehouse for you to limp. We'd draw attention, and that's not wise considering the guards will know within minutes that the palace was broken into."

Rhosyn grimaced. Ansel was right. Nate himself was probably already dispatching riders to the Royal Police stations throughout the city, putting the city on high alert. A man covered in soot helping a woman with glass in her leg limp down the street would draw attention, even in the mixed company of the lower city.

"Are there any exits closer to our safehouse?" Ansel asked.

Rhosyn shook her head. There was one close to her own house, but she was loathe to put the couple she rented from in the middle of things, after they had pursued a life away from crime. There was another option though.

"One path... It leads down out of the old sewer at the edge of the city. It comes out—"

"Near the circus." Ansel followed her train of thought. "It won't be hard to hide there."

"It was built to conceal people after all," Rhosyn observed dryly.

"And to do so in the best possible hiding place: in plain sight." Ansel's tone was proud.

It coaxed a chuckle out of Rhosyn, the sound chasing away some of the lingering tension from her chest. The further she limped from the palace, the more she believed they had gotten away with it, the sponsorship documents still safely tucked into the front of her shirt. With a jerk of her chin, Rhosyn directed them onto the path that would lead to the circus, and they slowly made their way through the tunnel.

However, the increasing clarity seeping through her brain gave her more of a chance to inspect her actions. She had chosen to stay and help Ansel even when she had a chance to leave the whole thing behind—to scurry back to her normal life as a police officer and try to forget this brief lapse back into crime. Yet, a string anchored beneath her ribs had yanked her forward, leaping to Ansel's rescue before she could fully consider the alternatives.

"Thank you." Ansel's voice broke the silence. Apparently, his mind had wandered down the same path.

"Yeah, well, I wouldn't have had to do anything if you hadn't sneezed," she quipped.

Ansel huffed. "It's not my fault the chimney was filthy and the ash got in my nose. It seemed like that place has never seen a chimney sweep."

"I'll remember to submit a complaint to the housekeeper when I get a chance."

Ansel chuckled, and a brief silence fell before he spoke again. "You could have run, though."

"I know." Rhosyn admitted. "Guess I just don't know how to walk away from a fight."

And that was the truth. She had never walked away from a fight that needed to be fought, even if it came back to bite her later. She hoped helping Ansel wouldn't end up being one of those occasions.

Chapter Ten

If Rhosyn could say one thing for the performers of Archer's Circus, it was that they didn't ask unnecessary questions. She and Ansel crept into the side of the circle of tents in the early hours of the morning, the sun just peaking above the horizon and casting the towering green and white striped structures in long shadows. The straw-strewn paths were nearly empty and quiet, absent of the exaggerated darkness and flickering lamp light that lent the feel of the fantastical at night, giving the whole place a sense of liminal space.

An early riser caught sight of them as they stumbled towards a tent and rushed over.

"We're going to need some bandages and something to wash up with. See if you can dig us up a change of clothes too," Ansel ordered. He had the same tone that Nate did when directing Lions or the King's Guard: with frank honesty and the insinuation that he respected his followers too much to waste their time with pleasantries. It had made people trust Nate with their lives, and now it had the same results.

Within minutes of collapsing in the tent where the Merry Men had performed before, the man reappeared with the necessary supplies.

Ansel thanked him and instructed. "Send a message to Little John. Tell him we're here and that I need to talk to him."

The man spared Rhosyn one long glance, tinged with curiosity, before backing out the entrance, letting the flap that would be tied open during the Circus's performing hours fall shut behind him.

With a sigh, Ansel sat down heavily on the edge of the stage. Now that they were alone, some of the persona that reminded her of Nate slipped away, revealing a man as tired as Rhosyn so often felt.

She sat down more gingerly next to him, extending her injured leg so as not to jostle it too much and dig the glass in farther. As it was, the shard didn't seem to be too deep. She let it be for just a second, limbs turning leaden as she finally relieved them of the burden of her weight. Her eyes fluttered shut, the sensations in her body—from the stinging in her calf to the throbbing on the back of her head that was sure to form a knot where it had collided with the wall—washed over her and carried her thoughts away in their current.

"Let me get this soot off myself, and then I'll help you with your leg." Ansel's voice interrupted her after a moment of quiet.

Rhosyn nodded, keeping her eyes shut. The air stirred, signaling that Ansel had stood, and his footsteps retreated towards the curtain separating the performing area from the backstage. After a minute, muffled splashing signaled to Rhosyn he was using the basin of water, supplied by his man, to wash up.

Finally, her eyes drifted open and she returned her awareness to what needed to be done. She crossed her injured leg over her knee, letting her see the back of her calf. Thankfully, the piece of glass that pierced the meat of the muscle still had a significant piece sticking out she could use to remove it. No need for tweezers.

She gritted her teeth, knowing there was nothing for it. Pinching the shard between her thumb and forefinger, she yanked. Her hiss of pain nearly drowned out the quiet squelch as it pulled free of her skin. She let it fall on the stage next to her, glad to be free of the twinge of sharp edges every time she moved.

Now that her pants were no longer pinned to her leg, she rolled them up to better inspect and clean the wound, shoving the cuffs all the way up to her knee. As she suspected, the wound was shallow, and most of the pain had come from having the glass still embedded in her leg.

She reached for the bandages and small glass jar the man had provided, but her hand was knocked away as familiar calloused fingers beat her to it.

"Let me help you with that."

Rhosyn had been too distracted with removing the glass to hear Ansel reemerge from behind the curtains. He knelt down before her and held out a hand expectantly.

The sight made Rhosyn's heart flutter. He had changed out of his soiled shirt, the new one slightly too big and threatening to slip off his shoulder, revealing the inviting chest Rhosyn had burrowed into the morning before—how had so much happened in twenty-four hours? His hair was slightly damp around the edges, as if he had dunked his face in the basin to try to get the soot off, and now a longer strand clung to his high cheekbone.

He raised a single brow in question at Rhosyn's hesitation. The action drew attention to a black smudge he had missed on his forehead. Her fingers itched to rub it away.

Instead, she leaned back on her elbows and placed her ankle in his outstretched hand. He set to dabbing the skin around the cut, and as he did, the fingers holding her ankle rubbed back and forth soothingly. Rhosyn wasn't sure if he even knew he was doing it, but she could scarcely think of anything else as he moved on to cleaning any debris from inside the wound.

She shifted, the movement causing the papers in her shirt to crinkle. The sound provided a welcome distraction from the warmth seeping up her chest to her face. Pulling them out, Rhosyn waved them at Ansel.

"These are yours, as promised."

His eyes flicked up from his task, and the concentrated furrow between his brow deepened into a true frown.

"What do you think about what we found in those contracts?" he asked.

"It...doesn't look good," Rhosyn admitted, wrinkling her nose.

"With that number of Talented at his beck and call, with those abilities, he could do some serious damage," Ansel agreed.

Rhosyn's stomach churned. While Mr. Gower had more polish to him than the powerful gangsters who lorded over the underworld, something about this setup smelled the same as when the Wolves collected Talented for their illegal fighting rings. Mr. Gower was clearly reaching for power, but how he would go about getting it, Rhosyn couldn't be sure yet.

"What do you think we should do?" Ansel asked, interrupting her thoughts.

Rhosyn frowned. "And why would you want the opinion of an officer of the Royal Police—and your hostage at that?"

Ansel's fingers stopped moving on her ankle, tightening so the pads of his fingers dug into the soft flesh on the inner part of her foot. She suppressed a shiver.

"I thought we might have moved past that, after the night we've just shared." Ansel bit the words out, as if saying them frustrated him.

The words hit Rhosyn in the chest, and she slumped. It was a hope she had indulged in too, although guiltily. But the fact that they had each saved each other tonight—even made a good team—didn't change the truth of their situation.

"I may be a police officer, and you might be a gangster I'm trying to arrest," Rhosyn started slowly, and Ansel's frown deepened. "But maybe we don't have to be enemies. Maybe we can just be…professional rivals."

"No, I don't think so." Ansel's dismissal came so quickly that it stung as tangibly as a slap across the face.

"Why not?"

Ansel lifted his gaze from where it had been fixed on her leg, and it pinned Rhosyn with its surprising intensity. "*Professional rivals* don't think about each other the way I think about you."

Rhosyn's breath caught in her throat, but Ansel didn't seem to want her to speak anyways.

"Professional rivals don't spend a whole day so distracted they can barely function, just from waking up to the smell of your hair. They don't admire the snarl on your face when you throw a punch or the way your smile is slightly crooked. They certainly don't spend hours agonizing over what it would be like to touch you everywhere—how warm you would be, if you would snap at me like you do in a fight or if I could make you into a mewling mess. How you would taste."

Ansel didn't break eye contact as he slowly deconstructed Rhosyn, piece by piece, with his words. All the barriers she had put up in her mind against him, the justifications that she *couldn't* want him, caught fire as the warmth under her skin burst into flames.

Rhosyn wet her lips, reaching for the right words. This wasn't their flirty teasing, hidden in the guise of adversaries, or even during a dance at a fancy party. This was something deeper. Heavier.

"I guess we aren't professional rivals then," she said, her voice hoarse.

Ansel let out a shuddering breath, mirroring the shiver that ran up her spine when the breath tickled the inside of her ankle, still held close to his face. His gaze tracked her movement, and slowly he lowered his head. His lips were a hairsbreadth away from her skin when he paused, eyes boring into her.

It was a bid for permission—a chance for her to recognize that this would change things for them, more than sleep-addled touches, that could be blamed on circumstances. Rhosyn still grappled with what she had done in robbing the palace, knowing it was a step she couldn't take back. But this...this decision was already made.

She nodded infinitesimally, and Ansel lowered his lips to her skin. At first, it was feather light, barely a kiss as he dragged his mouth up from her foot towards her knee. Rhosyn choked down a quiet, desperate sound at the contact, surprised how affected she was by the one simple action.

Something dark flickered in Ansel's eyes at the truncated noise. He nipped at the inside of her knee, startling a squeak out of her. That pulled a chuckle out of him, the sound lower and rougher than his usual laugh. She wanted to hear it again. She wanted to muffle it with her own lips.

At that thought, Rhosyn's body moved with all the speed of a trained fighter, acting on pure instinct. She lunged forward, grasping at the front of Ansel's shirt and crashing her lips to his.

He caught her, despite the suddenness of her actions, rocking back on his knees and arms wrapping around her easily. Rhosyn was distracted from the way he crushed her to his chest by the movement of his lips and the intoxicating taste of his tongue tracing the seam of her mouth.

Rhosyn pushed back against him, catching his bottom lip between her teeth. As she tugged on it, Ansel brought a hand up to her hair and grasped it firmly at the roots. It pinned her in place, letting him take control of the kiss.

Held like that, something heady washed over Rhosyn, the racing in her mind—the constant instincts to punch, run, *do*—quieted. All she could think about was Ansel single-mindedly devouring her mouth, as if he had thought about nothing else since she first chased him across rooftops.

So loud were the sensations of Ansel pressed against her in Rhosyn's mind that she at first didn't notice the shift in light that came from the tent flap swinging open. She only came back to herself when there came a commotion, jerking back as a familiar shout broke through the haze.

Her eyes snapped open at the same time Ansel whipped around, both turning towards the disturbance. Standing at the tent entrance, pistols drawn was—

"Kristoff," she gasped, still on her knees. She staggered to her feet, unbalanced by several rapid changes in quick succession.

The barrels of his guns were trained on Ansel, but he quirked a brow, and a mischievous twinkle sparked in his eye. He ignored the handful of other circus performers hovering at the entrance, clearly unwilling to make a move that could cause him to shoot their leader.

"I came to rescue you, Rhosyn, but based on the sight that greeted me when I got here, there was no need." He bent his arms, directing his aim up and away from Ansel and resting his guns on his shoulder. "I just didn't realize what kind of kidnapping this was."

"It wasn't like that." Ansel found his voice. "Well, not at first, at least."

"It doesn't seem wise to admit to the man holding the guns that you *did* kidnap his sister for less than honorable purposes...or at least the less amusing kind of dishonorable." Kristoff looked at Rhosyn with a question on his face, as if asking if he should go ahead and shoot Ansel anyways.

At his words, something between a sob and a laugh bubbled up in Rhosyn's throat, and she ended up releasing a hiccuping snort. Everybody looked at her questioningly, but a smile spread across her face.

She had been navigating protecting London and her little Lions using her own moral compass and ending up hopelessly lost. But here was Kristoff, calling her his sister and risking his life to find her. Nothing could feel that dire when faced with the sharp-shooter's crooked smile.

She darted forward and threw herself at him in a bone crushing hug. To Kristoff's credit, he managed not to shoot anybody or bang her head with his guns as he hugged her back. After a tight squeeze, he took her by the shoulders and held her back, looking at her.

"You're alright?" His gaze darted over her rumpled clothes and her bandaged leg.

She nodded. "Somehow less banged up than usual."

"That is saying absolutely nothing." Reassured that Rhosyn hadn't been mistreated, Kristoff's attention turned to Ansel, and his gaze narrowed. "I do still require an explanation."

Ansel's gaze fixed over Kristoff's shoulder, and Rhosyn followed it to the audience of circus members who had followed the commotion and now hovered, many of them seemingly unsure what to do with their hands now that violence didn't seem eminent. With a wave, Ansel dismissed them. While a few lingered for a moment, obviously curious, they did as he asked.

Rhosyn extricated herself from Kristoff, standing between the two men, who sized each other up.

"I didn't know you had a brother," Ansel remarked.

Rhosyn snorted, as nobody could mistake Kristoff for her real brother. Where he was tan and muscular with hair that always looked effortlessly mussed, she was lanky and pale with an unruly nest on the top of her head.

"He's a chosen brother," she clarified.

"Another Lion, I presume." Ansel raised a brow.

"Not just any Lion either," Kristoff answered. "And you might not have been around these streets long enough to remember, but the Lions used to be the most feared name in London. If I don't find out what you're doing with Rhosyn here soon, you'll find out why." Kristoff's tone was as casual as ever, but Rhosyn had known the sharpshooter long enough to know he didn't deal in idle threats.

"This is Ansel. He has Olivia and Paul," she interjected, hurrying to explain.

At that, Kristoff's grip tightened around his pistols, fingers drifting to the trigger. Rhosyn raised her hands, palms out.

"They're safe," she assured. "He's helping them get out of the city."

Kristoff's brow furrowed. "I thought they were joining proper society. They never struck me as the type to run away and join the circus."

Rhosyn shook her head. "It's...complicated." She looked back and forth between the two men, still looking at each other with narrowed eyes. A cord of tension ran between them, with her held taught in the middle. The thread anchored under her ribs pulled her in both directions at once—toward a past life that would never return but could not be forgotten and toward an impossible future that Rhosyn had only barely dared to dream of.

Shoving his hands in his pockets and shrugging, Ansel broke the moment, tension unraveling. "I suppose I should give you two a chance to catch up."

A breath rushed out of Rhosyn's chest, and finally, Kristoff holstered his guns. Given how quick he was on the draw, it barely made him any less dangerous, but it was clear he accepted Ansel's olive branch. Rhosyn shot Ansel a look that she hoped conveyed her gratitude.

He gave her the smallest nod and started strolling past them towards the entrance. "I am going to try to hunt down some tea. I'll be outside when you're done talking."

Kristoff kept his gaze trained on Ansel's back until it disappeared behind the fluttering tent flap. Then he turned back to Rhosyn.

"Even if he's standing guard outside, I can get you out of here right now," Kristoff said, voice low enough to not be heard through the thick canvas walls. "We can be at Nate's house in time for breakfast. You could be eating a fresh batch of Gregor's scones within the hour."

The watering of Rhosyn's mouth at the mention of Gregor's cooking did nothing to distract from the feeling of being punched in the chest. The rift inside her ached, having slowly been deepening inside her over the past days. In her subconscious, she knew she would be faced with the task of escaping from the Foxes, but that had been a problem for three days from now, when Olivia and Paul were safely out of London. Somehow, having an excuse to put it off allowed her to pretend that it was inevitable, but not immediate—not a decision she had to make, for it was not yet a reality.

But now, faced with Kristoff, who so earnestly offered to shoot his way out of this camp with her if he had to, her resolve shuddered.

"I'm not sure I can leave," she admitted, her voice smaller than she was used to.

"Is that man blackmailing you? If I need to—"

Rhosyn shook her head before Kristoff got any heroic ideas about setting things on fire, which was too often his first solution to any problem. "Ansel—all of the Foxes really—are trying to help the Talented who have been sponsored in the upper city. Something is wrong and...and I think I need to stay to help figure out what it is."

She didn't know it was true until she said it. Once the words were out of her, though, it felt like the wedge being used to crack open her chest was gone, allowing her to be a single person once more. As quickly as she could, she filled Kristoff in on what had happened since Ansel had kidnapped her at the circus, although she strategically left out the parts where she slept tied to his bed with him.

Kristoff's clear blue gaze pinned her as he cocked his head, surprisingly perceptive given how rarely he seemed to take anything seriously. "I take it you took my advice on investigating Mr. Gower, despite what the police said?"

"I think this might be another case where I need to let my instincts guide me, and those are hard to write up in a police report," Rhosyn admitted. "If I'm 'missing', then I can do these investigations off the record. I—" Rhosyn choked around the words she said next, "I'd appreciate if you didn't tell Chief Thorne you'd found me."

To his credit, Kristoff's face held no judgment. If anybody knew how to flirt with the line of what was legal and what was right, it was Kristoff.

"I have to tell Nate though," he said. "He's been going half mad since you went missing."

Rhosyn blinked, the back of her eyes suddenly stinging. "He has?"

"He nearly yelled at Joseph for not spending more resources on finding you, even though he knows the Royal Police are spread thin as it is and Joseph was doing everything he could," Kristoff said. "I've been searching for you ever since Joseph told us you didn't show up for your patrol, and Nate has joined me whenever he's not with the King. Even Contessa's had her ear to the ground, all her connections keeping an eye out."

Rhosyn's throat went tight. When the Lions had officially dissolved, it had felt oddly like losing a family, despite seeing all her friends constantly. She had felt the loss of the camaraderie that came from shared danger like a death in her heart. It was something she had never quite found in the police force, as much as she liked her new colleagues. Knowing the lengths Nate would go to filled her with the warmth of belonging once more.

"Then tell Nate and Contessa not to worry. I'll apologize for making them anxious later but for now...for now I have to figure out what the Gowers are up to."

"Is that the only reason you're staying? You and that Ansel chap seem...friendly." Kristoff's tone was playful, but she could tell his question was serious. Despite her relentless teasing of Kristoff over his affection for Gregor, he had never gotten to return the favor. There had never been any romantic liaisons in her life, and the physical relationships she allowed herself were brief and always beneath her friends' notice.

"That's new," Rhosyn admitted, kicking one foot against the ground.

"Seducing your would-be kidnapper…I must say I'm impressed." Kristoff elbowed Rhosyn playfully in the ribs.

She blushed and shoved him away. "That's hardly new for us. Didn't Contessa do the same thing?"

"Nate did *not* kidnap her. He married her."

"That's not how she saw it at the time," Rhosyn pointed out.

Kristoff chuckled. "Well, you don't seem to need my help getting Ansel on your side. But if you need my help with the other part, you know where to find me. You know I never like to miss out on a party."

"And by party, you mean all out brawl." Rhosyn's tone was dry.

"You know me too well." Kristoff smiled, but then his face smoothed into a rare serious expression. "Be careful, alright?"

"I will," Rhosyn promised. "And you be careful too."

"Never am," Kristoff quipped, making for the exit. With a jaunty wave, he stepped back out into the now bright sun of the spring morning.

Before the flap could flutter closed, Ansel ducked his head inside, eyes darting around the space before landing on her. He paused, his expression equal parts relieved and surprised.

"You stayed," he said, his tone unreadable.

A smile toyed at the edge of Rhosyn's lips. "Yeah, I guess I did."

"Well…" He seemed at a loss, but he smiled back at her, nonetheless. "I guess we better find you some breakfast."

Chapter Eleven

Rhosyn wouldn't have thought she would grow used to sharing a bed with another body in just a couple of nights. When she woke to late afternoon sun beaming in through gaps in the tent panels, though, her body instinctively stretched towards a form that wasn't there. As her fingers brushed against scratchy blankets, Rhosyn wrinkled her nose, scrunching her eyes shut.

She supposed privacy was an improvement on grinding herself sleepily on Ansel's thigh, but her body disagreed. After all, she had admitted she was staying, giving up an opportunity to leave Ansel and the Foxes behind, a sly voice in her mind reminded her. If she was already breaking the rules, what was the point in refusing to break this one? Especially when this transgression was so particularly enticing.

With a jerk, Rhosyn sat up. There was no point dwelling on things that might have been. She had slept alone, and it was likely to remain that way given that she was no longer a flight risk in Ansel's eyes.

Now, she needed to turn her attention to more important things, like the apparent army of Talented Mr. Gower had hired as household staff. The startling discovery was why she had sent Kristoff on his way, and she needed to focus on unraveling that mystery. It was how she would serve this city, even if she was betraying the Royal Police.

Rhosyn's boots lay where she had taken them off, haphazardly kicked aside as she collapsed face first onto the borrowed cot. With a groan, she shoved her feet back into them and began lacing them up with practiced fingers. Once they were on, she stood. Tilting her head side to side rewarded her with loud cracks, and she twisted her spine, adding a series of pops to the symphony as her vertebrae unlocked. Two days of forced rest had done her more good than she cared to admit, but her body still protested the previous long night. It had gotten a taste of a good night's sleep and now seemed to crave more. However, there was work to do right now.

Rhosyn poked her head out of the tent flap. The straw-strewn paths that had been relatively unpopulated this morning now carried a steady stream of people between tents, some bearing bundles, others chatting with each other easily. They seemed to be getting ready for another night of merriment and entertainment.

None paid her any attention as she stepped out fully onto the path. After Ansel had handed her off to a gruff man, who apparently ran the roasted nut stall, he had disappeared to get some sleep himself. Rhosyn had no idea where he might be or who to ask.

Instead of imposing herself on the busy performers, she meandered towards the largest tent again, where she and Ansel had sat this morning. It seemed like as good a place as any to start, and if he wasn't there, perhaps one of the Merry Men would recognize her and point her in the right direction.

The buzz of life in the city of tents bolstered her, adding more of a bounce to her previous trudge as she walked. Nobody shot her wary glances as she walked, and she felt light without the weight of a baton at her hip. To the tide of performers and staff, she could be anybody—certainly not an officer of the Royal Police or a notorious Lion. Just a woman, going to talk to a man. A man who had a tendency to tie her insides in knots.

The shade of the large central tent fell over her face as she approached, dulling the bright afternoon sun and cooling her skin. Rhosyn slipped her fingers into the gap in the closed tent flaps, which would be tied back to leave a wide entrance when the circus was open for business.

Pulling it open a few inches, she glanced inside for any signs of an occupant. A sudden *whoosh* almost had Rhosyn jerking back, before her eyes registered the blur whizzing through her vision.

Ansel swung from the trapeze over the stage, momentum slowing as his arc reached its peak. At the height of his swing, he let go, flipping easily in midair and twisting before catching the bar right as it started to descend again.

Rhosyn found herself unconsciously slipping into the tent, letting the flap close behind her. She stood transfixed with her back against the canvas, wide eyes following Ansel's dizzying dance. This next time he released the bar, he arched, head coming towards his feet as he flipped backwards, body making a perfect "c" shape in the air. The breath whooshed from Rhosyn's lungs as the trapeze swung away from him, out of his grasp. He was going to fall.

Instead, he caught an adjacent bar, weight landing on the tips of his fingers with little effort. Watching him, Rhosyn internally hit herself for ever thinking one of the Merry Men might have been the Hood. As skilled as they were, none of them held a candle to Ansel's ability...his Talent.

Now that she saw it, she didn't know how it hadn't been obvious to her from the first time she saw him flipping across lower city rooftops. Then again, many people thought Rhosyn's lockpicking and Kristoff's sharpshooting were Talents, when they were actually born of years of practice, interspersed with countless failures.

A particularly daring swing on Ansel's part snapped Rhosyn from her thoughts. She gasped audibly as he swung on a different trapeze, this one dipping so low Rhosyn feared he would crash into the ground. Instead, his toes just brushed the wooden platform that served as a stage, before he rose into the air once more.

In the cavernous and nearly empty space, her squeak of fear echoed. Ansel's head snapped up as he reached the height of his swing, and he caught her eye—although she had no clue how he could find his bearings so easily while hurtling through space.

He let go, floating as lightly as smoke on the wind before landing on one of the platforms at the top of the arena. He turned, looking down on Rhosyn from on high and smiling.

"I didn't know I had an audience." He raised his voice to be heard easily from such a height.

Rhosyn drifted forward, stepping up on the stage so she was nearly beneath him. "And I didn't think you performed anymore...not acrobatics, at least."

Ansel shrugged, and despite his usual bravado, something in the expression seemed sheepish. "I still practice sometimes, when nobody is around. It helps clear my head."

"Hurtling through the air at breakneck speed clears your mind?" Rhosyn propped her fists on her hips.

"I'd think you of all people would understand the appeal. After all, it seemed like throwing some punches at me the other day helped you think straight."

Rhosyn shrugged but couldn't deny that he was right. Letting fists do the talking tapped into a part of Rhosyn she spent so much time pushing down, because that brawler wasn't what London needed. Right now, though, maybe it was.

Instead of saying any of that, Rhosyn cocked her head in challenge. "Are you sure you don't like perching up there because it's the only time I have to look up to talk to you?"

"Bringing my height into it? I've never heard that before," Ansel scoffed, but his tone was playful. "I'm willing to level the playing field though."

Before Rhosyn could ask what he meant, Ansel cartwheeled, propelling himself backwards off the platform. Rhosyn clapped a hand to her mouth, seeing that his hands were nowhere near the closest trapeze. Instead, Ansel caught it with his legs, knees hanging over the bar.

Absorbing the momentum of his jump, the bar swung in a spiral around the stage, circling lower and lower around Rhosyn, making her pivot where she stood in the center of the platform. As if he had planned it perfectly—which he probably had, but Rhosyn was loathe to give him the credit—the trapeze drifted to a halt right before Rhosyn.

Still hanging from his knees, Ansel folded his arms, gaze level with Rhosyn's eyeline. She propped her fists on her hips, glaring at his upside-down smirk, just inches from her nose.

"Show off," she muttered.

Ansel's smirk only grew into a grin. Then he levered off the trapeze, righting himself as he did so, to land on his feet before her.

"I guess I can't help it. I'm—" In perfect juxtaposition to the easy confidence of his showmanship, Ansel looked to the side and pushed his now unkempt hair from his face. "I'm just happy you're still here."

It was Rhosyn's turn to look down at her feet. "I am too, although I'm not sure I should be."

Ansel's gaze snapped up at that. "Why not?"

"I just..." Rhosyn grasped at words that seemed to allude her, her frustrations always better spoken with actions than breath. "Who am I anymore? I'm not really a Lion, but that part of me isn't gone. I'm not really a police officer anymore either, am I?"

"You're..." Ansel gestured at her incomprehensibly, but fervently as if it were of the upmost important that she understood his meaning. "You're Rhosyn."

Her frustration flared, and she thrust her hands into her hair. "Who even is that?" she demanded. "How am I supposed to know what I am when I've spent my whole life being whatever it was people needed most? A sister, a nursemaid, a lockpick, a thief... I became these things because that's what Nate and Kristoff—my family—needed, and the Lions needed somebody to care for them. Then I became an officer of the Royal Police because Contessa and Nate needed somebody they could trust. Now...I fear this city needs something else, and I will become whatever it requires of me. I just wish I knew what was really *me*."

The tirade poured out of her, unbidden. By the time Rhosyn finished, she was breathing heavily, as if the words had ripped free of her chest with great effort. The heat of embarrassment at such an emotional outburst began to compete with the burning of tears behind her eyes, until she met Ansel's gaze.

His face held compassion but no pity. And deep in the pools of his emerald eyes, she found what she hadn't even realized what she was searching for—understanding. After all, hadn't Rhosyn known that both the Hood and Mr. Blakely were masks Ansel wore? Parts of him, but not the whole truth of the man beneath?

A breath shuddered out of her, goosebumps dancing over her skin at the thought that Ansel was looking at Rhosyn and truly seeing her and not just the role she filled. In that moment, she saw him too.

He took an intentional step, the sparse distance between them shrinking to nothing.

"I can tell you one thing you are," Ansel said. His breath puffed across her face, warm and sweet.

Rhosyn's eyes drifted to his lips, and for the first time since they met, Rhosyn didn't fight the way her body pulled her to him.

"What's that?" she prompted, nerves drawn so taut that she could barely follow the thread of the conversation but needing to know what he would say regardless.

"You're everything I want."

The words were spoken nearly against Rhosyn's lips, and she closed the rest of the distance between them so quickly, he barely finished his thought. Close as they had been, Rhosyn dove into the kiss with such force that it knocked him back a step. He took it in stride, arms wrapping around her back and crushing her nearer still.

Her hands braced on his shoulders, fingertips digging into his shirt, slightly damp with the sweat of his earlier exertion. Rhosyn wanted to taste it. She groaned, and it gave Ansel room to deepen the kiss, tilting her head and delving into her mouth with a singular focus.

It was far from gentle and sweet, but neither was it the rapid, selfish kiss of a man seeking a vessel for his own pleasure. No...this was the kiss of a man who wanted to devour her piece by piece. To learn exactly what took her apart, from the way she whimpered when his tongue slid against her own to the way her legs began to shake when he nipped at her bottom lip.

Ansel's hands traveled up and into her hair, pulling free what remained of the haphazard braid she had slept in. His blunt nails raked against her scalp with none of the shyness of his previous morning explorations, and she whined unconsciously.

Fisting the roots of her hair, Ansel pulled her head back, gently but insistently. Her eyes fluttered open to stare sightlessly at the striped canvas of the ceiling as Ansel's lips traveled down the column of her throat. His mouth was so hot against her skin, she imagined it would burn marks into her pale skin. She almost hoped it would.

Not one to let Ansel have all the fun, Rhosyn pushed her pelvis forward, grinding into the growing hardness against her hip. The choked grunt that rewarded her actions pulled a mischievous smile from her. She dragged her hands down his chest, nails catching on Ansel's shirt as her fingers traced a path to his belt. Before she had struggled with it for more than a few moments, one of Ansel's hands flew to her wrist to stop her.

"No." His tone was firm.

Rhosyn began to pull away in stinging confusion, but his hand in her hair pinned her firmly where she was.

"No," he repeated, softer this time. "You just said you have spent your life doing things for other people. I don't want this to be about that. I just want you to feel."

Rhosyn stilled, one of her fingers still stroking the notched leather of his belt. She itched to push him back, rip off his belt and drop to her knees, just to show him she could give as good as she got. And he would let her. If that was what she truly wanted, Ansel would let her control this encounter and take her pleasure from him.

Instead, she paused, a shiver running up her spine at what he proposed. *Just feeling*. She was no stranger to sex, but even in her brief encounters, she had found herself drawn into being what her partners desired—normally the untamed spitfire that treated everything, even pleasure, like a competition.

But with Ansel...the proposition was as terrifying as it was delicious. And Rhosyn wasn't one to scare easily. Slowly she nodded.

She was rewarded by the movement of Ansel's lips curving into a smile against the hollow of her throat. "Good girl."

A shudder trailed down Rhosyn's body in the wake of Ansel's hands, trailing over her flanks towards her hips. She let her own hands fall to her sides, clenching into fists as she endeavored to do as Ansel asked, and just feel what he was doing to her.

So slowly that Rhosyn thought she might scream, Ansel inched her shirt up, sliding his warm, rough palms against the planes of her stomach. She sucked in a sharp breath, wanting to pull away from the all-consuming heat that ran through her, while also craving more.

Ansel continued to lift her shirt until he pulled it off over her head and let his fingers trail back down from her shoulders to her clavicles.

"You even have freckles here," he murmured as he traced over the swell of the top of her breast.

"Comes with the territory." Rhosyn intended to joke, but the breathless rasp of her voice detracted from the effect. Any further teasing gave way to a gasp as Ansel's lips replaced his fingers on her sternum.

He dragged his mouth sideways, tongue darting out to taste her skin until his mouth latched around the peak of her breast. Her mind fixated on the exquisite pleasure so adamantly that she barely even noticed his hands drifting lower to the button of her pants.

He switched his attention to her other breast, and she couldn't help herself. She plunged her fingers into his hair, pulling him closer at the same time she arched towards him, not sure what she was chasing except *more*.

He pulled back, looking up at her with already glassy eyes, lips red and wet in a way that almost undid Rhosyn right there.

"You really can't stay still unless I tie you to a bed, can you?" Ansel asked. His tone was teasing, but with the hoarseness in his voice, Rhosyn couldn't help but picture what it would be like to be tied in his bed again, this time in a completely different context.

Already flushed, a fresh wave of redness rushed down from Rhosyn's face to her chest. Ansel's gaze flickered over her, taking in her visceral reaction to his words. His eyes darkened as he looked up at her through his lashes, pressing an open-mouthed kiss to her sternum.

"Maybe some other time," he murmured.

Rhosyn refused to wonder if they would have a chance for *some other time*. Not when her mind was occupied being melted by the heated expression on his face.

"For now, reach up and grab the bar."

Momentarily confused, Rhosyn glanced up to find the trapeze Ansel had descended on so gracefully dangling over her head.

"I'm not much of an acrobat," she huffed.

"I know, but it'll give you something to do with your hands," Ansel murmured into her skin. "Be good for me and grab the bar."

When he put it like that, Rhosyn was of no mind to disobey. Her arms stretched above her, fingers wrapping around the solid wood of the handle, the grain against her palm grounding her. She didn't have to go on her tiptoes to reach, but only just, the position leaving her fully stretched out and vulnerable.

"Perfect," Ansel murmured, so low it might have been more for his own benefit than Rhosyn's. Then, he proceeded to systematically drive her towards the brink of insanity, alternating dragging his teeth over her nipples before soothing over them with the flat of his tongue.

Rhosyn's chin fell forward onto her chest and she whimpered. The wooden bar dug into her palms as she gripped it tighter, a throbbing starting in her core that she was helpless to do anything to relieve.

Seeming to sense her growing desperation, Ansel smirked against her skin before falling to his knees. He pressed a kiss to her lower belly as he undid her pants and dragged them down her thighs, soothing some of the feeling that she was going to vibrate out of her skin, which Rhosyn tried desperately to contain.

When he finally tossed her trousers over his shoulders and let his gaze rest on the apex of her thighs, a low curse escaped Ansel. "Your hair is even red here."

"What color did you think it would be?" Rhosyn tried to retort, the bite completely drowned out by the urge to beg him to finally touch her there.

"Honestly?" Ansel pressed a kiss to her hip bone. "I tried not to think about it. Because I knew when I started imagining what it would be like to have you, I wouldn't be able to stop. And up until yesterday, I never thought I'd get the chance to see you like this at all."

Rhosyn's breath stuttered as he drew his nose across the crease of her thigh. "But you hoped?" The question came out more desperate than Rhosyn wanted, but she had to know.

"Oh, how I hoped."

The warmth that suffused her chest at his answer only registered for a moment before she arched her back in pleasure at the kiss Ansel planted directly over her sex. She tried to spread her legs to give him more access, but Ansel had other ideas. A broad hand grabbed her thigh, pulling it over his shoulder and leaving her completely open to him.

She squeaked in a most undignified manner, suddenly glad to have the bar for support as she balanced on one leg. Ansel chuckled against her heated flesh before returning to his task.

His tongue parted her in one long stroke, and suddenly it was all she could do to stay upright. He repeated the motion, finding a cadence that made her squirm. She tried to pull him closer to her with the knee draped over his shoulder.

When he sucked at the most sensitive part of her, Rhosyn's standing leg gave out completely, leaving her nearly hanging from the trapeze above her. Ansel didn't relent, throwing her other leg over his shoulder as well, leaving her supported only by her arms and his hands on her ass, spreading her open as his mouth did unspeakable things to her.

The peak of her pleasure was at the tips of her fingers, beginning to spark through her limbs. Desperately, she bucked forward, trying to grind herself against his face and finding she had no leverage as the trapeze she hung from wobbled.

Ansel pulled back, and Rhosyn whined high in her throat as the pleasure that had been about to crest over her dissipated.

"What did I say about just feeling?" he scolded, turning his head to nip the sensitive skin of her inner thigh.

With concerted effort, Rhosyn relaxed her hips, letting herself settle in his hands again. She was rewarded with a satisfied hum and a soft kiss to her inner thigh. Then, he began working her up anew, and Rhosyn fought every instinct to buck against him and chase her own pleasure. She squeezed her eyes shut, and her fingers grasped the trapeze bar so tightly it creaked, as if it might splinter in her hands.

Ansel worked her higher and higher until Rhosyn feared she might float away. Finally, Ansel sucked her flesh into his mouth once more, and she came undone with a voiceless shout. One of her hands let go of the bar to fist his hair, just to ground her to the man who had brought her such pleasure as she shuddered uncontrollably.

Unable to hold herself up with one arm as the pleasure started to ebb from her, leaving her boneless, she began to slide down. Ansel helped her, cushioning her descent until she straddled his lap where he kneeled on the floor, cradled to his chest.

She panted there, the spicy sweetness of him mixing with the heady rush of pleasure in an indelible mix in her mind. Mindlessly, she nuzzled into the "v" of skin visible on his chest, the rough fabric against her cheeks reminding her that he still had all his clothes on.

Now that Rhosyn was boneless with pleasure, she assumed Ansel's request for her to *just feel* was fulfilled. She wanted to do much more than feel right now.

No sooner had her fingers slid under the collar of Ansel's shirt, ready to feel the solid warmth she knew hid beneath, than a loud cough sounded from the door. Before Rhosyn had even registered they were no longer alone, Ansel dove forward, covering Rhosyn's exposed form with his own, substantially more modest body. Rhosyn buried her face in his shoulder with a squeak, half embarrassment and half-surprise.

"Sorry, Boss... I—" Little John's deep rumble sounded by the door along with some shuffling as if attempting to make a hasty retreat and stumbling over his own feet.

"You've already interrupted, John," Ansel growled, his back hunched over Rhosyn protectively as she tried to cram herself into as small a ball as possible, to stay hidden beneath him. "Just spit it out."

"I've made the arrangements you asked for and have all the volunteers gathered. They'll meet you in the office." John spat the words out as if it were a race before a swish of canvas and retreating footsteps indicated they had fled.

With a sigh, Ansel dropped his head to Rhosyn's collarbone. It was a position of such abject defeat that Rhosyn couldn't help but chuckle. The motion jostled Ansel's forehead where it rested on her chest, and he began to laugh as well. Maybe it was the fizzling pleasure still running through her veins making Rhosyn feel light, or the shock of suddenly being discovered, but in a matter of moments, she had descended into full on cackles.

To his credit, Ansel joined her in her mirth, lifting his head and laughing along. His eyes crinkled at the corner as he smiled sheepishly.

"We should...probably talk."

Rhosyn nodded in agreement. The heat of the moment had dissipated, and as humorous as the situation had suddenly become, reality was sleeping back in. She had chosen to join Ansel in uncovering Mr. Gower's plots, but there was no guarantee of where they would stand once the issue was resolved. And there were still sponsored Talented to help to their freedom.

Bracing her hands on Ansel's shoulders, she pushed him back lightly, and he went easily. His hands patted the floor around him until he located her clothing. She sat up and began pulling them on, trying to make herself look as unruffled as possible, although she knew it was a lost cause. Her disarrayed hair and crimson flush spoke volumes—not to mention that Little John would clearly know what had been happening between them.

Still, Rhosyn stood and arranged herself as best she could, but she couldn't help the flutter that ran through her as Ansel wiped his still-glistening mouth with the back of his hand.

She cleared her throat. "What are these arrangements Little John mentioned?"

Ansel ran his hands through his own hair, pushing it back out of his face, although the single silver strand fell forward defiantly again. He glared at where it hung between his eyes in frustration, the expression so endearing that Rhosyn felt herself smiling despite her efforts to be serious.

"Archer's Circus was lucky enough to get a fortuitous invitation during our trip to the palace," Ansel explained. "I thought accepting might give us a chance to get more information about Mr. Gower."

Rhosyn lifted an eyebrow. "Do tell."

"It seems the King enjoyed our performance at his ball—so much so that he wants the circus to provide some entertainment for an excursion to his country estate that he is planning with some members of society. I had some of the Foxes do some digging, and it appears that Mr. Gower is on the invite list."

"Do socialites really have nothing to do but throw parties and attend balls? What about their supposed business?" Rhosyn mused.

"Parties are where their daughters find wealthy marriages and influential men find women with dowries to support them. That *is* their business," Ansel pointed out.

Rhosyn frowned. It was such a strange way to think of things, but she supposed Ansel was right. "I suppose the Circus is going to another party then."

"We are. And you're coming with."

Chapter Twelve

The glass chilled Rhosyn's nose as she all but smashed her face against it, watching the countryside roll by. She had never known there was so much green so near the incessant grays and browns of London. In the clearer air of the country, the leaves seemed even brighter than those on the sparse trees outside the manors in the upper city, where the smokey air from the nearby factories made everything muted.

A dry chuckle from the bench across from Rhosyn made her pull back.

"One would think you'd never seen a tree before." He teased.

"One tree? Yes," Rhosyn conceded. "This many in the same place? No."

Ansel tilted his head. "You've really never been out of the city before."

Rhosyn shook her head, looking away towards the window to avoid the feeling in Ansel's eyes as he observed her. They still hadn't talked about what had happened between them in the Merry Men's tent, and Rhosyn was loathe to bring it up. After all, what was there to say? It couldn't possibly mean more than a simple physical release. Not when Ansel would leave with the circus and Rhosyn would go back to the police after Mr. Gower's plans were uncovered.

"I never had the chance to travel," Rhosyn admitted. "When I was with the Lions, none of us had much time to do much but stay alive and keep the young ones fed."

Of course, after the Lions had dissolved, life had been different. Nate had taken Contessa to a cottage by the ocean, and even Kristoff and Gregor had managed to steal away for a holiday. But Rhosyn had entered training for the police as fast as she could and never taken more than one consecutive day off since. Not until her time with the Foxes.

"But you wanted to?" Ansel asked, drawing her from her thoughts.

She turned back to him. "Yes," Rhosyn admitted.

"Where did you want to go?"

It wasn't a question Rhosyn had expected, so much so that it surprised the truth out of her without a second thought. "The ocean."

"Really? The consummate city girl has a taste for exploring?" Ansel's brows rose, and a smile toyed with the edges of his lips.

Rhosyn sighed. "My father. He was a sailor on transatlantic steam ships. I barely remember him, but the images I do have of him are always headed off to another adventure. All the time away from London was probably what let him hide his Talent for so long. I've always wanted to see where he was running off to for all those years."

Rhosyn swallowed, looking down at her hands in her lap, unconsciously popping her knuckles. The sound was loud in the quiet carriage at the end of her speech. She had once admitted to Contessa that her dream had been to follow in her father's footsteps. At one point, when she was barely more than a child, she had inquired about jobs on one of the steam ships down at the port. Rhosyn had even gone so far as to gather up her meager belongings, to leave the perils of London and the lower city behind.

Then Nate and Kristoff had come to check on the overcrowded Den, looking hopeless and harrowed by the monumental task they had set for themselves, and Rhosyn knew she couldn't go. They were her family, and she owed them her life after they had broken her out of the textile factory she lived in after her parents' deaths. So, she stayed. Only Contessa had ever heard that she dreamed of something else for her life at one point. It wouldn't be fair to lay that responsibility at the feet of the men who had loved her like a sister for so many years.

"You know," Ansel said with purposeful casualness, "I've thought about taking the circus to America for a tour before. Talents are so much more widely accepted over there, after all."

Rhosyn blinked. The way Ansel said it almost sounded like an invitation—like a chance for a new life where her mixed past wouldn't have to constantly be locked in eternal battle for her future. But that would be impossible.

Rhosyn hummed noncommittally and turned her attention back to the countryside rolling by outside the window. In the absence of conversation, the rattling wheels of the carts traveling with them permeated the enclosed space. Alongside the modest carriage carrying Ansel and Rhosyn, Archer's Circus had sent several wagons of performers, whose equipment could be easily packed up and transported without the train. They had been on the road for an hour now and should be just over halfway to the estate where the King's gathering was to be held.

"We only have a little while until we get there." Ansel broke the silence to echo her thoughts. "We should finish getting you into your disguise, just in case."

Rhosyn turned towards the bundle at her side, containing the remainder of the accessories for her ensemble. She already wore a deep purple dress with sleeves more flowy than were strictly fashionable, but that gave her the appearance of drifting through water when she walked.

A muffled jingle came from the bag as she opened it, and she raised her eyebrows.

Ansel shrugged. "It's not like I haven't hidden somebody in plain sight by dressing them up as a circus performer before. When people are used to seeing you in a Royal Police uniform, they will barely notice you at all bedecked as an eccentric fortune teller."

"Hopefully, most of the people at this gathering will only ever have seen me in passing, on one of the few occasions Contessa and Nate took me to a party." Rhosyn pulled out a long navy scarf embroidered with silver moons and stars.

"For your hair," Ansel explained. "It's...rather distinctive. I thought it would be best to cover it up."

Rhosyn sighed, but he was right. She piled her curls on top of her head and began winding the fabric around it. The reason she and Ansel had decided on a fortune teller for her disguise was so she could mingle easily through the party, giving her better chances to eavesdrop on any important conversations Mr. Gower might have. It wouldn't do for him to spot her from across the room based on the top of her head.

She fumbled as she reached the end of the length of fabric, fingers struggling to tie the short ends into a knot at the base of her skull.

"Here, let me." Ansel shifted across the carriage, sliding onto the same bench as Rhosyn.

She turned her back to him, to give him a better angle to help. His warm hands came up to cover hers and she let them fall back into her own lap. His nimble fingers made quick work of the knot, but his touch lingered. The pad of one callused finger ran down the nape of her neck, so lightly she questioned if it was intentional.

A shudder washed over her. Ansel snatched his hand away, as if Rhosyn's response shocked him out of a trance.

"Sorry, rough hands." He cleared his throat.

Rhosyn turned on the seat, so her back was no longer to him, busying herself with the bag once more. "Between the trapeze bars and the knives, I'm surprised your skin hasn't turned to stone."

"I'd think the calluses are more from the knives at this point," Ansel admitted. "I almost completely stopped doing acrobatics for many years, when I was afraid my Talent would be too obvious. Not to mention, I'm not actually Talented with knives, so building that skill required a lot more practice...and a lot more accidentally slicing myself. I count myself lucky I still have all my fingers."

As Ansel spoke, Rhosyn fished a handful of silvery bangles out of the bag, explaining the earlier jangling. She slid them on and let them settle on her wrists, where they threw sparkling lights all over the carriage every time she moved her hands.

The bracelets jingled like tiny bells as she dug around in the bottom of the sack for the last few items. As she fished out a pencil of kohl and a small pot of rouge, she raised her brows curiously at Ansel.

"It'll make your face less familiar," he explained.

"It will just make it clear how much I don't know what I'm doing with this." Rhosyn frowned at the objects in her hand. The only times she had ever gone anywhere where her appearance might matter, Julia had helped her with her hair, only applying the most minimal amount of powder to her nose. Otherwise, whenever Rhosyn looked in the mirror, the lack of freckles made her feel like a ghost.

"I can help you." Ansel gestured for her to hand him the makeup.

Rhosyn's brows rose even higher. "You're going to help me with my makeup?"

"I run a circus. You don't live with this many clowns and not know how to paint up your face." Leaning in close, Ansel motioned for her to close her eyes.

When she did, he began smudging the kohl sticks on her eyelids, fingers sure despite the jostling of the carriage. With her vision gone, Rhosyn's ears pricked, zeroing in on the sound of Ansel's breath so close to her own.

A finger pressed into her top lip and her eyes snapped open, to find Ansel's gaze fixed on her mouth. He pushed at it again, smearing the rouge on it. As he moved towards the bottom lip, the pressure forced Rhosyn's mouth open slightly. Her breath caught, and Ansel's gaze flicked up to her eyes.

The glimmer she saw there made her bold. Quickly, she flicked her tongue against the tip of his finger where it rested against her lip. His gaze darkened.

"Be good," he purred.

Something in Rhosyn's core melted at the words. Where so often she rose to every challenge presented to her with bared teeth and flying fists, something about the way Ansel said it made her pliant. She ached for more, and the way Ansel looked at her told her he did too.

Rhosyn sat perfectly still as he finished applying the tint to her lips before pulling back to admire his work. "Dramatic and eccentric. Nobody will suspect a straight-laced police officer under that get up."

"I'm not sure I ever would have called myself straight-laced, even when I wasn't running with a gang of thieves," Rhosyn countered, her voice only slightly hoarse from Ansel's recent touch. She cleared her throat and shook herself free of his spell as he retreated to the far side of the carriage.

"Good, because you're going to have to be creative and have a little fun with your fortune teller ruse," Ansel said. "In fact, why don't you do a little bit of a practice run on me."

He dug in his coat pocket and produced a small packet, which he held out to Rhosyn. Seeing what it was, she stared at him quizzically.

"Playing cards? Shouldn't I be reading tarot cards or something a little more...mystical?"

"Do you know anything about tarot cards?" Ansel countered.

Rhosyn shook her head.

"In my years of hiding Talented in the circus, I've learned that it's best to stick to what people know. That way their ruse isn't completely a lie. Besides, I'm pretty sure you already know a few card tricks that could convince people you can read their minds." Ansel's look was pointed.

Rhosyn grabbed the deck from his outstretched hand with narrowed eyes. "Alright then."

She pulled them from their paper packaging and began shuffling. They were clearly new cards, snapping energetically as they jumped in her hands. She bent them in a rippling bridge, using the motion as a distraction as she palmed one card, surreptitiously glancing at it.

Keeping the one card in her hand, she restacked the deck and held it out to Ansel to cut. He did, and as she restacked it, the card in her palm found its way to the top of the deck.

"Draw your card," Rhosyn instructed, adding a dramatic timbre to her voice.

He did, the ghost of a smile playing over his lips before he schooled his features again.

"Now, think hard on your card, and I will tell you what it is and what it means." Rhosyn closed her eyes, breathing in deeply with a look of upmost focus on her face.

"You are holding...the three of spades."

Ansel huffed in amusement, and Rhosyn smiled slightly, although she kept her eyes closed.

"This card carries great weight. You have an important trial before you, and the fates of many others lie in your hands," Rhosyn intoned with as mystic of a tone as she could manage.

"That's hardly hard to figure out," Ansel snorted.

Rhosyn opened her eyes to glare at him. "Isn't that the trick of this sort of thing anyways? Be just vague enough and base your predictions off what you already know of somebody? Unless you have somebody with a Talent to actually predict the future..."

"That I do not. I'd think that would be much too powerful a Talent," Ansel admitted.

"I have a friend who can predict danger but nothing specific."

"Even if all those who tell fortunes at Archer's Circus are using tricks, you definitely used some slight of hand to make me pick the three of spades," he pointed out.

"It's not like you didn't know I knew my way around a deck of cards." Rhosyn shrugged one shoulder, smiling crookedly.

Ansel reached out and snatched the deck from her fingers. "Well, since you used that to swindle me out of a bet, I think I should have a chance to even the playing field."

"What did you have in mind?" Rhosyn's curiosity piqued. She watched his deft fingers manipulate the cards, and although his shuffling wasn't as elaborate as hers, the nimbleness of his fingers still held her attention. Realizing she was staring, she snapped her gaze back up to his.

"You draw a card," Ansel purposed. "If I guess the correct card, you have to answer a question."

"What kind of question?"

"Any question I want. And you have to answer honestly."

Rhosyn swallowed, her eyes drifting back the deck, which he now held out to her. It was a dangerous proposition.

And Rhosyn loved danger.

She reached out and slid the top card off the deck. Flipping it towards her, the perfect face of the Queen of Hearts stared back. Rhosyn glanced up to find Ansel smirking at her knowingly, and she grimaced. She wasn't the only one with tricks up her sleeve.

"You're holding the Queen of Hearts," he said.

"Yes," Rhosyn admitted, "But you already knew that."

"Now to figure out what to ask." Ansel leaned back in his seat and folded his arms.

Rhosyn wrinkled her nose. "You don't just want to know my favorite color? Or maybe my favorite food?"

"You might tell me that without a wager. I need to use this on something you wouldn't answer otherwise."

It was Rhosyn's turn to fold her arms. "Bold of you to assume I'd tell you my favorite color."

"Even more reason to make this question count." Ansel narrowed his eyes. "Would you rather be a Lion or an officer of the Royal Police?"

Rhosyn sat back in her seat as if she had been slapped. To answer Ansel's question would be to dive off the knife's edge that her life was currently balanced on. She had been picking her way through every situation on tip toes, precariously balanced between upholding the law and thwarting it based on what the situation required.

In the secret tunnels, Ansel had asked her what she truly was. But which one did she *want* to be?

"Both."

Neither.

She wanted all of it, yet something beyond what either position had offered. Something, that Ansel seemed to offer more with every moment they spent together, yet Rhosyn remained terrified to grasp onto it.

"That's not an answer," Ansel argued.

Rhosyn opened her mouth to respond that it was the most honest answer she had when the carriage jolted to a stop, cutting her off. After a moment, the door to the carriage swung open, late afternoon light spilling into the darkened space.

Rhosyn squinted past the coachman, who pulled down the stairs on the carriage, towards a sprawling estate.

They had arrived.

Wearing the face of somebody else was simultaneously stifling and liberating. Rhosyn drifted around the party, shrouded in an air of mystery. She stole glances at guests under hooded, heavily kohled eyes and talked with her hands so that the bangles on her wrists glittered in the lantern light.

The persona of Archer's Circus's newest fortune teller sat heavily on her like a mask, allowing her to be less self-conscious than she had been on accompanying the Woodrows to parties in the past. Still, the evening of putting on airs gave her new appreciation for the exhaustion she found in the crinkles of Ansel's eyes, and the slump of his shoulders when he shed the personas of the dashing Mr. Blakely or the devil-may-care Hood.

At the thought, Rhosyn's gaze darted across the milling crowds scattered across the lawn to where Ansel stood. He was currently engaged in conversation with several posturing gentleman, who had paused in front of one of the many performers stationed around the garden.

Rhosyn recognized the girl who juggled the glasses at the Foxes hideout, now fully made up and in top form as she tossed flaming clubs in the air. The men gaped as the performer spun, tossing the clubs behind her back for a few passes before turning back around and grinning.

As if Ansel sensed Rhosyn looking in his direction, he glanced up from the partygoers he was entertaining, his gaze catching hers. The silken sheen of his top hat and his glittering eyes reflected the flames from the juggler beside him, giving him the appearance of incandescence.

Rhosyn tore her gaze away in favor of focusing on the knot of people approaching her. The group was mostly composed of young women who giggled and whispered behind their hands. It was several minutes before the ladies drifted away, all pleased with promises of marrying for love. Rhosyn hoped the fortunes she gave them would come to pass, fabricated as they had been.

Unengaged again, she glanced over to where Ansel had been, to find him gone. A furrow formed between her brows as she scanned the crowd for him. While the gathering had been underway for almost an hour and the revelry was gathering steam, neither of them had encountered Mr. Gower yet.

The gleam of Ansel's top hat finally caught her attention, his silhouette almost completely hidden in a tight knot of people. The man standing next to him explained the eagerness of the crowd in that area. The King.

Hovering just over King Byron's shoulder was a scarred and scowling face that Rhosyn knew almost better than her own. Internally, Rhosyn cursed. She had known there was a chance Nate would be serving as the King's bodyguard this evening, but she had hoped it would be another of the King's Guard in rotation, so she could avoid being recognized and having Nate accidentally ruin her cover.

Maybe if she could catch him alone, she could explain the situation to him and get Nate to play along. Rhosyn spun on her heel, dress swirling in a rippling pool around her, and walked towards the servants' entrance at the edge of the garden.

She slipped past white gloved footmen carrying silver trays of food and drink into the staging area. Some of the servants shot her odd looks, but she strode past with confidence, and nobody stopped her. Once she was hidden from view of the main garden by a dense wall of hedges, she paused, evaluating her next move.

One of the servants could pass Nate a message asking him to meet her away from the main party. Before she could grab one of them to ask a favor, an eddy in the flow of activity in the staging area caught her attention.

Off to one side, three men stood bent in close conversation. Rhosyn recognized with a start the impressive silver mustache of Mr. Gower. From the redness of his face and the sharp gesticulations of his hands as he talked, Rhosyn could guess he was arguing with the two other men. She was unsure what he might have to argue with his servants about, as the other two men were clearly his staff—not dressed nearly as finely.

Rhosyn drifted closer as subtly as she could manage, straining to hear their words, although the ambient buzz of party made picking out a single conversation nearly impossible. As she approached, it became apparent that Mr. Gower and one of the men were in disagreement with the third.

Mr. Gower snapped something at his companion, and the conversation stalled for a moment. Then, the man who appeared to be on Mr. Gower's side said something, and the third man stiffened, standing as straight as a board. Mr. Gower said something next, but the stiffened man barely reacted at all, only blinking slowly.

Something about the blank expression on his face trickled cold down Rhosyn's spine. It reminded her of something she had seen before.

It reminded of her of Paul's listless appearance when she had seen him at the Gower's house.

Mr. Gower and the second man each said a few more words before turning around and striding purposefully back towards the party. Rhosyn moved to follow them, sure that whatever was happening with Mr. Gower's servants was untoward and likely held the answers to what he was trying to accomplish with such a dangerous group of Talented. Her gaze clung to the third man, though, who remained oddly inanimate.

Before Rhosyn could follow Mr. Gower and the second man to the main garden, the third man turned on his heel and marched from the side garden, motions as mechanical as a tin soldier. He strode quickly in the direction of the manor house, and Rhosyn frowned.

Something about the oddity of his behavior called to her instincts. She hovered for a split second of indecision before trailing him in the direction of the house. Ansel was still at the party, where he could keep an eye on Mr. Gower.

On light feet, Rhosyn followed the servant out of the side garden towards the manor. She held her wrists with her opposite hands to keep her bangles from jangling and giving her away. The servant ducked in a side door, and she waited for a moment before following suit.

She thanked luck for hinges kept well-oiled by the royal housekeepers as it shut silently behind her. The quiet in the empty hallway lay heavily after the liveliness of the party. Rhosyn took short steps, afraid even the quiet swish of her skirts would alert the man to her pursuit, but he didn't react.

In fact, he seemed blind to all around him, marching with purpose towards his unknown destination. He led Rhosyn up a flight of stairs, out of what appeared to be the servants' quarters and into the manor proper.

The halls here were richly appointed, paintings in gilded frames decorating every wall and elegant furniture upholstered in brocades and velvets. The man clearly wasn't here to steal, for he easily would have been able to pocket a fortune, unattended as they were. He instead made a beeline for the stairs.

Up on the second floor, they passed several closed doors that Rhosyn assumed concealed bedrooms, until the man opened one and strode inside. There was nothing marking this door as distinct from the others, and Rhosyn might have thought it was chosen at random if not for the purposefulness of his stride.

Rhosyn stopped outside the closed door, weighing her options. Looking up and down the hallway for anybody who might be watching, Rhosyn found the place deserted, everybody apparently at the party. She leaned forward and pressed her ear to the door. Only a faint shuffling greeted her, the absence of voices indicating he had not come up here for a surreptitious rendezvous.

In a rustle of skirts, Rhosyn fell down onto her belly so she could peer through the slight gap under the door. She squinted, as she tried to concentrate her vision through the narrow slit. As the man's silhouette came into focus, her stomach dropped.

In his hands was the long, thin length of a repeating rifle. A metallic click told Rhosyn he was loading it.

The time for secrecy was at an end.

She sprang to her feet and grabbed the door handle, only to curse when it didn't turn. He had locked the door behind him. Bending over to get a better look at the lock, she was momentarily distracted by a distant cheering from the party.

Something told her she didn't have much time. Rhosyn didn't know what the man planned to do with the rifle, but she doubted he was using it as a back scratcher. With a grimace, she took a step back. Then she drew her knee up into her chest and kicked out, foot hitting the door firmly, just above the handle. The blow rattled her teeth, and a shock ran from the sole of her foot up to the top of her head, the slippers she wore not offering nearly as much protection as her usual boots.

Still, it was enough for the lock to give way, and the door crashed inwards.

The sight that greeted her left her with no time to think about the jolt echoing through her. Seemingly unperturbed by the interruption, the man stood in the window, back to her with the rifle raised. He stared down the sights through the open window, which offered a clear view of the garden where the party was being held.

At the near end of the garden was a small platform, erected by Ansel for some of his performers, and standing on it, with his arms raised as if in speech, was King Byron.

The safety on the gun clicked, the sound echoing as time stretched. Rhosyn bounded across the room in three long strides. The man's finger was already tightening on the trigger by the time she reached him, giving her only enough time to crash into him. She grabbed him around the chest, forcing his arm up as the gun fired.

The volume of the shot shattered through her, leaving both her and the gunman momentarily frozen. The ringing in her ears quickly gave way to screams from the party. Over the gunman's shoulder, she spotted Nate hustling King Byron off the stage, both seemingly uninjured.

Before she could process anything else, the man lurched back into her, trying to throw her off. The motion loosened her grip just enough for him to spin in her grasp. He tried to lower the gun to point it at her, but the close quarters gave him very little room to maneuver. Rhosyn grabbed the rifle, keeping the barrel pointed at the ceiling and trying to wrest it from his grip.

He was deceptively strong and tugged back. Rhosyn grit her teeth and held on with all her might, knowing that her chances for survival were infinitesimal if he controlled the weapon. She kicked out savagely, foot catching him in the shin.

He grunted in pain, and she gained the advantage. As she tried to get a better grip on the gun, her finger slipped onto the trigger.

A blast echoed through the room as the gun discharged, so loud and so close that Rhosyn's vision swam. Stunned, she staggered back, letting go of the gun.

A heavy object plummeted past her, missing her by inches as she stumbled away. The gunman wasn't so fortunate, a heavy light fixture dropping from the ceiling, knocked loose by the accidental shot.

One of the wrought metal arms caught him square in the forehead, and he crumpled like a marionette whose strings had been cut. Rhosyn took the opportunity to lunge across the destroyed light fixture to where he lay on the floor.

She pinned him to the ground and wrenched the rifle from his slack fingers as he blinked dazedly.

In the few seconds of relative calm, shouts drifted in through the open window.

"—tried to kill the King!"

"On the third floor!"

Slamming doors and pounding footsteps accompanied the voices.

Rhosyn's attention was drawn away from the commotion by gunman's expression going from dazed, to confused, and finally settling on horrified.

"What happened?" he gasped.

"What do you mean what happened?" Rhosyn snarled. "You tried to assassinate King Byron. Did Gower put you up to this?"

His eyes widened so far that white showed all the way around his irises. "He wanted me to do something... I told him I wouldn't," the man sputtered. "But then the groom, Hamish—the one with the unnerving eyes—he said something to me. I...I don't remember."

Rhosyn froze. Mr. Gower's groom. Something began to click into place in her mind, only to be blocked by shouting from the hall.

"Down there! That's where the shot came from."

Panic overtook the man's expression. "No...no! I'll hang."

Before Rhosyn could do anything, the man shifted beneath her. She moved to press her weight into him so he couldn't escape, but he didn't try to push her off. She had the odd feeling of sinking and blinked incredulously as the servant beneath her appeared to sink into the floor as if being submerged in water.

In a second, he was gone. Rhosyn patted the floor where he had been in disbelief before an image flitted through her head: Sponsorship papers for a Talented who could walk through walls.

She shot to her feet, ready to dash out into the hallway and try to cut the would-be assassin off downstairs. Before she took one step, several King's Guard and Royal Police piled through the door, shouting.

There she stood, alone in the very spot the shot had come from, holding the weapon that had been used in an assassination attempt on the King.

"There she is. Arrest her!"

Chapter Thirteen

Rhosyn's brain tumbled to a halt, like a carriage meeting an unfortunate end in the street races that crashed through the lower city. In the smoldering wreckage of her plan, her mind fixated on one thing: The widened eyes of Royal Police, taking in the person who had attempted to take the life of their country's leader.

The scarf that had been tied around her head fluttered to the ground at her feet, having come loose in the mayhem. Even without her hair showing, she would have been recognizable to those who had crossed paths with her at the station for years.

Fletcher and Davies stood to one side of the bunch, expression morphing from open in shock to contorted in fury as the moment stretched.

"I... It wasn't—I didn't..." Rhosyn searched for words to deny the appearance of the situation.

But it wouldn't change what was about to happen. They would arrest her as the real killer ran away. After she had disappeared from the Royal Police with no explanation—and was clearly no longer a hostage—they wouldn't be quick to believe any of her explanations.

The shock that held the room in temporary suspension was shattered by a ripple that ran through the assembled guards and officers. A tall figure pushed its way towards the front of the crowd.

Rhosyn swallowed as she caught sight of shaggy auburn hair. Then, Nate stood before her. A long moment stretched, where she was sure everybody assembled could hear the pounding of her heart. Nate's good eye widened slightly before his face became unreadable, his mouth set in a hard, straight line.

"You are under arrest for attempting to assassinate King Byron."

Rhosyn's ears rang, and her knees trembled. Even Nate—the closest thing she had to a family—believed the worst of her right now. She expected the rage of betrayal to burn like fire in her veins, but instead an icy cold washed over her. She nearly crumpled where she stood, but a flicker of Nate's eyes caught her attention.

He glanced back and forth between her face and the rifle still clutched to her chest. He took one slow step forward. Surely he didn't think she would shoot him?

No. Nate could have had her disarmed and on the ground by now, and never shied away from jumping into danger to protect his family or his King.

He was dutiful and proud of his position, and he wouldn't refuse to arrest her in front of all these onlookers. But he would give her a chance to escape. Rhosyn's fingers tightened on the gun. Nate's chin dipped in the tiniest of acknowledgements.

Before she could second guess herself, Rhosyn angled the gun forward slightly and pulled the trigger at the same time. Plaster exploded everywhere as the bullet hit right at the base of a second chandelier. People shouted as the chain holding the light fixture detached, but Rhosyn didn't stay to watch it plummet to the floor between her and her would-be captors, momentarily blocking them from view.

She dropped the gun, knowing she was unwilling to actually shoot anybody to escape, and spun towards the window. Not breaking her stride, she jumped up onto the sill and twisted in midair, catching the overhang above the opening with her fingers.

If she descended, she would be throwing herself into the path of more guards. The roof was her best chance to make a getaway, and she only had a few seconds head start. Wishing for Ansel's agility and thanking the royalty's gaudy architecture for its ample handholds, she scrambled up the last story to the roof.

As soon as her feet hit the slate tiles, she took off, dashing up the steep slope of the gable. The garden where the party had been was in the back of the manor, but her best chance of escape from the property would be through the gates at the front, left open for all the comings and goings of guests.

She reached the towering peak of the roof and crested to the other side. Instead of running down hill, she fell to one hip, sliding down feet first. The tiles rucked her skirts up and skinned her legs, leaving a stinging in their wake, but Rhosyn didn't stop. She let gravity build her momentum, gaining speed—and hopefully distance on her pursuers.

At the end of the steep slope was a small flat section of roof over the front entrance. She tumbled onto it, descent halted with enough force to knock a grunt from her. A few stumbling steps took her to the very edge, when her eyes lit on exactly what she was hoping for: carriages.

She had never driven one before, but there was no better teacher than necessity.

Her gaze lit on a sleek navy coach with gold accents, hitched to a pair of brown horses whose muscles rippled under shining coats. They would do quite nicely—not that she had time to shop for options.

Already, shouts of pursuit were echoing from the side of the house as people on the ground ran around the manor to stop her. Rhosyn crouched before springing forward. Her heart flew up into her throat as she fell for one extended second. Then, she landed in a crouch on the top of the carriage.

Before she had a chance to catch the breath the impact knocked out of her, the carriage lurched, sending her sprawling, and nearly knocking her off. A sharp whinny told her that her sudden appearance had scared the horses. They took off, and she rolled, not having a good grip, only managing to keep herself from tumbling to the ground by grabbing the edge of the roof before she toppled over it.

The vehicle bumped as it picked up speed, the horses seemingly only spurred on further by the yelling behind them, as Rhosyn's pursuers commandeered carriages of their own. The clatter of wheels over the cobblestone drive echoed through her skull as she crawled over the roof towards the driver's seat, remaining flat on her belly lest the bumping knock her loose.

Wind whipped at her unbound hair and stung her eyes as she dragged herself on her elbows, until she at last tipped over the front edge and collapsed onto the driver's bench.

Her fingers scrambled for the reins, but even as they closed around the worn leather, her heart sank. Any hopes of driving the carriage were a lost cause. She had never handled a horse before, and the shock combined with shouts from behind of "Halt in the name of the crown!" seemed to have whipped them into a frenzy. The horses would gallop until they deemed it appropriate to stop, and Rhosyn was at their mercy.

By now, they had already charged down the long drive leading to the manor and careened through the front gates of the property. The horses followed the road through a sharp bend. Rhosyn's nails bit into the reins so hard they would leave marks in the supple leather, as the carriage rocked precariously at the suddenness of the turn.

As it righted itself, falling back onto four wheels after skittering on two for a moment, Rhosyn chanced a glance over her shoulder. She had gained considerable distance from her pursuers thanks to the horses' reckless speed, but she was likely to end up thrown from the carriage with a broken neck if this went on much longer.

Dust rose from the pounding of hooves on the country lane, stinging Rhosyn's eyes and burning her throat as she fought to think. The rattling wheels drowned out her thoughts, and she gritted her teeth so hard she thought they might crack in an effort to focus.

Her gaze caught on a dense wood off to one side of an upcoming turn in the road. It could provide good cover.

Especially if her pursuers thought she had continued down the road.

The bend approached quickly, as did her opportunity to decide: jump voluntarily from a hurtling carriage or wait until she was either thrown from it or captured and thrown in jail.

Rhosyn always liked to play the odds.

The horses thundered around the corner. As soon as they rounded the bend, hiding the carriage from view for mere seconds, she jumped.

She threw her arms up over her head and tucked herself into a ball as best she could. The ground hit her with all the force of a steam engine, and the world twirled sickeningly as she tumbled through brambles into the ditch. The sharp scratch of thorns against her skin cut through the haze of disorientation as she rolled into the thicket of the forest, and the clattering wheels of her stolen carriage moved away. Hopefully her pursuers thought she continued with it.

As she reached the bottom of the downhill slope away from the road, she threw her hands out, but the trees approached too fast. Her forehead smacked against the base of one, bark cutting into the skin of her temple.

The brown and green of the trees around her swirled together as she tried to grapple onto consciousness, only for it to slip through her fingers like smoke. The last thought before darkness took her was that she hoped Ansel found her before the Royal Police.

Cool fingers stroked her temples. Rhosyn's eyelashes fluttered in pleasure, the touch soothing enough to counteract the mild throbbing on her forehead. The knot there was not nearly as bad as it could have been for running headfirst into a tree, mostly stinging from the abrasion left by the bark.

At the memory of tumbling into a forested ditch, Rhosyn's eyes snapped open. Instead of the dappled light of trees at night, or the dingy gray of a prison cell, her gaze focused on concerned green eyes.

"Ansel," she sighed, her voice a breathy croak.

"Rhosyn." Ansel's voice was hardly any better.

Movement beneath her drew attention to the firm thighs cradling her head, flexing as Ansel bent over his lap where she rested. Rhosyn had been knocked out more times than she cared to admit, and all those occasions would have been vastly improved by waking like this. Her instincts pushed her to rise and get back in the fight as soon as possible, but Ansel's gentle touch pulled her even more insistently to stay right where she was.

Although she wasn't entirely sure where here was.

"What…"

"We're back at the safehouse in the lower city," Ansel explained. His fingers drifted to her hair as he spoke, twisting a ringlet around his finger absently. "After the commotion died down and I put together what had happened, the performers and I started combing the area for you. Once we found you in the ditch, we snuck you into our carriage. We figured you were the least likely to be found out here."

"You found me," Rhosyn echoed. Ansel had known she would be wanted for trying to assassinate the king—a treason punishable by death—and he had hidden her among the Foxes anyways. He and his people would be seen as accomplices if she were caught, likely suffering the same punishment, but he had recounted the events like it hadn't been a choice. As if he hadn't even considered that it might have been an opportune time to sever their unlikely alliance.

"You could die for helping me," she croaked, the hoarseness in her voice no longer just from disuse. "Why would a gang leader risk himself for one crooked cop?"

Ansel's hands drifted down to cup her cheeks, so gentle that Rhosyn thought she might shatter. "I would think it was obvious."

Rhosyn stared up at him, a bubble of something warm forming in her chest as she waited for him to continue.

"I love you. Isn't it awful?" He chuckled dryly, with no small amount of affection, as though he couldn't conceive of how they had possibly ended up in this situation.

Rhosyn's breath caught, and she had a moment where she understood how Ansel must feel on the trapeze, right before letting go and trusting his fate to gravity. "The worst part is, I love you too."

All of this consternation about whether she was a Lion or an officer of the Royal Police faded to the background with the admission that she was a woman who had fallen in love under the most inconvenient circumstances.

"What are we going to do about it?" Ansel asked, seemingly half to himself.

A simple question held so much weight. With the disaster at the King's party and the horrible revelation that Mr. Gower appeared to be using his Talented servants to try to kill the King, the world outside this room held nothing but chaos for Rhosyn and Ansel.

"It certainly is problematic, given that my life is pretty much ruined and I'm well on my way to bringing you down with me," Rhosyn said.

Ansel smiled softly down at her. "Love is hardly ever convenient, but something tells me it's worth it, despite the trouble it causes."

Rhosyn's heart fluttered up into her throat. "Well then, I guess we'll just do what people in love do."

Before Ansel could ask her what she meant, Rhosyn surged upwards, crushing her lips to his. In an instant, his arms went around her shoulders, supporting her as she draped across his lap, holding her to him with a heady mix of firmness and gentleness.

Her lips moved over his, searching and insistent, but he did not yield to the franticness of her kiss. Instead, one hand came to hold her jaw, tilting her head to give him better access to her mouth. With her at his mercy, Ansel deepened the kiss, slowing the pace as his tongue slid against hers with single-minded focus.

Rhosyn whimpered, and Ansel drew back. Her lips chased his, but his hand at her jaw held her firmly in place.

"We shouldn't. Your head..." The rasp in Ansel's voice sent tingles all the way down to Rhosyn's toes.

"Is fine." Rhosyn insisted. She took advantage of their momentary pause to sit up all the way and throw one leg over Ansel's hips, so she straddled him. "Once we leave this room, there will be no escaping reality. But for now, I'm a woman in bed with a man who just told me he loves me. If this is all we will ever have, let me have this. *Please*."

Ansel let out a groan, the rumbling of his chest vibrating against Rhosyn's nipples. She squirmed, increasing the friction so they grew hard, begging for more attention.

"If you say 'please' like that one more time, you won't be leaving this room until you are mine in every way."

"Show me," Rhosyn breathed.

Ansel obliged, diving forwards to nip and suck at her neck. The heat of his mouth drew a shiver from her. She squirmed, working to ruck up her skirts, still wearing the fortune teller dress. Hands grabbed her wrists, rough skin against her sensitive skin halting her.

"You asked me to show you, and that means I give you everything." His thumb drew small circles around the inside of her wrist, her pulse hammering against his touch. "Which also means you have to be patient."

Rhosyn's breath caught in her throat. The strange shimmering warmth that Rhosyn had felt before when he told her to *be good* washed through her again. Slowly, she nodded. Ansel smiled, the brightness of the adoration in his gaze doing nothing to detract from the feral edge of desire seeping into his posture.

Carefully, he unlaced her bodice, each drag of his fingers across the fabric tortuous as she waited for him to reach skin. When he finally pushed it off her shoulders, leaving her bare from the waist up, her hands flew to his shoulders.

Her fingers dug into the firm muscle there, needing to hold on, as if she might fly away from the intensity of his gaze on her alone.

"Perfect," he murmured, before lowering to press an open mouth kiss to the valley between her breasts.

Rhosyn tipped her head back, eyes staring unfocused at the dingy wood ceiling. The single word echoed through her. Here with Ansel, she was not a Lion, a police officer, a brawler, or a thief. She was Rhosyn, and all she had to do to be perfect was just *be*. She wanted—needed—to watch Ansel come undone. Not because he expected anything of her in this moment, but because if she didn't give this man beneath her, who had given her so much, all the pleasure as she was capable of, she would regret it forever.

In one motion, she slid off Ansel's lap, landing on the floor between his thighs in a puddle of skirts.

"Rhosyn—"

"*Please.*"

"Anything."

A fine tremor ran through Rhosyn's fingers as she undid his trousers, pulling them open and finally pulling Ansel's hard length free. As her fist closed around him, the guttural groan that ran through him sent heat rolling down her spine and into her core. While her gaze remained fixed on her hand around him, his fingers in her peripheral vision clenched the edge of the bed so hard they turned white.

Rhosyn's tongue darted out to lick her lips and glanced up at him through her lashes. He wore a thoroughly wrecked expression, even though she had just started touching him. His eyes went wide as she leaned forward, wrapping her lips around his head.

"*Fuck.*"

Rhosyn was drunk on his reactions, the twitch of his manhood against her tongue and the strangled grunt of pleasure as she took as much of him into her mouth as she could. She began to slide up and down, but her gaze remained fixed on his face. Her eyes desperately catalogued every twitch of his jaw and the way his teeth dug into his lower lip as he tried to contain his desperate noises. Her rhythm faltered as she stared.

One of Ansel's hands came to hold her jaw, guiding her gently as his hips twitched.

"You're incredible like this," he growled. "I can't decide whether I like you better when you're throwing punches at me or when you're on your knees with your lips stretched around my cock."

Rhosyn whimpered around him, the noise unadulterated desperation.

"Maybe that's why I love you. Because I don't have to choose."

And I don't have to choose either, Rhosyn echoed in her mind, her mouth too busy to speak the words out loud.

Ansel pulled her off his length, and Rhosyn stared up at him with her mouth still hanging open. She only had a moment to admire him, his flushed face and the way his hair had fallen into his eyes, the silver piece gleaming in the lamplight, before he gathered her up into his arms and swung her onto the bed.

Her back landed on the mattress with enough force to make the ancient springs creak, but Ansel paid no mind, already prowling up her body. He shucked off his pants completely along the way, sitting up above her to pull his shirt off as well. Rhosyn took the cue to shimmy the dress the rest of the way down her hips, until their clothes lay in a discarded heap at the foot of the bed.

Once they were both completely bare, Ansel fell to his forearms, elbows bracketing her head. He circled his pelvis against hers, dipping into the considerable moisture that had gathered there, but not entering her yet.

Rhosyn bucked her hips, but one of his hands fell to her waist, pinning her down.

"Patience, love." He breathed the words into her neck before nipping at her collarbone.

Ansel sat back on his heels, pulling Rhosyn's hips into his lap. As he lined himself up at her entrance, a breathy moan escaped her, just the feeling of his tip stretching her open enough to drive her to the brink of madness she had been flirting with for so long.

The noise snapped his gaze to her face, and he pinned her there with it. Holding her eyes, he slowly pushed forward, sliding himself inside her inch by glorious inch. The tortuously slow drag made her eyelids flutter, but she dared not look away from the intensity of his expression. The expression that told him he saw *her*, not the mask of whatever role she was wearing, in this moment and all others.

Just as she saw him.

His hips met hers, and his mouth fell open in pleasure.

"So good. You take me so well," he panted.

Rhosyn hardly had time to register the zing of pleasure his words sent through her before he rolled his hips. At this angle, with her hips raised, his pelvis ground against her most sensitive spot and she gasped.

He repeated the action, grinding against her before withdrawing. He repeated the motion again and again, picking up speed until every thrust punched a breathy moan from her. As his hips pistoned into her, Ansel fell forward, bracing one hand on the wall above the headboard. The other gathered her wrists, bearing down on them with his weight and pinning her hands to the pillow above her head.

She rolled her hips against his, her world narrowing to the rising heat radiating out from her core, threatening to liquefy her into a pool of pleasure. But Ansel slowed, denying her the last bit of friction that would send her spiraling in pleasure.

She whimpered, and Ansel planted a kiss in the hollow just behind her ear. "Just a little more, Rhosyn."

The sound of her name on his lips, dripping with adoration and desperation, was all she needed to dive deeper into the well of pleasure he was driving her into. She tunneled further and further into the roiling inferno of her impending release as his hips snapped against hers relentlessly.

Rhosyn tossed her head side to side, as if it could help her contain the intensity of the moment. But at that instant, Ansel picked up his pace, his own control snapping as he chased his release.

The tension within Rhosyn shattered, so hard it bordered between pleasure and pain as she cried out her release. Her back arched and fireworks danced behind her eyes. She convulsed around Ansel, making it almost impossible for him to withdraw as he stuttered through a few more thrusts before spending himself inside her with a broken groan.

"Rhosyn."

They both drew in long, shuddering breaths as Ansel's forehead came to rest on her collarbone. He released her wrists from his grasp, and she moved her hands to his head, where she gently carded her fingers through his hair. The thin sheen of sweat covering both of them glimmered ethereally in the flickering lantern light. It combined with the deep quiet of early morning, amplified by the rushing of blood finally calming in Rhosyn's ears, to give the moment an otherworldly effect. As if the world beyond this room didn't exist, and they were held in the perfect bubble of this moment.

When it popped, the direness of their situation would sink back in. But for now, Rhosyn let Ansel bundle her into his arms as he rolled off her onto his side. For now, there was nothing besides his fingers in her hair and whispered praises between the kisses he pressed to the top of her head.

Chapter Fourteen

The smell of bacon roused Rhosyn from her doze. Her stomach growled before she even had a chance to open her eyes, prompting a low chuckle from somewhere across the room. She cracked one eye open to find Ansel standing at the foot of the bed wearing a bemused expression.

In his hands was the source of the smell: a plate of breakfast and a cup of tea. It looked almost as delicious as he did in that moment, his hair mussed from bed and his shirt open at the neck, exposing one shoulder.

Rhosyn opened both eyes to appreciate the sight and reached her arms over her head in a long stretch that drew attention to several sore spots in her body, both from her enjoyable night with Ansel and the much less enjoyable chase before that.

"Breakfast in bed? You're giving me the real princess treatment," she remarked as she sat up.

"I knew you must be hungry, but I figured we should let as few people know you're here as possible. There is a substantial reward for your capture, and people can't let slip a secret they don't know," Ansel explained, passing off the plate before setting the teacup on the rickety side table.

"Ah, so not a princess. Just a wanted criminal." Rhosyn grimaced, any illusions of domesticity in Ansel's breakfast delivery thoroughly shattered.

"Speaking of, we need to discuss why you're a wanted criminal. I'm assuming you didn't actually try to shoot the king?"

Rhosyn shook her head, mouth already full of bacon and a hefty slice of toast.

"Then, what actually did happen?"

"I was following one of Mr. Gower's men who was acting strange." Rhosyn explained the odd argument she witnessed in the garden, and how she had jumped in to thwart the assassination. She furrowed her brow when she began to recount how she had been the one left at the scene of the crime with a weapon. "It was so strange, though. Like he didn't even remember how he had gotten there."

Ansel's face grew pale. "So, Mr. Gower wants to use the Talented he's sponsored to get rid of the King."

Rhosyn grimaced even as she nodded in agreement. The cadre of Talented with violent abilities, combined with the assassination attempt at the party, painted a clear picture of what Mr. Gower wanted. "It's bold, considering that King Byron is wildly popular among the Talented after ending the Inquiries. It would be hard to convince them to take violent action against him."

Ansel's mouth formed a hard line, the look in his eyes causing the breakfast in Rhosyn's stomach to turn leaden.

"I had Little John look through the sponsorship papers we stole from the palace, and Rhosyn...one of the Talented he sponsored almost two years ago had powers of extreme persuasion, even to the point of being able to control somebody's actions."

Bile rose in Rhosyn's throat. "The groom."

Ansel nodded grimly. "His name is Hamish. It would explain what we overheard that night in the stables. Why they thought Olivia and Paul might come back of their own accord."

"And why they hardly seem to remember their time there. When the groom persuades them, it seems to put them nearly in a trance to force them to obey." Rhosyn's throat burned, and she put aside the plate of breakfast, food suddenly unappealing. All those Talented thinking they were getting a chance at a better life, only to be turned into thralls and set to a violent purpose.

"If Mr. Gower was willing to go to such lengths to oust the King, he won't give up after one failed attempt," Ansel pointed out. "He needs to be stopped. If a

Talented assassinates another king, and one who was their best hope of equality, it would start the Inquiries all over again. Fear of the Talented hasn't abated, especially among the rich and powerful, and this would stir things up again."

Ansel's words picked up in pace as he spoke, signaling to Rhosyn that under the surface of his analytical approach stirred the beginnings of panic. It was panic she recognized all too well in the young Lions who started to show Talents, afraid that it would end with them at the end of a noose. A fear that she had felt responsible for protecting them from, as she had been lucky enough to have no Talent to hide.

"Mr. Gower *will* be stopped," Rhosyn promised. "But we can't do it just the two of us."

Ansel grimaced. "Do we have a choice? With you neatly framed for the attempt, I don't think many people would believe us."

She cracked her knuckles one by one as she thought. "I didn't escape the estate without a little bit of help. I know somebody who would give us the benefit of the doubt."

Rhosyn had never wished more that Nate had not bricked up the secret passage into his office. The darkness was thick tonight, wind blowing the smog from the factories back into the upper city so that it blocked out the light of the stars. Still, Rhosyn wished for Scarlett's powers to thicken the shadows even further as she and Ansel crept over rooftops.

Ansel had donned the outfit of the Hood, face and hair covered, with a wrist bow strapped to his forearm. Rhosyn hoped he wouldn't have to use it.

He had leant her a spare hood too, and together they stole like shadows up through the middle city. Below them on the streets, Royal Police prowled between pools of flickering lamplight, out in force after Rhosyn's perceived betrayal.

She paused on the edge of one roof, waiting for a pair of officers to pass by on the street below, before jumping the gap to the next building, Rhosyn tried not to wonder if she knew the officers—if she had worked with them before, and what they might be saying about her now. Ansel's shoulder brushed hers as he crouched beside her, and the warmth of his touch dulled the chill of those thoughts.

It took the pair longer than it might have to make their way to the upper city, as careful as they were to not be spotted. Once they reached the affluent neighborhoods where the manors were too far apart to travel directly from roof to roof, they picked their way between shadowy hedges in back gardens, heading for a familiar house.

Rhosyn dropped to her belly next to a familiar hedge and dragged herself by her elbows through a narrow gap below the thick shrubbery that served as a natural wall. She cursed quietly as brambles snagged on her hood, nearly ripping it free.

When she emerged from the leaves, the familiar sound of tinkling water in a fountain drifted through the air. She pushed to her feet, waiting for Ansel to follow. However, no rustling signaled that he was following her through the shrub. She frowned with concern, only to start when a dark shadow flew overhead.

Ansel landed neatly before her on the balls of his feet, as if he hadn't just flipped easily over a hedge that stood as high as she did.

"Showoff," she muttered under her breath as she turned towards the house. As always, the back garden was a veritable Eden, flowers all at full bloom, dripping with the verdant life that Gregor coaxed from them so lovingly.

Rhosyn hadn't been here in too long, but she didn't have time to admire the roses.

As she had known they would be, the back door on the ground floor was locked. She didn't want to draw attention by knocking, in case they had company over, so they would have to climb. Rhosyn gestured to a window on the second floor, indicating to Ansel that it would be their point of entrance.

As picky as Nate was about security, he had a habit of leaving the entrance to the rose room unlocked so Scarlett could come and go as she pleased, without the apparent indignity of using the front door. Ansel started up the wall first, the agility from his Talent offering him incredible speed. Rhosyn's toes had barely left the ground by the time he pushed at the glass, swinging it open easily as she had hoped.

Rhosyn continued climbing as Ansel disappeared inside the house. Just as her fingertips reached the sill, a crash and a shout echoed from inside. Lightning shot up Rhosyn's spine and she flung herself over the ledge, tumbling into the bedroom.

Nate stood on the far side of the bed, knives drawn and a snarl on his face. Ansel had his wrist bow raised, pointed squarely at Nate. One bolt already quivered in the wall just over Nate's ear, the glass shade of a decorative sconce that had been there shattered on the ground.

"Stop!" Rhosyn shouted, throwing up her hands.

Nate froze, his gaze darting to her for a split second and then back to the threat before him. In one movement, Rhosyn stepped between them and ripped her hood back so Nate could see her face.

"It's me," she said. For half a second, everybody was still and Rhosyn stood frozen at the sight of the assassination again. Nate's eyes flickered gold in the lamplight, and her heart stuttered at the reminder of how truly dangerous he could be, even though she had never before been on the receiving end of his blade.

"We're here to ask for help." Rhosyn raised her hands to communicate that they came in peace, giving Nate a chance to feel her intentions.

Nate moved so fast Rhosyn couldn't react. His knives clattered to the floor and he crossed the room in two strides, before his arms came around her with enough force to knock the wind out of her. Still, he squeezed relentlessly, lifting her feet off the ground.

Rhosyn's arms wrapped around his shoulders, and for a moment, she was just a girl again, desperately holding onto one of the only people who had been able to make her feel safe in a city torn apart by hate.

She made a sound that was half chuckle half sob. "Nate, you're going to break my ribs if you keep on like this."

He put her on her feet and promptly punched her in the shoulder, not hard enough to hurt, but still enough to mean business. "Don't ever scare me like that again."

Rhosyn rubbed her shoulder and grimaced. "I would rather not have done it the first time."

Nate looked over her shoulder to where Ansel stood just behind her, weapon lowered, watching the reunion.

"You're lucky your friend missed, or I might have hurt him before you stopped me," Nate grumbled as he gestured to the bolt in the wall.

"I didn't miss," Ansel retorted, pulling his hood back now as well. "It's called a warning shot."

The two eyed each other appraisingly, each puffing out their chests and squaring their shoulders. Rhosyn resisted scolding them for their posturing by reminding them that she had beat both of them in a fist fight at one point or another.

"Nate, this is Ansel Blakely," she gestured between them. "You can trust him."

"I take it you're the one the Royal Police have taken to calling the Hood." Nate folded his arms across his chest.

"I do have that dubious honor," Ansel admitted. He opened his mouth as if to say more when a swishing sound came from the doorway.

"Rhosyn!" Contessa crashed into the room, still managing to have her skirts drift around her elegantly as she threw herself at Rhosyn. She hugged her around the waist tightly but briefly before holding her at arm's length to inspect her.

A slight glassiness in her eyes and pallor in her complexion took Rhosyn off guard, as Contessa's polished exterior rarely showed a scratch. Especially now that Rhosyn didn't have the chance to knock her guard down by training her in self-defense.

"Sorry to stop by unannounced." Rhosyn smiled ruefully.

Contessa's lips pulled up at the corners slightly. Behind her, the rest of the tension in Nate's posture relaxed. If Contessa's Talent wasn't signaling any danger, then he would be convinced that Ansel wasn't planning any betrayal.

Contessa's eyes darted to Ansel.

He sketched a small bow. "Ansel Blakely. I do apologize for the light fixture."

With a frown, Contessa stared at the broken glass on the floor. "No apology necessary. Everything in this room is hideous. I'm just sorry I wasn't the one who got to smash it. But we'll be redecorating soon enough anyways."

Rhosyn caught Nate's eye over his wife's shoulder and snorted. The gaudy wallpaper of the rose room was a running joke, but no matter how many times it came up, they had never gotten around to changing the décor in Contessa's old bedroom.

"We've been saying that for years," Nate pointed out.

Contessa hummed noncommittally before turning back to Rhosyn and Ansel. "Come downstairs and I'll have Gregor make some tea. Although, I assume you're here for more than a polite visit."

Rhosyn's gaze flicked to Nate. "I have an explanation…and some information."

The four cups of tea on Nate's desk were empty by the time Rhosyn finished her tale. Nate's knives were unsheathed and spread across the desk, glimmering almost as lethal as his golden eyes in the lamplight. The metallic *shink* of a whetstone being drawn across a blade punctuated the heavy silence. Rhosyn wasn't even sure Nate realized he had begun sharpening his knives, just falling into the habit as Rhosyn informed him of Mr. Gower's treachery.

Even worse, though, was the complete absence of color in Contessa's already pale complexion. Her gray eyes were as cold as ice, reminding Rhosyn the woman could be even more intimidating than her husband in the right circumstances. The twisting of Contessa's hands in her lap, knuckles white against the blue fabric of her dress, gave away her distress, though.

Nate set his knife down and put one hand in Contessa's lap, interlacing his fingers with hers so she let go of the now wrinkled silk of her skirt.

"They'll try again," Nate broke the heavy silence. "Especially since he can use you as a scapegoat." He nodded at Rhosyn.

She nodded in agreement. "You need to keep the King safe at all costs."

"The sponsorships were supposed to help the Talented. Instead, Mr. Gower is using them to try to start the Inquiries all over again. To turn people against the Talented." Contessa's voice cut through the stillness of the night like a blade, so sharp Rhosyn nearly flinched.

Her heart squeezed at the anger in Contessa's words—how much it must hurt to have her life's work turned against her, when she had put her own father in jail to put a stop to the persecution of the Talented.

Before Rhosyn could offer any words of comfort, Nate squeezed his wife's hand. "We'll arrest Mr. Gower."

Contessa shook her head. "He'll be out of jail in no time without hard proof. You know that better than anybody." She fixed Nate with a pointed look and he ducked his head, acknowledging that she had married him in the first place to get a hold of hard evidence necessary to send a known gangster to jail.

"The only proof we have is the testimony of a person already wanted for the attempted assassination and documents that were stolen from the palace by a gangster. Even then, the sponsorship contracts are circumstantial at best," Contessa explained.

"We have to prove he was behind the attempt at the party to clear Rhosyn's name," Ansel chimed in.

Rhosyn twitched in surprise, as he had been silent through her whole story, letting her tell it uninterrupted. She glanced at him to find his gaze fixed on her.

"And what do you have to gain from all of this?" Nate asked, fixing Ansel with a deep stare, sharp enough to look into Ansel's soul. Knowing Nate, he probably was.

Ansel raised his chin. "I've spent my life trying to give the Talented a better life too, albeit in a different way than you. This is my fight as well."

Nate's eyes narrowed. "And clearing Rhosyn's name?"

Rhosyn cleared her throat and glared at Nate, clearly trying to intimate that now was not the time for such discussions. His eyes darted over to her, and she detected the slightest hint of amusement in them before they landed on Ansel once again.

She supposed this was his payback for the way she ruthlessly teased him about Contessa when they were first married.

"Rhosyn should have the chance for the life she wants too," Ansel said firmly.

Crimson climbed up Rhosyn's neck to her face, and she looked down at her hands. Somehow, she felt more exposed than if Ansel had admitted to their truly debauched activities on a trapeze a few days earlier. But this statement went farther than skin deep, flaying her open more thoroughly than something that would just result in incessant teasing from Nate and Contessa. Rhosyn had fallen for her kidnapper, and the feelings were reciprocated.

"Then we will bring to justice the people really responsible for the plot against our king." The voice was Contessa's, proud and firm. Rhosyn glanced up at her friend, finding some warmth returned to her steely gaze.

If anybody understood falling in love with somebody you didn't intend to, it was Contessa.

"What we need is to catch Mr. Gower and his Talented in the act, so there is no way he can wiggle out of the charges," Contessa mused, her brain whirring almost visibly as she turned her mind to planning.

"If we set up a prime opportunity for the King to be assassinated, we might be able to entrap Mr. Gower into trying again." Ansel nodded along.

Nate frowned. "I'm not sure it would make me a good bodyguard if we used the king as bait in a setup."

Contessa shook her head. "We won't use him as bait. The king needs to go into hiding. Get out of the line of fire until we know the threat on his life has passed. We need to come up with a way to sneak him out of London."

"I think we might have a way," Rhosyn interjected. She looked over at Ansel, and understanding dawned across his face.

If he could dress Talented up as acrobats and clowns and smuggle them out on his circus train, then he could certainly sneak out a king.

"Archer's Circus," he chimed in. "We've been offering Talented safe passage out of the city with our performers for years. Our train is scheduled to leave the day after tomorrow. We may just have picked up another act while we were in town."

Nate's unscarred brow raised in curiosity at the admission, but there was no time to get into the hidden history of Archer's Circus—not when Contessa's eyes were already narrowing in renewed calculations.

"Then the King will take the train to his country estate where he will stay until Mr. Gower is arrested. Who knows how long he will have to rule from there, so I'll have to accompany him," Contessa thought out loud.

"And I'll be going to guard him," Nate added.

"No." Contessa's voice was firm, causing her husband's gaze to snap to her. "You'll be needed here to make it seem like the King never left and apprehend anybody who participates in the next assassination attempt."

Nate scowled—an expression known to send grown men running away with their tails between their legs—but Contessa stared him down coolly.

"I won't leave you unprotected," Nate growled. "Not when you've been ill recently."

"I'm not ill." Contessa looked down at her lap.

"But—"

"You can tell I'm not lying," Contessa snapped.

Rhosyn looked at her friend more closely, seeing her pallor and the circles under her eyes in a new light. Guilt began to gnaw at her belly for not noticing how drawn she appeared and for laying these concerns at Contessa's feet when she already shouldered too many troubles. Maybe she and Ansel could solve this problem without bringing Contessa into it.

"I can tell you're not telling me everything though," Nate argued, standing and squaring on his wife, completely ignoring the others in the room. "You barely gave me any information on what the doctor said last week."

"I wanted to wait to tell you until you weren't so busy worrying about what happened with Rhosyn," Contessa said softly.

"Tell me what? If you need treatment, I want to know as soon as possible. We can go anywhere you need for the best—"

"We're having a baby."

The room froze as Contessa stared up through her lashes at her husband. Nobody breathed at all. The thuds of Nate's boots against the floor echoed loudly as he stumbled back a few steps, before sitting down heavily on the top of the desk.

"You're…pregnant?"

"We've been trying so long. I just wanted to be sure before I told you," Contessa's voice had softened to something full of hesitant joy.

Rhosyn looked over to Nate, his scowling face blooming into an expression softer than it had any right to be, with the fearsome scar bisecting his face. It was the way he looked at Contessa when they were first married, every time he didn't think anybody was looking—back when he didn't think there was any way she might love him.

Warmth bloomed in Rhosyn's chest—a delicate tendril of hope springing forth amid the darkness of recent events.

"I guess we do really have to redecorate the rose room," Nate mumbled, shell shocked. "We're going to need a nursery."

Contessa stood slowly and took a few steps forward, to stand between his knees. Nate's hands drifted to her waist and pulled her closer. He buried her face in her hair and breathed in shakily, paying no heed to the delicate mass of braids that must have taken hours to weave together.

"You're definitely not going anywhere without me," Nate declared into Contessa's hair.

At that, she stepped back, not far enough to force him to let go of her waist, but enough that he had to lift his head and meet her gaze.

"No. This is exactly why we have to do this." Contessa's tone brooked no argument. "I want our baby to know that we always do what must be done. They are likely going to be Talented, with the two of us as their parents. I do not want them born into a world where they have to fear their Talent, like we did. If we fail to catch the Gowers, that is exactly what might happen."

"I won't let you go alone," Nate said, his voice the closest to pleading it had ever been.

Rhosyn sprang to her feet. "She won't be alone."

In a few strides, she had crossed the room and slung her arm around Contessa's shoulder. The shorter woman smiled up at her fondly.

"You know I would walk over broken glass for both of you, and my future niece or nephew," Rhosyn added.

"You have also done much stupider things for much less important reasons," Nate pointed out, but his gaze softened.

"Even more proof that I won't hesitate to do what needs to be done."

"I'll be there too," Ansel volunteered, joining them all in standing, stepping up at Rhosyn's shoulder.

"And you think you have what it takes to protect my wife? And my sister?" Nate looked at Ansel appraisingly.

Before he answered, Ansel leaned forwards and picked up one of Nate's knives off the desk before him. He tossed it in his palm a few times as if testing its weight. Then, his wrist whipped forward faster than Rhosyn could blink.

A thud punctuated the air as the tip embedded itself into the wall above the shelf that served as a bar. Pinned to the knife was the cork of a bottle of whiskey, neatly removed by Ansel's throw.

Nate's eyebrows rose in admiration, a feat rarely achieved by anybody when it came to knife handling. "You certainly know your way around a blade."

"That's settled then," Contessa said, with finality in her tone. "I'll have plenty of protection."

Rhosyn clapped her hands and rubbed them together. "Let's go catch a king killer."

Chapter Fifteen

Steam drifted through the early morning air in thick blankets, turning all the busy figures in the train-yard into hazy silhouettes. Rhosyn lifted another crate, this one labeled "Fire Whips", onto the Archer's Circus train.

Her hair was hidden under a woolen cap to conceal the color, but the hazy dawn made it seem unnecessary, even the garish green and yellow on the train cars appearing dull and muted. Her eyes darted down several cars to where Ansel stood, directing traffic as the circus loaded up their supplies for a supposed tour. The confident clip of his voice and sureness in his gestures as he pointed to where things should go painted him as in his element, but Rhosyn could just make out the outlines of weapons through his sleeves. She had even watched him shove a small pistol into the waistband of his pants before they left the safehouse this morning.

They had to be prepared for anything.

Two figures emerged from the mist and approached Rhosyn. The shorter of the two peeked up from under a hat, revealing Contessa's determined face. The taller silhouette paused just behind her, and Rhosyn couldn't help staring at the king's face for just a moment.

Dressed in a worn, striped shirt and gray trousers, a cap pulled low over mussed hair, it was hard to believe he wasn't just another lower city worker. Still, Rhosyn's throat stuck with nerves as she went to speak.

"Grab that crate and take it to Ansel over there. He'll tell you where to put it." If the King took offense to being ordered around, he didn't show it, doing as

Rhosyn ordered. Apparently, Contessa had prepared him for the situation well, and he understood how important it was for him to get on the train undetected.

The pair disappeared into the mist, and the circus performers made quick work of loading the remaining crates and barrels in an organized dance, speaking of how used to being on the road they were. Before the sun had risen a few more degrees, Ansel was at her elbow, jerking his head to tell her it was time to get moving.

As he stepped up into the rearmost car and offered a hand to help her in after him, she opened her mouth to admit she had never been on a train before. Instead, she snapped her mouth shut as he helped her into the passenger car. This was too important a moment to admit to her inexperience.

Still, he saw her hesitation and interlaced their fingers, even when she was inside, his thumb rubbing a soothing circle on her skin.

"Nate will catch Mr. Gower," he assured, voice soft enough to not be heard over the hustle and bustle of all the performers finding a place to wait out the journey. "Mr. Gower already accepted an invitation to go to the palace today to discuss his sponsorships and to bring his Talented servants with him. Once he has his entire Talented army at the palace, he won't be able to resist taking another crack at the king...or the decoy who will be stationed in his study at least."

Rhosyn nodded, but a lump still rose in her throat. "So many things could go wrong."

"And he's got the best possible team for thinking on his feet." Ansel's arm dragged up to her shoulder, warm against her skin that had been chilled by the morning air. "From what I heard of your friend Scarlett, I wouldn't bet against her in any situation. She'll be keeping a close eye on the situation from the shadows, especially given that her husband volunteered to be the decoy."

Ansel pulled Rhosyn further into the train car, toward the cabin Contessa and the king had disappeared into. "By this time tomorrow, it will all be over, and you'll be free to live your life."

Rhosyn tugged his arm, stopping them in the hallway, now sparsely populated as people had hurried to find their place on the train. Slowly, the steam engine rumbled to life, and they started to trundle down the tracks. The train whistle blew, and Rhosyn paused what she was going to say until she could be heard, the locomotive picking up speed beneath her.

"What is the life I'll be going back to?" Rhosyn asked.

"Well, you don't have to go back to the exact same life you had, if you don't want to." Ansel hesitated. "You have some...new opportunities now. Archer's Circus is always looking for more security and I—I would like to have you around."

Rhosyn swallowed. It was such a momentously huge decision—to leave behind the life she had built to follow this thief, who had plucked her heart out of her chest as easily as she picked purses from pockets. But maybe it didn't have to be. Maybe, for once she could make a decision based on her heart, instead of just volunteering herself to solve the biggest problem she could find.

She opened and closed her mouth, trying to find the words to say this to Ansel. Before she could speak, an echoing *thud* ran through the train car. Rhosyn threw her hand out to catch herself on the wall as it rocked side to side, nearly throwing her off balance. Ansel frowned as the lamps hanging from the ceiling swayed in response.

Contessa's head poked out of the compartment she had disappeared into with the King. "Did we hit something?"

"It sounded more like something hit us," Ansel said.

Rhosyn moved to ask what would hit a train, but he held up his hand to silence her, looking up at the ceiling. They all froze, when over the rattle of iron on rails came the tromping of footsteps on the roof.

Rhosyn's heart leapt into her throat. Contessa's eyes widened.

"Stay in there, and bar the door," Ansel ordered Contessa.

Then, he marched off down the hallway. Rhosyn wasted no time in hurrying after him, towards the door between cars. When he reached it, he slid it open and stepped onto the narrow metal platform between the two bobbing compartments. Rhosyn tried not to look down as she joined him, but the blur of rails flying by, just inches below her feet, made bile rise in her throat. She had enough fear about being thrown from a carriage, it hardly bore thinking about what would happen if she fell from a train.

With little hesitation, Ansel turned to the short ladder leading to the top of the car and began to climb. As his fingers reached the top rung, Rhosyn looked up and gulped. She might not have the advantage of his Talent for balance, or years of experience on a trapeze, but she would not let him face whatever was up there alone.

She scrambled up the ladder, knuckles white as she gripped each rung with all her might, following Ansel as quickly as possible. When she crested the edge to crouch on the swaying roof of the train, any fear of the climb was overshadowed by the sight that greeted her.

Four men in dark clothes crouched at the far end of the car. The silver of knives and pistols glinted in their hands, and while three of them were unfamiliar, the face of one stood stark in her mind.

The man she had stopped from killing the king, who had sunk through the floor as if it were water.

"They're Mr. Gower's men," she hissed, barely audible over rumble of the steam engine. "Our plan."

Somehow, they had been found out. Nate, Scarlett, and Benedict were waiting for an assassination attempt at the palace, but the real danger was here, on the train that was supposed to be their safe getaway.

Rhosyn didn't have time to wonder how Mr. Gower had discovered their deception, as the man in the rear of the pack stood and pointed towards her and Ansel.

"Get rid of them first, then find the King."

When he spoke, his voice had an odd echoing quality. Rhosyn found herself blinking in a moment of stunned stupor, when it hit her. It was similar to the effect of Paul's voice when he lulled somebody to sleep, but the tone underneath was different.

Hamish, the groom with the power of persuasion. These other Talented were under his thrall as they stood and began prowling towards her and Ansel.

"Don't hurt them if you can help it!" Rhosyn shouted to be heard over the train whistle, sounding again as they trundled towards the edge of the city. "They aren't in control of their actions."

Ansel stood as well, and knives slid into his hands. Rhosyn dipped her hands into her pockets and slipped on the pair of brass knuckles, which Nate had handed her with a heavy look before she set out.

Then, Ansel charged. She was hot on his heels, dashing across the roof of the train towards the attackers. Before Ansel clashed with the first one, he jumped, flipping over his head and landing on the far side as if gravity were just a suggestion. Before his opponent could get his bearings and turn, Ansel kicked out at the back of his leg, forcing him down to his knee.

As much as Rhosyn's heart jumped into her throat, she didn't have time to worry about Ansel, her own assailant facing off against her.

He swung first, broad and wide against her, as so many did when faced with a willowy woman. She ducked under his meaty arm before driving her shoulder up into his diaphragm. He stumbled back, lifting one hand palm out.

For a moment, Rhosyn was impressed with herself for forcing her opponent to surrender in one hit, until a ball of light started forming in the palm of his hand.

Name: Thomas Pemberton

Power: Combustion

The sponsorship paper flashed through Rhosyn's mind for a split second before she threw herself sideways to avoid the blast. A strangled yelp escaped her as the force of the explosion clipped her right shoulder, sending her spinning out of the way. Her feet slipped on the roof, slick with droplets of condensed steam. She scrambled for a foothold, but it was too late. She landed hard on her side, and the gentle slope of the roof sent her sliding towards the edge.

The world whirred by in a sickening mix of steel and smoke as she scrabbled for purchase on the hard surface with her fingernails. Her grasp caught on the edge of the roof as she reached it, but her momentum was too great to stop.

Her body swung over the edge, and for a sickening moment, the rails flew by beneath her dangling feet. Then, her weight caught with a jerk as she managed to hang on, body colliding with the side wall of the train car with enough force to make her eyes water. Her toes scraped against the surface, trying to get enough purchase to adjust her grip and climb back up.

Every sensation in her body screamed for attention, from the howling of wind in her ears to the sharp pinch in her shoulders as she tried to haul herself up. She tried not to think about the certain death, splattered on the cobblestones, if she were to lose her grip.

She had just managed to get enough traction to start inching up the wall when a shadow darkened her vision. She craned her neck upwards to find her opponent standing above her, looking down at where she dangled precariously on the edge of life and death.

Bile rose in her throat as he opened his palm, pointing his arm straight down at her.

He was going to blast her off the side of this train. She wasn't going to be able to protect Contessa like she promised Nate. And she wasn't going to be able to tell Ansel that she wanted more than anything to see the world with him and his circus.

Light began to coalesce in her attacker's palm, but a new bolt of fire shot through Rhosyn.

Their plan had gone to utter hell, but when had that ever stopped Rhosyn before? Chaos was where she thrived, and she could cause a little of her own.

Gritting her teeth, she peeled the fingers of her left hand free of their death grip, so she dangled by just her right. The train shook, nearly knocking her free, but she gritted her teeth as she dug her free hand into the inside of her jacket.

Praying that some of Ansel's skill had rubbed off on her, her fingers wrapped around the smooth handle of a knife. In the same motion that she drew it out, she threw it forward, aimed squarely between her attacker's eyes. The pommel struck him in the forehead, and he stumbled back. As he fell, his arm shot up, and his explosive burst shot straight into the sky, shimmering like a silver firework.

Rhosyn struggled to climb back up, but before she could get a hold of the lip of the roof once more, Ansel's worried face appeared above her. He grabbed her by the elbows, hauling her back onto the roof. As she tumbled over the edge, she landed on her knees, one of his arms wrapped firmly around her to keep her from toppling off once again. Adrenaline from her brush with death left her shaky, but ready for another brawl.

Her eyes darted around the roof, finding three thugs lying unconscious. One was conspicuously missing.

"The groom," she shouted, just as her eyes caught on a silhouette running towards the front of the train. His form was obscured by the steam billowing from the engine and wafting in thick clouds towards the back, and he disappeared into the thickening haze.

Without hesitation, Ansel hauled her to her feet and they took off after him. When they reached the end of the car, he didn't break his stride before leaping over the gap onto the next one. Rhosyn refused to falter as she followed, her mind offering her an image of how she did the same chasing the Hood over rooftops during their first encounter weeks ago.

She didn't waver then, and she wouldn't now.

Before they were halfway across the second car, Ansel skittered to a stop in front of her so suddenly she nearly crashed into his back. She was about to shout at him when she saw why.

The front of the train passed under a bridge, and as it did, several figures jumped off it, landing on the roof before them and cutting them off. Heavy thuds sounded behind Rhosyn, and she spun, finding at least half a dozen more adversaries there as well.

They were surrounded by Mr. Gower's army of Talented, and all Rhosyn had was her fists and a few spare knives.

She backed up a few steps, until her shoulders hit Ansel's. Standing back-to-back with him, she raised her fists. The thugs started closing in like a noose, and Rhosyn's heart hammered in her chest.

"Think we can take them?" Ansel asked over her shoulder.

Despite it all, fondness tugged like a string below Rhosyn's ribcage. If she was going to go down, then she wanted it to be fighting side by side with Ansel.

"You kidding?" she quipped back. "If I were you, I would be worried that there weren't enough for both of us."

"I'll be sure to leave plenty for you," Ansel promised. He shifted his weight against her back, ready to leap into action.

Rhosyn bared her teeth, a growl building in her throat, when a screech of horses and clatter of wheels drew her attention. An open-topped phaeton crashed along the street running parallel to the train tracks, and Rhosyn started as she recognized the man in the driver's seat.

She hardly had time to register Benedict's reckless driving before two figures jumped from the back of the speeding vehicle. A cloud of shadow fell over the train as wings of darkness formed around the figures, helping them sail onto the train.

Nate landed in a crouch beside her, the Beast in action. As knives sprang into his hands and he snarled, the thugs around them couldn't help but back up a few steps.

Scarlett stepped out of the dissolving shadows, the darkness clinging to her like morning dew. Her expression was no less feral than Nate's as black daggers of pure night formed in her hands, turning her into the dark shadow only referred to in feared whispers.

The hope that had sputtered in her chest flared again.

"Well, now there definitely aren't enough for all of us," Rhosyn mused dryly.

Scarlett leaped into action first, Rhosyn only a beat behind her. The satisfying thud of knuckles against flesh overtook her mind as she took on her first opponent. She struck his cheek first, before he landed a kick to her shin. The sharpness of the pain shooting up her leg honed her senses, and she threw a vicious uppercut. He crumpled like a sack of potatoes, but she spun to find her next enemy before he hit the ground.

Her gaze caught on Nate, currently warding off three enemies. Rhosyn's vision swam as one of them seemed to waver in and out of existence, as if the light around him bent out of his way. Lightning danced at the fingers of a second, while the third loomed large enough to eat Scarlett for breakfast.

Rhosyn darted forward to come to her aid, but Nate caught her eye and shook his head.

"Follow that one!" he shouted, jerking his head towards the front of the train. "Contessa—" he shouted before he was cut off by a bolt of electricity that forced him to dodge out of the way.

Rhosyn didn't wait to be told twice. She darted through the mayhem, following the shadow of the man who continued running towards the front of the train. She couldn't quite make out who it was, but her gut told her it was the groom. With the Talent of persuasion pulling all of these Talented into his thrall, Hamish was sure to be the leader of this whole operation.

Rhosyn pumped her arms, feet pounding against the metal roof as she gained ground on him. Up closer to the engine as they were, the smoke grew thicker, burning her eyes and nose as she panted for breath.

She could barely make out the groom's silhouette, forced to squint against the billowing haze and the roar of the engine in her ears. Then, he dropped down and disappeared, and Rhosyn skittered to a stop at the edge of a car.

He had gone inside the train.

Rhosyn hurried down the ladder, fear of falling far outweighed by the fear of what would happen if the groom made it to Contessa and the king before she did. She burst inside to find that the chaos in the train was nearly as dense as the pandemonium outside.

Some of Mr. Gower's Talented army had managed to get into the cars, but the circus performers seemed to share Ansel's fighting spirit. One armed man was cowering on his knees, arms over his head and two men pummeled him with juggling batons. Rhosyn tore her eyes away from the spectacle to search for the groom, only to find him slipping through the door at the far end of the hall, back towards where the king was.

Rhosyn pushed through the mayhem, ducking around a clown armed with a pie, which he enthusiastically smashed into the face of another of Mr. Gower's thugs. She crashed through the car, following the groom into the next. In this one, one of the Talented assassins had been backed into a corner by a snarling lion, while the lion tamer stood next to him with folded arms in satisfaction.

She gained on the groom, but he was still half a car in front of her when he slipped through the door to the train car containing Contessa and the king. Rhosyn shoved through as fast as she could, lungs burning and heart hammering.

The door slammed open as she shouldered through it, only to find the hallway...empty.

Rhosyn froze, head whipping back and forth to locate the missing groom.

A hand landed on the back of her neck, and her shoulders hunched up.

"Stop."

The word rung through the air with crushing weight and settled into Rhosyn's limbs like lead. She struggled, but it was as if the connection between her brain and body had been cut, leaving her dangling like an abandoned marionette.

A rough chuckle sounded behind her, grating against her skin like stone.

"Usually it takes me weeks of building influence over somebody to be able to command them with my Talent so thoroughly. But if somebody lets their guard down enough to let me touch them, skin to skin, well..." Hamish chuckled again, Rhosyn's current helplessness clearly illustrating his meaning. "It's how I got one of the King's Guard to tell me where he had gone when I suspected a trap."

"Why are you doing this?" Rhosyn growled, seemingly still capable of speaking, despite being otherwise immobilized.

"Why shouldn't I?" he spat. "King Byron is like any other powerful man, willing to step on the rest of us to maintain control."

"You don't have to do this," Rhosyn insisted, voice taking on a pleading edge. "Whatever Mr. Gower has told you, it doesn't have to be this way. King Byron ended the Inquiries... You're safe now."

"I'll never be safe while my Talent makes me useful," Hamish growled, but his voice broke on the last word. "Mr. Gower...he has my son somewhere. I don't know where, but if I fail, he'll hurt him."

Rhosyn's heart sank. Another parent and child separated by a Talent. As much as her heart stuttered in sympathy though, she fought against his mental hold. If he succeeded, the Inquiries would start anew, and many more children would be ripped from their parents.

"I can help you," Rhosyn insisted. Her fingers started to wiggle, as if her paralysis eased, but then his grip tightened at the nape of her neck once more. She went rigid.

"Oh, you will. You're going to kill King Byron for me. You were already blamed for the last attempt, and I can't very well get my son back if I'm in jail."

His words doused Rhosyn in cold like ice. She tried to shout, but her voice seemed taken from her now too.

"Go on," he urged. "Knock on the compartment door. Your friend will recognize you and let you in. Then one slice with one of your knives, and it'll all be over."

His grasp on her nape loosened, but the claws that gripped her mind only dug in further. Rhosyn's feet took one step forward, then another. It was the sensation of being in a dream, her unconscious mind taking charge and leading her down a perilous path while her conscious self screamed helplessly from the sidelines. But there would be no waking from this dream. Not until the King's blood stained her already dirty hands.

Her arm raised, knuckles poised to knock on the entrance to the compartment holding Contessa and King Byron.

A crash interrupted her actions. She managed to turn her head to see Ansel crash into the car from the same direction she had come, although she couldn't move away from her position. Ansel froze in the doorway, panting heavily as his gaze darted over the scene in front of him, rapidly cataloging the situation.

"Ah, the infamous Hood, I presume. You've caused too many problems already," Hamish mused. "I suppose I can knock out two birds with one stone here. Kill him first."

Horror rose in Rhosyn's throat, a palpable thing making her unable to draw breath. Still, her hands slid into her sleeves, the knives within settling on her palms with the weight of finality. Rhosyn might not be the knife fighter Nate was, but she had brawled with Ansel enough times to know that in a fair fight, his odds were slim. If he were holding back for fear of hurting her... Rhosyn could only hope help came in time.

Ansel raised his hands, but Rhosyn advanced on him as if pulled forward by a string. With her eyes, she begged him to arm himself—to grab his blades before she was forced to drive her own into his flesh.

She raised her arm, and in the instant before it came down, silver flashed in his hand. He grabbed his knife just in time to catch her blow on the hilt of his weapon. In a flurry, Rhosyn disengaged. Rhosyn swung again and again, but Ansel only dodged, making no attacks of his own.

Her mouth was not under her control enough to form words, but she managed to squeeze out a choked sob. She hoped it conveyed all that her voice couldn't say right now.

Fight back. Please. I'd rather die here than have to watch myself kill you.

When she raised her arm next, Ansel took his shot. A blade *thunked* into the wall behind her. As her arm swung forward, she was jerked back, Ansel's knife pinning her to the wall by her sleeve—just as he had the first time they'd met.

Another *thunk*, and her other arm was pinned.

"Break free! Kill him!" the groom shouted, his voice clawing into her mind as she started to struggle against her restraints.

Ansel rounded on him, advancing when a ripping split the air as Rhosyn's sleeve gave way. To her horror, she brought the blade in her hand to her own throat.

"Stop," the groom commanded Ansel. Hamish's voice was his own, with no Talent behind it, but he didn't need it. Ansel froze as Rhosyn's movement caught his eye.

"If you attack me, I'll have her kill herself," the groom announced triumphantly.

Ansel's gaze met hers, his deep emerald gaze pleading. Her hand trembled, against her throat, the tip of the knife scratching the delicate skin there. A warm rivulet of blood trickled down to pool in the hollow of her collarbone. The sensation did something to cut through the odd haze of her mind.

"Rhosyn."

Ansel had said her name many times before. To get her attention. In frustration when she challenged him. At the peak of his pleasure.

But this was different. This was both a prayer and a plea. Full of love and a promise that Rhosyn didn't want: that he wouldn't hurt her even to save himself.

It struck something within her, the blow forming cracks in the stone grasp around her mind. She squirmed physically, her muscles twitching in response to her commands, although not yet fully responding.

"End this," the groom growled.

His orders pulled at her muscles, but Rhosyn knew now she could break free. She had to.

An image flew to her mind unbidden. The last assassin's eyes clearing of their odd haze as the chandelier knocked him squarely in the forehead. A blow to the head had freed him of the grip of the groom's Talent.

If Rhosyn knew how to do anything, it was take a hit.

With an almighty roar, she lunged forward, ripping her sleeve free and leaping at Ansel. The groom still compelled her to fight him, but she used the foothold of control she had to lead with her head.

Her forehead connected with Ansel's with a resounding crack. They both stumbled back, Rhosyn hitting the wall behind her and sliding to the ground. The groom screamed at her to get up. To kill Ansel.

But Rhosyn didn't move.

Her mind was free.

Her vision swam and her limbs flailed uncoordinatedly as she tried to recover from the blow to her head. Her vision cleared and she looked up, only for her heart to stutter once again.

The groom had drawn a pistol from his coat, and she now stared down the barrel of it.

"I'll have to do this the hard way then," he growled.

Rhosyn stiffened as a bang split the air, but no pain bloomed in her chest. Instead, the groom's face smoothed in shock. He wavered where he stood, crimson blooming across his chest.

He looked down at the spreading stain, but no horror crossed his expression. Instead, his eyes filled with something like relief.

"It's over then."

That was all he said before he toppled sideways, dead before he hit the ground. Behind him sat Ansel, back propped against the wall as he held a small pistol in a shaking hand. Rhosyn met his gaze over a bloody and already horrendously purple nose.

The gun fell from his hand, and Rhosyn was on him before it clattered to the ground. Blood dripped over his lips, streaming from a crooked nose, clearly broken by Rhosyn's inelegant attack. But his eyes were full of life, and his arms were warm and solid as he wrapped her in them.

She sat there in his embrace, and she wasn't sure if the shaking in her limbs was from the rumbling of the train or the trembling relief running through her body.

"You saved me," she murmured into his chest.

He nuzzled into her hair, smearing blood all over it, but she didn't care. "You did that yourself. You fought tooth and nail, like you always do. And you won."

They inhaled each other's presence in silence for a moment, only for it to be broken by the creak of a door sliding open.

Rhosyn raised her head to find Contessa, standing in the doorway, a look of utmost relief on her face. If Contessa's Talent told her it was safe to come out, then the fight must be over.

Contessa nodded at the question in Rhosyn's eyes. "We're safe now."

Chapter Sixteen

Rhosyn stared down the line of her friends and family, pride blooming in her chest. To her right stood Contessa, resplendent in silver silk, although when she looked closely, she could see it wasn't nipped in as close at the waist as usual. Nate hovered off her shoulder, unable to look away from his wife, even as King Byron stood before his throne, thanking them for serving King and Country.

Rhosyn snuck a glance to her left, looking past Ansel to Scarlett and Benedict. She nearly chuckled at the pair they made, Benedict's charming smile a perfect contrast to Scarlett's perpetual scowling at all the pomp, made even fiercer by the knot of scar tissue on the side of her head where one of her ears should be.

Ansel's shoulder bumped against hers, and he shot her an amused glance as if saying to her, "You only get inducted into the Royal Order once."

Rhosyn returned her attention to the King's words, but as he thanked each of them for their fearless actions to foil the plot against the crown, her mind kept drifting to Ansel's warmth at her side.

The week following the fight on the train had been a whirlwind, but Ansel stood by her through it all. Despite the bandage on his nose and the dark circles of bruises under his eyes, he sat with her through Mr. Gower's trial, squeezing her hand before she took the stand to testify against him.

Although Rhosyn had put many criminals behind bars in her life, no guilty verdict had given her as much satisfaction as Mr. Gower's. As they dragged him away, he hissed and spat that King Byron had ruined this city by allowing the

Talented to run free—that he should be removed from power for ending the Inquiries.

As the Royal Police hauled him past the box where Contessa sat, he had momentarily pulled free to spit in her face.

"You're no better than your father," he snarled, turning purple under his impressive mustache.

Everybody surrounding Contessa froze at that, and Nate nearly leaped out of the box and strangled Mr. Gower where he stood. But Contessa had stayed him with a hand on his wrist. Instead, Contessa stood and stalked to the front of the box, somehow towering over him despite her slight stature, as always, her poise making her larger than life.

"I am *not* my father, and I know this because I am willing to change course when something I've done is being used for evil. My father let the Inquiries, which were meant to protect his people, warp London into a place of hatred and fear. You tried to abuse the Talented through their sponsorships, but I won't let the work I've done in protection of the city be twisted into something violent and hateful. I *will* stand up for what is right, and I won't let you abuse the Talented of this city any longer."

She watched with ice in her gaze as he was dragged off to prison, where he would await execution for high treason. Anybody who heard of the display at the trial would think twice before challenging the king's advisor and bodyguard.

A search of Mr. Gower's study had also uncovered his co-conspirators, and although more trials would come, the evidence would allow King Byron to rip out the dissent against his support for the Talented by the roots. At last, the future of the Talented in London seemed bright. The King had even pardoned all the Talented Mr. Gower had sponsored for their involvement in the assassination, knowing they hadn't acted of their own free will. When the groom died, it was as if they had woken up from a trance, and they all immediately dropped their weapons and surrendered.

Scarlett had used her network of whispers to track down the groom's son at a hidden house in the country and bring him back to the city. Rhosyn sat in Nate's old office next to Contessa as she drew up papers for him to be adopted to a couple who wanted nothing more than to raise a child.

Her eyes were glassy as she stamped the paper with the King's seal.

"I hope this is the last orphan of Talented parents."

Rhosyn squeezed her friend's hand and sat with her late into the night.

In the past week, Rhosyn had also not returned to her rented room, staying in Ansel's bed with him at the Foxes' safe house. They didn't need to hide anymore, given that King Byron had personally exonerated them of any crimes, given their involvement in saving him. Still, she didn't feel like she could go back to her old room and her old life like nothing had changed.

Not to mention, knowing that time in bed meant being wrapped in Ansel's arms helped her get more sleep than she ever had in the past.

Now, she puffed out her chest proudly as King Byron pinned a medal to her jacket, smiling at her kindly before moving on to do the same to Ansel. She had come a long way from a rough and tumble Lion to having bestowed upon her the highest personal honor that royalty could award.

The audience behind them roared, and as the six of them turned to smile at the crowd, Ansel slipped his hand in hers. He didn't let go even as they walked down into the audience to receive their congratulations.

So many people shook Rhosyn's hand and patted her on the back that she stopped recognizing faces or remembering names until a familiar voice drew her from the haze of celebration.

"Officer Walsh." Joseph stuck out a hand.

Hesitantly, Rhosyn took it, but his smile was warm as he clasped it back.

"You don't have to look at me like I'm going to discipline you. I'm proud," he admitted.

"You are?" Rhosyn asked. She may have saved the King's life, but she certainly hadn't been following protocol when she did it.

He smiled, something softer and less tired in his gaze than it had been the last time she had been in his office. Rhosyn briefly wondered if it had something to do with the way Benedict's sister, Lottie, had been hanging on his elbow during the ceremony.

"You know, when I inherited the Royal Police, they may have followed the law, but they certainly weren't good. Even though something isn't perfect, and may never be, doesn't mean it isn't worth fighting to make it better. And you always fight to make things better," Joseph smiled wryly, "even if you tend to break a few rules along the way."

"Well, thank you," Rhosyn struggled for words. "I didn't think you'd want me back on the force after the things I did."

"I would always want to have somebody like you in my corner, but I think you would be whether you wear a uniform or not," Joseph admitted. "The question is, do you want to come back to the Royal Police? It would seem to me you might be looking for a…change in pace."

A smile crept across Rhosyn's face as she turned to look at Ansel—he was eyeing her curiously. Mischief twinkled in his eyes as her smile grew into an unrestrained grin.

"I've always wanted to run away and join the circus."

Epilogue

Even after more than a year, the sparkling lights of Archer's Circus still dazzled Rhosyn. Every time they stopped in a new town, she felt like one of the visitors drinking in the spectacle for the first time. The sweet warmth of roasted nuts and spun sugar made even the air seem magical. At night, the flickering lamplight gave the whole place an enchanted quality, as if magic and adventure might lurk around any corner.

And at Archer's Circus, it did.

Tonight's performance, though, was particularly electrifying. They were back in London after touring most of Europe, and Rhosyn had convinced Ansel to celebrate the occasion by performing with his Merry Men.

He hadn't had time to perform before, when he was so busy running the business side of the circus and leading a secret Talented smuggling train. Now, though, with Rhosyn helping him, he had some time to spare for acrobatics.

Although, they still managed to find trouble—legal and otherwise—in almost every city they visited.

Rhosyn peeked out from her post backstage to the box where their most honored guests sat. She smiled at the sight of Contessa and Nate, baby Eliza, who was named after Contessa's mother, perched happily on Nate's lap. The child watched with wide eyes as the colorful acrobats flew and arced through the air, gravity having loosened its hold in the confines of this tent.

Even Scarlett was wide eyed with wonder, leaning into Benedict, who wrapped an arm around her obligingly. Kristoff and Gregor sat in the back of the box, but based on the way Gregor blushed after Kristoff whispered something in his ear, they were paying far less attention.

The sight of them all warmed her heart. She loved being on the road with Ansel, and each homecoming was sweeter knowing she had a family to come back to.

Rhosyn ripped her eyes away from her friends in the box, and she turned her attention to the performers on stage. As always, the Merry Men were consummate performers, but her gaze fixed itself on Ansel as he flipped and twisted through the air.

Her eyes tracked him through every improbable maneuver until at last he landed on the stage and the audience exploded in wild cheers. He bowed several times at their appreciation before ducking behind the curtain to the backstage area.

Rhosyn jumped on him in a heartbeat, never able to contain herself after watching him perform—something that had played no small role in Ansel's eagerness to appear regularly with the Merry Men once more.

He caught her easily as she jumped into his arms, and the rest of the acrobats groaned and chuckled good-naturedly.

She kissed him soundly, not discouraged in the slightest by the thin sheen of sweat coating his skin, but he pulled away in favor of nipping her earlobe.

"What have I told you about being patient?" he murmured, his voice taking on the deep, teasing timbre that made her shiver.

"You know I'm not very good at being patient," she quipped, but he just smiled and kissed her again before putting her down.

"Then it's a good thing I have all the time in the world to work on that."

As always, Rhosyn couldn't wait.

The Gardener and the Sharpshooter

A Gregor and Kristoff Prequel Story

Chapter One

Running his fingers over the smooth leaf of a parlor palm, Gregor looked over his shoulder at the group of young men throwing dice in the corner. They weren't paying him much mind, laughing raucously at something one of them had said.

Turning back to his plant, he muttered encouragements to it softly. In response, the limp leaf grew greener, the sickly yellow cast around the edges fading. He supposed it didn't truly matter if the other young Lions saw him use his Talent, but years of habit made him look over his shoulder before coaxing a plant to reach its potential, even if it had only been a dandelion struggling to sprout between the cobblestones of a London alleyway.

He released the palm leaf with a sigh, turning the plant to get what little light it could from the narrow window in the Lions' safehouse, thinned even further by the smoke perpetually belching from the factories this close to the port. As much as Gregor itched for a full garden to tend, he wasn't going to turn up his nose at the opportunity to at least have a potted plant.

Just before he was about to turn away from the window and join the other young men in their game, a shape on the opposite rooftop grabbed his attention. He leaned in to get a closer look at the man running across the slate tiles, straight towards the safehouse. Gregor threw himself backwards just in time for the figure to crash through the window.

Glass exploded into the cramped room, all the occupants jumping to their feet with a shout. The intruder rolled across the uneven floorboards before stopping on his back with a *whump*, arms and legs spread wide as he took up most of the floorspace in the crowded room.

Stunned silence fell.

To his surprise, Gregor was the first to edge forward. The other young Lions Gregor shared this safehouse with were usually more prone to throw themselves into adventure, while Gregor preferred to stay home and patch up the crew when they returned if the mission didn't require an extra set of hands. Even then, he tended to be relegated to being a lookout, or the bait as another lifted a distracted mark's purse.

Now, Gregor stepped towards the man on the floor, drawn forwards before he fully realized his feet were moving.

The man's dark hair curled around his head in a way that would have looked windswept, like a pirate from a storybook, if it hadn't been matted and dark at one temple. A trickle of blood ran down from his forehead across tanned skin and high cheekbones. Dressed in shirtsleeves, black whirls of tattoos poked out from beneath his collar and around his wrists. The handles of twin revolvers were just visible at his waist. He looked somewhat familiar, but Gregor couldn't place where he would have seen him. He had a feeling he would remember having met this man.

Gregor swallowed, mouth dry.

He fell to his knees, reaching out to find the source of the blood at his head. Just before Gregor's fingers made contact, the man's eyes opened, and Gregor snatched his hands back.

The man blinked several times, as if trying to focus his vision, giving Gregor time to admire the striking blue of his eyes.

"I must have hit my head harder than I thought if I'm waking up to an angel," the man said.

Gregor instantly choked on his tongue, making a very un-angelic noise. Thoughts of the man's injury and the guns at his waist flew from his mind as he struggled to process such shameless flirtation from a man who had just made such a bold entrance.

"Kristoff Mainsworth, at your service." The man on the ground shoved out a hand in greeting, although otherwise stayed laying flat on the floor.

The name rang a familiar bell in the back of Gregor's mind—the second in command of the Lions. That would explain why he found him familiar, even if he had only ever seen him at a distance.

"Gregor Topps." He shook the proffered hand, the touch of skin-warm metal from the rings Kristoff wore on every finger unexpected and pleasant. Gregor's face warmed and he internally cursed his tendency to blush at any interaction this side of friendly.

"Kristoff!" Voices murmured in recognition behind Gregor, and there was a sudden flurry of activity as everybody hurried to aid their sudden guest. After all, Kristoff had personally liberated more than one person in this room from rough factory work, and likely saved them from facing the gallows for their Talents in the process.

The voices of his friends murmuring in anxious admiration yanked Gregor from his stupor, and he pulled his hand from Kristoff's grip.

"My kit," he mumbled to himself, heading over to his narrow bed and fishing beneath for the battered leather case that held a meager supply of medical equipment. He hurried back to Kristoff's side. Although his roommates jostled to be closer to the legendary Lion's side, they made room when they saw what Gregor held.

He'd patched all of them up once or twice before after a territory dispute with another gang or a job gone wrong. Gregor may be abysmal at picking pockets or dealing stacked hands of cards, so he endeavored to make himself useful to the Lions in the ways he could.

"Ah, my angel is here to save me!" Kristoff proclaimed as Gregor dug through the leather case for a clean cloth and a small glass vial.

"Gregor is fine, sir," he mumbled, hands fumbling among his tools

"If you insist on calling me sir, then I will have to insist on calling you angel."

Gregor succeeded in wetting the cloth with the contents of the vial and the pungent sting of alcohol filled his nose. He wasted no time pressing it to the wound at Kristoff's temple, making the handsome man hiss at the sting. At least that way he couldn't say anything that deepened Gregor's already embarrassing blush.

Gently, Gregor kept gently dabbing at Kristoff's temple until the worst of the blood was cleaned from the area. If his breath stuttered each time his fingers made contact with Kristoff's skin, then that was his business.

Eventually, the wound was clean enough for Gregor to see that it was a relatively shallow cut, the amount of blood seeming disproportionate to the damage as it often was with cuts to the scalp. He wouldn't even need stitches, just a small bandage.

"What's the prognosis?" Kristoff asked.

"I'm afraid we'll have to amputate," Gregor quipped back.

"And deprive the world of my handsome face? This is a tragic day," Kristoff lamented.

Before Gregor could grasp at an adequately clever response, pounding sounded at the door downstairs. Everybody in the room stiffened. The fluttering that had begun in Gregor's belly solidified into icy apprehension.

The banging sounded again. "Royal Police! Open up!"

The room sprang into panic. Kristoff used his hands to push to sitting, wavering slightly, obviously still jarred by the impact of his sudden entrance.

"That'll be for me." Kristoff started to push to his feet, but Gregor stopped him with a hand on his chest. He was his patient after all, and it was his responsibility to see he made a full recovery.

"Stay," Gregor commanded, his voice more forceful than he had ever heard it before.

Kristoff raised a single brow in question, but did as Gregor asked.

Before he could second guess himself, Gregor pushed to his feet and scurried down the stairs to the ground floor while banging continued on the door. By now, it had progressed to a volume indicating that it was soon to fly off its hinges.

Gregor yanked the door open to be met with a trio of Royal Police officers, all scowling. Their navy-blue uniforms, pressed to perfect creases, contrasted wildly with Gregor's own rumpled shirt.

"We're looking for a thief running from the scene of a crime," the clear leader of the group stated without preamble. "We have reason to believe he is hiding here."

"You're right." Gregor steeled himself before saying the stupidest and bravest thing ever to pass his lips. "It's me."

Chapter Two

Gregor had known in an abstract sort of way that him ending up in prison at some point in his life was a distinct possibility. After all, he proudly called himself a member of the most notorious gang in London. However, if you had asked him when he woke up that morning if today was the day he would find himself behind bars, he would have laughed.

Apparently a set of pretty blue eyes changed things.

Gregor tightened his arms around his knees and tried to make himself as small as possible in the back corner of his shared cell. It wasn't hard to make himself seem to be the least threatening person there, as the other six or so criminals all seemed to be bruisers and enforcers from competitor gangs. He had already spotted a scorpion tattooed on one bicep, and a raptor peaking out under another collar.

A larger concern than his cellmates though, was Gregor's Talent. For now, it remained safely hidden, but he knew the Royal Police would question him. His bravery had been a fleeting thing, flaring to life as he turned himself in to save Kristoff in a sudden fit of inspiration. Now though, it stuttered in the face of what the police might do. He didn't know what ways they might have of wheedling out the truth of his Talent, but the Royal Police had a reputation of cruelty in the lower city.

If they did uncover his Talent, he would be hanged.

Even now, concentrating on keeping a tight leash on his ability, he could feel the moss between the stones of the cell threatening to spread from his presence alone. Subtle as his ability was, plants tended to spring to sudden life around him whenever his emotions washed over him with particular intensity.

Now was one of those times.

Gregor screwed his eyes shut, trying to control his breathing.

Two seconds in, two seconds out. Two seconds in, two seconds out.

Instead of calming, his heartbeat got faster, banging so loud it echoed in his ears.

His eyes snapped open. That clanging wasn't his heart, it was coming from outside the cell. Gregor sprang to his feet just in time to see Kristoff emerge around the corner of the shadowed hallway.

A bandage wrapped around his temples, but otherwise he looked no worse for wear as he pulled a pistol and fired off a shot into a police officer's knee before he could so much as pull his baton from his belt. Another officer came charging down the corridor, drawn by the noise, but Kristoff spun on his heel, lashing out so the butt of his pistol hit his temple with a solid *crack*. The Royal Police officer crumpled to the ground.

By now, the prisoners were all cramped around the bars watching the mayhem with cheers and shouted encouragement. Kristoff might not run with any of their gangs, but in moments like this, an enemy of the police was a friend of theirs. All of the thugs were taller than Gregor and he lost sight of Kristoff behind the wall of muscley bruisers.

He held his breath and prayed that Kristoff didn't do anything stupid.

After a moment, the immediate commotion died down, although pounding footsteps above their heads indicated that reinforcements would be arriving soon.

"One of them has to have the keys—" Kristoff's voice drifted into the cell.

With a few metallic clangs and a earsplitting shriek the door to the cell swung open. Kristoff stood at the entrance, gesturing for everybody to leave like a footman welcoming honored guests to a dinner party.

"If you wouldn't mind, friends, please go cause some chaos," Kristoff said cheerily as the various thugs barreled past him into the hallway.

Gregor found himself frozen to the spot in the middle of the now empty cell, as Kristoff fixed him with a crooked grin.

He had come back for him: the Lion who couldn't even hold a gun, let alone fire it.

"Are you coming?" Kristoff asked with a crooked brow.

The casual question roused Gregor from his awestruck state, and he rushed forward. He turned to follow the way the other escapees had gone—the direction he had been brought in—but Kristoff grabbed his hand, stopping him.

"I know a better way," he explained before tugging him the other way.

Gregor followed curiously, noticing that Kristoff kept ahold of his hand even though it wasn't strictly necessary. They reached what appeared to be a dead end, and despite the feeling of Kristoff's callused palm against his own, Gregor began to panic anew.

Now they were both going to be caught and Gregor's brave stupidity would have gotten them both killed.

Before Gregor could take two hyperventilating breaths, Kristoff reached up and pushed a stone among the wall that didn't quite fit with the rest of them. A quiet cracking echoed through the hallway, nearly drowned out the growing noise of fists meeting flesh and pained shouts at the far end of the prison. Kristoff's planned diversion seemed to be taking off with enthusiasm.

Kristoff let go of Gregor's hand to throw his shoulder into the wall, only for it to swing open, revealing a dark passageway behind. It inched open, as if it hadn't been used often, and Gregor joined in. As soon as a gap wide enough for somebody to slip through formed, Kristoff stopped and shooed Gregor inside.

As quickly as possible, Gregor and Kristoff shoved the hidden door closed behind them, plunging them into utter darkness. Gregor's thoughts began to race again, wondering how they were ever supposed to navigate...wherever they were...without being able to see. Then Kristoff's hand slipped into his once more and gave a gentle tug.

"Time to make our exit."

They emerged from the hidden tunnels into what appeared to be an abandoned warehouse. A thick layer of dust covered wooden crates, some of which were broken, splinters of wood scattered across the floor. Quiet skittering and squeaking indicated more rodents called this place home than humans.

As Gregor blinked, become used to indoor daylight again, a thousand questions for Kristoff jostled for space in his mind. There was something much more important to say first though.

"Thank you," he panted, still somewhat winded from their dash through the tunnels.

Kristoff looked at him incredulously. "Thank me? Thank you! You went to prison for me and I have never even said your real name."

Maybe it was the lingering adrenaline from their near escape, but Gregor found himself mumbling, "Maybe I liked it when you called me angel."

Perhaps Kristoff didn't hear him, or maybe he decided to spare Gregor from the embarrassment of commenting on such an admission, but Kristoff pressed on. "Honestly, you must let me do something to thank you. After you were arrested, your friends told me about your Talent. If they had found out…"

Gregor swallowed at the gruesome end implied by Kristoff trailing off.

"I didn't think about that at the time," he admitted. "I only knew you were likely wanted for other crimes, while I was a nobody."

Kristoff shrugged, a bit of dancing mischief returning to his gaze. "Yes, but you don't become notorious by being arrested only once. You get that reputation by continuing to get away."

Gregor smiled at that.

"Seriously though," Kristoff insisted, "There must be something you want."

"Not unless you can get me a garden," Gregor chuckled. "Knowing I was actually helpful for once is enough."

Gregor expected Kristoff to laugh along with him, but instead, the handsome man froze, a pensive expression taking over his fine features.

"A garden you say?" he mused.

"They're hard to come by in the lower city."

"Indeed," Kristoff agreed, "but I may know somebody who has just bought a house in the upper city. He hasn't hired any staff yet, because he is concerned about people around him being discrete. Given your affiliation though, I doubt that would be an issue."

Gregor's heart stuttered. A real garden, with a fine house to match? Still, he didn't let his hopes rise too fast.

"I don't have much experience beyond my Talent," Gregor admitted.

Kristoff was not deterred, instead looking him up and down with an appraising gaze. Gregor's skin warmed and he tried not to fidget.

"Besides gardening and knowing your way around a medical kit, what other hidden skills do you have?" Kristoff asked.

"I can cook," Gregor admitted.

"That would get you the job right there. Nate desperately needs to eat real meals."

Gregor choked on his saliva. "Nate? As in... Nathanial Woodrow, the Beast?"

"Don't call him that to his face," Kristoff advised. "But yes, he desperately needs somebody to help him keep the mansion of a house he just bought. Come, we'll go see it right now."

Chapter Three

Apparently, the tunnels they had used to escape from the prison also led to a secret hatch in the back of Nathanial Woodrow's house—a large part of the reason the Beast had bought the building, according to Kristoff. It also seemed that Kristoff was welcome to come and go as he pleased with no warning.

As Kristoff lead Gregor from the small study, he called out "Nate!" not seeming to care for propriety. Gregor, on the other hand, did his best to brush the grime of the prison off his rumpled shirt and smooth his hair as he took in the grand but empty house.

They came upon Nate in a parlor that was empty but for a single chair which looked much too small for the hulk of a man occupying it. Even though the Beast was responsible for the freedom of all the Lions and was rumored to be a kind man, Gregor's spine straightened involuntarily at the sight of his scarred face. Respected leader as he might be, the Beast was still one of the most dangerous men in London.

"Nate, I have a solution to your problem," Kristoff announced cheerily.

"Which one?" Nate grumbled before looking up and catching sight of Gregor. Gregor thought his expression might be one of surprise, but it was hard to tell with one half of his face completely frozen by scar tissue, running from his temple to his jawline. The twisted shape of it made Gregor think the wound that caused it must have festered.

"The problem of how to keep such a grand house without besmirching your spotless reputation." Kristoff gestured grandly to Gregor as if presenting a piece of art. "One of our Lions has a knack for domesticity, and I owe him for getting me out of a tight scrap."

Nate looked back and forth between Gregor and Kristoff a few times appraisingly, taking in Kristoff's wide-eyed pleading expression. The thought flickered through Gregor's head that he wouldn't be able to deny Kristoff anything when he wore that expression, but he dashed it away.

"You promise to keep my business to yourself?" Nate asked suddenly.

Gregor nodded quickly. He wouldn't dream of crossing the Beast, especially when he was the reason Gregor wasn't suffering under the cruel eye of a factory owner at this moment.

"Then congratulations, you have a job. Sorry it'll be a lot of work though. I don't have any other help," Nate admitted. He hesitated for a moment and then made to leave the room, clearly at a loss for what to do with an employee.

Gregor surprised himself by interrupting. "Do you have a garden?" he blurted.

Nate paused. "Yes. You can do with it whatever you like."

Gregor's soul lifted as Nate pushed from the room.

"He'll make it lovely for when you get around to having a wife!" Kristoff called after him.

"There will be no wife," Nate shouted from the hallway.

Gregor would have laughed at the friendly banter if he wasn't already too busy imagining all the flowers he would plant in his new garden. He would start with roses—as many kinds as he could find.

He jolted back to himself when he realized Kristoff was looking at him with a soft smile. Even more than his mischievous grins, something about the expression made Gregor's insides flip. Before he could think better of it, he threw his arms around Kristoff in a tight hug. It was the only way he could think of to properly thank him for what he had given him.

Gregor didn't miss the way the embrace lasted a beat longer than was strictly proper, or the tiny circle Kristoff traced on the small of his back with his thumb.

When Gregor pulled away, he was sure his blush trailed all the way down to his chest.

"There's another advantage to your employment here," Kristoff observed, some wickedness returning to his gaze.

"Oh, and what's that?" Gregor asked.

"I come to visit often."

Gregor grinned. He was counting on it.

Acknowledgements

Staring at the book that contains my first completed series is surreal, and I know I wouldn't be here without an incredible amount of support. First, a huge thank you to the group of authors that has become my cheering section. I wouldn't be where I am without the help of each and every Discordant Owl. A special shout out goes to Lily, for being the author bestie I never knew I needed.

I would be remiss not to acknowledge my amazing family. Without their support in every aspect of my life, I wouldn't have even put my first words on paper, let alone be releasing a special edition omnibus of a completed series. I also want to offer all the thanks in the world to my husband, Rhys, who is always the first to tell me to "*Do the thing*" whenever I'm facing down a goal that scares me.

And most importantly, thank you to my readers, who have stuck by me through book one and encouraged me to continue the journey of The Talented Fairy Tales. This one is for you.

About the author

S.C. Grayson has been reading fantasy novels since she was a little girl, and that has developed into a love of writing and storytelling. She is currently focused on fantasy and paranormal romance. She has written several Gaslamp fairytale retellings, and looks forward to publishing additional epic fantasy, paranormal, and science fiction romances.

When she is not sitting in a local coffee shop writing and consuming an iced americano, Grayson is a nurse researcher, focusing her efforts on breast cancer genetics. She lives in Maryland with her loving husband and their two cats, who enjoy contributing to her work by walking across her keyboard at inopportune moments (the cats, not the husband).

www.scgrayson.com

Printed in Great Britain
by Amazon